"By the Blood of the Seven," Falken said through clenched teeth. "She's led us into a trap. We have to find a way to open that door."

But it was already too late. Grace heard the echo of low grunts, the scraping of talons on stone. They froze as misshapen forms slunk into the kitchen, five, six, seven of them. Their backs were humped, their gray fur matted, their yellow eyes filled with pain and hunger. A stench like spoiled meat rose from them, making Grace's gorge rise.

The *feydrim* arranged themselves in a half-circle on the far side of the room, looking like nothing so much as spider monkeys crossbred with wolves: feral, intelligent, tortured. What were they waiting for? Why didn't the creatures leap forward and rip out their throats? Then the half-circle parted, and two figures stepped through, one slightly in front of the other, and Grace understood. The *feydrim* had been waiting for their mistress.

"You cannot escape," the old countess said.

The *feydrim* crouched, ready to spring.

BLOOD OF MYSTERY

BOOK FOUR OF
THE LAST RUNE

MARK ANTHONY

BANTAM BOOKS

NEW YORK TORONTO LONDON SYDNEY AUCKLAND

BLOOD OF MYSTERY

PUBLISHING HISTORY
A Bantam Spectra Book / April 2002

0-553-58332-8

Published simultaneously in the United States and Canada

PRINTED IN THE UNITED STATES OF AMERICA

OPM 10 9 8 7 6 5 4 3

for Ésther Elizabeth Anthony

In Loving Memory

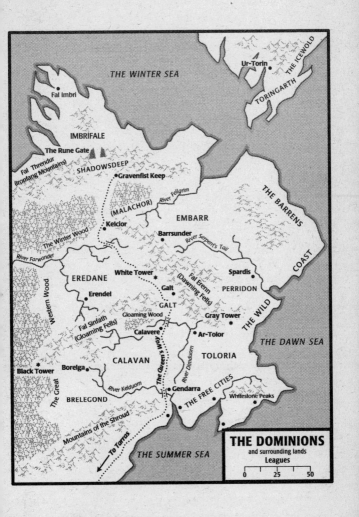

THE DOMINIONS
and surrounding lands
Leagues

0   25   50

breathe the wind
walk the fire
Raven be your master

chain the flesh
free the heart
Raven flies forever

—FIRST PRAYER OF THE RAVEN

drink the ice

breathe the fire

Shadow be your lover

chain the mind

still the heart

Darkness rules forever

—THE RAVEN REBORN

PART ONE

LOST

1.

The raven sprang from the edge of the precipice, spreading dark wings like shadows, and soared into the fiery dawn sky.

A wall of peaks fell away behind it, sharp as dragons' teeth, an impenetrable barrier of stone that stabbed at the sky. A wind howled off the mountains, slicing through the raven's feathers. It seemed the king toyed with his Stone again. The raven beat hard against the blast, righted himself, and fixed his eyes on the leafless forest that clung like mist to the land below. He had a message to deliver before the day died, to one in a place far to the south, and he would not fail in his task.

The raven's name was Gauris. Eleven and one hundred times the ice floes of the Winter Sea had cracked, thawed, and frozen again since the day of his shell-sundering. Through all of those years, Gauris had served the king faithfully. True, his feathers were not so glossy as they once had been, and his beak and talons were duller. However, his black eyes were still keen, and not even the young ones of the brood, for all they puffed their sleek breasts in pride, could fly so far in a single day as Gauris. That was why this message had been entrusted to him, for it was a missive of particular importance.

Or at least, so Gauris supposed. For no one, not even the king's closest minions, could know the king's thoughts and will. His heart was made of cold, enchanted iron, and some said the mind beneath his icy crown was forged of the same stuff. One thing Gauris knew for certain: The winds of war were blowing. And like a knight sharpening his blade and searching for chinks in his armor, the king needed to be sure all of his tools were at the ready. It was one of those tools—one of the most precious of them all—to which Gauris flew now.

He swooped toward the forest, skimming just above the tops of the bare, silvery trees. It was still only early Sindath, but winter had already come to this part of Falengarth, and it would never depart again if the king had his way. Gauris awaited that day with great anticipation. Surely there would be need for swift couriers in the New Times: messengers to carry the king's commands throughout his vast realm, which would claim all of Falengarth from shore to shore. And none were swifter than the king's ravens, fed with dark meats over the centuries to grant them speed and strength.

True, it was whispered by some that the king had his own master who would return in the New Times, a master whom some called the Nightlord and who had been wrongfully banished long ago. If this were so, would not the Nightlord be ruler of all things when the war was won? But surely the Nightlord would be grateful for the king's service, just as the king would be grateful for the swiftness of his ravens. Surely, in the New Times, there would be rewards for all who served on the victorious side.

The forest fell behind him, and Gauris pumped strong wings as the sun edged higher. Sere fields slipped below, dotted by lakes that flashed like coins before vanishing behind. Another range of mountains hove into view. It was a weathered jumble of rocks far lower than the wall of bitter stone that barred the way into and out of the king's dominion (and which were woven with spells of madness, so that only his ravens and a few of his other servants could pass beyond them). Gauris struck toward the line of muted peaks and followed them southward.

After a few more leagues, he spied a bowl-shaped valley in the mountains. In the valley was a lake; and in the center of the lake, on a jutting spur of rock, was a half-ruined fortress. Smoke belched up from the keep's towers, as if from arcane engines, and steam boiled from the nearby waters of the lake. A crimson flag snapped atop the keep's highest turret, its bloody field marked by a black crown encircling a silver tower. Tiny figures moved outside the walls of the fortress; light glinted off helms and swords.

Gauris didn't know exactly where he would find the one to whom he was to deliver the king's message, but he knew the signs to look for: strife and destruction; smoke and fear. Wherever she was, shadows would gather. He folded his wings and dived toward the fortress below.

Moving so swiftly that the men in the keep's main yard

would perceive nothing more than a dark flicker in the corner of their eyes, Gauris darted through a gap in the side of a crumbling watchtower. He settled on a rotten beam and took care to keep to the gloom of the ruin.

In the yard below, a score of knights marched to the fierce beat of a drum. The knights wore suits of plate armor as black as Gauris's feathers. Each carried a red shield marked with the same black crown and silver tower as the flag above the keep. Broadswords slapped against their thighs.

As the dark column of knights drew near, gaunt men, women hunched in rags, and children with scab-crusted legs hastened to get out of the way, clutching buckets of water or lumps of peat to their chests, their eyes hazed in fear. Puckered brands marked the backs of their hands.

As the knights reached the center of the yard, the gates of the keep flew open, and three more of the onyx warriors thundered through on sooty chargers. The horses pounded to a stop. One of the knights on foot approached the horsemen. Cocking his head, Gauris listened.

"Hail to the glory that once was," said the knight who stood on the ground, holding a fist against his breastplate, voice deep and hollow inside his helm.

One of the horsemen nudged his mount forward and mirrored the salute. "Hail to the glory that will be once more."

Both men lowered their fists.

"Did you find the fugitive's hiding place?"

The horseman grunted in disgust. "The wildmen who follow him are little better than dogs. But they are clever dogs, and there are witches and workers of runes in his band of rabble. There is no telling what tricks and deceptions they have fashioned to hinder us."

"Magic," the other spat. "Such perversions will not be suffered when the ancient order is restored. The witches and runespeakers will be put to the torch, and the land of our ancestors will be polluted no longer. It cannot happen too soon."

"Have faith, brother," the horseman said, laying a gloved hand on the other's shoulder. "The miscreant dared to call himself king of this place. We will find him and his motley band soon enough. And they will pay for their sins."

The men continued to exchange words, but Gauris had heard enough. Before any wandering eyes might notice the shadow in the ruined tower, he sprang from the rafter and darted into the sky. He wondered who these onyx knights were. Surely they were men of war. But in the coming battle, which side did they serve?

It didn't matter. Clearly the one to whom he was to deliver his message was not among them. Gauris flew on.

Again he followed the tumbled line of mountains south, searching for the telltale signs of strife and panic. His wings had begun to ache, but he ignored it. In his younger days, he could have flown twice this far without so much as a twinge.

Far below, the thin line of a road snaked over hills and vales. Gradually the road grew wider, linking together gray blots on the land that Gauris knew to be towns of men. A dark cloud billowed up from one of them. He swooped nearer.

The town burned.

Flames leaped among shabby buildings, consuming thatch roofs, cracking stone walls. Cries of suffering rose with the smoke, along with the ringing of swords. It seemed dark figures moved with swift precision through the streets, although Gauris couldn't be sure; it was hard even for his eyes to pierce the veil of smoke. Besides, his heart told him this was not the place. From what little he knew of the one he sought, such a mean collection of hovels would be far beneath her attention. He rose again toward the sky.

The aching in the raven's wings grew steadily as he flew southward. When he could, he caught an updraft of air, floating upon it for a while so he could rest. Then, when the air shifted, he beat his wings once more. More towns and castles passed below, and stone-walled fields where crops lay rotting. The spidery web of roads that connected the keeps was empty. Then Gauris's black eyes caught a speck of motion. He forced his stiffening wings to bend and wheeled closer.

A line of people moved along the road, three hundred strong, all clad in black. Was this an army of some sort?

No. Gauris circled lower and saw that over half of the people were women and children, and instead of armor they wore robes of rough, black cloth. A feverish light shone in their eyes, so that Gauris wondered if they were refugees of plague. Then he saw the symbol drawn in ashes upon the brow of each man, woman, and child: the shape of a single, staring eye.

So this was an army after all, but an army of pilgrims, not warriors. Their toneless chant rose on the air.

> *drink the ice*
> *breathe the fire*
> *Shadow be your lover*
>
> *chain the mind*
> *still the heart*
> *Darkness rules forever*

Gauris's heart swelled in his breast. Yes, he understood. There was a gate in the northern mountains, a gate of iron a hundred feet high, bound with runes. But soon the last of the hated runes would crack, the gate would open, and the king would at last ride free. Then it would be just as the people chanted. The king would rule forevermore.

Whoever these pilgrims were, surely they were on the side of right in the coming battle. His spirit rising, Gauris forgot the pain in his wings and soared onward.

Just as the sun reached its zenith, the line of mountains he had been following ended in another wall of peaks that ranged east to west. The raven propelled himself upward, then across a bare, rocky highland. The air here was terribly thin, so that he had to beat his wings twice as often just to move the same distance. At last, blood pounding, he spiraled down the other side of the pass, to greener lands below.

He strayed both east and west, searching. Below him, all appeared peaceful and prosperous; these realms had not yet been gripped by early winter and war as had the lands to the north. All the same, Gauris's keen eyes could make out the subtle but unmistakable signs of growing strife. Here and there he paused—on a branch, a window ledge, a stone wall—an unseen shadow, listening.

Atop a hill, hidden in a labyrinth of standing stones, a dozen men gathered. They sat in a circle, naked save for linen kilts, sweating in the heady smoke of herbs thrown on a fire. One of them, a man with powerful arms, wore a wooden mask shaped like the head of a bull. A sword lay across his knees.

"Tell us of the Hammer and the Anvil," the men in the circle said to the one in the mask.

A rumbling voice issued from behind the mask. "The Hammer and the Anvil are the tools of Vathris. With them he will fight the Final Battle, and their deeds will be glorious."

"And when will they come?" the men asked.

"They are already here. At least, so say the priests of the innermost circle. They believe that the Final Battle has already begun."

A thrill ran around the circle.

"Will we win it?" said a young man, gazing into the fire, his beard no more than a soft down on his cheeks.

The one in the bull mask shrugged massive shoulders. "Win or lose, it does not matter. Even in defeat there is glory, if one fights with honor. All who die in the Final Battle will have a place in Vathranan after the world ends. Now, if you would fight for your god, you must draw from yourself the blood of his Bull."

He took up the sword and ran his hand across the edge, so that crimson flowed, staining the steel. He passed the sword to the next man, and the next. All drew blood, the young one with the greatest fierceness of them all. . . .

The raven flew on.

In a castle with nine towers, a king paced and fumed.

"What do you mean she's no longer at Ar-tolor?" the king bellowed.

He was a powerful man, clad in black and silver, his beard glossy with oil. Blue eyes sizzled like lightning. The guardsman took a step back.

"Forgive me, Your Majesty. That is the news brought by Sir Dalmeth, who returned from Toloria not a quarter hour ago."

The king clenched a fist. "Then by all the Seven, where in the Dominions is she?"

The guardsman swallowed. "It seems she's not anywhere in the Dominions, Your Majesty."

The king stopped in his tracks. The mastiffs by the hearth whined and cowered. *"What?"*

"Tarras," the guardsman managed to blurt out. "She went south to Tarras, Your Majesty. With Lord Falken, Lady Melia, and others. Two moons since."

The king's blue eyes narrowed. "It is not like my ward to run off on foolish adventures. At least, it wasn't until she made the acquaintance of Ivalaine. By the Bull, this has the mark of the Witch Queen in it. But I'll put a stop to it." His gaze returned to the guard. "Send a messenger to Tarras at once...."

Still the raven flew on as the sun sank toward the western rim of the world.

Not far from the castle, beyond a circle of standing stones, in a dense fragment of primeval forest, soft lights danced beneath gold and copper trees. High laughter rose on the air, along with wild music and the chiming of bells.

All at once, both laughter and music ceased. Around the eaves of the wood, gangly shadows prowled back and forth, seeking entry. Lights flashed again—brilliant silver now, near the edges of the wood. Shrill cries drifted upward. The shadows retreated; all was still....

Onward the raven flew, each beat of the wings a stab of pain in his breast.

In the grotto of a secret garden, a trio of young women gathered, eyes bright, gowns smudged with dirt, and leaves tangled in their hair. An iron pot suspended from a tripod of green sticks bubbled above a fire.

One of the young women held a handful of leaves above the pot. "How many should I put in, Belira?"

"All of it. And the moonbell root, Carsi."

The other two complied, dropping the herbs into the pot.

"You still haven't told us what this spell will do, Belira."

The brown-eyed one drew closer to the pot, breathed in the fragrant steam. "I learned it from Sister Liendra herself. It's a potion of vision. With it, we might gain a glimpse of one who is far away."

The other two gripped each other, giggling.

"And whom will you see, Belira? Lord Teravian?"

The one called Belira looked up, expression hard. "We haven't spent all day working this spell for girlish fancies. There's another I would see, one of far greater importance. And if we were the ones to find him, surely we would be drawn to the center of the Pattern."

The others frowned prettily. "Whom do you mean?"

The brown-eyed one gazed into the pot and murmured a single word. "Runebreaker..."

Gauris rose upward—then began to sink again. His wings were molten with pain; he could hardly move them. Never had he flown so many leagues in a day. But he had not found her, the one to whom he was to give the king's message. Better to fall than to return to the king's dominion having failed.

As the sun neared the western horizon, a cruel wind rushed over the land. The wind caught him, buffeting him about. By the time he righted himself, he was dizzy and lost. Which way was north? He whirled around, searching...

...and saw a shadow on the land.

It was subtle yet unmistakable: a premature gloom clinging to a hill that should yet be bathed in the last rays of the sun. There could be only one answer; no matter where she went in the light, a tatter of darkness would always follow her.

Gauris fluttered downward. The hill was perfectly circular, its slopes green, its summit crowned by a ring of pitted stones. A burial mound, then, perhaps a relic of the king's first war. Gauris let out a croak of laughter. He should have known he would find her in such a place.

All life and feeling went out of his wings; he could move them no longer. His wheeling descent became a plummet. Just as the bloody circle of the sun touched the horizon, Gauris crashed to the turf in the center of the stone circle. He lay crumpled in a heap of black feathers, dazed, unable to move.

A shadowy figure approached him.

"Well, now what have we here?"

The words were cooing, the voice feminine, but the sound of it was hard and lifeless.

Another figure drew near. "It's just a bird, Shemal. That gust of wind must have caught it and dashed it down. If I'm out here too long, my absence from the castle will be noticed. Toss it down the hill and let it die."

"Truly, Liendra?" crooned the icy voice. "And here all this time I believed you and your sisters considered every living thing precious. I'm so pleased you've shown me otherwise. However, this is certainly not 'just a bird.'"

The one called Shemal knelt beside Gauris, encircled his body with thin fingers, and picked him up. He struggled weakly, then gave up; he did not like being held, but he could not escape her clutch. He craned his head to look at the one who gripped him. All he caught was a fragment of a sharp, white smile inside the heavy black cowl of a robe.

The other, the one called Liendra, stepped closer: a tall, regal woman with red-gold hair, a cloak of pale green thrown over her shoulders against the evening chill.

"Why can you never speak plainly, Shemal? If the bird is important, then tell me."

"Come now, Liendra. I know your magics are feeble compared to those of your sisters. That isn't why I chose you. But surely your spells are enough to sense this is no mundane bird."

Liendra frowned; either she did sense it, or she didn't wish to admit otherwise.

"This raven is one of his messengers," Shemal said, stroking Gauris's feathers. He shuddered under her touch.

"Whose messenger?"

"And now you're willfully misunderstanding. A messenger of the one who will have you trade your heart for iron the moment you show the first sign of weakness."

Liendra shivered despite her cloak, tightening her arms across her breast. "Your master...."

"My master?" Shemal laughed, a sound like glass shattering. "Yes, I suppose he believes he is my master still. But in the end, we both serve the same master, that is all. Sometimes I believe, over the centuries, he has forgotten that—that he has become used to ruling in our master's absence." A colorless eye peered from the cowl of the robe. "And recall, Liendra, my master is your master as well."

Liendra swallowed. "If it is a messenger, then what is its message?"

Shemal stroked Gauris's feathers, harder this time. "Speak, raven. What did your pale master bid you tell me?"

The message. He had to speak the message. Gauris opened his beak, but only a low croak came out.

"Hush," Shemal said, a sound like a flame dying. She pinched his beak shut with two fingers. "You need not bother to speak the words. I know the message he would send me. It has been long years since I have journeyed to his dominion. He bids me go there and abase myself before him, so that he can be certain he rules me still. He, who was born a mortal, while I was once a goddess!"

"Shemal? I . . ."

The robed one shuddered and released Gauris's beak.

"Yes, Liendra. I have not forgotten. It would not do for that wench Ivalaine to discover you here. Soon she will be nothing, a doll for us to play with, but not just yet. So run along to the castle."

"But you haven't told me why you called me here."

Again Shemal laughed. "I fear our feathered interloper has quite distracted me. I simply wished to tell you this, Liendra: I have found the one whom we seek."

Liendra's eyes flashed. She took a step forward, her voice quavering. "You don't mean . . . the Runebreaker?"

"No, not quite. But close. You see, I've found *a* Runebreaker."

Liendra's frown returned. "I don't understand, Shemal. You mean to tell me there's another who can break runes?"

Shemal's voice was triumphant. "Yes, a second Runebreaker! And this one has pledged himself to me."

"But the prophecy of the Witches . . ."

"The prophecy says only that Runebreaker will shatter the world. It does not say which Runebreaker. And now this one is under our control, a tool we can use toward our ends."

Liendra opened her mouth to speak, but Shemal shook her head.

"That's enough, dearest. I will tell you more later, when you have need to know. For now, keep watch over Ivalaine, and if she hears any more from your two sisters in the south, let me know at once."

The sun was gone; dusk had fallen over the mound. Despite

the dimness, Gauris could see the hate in the eyes of the gold-haired woman. Liendra wrapped her cloak more tightly around herself and slipped between two stones, into the gloom.

Shemal held the raven to her breast. "Soon, my little messenger. The signs fall into place. The war comes. But it may not all go as your master believes it will."

Gauris struggled in her grasp. Something was wrong here. He had to return to the north, to tell the king.

The other held him tightly. "No, little brother. I can't let you tell your master what I've spoken here. It wouldn't do. It wouldn't do at all. And you are weary; you have no strength left to fly." Her cold fingers encircled his neck. "It's time for you to rest."

One last time he fought against her, but it was no use. She was right. He was weary, so terribly weary.

The fingers tightened around his neck. A popping sound echoed off the circle of stones. For a moment Gauris flew into an eternal sky of darkness.

Then he was lost.

2.

Grace Beckett had never really believed in fate.

After all, it wasn't fate that brought people through the doors of the Emergency Department of Denver Memorial Hospital. It was cruel luck. They happened to cross a street just as an oncoming driver—who had never been sick a day in his life—had a brain aneurism. Or they didn't notice the electrical cord was frayed as they plugged it in. Or they got a phone call when they were unpacking groceries and forgot to put the box of rat poison they had bought on a shelf where their toddler couldn't reach it. In an instant, for no reason at all, their lives were changed forever.

Nothing was destiny; things simply happened. And if sometimes prophecies came true, it was only because they were self-fulfilling by nature. *Oedipus Rex* wasn't an affirmation of the existence of fate; it was a warning about heeding warnings.

Oedipus would never have killed his father if the seer's words of doom hadn't set the whole thing into motion. The only real fate was what people made for themselves.

At least, that was what Grace had always believed back in Colorado. Only now she knew another world. A world where gods appeared to the naked eye. A world where magic was a force as real as electricity. A world where maybe, just maybe, prophecies really did come true.

It had been over a month since the demon freed by Xemeth was destroyed, transformed to a dead lump of rock by the touch of the Great Stone Sinfathisar. Over a month since they fled the destruction of the Dome of the Etherion only to find that not all of their number were present. And over a month since they had begun the impossible search for those who were lost.

The villa where they had been living stood atop a hill a half league from the outermost wall of Tarras. The tile-roofed building was shaped like a horseshoe, encircling a courtyard filled with fountains and fragrant *lindara* vines, and the entire house was surrounded by a circle of *ithaya* trees that made Grace think of green-gold columns. The emperor had rented the villa for them when he learned of their intention to take rooms at a hostel in the Fourth Circle.

"I won't have my cousin dwelling with the unwashed rabble," Ephesian said, jowls waggling in outrage. He had taken to calling Grace *cousin*, much to her chagrin and—she was forced to admit—her secret delight.

"Nonsense, Your Excellency," Melia said soothingly, "there are a large number of bathhouses in the Fourth Circle, and your subjects appear to be admirably well washed. We shall be quite comfortable at the hostel."

"Absolutely not!" Ephesian pounded the arms of his throne with chubby fists, and his attendants—he was back to eunuchs now, all fully clothed Grace was glad to see—edged away, eyes wide. "You already have something of an irregular reputation, Lady Melia. But for Lady Grace to stay in the Fourth Circle would besmirch the exalted station of the empire."

Melia raised on eyebrow. "You mean unlike the centuries of pillaging, corruption, and slaying of innocents?"

However, despite their protests, there was no swaying Ephesian. Nor was Melia about to give in to his demands; she refused to take an apartment in the First Circle. "You're every bit as bossy as a mother hen, Ephesian. You'd never stop pecking at us if we didn't do exactly as you wished."

It was Grace who finally came up with a compromise. She asked Ephesian if there might be some accommodation outside the city that would be of both appropriate station and suitable distance. After Melia's caustic remark, Ephesian seemed none too keen on the idea of having her nearby, and the idea of the villa was settled on.

"That was very diplomatic of you, Your Majesty," Beltan whispered with a grin as they left the palace.

These words took Grace by surprise. On retrospect, she had to admit it *was* a good solution. Maybe she was better at this whole royalty thing than she gave herself credit for. Maybe it was in her blood.

Sometimes, long before the others awoke, Grace would slip from her bed, part the gauzy curtains that were the only barrier between her and the last breath of night, and step onto a balcony outside the room. She would touch the steel pendant that hung at her neck—a pendant that was in truth a fragment of a sword—and ponder that thought. Could fate really be contained in the suspension of one's blood?

Once there was a patient in the ED whom she diagnosed with symptoms of leukemia. She remembered him clearly. He was one of those big, burly men who moved with exaggerated care, as if afraid he might accidentally break someone. He taught high school, still lived with his elderly mother, and had a gentle laugh. Grace had liked him.

They put him on a list for a bone marrow transplant. But a few months later Grace learned that no donor match was ever found, and he had died. She felt a pang of sorrow, but his fate hadn't been up to her. The answer of whether he would live or die had been locked in his blood, determined by his genetic code, and there was nothing anyone could have done to change it.

Maybe she had been wrong all of those years. Maybe everything really was fate.

For a while Grace would stay there on the balcony, gazing at the distant city. The white houses of Tarras glowed in the ghost light that always came a full hour before the sun, and low in the sky, just visible over the chalky cliffs south of the city, pulsed a single spark of crimson.

The red star.

Once the star had been a harbinger of change and death; it was the Great Stone Krondisar, first raised into the sky by the Necromancer Dakarreth to spread a plague of fire across the land. But Travis Wilder had defeated the Necromancer, and the mute, red-haired girl Tira had taken the Stone and risen to the heavens: a goddess newly born. Now the star was a symbol of hope, and a reminder of a closeness Grace had felt, if only for a fleeting time.

"I love you, Tira," she would whisper.

While it all seemed as if it had happened long ago, the red star had appeared just that spring. It was Sindath now; back in Colorado it would be November. Impossible as it was to believe, it had been barely over a year since she encountered the preacher Brother Cy outside the burnt husk of the Beckett-Strange Home for Children. Barely a year since she came to Eldh.

Came *back* to Eldh.

Whether it's fate or not that you're here, Grace, this is where you belong. You know it is. Just like you know you're going to find them, wherever they are.

She would wait until the red star set beneath the line of the cliffs. Then she would step back inside, to wait for dawn and the others to rise, so they could begin their search anew.

"You never did tell us where you went yesterday, Falken," Melia was saying, as Grace stepped into the courtyard where they gathered for breakfast each morning. It was the ninth day of Sindath. Over a month they had been searching; over a month without any sign.

Melia, clad in a silver-white shift, was filling cups from a pitcher of *margra* juice. She glanced at the bard. "I wasn't even certain you were back."

"He came in late," Beltan said. The blond knight cracked a great yawn. "And might I suggest, the next time you try sneaking across a tile floor, take your boots off first. Or get a pair of sandals, like everyone else in this city."

The knight was dressed in the fashion Tarrasian soldiers adopted when not on duty: sandals, a kilt that reached below the knees, and a loose white shirt.

Falken winced, running his black-gloved hand through his hair. While he wore a long tunic and loose breeches in the Tarrasian fashion, he still hadn't given up his northern-style boots. "Sorry about that. I suppose I was a bit tired myself. I was up in Tyrrinon all day yesterday."

"Tyrrinon?" Aryn said. "Where's that?" The young baroness wore a flowing Tarrasian gown of soft azure that contrasted with her dark hair. She accepted a cup of juice from Melia.

"It's a village a few leagues west of Tarras, dear," Melia said. "It's up in the hills, and other than shepherds and their flocks there's not much there." She shot Falken a speculative look. "Except, of course, for the old monastery of Briel."

"Briel?" Beltan said around a mouthful of bread. "Who's that?"

Grace couldn't help a smile. These days she could hardly keep food down for worry. However, in the year she had known him, no matter what was going on, Beltan's ability to eat never waned. As far as she could tell, the appetite of Calavaner knights was a universal constant.

"Briel is one of the minor gods of Tarras," Falken said.

Melia shot him a piercing look. "Please, Falken. That's such a demeaning term. No god is *minor*."

"Then what term should I use?" the bard said with a scowl.

Melia tapped her cheek. "How about penultimately glorious?"

"How about I just keep talking?"

Melia let out a pained sigh but said nothing more.

"Briel is a minion of Faralas, the god of history," the bard went on. "He's known as the Keeper of Records, and it's said he possesses a book in which he's written down every significant event since the beginning of Tarrasian history. I heard some years ago there was a good library at his monastery in Tyrrinon."

"And was it still there?" Aryn said.

"I'm afraid things were in something of a state of disrepair. It turns out there aren't many monks left at the monastery. I suppose people aren't really all that interested in history these days."

"Which only means they're bound to repeat it," Melia said.

Beltan brushed bread crumbs from his sparse gold beard. "Falken, you still didn't say what you were looking for in the Library of Briel. Was it something about gates?" A light glinted in his green eyes. "Something that might help us find—?"

"No," Grace said, the smile falling from her lips. "It was Mohg, Lord of Nightfall."

The others looked up, faces startled.

"Good morning, dear," Melia said, recovering first. "There's hot *maddok* for you."

Aryn's sapphire eyes were concerned as her voice sounded in Grace's mind. *Are you all right, sister?*

"I'm fine," Grace said aloud. While Lirith and Aryn seemed comfortable speaking across the Weirding when others were present, Grace avoided it if she could. Despite what King Boreas might think, she really wasn't all that adept at intrigue; it took so much more energy than being obvious.

She sat down—adjusting the folds of her gown, which was similar to Aryn's but a pale green—and poured a cup of *maddok*, breathing in the slightly spicy fragrance. Only after she took a sip did she realize that the others were still gazing at her. She glanced at Falken. "You were hoping to learn something more about Mohg, weren't you? Something that could help prevent his returning to Eldh."

Falken nodded, his faded blue eyes grave. The sun in the courtyard seemed to go thin. Grace could feel it: the shadow attached to the thread of her life. They all had their shadows, she knew. She had passed through hers when the demon tried to consume her, and while she hadn't defeated it, it was behind her now. The shadow might have made her who she was, but it was up to her to determine what she would be.

However, in passing through her shadow, she had exhumed memories she had forgotten as a means to survive, memories from twenty years ago: the night the orphanage had burned down. She knew now what she had seen that night. The orphanage's cook, Mrs. Fulch, being made into an ironheart. The bright, baleful form of the wraithling. And the figure emblazoned on the tapestry in the forbidden upstairs room: ancient, primal, its one staring eye filled with desire and hate.

It was Mohg, Lord of Nightfall. The Old God who feared the coming of men and tried to claim Eldh for his own, only to be banished from the world by the alliance of the Old and New Gods—an alliance that could never happen again, for the Old Gods had since faded into the Twilight Realm. Somehow Mohg had found his way to Earth; his likeness in the Beckett-Strange Home for Children had proved that. He sought to use Earth as a bridge to Eldh, to lay claim to it once again, and to cast it under the gloom of night forever.

"Well," Melia said, regarding Falken, "did you find anything at the library?"

He gazed into his empty cup. "Nothing that we don't already know: how Mohg drank the blood of the dragon Hriss to gain the dark wisdom of how to claim Eldh for his own; how he tried to reach the Dawning Stone, to break the First Rune and remake Eldh in his image; and how the New Gods and Old Gods banded together, tricking Mohg into stepping beyond the circle of the world, then closing the way behind him, banishing him forever."

Aryn clutched her good left arm around herself, shivering despite the sunshine. "Only he wasn't banished forever. Not if he finds a way back."

Beltan wrapped his arm around her shoulders. "Don't worry about what hasn't happened yet, cousin. Mohg won't get back—not if Falken has his way."

A small, black form hopped up onto the table—Melia's kitten. Somehow, Grace had gotten used to the fact that the kitten never seemed to get a day older. Its golden eyes gleamed as it started stalking toward a bowl of milk. Melia picked the kitten up, and it let out a petulant *mew*.

"So you found nothing else, then?" Melia said, petting the kitten as it struggled to get free. "I thought Briel would be a better record keeper than that."

The bard grunted. "You're not the only one. Most of the books were falling apart or never finished at all. And there was one thing I found especially confusing. In the oldest of the books that recounted the story of Mohg, there was a passage that mentioned 'those who were lost beyond the circle.' But the book never said who they were. Do you have any idea what it might mean?"

Melia lifted the wriggling kitten to her cheek; the little creature seemed to forget its displeasure and began to purr. "I'm not certain. As far as I know, none of the gods were slain in the war against Mohg. At least, none of the New Gods. The Old Gods were so strange and distant to us. Even though we worked with them, we understood them little. Then, so soon after the war, they faded away, back to their Twilight Realm. I suppose it's possible some Old Gods perished in the battle, and that we didn't even know about it."

Falken scratched his chin—in need of a shave, as usual. "Maybe," he said, but that was all.

They finished breakfast, then made their plans for the day. Melia mentioned that a message from the emperor had arrived just after dawn, inviting them to the palace tomorrow night.

Falken rolled his eyes. "I haven't been to so many feasts since we stayed at King Kel's court."

"Or seen such poor manners," Melia said with a look of displeasure.

"Please," Falken snorted. "That's an insult to Kel's wildmen. Have you seen how Ephesian's courtiers eat? It must be high fashion to forgo using a napkin in Tarras."

Aryn shuddered. "Don't remind me! My hand was so sticky after the Minister of the Treasury kissed it that I had to peel it away from his lips."

Grace supposed the invitation was largely her fault. In the absence of Lirith, it had been up to her to fulfill Ephesian's ravenous new appetite for knowledge about morality and virtue. Grace wasn't certain she was the best model in those topics, but she had enlisted Aryn's help, and the emperor had gobbled up everything they had to tell him. Unfortunately, Ephesian had had a more difficult time convincing the members of his court—or the staff of his kitchens—of the value of moderation.

"I really don't see what you people have against feasts,"

Beltan said in a wounded tone. "What could be wrong with eating until you burst?"

Melia patted the big knight's hand. "I think you just answered your own question, dear."

"Besides," Grace said softly, "we have other things to do."

At once Beltan's visage grew solemn. He nodded, as did the others. It was time to start searching again.

In the ED, Grace had seen cases of phantom limbs: amputees who still felt the pain of appendages that were no longer there. In a way, what they were feeling was the same. Every time they sat at the table, it was agonizingly clear that some who should be there were not.

What had happened those last seconds in the Etherion, they could only conjecture. The dome had been on the verge of collapse. Trapped on the other side of a chasm, Travis, Lirith, Durge, and Sareth had intended to use the gate artifact and a drop of blood from the Scarab of Orú to make their escape. But as Grace and the others waited outside, the four never appeared. Vani said transport through the gate was instantaneous. Which meant something had gone wrong.

For a fortnight she had feared there hadn't been enough time, that the Etherion had come crashing down upon the four before they had a chance to activate the gate. But the emperor's army of laborers had worked swiftly, carting away the broken rubble of the Etherion so it could be built anew. Dozens of bodies were found in the destruction, some human, some not. But there had been no sign of Travis, Lirith, Durge, or Sareth.

Which means they made it through the gate, Grace. They're alive, they have to be.

But where? The gate artifacts had the power to whisk one between worlds, and with blood as powerful as that in the scarab, there was no telling where the four had ended up.

As servants—more gifts from the emperor—cleared away the remains of breakfast, Melia announced she was going to visit the temple of Mandu the Everdying. Some of the gods had begun to accept followers of Ondo, Sif, Geb, and Misar into their temples, which meant the lost sheep no longer needed Mandu to care for them.

"Mandu's work is nearly done," Melia said, "and I fear when it is, he'll pass on to another circle. I need to talk to him before he goes. He might have some wisdom that can help guide us in our own search."

Aryn, in turn, said she intended to visit the witches of Tarras that day. She had sought them out a few weeks before, in the grotto where Lirith had first found them.

It had been difficult for the young baroness to get close to the witches, for they were secretive—there in a city that did not favor the old ways like those of Sia—but gradually she had gained the trust of Thesta, the leader of the coven. Several in the coven possessed the Sight, and Aryn hoped they might have seen something in their dreams.

The baroness sighed. "If only I had the Sight like Lirith, maybe I would have seen something myself."

Grace squeezed her good hand. Aryn had her own powers, ones that seemed to grow by leaps and bounds every day.

"Grace," Falken said, "do you think I could borrow your necklace again today? Just for a little while?"

Twice before, Falken had asked to study the steel shard of her necklace. Grace wondered what he did with it. He had said he was going to spend the day examining some of the notes he made at the Library of Briel. What did that have to do with her necklace? Grace didn't know, but all the same she carefully removed the necklace and handed it to Falken. She felt strangely naked without it.

Beltan was looking at her, his expression serious but eager. "Are we going to the university again today?"

She drew in a deep breath, gathering her strength, knowing she was going to need it. "If you'll come with me."

"Lead the way, my lady."

3.

The University of Tarras occupied almost an entire quadrant of the city's Second Circle. At first, when passing the high arch of its gates on the way to and from visiting the emperor, Grace had mistaken the precisely arranged quadrant of buildings—with their columned facades, elaborate friezes, and plethora of marble statuary—for a complex of temples. It was only one day when she stopped to ask a man approaching the gates to which god these temples were sacred that she learned the truth.

Since that day, Grace had come to the university several times a week. Ephesian had given her a gold ring marked with the signet of the empire: three trees crowned by five stars. The ring possessed near-magical abilities to open doors in Tarras. The gatekeeper of the university had looked at her in suspicion when she first requested entrance. However, one flash of the ring, and he had hurriedly escorted her inside.

On her first few visits, Grace had been content just to wander, eavesdropping on scholarly debates or speaking to those students or professors who seemed amenable to interruption. She soon gathered there were four main colleges in the university, each centered around one general topic: rhetoric, logic, mathematics, and history. While all of the colleges interested Grace, it was to the College of History that she directed her attention. It was the smallest of the four, located on the south end of the quadrant.

In the college's library, she discovered its focus was history in the broadest sense: both natural and civilized. Many of the library's tomes and treatises concerned biology, comparative anatomy, and a rudimentary kind of chemistry. In addition, a large portion of the library was devoted to a collection of animal specimens that had been caught over the centuries and preserved for study. Grace opened drawer after drawer, encountering the skins and blindly staring skulls of animals she could not name, and which looked almost but not quite like primates, rodents, and marsupials.

The faunas of Earth and Eldh are similar, Grace. Too similar. There's simply no way they could have evolved this closely in parallel. But certainly things here have diverged, just like the animals of Australia did in isolation from the rest of the continents.

But if it was true that the creatures of Earth and Eldh had diverged, then it was also true they shared a common ancestry. So when were the faunas of the two worlds exchanged?

Intriguing as that question was, Grace forced herself to shut the specimen drawers and focus instead on the shelves of books. Her reason for coming to the university was simple: to learn something that could help them discover what had happened to Travis and the others.

She spent days poring through tome after tome. Grace was particularly interested in any book that concerned the history of the southern continent of Moringarth and the ancient city-states of Amún. Morindu the Dark had been one of those city-states, and it was the sorcerers of Morindu who first learned of the world beyond the void—the world Earth—and created the gate artifacts to get there.

Why they had wanted to find a way to Earth, Grace had no idea. Nor did the Mournish seem to know the answer—at least not any they had voiced—and they were the descendants of the people of Morindu. But it didn't matter. Grace just wanted to learn more about how the gate artifacts functioned, not why they were created.

Grace was surprised when, after her first few visits to the university, Beltan asked if he could help her. It wasn't that she didn't care for his company; it was simply that she knew the knight's career had left him little time for more scholarly pursuits. However, once she recovered from her astonishment, she gladly accepted his help.

Now, as they once again sat at a long table scattered with books they had pulled from dusty shelves, Grace regarded the big man. A hand held his thinning, white-blond hair back from his high forehead, which was furrowed in concentration. His lips were moving, and Grace knew he was sounding out the words scribed by hand on the page before him.

Beltan was literate, but only barely. Of course, even that was something of an accomplishment for a man of war living in a medieval world. However, Grace had spent some time coaching him, and since then his reading had improved rapidly. His eyes moved eagerly over the page. Whatever Beltan thought of himself, he was not stupid. Still, Grace wondered why he really wanted to join her on her forays to the university.

Maybe he's coming for the same reason you are, Grace. To

have something to do that at least seems constructive, even if it's a long shot.

Tired of her own book, and having found nothing in it about gates, Grace rested her chin on a hand, watching the knight. "So, are you planning to trade in your sword for a student's robe?"

He looked up with a grin. Beltan's face was plain except when he smiled, and then it became brilliantly handsome. "I just might at that," he said, then bent back over his book.

Smiling, Grace returned her attention to the tome before her. Beltan wasn't the only one whose reading skills were improving. While it was still easier to read when the silver half-coin was about her person, she found that even without it she could pick her way through just about any book in the library, even those written in archaic dialects. What's more, she was nearly fluent in spoken Eldhish now, although one day when she experimented with this, Beltan told her she had a peculiar accent.

"It's like you're talking with your nose pinched shut. Underwater. And with a mouthful of bread. But otherwise you sound wonderful, Grace."

After that, she stuck to keeping the half-coin in the small pouch at her belt—although it was nice to know she'd be able to make do in a pinch.

A thought occurred to her. The silver half-coin granted her the ability to speak Eldhish. And she knew the fairy blood Beltan had been infused with, and which had healed him, had also allowed him to speak English when he was in Denver.

So maybe his newfound skill at reading isn't exactly a co-incidence, Grace.

As the sun crept across the mosaic floor, and students in brown robes shuffled quietly in and out of the library, Grace worked her way through several more tomes, including *The Rise and Fall of Amún, The God Kings: Holy Tyrants of the South,* and *Blood Ritual in the City States of Moringarth—Myth or Magic?* However, as interesting as some of them were, none contained anything about gate artifacts.

At last, head aching and eyes bleary, she shoved aside the books. How many tomes had she read these last weeks? A hundred? Whatever the number, it was only a fraction of what lined the precisely organized shelves that were the antithesis of Falken's description of the Library of Briel. There was so much knowledge here—there had to be something that would help them. They just needed a better system for finding it.

"I wish Durge were here," she said, not realizing she had spoken aloud until Beltan looked up.

"It's all right, Grace." He reached across the table, covering her hand with his. It was large and marked with white scars. "We'll find them somehow."

Grace smiled, and amazingly the expression wasn't forced. The knight's strength these last weeks had been a crutch all of them had leaned upon. Beltan loved Travis; the knight should have been a wreck. Only somehow he wasn't.

After they returned to Eldh, after the fairy healed him, Beltan had been empty and broken, consumed by the shadow of his past, whatever it was. She knew only that it had to do with someone the knight said he had slain; although, as a warrior, certainly he had been forced to kill many in battle. Yet ever since they faced the demon in the Etherion, it seemed Beltan had left his shadow behind him just as Grace had. Now the knight was as bright and full of humor as she remembered him, as if Travis's vanishing had not caused despair, but instead had granted him new life and purpose.

What knight doesn't need a quest, Grace? And now he has one: to find Travis, no matter what it takes.

No matter the reason for his transformation, it was good to have the old Beltan back. Although, whether it was the strange blood that now ran in his veins or something else he had gained along the way, there were changes in the knight. Sometimes she could glimpse the hidden light of his face even when he wasn't smiling, and there was a depth to his green eyes she had never seen before.

He cocked his head, and only then did she realize she had been staring.

"What is it, Grace?"

She fumbled for words. "It's nothing. I was just—"

"You can see it, can't you?" His words were soft. "But I suppose it makes sense. After all, you saw it in me before, on the road to Spardis. My shadow."

She shook her head. "Beltan, you don't have to—"

"No, it's all right, Grace. The past doesn't own us. That's what we learned in the Etherion, isn't it? And I think I've wanted to tell someone for a while now. I think maybe I have to."

Grace couldn't move. The knight tightened his grip on her hand. He didn't look at her as he spoke, but instead at a half circle of cobalt sky outside a high window.

"For so many years, I searched for the man who murdered my father, King Beldreas. I suppose I thought if I avenged his death, I might somehow finally win his approval. Vathris knows, I never could seem to get it when he was alive, as much as I longed for it. Only then, in Spardis, I learned the truth. I had known my father's murderer all along. You see, it was me."

For several hushed minutes, Grace listened, frozen, as the knight described what the Necromancer Dakarreth had revealed to him in the baths beneath Castle Spardis: how the Pale King had ordered Dakarreth to go forth and sow strife in the Dominions; how Dakarreth had stolen into Beltan's dreams, compelling the knight to take up a knife and drive it into his father's back; and how, as he reopened Beltan's old wound, the Necromancer had at last let Beltan relive the terrible moment in his memories.

The knight fell silent, and Grace found the power to move, laying her other hand atop his. "Oh, Beltan . . ."

He shook his head. "Don't worry, Grace. I know it wasn't my fault. I was just a sword in Dakarreth's hand; he was the killer, not me. And no man could have resisted the Necromancer, not even Falken. After all, he did something to Falken's hand a long time ago. Well, this is what he did to me. But I won't let Dakarreth win, not after Travis gave up everything to defeat him."

Despite her sorrow, Grace found herself smiling. How could she not? Beltan had every reason for rage, or despair, or madness. Instead, he had chosen life and love.

The knight pulled his hand from hers and gently brushed a tear from her cheek. "You'd better stop that, Grace. The librarian will toss you out if you get one of his books wet. You saw the fit he threw when I brought that bottle of wine in. Now, let's get some more books so we can keep working."

The knight scooped up an armful of volumes and headed across the library. Grace drew in a breath, then rose and turned around.

And found herself gazing into a pair of golden eyes.

A woman stepped from the shadow between two bookcases, into a beam of honey-colored light. As always, she wore clinging black leather, and her dark hair was slicked back from the striking oval of her face.

"Vani," Grace breathed. "How long have you been there?"

"Not... long."

Grace studied the Mournish woman. She knew Vani was a princess, descended from the royal line of the city Morindu the Dark. And she was also *T'gol*—an assassin, trained since childhood in the art of killing others.

"You heard everything, didn't you?" Grace said.

"I did."

Grace licked her lips. "You have to understand, Vani. It wasn't his fault. Just because he—"

Vani held up a hand. "I will not judge him for his deed. That is not for me to do."

Grace winced. Like Beltan, Vani loved Travis—although for different reasons. For the knight, it was a matter of his heart. For Vani, it was a matter of fate. And they had both lost him.

A weight pressed down on Grace. She turned away. "Beltan is a good man, Vani."

"I know."

They were silent for a time.

"The Mournish will be leaving Tarras soon," Vani said at last. "They usually travel farther south this time of year, to the cities south of Tarras."

Grace turned back, startled. "Are you going with them?"

Vani smiled, but it was a bitter expression. "I would think my fate lies with you and your companions. If you will have me, that is."

Whatever the tension between the *T'gol* and Beltan, Vani was her friend. Grace felt an impulse to rush over and catch the other in an embrace, but she supposed making sudden moves around an assassin wasn't a good idea. She settled for a warm grin instead. "I'm glad you're not leaving."

Vani moved to the table and brushed a finger across one of the open books. "You seek knowledge of the gates in these?"

"We're trying," Grace said.

"The sorcerers of Morindu kept their secrets close. It's not likely you'll find revelations here, however old these may be."

Grace let out a sigh. "I know. But I have to do something. I suppose I was just hoping."

Again a smile touched Vani's lips, only this time it seemed a secret expression. "There is always hope."

The two spoke for a few more minutes, and Grace learned that the Mournish intended to have one more feast before they packed their wagons and began their wandering once more. Vani's al-Mama had invited Grace and the others to the Mournish camp the next night to take part in the festivities. Grace accepted the invitation, knowing they could all use a break. Besides, it would give them a reason to decline the emperor's invitation.

"We'll see you tomorrow night," Grace said.

The dusty library air was already rippling, folding back in on itself. Vani was gone.

Beltan was still off somewhere putting away books. Grace picked up a stack to do the same. She wandered through the dim rows of bookcases, making sure she put each tome back in its proper space, fearing what one of the librarians would do to her if she didn't, emperor's ring or no. Soon she had one book left. After much searching, she found the gap on the shelf where it belonged. She slid the thick volume into place.

Or at least she tried to. The book stopped with two inches to go. Grace pushed, but the book wouldn't slide in any farther. Now that she thought about it, it was because the book had been sticking out slightly that it had caught her eye in the first place. She pulled the tome back out and peered into the gap.

Something was in there. Grace reached in, and her fingers found something flat and hard. She pulled it out. It was a book.

She convulsed in a powerful sneeze. *Make that a dusty book.*

She set down the other tome and regarded the volume she

had pulled from the gap. It was uncharacteristically slim. She supposed it had gotten pushed behind the others on the shelf and lost there. A long time ago, by the looks of it. Grace used a corner of her gown to wipe the dust from the leather cover. On it, written in tarnished gold, was the title *Pagan Magics of the North*.

She flipped through the yellowed pages. All the books she had looked at so far were composed in a bold, blotchy, flowery script on thick vellum, but this book was penned on crisp, smooth paper in a spidery but even hand. A few words caught her eye as the pages fluttered past: *Malachor, Runelords, Eversea* ...

"What have you got there, Grace?"

She turned around. Beltan's face was smudged with book dust, and his green eyes were curious.

"I'm not exactly sure," she said. "It was lost behind the other books on the shelf. And it's not a history of Tarras. It seems to be about myths and legends of the north."

"That's probably why it was lost. I don't know if you've noticed, but these Tarrasians seem to think they're the center of the world."

"That's probably because, for a millennium, they were."

Beltan grunted. "Old habits die hard."

Grace glanced out one of the high windows. The sky was fading to slate; it was time to go. However, she was loath to leave this book. What if one of the librarians filed it away in a place where she couldn't find it? True, she was searching for knowledge of the south, not the north. All the same, her hand tingled as she pressed it against the cover.

"I'm going to check out this book," she decided aloud.

Beltan raised an eyebrow. "Check it out? What does that mean?"

"I mean borrow it," Grace said, heading toward the main desk near the entrance of the library.

Beltan gave her a sly wink. "Now I get it." He dropped his voice to a whisper. "I'll just create a little distraction while you make off with the book."

She shot him a horrified look. "Beltan!"

Several students and a passing librarian looked up as her

voice echoed throughout the library. Grace winced and steered Beltan quickly away.

"Listen to me," she said, this time keeping her voice low. "I am *not* stealing the book. So no distractions of any kind. Do you understand?"

The blond knight looked slightly hurt. "Whatever you say, my lady. But if you get caught pilfering, don't blame me."

They had reached the front desk; there was no more time for whispers. Grace handed the book to one of the librarians behind the expanse of glossy wood.

"I'd like to borrow this please."

The librarian took the tome. "What is this?" She flipped through the book, and her pinched face grew even tighter. "Wizards? Spells? Dragons? I had no idea there was such rubbish in this library. I'll take care of this."

She started to turn away, but Grace was faster, snatching the book out of her hand.

"If I could just check it out now," Grace said, trying to sound demure.

The librarian's eyes narrowed. "You're not a student here, are you? Do you have a library token?"

Grace swallowed hard. "No, but I do have this." She lifted her right hand, displaying Ephesian's gold ring.

The librarian appeared unimpressed. "Madam, even the emperor himself cannot borrow a book without a library token. You'll have to petition the archdean for a token and come back—"

"Wait," Grace said. She hated to do this, but there was no choice. "I forgot. I do have a token. Right here."

Hastily she reached out with her mind and touched the Weirding—the shining web of power that flowed through all things. She wove several threads together into a hasty spell and held out her hand.

The librarian blinked, staring at Grace's outstretched hand, then gave a curt nod.

"So you have a token after all." Her dry voice bore a note of disappointment. "Very well, you may borrow the book. But you must sign for it first."

With a quill pen, Grace scratched her name and the title of

the book on a piece of parchment, then turned, leaving the fussy librarian at her desk.

"What just happened back there?" Beltan said, as they stepped out the door of the library. "Your hand was empty, but she acted like she was seeing exactly what she wanted to see."

Grace could still feel the faint hum of power in her hand. "So she did."

Beltan gave her a sharp look. "And using magic is different from stealing how, my lady?"

Grace laughed and took the knight's arm. "It's far more polite," she said, and they started across the university grounds as purple dusk fell.

4.

It was late, and Grace's head ached.

She lifted her gaze from the book on the table and rubbed the back of her neck. Her eyes seemed to have forgotten how to focus. The others had gone to their rooms an hour before, and Grace knew she should go to sleep as well if she intended to have the energy for the next day's revel with the Mournish.

At supper, she had told the others of Vani's visit at the library. When she mentioned that the Mournish woman would not be leaving with her people, Beltan had turned away, so that Grace could not read his expression. As if she would have had the power anyway. She was still a neophyte when it came to the subject of human emotion, and unlike medicine or history, it was not something she could learn in a book.

Grace had planned to show *Pagan Magics of the North* to Falken, but he had spent the day going over the notes he had made at the Library of Briel, only without much to show for it. After accepting her necklace back, she decided to show him the book in the morning. Providing he woke in a better mood.

A warm zephyr fluttered the gauzy curtains. Outside the window, Grace could see a pulsing crimson spark low in the sky. Tira's star was rising, beginning its nightly sojourn across the heavens.

Just one more page, Grace. Then bed. Doctor's orders.

Falken had told them much of the War of the Stones, and Malachor, and the Runelords. However, the book contained more details than Falken's stories. She was especially fascinated by references to Eversea—a land far to the west in Falengarth, where it was said many who fled the destruction of Malachor went after that kingdom fell. Could it be that people of Malachor—distant cousins of hers—still dwelled there?

Another question occurred to her. She doubted any of the scholars at the University of Tarras were experts in northern mythology. So who had written this book? The binding seemed somewhat newer than the rest of the volume; Grace suspected the title page had been lost when the book was rebound, along with the identity of the author. Regardless, it was riveting. Stifling a yawn, Grace flipped the page.

The yawn became a gasp.

It was faint, faded by time, but clear. Someone had marked in the book with what looked like black pencil. A brief passage of text was underlined:

> *...that gods, dragons, and witches of the Sight have all foretold his coming. The one named Runebreaker will shatter the rune Eldh, which was the First Rune spoken by the Worldsmith, who bound it in the Dawning Stone at the very beginning of the world. And so the First Rune shall also be the Last Rune, for when it breaks, the world shall end....*

Disturbing as they were, it was not these lines that froze Grace's blood. Instead, it was the three words penciled hastily, almost desperately, in the margin next to them:

IS IT ꟻATE?

"No," Grace whispered. "No, it can't be."

She dug in the pouch tied to her sash, pulled out the silver half-coin, and shoved it across the table. Again she looked at the book. Even though she could still read it with effort, the text on the page was now strange and archaic-looking, written in Eldhish letters. But the penciled words were written in English.

Eyes wide, Grace looked up. This was impossible. And there was something else. There was something about the words in the margin—the way the letters were shaped—that disturbed her even more. Only what was it? She stared at the window, thinking. Outside, the red star gazed back like a fiery eye.

The eye blinked shut.

Paralyzed, Grace kept watching, waiting for the crimson spark to shimmer back to life.

Nothing happened. Dread flooded her chest. Trembling, she rose and moved to the window. There were no clouds. The moon was a great sickle, and stars scattered the night sky like shimmering chaff. But where the crimson spark had shone moments ago there was only a black void in the heavens.

The red star—Tira's star—had vanished.

Grace jumped at a sharp knock on the door. After a moment she gathered her wits enough to stumble to the door and fling it open. It was Falken.

"Melia wants you. Downstairs." The bard's eyes were every bit as startled as she knew her own to be.

They found Melia at the table where they took their meals when rain precluded dining in the courtyard. The lady looked up, the expression in her amber eyes far too deep for Grace to fathom. Aryn and Beltan appeared moments later.

The knight yawned. He was clad only in a long nightshirt. "What's going on? I was dreaming about ale. And not the feeble stuff they make down here, mind you, but real, Galtish ale—the kind that socks you in the gut, then picks you up off the floor, puts a strong arm around you, and walks you back to the bar, grinning all the way."

Aryn adjusted the diaphanous robe she had thrown on and frowned at the blond man. "Are you sure you weren't dreaming about Galtish men rather than Galtish ale?"

"Either way, I'd still rather be sleeping."

"What's going on, Melia?" Falken said.

Melia's visage was tightly drawn. "I was hoping Grace might have an idea."

Aryn glanced at Grace. *What is it, sister?*

"Tira's star," Grace croaked aloud, struggling for breath. "It's gone."

They talked as the crescent moon arced outside the high windows. Melia's kitten soon made an appearance, prowling across the table, begging affection from each of them in turn. At some point the servants must have come in, for cups and a steaming pot of *maddok* appeared on the table. Grace gladly accepted a cup when Aryn handed her one. Despite the balmy night, she felt cold.

Of them all, only Grace had actually been gazing at the red star the moment it vanished—although Melia had evidently noticed its disappearance within moments, given how quickly Falken came to Grace's door. Unfortunately, none of them had an explanation for what had happened.

Aryn's blue eyes were bright with worry. "You don't think . . . you don't think Tira is . . ."

"She's a goddess, dear," Melia said, her tone reassuring. "I'm sure she's fine."

Beltan scratched his chin. "What about the Stone of Fire? Tira was supposed to protect it. What if she's lost it? That would be bad, right?"

"More than bad," Falken said. "It would be disastrous. The Pale King still seeks the Stones of Fire and Twilight to set beside the Stone of Ice in the iron necklace Imsaridur. And his master, Mohg, is trying to get back to Eldh. There's no doubt this comes at a dark time."

Melia looked at Grace. "You were gazing out the window at the time, dear. Did you see anything strange in the moments before the star vanished? Anything that might have presaged what happened?"

Grace wished she had, but she shook her head. "I was reading a book I borrowed from the university. My eyes were tired, and I looked out the window to rest them. I saw Tira's star. And then it was . . . gone."

Falken gave her a sharp look. "What book were you reading?"

"It's called *Pagan Magics of the North*. I was going to show it to you earlier, only after the Library of Briel you didn't seem in a very probook mood."

Falken grunted. "I can't argue with you there. But I have to say, I know most of the books ever written about northern magic, and I've never heard of that one. Could I look at it?"

Glad to have something to do, Grace hurried upstairs and retrieved the book. She returned to the others and handed it to Falken. The bard turned it in his hands and thumbed through the pages. Grace explained how she had found it.

"Interesting," he said with a frown that said *strange*. "The text is definitely written in High Malachorian. But I've never seen paper of such fine quality, and the binding is Tarrasian. I doubt *Pagan Magics of the North* was the volume's original title. It's far too condescending to be anything but the creation of a Tarrasian scholar. I suppose whoever renamed the volume tossed out the original title page." He shut the book. "I doubt we'll ever know who wrote it, but it does look interesting. Would you mind if I borrowed it, Grace?"

"No, but there's something I want you to look at, something I saw just before the red star vanished." She sat next to him and tried to keep her hands from shaking as she turned to the last page she had been reading.

Falken's eyebrows drew down in a glower. "I find it despicable when people mark up books that aren't their own. And what's this written here in the margin? It's gibberish."

Grace reached into the pouch at her sash and took out the silver half-coin. "Here," she said, pressing the coin into Falken's hand. "Now read it."

He glanced again at the book, and his eyes went wide. He looked up at Grace. "It can't be."

"What does it read, Falken?" Melia asked.

Grace licked her lips. "It reads, 'Is it fate?' The words are written next to a passage about the prophecy of the one called Runebreaker."

Aryn sat up straight. "Runebreaker?"

"Yes, but that's not what's important. What's important is that—"

Falken brushed the page. "—the first letter of 'fate' is written backward."

Beltan leaped to his feet and pounded the table. "By the blood of the Bull, it's Travis! He's a mirror reader—you said so yourself, Falken. And this was written backward. It has to be him. He's in Tarras somewhere."

"Calm yourself," Falken said in a warning tone. "We don't know for certain that Travis wrote this."

Except Grace knew the bard didn't believe that. A note in English with one of the letters reversed, scribbled next to a passage about Runebreaker. Who else could it be but Travis? Only how could he have written a note in a book that had obviously been lost for years at the University of Tarras?

Grace took the half-coin back from Falken, then flipped to the front of the book. A slip of paper was pasted inside the cover. On it, the librarian had written the date Grace was to return the book to the library—a fortnight hence. Above it, crossed out, was a list of previous due dates. Grace looked at the one just above hers in the list.

Durdath the Second, in the thirty-seventh year of the blessed rule of His Eminence, Ephesian the Sixteenth.

A gasp came from behind Grace. It was Melia; she had risen to read over Grace's shoulder.

"But that's impossible," the lady said. "The sixteenth Ephesian died well over a century ago."

Some of Beltan's exuberance gave way to confusion. "What are you talking about, Melia? Even I know Travis couldn't have written something in a book that's been lost behind a shelf for more than a hundred years."

"No," Melia murmured. "No, I don't suppose he could have."

More conversation and cups of *maddok* ensued. However, at the end of it all, they were no closer to unraveling either mystery. They could only guess why Tira's star had vanished—and could only hope both the child goddess and the Stone of Fire were still somehow safe.

"Maybe the star will rise again tomorrow," Aryn said, but even the young baroness seemed unconvinced by the hopefulness of those words.

Somewhere in the distance, a rooster crowed. Outside the windows, the moon and stars had vanished, replaced by flat blue light. Aryn was nodding in her chair, and Falken wrapped his faded cloak around her shoulders.

"Come, Your Highness," he murmured, rousing her with a gentle shake. "It's long past time for bed."

Grace pushed a half-finished cup of *maddok* away. Her nerves buzzed like wires. Exhausted as she was, there would be no sleep for her.

Melia glanced at Beltan. "I know you're no longer officially my knight protector, dear. But would you mind helping a weary former goddess up the stairs?"

Beltan nodded and moved to her. However, his green eyes were haunted, and Grace knew of whom he was thinking.

She pushed herself up from the table. "I think I'll go see if the milk has been delivered yet."

Grace had found it amusing when she discovered that, just like on Earth in a bygone era, clay jugs of milk and cream were delivered to the villa's doorstep each morning. She knew the servants would be tired from having to stay up so late serving *maddok*; if the milk had arrived, she could take it to the larder in the kitchen and save them some work.

As Melia and Beltan followed Falken and Aryn to the stairs, Grace headed for the front door of the villa. She pushed back the iron latch and opened the door, letting in the moist grayness of morning. She looked down. Something indeed lay on the doorstep, only it wasn't a jug of milk. It was a man in a brown robe.

"Beltan!" she called out on instinct.

In moments the knight was there. "What is it, Grace?"

She knelt beside the figure that slumped facedown on the stone step. Beltan let out an oath, then knelt beside her. Grace was dimly aware of the others standing in the open doorway, but she focused on the man before her.

His brown robe was rent in several places, and the fabric was damp with blood, but he was breathing. She pressed two fingers to his wrist. His pulse was weak but even. All of her senses told her his injuries were not critical. But he was cold, suffering from exposure.

And how is that possible, Grace? It barely got down to room temperature during the night. A naked baby could have slept outside and been fine.

That thought could wait until she was sure the patient was

out of danger. She started to turn him over so she could check for more wounds.

"Beltan, help me."

With strong, gentle hands, he turned the man over while she held his head steady. The front of his robe wasn't torn; whatever had caused the injuries had come at him from behind. A heavy cowl concealed his face. Grace pushed it back.

For the third time since the sun last set, shock coursed through her. He was a young man, mid-twenties at the most, his eyes shut. His face was broad, with a flat, crooked nose and thick, rubbery lips. However, despite its homeliness, there was a peace about his visage that was compelling.

"By Vathris, I recognize him!" Beltan said, and by the gasps of the others they did as well.

But how can it be, Grace? He helped you save Travis from being burned by the Runespeakers at the Gray Tower. Only then he vanished, and you never saw him again.

Until now.

Grace brushed damp hair from his heavy brow, and his brown eyes fluttered open. For a moment she saw fear in them, then they focused on her, and his lips parted in a grin. He mouthed the words *Lady Grace*, and she glimpsed the stump that was all that remained of his tongue.

He lifted bloodied hands, moving them in a gesture that communicated with uncanny eloquence. *Good morrow, my lady. I hope you'll forgive my appearance.*

Grace didn't know if he meant his sudden arrival, or the state of his robes. Nor did it matter. This was utterly impossible. But maybe that was all right; maybe sometimes the impossible did happen.

She flung her arms around Sky's thick shoulders and laughed.

5.

If he didn't look too hard, Travis Wilder could almost believe he was finally, impossibly home.

Panting for breath, he paused at one of the numberless

switchbacks the trail made as it snaked its way up the eastern escarpment of Castle Peak. He wiped sweat and grit from his stubbly bald head with a handkerchief and adjusted the lumpy canvas pack slung over his sore shoulder. A thousand feet below, the valley trapped the last rays of late-afternoon sun like flecks of color in a Fifty-Niner's gold pan. The thin sigmoid of Granite Creek flashed in the light, sleek and silver as a trout, but purple shadows already made pine-thick islands of the moraines at the foot of Signal Ridge.

He knew he should ignore the fire in his lungs and keep moving. Night came early to the mountains, and it wouldn't be long before he was no longer sweating. Even in July, frost was no stranger at ten thousand feet once dusk fell, and they didn't want to spend a second night like the first. For what seemed an eternity the four of them had huddled together on the dirt floor of the abandoned miner's cabin, silent and shivering, while wind sliced through the chinks in the logs.

You could have used a rune, Travis. He touched the hard lump in his shirt pocket. *Sinfathisar let you speak runes the last time you were on Earth. Just because this is a different century doesn't matter. You could have spoken* Krond *and lit a fire. Lirith was blue this morning, and there was ice on Durge's mustache. And Sareth...*

However, the idea of trying to speak the rune of fire had been more terrifying than the possibility of freezing to death. When he used magic, things had a tendency to get burned and broken. And sometimes those things were people. He didn't know if he was really the one Lirith and the Witches called Runebreaker, but he knew they were right to fear his power. He did.

You need to get back. Sareth didn't look good when you left. He's probably coming down with altitude sickness, and the others won't know what that is. He needs to drink a lot of fluids, but the water up here isn't safe until you boil it, and that's not going to happen until you get there with the matches.

His boots of Eldhish leather stayed stuck to the trail. If he half shut his eyes, the valley didn't look much different than the last time he had gazed out over it. The stegosaurus-backed silhouette of the mountains hadn't changed, and the high plain at their feet was speckled with the same dusty green sage. However, when he opened his eyes fully, his preternatural vision quickly picked out everything that was wrong.

Below and to his right, the southern flanks of Castle Peak were populated with cabins and rough-milled mine shacks that, in his memory, were no more than weathered gray splinters. Heaps of tailings, red and umber, oozed down the mountainside like the discharge from fresh wounds. A heavy mist of pulverized rock drifted on the air, and the sound of the last powder blast still echoed off the peaks like late thunder.

Across the valley, a thin line of steam rose from a train just pulling into what must be a temporary depot. Travis could make out the pale line of the railroad grade that reached toward town. Just ten more miles of narrow-gauge track to lay, and the engines would be pulling into Castle City proper, bringing more people and cheaper goods from Denver, and taking raw ore from the mines back to the rock mills, where bright silver was freed from black carbonate of lead.

Castle City itself was far bigger than he had ever seen it. But then, it was a strange trait of Colorado mountain towns that, unlike most cities, they grew backward. A rich gold or silver strike could turn a small mining camp into a clapboard city of five thousand people overnight. Then, as one by one the mines played out and shut down, people moved on, and the city shrank. A few such towns found rebirth a century later as winter playgrounds for the wealthy. Castle City was one of the rest—a patchwork of Victorian frame houses, rust-roofed shacks, and not-so-mobile homes where just a few hundred souls dwelled, a ghost of its former splendor.

At least, that was how things were in Travis's memory. But just then, in the valley a thousand feet below him, that ghost was alive and well.

He still hadn't gone all the way into town. That thought had frightened him as much as speaking the rune of fire. This was every bit as much an alien world as Eldh was the first time he had set foot in the Winter Wood. How would people react to his Mournish clothes or his twenty-first century accent? Would he even be able to communicate with them?

His fears hadn't been entirely unfounded.

While in this era, as in his own, McKay's General Store would have had everything he needed, he had instead stopped at the first shop he came to a half mile outside Castle City. Its square false front couldn't hide the crude cabin that skulked behind, but Travis didn't care. The store was situated close to the mines of Castle Peak, and—no doubt like a lot of the miners—Travis was more concerned with proximity than selection.

He pushed through the door into a dim space, the air stinking with smoke. Wooden crates made a haphazard maze. Guns, tin lanterns, hams, and pickaxes hung from low rafters. The only person in view was a short, dour woman who stood behind a counter fashioned from a plank slapped over two barrels. Her oily hair was pulled back in a severe knot, and she wore a heavy black dress, its shoulders dusted with white flakes of dandruff. She looked up from the ledger open before her and gazed at him with narrow eyes in a puffy red face.

"So what are yeh now, some kind o' bilk?" Even with the help of the silver half-coin, her high, nasal words were only barely understandable. "An' here I was thinkin' the Cousin Jacks out o' Cornwall were a queer lot, what with their tales an' all. Well now, I cain't help yeh if yer grubstake is already bust. I don't give nothing away for free. 'Cepting for lead, that is." She nodded to the gun lying on the counter within easy reach of her hand—a small derringer with a mother-of-pearl grip.

Travis started to brush the dust from his flowing Mournish garb, then forced himself to stop. He didn't want to draw more attention to his outlandish clothes. He cleared his throat and tried to speak in as plain a voice as possible.

"I have these." He held out the small hoard of thick gold coins he and the others had collected by rummaging through their pockets. It wasn't much. All the same, a fire lit in the woman's eyes.

"Well, don't jes' stand thar. Give me them eagles."

He gave her the gold pieces, and she frowned, no doubt realizing they weren't U.S. coins after all. Taking up a small knife, she scratched several flakes off the edge of one of the coins. She grunted, then placed the coins on one side of a small scale and piled brass weights on the other. Travis noticed her thumb lingered along with the weights, but he said nothing.

"I'll give yeh fifty dollars for 'em. Well go on." She waved her stubby hand. "Take yer pick o' the store. I'll tell yeh when yeh've hit yer limit."

By the chortling in her voice, Travis knew she was getting the better end of the deal, but it didn't matter. He just wanted to get out before someone else came along. Hastily, he gathered an armload of goods and brought them to the counter. She was clearly disappointed when, after totaling the bill, she still owed him twenty dollars. Curtly, she counted the large, rumpled banknotes into his hand. He loaded the canvas pack he had bought and headed for the door.

"That's all the gold yer likely to see on that thar mountain," she called after him.

He hesitated. "I'm not looking for gold," he said, then stepped outside.

Now the sweat had dried on his head, and the wheezing of his lungs had subsided to a faint rattle. Travis turned and continued up the trail.

By the time he reached the abandoned cabin, the whole valley lay in the shadow of the mountain. Travis was the one who had spotted the cabin the previous afternoon. Weary after their battle with the demon in the Dome of the Etherion, and dazed at finding themselves on Earth, they had fled the people and noise of Castle City. They needed a place where they could think and get their bearings. Then Travis had looked up and had seen the small, boxy shape perched above them on the slopes of Castle Peak. The cabin had been abandoned, no doubt by a miner whose claim had yielded not silver, but worthless rock.

Travis opened the cabin's sun-beaten plank door to find that the others had been busy while he was gone. Durge, in a bout of good Embarran industriousness, had chinked the walls with the mud from the tiny creek that trickled past the cabin, shutting out most of the drafts. Lirith had swept the hard-packed floor with a bundle of sticks and cleaned out the crude stone fireplace, laying a neat stack of wood inside. However, Sareth sat in a corner, his usually coppery face ashen.

"It's good you're back," Durge said, not voicing the words Travis could see in the knight's deep-set brown eyes. *We were worried about you.*

Travis eased the pack off his shoulder, which immediately began cramping. "How are you doing, Sareth?"

The Mournish man grinned. "I keep trying to tell Lirith my head has cracked open, but she refuses to believe me. By now she's probably swept my brains out the door. And my breath seems to come but grudgingly."

Durge nodded. "The air seems strangely thin here. Is it always so on this Earth of yours?"

"It's the altitude," Travis said. "We're the better part of a league higher up than we were in Tarras. Everyone needs to drink lots of water."

"But you told us earlier not to drink the water," Durge said, glowering.

"That's because we need to boil it first." He started to say more, then stopped. He was too tired to explain about microscopic amoebas and how they could play havoc with your intestines. Right now Durge could simply think he was contradictory.

Lirith knelt beside the pack. "Did you get the . . . *mashes* you talked about, so we can make a fire?"

"Matches. Yes, and more."

Travis knelt beside her, and they unloaded the contents of the pack. It looked like less than it had at the store. Even in 1883, thirty dollars didn't seem to buy much. Of course, Travis knew prices had been outrageously inflated in the booming mining towns. A sack of flour could go for a hundred dollars. But with the nearing of the railroad, prices were probably on their way down.

Along with a tin kettle for boiling water and a single cup they could share, he had gotten some food—soda crackers, a small wheel of cheese, a lemon, and a few cans of sardines. The cans probably had lead in them, but that was the least of their worries at the moment.

There were also new clothes for each of them, garb that would hopefully keep others from thinking they were *bilks*, whatever those were. There was a pair of canvas jeans and a calico shirt for each of the men, and a brown poplin dress for Lirith. Their Eldish shoes would have to do, but Travis's and Durge's boots were plain enough to go unnoticed, and the low shoes Lirith and Sareth wore weren't so far off from moccasins. The handkerchief Travis had used to mop his head had been a last-minute luxury. He wasn't certain why he had gotten it; he just seemed to remember something about how you weren't supposed to run off on an adventure without one.

"I also got this," Travis said, pulling out a small purple bottle. "They didn't have any aspirin."

Lirith frowned at the bottle. "Aspirin?"

"Don't worry about it—I'm pretty sure it hasn't been invented yet. But I think this is almost the same thing."

The small label glued to the bottle read *salicylate of soda*. Lirith took the bottle, unstopped it, and held it beneath her nose. She raised an eyebrow and looked up.

"It smells like tincture of willow bark."

Travis nodded. "It should help Sareth's head."

Soon they had a fire going, and the kettle of creek water hung from an iron hook over the flames. However, Travis was a bit disappointed the others didn't seem to regard the matches as magical in nature.

"I see," Durge said, studying one of the matches. "It's an alchemical reaction. The sulfur acts as a catalyst for the fuel, and fire results."

"They do seem handier than flint and tinder," Lirith said, adding a stick to the fire, and Sareth nodded in agreement.

Travis groaned. "You're all boring. Matches are totally cool! When I was a kid, I liked seeing how far I could flick them while they were burning."

Durge gently but insistently took the box of matches away from Travis.

Full night found them, if not exactly comfortable, at least far less miserable than they had been the night before. Their new clothes were stiff and chafed at the seams, but were warmer than the garb of the Mournish, intended for southern climes. The fire gave off cheering light, and somehow Lirith made the sardines and crackers look appealing, although getting the tin cans open hadn't been easy at first. It was only when Durge unsheathed his greatsword and pointed it at one of the cans that Travis remembered his Malachorian stiletto. He pulled it from the small bag of things he had managed to hang on to in the

Etherion, and the blade cut through the lid of the can like butter.

All of them drank water once it cooled, and Lirith made a tea with several drops of the salicylate of soda. This seemed to ease the pain in Sareth's head. Not in immediate fear of survival, their minds turned to other, no less pressing, worries.

"So how are we going to get back to Eldh?" Lirith said. The witch's dark eyes gleamed in the firelight.

"I have a better question, *beshala*," Sareth said. His color had gotten better, and he sat up straight. "*When* are we going to get back to Eldh?"

The day before, after much struggling, Travis had managed to explain to the others that, while this was his world, it wasn't his world as he had known it. The date in the *Castle City Clarion* had read June 13, 1883. They knew the demon had altered the flow of time in Tarras. Somehow its lingering influence had also affected the gate artifact when they tried to escape the Etherion, and as a result they had traveled over a hundred years into Earth's past.

"Can the gate artifact not help us?" Durge said. "It was able to transport us to a time long ago. Logic dictates it must also be able to take us to a time yet to be. And there remains one drop of blood in the Scarab of Orú."

"I'm not sure logic applies this time, Durge." Travis reached into the sack and pulled out the gate artifact. He set it on the dirt floor, and a tiny, gold shape crept to the top of the obsidian pyramid, reaching out one of its eight slender legs to stroke Travis's hand.

As always, Travis was entranced by the scarab. It looked like a real spider, except that it was fashioned of gold, and on its abdomen glittered a teardrop-shaped ruby. It seemed truly alive, but what would happen when they used the last drop of blood contained within? Would the scarab die?

"I don't think the gate can move us through time on its own power," Travis went on. "I think it was only because of the demon that we traveled across time as well as worlds."

Lirith combed her black, curling hair with her fingers. "Which means if we used the gate, we'd arrive in Tarras a hundred years before any of us were born."

"Maybe it's not so bad as it sounds," Sareth said, flicking a bit of dirt from the wooden peg at the end of his right leg. "I used to dream sometimes about going back to the past."

"So there is nothing in the present to keep you?" Lirith said, her words sharp.

Sareth looked up at her, coppery eyes startled, but she had turned her gaze to the fire.

"It seems we are lost," Durge rumbled. In his jeans and calico shirt, the knight looked exactly like nineteenth-century miners Travis had seen in old photographs. The Embarran's mustaches and longish hair, swept back from his somber brow, only added to the effect. "If a demon is required to move through time, then your fancy has come to be, Sareth, and we have no hope but to remain in the past—on this world or our own."

"No," Travis said, standing up to pace back and forth. "I don't think we have to give up yet. I think there's someone who might be able to help us—the one who got me mixed up in all of this in the first place. Only I don't know if he's here yet."

Lirith looked up from the fire. "Who are you talking about?"

"The man who gave me this." Travis pulled the Stone of Twilight out of his pocket. It gleamed silver-green in the palm of his hand. "Jack Graystone."

Travis had never spoken a great deal about Jack Graystone with anyone but Falken and Melia, so he started at the beginning: how a year ago, on a windswept October night, his old friend Jack had called him to the antique shop just outside of town, and everything in Travis's life had changed forever. Jack had given him Sinfathisar and had told him to run from perilous beings that came in light—beings Travis only later learned were wraithlings. Travis had run, and somehow, impossibly, he had stepped through a billboard into the world of Eldh. It was only later, when Travis returned to Earth, that he learned that what he had feared was true: Jack Graystone had died in the fire that consumed his antique shop that wild October night.

Durge stroked his mustaches. "So, like Mindroth, this wizard Graystone was one of the three runelords who fled with the Great Stones after the Fall of Malachor. Only he found his way to your Earth. And you believe he might be able to help us get back to the time in which we belong."

"That's right," Travis said.

"And it was because of Graystone that you gained the Stone Sinfathisar and sealed the Pale King behind the Rune Gate last Midwinter's Eve. And stopped the Necromancer last summer."

"And defeated the demon," Lirith said. "As well as the sorcerers of Scirath."

Sareth let out a low whistle. "It seems a lucky thing that you met this Jack Graystone."

Travis gripped the Stone. "I suppose you could call it that." After all, it couldn't have been fate. Not if he was *A'narai*, one of the Fateless, as Sareth's grandmother had said.

"So you think there is a chance the wizard Graystone is here in this time?" Durge said.

Travis sat back down and flicked at a sardine head in one of the opened cans. "I'm not sure. He might be. I'm trying to remember how it all happened. You see, Jack had lived for several centuries in London—that's a great city far from here, across an ocean. He owned a bookshop there called the Queen's Shelf. Only then the bookshop burned, and after that he came here, to Castle City. I know the Queen's Shelf burned down in 1883—that's this year. But I don't know exactly when in 1883 it happened."

"So this Jack Graystone could already be here," Sareth said.

Travis shrugged. "Maybe. Or it could be months before he comes. Either way, we need to find out. I suppose I'll have to go into town tomorrow and ask around."

"There is a way we could find out tonight," Lirith said softly.

The others stared at the witch.

Lirith went on. "If I knew this Graystone, perhaps I could sense the presence of his life thread. I imagine a wizard's thread would shine brightly in the Weirding."

Sareth was studying her. "Can you do that, *beshala*?" It was not doubt in his voice, simply quiet wonder.

"I think so. The Weirding is weaker on this world than on Eldh. But I think it is strong enough to work this magic. Although there's something wrong as well. It's as if the land cries out in pain."

Travis thought he understood. In modern Denver, where Grace had tried to work magic, the natural world to which the

Weirding was connected had been all but smothered beneath concrete, steel, and asphalt. But in the mountains, in 1883, the land was still mostly wilderness. Only it had been wounded: mines gouged into its flesh, railroads sliced across its skin.

"Forgive me, my lady, but there seems to be a problem," Durge said, making a clear effort not to look queasy. The knight never had seemed to care for witchcraft. "You said you could see the wizard Graystone's thread if you knew him. But you have never met him."

Lirith looked up. "Travis could help me."

Travis knelt beside her and held out his left hand. Lirith took it between both of her own. Durge's eyes widened in an expression of horror, and he quickly moved away. Travis wondered what had caused the knight's strong reaction, but before he could ask, Lirith shut her eyes and a voice spoke in his mind.

Picture your friend Jack.

Travis shut his eyes and did as Lirith's voice instructed. He visualized Jack as he always remembered him: a handsome and professorial older gentleman, clad in a rumpled gray suit and green waistcoat, his wispy hair flying about his head and his blue eyes sparkling.

Travis felt a tingle in his hand, then Lirith let go. He opened his eyes, but the witch's were still shut. The three men watched her, holding their breath.

"I don't think he's come here yet," Lirith murmured after a minute. "The vision you gave me was clear, Travis, and his thread should be easy to see. But it's nowhere in sight. He must still be in—oh!"

Lirith's eyes fluttered open. Sareth hurried to kneel beside her. "What is it, *beshala*?"

"I saw something," she whispered. "A shadow. Close."

Durge was already on his feet. He gripped his greatsword in two hands and stalked to the door. There was a long moment of silence, then all of them heard it: the sound of a small pebble skittering over rock.

In one swift motion, Durge jerked open the door and lunged outside, sword at the ready. Travis was right behind him, Malachorian stiletto in hand.

Cold wind swept through the empty night. The moon shone

down from the cloudless sky, revealing bare rock and nothing more.

Durge lowered his greatsword. "It must have been an animal. One of those little striped *chippucks*, as you called them."

Travis started to answer the knight, then a glint of crimson caught his eye. He glanced down at his stiletto just in time to see the ruby set into its hilt flicker dimly, then go dark.

6.

Travis woke to the boom of thunder.

Grit sifted down from the rafters of the cabin, falling onto his face. He rubbed the stuff from his eyes and sat up. Sunlight shafted between the planks of the door, carving hot slices out of the dusty air. Morning.

Another report shook the cabin.

Next to Travis, Durge sat up, eyes wild, sand in his tangled hair. "We must hurry!" the knight sputtered. "The dragonsfire is spreading. The castle is going to collapse!"

"Wake up, Durge," Travis said, shaking the knight's shoulder. "There's no dragon. And believe me, this is no castle."

"Is it a storm, Travis?" Lirith said. She was curled up on the floor under Travis's gray mistcloak. Sharing the cloak was Sareth, who still appeared to be sound asleep.

Travis stood, stretching stiff limbs. "It's blasting. Over on the south ridge of the mountain I suppose."

Durge's forehead furrowed. "Blasting?"

Lirith sat up and wrapped her arms around herself. "They're making more holes in the land. But what magic do they use to work such a feat?"

"It's not magic," Travis said. "It's explosives. Dynamite, maybe nitroglycerin. I'm not sure what they would have used back then—I mean, now. I do know they can blow out tons of rock with a single charge."

Durge shook the grit from his brown hair. "I think I should like to see this *blasting*, as you call it."

Sareth let out a groan. "These are without doubt the loudest dreams I've ever had. Would you all go away so I can sleep? And take your blasting with you."

The night had been better than the first, but not by much. Even with the chinking and the fire, the cabin was wretchedly cold not long after dark. Travis hadn't bought any blankets at the store, and the only cloak they had was his frayed gray mist-cloak, which had been wadded at the bottom of his sack of belongings. He gave the cloak to Lirith and Sareth, after the two lay down close to one another, huddling for warmth.

As the two curled together under the cloak, Durge had given Travis an appraising look.

Travis had done a double take. "You're not serious?"

The practical Embarran had let out a snort. "Last I knew, Goodman Travis, you favored knights with fair hair rather than dark. And I favor knights not at all. So I think we are safe on both accounts." He lay down on the floor. "Now put your arms around me before we freeze solid."

Travis had spent the night pressed close to Durge's hard, compact body, and he supposed that had saved him from the worst of the cold. But he still felt as stiff as if he had spent the last eight hours hanging from a hook in a meat locker.

Another boom rattled walls and roof. A chunk of wood fell directly on Sareth's head. With a hot Mournish oath that required no translation, he flung back the cloak and sat up.

"I see fate has decided it is not my lot to sleep."

Travis couldn't help laughing. "Feeling better, Sareth?"

The Mournish man's glare transmuted into a look of mild amazement. "As a matter of fact, I do."

Durge rose from the floor, joints emitting a symphony of pops and snaps. "My lady," he said to Lirith, "is there any sign that the . . . snare you set was sprung?" The knight tried not to look uncomfortable as he spoke, which of course had the opposite effect.

Lirith stood and dusted off her dress, which bore hardly a wrinkle. Before sleeping she had woven a small rope of dried grass, which she laid across the threshold. Now she knelt to examine the grass rope.

"No, the spell was not broken. Nothing tried to enter here last night."

"Save the cold," Durge said, flexing raw-knuckled hands.

"And loud noises," Sareth said sourly.

Travis ignored them and looked at Lirith. "What do you think it was you sensed last night?"

The witch shook her head. "I'm not sure."

"Could it have been an animal? A bear maybe, or a mountain lion? There are probably dozens of them up here."

"No, the presence of an animal would not have affected me so adversely. But whatever it was, I only glimpsed it for a moment." She lifted a hand to her chin. "In a way, it reminded me of . . . but, no, that's impossible."

"What is it?" Travis said, feeling a gnawing in his gut that wasn't just hunger.

"In a way, it reminded me of the way I felt in the Etherion."

They all exchanged startled glances. Could some of the demon's magic have followed them through the gate?

Travis made a decision. "It's too isolated up here, and we still have some money left. I think we had better try to find a place to stay in town."

"Is that wise?" Sareth said. Two days' worth of beard shadowed his bronze cheeks, imparting a sharpness to his expression. He gestured to Lirith and Durge. "We are strangers to this world."

Travis sighed. "So am I. At least in this century. But I still think we should go. If something is stalking us, I'd rather not be such an easy target. Besides, there's a chance someone in town might have an idea of when Jack is going to arrive. He might have written ahead to arrange for a house. And don't tell me you really want to spend another night in this palace."

As one they gazed down at the hard dirt floor, and that settled it.

They made a dull but welcome breakfast of most of the remaining foodstuffs Travis had bought; the cold had made them all ravenous. Travis would have done anything for a pot of steaming coffee, but he hadn't bought any at the store, and as far as he knew there was no rune for *maddok*. He started to ask Lirith if there was any witchcraft that could conjure a cup, but as soon as he mentioned the word *maddok* she snarled at him, then stalked away, clutching a hand to her head. In the end, he and Lirith each settled for a cup of hot water with a few drops of salicylate of soda added in hopes of easing their throbbing skulls.

It didn't take long to pack up their few belongings, and an hour after dawn they set out. The high-altitude sun was already bright, and Travis was glad for the straw hat on his head. With his shaved cranium and sensitive skin, it was a necessity if he didn't want to immediately turn into jerky. He had bought hats for all of them. Didn't just about everyone wear hats back in the 1880s?

They saw no people on the narrow trail that snaked down the mountainside, and the few cabins they passed were in even worse repair than the one where they had stayed the last two days. From his years in Castle City, Travis knew most mines were abandoned not long after they were claimed, once the easy-to-reach blossom ore was hauled off. By now, the only operations still running in the valley would be the big mines, the ones that had enough capital to buy the equipment and hire the men needed to dig down deep to the bones of the mountain.

Once it reached the floor of the valley, the trail met up with a rutted dirt road. As they approached, Travis could see it was busy with people: mostly miners on their way to the diggings, although the first mule-drawn carts filled with ore were already lurching down the road, making their way to the train depot.

It was only when he saw the people that a troubling thought occurred to Travis. He supposed he would be able to communicate in Castle City—despite the fact that, if the woman in the store was any indication, the English they spoke wasn't quite what he was used to. However, Lirith, Durge, and Sareth didn't speak English at all. What if someone tried to talk to one of them?

You could give one of them the half-coin, Travis. Except that wouldn't help the other two. And then you wouldn't be able to talk to the three of them, unless your Eldhish is a whole lot better than you think it is.

The four had stopped on the trail, about a hundred yards from the road where the men and wagons moved past.

"Is something amiss?" Durge asked. "These men look to be a rough lot. I suppose they'll attack the moment they see us."

The knight reached over his shoulder for his greatsword, now wrapped in Travis's mistcloak.

"No, Durge. I don't think they'll attack us."

In fact, the road was so crowded—and with such a variety of people—that Travis doubted anyone would even notice them. Mixed liberally among the tide of pale Europeans were faces of black, brown, yellow, and red. But then, from what Travis knew, the Old West had been a true melting pot. Just about everyone had heard the twin siren calls of gold and silver.

There were people from the old colonies—Georgia, the Carolinas, New England—as well as from the states that had made up the country's first western frontiers: Kentucky and Ohio, Kansas and Missouri. Others sailed over the Atlantic, from England, France, Prussia, and Sweden. There were Russians by way of Alaska, and Mexicans who had not so long before held claim to this land. Most of the Indians had been forced south and west to the ever-shrinking reservations; still, a few remained. And there were people of African descent, many freed from slavery not twenty years earlier.

You'll have to tell Lirith about that, Travis. Only he wasn't certain how he could explain that, not so very long ago, people like her had been held in bondage against their wills in his country. He would have to find a way.

Just like he would find a way to help the others manage in this time. He took out the silver half-coin, turning it over in his hand. If he only he had three more of them.

Then why not make more, Travis? After all, you only have half of the coin, and its magic works fine. What's to say smaller pieces won't work as well?

There was only one way to find out. He closed his fist around the coin, and with his other hand reached into the pocket of his jeans, brushing the smooth surface of the Stone of Twilight.

"Reth," he murmured. He felt a surge of power and a sharp tingling in both hands.

Lirith gave him a sharp look. "What did you just do?"

Travis held out his hand and opened his fist. On it lay four small pieces of silver.

It didn't take long to verify the slivers of coin were working.

Travis was able to understand Sareth when he swore in Mournish after his peg leg caught in a rut in the road.

"By the bloody milk of Mahonadra's teat!" he said in the hot, lilting tongue of the Mournish. By the looks on their faces, Durge and Lirith understood as well.

"Sorry," Sareth said, noticing their stares. "That's one of those oaths that's better when others can't understand it."

Lirith raised an eyebrow. "Indeed. And just who is Mahonadra?"

"She was the god-king Orú's mother. And believe me, I'm not going to tell you anything more."

As Travis hoped, the miners paid them little heed as they started down the road toward town, although a few of them grinned and doffed greasy hats in Lirith's direction, some seemingly out of politeness, others with leering looks on their smudged faces. Lirith kept her gaze fixed ahead.

The crowd thinned as they passed the last few miners who straggled to their work, eyes still red from too much whiskey the night before. However, the road soon grew busy again—as well as broader, straighter, and dustier—when they reached the end of a long line of false-fronted buildings.

Travis was astonished how little things had changed in his time. There was the Silver Palace Hotel, a long brick edifice three stories high, and McKay's General Store, neither looking significantly different than he remembered. Just beyond was the Castle City Opera House, with its stately Greek Revival columns, and the assay office—although it was not abandoned as Travis had always seen it, but instead had men lined up at the door, each holding a small sack of ore to be tested. Travis knew what his sharp eyes would see if he gazed a little farther up the street, but he forced himself not to look. Not just yet.

You won't own the saloon for more than a hundred years, Travis. So don't even think about it.

He took a step forward, then stopped, dust swirling around his feet. A nervous breath fluttered out of his lungs.

Lirith gave him a concerned look. "What's wrong, Travis? Isn't this your home?"

"I suppose so. Only this is how it was a hundred years before I was born."

Durge let out a grunt. "I'm sure Stonebreak Manor has altered little in a century's time, save for the trees' growing taller. What could be so different in just a hundred years?"

As if to punctuate the knight's words, a stagecoach hurtled past, wheels rattling, driver's whip cracking. The four of them stumbled back just in time to avoid being trampled. Travis knew just enough about history to be sure that, for everything that seemed familiar, a dozen other things would be dangerously different. People had perished every day in the Old West—from disease, from mishaps, from bullets.

Another coach rushed by as they started down Elk Street. A few more months, Travis supposed, and the narrow-gauge would reach Castle City; until then, the coaches would ferry people from the end of the line to the town's main street. The coach lurched to a stop in front of the Silver Palace Hotel. Its door opened, and a man in a fine gray suit stepped out. He turned to help a lady down the coach's steps. She was clad in yards and yards of black and maroon, with a massive bustle behind and peacock feathers trailing from her tiny hat.

Lirith brushed her plain brown dress, her dark ruby lips twisting in a wry smile. "Well, that certainly puts things in perspective for a woman."

"Are those two the lord and lady here?" Durge said. "If so, we must go beg their hospitality."

The man in the gray suit looked from side to side, his eyes shadowed beneath the brim of his bowler. The woman adjusted the netting that hung from the brim of her hat. He slipped an arm around her waist and whisked her inside the hotel.

Sareth let out a low chuckle. "Something tells me they're not from around here. And that for all her finery, she's no more a lady than he is a lord. Or at least not the kind of lady you mean, Durge."

Crimson tinged the Embarran's craggy cheeks. Sareth started to laugh, but Lirith turned her back, and the mirth died on his lips. He gazed at her, confusion in his dark eyes.

Durge regarded Travis. "If that is not the lord of this land, who is?"

"There are no lords here, Durge."

"But who serves the king and queen?"

"There isn't a king or queen, either." Travis reached under his hat to scratch his head. "Well, there *is* a queen in England—the country across the ocean I was talking about last night. Her name is Victoria. And nobles from Europe did visit Colorado back then—I mean, in this time. I seem to remember something about a Russian grand duke who came to the West to hunt buffalo." He sighed. "Although I suppose they're already just about gone by now, aren't they?"

Durge seemed to consider these words. "If you have no king in this land, how is order kept?"

Travis hadn't considered how strange things here would be to people from a medieval world. He tried to think of a simple way to explain it. "Well, we have a president. I'm not sure who it would be right now. Grover Cleveland? No, he was a bit later—he was the one who made all of the silver miners go broke." He shrugged. "Anyway, the people of the country elect a president every four years, along with a number of lawmakers. And each state has a governor. And there are local officials like mayors and sheriffs who are elected as well."

"A curious system," Durge rumbled in obvious distaste. "And who votes for these officials? Peasants?"

"Anyone over eighteen." Travis rethought that. "Well, in my time, at least. Right now, women aren't allowed to vote."

Lirith turned back around and let out an exasperated sound. "I see some things are the same on any world."

"I think this place is more like the Free Cities," Sareth said to Durge and Lirith. "It's not royal blood that matters, but gold and silver."

Travis couldn't argue with that. In his time, Castle City was a quiet town, especially when the handful of tourists left for the summer. However, the small city before him was alive with action.

People jostled past each other on the boardwalks that lined the streets, some in the dusty garb of miners and cowboys, others in black coats and stiff white shirts, checking gold pocket watches as they went. Some women trudged by in elaborate, heavy dresses, while others wore the drab pinafores of laundry-women and workingmen's wives. A flock of children in shabby shoes followed a prim schoolmarm, and young men wearing caps ran past carrying stacks of freshly printed newspapers. The street itself was a circus of horses, mule-drawn wagons, and more coaches. On rainy days it was probably a quagmire; today it was a dust bowl, and a fine layer of grit covered everything and everyone.

The buildings that lined the street were every bit as diverse and industrious-looking as the people. Some were brick or stone, but most were slapped together from wood planks, each wearing its false front like a miner who had donned an opera coat. Travis saw banks, restaurants, barbershops, grocers, tack stores, booksellers, and clothiers. And every third storefront looked to be some sort of saloon or drinking house. Silver flowed freely from the mines, and the wealth was everywhere.

Only it wouldn't last. By 1883, the mines were already starting to play out. And Travis had heard stories of the crash of 1893, when President Cleveland finally revoked the Bland-Allison Act, which had created an artificial market for silver. Overnight, the price of silver fell to a fraction of what it had been, and just about every mine went bust. Vast fortunes were lost in a day. Henry Tabor, who had been the richest man in Colorado, would spend the last year of his life grateful just to be postmaster of Denver. His wife, the fabled Baby Doe, would die years later, a solitary madwoman. They would find her body frozen so hard to the floor of her shack in Leadville they would have to wait until the spring thaw to take it away.

"So where do we go for lodging?" Lirith said, eyeing the buildings on either side of the street.

Travis was pretty sure they couldn't afford the Silver Palace Hotel. "I'm not sure. Let's just walk down Elk Street and see if anything looks—" He swallowed the word *cheap*. "—affordable."

They moved onto the boardwalk, jostling their way past workingmen, miners' wives, and clerks running errands. They passed several establishments that bore signs in the window, offering rooms for rent. However, the prices shocked Travis. Some wanted as much as five dollars a day. At that rate, their remaining twenty wouldn't last long. They kept moving.

Travis supposed it was nine in the morning, but as far as he could tell all of the saloons were open. Most of them had swinging doors, just like in Western movies, but a wooden screen or panel just beyond kept anyone from seeing inside. All the same, the sound of laughter and the rattling of dice spilled out, along with the occasional man who squinted bleary eyes—obviously astonished to see the sun was well risen—before stumbling away down the boardwalk.

Soon Travis caught sight of a familiar sign hanging over the boardwalk. The sign looked almost the same as the last time he had repainted it, its lettering so familiar he could read it without the usual effort: THE MINE SHAFT. The saloon. His saloon—at least one day. What would it be like to walk through those doors?

Hard laughter interrupted his thoughts. Three men leaned against the boardwalk railing just ahead. They looked to be in their twenties and were dressed in white shirts and dark three-piece suits with silver watch fobs dangling from their vest pockets. Black Stetsons crowned their heads, and black boots shod their feet. One of the men was clean-shaven, one had a downy red beard, and the other a neatly waxed mustache.

The clean-shaven one spat tobacco juice, then made a lewd gesture and pointed a finger. As he did, the front of his jacket parted so that Travis could see the gun holstered at his hip—some kind of revolver. However, it wasn't the gun that made Travis's blood go cold.

The man was pointing straight at Lirith.

Travis felt the witch go rigid beside him. She must have seen. The three men laughed again, louder this time. The one with the sparse red beard—the handsomest of the lot—blushed and dropped his head. However, the mustachioed one stared at Lirith, a salacious look on his sharp face, and the clean-shaven one just grinned, a cold light in his blue eyes.

"May the starving spirits of the *morndari* consume their manhood," Sareth hissed.

Travis winced. He had a feeling that was another of those Mournish oaths that was better without translation. Sareth took a step toward the men, but Travis grabbed his arm.

"Forget it, Sareth. They have guns."

But the Mournish man wouldn't know what guns were. He started forward again. However, Durge moved in front of him. The knight's visage was stern.

"Travis is right. We are strangers here—we must not make trouble. And I know something of these guns he speaks of. They allow a man to kill another without even drawing close."

Sareth's eyes blazed. "But those bastards—"

"Mean nothing to me," Lirith said, stepping between Durge and Sareth. "They are foolish boys, nothing more. And we still must find a place to stay. Please. *Beshala*."

Some of the anger left Sareth's eyes, replaced by a softness as he gazed at Lirith. He nodded.

Together, the four continued down the boardwalk at a steady but not too-swift pace. Travis and Durge kept Lirith and Sareth between them. Catcalls rang out as they passed the three men, but they kept their gazes fixed ahead, and soon the whistles and whoops fell behind and were gone.

After walking two blocks, they stopped. Travis risked a glance over his shoulder, but the three men were nowhere in view. They had passed the Mine Shaft a block or so back, but he wasn't about to retrace their steps. He turned toward the others—then frowned.

"Where's Lirith?"

"She was right here," Durge rumbled.

Sareth pointed. "There."

They hurried after Lirith, who had moved a dozen paces down the boardwalk. They reached her just as she approached a wooden table covered with small blue bottles. Beside the table stood a man with frizzy gray hair, clad in a shabby suit. A painted canvas sign hung on the wall behind him:

DR. WETTERLY'S MEDICINAL BITTERS $1
CURES MANY AND SUNDRY ACHES AND AILMENTS,
INCLUDING BUT NOT IN ANY WAY LIMITED TO
BRUISES, CORNS, CROSSED EYES,
NEURALGIA, HALITOSIS, BOILS,
DROPSY, A LAZY TEMPERAMENT,
RHEUMATISM, GOUT, MELANCHOLIA,
AND HICCOUGHS.

The man in the suit spoke in a ringing voice, addressing the half dozen or so people who stood around the table as if they were a great throng, extolling the virtues of his patent medicine. Lirith picked up one of the bottles, unstopped it, and took a sniff. Her brow creased in a frown.

The medicine seller turned to her. "If you want to do more than smell, miss, lay down your dollar and take yourself a drink. It'll cure anything that ails you."

Lirith restopped the bottle and set it down. "You're lying," she said in a calm voice, and a murmur ran through the gathering of people.

The man spread his arms, chuckling. "Now, miss, I can understand why you're a skeptic. But rest assured that in this little blue bottle—"

"Is nothing but crude grain spirits flavored with pepper and colored with burnt honey," Lirith said, her voice sharper now. "I can sense no herbs, no oils, no tinctures—nothing that might cure even the simplest ailment. In fact, this *medicine* as you call it is little better than poison, and anyone would be a fool to drink it, let alone pay for it. You should be ashamed of yourself."

The people at the table snatched their silver dollars back, disgust on their faces, and hurried away. Befuddlement gave way to anger in the medicine seller's eyes.

"Why, you little trollop," he growled, all traces of good humor gone. "Look what your words have done. You've cost me a morning's income. And you're going to make up for it."

Lirith started to step back, but before she could the man grabbed her wrist, twisting it. She let out a soft cry.

Travis and Durge both lunged at once for Sareth, but they were too slow. In a second he was at the table, dark eyes smoldering. Sareth gave the man's outstretched arm a sharp blow. The fellow let out a yelp, letting go of Lirith and clutching his arm to his chest as he stumbled back against the table. Bottles tumbled, breaking against the boardwalk. The sharp reek of cheap alcohol suffused the air.

"Let's go," Sareth said, steering Lirith away from the table.

"Thief!" the gray-haired man shrieked. "You have to pay for what your harlot's broken. Thief!"

Heart pounding, Travis hurried to Lirith and Sareth, Durge just behind him. They needed to get out of there. Fast. As one, they turned around—

—and found themselves facing the trio of men in suits.

The beardless one grinned the same grin they had seen before, although the expression didn't reach his cold blue eyes. "What have we got here, Doc? A bunch of bummers? Well, we know what to do with the likes of them in this town."

He pushed back his suit coat, displaying the revolver at his hip, and the two men flanking him did the same.

7.

Dusty air swirled through the empty space that seconds ago had been a crowded section of boardwalk. Frightened faces peered from across the street or through shop windows, but no one came near.

Travis drew in a gritty breath. Out of the corner of his eye, he saw Durge start to reach over his shoulder for his greatsword, then stop. The blade was wrapped in the cloak and bound with rope; it would do the knight no good.

"Are you all right there, Doc?" asked the youngest of the three men, the one with red fluff on his cheeks.

The gray-haired man—evidently Doc Wetterly himself—scrambled on his hands and knees on the boardwalk, grabbing stray bottles and stuffing them in his coat pockets. "Yes, yes, Mr. Murray. I assure you, I can manage just fine." He hopped to his feet, clutching several bottles to his chest. A number of them were leaking, dribbling down his suit, onto the boardwalk. "Now, if you'll just—"

Before Wetterly's lips could finish excusing himself, his legs were already carrying him at a fast clip down the boardwalk. He ducked around a corner and was gone.

The blue-eyed man shifted his weight and rested his hand on his hip beside his gun. "I thought these four had a shifty look about them the moment I laid eyes on them. Didn't I say so, Mr. Ellis?"

"That you did, Mr. Gentry," said the mustachioed man, the one with the sallow face. He lifted a thin cigar to his lips and took a long puff.

"I thought for sure I did," the one called Gentry said in a melodious drawl. "I suppose these two don't look all that peculiar." He nodded at Travis and Durge. "Though the tall one's a mite on the pale side—must be he's fresh from the East. And the short one has a perilous look about him. I know a man-killer when I see one, and I'd say by the look in his eyes he's taken a life before, maybe more than just one."

Travis could see muscles bulge along Durge's jaw. Next to him, Lirith pressed close to Sareth. Was she speaking to him with a spell? Travis wanted to say something, anything, but his tongue had bonded to the roof of his mouth.

Gentry moved toward Sareth and Lirith. "Now these two, Mr. Ellis, Mr. Murray, they stood out right away. We don't see too many Negresses in this town, and the only ones I know of can be found for a dime a dance down at Morgan's Variety. But you ain't dressed like a hurdy-gurdy girl, though I reckon you're more than pretty enough to be one."

Anger flashed in Sareth's eyes. He started to speak, but Gentry was faster.

"And you," he said, his voice growing hard, "you're the one that really troubles me. When I seen you, I thunk to myself, 'Lionel Gentry, what in tarnation would a good man be doing with a peg leg?' And then the answer came, 'Well now, a good man wouldn't have a peg leg. Them are for pirates and the like.' And then I thunk, even without a peg leg, you're an odd fellow. You don't quite look like a Mexican, and you sure ain't an Indian. So just what are you, boy?"

"He's a gypsy," Travis blurted out before Sareth could speak. He didn't want Gentry to start asking what a *Mournish* was.

Gentry's eyes narrowed to icy slits. "A gypsy? Well now, seems I was right about you. I've heard your kind are nothing but a lot of liars, thieves, and murderers. That's why you're always a-wandering."

Motion caught Travis's eye. He could see Lirith's fingers moving at her sides. Was she trying to weave a spell? Maybe, but didn't she need to close her eyes to concentrate?

What about you, Travis. Why don't you speak a rune?

Only what rune could he speak without killing them all? This town was practically made of kindling; speaking *Krond* would burn it to the ground. What about *Meleq* then, the rune of wood? Could he make the planks of the boardwalk obey his commands? He had done something similar once with *Sar*, the rune of stone—forging shackles from a stone wall to bind an ironheart who tried to kill him in Calavere.

And what would Meleq *do to Sareth's leg, Travis? And all the shops around us, and the people in them?*

Durge started to reach again for his greatsword, then forced his hand down.

The man called Ellis let out another puff of smoke. "What does that one there have on his back?" He pointed with his cigar at Durge.

"That's right," said the young one, Murray. "I keep seeing him reach for it, like it's important to him."

Gentry stood in front of Durge. "What do you have wrapped up in there, mister? A shotgun, maybe?"

Durge's brown eyes were grim. "It does not concern you."

At this, Gentry let out a soft laugh. "On the contrary, everything in this town concerns me. And right now, that includes you and your friends here. You see, this ain't like some places you might have been. We believe in law and order here in Castle City. Good folk live here, peaceable folk. We've got no place for bummers or bilks or shootists. Or gypsies. Those types better learn to behave themselves. Or better yet, they should just get on out of town." He touched the grip of his holstered gun. "You see, around here, bad things have a tendency to happen to bad folk."

Travis tried to swallow the dusty lump in his throat. They couldn't leave town. Not yet. They had to wait for Jack to come. Jack was the only one who could help them get back to where they belonged.

"I think they get your meaning, Mr. Gentry," Ellis said, his lip curling in a smile. He took one last drag on his cigar, then poised his fingers to flick away the butt.

Lirith's fingers froze. "I wouldn't do that." Her gaze flickered down to the boardwalk.

Travis looked down and saw the wet stains seeping across the wood planks.

Ellis's visage darkened. "I won't have the likes of you telling me what to do, miss." He flicked the butt from his finger, and the glowing stump of the cigar hit the boardwalk.

Blue flames roared upward.

Travis, Lirith, Durge, and Sareth had already taken a big step back; even without a magical communication from Lirith, each had known what was going to happen. Not so the others. Murray scrambled back, kicking out the flames dancing on the toes of his boots. Ellis stared, mouth gaping. Gentry grabbed his arm, jerking him away from the fire.

"You idiot," he snarled. "You know Doc Wetterly's stuff is just about strong as kerosene. Now help me get this fire out."

He took off his coat and started beating at the flames. Ellis and Murray did the same. However, the dry, weathered wood had been soaked with the alcohol from the broken bottles of patent medicine. The flames raced along the boardwalk. Shouts rang out up and down Elk Street.

"Sareth!" Lirith shouted. "Water!" She pointed to a rain barrel a few paces away, near the entrance to an alley. As one, Sareth and Durge lunged for it.

Yes. That was what they needed. Water. Travis reached into his pocket and touched the Stone of Twilight. Just as Durge and Sareth tipped the barrel, Travis whispered a word.

"Sharn."

The rain barrel was only half-full. A thin sheet of water poured forth and struck the flames, but it wasn't nearly enough. It should have evaporated in an instant.

It didn't. Suddenly, more water than a single barrel could possibly have held flooded the boardwalk, washing over the tops of their boots, quenching the flames in a cloud of hissing steam. By the time the steam began to clear, the fire was out, and the water had run off the boardwalk, where it was drunk by the thirsty dirt of Elk Street. Murray and Ellis stamped the water from their boots; the cuffs of their pants were sopping.

"What the hell?" Gentry said, gazing at the barrel. "That just ain't possible."

He looked up, and his blue eyes narrowed as they locked on Travis. Travis opened his mouth, but before he could speak, Gentry lunged forward and grabbed the neck of Travis's shirt.

"Let him go, Mr. Gentry," said a deep voice.

Both Gentry and Travis froze as a man stepped through one last curl of steam.

He wasn't a big man, no taller than Durge and slight of build. His face was plain, largely lost behind a sandy mustache, and his eyes were a watery color beneath the brim of his gray hat. All the same, there was something about the way the man stood that lent him an air of gravity. He wore a navy blue suit similar to those the other men wore. The suit was free of dust, but somewhat threadbare and frayed at the cuffs.

Gentry didn't move; he still gripped Travis's shirt. It was getting hard to breathe.

"I said let him go."

Gentry released Travis and took a step back, his smooth face bearing no trace of expression.

"You don't understand," Murray said, stepping forward. "They're a bunch of bummers, Sheriff Tanner."

Only as Murray spoke did Travis finally see the polished silver badge pinned to the breast of the newcomer's suit.

"Is that so, Calvin Murray?" Sheriff Tanner let out a quiet laugh that was somehow more damning than the sharpest reproach. "Of course, it looks to me like they just kept the whole town from burning down. Pretty good for a lot of bummers, wouldn't you say?"

Murray hung his head, his cheeks as red as his whiskers.

The sheriff took a step forward. "What I'm curious about is how this fire got started in the first place." He eyed the broken medicine bottles on the boardwalk, then kicked something with the toe of his boot. It was the charred stump of a thin cigar. "Well now, I'd say that looks like your brand, Eugene Ellis. You know, you shouldn't throw your live butts down on this old boardwalk. It's dry as tinder."

Ellis gave the sheriff a sour look, then bent down, snatched up the cigar butt, and turned away.

Travis cast a glance at Durge, Lirith, and Sareth, but all of them were watching the sheriff. Tanner took another step toward Gentry, so that only five paces separated the men. Gentry's hand rested near his right hip. In what seemed a completely casual gesture, Tanner brushed back the front of his jacket, revealing a gleaming revolver.

"Why don't you just move along and get you and your boys a shot of whiskey, Lionel Gentry?" Tanner said. "It'll steady your nerves."

Now an expression did touch Gentry's face: a grin as curved and cutting as a bowie knife. "I don't think I'm the one who needs steadying, Sheriff."

Hovering an inch above the grip of his gun, Tanner's hand vibrated with a resonance too rapid to be voluntary.

The sheriff let his jacket fall back, concealing the gun, and balled his right hand into a fist. "I said move along, Gentry."

Gentry nodded, still grinning. "C'mon, boys. You heard the sheriff. It's time for a drink."

The three men started down the boardwalk, sooty coats slung over their shoulders. After a few paces, Gentry cast a glance back, only it wasn't the sheriff he looked at. Instead, his icy gaze fell on Sareth. Then the trio stepped through a pair of swinging doors, vanishing into the dimness of a saloon.

"Are you folks all right?"

The sheriff was eyeing them, although not with an air of suspicion like Gentry and his cronies. Instead, his watery eyes were curious.

"We're fine," Travis said, letting out a breath of relief. "Thanks for your help, Sheriff."

"No problem, mister. Men like Lionel Gentry want to think they're in charge here in Castle City." He blew a breath through his mustache. "I'm afraid it's my job to keep reminding them otherwise."

Durge nodded. "A sheriff is a kind of knight, then."

Tanner tipped up the brim of his hat. "You haven't been reading dime novels, have you, mister? If so, don't believe a thing you've seen in them. There isn't anything romantic about being a sheriff in the West. It's a dull and dirty job, and not one I asked for."

"Then why are you sheriff?" Lirith asked.

Tanner laughed. "That's a story in itself, ma'am. Although nothing so entertaining as you'll read in one of your pal's dime novels."

Sareth frowned. "What are these 'dime novels' you keep speaking of?"

"Please forgive my friends," Travis said hastily. "We're not from around here."

Tanner let out a whistle. "That's for sure. Castle City's gotten too big for me to know everyone in town, but I could tell in a second you're not locals. There's something different about all of you, though I can't quite put my finger on it. What parts do you hail from?"

"Back East," Travis said, hoping that was both vague and specific enough.

"You got a place to stay in town?"

The four were silent.

"Thought as much," Tanner said. "Well, you won't find anyplace to stay here on Elk Street." He cast a sidelong glance at Lirith. "But there's a boardinghouse two blocks over, on Grant Street, called the Bluebell. I know the woman who runs it. She's a good gal, despite what some folks might say. Tell her I sent you, and she'll fix you up with a couple of rooms."

Travis gave him a grateful smile. How old was the sheriff? It was hard to tell. He didn't look any older than Travis; all the same, there was an air of weariness about him, frayed at the edges just like his suit.

Lirith stepped forward and took the sheriff's right hand, pressing it between her own. "Thank you," she said, gazing at him with dark eyes.

"You're welcome, ma'am. Now go on over to the Bluebell, and get yourself off of this dusty street."

Gentle as the words were, their intent was clear: Eyes still watched, and the sheriff wanted this show over. He tipped his hat, and the four headed down the boardwalk, which in moments was crowded once more.

They didn't speak until they reached Grant Street. It was narrower than Elk Street, and not a fraction as crowded, although it was just as dusty.

"That was close," Travis said with a sigh.

"I have met men such as this Gentry before," Durge said in his rumbling voice. "They are bored and dangerous, and they are not merely simple brigands. We should take care not to run into him again, else I will have to unwrap my sword."

Travis tried to imagine the public reaction to Durge wielding his Embarran greatsword in the middle of Elk Street. "Let's stick to the not-running-into-them-again option."

"Why did that one hate me so much?" Sareth said, shaking his head. "Was it really because of my leg?"

Travis laid a hand on the Mournish man's shoulder. "Men like that don't need a reason, Sareth. They just pick someone out of a crowd and decide that's someone they don't like, and nothing will change their minds."

Sareth nodded, but his expression remained somber.

"The Sheriff Tanner," Lirith murmured. "There's something wrong with him. You saw the way his hand shook, didn't you? When I took it in my own, I tried to sense what was the matter. I did feel something inside of him, almost like a shadow, but there wasn't enough time for me to tell what it was."

Travis knew it could be almost anything. There had been countless diseases to die of in the Old West—tuberculosis, smallpox, cholera, dysentery.

"Come on," he said. "I think I see the sign for the Bluebell just up ahead."

The Bluebell was the largest house on its block of Grant Street—a three-story Victorian with a full dozen cupolas and a wrought-iron widow's walk topping its roof. In all, it seemed a little grand for a boardinghouse. Had Tanner overestimated their ability to pay? Then, as they drew closer, Travis saw the peeling gray clapboards, the sagging shutters, and the witch-grass tangling its way through the lattice beneath the front porch.

They headed up creaking steps to the front door and found a scattering of cats lounging in stray sunbeams or perched on the porch railing. All of them looked well fed. Lirith stopped to pick up a little calico. She held the cat to her cheek, and it let out the tiniest *mew* Travis had ever heard.

The front door opened with the sound of chimes.

"Watch out for Guenivere there, miss," said a woman's voice, rich and smoky as whiskey. "I think she's got a bum paw."

Lirith didn't look up from the kitten. "Yes, she does. I think she's gotten a thorn."

"Does she now? I thought I had checked."

"You can't see it—it's worked down between the pads."

A low laugh, and a jangling sound Travis couldn't place. "Well, bring her on in, then. And don't forget your menfolk. You must be a lucky lady to have three such likely-looking gents in tow."

The door opened wider.

Lirith laughed and, still holding the kitten, stepped through the door. Blushing, the three men followed.

They moved through a small foyer and entered a parlor. The walls were papered with a crimson fleur-de-lis pattern, although the wallpaper was faded and water-stained. A threadbare Persian rug covered a scuffed wood floor, and lace curtains, darkened to ivory by the sun and soft with dust, draped the windows. Just like the exterior, the parlor seemed oddly fine for a boardinghouse, yet worn as well, as if everything had been used far too heavily in its short time.

Travis could have said the same thing about the woman who stood in the center of the room. She couldn't have been older than Grace—in her early thirties—and there was a fineness to the oval of her face. However, she was every bit as faded as her green-velvet dress. She made Travis think of a portrait of a young woman left too long in a dusty attic, so that the painted hues—the yellow of her hair, the blue of her large eyes, the pink of her cheeks—were all muted with gray.

"I suppose you all need rooms," the woman said, her voice like smoke—but not harsh and acrid. More like the heady smoke of cherry tobacco. "Do you have references?"

Travis glanced at the others, then swallowed. "Sheriff Tanner told us to tell you—"

She held up a hand. "Stop right there. If Bart sent you, that's good enough for me. Now, on to more important matters—Miss Guenivere's paw."

The woman moved to Lirith. As she did, Travis heard again the metallic jingling sound. She stopped beside the witch, and only as she propped a polished mahogany cane against a battered horsehair sofa did he realize she had been using it to walk. The two woman sat on the sofa, cooed over the cat, and in a minute the offending thorn was plucked free. The patient was placed on a pillow, where it curled up, licking its paw.

Leaning on her cane, the woman stood. This action seemed to take the wind out of her. Lirith hurriedly stood beside her, but the woman gave her a warm smile.

"Now," she said, still a bit breathless, "let's see to your rooms. Since you were so kind to Miss Guenivere, I'll give you a good rate—a dollar a day for room and board for each of you." She gave them an appraising look. "You can pay, can't you?"

Travis gave a quick nod and started to reach into his pocket for their last twenty dollars.

She laughed. "Not now, partner. All I need is your names. I'll sign them in the ledger for you, if you can't write them yourselves."

Travis took the job of dipping a steel-tipped pen in an ink pot and writing their names in the book that lay open on a small marble table. He wasn't sure he was the best choice, but he didn't know if the coin pieces would let the others write in English. However, some magic seemed to be at work, for as he put down the pen, the names didn't look as he had intended, and it wasn't because of reversed letters.

The woman picked up the book. She smiled and glanced up at Lirith. "Lily. Now that's a pretty name for a pretty gal. And let's see if I can guess these others right." She pointed at Durge, Sareth, and Travis in turn. "That's Dirk, that's Samson, and that would have to be Travis."

The others shot Travis confused looks, but he simply shrugged and grinned. "That's right."

"And what's your name?" Lirith asked.

The woman lifted a hand to her forehead. "Where have my wits gotten to?" She thrust out a hand. "Call me Maudie. That's Maudie Carlyle. No matter what folks might tell you, I don't go by Ladyspur anymore."

Ladyspur?

She gave each of their hands a firm shake, and when she turned away, Travis glanced down and saw them just peeking out from beneath the hem of her dress: the brass wheels of a pair of spurs.

Of course, Travis. This is Ladyspur. You know her story. She was a prostitute and later a madam, and once she won a fair gunfight in Elk Street. He glanced up and saw a pair of six-shooters mounted above the fireplace. *After that, she gave up the profession and tried to become a proper lady in Castle City. Only none of the society ladies would have anything to do with her. And then not long after that—*

His heart skipped a beat in his chest. He noticed again the thinness of her hand that gripped the cane.

—she died of some disease, like cholera or consumption.

Maudie hardly seemed to use her cane as she moved back into the hallway. "You've missed dinner, but let me know if you need a biscuit to tide you 'til supper. We sit down at 6 P.M. Don't be late." She gave the men a stern look. "And be sure to wash up first. You'll find your rooms on the third floor, first two doors on the left at the top of the stairs. The first one is for the lady."

"Two rooms?" Durge said. He looked at Travis. "Is that within our means?"

"Of course it is!" Maudie said before Travis could answer. "The rate's the same. And you don't expect Lily here to share a room with a bunch of louts like you. She's far too lovely for that."

Sareth grinned, his coppery eyes gleaming. "That she is."

Lirith lowered her head and started quickly up the stairs, but not before Travis saw the glow of her cheeks. The three men gave their thanks to Maudie, then followed Lirith.

8.

They spent most of the next three days in their rooms at the Bluebell, coming downstairs only to take meals or to use the attached outhouse in back, or to sit on the porch while a thunderstorm passed over the valley—as it did most afternoons—breathing moist, sage-sweet air, one of Maudie's cats curled in each of their laps. Except for Durge. Somehow the somber knight always found a way to accommodate two or three of the purring felines.

"It's not that I fancy them, mind you," Travis overheard

Durge say to Lirith. "It's simply that they're frail, foolish creatures and cannot endure the elements. If one were to take ill,
Lady Maudie would no doubt become distressed, and that
would impair her ability to see to the needs of her guests, including ourselves. It's quite practical, you see."

"Yes, I think I do see," Lirith said, dark eyes gleaming, as
Durge gently petted Miss Guenivere with a rough hand.

Usually they gathered in the room Travis shared with Sareth
and Durge, as it was a good deal larger than Lirith's, if not
nearly as comfortable. Lirith's room was decorated in pinks and
crimsons, with tassels and lace doilies adorning every available
surface—all bespeaking Maudie's personal touch. In contrast,
the room the men shared was spartan and slightly drafty, occu-
pying as it did the north half of the third-floor attic. The rafters
were soot-stained and bare, and the only furnishings were four
narrow beds, four rickety chairs, and a massive pine bureau
with a chipped pitcher and basin for washing.

All the same, the room was clean, and it bore a certain rustic
charm that would not have been out of place in a manor house
on Eldh. Nor did they need any more than the one bureau.
None of them had a change of clothes, and Travis had just his
few things to put in one of the drawers—his Malachorian
stiletto, the rune of hope talisman, and the wire-rimmed spectacles Jack had given him. Durge's greatsword wouldn't fit in a
drawer, so they tucked it, still wrapped in the mistcloak, up in
the rafters.

As Maudie had warned, meals were served at precise intervals. All of them were famished by suppertime that first night,
and they devoured the ham, corn bread, wilted greens, and
cherry cobbler Maudie and her sole helper at the boardinghouse—a young, quiet, sweet-faced woman named Liza—laid
on the table. Even Lirith tucked away several helpings, although somehow the witch made the act of gorging look almost
delicate.

There were only a half dozen other guests at the boardinghouse at the moment. All were men, and none seemed interested in talking. Each was freshly scrubbed, their still-wet hair
slicked back, and they wore clean white shirts and denim pants.
However, no amount of scrubbing could have removed the

black dirt embedded in the skin of their hands. They ate swiftly, and when they were done scraped their chairs back from the table, put on their hats, and left without a word.

"Where do you think they're going?" Sareth said.

"To the poker and monte and faro tables," Maudie said, as she and Liza cleared away plates. "It was payday at the mines today. They'll all come back in the morning, heads aching and pockets empty."

After supper that first evening, Travis discovered a stack of newspapers—copies of the *Castle City Clarion*—in the front parlor. He asked Maudie if he could take some of them upstairs.

She gave him a sharp look. "No fires in the rooms. Not after what happened before."

So that explained the sooty rafters. "No fires," he promised. "I just want to read them."

"Well, then help yourself. None of the other men seem to have much of a care for reading. I suppose that would take time away from their gambling and drinking."

Travis picked up a stack of papers. Before he could head upstairs, Maudie placed a bundle tied in a cloth napkin atop the stack. A warm scent rose from the napkin: biscuits.

"Take those up to Mr. Samson. He didn't eat much at supper, and I don't like the circles under his eyes. Has it been long since he lost his leg?"

"A while," Travis said. "I think it's the altitude that's bothering him."

"Well, that's no surprise. It bothers everyone. Lately, it seems like the air's so rarified up here I can hardly breathe." Gripping her cane, she headed back to the kitchen, spurs jingling, and Travis bounded up the steps with his prizes.

"I like Lady Maudie," Durge said as he munched biscuits in their room.

Sareth was too tired to eat, and had lain down on one of the beds after taking more of the salicylate of soda at Lirith's prompting.

"She's sick," Travis said.

Lirith met his eyes. "I know. I saw it in her. Her lungs are wasting."

Durge stopped eating and stared, and Sareth propped himself up on an elbow, his coppery eyes thoughtful.

"You know how long she'll live, don't you?" Lirith said. "You know it from the histories of your day."

Travis gave a reluctant nod. "There were still stories told about her. She was pretty famous in her time—in this time. They used to call her Ladyspur, just like she said. It was because she always wore boots and spurs while she danced."

"She danced?" Lirith said, her voice suddenly cool.

"Yes, she was a variety hall girl. Well more than that, really..."

"So she was a whore," Sareth said. The words was not a condemnation, merely a statement.

"And later a madam," Travis said. "I'd guess Liza is one of her former girls. But she gave up her profession after winning a gunfight against a man who insulted her honor. After that, she decided to change her ways."

Durge finished the last biscuit. "I still like her."

Travis noticed that Lirith had turned away, hands pressed to her stomach. Had the heavy supper disagreed with her after being so famished?

"Lirith?"

She turned around, her gaze stricken. "When," she said quietly. "When does she die?"

"I don't know exactly. All I know is that she died of consumption a few years after she won the gunfight and turned her brothel into a boardinghouse."

"It's already been a few years," Sareth said. "She told me she's been running the boardinghouse for three years now."

They were silent after that. Travis knew there was nothing they could do for Maudie. And he supposed he and the others were in danger of catching tuberculosis just staying there, although he didn't know how contagious it was—he needed Grace for that. Anyway, that felt like the least of their worries.

Travis turned his attention to the newspapers, and that evening—and over the next two days—he pored through the murkily printed sheets of newsprint, concentrating to keep the letters from doing a do-si-doe.

Travis wasn't exactly sure what he was hoping to find in the papers. Maybe, he reasoned, there would be something that might give him a hint about Jack—whether he had ever visited there, or when he might be coming. From everything Travis knew, Jack had always been a prominent figure in Castle City society. If anyone knew he was coming, surely the *Clarion* would have an article about it; there were stories about nearly every happening in town, from who had opened up a new shop to who had just robbed it.

However, as Travis dug further and further back in the stack, he found no mention of Jack Graystone. All the same, there were countless fascinating articles that caught his attention— and which served to remind him just how different this world really was from the Castle City he remembered.

Not surprisingly, much of the news was about the mines. Countless articles talked about the amount of ore each of the mines was producing, and how much silver was assayed to each ton of rock. One story quoted a geologist who warned that the veins of carbonate of lead were pinching out—although the editors of the *Clarion* were quick to reject this, denying all rumors that the boom was anywhere near over. Of course, Travis knew it was, but people were never so vehement as when defending their most beloved delusions.

In addition to stories about the mines, there were frequent updates on the spur of the Denver & Pacific Railroad, which was inching its way toward town. And, to Travis's morbid fascination, each issue included a column called "Morning Mayhem," which reported the previous day's crimes. They ranged from public drunkenness and fistfighting to robbery and murder.

Before long, Travis began to notice a trend in "Morning Mayhem." In the papers near the bottom of the stack, the crime report took up only a section of one page. But the column grew larger the higher up he went, so that by the middle of the stack it consumed a full page. However, after that, the column shrank again, and in the most recent editions it was smaller than ever. It looked as if, after a steady climb, crime was on the decline in Castle City.

At least petty crime. While there were fewer crime reports in the more recent newspapers, the reports there were tended not to be about robbery and whiskey-related assaults, but more serious crimes—like horsethieving and murder. Only, strangely, the column seemed to have stopped reporting just how the victims were killed or who the main suspect was.

Homer Tattinger, late out of North Carolina, read a typical report, *was found dead on Saturday afternoon on the north bank of Granite Creek about a mile downstream from town. He was found by Sheriff Bartholomew Tanner and had been dead a good day or so. Mr. Tattinger was known as a ruffian and hard drinker, and was said by some to be a shootist, and thus it is little wonder for him to be found in such a grim state. The Editors must trust others of similar nature will take note.*

Travis wasn't the only one who was interested in the newspapers. Durge seemed fascinated by them, although for different reasons than Travis.

"These could not possibly have been penned by hand," the knight pronounced the afternoon of their second day, setting down one of the newspapers. His hands were smudged with ink, and there were gray fingerprints on his craggy brow. "The letters are too small, and each is shaped precisely the same. I cannot fathom its nature, but I believe some sort of mechanical process was used to place the words on these sheaves."

For the next hour they sat in the parlor, drinking tea, while Travis explained what little he knew about the invention of movable type and the printing press.

Durge's brown eyes were thoughtful. "I have seen the peasants who dwell on my lands create pictures in a similar way, carving a shape on a block of wood, painting the block, and pressing it to cloth or sheepskin to make an image. This printing press you speak of is not so very different."

"No, it isn't," Travis said with a grin, wondering if he had just forever altered the march of technological progress on Eldh.

Only if Durge ever gets back to Eldh, Travis.

He sighed and kept reading.

Sareth and Lirith were also curious about the newspapers, although they seemed more interested in the advertisements than the articles. Sareth constantly asked Travis about various items advertised for sale. However, Travis was hard-pressed to explain what some of them were for. Lirith, in turn, liked the pictures of ladies' fashions. Although she seemed horrified once she grasped the concept of a corset.

"Why, this would squeeze the life right out of you," the witch said indignantly. Whatever had troubled Lirith their first night in the boardinghouse, she seemed to have set it aside. Although Travis noticed that Sareth cast frequent looks of concern at her—looks she seemed unwilling to return. "Only a man could have devised such a thing," Lirith went on. "The women of this world ought to rebel against such torture."

"Actually," Travis said, "they will. In fact, in about another eighty or ninety years, women will be burning their underwear in protest."

Durge glowered. "That sounds dangerous."

"I think he means after they've taken it off," Sareth said with a grin.

Sareth seemed to be doing better again—the shadows beneath his eyes were reduced, if not entirely vanished—and Travis hoped the Mournish man was getting accustomed to the altitude.

Sareth flipped the page in the newspaper, and his smile faded. Travis glanced over his shoulder, and his heart sank. On the page was an advertisement filled with pen-and-ink drawings of prosthetic devices: wax hands and glass eyes. And wooden legs. *Feel like a whole man again!* proclaimed the advertisement. And, farther down, *So lifelike, the ladies will never guess the truth!* Sareth hesitated, then brushed a picture of the false leg.

Durge was talking to Lirith about printing presses, and she listened with an attentive though slightly pained expression. She hadn't seen what Sareth was looking at.

By breakfast of their third day at the boardinghouse, as he counted out four more dollars into Maudie's outstretched hand, Travis was finally forced to admit what he had known all along: They needed more money. They had only enough for two more days at the boardinghouse, and for all Travis knew it could be months until Jack came to town. What were they going to do for money in the meantime?

Maudie must have noticed the worry on his face. "You'll be wanting to find a job, I imagine."

He gave her a sheepish smile. "That obvious, is it?"

She patted his stubbled cheek. "Do forgive me, my boy. But you don't have the air of a silver baron about you. I'm afraid you look more like a workingman—not that there's anything to be ashamed of in that."

"I suppose I could ask at one of the mines and—"

"Not on your life!" Maudie shook a finger at him. "Those mines are pits of doom and despair, that's what I say. I won't have you or your boys working in them. Mr. Samson wouldn't last a week in one of those holes."

Travis couldn't disagree. But what else could he do?

"Surely you've got some skill or trade," Maudie said.

Travis almost laughed. Would anyone in town want to hire a dyslexic runelord? "I used to be a saloonkeeper."

Maudie gave an approving nod. "Now that's something that will earn you a dollar in this town. Go talk to Mr. Manypenny. I know he's always on the lookout for a good bartender. They're hard to keep hold of."

"Why is that?"

Maudie winked. "I suppose they're faster at pouring whiskey than they are at reloading shotguns."

Travis gulped; he wasn't certain this proposal sounded any safer than mining. "Who's Mr. Manypenny?"

"He operates that Mine Shaft over on Elk Street. It's one of the more respectable establishments in town. Arthur Manypenny is an old customer . . . that is, he's an old acquaintance of mine. Let him know you're staying here, and that I'll vouch for you."

Travis stared, Maudie's words buzzing in his ears. *He operates the Mine Shaft . . .*

Before he knew what was happening, Maudie had sent him upstairs with a borrowed straight razor, strop, and shaving mug, along with orders to get cleaned up.

An hour later, Travis stood on the boardwalk in front of the swinging doors that belonged to the Mine Shaft Saloon, as clean as he could get with a pitcher and basin. His head and cheeks were freshly shaved—without severe loss of blood, thanks to Sareth's skilled hand. Travis watched a dozen men pass through the swinging doors of the saloon—more going in than out—but he couldn't see past the screen that hid the interior.

You can do this, Travis. After all, you've done it before. Or you will do it, anyway. If there's anywhere in this town you belong, it's here at the Mine Shaft.

He drew a deep breath and stepped through the doors.

It was like stepping forward in time. Of course, the differences were immediately apparent. Kerosene lamps hung on the walls rather than electric lights, and there were no neon beer signs behind the bar. The tables at the back of the saloon were covered in green felt and were obviously intended for gambling, although they were quiet at the moment.

What was more shocking was what hadn't changed. The pine floor strewn with sawdust, the deer and elk trophies on the walls, the player piano on the little stage, and the twenty-foot, brass-trimmed, glossy walnut bar imported from Chicago, with its diamond dust mirror behind—all of it looked just like Travis remembered, if a little newer and shinier.

It wasn't hard to locate Mr. Manypenny. Everyone in the saloon was dressed in either the dusty denim and calico of a miner or a three-piece suit—everyone except the man behind the bar. He was a big, red-faced gent, probably athletic in his youth, now growing corpulent in his forties. He wore a crisp white shirt with black garters on his upper arms, and his slick hair was parted precisely in the middle—all the way down to the nape of his neck, as Travis could see in the mirror. He wore an elaborate handlebar mustache, carefully curled and shaped with what had to be enormous amounts of wax.

A pair of men stepped away from the bar, their whiskey in hand. Manypenny wiped the bar with a towel. Now was Travis's chance. Hands sweating, he stepped forward.

Three minutes later, Travis had a job.

At first, when Travis said he hadn't come for a drink, Manypenny gave him a scowl. However, as soon as Travis mentioned he had owned a saloon before, Manypenny's scowl turned into a jovial grin. He asked Travis to pour a whiskey and, starting to feel more confident, Travis risked showing off a bit. He flipped the shot glass into the air, caught it behind his back, and poured over his shoulder before slamming the shot on the bar—without spilling a drop.

This elicited a laugh from Manypenny, and he slapped Travis on the back—hard enough that Travis took a staggering step forward. He was going to hurt in the morning.

"You have won yourself a position, Mr. Wilder," Manypenny said in a surprisingly high-pitched and refined voice. "I haven't witnessed such fancy pouring in a dog's age. It seems that all my best bartenders are always doomed to hear silver's siren call and run off to stake a claim for themselves. You don't have a yearning for the mining life, do you? If so, tell me now."

Travis assured him he didn't, and Manypenny said he could start that evening. Travis had to promise to buy a white shirt and black-wool pants; that would use up more of their money, but now that he had a job, that wasn't a worry. The wage was four dollars a day, which would just cover their expenses.

"I'll provide the apron," Manypenny said. "But you'll need to purchase your own pomade in order to properly coif your head. I find Prince Albert's works most satisfactorily."

Travis gave a sheepish grin, then took off his hat, displaying his shaved pate. This elicited another hoot of laughter and slap on the back. Then Manypenny walked him to the back of the saloon.

"Employees always use the back door," the saloonkeeper said. "I find that it's useful to maintain a discreet distance from the clientele."

Given the way most of the men in the saloon smelled, Travis couldn't disagree. He promised to be back at seven, then shook Manypenny's hand.

"I shall send my thanks to fortune fair you came in," Manypenny said, pumping Travis's hand energetically. "What saloon did you say you used to travail at?"

Travis grinned. "It was one a lot like this."

Manypenny laughed again and opened the back door. Travis started through to the alley beyond—

—then froze.

It was plastered to the wall next to the door—a yellowed poster. It read in bold letters:

WANTED DEAD OR ALIVE
FOR SUNDRY AND TERRIBLE CRIMES AGAINST MEN
TYLER CAINE, THE MAN-KILLER
REWARD $500

However, it was not those words that made Travis's knees go weak. It was the crude sketch beneath them. The drawing depicted the face of a man. He wore a handlebar mustache instead of a goatee, as well as a black hat, but the only other difference was a pair of round, wire-rimmed spectacles.

It's you, Travis. It's you with a black hat and a mustache. And wearing the spectacles Jack gave you.

The spectacles Travis had found in a box in Jack Graystone's antique shop, and which Jack had told him had once belonged to a gunfighter.

A gunfighter named Tyler Caine.

That's impossible, Travis. It can't be.

Except it was.

"Is something wrong, Mr. Wilder?" Manypenny was looking at him, concern on his red face.

Travis licked his lips. "That poster . . ."

Manypenny's eyes lit up. "That's Tyler Caine, the famous civilizer. Surely you've heard tell of him? He's wanted for shooting men in five different states and territories. The law brands him a villain, but the people know better. Not since Ivanhoe or Robin Locksley of Sherwood has there been such a protector of justice, such a defender of the common man."

Travis frowned, forgetting some of the sickness in his stomach. He wondered if Manypenny had been reading those dime novels Sheriff Tanner had talked about.

"I've heard he always wears his spectacles," Manypenny went on. "Even in his sleep. That's how you can recognize him. Of course, the stories say he died a few years back of diphtheria up in Virginia City. But I don't believe that for a moment. I wish he'd come here to Castle City. By Jove, I imagine Tyler Caine could put an end to these—"

Manypenny bit his lip and glanced over his shoulder at the front door of the saloon. His shoulders were hunched, and the big, good-humored saloonkeeper seemed suddenly fearful. What had he been about to say?

Better yet, Travis, who is he afraid might have overheard him?

However, Travis didn't get a chance to find out. Once more Manypenny bid him good-bye, and the next thing Travis knew the door shut behind him, leaving him alone in the alley behind the Mine Shaft. He reached up and touched his face, but the wire-rimmed spectacles he had worn for so many years weren't there. His new eyes—reborn in the fires of Krondisar—had no need for spectacles. But in the poster he had been wearing them. What did it mean?

No answer came but the lonely moan of the wind between the buildings. Hands in pockets, Travis headed back to the boardinghouse to wait for seven o'clock and his new job to begin.

9.

Grace helped Beltan carry Sky to the small sitting chamber just off the villa's main room. Either shock had granted her an uncanny strength, or life on a medieval world had made her tougher than she thought. Whatever the reason, though Sky was nearly as tall as she was—and far denser—Grace lifted his legs as easily as Beltan did his shoulders. They laid the wounded young man gently on a chaise.

"Place him on his side, Beltan," Grace said.

Beltan cast her a quick grin. "Yes, Your Majesty."

She glared at him, then returned her attention to Sky. What on Eldh was he doing here? They hadn't seen him since he disappeared from the Tower of the Runespeakers. And who was this peculiar young man really? At the Gray Tower, she had never had a chance to find out; she had never understood why he risked everything to help her save Travis. Maybe now she would.

First things first. Grace probed his back, neck, and head with expert fingers. His wounds were still oozing blood, and he was unconscious, although a quick check of his life thread revealed that this was not shock, but merely the sleep of exhaustion.

"How is he, dear?" Melia stood in the door of the chamber, along with Falken and Aryn.

"The lacerations on his back are deep, but I don't think they're life-threatening," Grace said, speaking in the same brisk tone she had always used in the ED at Denver Memorial. "But he's suffering from exposure, and he's lost a fair amount of blood."

"What can we do?" Falken said, faded blue eyes grave.

"You can get me some things." Grace ticked off the items. "I need warm water, a bottle of wine, a blanket, and clean rags for dressing his wounds. A knife, too. Needle and waxed thread. And a candle."

"What about me, Grace?" Beltan said, as the others hurried from the room.

Grace took the blond knight's hand and wrapped it around Sky's wrist. "Do you feel his pulse? Good. If the rhythm starts to get faster or weaker, let me know at once."

When the others arrived with the things she had requested, Grace got to work. She cut Sky's rough brown robe away from his wounds; his back and shoulders were broad and powerfully sculpted with muscle. Beltan let out a surprised grunt, and Grace met the knight's eyes. She knew they were both thinking the same thing. One didn't get a physique like this by cooking dinner for runespeakers.

She dipped a rag in the warm water, and the sharp, clean scent of *alasai* wafted upward. Melia or Aryn must have crumbled some dried green scepter leaves into the bowl. That was good; *alasai* seemed to have antiseptic properties. Grace cleaned away the caked blood and dirt from Sky's back. There was a set of three gashes on his right shoulder, and another set just beneath the left shoulder blade.

They look like claw marks—like wounds from a mountain lion or another predator.

Except what predator had only three talons? None that she could think of.

And what about feydrim, *Grace? How many digits do they have on their forelegs?*

But she couldn't remember; she had only ever gotten to examine one of those twisted creatures up close once, after she and Travis barely fended it off in her chamber in Calavere. Besides, *feydrim* were creatures of the Pale King, and Berash had been sealed behind the Rune Gate last Midwinter's Eve.

She kept cleaning away the blood—then stared as her work revealed something else on the young man's shoulders.

"What in Sia's name is that?" Aryn said.

Grace leaned back, staring. "I'm not sure."

In the center of the young man's upper back, just below his neck, was a tattoo. Drawn in swirling, blue-black ink, the tattoo was about as large as Grace's two splayed hands. It consisted of a trio of intertwined circles, each one rimmed with symbols she supposed were runes. Inside the center of each of the three circles was a single, larger rune.

Beltan let out a grunt. "I've seen marks like that before—on wildmen of the north, like the ones in King Kel's court. The warriors in those tribes often take such tattoos to signify the chief for whom they fight."

Aryn's blue eyes were startled. "Warriors? But Sky is a servingman."

"I'm starting to doubt that," Grace said.

"Do you know what these runes signify?" Melia said to Falken.

The bard drew closer. "I'm not sure about the smaller runes around the edges of the circle. I'd need time to study them. But I recognize the larger runes. This one here, on top, is the rune for sky. That makes sense, I suppose. It's his name. But the one inside the right-hand circle is the rune for Olrig, and the one on the left is the rune for Sia."

Aryn looked up. "There's a rune for Sia?"

"Of course," Falken said. "As well as for each of the Old Gods. Everything under creation has a rune. Except for the New Gods, of course, and the dragons."

The baroness chewed a knuckle. Grace understood her conundrum; according to the Witches, Sia was the Mother of Eldh, and she had nothing to do with the Old Gods or rune magic. In turn, the Runespeakers believed that the Worldsmith spoke the runes that brought Eldh and all things on it into being. And it was the Old God Olrig who stole the secret of those runes from the dragons, who had dwelled in the gray mists that existed before the world, and who had heard the runes as they were spoken. So how could Sky serve both Sia and Olrig at the same time?

"I've not seen these two runes in a long age," Falken went on. "And even then, they were already ancient."

Melia's amber eyes gleamed. "Fascinating," she murmured, although she did not elaborate.

Grace pushed aside the questions burning in her mind and focused on her patient. With automatic efficiency, she irrigated and sutured the lacerations.

"Beltan, help me sit him up. I need to bind these bandages around his chest to hold them in place."

With Beltan's help, they sat the young man up and folded the shreds of his brown robe down to his waist. Like his back, Sky's chest and arms were massively built.

"By Vathris, I'd say he could swing a sword if he had to," Beltan said.

Grace nodded. But for some reason she wondered if that was really the kind of warrior Sky was. More tattoos snaked up the smooth skin of his chest and encircled his biceps. Most of them were runic symbols Grace couldn't decipher, but directly over his heart was an elaborately drawn picture she could clearly make out. It showed the jagged outline of a black tower with three circles floating above it.

No, not circles, Grace. Three moons.

One of the moons was a waxing crescent, one was full, and the last was waning to dark. Skillfully drawn in the circle of each moon was the faint image of a woman's face: a girl, a beautiful woman, and a withered crone.

Grace heard a gasp. It was Aryn; she was staring at the tattoo on Sky's chest. Grace didn't like speaking secretly, but there was something in Aryn's blue eyes—a deep expression of shock—that compelled her.

Aryn? she said, her voice thrumming across the web of the Weirding. *Aryn, what is it?*

It can't be, came Aryn's astonished voice. *By the three faces of Sia, it can't be. A black tower—didn't they raise a black tower?*

Who did, Aryn?

The Runebreakers . . .

What was Aryn talking about? What did she mean about the three faces of Sia? Grace started to form another question in her mind, but before she could send it along the threads of the Weirding, Beltan spoke in a low voice.

"Grace."

Her gaze came into quick focus as she ceased reaching out with the Touch. Sky gazed at her with gentle brown eyes.

She lifted a hand to her heart, and his homely face crinkled in a weary grin. He made a quick, elegant gesture with a hand, then pantomimed a stitching motion. *Thank you, my lady. For sewing me up.*

Startled, she couldn't help returning his smile. "You're welcome, Sky. I don't think your wounds are too serious, not if we keep them clean. But who—what did this to you?"

His grin faded, and he shook his head. He seemed to grasp her words from the air with a hand and set them gently but firmly aside. *That's not important right now, my lady.* He made another set of pantomimes, using a finger to mimic writing on his palm, then holding his hand out to Grace.

"I don't understand," Beltan said with a frown. "What's he trying to say?"

However, Grace caught the meaning of his gestures as clearly as if the words had flown to her across the Weirding.

"A message," she softly. "He says that he's brought us a message."

Melia stepped closer, her eyes locked on Sky. "A message? But from whom?"

Again Sky made a series of eloquent gestures.

From those who are lost.

For a long moment they stared at the young man in stunned silence.

It can't be, Grace. He can't know they're missing.

But who else could Sky be talking about? Who else was lost? No one except Travis, Lirith, Durge, and Sareth.

The others seemed to recover their wits at once, and all began talking at the same time, questioning Sky. A shudder coursed through the young man's body.

He's lost blood, Grace, and he can't keep warm. If he gets too cold, he could still slip into shock.

She held up a hand, and she was somewhat surprised to see this had the effect of silencing the others. Her lessons in imperiousness with Ephesian seemed to be paying off. She handed Beltan the blanket the others had brought, and while she and the other women turned their backs, Beltan and Falken helped Sky out of the last shreds of his robe. When Grace turned around, the young man lay again on the chaise, tightly wrapped in the blanket. He was still shivering, but not so severely.

"Drink this," Grace said, handing him a cup of watered wine, and he complied. The alcohol would act as a mild sedative, and it would also help control any bacteria or amoebas in the water. The last thing he needed now was a secondary infection.

After he handed her the empty cup, Sky motioned with his hands, and as always the meaning of the gestures was strangely clear.

"You want your robe?" Grace said. "But I'm afraid there's not much left to it."

However, Sky gestured again, and she picked up the heap of rags from where it had fallen and handed it to him. He rummaged through the garment, then let it slip back to the floor. In his hand was a key. The key was large and looked to be forged of black iron. He held it out.

You must take this, my lady. You must take it and go there.

Falken rubbed his chin with his gloved hand. "But go where? What does that key open, Sky?"

The young man shrugged, letting the blanket slip off his left shoulder. He pointed to the tattoo just above his heart—the tattoo of the dark tower.

The bard let out an oath. "By all the Old Ones, it's the Black Tower, isn't it? That's where you want us to go. The Tower of the Runebreakers."

Sky nodded. Aryn clamped her left hand to her mouth too late to stifle a gasp. Grace glanced at her. Why did Sky's words disturb the young witch so? There was something about the Runebreakers—something the baroness knew and had not told Grace. But what?

It would have to wait. Grace knelt beside the chaise and grasped Sky's hand. "I don't understand. I thought the Black Tower had been abandoned for centuries, that there were no more Runebreakers. Why should we go there?"

He pressed the iron key into her fingers. *To find what has been lost.*

Grace froze. Maybe, just maybe, she understood. Falken had told her the stories: how the Runebreakers had vanished from Falengarth long ago, and how the members of the other two runic orders—the Runebinders and Runespeakers—had turned against them, blaming the Runebreakers for bringing the fear and hatred of the people upon all wizards and workers of magic.

But there is still one Runebreaker left, isn't there, Grace?

Beltan spoke the word before he could. "Travis. It's Travis isn't it? Somehow he's there, along with the others, at the Black Tower. We have to go find them." The big knight started for the door, as if he would leave on the journey that very moment.

Sky held out a hand. *Wait.*

"What is it, Sky?" Melia said softly.

He gestured again to the tattoo of the tower, then made his hands into two fists and circled them around each other several times. Then, at the point in the circle when his fists were farthest apart, he halted.

These gestures were too much for Grace. "I don't understand, Sky. What do you mean?"

"I think I know," Falken said. "It's Midwinter's Day. That's when you want us to go to the Black Tower."

Of course. When the sun appeared to be its farthest from

Eldh. "But why?" Grace said. "Why go there on Midwinter's Day and not now?"

Once more Sky made motions that bespoke words. *Because that is when the lost may be found again.*

Falken started to ask more questions, but the young man's eyes fluttered, and he sank back against the chaise. Instantly, Grace's medical instincts superseded any desire to learn more about Sky's mysterious message.

"He's exhausted," she pronounced. "You can talk to him more later. Right now he needs to rest."

Falken started to protest, but Grace gave him a look as piercing as a hypodermic needle, and the bard clamped his mouth shut. After the others departed, she smoothed Sky's hair from his heavy brow. She was full of questions herself, but they could wait. "Will you be all right?"

He gave her a faint smile, then reached up and gripped her hand, pressing her fingers tighter around the iron key.

I will be now, my lady. I will be now.

She returned his smile, but he had already shut his eyes, and in moments his breathing grew deep and even. Grace slipped from the room, shutting the door behind her.

The others were gathered around the table in the villa's central room—although Beltan was pacing rather than sitting.

"I don't see why we can't leave now," the knight was saying. "How far is it? Maybe eightscore leagues? We could be there in three weeks."

"You heard Sky," Falken said, then scratched his head. "Or saw him, I suppose. He says that whatever it is that we'll find in the Black Tower, it won't be there until Midwinter's Day. Or perhaps the key won't even work until then. If we go now, we could end up sitting around for weeks. And even before the Black Tower was abandoned, those were wild lands. It wouldn't exactly be a safe place to set up camp for that long."

Beltan clenched his hands into fists. "But Travis and the others could be wounded or starving. They could die waiting for us."

"You're raving, dear," Melia said affectionately, touching the knight's arm. "Certainly Sky would not direct us to delay our journey if the others were there and in need of our aid."

"Why there of all places?" Aryn murmured. The baroness's

gaze seemed turned inward. "Why must we go to the Tower of the Runebreakers? And why now? This can't be good. It can't."

Grace stared at the young witch. Why was Aryn so upset at this news? Grace started to speak—

—and a pounding emanated from the front door of the villa.

For a moment all of them were too startled to move. The pounding came again, hard and urgent. Then Beltan crossed to the door in three strides and threw it open.

The man in the doorway was not one of the emperor's men; he did not wear the bronze breastplate or leather kilt of the Tarrasian imperial soldiers. Instead, he was clad in a chain-mail shirt over gray tunic and hose, along with a forest-green cloak spattered with mud. The man pulled his hand back just in time to keep from pounding on Beltan's chest. Only as a grin crossed his handsome face did Grace realize she recognized him. The man was not so tall as Beltan, but well shaped. And with his short, wild red hair and the pointed red beard on his chin, it could only be—

"Sir Tarus!" Beltan exclaimed.

The blond knight threw his arms around the other man and caught him in a fierce embrace, dragging him over the threshold and into the villa in the process. The red-haired man seemed to hesitate, then returned the gesture.

Finally, Beltan released him. "By the tail of Vathris's Bull, you reek, Sir Tarus."

The young man laughed and scratched his beard, as if digging for unwanted trespassers within. "I've been riding as fast as I could for more than a week, Sir Beltan. And I fear there wasn't a lot of time for niceties like bathing or sleep. I was going to warn you, but—"

"—but as usual," Melia said, gliding forward, "Sir Beltan's enthusiasm has gotten the better of him. Of course, in your case, it's easy to see why, Sir Tarus."

The knight's cheeks flushed as crimson as his beard. He bowed before Melia, chain mail jingling.

Grace remembered the first—and only—time she had met Sir Tarus. It had been on their journey to the Gray Tower earlier that year. They had encountered Tarus and Beltan, along with the other Knights of the Order of Malachor, in the forests of western Calavan. She had guessed then that Tarus and Beltan had been lovers, at least for a time. Clumsy as she was at reading others' emotions, even she could see it now when Tarus rose and glanced at Beltan—a shy light in his eyes.

However, his smile was strong and genuine, and—it seemed to Grace—bore no hint of heartbreak. She supposed it had not been hard for a man as good-looking as Tarus to find another to warm his bed. But it was more than that. There had been a boyish ebullience to Tarus when she met him last—she could see it still in his face. Yet there was a strength there now as well. Beltan had left him in command of the band of Malachorian Knights; it seemed being a leader suited him.

"It's good to look upon you again, too, Lady Grace," Tarus said, bowing in her direction.

She winced. He must have seen her staring. Hastily she returned the bow, only belatedly realizing she should have curtsied instead.

And be grateful for your goofiness, she told herself with a wry smile. *In case you ever start to delude that you really are a queen...*

"Thank you," she said. "Now, are you going to tell us why you've ridden so hard to Tarras?"

"To find us, obviously," Falken said. "But for what is the question?"

In an instant, Tarus's demeanor changed. He threw his shoulders back and spoke in a formal voice. "I bear a message from King Boreas for Her Highness, the Lady Aryn, Baroness of Elsandry."

Aryn clutched the back of a chair with her left hand. "A message for me? From the king?"

Grace understood the shock in the young woman's blue eyes. She had stolen away from Calavere six months earlier and had not been back since. Nor had she asked for King Boreas's permission before traveling south to Tarras, even though the king was her foster father. Suddenly, Aryn didn't look so much like a regal young woman as a teenager who had gotten caught sneaking out her bedroom window.

Tarus bowed in Aryn's direction, then straightened. "This message comes to you by the hand of His Majesty, King Boreas of Calavan, Lord of the Land Between the Two Rivers, Bearer of the Sword of Calavus, and—"

"Yes, yes," Falken said, waving his black-gloved hand, "we're all aware of Boreas's overwhelming magnificence. Could you just get on with the message?"

Tarus bit his lip to hide a grin. He moved closer to Aryn, speaking more casually now. "I have a summons for you from the king, my lady. Boreas has commanded you to return to Calavere at once, making all possible haste."

Aryn still clutched the chair; she looked as if she would fall if it were snatched away. "Return to Calavere? But why? Am I to be . . . punished?"

"Punished?" Tarus frowned. "No, my lady, it is for a much happier reason that Boreas has bid you return. You see, the king has finally found a husband for you."

Aryn stared, mouth open, as did the others.

"Congratulations, Lady Aryn," Tarus said with a big grin. "You're going to be married."

10.

"It seems to be a day for messages," Falken said, setting down his empty wine cup on the table in the villa's main gathering room. He looked up as Grace quietly shut the door to the side chamber. "So, how's our first courier doing?"

She sat down at the table. "He's still sleeping. I think he'll be out for a while. Whatever happened to Sky on his journey, he's utterly exhausted."

"I'd like to know exactly where it was he journeyed from," Falken said. "And I have a dozen other questions for our mysterious friend. But I suppose that will have to wait until he wakes up."

"Yes," Grace said firmly, "It will."

She reached for the wine bottle in the center of the table and upended it over an available cup.

Exactly two drops poured forth.

She set down the bottle and shot a dark look at both Falken

and Beltan. The bard feigned a look of surprise, and the blond knight gave her a sheepish shrug before hastily quaffing the last swallow in his own cup.

"So where are the others?" Grace said with a sigh.

"Tarus is taking that much-needed bath," Beltan said. "And I think Melia is upstairs with Aryn."

Grace sighed again. It was good the lady was with Aryn. Tarus's message from King Boreas had stunned them all—although maybe it shouldn't have.

She had learned not long after meeting Aryn that Boreas intended to find a husband for the young baroness by her twenty-first birthday, someone who could help rule the barony of Elsandry and who would be a loyal vassal for the king. However, in the upheaval of these last months, it had been easy to forget about such matters. One thing Grace had learned in her time on Eldh was that, while being a noble brought many privileges, it also brought far less welcome duties and responsibilities. Aryn's marriage was of great political importance to Boreas; her heart—and her wishes—had nothing to do with it.

Aryn had only nodded at Tarus's message; she had not cried out in protest or thrown a tantrum or refused in any way. The young woman knew her station. All the same, Grace had seen the stricken look in her blue eyes.

"Well, isn't this a lively crowd," Tarus said with a grin, striding into the room.

Grace managed a weak smile. The young knight was much improved for his bath, both the dirt and weariness gone from his face, the beard on his chin trimmed to a neat point. The servants had cleaned the road grime from his cloak and tunic, and no doubt his mail shirt was off being polished.

Beltan gave the red-haired man an admiring look. Grace knew Beltan loved Travis more than anything. But Travis was a world away, and Grace was beginning to get the sense that, on Eldh, there was a distinction between love and sex. The former was an exalted ideal, to be treasured and cherished; but the latter was regarded as more akin to food—or in Beltan's case ale—a staple nourishment that one could do without for only so long before ill effects resulted.

And what about you, Grace? If physical intimacy was really such a necessity for life, you'd be six feet under by now.

Of course, most people hadn't spent ten years of their life in an orphanage run by people with hearts made out of iron. While she had left the shadow of the past behind her, she couldn't change what the past had made her. Or at least, she hadn't changed yet. And whatever Beltan's look portended, Grace noticed that Tarus studiously avoided it.

A full bottle of wine had appeared on the table, brought by a servant. Grace poured a cup for herself, then filled another and held it out toward Tarus.

"Thank you, my lady," he said. "And how did you know I could use a drink?"

"Doctor's instincts."

Tarus started to reach for the cup—

—then spun around, jerking the dagger from his belt and holding it at the ready. The air in front of Tarus rippled, then grew smooth again. A lithe figure clad in black leather stood before him, golden eyes gleaming.

"Not bad, Servant of the Bull," Vani said, a sharp smile slicing across her angular face. "You are swifter than most I have met."

Tarus let out a cry of alarm. Grace tried to call out, to tell him it was all right, that Vani was a friend, but she was too slow. Tarus thrust forward with his dagger hand.

The hand was empty.

Vani cleared her throat. Her eyes flickered downward, and Tarus followed her gaze. She tapped a dagger against the inside of his thigh. His dagger.

"What the—?" Tarus said, eyes wide as he took a quick step back.

Vani grinned, flipped the dagger in the air then tossed it hilt first at Tarus, who, despite his startlement, caught it in a swift hand.

Finally, Grace found her voice. "Tarus—I'd like you to meet our friend Vani."

The young man glanced at Beltan. "Friend?"

The blond knight hesitated, then gave a curt nod. "She's a far better warrior than most men will ever be, Tarus. Be glad you aren't her enemy. If you were, right now you'd be joining those fanatical new priests I've heard about here in Tarras—the ones who've offered up the jewels of their manhood in a golden bowl at the altar of Vathris."

Tarus swallowed hard, and Grace tried not to notice the quick check he made of his equipment.

"Vani," she said, rising, "we didn't see you come in."

"Do we ever?" Falken said with a pained look.

The bard had a point. "Is it time?" Grace said to the assassin.

Vani nodded. "My al-Mama is waiting for you."

Just as the last rays of the sun turned the gold domes of Tarras to copper, they reached the circle of slender *ithaya* trees atop the white cliffs north of the city. Here, a thousand feet above the harbor, the Mournish had camped for the last two months. Half-lost in the gathering shadows among the trees, Grace could just make out the fantastical shapes of their wagons: a hare, a snail, a crouching lion, and—coiled like a serpent ready to strike—a dragon.

Part of Grace had been reluctant to leave Sky at the villa. But he was sleeping, and all of her instincts as a doctor—and as a witch—told her his wounds were not serious, that he would recover. She had left one of the manservants outside the door of Sky's room with strict orders not to let anyone in.

Despite being weary from his long journey, Sir Tarus walked with them up the trail to see the Mournish.

"King Boreas ordered me to return to Calavere with Lady Aryn," the young knight said. "I'm not about to let some bunch of vagabonds steal her away. I've heard stories about the Mournish, and how they . . ."

His words trailed off as he noticed Vani's hard, golden stare.

Beltan clapped his hand on Tarus's back. "And you've heard how they throw the best parties, and you don't want to miss your chance to see one."

As they entered the circle of trees, the last sliver of the sun vanished beneath the western horizon. At the same moment, to the east, the full circle of Eldh's enormous moon sailed above the edge of the sea. It looked to Grace as if the moon had actually risen out of the water, and its light made a silver road on the surface of the ocean.

Melia stopped and curtsied in the direction of the moon, murmuring something. Grace wasn't certain, but it might have been, *It's good to see you as well, dear.* Before she could wonder more, brown hands touched her arms, drawing her and the others into the circle of firelight in the center of the grove.

One thing hadn't changed: The Mournish still knew how to throw a party. Wild music swirled all around, and dancers leaped and darted like the flames. The smell of rich, roasted meat was thick on the air, and the cup in Grace's hand seemed eternally filled with fiery red wine. However, she wasn't really hungry, and she had never been much of a dancer, so she was content to sit on a pillow beside Aryn and Beltan and stare into the fire while the wine did its work.

At one point during the revel, one of the dancers—a voluptuous woman with smoky eyes—approached Grace.

"Where is your friend?" she said in a lilting voice.

"My friend?" Grace said.

"Yes, the dark-haired one with the solemn face and many muscles."

Grace blinked. "You mean Durge?"

"Yes, D'hurj." The woman smiled. "That was his name."

Grace felt a pang in her heart, and she wondered if that fragile organ could bear much more pain. "I'm afraid he's not here."

The woman was clearly disappointed. "I am sorry to learn it. He was a fine . . . dancer."

With a flash of scarves, the woman spun away.

The feast continued as sparks rose up to glimmer among the stars. Then—at some signal Grace could not detect—it was over. The dancers and musicians slipped away into the shadows. The doors of the wagons opened and shut. The companions were alone in the circle of firelight.

Not quite alone, Grace.

Gold eyes shone in a withered face, gazing at Grace. Propped on a heap of pillows beside Vani was a figure Grace had not noticed in the wildness of the revel. Her neck was as thin and crooked as a vulture's, and hair like cobwebs floated about her knobby head.

The ancient woman smiled at Grace, baring her one fanglike

tooth. "I told you, did I not, that you would be the strongest of them all?"

Grace licked her lips. "Thank you for inviting us here. It was you who invited us, wasn't it?"

The old woman let out a cackle. "I had the idea, yes, though Vani spoke it before I could. I wished to speak to you before we departed. We will begin our wanderings again on the morrow. Such is our fate." Her eyes narrowed. "Just as you will begin your own journey soon—for such is yours."

Grace lifted a hand to her throat. "How do you know about that? Did Vani tell you?"

The old woman scowled. "Surely you must know the portents are clear and strong. The ruby star vanishes as suddenly as it appears; things go lost that must be found once more. And no matter how I shuffle them, the cards I draw are always the same. The Wagon, the Spire, and the Queen of Blades. I know not what this tower is, or what you will find. I only know that you will go there."

Falken jerked his gaze up from the fire. "Why did you call her that just now? The Queen of Blades?"

The crone shrugged knife-sharp shoulders. "It is her fate, is it not? Even I can see that much, dim though my eyes have grown. And I would have thought you of all people would know that, Falken Blackhand." She cackled again. "But not Blackhand for long. For that I've seen as well."

Falken flexed his gloved hand, but what he thought of the old woman's words he didn't say.

"Do you truly believe they can find Sareth and the others, al-Mama?" Vani said to the old woman.

"It is their fate to seek your brother and the rest. However, whether it is the fate of the lost to be found, I cannot say. Would that I could see what will become of the *A'narai*. But he has no fate, and my cards are useless in this. He is a mystery to me, as are all those near to him."

Tarus, who had been sitting quietly throughout the revel, glanced at Beltan. "Either I'm denser than I've always liked to believe, or the Mournish really do know how to cast spells of befuddlement. I don't understand a word of any of this."

"Don't you?" the old woman said before Beltan could answer. She turned piercing eyes on Tarus. "Have you not seen signs of the coming darkness yourself?"

Tarus sat up straight, his blue eyes wide.

Beltan laid his hand on the young man's knee. "What is it, Tarus? I'd bet my sword you bring more news than just King Boreas's message for Aryn. What's happening in the Dominions?"

Tarus sighed. "I wish I could tell you. All I know are rumors. They started around the beginning of Revendath. At first it sounded like the kinds of stories peasants in the backwoods always tell—shadows in the wood, strange noises, weird lights on hilltops—that sort of thing. Only then..." He cocked his head. "You know the borders of the Dominion of Eredane have been closed ever since last Midwinter's Eve?"

Falken nodded. "Queen Eminda was murdered at the Council of Kings. Her chief counselor was an ironheart. We have no idea who's ruling Eredane now."

"Except I think we do," Tarus said. "For now it's not just Eredane whose borders are closed, but Brelegond as well. No one is allowed in or out. And it's said that guarding the roads are knights who wear black armor and black visors on their helms, and who strike down anyone who strays a half a league into that Dominion."

Tarus's words were a cold dagger in Grace's chest. A year ago there had been rumors of shadows like this, and the rumors had turned out to be true. Wraithlings and *feydrim*—servants of the Pale King—had stalked the land. And the Raven Cult that had swept through the Dominions had proved a front for the Pale King as well. After Midwinter's Eve, when Travis sealed the Rune Gate, the wraithlings and *feydrim* had vanished, and in the weeks that followed the newly founded Order of Malachor had stamped out the activities of the Raven Cult. It had seemed the dark days were over.

Except maybe now the dark days are returning.

"What of the other Dominions?" Falken said to Tarus.

"Things seem well enough," the knight said. "Calavan awaits the happy marriage of Lady Aryn. Galt stands uneasily in the shadow of Eredane, but I've heard naught of trouble there. Toloria is as you left it. And the word is that young

Queen Inara has proved to be a strong leader in Perridon, ruling well in her infant son's name."

Melia smoothed the fabric of her kirtle. "You have forgotten Embarr, Tarus."

He shook his head. "No, my lady, I believe it is Embarr who has forgotten us—as well as the pact it made at the Council of Kings. The stories say that King Sorrin grows madder by the day. That I can't vouch for. But I do know he's pulled all of his knights from the Order of Malachor. Some say he's created his own order of knights, although what he names it, and what its purpose is, I cannot say."

Falken's expression was troubled. "That's strange news."

Tarus gazed at the old Mournish woman, boldly returning her stare. "So what does it all mean, if you can see so much in those cards of yours? Are these black knights connected to everything else that's changing?"

"All things are connected," the crone murmured, as if she had spoken the most profound truth. And perhaps she had at that.

Tarus, however, seemed less than satisfied. He glanced at Grace. "I have not seen Lady Lirith among you. Am I to take it she is one of the ones who was . . . lost?"

Grace's throat was too tight for words, so she nodded instead.

Tarus gazed down at his clasped hands. "I hope she wasn't right, then. I hope it's not already come to this. By Vathris, I thought they were just tales told by the priests. I never thought I'd be alive to see the Final Battle myself."

Grace didn't understand Tarus's words. However, she noticed that Beltan, Falken, and Melia all stared at the young knight with the same look of astonishment.

It was Beltan who recovered first. "This is dark news about the Dominions. But our task is still clear. We have to journey to the Black Tower."

"That may not be so simple as we think," Falken said. "The Tower of the Runebreakers stands where the range of the Fal Sinfath ends at the Winter Wood."

Beltan frowned. "But that puts it on the other side of Brelegond from us."

"Exactly," the bard said, expression grim. "And from what good Sir Tarus here tells us, journeying through Brelegond is not an option right now."

Beltan pounded a fist on his knee. "This is one time I'll agree with Vani's al-Mama and her cards. We all have to find a way to get there."

"No, not all of us," Aryn said in a soft voice.

The baroness sat on the edge of the firelight. Her face was touched by sorrow, yet there was a resoluteness to her expression. Grace let out a breath. In all their talk, they had forgotten about Tarus's message and what it portended for the young woman.

"My dear one," Melia said, taking Aryn's hand in her own. Aryn gave her a faint smile.

Grace reached out and touched the Weirding. It was easy to pick out Aryn's brilliant blue thread.

Please don't worry, Aryn. I'm sure it'll be all right.

Grace winced. The words were utterly worthless. But hopefully Aryn could feel what she meant.

I know it will, Grace, came Aryn's voice, strong across the web of the Weirding. *Ever since I was a little girl, I always knew this would be my duty. And I won't fight it. It's just that so much is uncertain right now, and I promised Ivalaine—*

Grace felt a tug in her mind as Aryn hastily pulled her thread back, breaking the connection. What had the baroness been about to say? And why didn't she want Grace to hear it?

Maybe it's because you weren't the only one who was listening, Grace.

Melia's golden eyes were fixed on Aryn, her visage unreadable. Aryn pulled her hand from Melia's and gazed into the fire. There was something the baroness knew, something she wasn't telling. Ivalaine had commanded Aryn to do something. Only what?

"We can't go through Brelegond," Falken said, "so we're going to have to find another way to the Black Tower."

Melia raised an eyebrow. "And why do I have the feeling you already know what that way is, Falken?"

The bard couldn't quite hide a wolfish grin. He reached into the case that held his lute and pulled out a book. It was *Pagan*

Magics of the North, the book Grace had found in the university library.

"I've been reading this interesting little volume," Falken said, thumbing through the yellowed pages. "I'm still not certain who wrote it, but whoever it was, he or she knew a great deal about both magic and history."

Melia let out an exasperated breath. "Do spare us the dramatics, Falken. You've learned something in the book, and you know you can't resist telling us, so out with it."

The bard shut the book and looked up. "I know where we can find the shards of Fellring."

Grace listened in growing numbness as Falken explained what he had read in the book: how after the first War of the Stones, the broken shards of Ulther's magic sword Fellring—with which he had defeated the Pale King—were taken back across the Winter Sea, to his homeland of Toringarth.

"So you think we should go to Toringarth?" Beltan said dubiously.

The bard nodded. "Whatever Tarus's troubling stories mean, there's one thing we do know. Mohg, Lord of Nightfall, seeks a door back to Eldh. If we could find a way to reforge Fellring, we would have a powerful weapon we could use to fight him."

Grace nearly choked on her tongue. She knew very well what Falken had failed to say—that, according to the legends he loved so much, only Ulther's heir could wield Fellring. But whatever he might think, Grace knew she was not up to the task of slaying gods, no matter how old and decrepit they might be.

"It's nearly two months until Midwinter," Falken went on. "What's more, we know we can't journey through Brelegond—and it's not any farther to the Black Tower from Toringarth than it is from Tarras. We can sail to Toringarth, then make our way to the tower in plenty of time for Midwinter's Day."

"But what about Eredane?" Beltan said. "Are not the black knights in command there? And what of Toringarth itself? No word has come from that land in centuries."

"We can stay between the River Silverflood and the Western Wood on our way south to the Black Tower," Falken said. "We won't have to set foot in Eredane."

"Yes, Falken of the Blackhand," al-Mama said in her hoarse

voice. "Your words feel like fate to me. I believe you all must do as he says."

Grace touched the necklace at her throat. "These black knights." She glanced at Falken. "Do you think they're related to the Pale King somehow? I mean, they—"

She couldn't voice the rest of her thoughts, but she knew Falken would understand. It was the bard who told her the story, how a band of black knights had murdered her parents. And it made sense, didn't it? Wouldn't the Pale King want to stamp out all of the heirs to the throne of Malachor?

"I don't know, Grace," Falken said. "But if the black knights are linked to the Pale King, then it's all the more important we find a way to forge Fellring anew."

Grace tried and failed to swallow the lump in her throat. The idea of playing a fabled hero was absurd. However, when she saw the light burning in the ageless bard's eyes, she found she had no words to tell him he was wrong.

The last flames flickered atop the coals, then in a sizzle they vanished; it was time to go. They bid Vani and her al-Mama farewell, then rose and made their way from the circle of wagons to descend the trail in darkness.

"Don't worry, Grace," Beltan said, clasping her hand in his. His grip was rough and strong. "Falken's plan is a good one, I'm sure of it. We'll find the pieces of your sword, and we'll still get to Travis in time."

Grace started to answer him, only she caught the flash of two gold eyes gazing in the darkness. Then the night rippled, folded, and the eyes were gone.

The moon was high in the starry sky when they reached the villa again. They had made their way back in silence. Grace had wanted to talk to Aryn, but she hadn't known what to say. As they stepped into the main room, Grace saw that the manservant still stood before the door to the side chamber.

"Thank you, Mahalim," she said, touching his arm. "Go get some rest now."

The man gave her a weary smile, then bowed and departed. Quietly, Grace pushed open the door and entered the room to see how her patient was doing.

"Oh," she said, stopping halfway into the room.

"What is it, Grace?" she heard Falken say behind her. Then came the bard's soft oath, and she knew she didn't need to explain anything.

Mahalim had guarded the door; she didn't doubt that. And the room's only window was small and barred with iron. All the same, the chaise was empty, and the blanket lay crumpled on the floor.

Sky was gone.

11.

At dawn two days later, they gathered on the docks of Tarras to say good-bye.

They had already made their hasty farewells to Ephesian the evening before, in the vast throneroom of the imperial palace in the First Circle. The emperor hadn't taken the news of their departure well.

"This is ill news indeed, cousin," he said, glaring at Grace and crossing his arms over the great bulk of his body. "I should have you tossed in prison so you can't leave."

Grace bit her lip. "That isn't how one treats family, Your Magnificence."

"On the contrary—that's exactly how one treats family. Especially if one doesn't wish to wake up one morning to find a dagger in one's back." Ephesian sighed and adjusted the eternally crooked circle of gold *ithaya* leaves on his brow. "Consider that my last lesson in imperial rule to you, cousin. I shall miss you indeed."

"And I you," Grace said, almost surprised to realize how much she meant it.

She moved a step up the dais and leaned forward to kiss his cheek—only belatedly realizing this could well be an offense punishable by death. However, the emperor only held a hand to his cheek as they departed.

As luck would have it, the ship Falken had hired to take them north belonged to one Captain Magard—the very same captain, Grace learned, who had brought the others south to Tarras. Magard had bought a new cargo of spices and was heading to the Dominion of Perridon for trade. Falken's gold had convinced the captain to extend his journey northward a bit farther.

"Magard has agreed to take us as far north as Omberfell," Falken said, picking up his lute case from the dock and slinging it over a shoulder. "That's a city on the northwest coast of Embarr, at the mouth of the River Fellgrim."

Melia's eyes glinted in the morning light like the gold domes of Tarras. "And why will Magard only go as far as Omberfell? Does not Toringarth lie farther north, across the Winter Sea?"

"It does," Falken said. "But Magard's ship was built for southern waters. The Winter Sea will be thick with ice this time of year. It would crush the hull of Magard's ship like the shell of a nut. We'll have to find a new ship in Omberfell to take us the last leg."

"Maybe we should wait for spring," Beltan said.

Falken's blue eyes were hard. "And maybe spring will be too late. Come on, Beltan—help me load our things on the ship."

The bard started toward the gangplank, carrying nothing but his lute case. Beltan eyed the large heap of bags on the dock, sighed, then started to gather them up.

"Not those, dear," Melia said, pointing to two small leather satchels Grace knew belonged to the lady. "You can leave those with Lady Aryn's and Sir Tarus's things."

Beltan frowned. "Why?"

"Because I'm not going to Toringarth with you, dear. I'm going to accompany Aryn to Calavere."

"What?" came Falken's sharp voice. At once the bard turned and hurried back toward them. "What do you mean you're not coming north with us?"

A pained expression crossed Melia's face. "Let me try again, dear. You run along to Toringarth just as you've planned. Only when you arrive, I won't be with you. That's because I'll be in Calavere. With Aryn." She patted his arm. "Do we have it all sorted out now?"

The bard glowered at her. "I know what you meant, Melia."

"Really? Then why did you ask?"

"Because it doesn't make any sense," Falken growled.

The lady's expression softened a fraction. "Actually, it does, dear one. You know that the sea and I don't mix very well. And besides, a lady of Aryn's station cannot travel alone with a man. It would not be seemly."

Tarus grinned. "I think Lady Aryn's virtue is quite safe with me. I suspect that's why King Boreas chose me for the task."

Melia gave the young knight's cheek a fond but firm pat. "Don't ever disagree with me again, dear, and we'll get along famously on the road to Calavere."

Tarus hastily picked up Melia's bags. "I'll put these with Aryn's things," he said, and hurried across the dock to where their horses waited.

Only as he reached the horses did Grace realize there were not two, but three. The third was a mist-white mare that looked exactly like the horse Melia had ridden east to Perridon earlier that year.

It was all decided then. Beltan gave Aryn a great hug, then lifted their bags, staggered under the weight, and started up the ship's gangplank. Melia and Falken moved a short distance away to exchange their final words in private. Tarus was with the horses. That left only Grace and Aryn.

"It seems so strange," Grace said. "Saying good-bye."

Aryn reached out and took her hand, her blue eyes shining. "Then let's not say it, Grace. Let's not even think it. After all, it's just for a short time. And when I see you next, you'll have the shards of Fellring, and I'll lay my head on your knee and listen while you tell me all about your marvelous adventures in the north."

Grace squeezed her hand. "And when I see you again, you'll be . . ."

Aryn's smile was brave, but it couldn't quite mask the trepidation in her eyes. "I'll be your friend just as ever, and far more than glad at the sight of you."

Grace embraced the baroness. Aryn had been her very first friend on Eldh, and the young woman would always be her best. Without even thinking, Grace spun the words over the threads of the Weirding. *I love you, Aryn.*

The reply came back, nearly overpowering in its strength. *And I you.*

At last they started to let go. Then, just before the connection was broken, Grace spun one last question along the Weirding. *Aryn, I don't mean to pry, but I think something's been troubling you lately—something about the Witches and what Ivalaine bid you to do. What was it?*

She felt Aryn stiffen in her arms, then hastily the young woman pulled away. "The others are coming, Grace," she murmured. "It's time for us to go."

Soft as they were, the words were like a slap. Grace stared as Aryn moved quickly toward Tarus and Melia. Then Beltan and Falken were beside Grace. A high, aching note sounded on the air. A sailor in the rigging of Magard's ship blew on a large seashell.

"It's time, Grace," Falken said.

They bid their last farewells quickly. Then, together with Beltan and Falken, Grace walked up the gangplank of the ship. She turned at the top to wave one final time, but Aryn, Melia, and Tarus had already mounted their horses and were gone.

Grace didn't have the Sight, not like Lirith did. All the same, she felt a strange premonition of fear and darkness. Aryn was hiding something—something that would lead to trouble in the end. She was sure of it. Grace felt the urge to run down the gangplank and dash after the baroness.

It was too late. As the piercing note of the shell horn sounded again, Magard's crew leaped into swift action. The plank was pulled in. Ropes hissed in all directions. The furled sails fluttered, as if anxious to fly free from their bindings. First, the ship had to be rowed out of the harbor. Two dozen oars lapped into the water, and the ship moved smoothly away from the dock. Grace gripped the railing as the deck rose and fell beneath her.

It'll be all right, she told herself with a fierceness that almost felt like conviction. *Aryn isn't a girl anymore. She can take care of herself. Besides, Melia is going with her.*

Then again, Grace had a feeling it wasn't just out of a sense of propriety and a dislike for seasickness that Melia had decided to go north with Aryn.

Tarus's stories last night troubled both her and Falken. Melia plans to keep an eye on things in the Dominions—just in case the shadows really are gathering again.

"What's wrong, Grace?" Beltan said next to her. "You're not getting seasick already, are you?"

The salty wind blew the knight's hair back from his brow, and his green eyes were concerned. Falken was nowhere in sight; he must have gone down to see to their quarters.

Grace reached out and found the knight's hand. "It's nothing, Beltan. It's just that—"

Nearby, a stray edge of one of the sails fluttered outward from one of the ship's two masts. Then it fell back, revealing a dark, lithe figure that had not been there a heartbeat before. She stalked forward, moving sleekly as a cat despite the movement of the deck. Her short black hair was slicked back, and she wore the same tight black-leather garb as the day Grace first met her.

Beltan's eyes narrowed. "Vani. What are you doing here?"

"As I said, it is my fate to come with you on this journey," the Mournish woman said, her gold eyes fixed on Grace rather than the big knight.

For a moment Grace's heart leaped in her chest. What they were trying to do seemed so daunting; maybe having Vani with them made it all just a little less impossible. Then she saw the hard look of suspicion in Beltan's gaze, as well as the way Vani cocked her shoulders so that she was turned slightly away from him, and Grace's heart sank again.

The ship moved out into the shimmering waters of the harbor, and Grace felt the first hints of churning in her stomach. Something told her this was going to be a long journey.

12.

Captain Magard's ship was named the *Fate Runner*. Grace couldn't have thought of a more appropriate name. But were they running from fate, or directly into its arms?

They sailed north through the sparkling waters of the Dawn

Sea, the coast always just visible as a hazy green line far off to port. Grace knew it made sense for ships to stay close to the shore. After all, there were no global positioning satellites orbiting Eldh to tell them where they were. Their first day out at sea, she saw Captain Magard use an instrument she supposed was some sort of sextant to measure the angle of the sun. That would give him an idea of their latitude. However, without an accurate clock—something Grace had yet to see on Eldh—there was no way to measure longitude. Sailing away from the shore meant sailing off the edge of the map.

Then again, the Polynesians found Hawaii, and the Vikings made it all the way to Newfoundland in their dragon ships. Perhaps there were other continents on Eldh; perhaps ancient navigators had already discovered them.

That first evening, as the sun touched the sea and set it afire, she decided to ask Captain Magard about it. There wasn't much else to do. It hadn't taken long to get settled in their two cramped cabins belowdecks—one for Beltan and Falken, and one for Vani and Grace. While none of them were violently seasick, the other three were made more than a little queasy by the motion of the ship. Beltan and Falken lay on their cots, occasionally groaning like the planks of the hull when the ship struck a particularly large wave. Vani sat cross-legged on the floor of the cabin she shared with Grace, remaining very still.

"I'm meditating," the Mournish woman said. "A *T'gol* must practice the art of concentration, so that she is never caught unaware."

Given the greenish tinge to her coppery skin, Vani was concentrating on not vomiting more than anything else. Grace forced herself not to smile as she left the cabin.

Unlike the others, Grace felt no trace of seasickness. The sourness in her stomach that morning had been a result of anxiety rather than the tossing of the ship, and while it wasn't entirely gone, the feeling had subsided. It would be impossible to turn back now, so there was no use worrying about the journey.

It was obvious her legs were going to take longer to adjust than her stomach. Just walking on the deck without toppling over the rail was a challenge, and she held on to everything in her reach as she inched along.

She found Magard on the aft deck, leaning against the rail and watching the ship's swirling wake. She hadn't been formally introduced to the captain—there had been no time in the bustle of leaving port—but Falken had spoken well of him.

"Excuse me." She searched for something polite to say but found nothing and so decided to dive in. "I was wondering— are there lands on Eldh beside those of Falengarth?"

The captain turned around. His skin was creased like old leather, but his eyes were bright as a gull's. With them, he seemed to size her up in a single look.

"There's Moringarth to the south," he said after moment. "But, save for the sultanates of al-Amún on the north coast, it's nothing but a blasted desert and fit for no man. Then there's Toringarth to the north, but the stories say it's mostly ice. The Black Bard tells me that's where you're headed." Magard rubbed his chin with a hand that bore only four fingers. "Though, by the salt of my blood, I can't fathom why you'd want to go there."

Grace decided it was easier not to reply to that. "Are there any other lands?"

"None I know of. My men think if you sailed too far east, you'd sail right off the edge of the world. But you know what I think, my girl?" His eyes crinkled as he grinned. "I think if you sailed far enough, you'd hit Falengarth again—only the west coast, not the east."

Grace returned his smile. "I think you might just be right, Captain."

"Now you're humoring me. It's a mad idea. But I'll have to write it down someday, when I'm too old to sail anymore and have to spend my days in a tavern near the sea, sitting by a fire with a cup of spiced wine in my hand."

"I think you should," Grace said, and she meant it.

Magard turned, gazing across the ocean. The first stars were just coming out. "It's said there's a whole kingdom there, in the far west of Falengarth."

A cool night wind sprang up off the ocean. Grace crossed her arms, shivering. "What kind of kingdom?"

Magard shrugged. "Who can say? It would be a fool's errand to try to get there overland. They say the way was open once, but if it was, it's closed again long since. Now there's only the Great Western Wood, which goes on for a thousand leagues. And there are queer things in the woods, if you believe the tales. Old things. Yet if you journey all the way west, some say you'll find a kingdom where the streets are paved with silver, and children play with baubles made of gold and jewels. If I could find a way to sail there and start a trade route, I'd be . . ."

His words trailed off in a sigh. For a time they watched the sea change from copper to smoky amethyst.

"I hope you do," Grace said softly. "Find a way to your golden kingdom someday."

Magard's teeth flashed in the darkness. "And what would I do with a kingdom full of silver and jewels? I have all I need right here."

He gestured to the sea. The reflection of countless stars danced on its surface, like diamonds on black silk. Grace smiled, then turned to stumble her way back to her cabin.

The days that followed were peaceful if not quite pleasant, although in their utter sameness one blurred into the next.

Grace rose early each morning. Not that there was anything for her to do. It was just that, between the rolling of the ship and the constant scrabbling of rats in the hull, sleep was a near impossibility. This fact didn't seem to keep Falken and Beltan from spending most of their time lying in their cabin—but both rose quickly enough and scrambled abovedecks when the sound of the horn announced the distribution of the daily ration of ale.

In addition to a generous dipper of ale, every day Magard gave each person on the ship a half of a lemon to eat. It seemed the captain was familiar with both the perils and prevention of scurvy. Grace made sure the others ate every bit of their lemons, although Beltan made such horrible faces one might have thought he was eating a handful of alum.

Meals were served twice daily and consisted mostly of hardtack and salt pork; Grace couldn't help but wonder if that didn't have something to do with all the vomiting. Not all of Magard's crewmen were immune to seasickness, as she would have thought. When the smell became too much, Grace would stand in the cargo hold and breathe in the fragrance rising from the crates filled with spices, letting the aromatic scent clear her head until she felt ready to venture forth again.

Despite the fact that they shared a cabin, Grace spoke little with Vani. The Mournish woman appeared and vanished without warning. Magard's ship wasn't large; it had only two masts and was not much more than a hundred feet from stem to stern. All the same, Vani could disappear for hours on end, and one day Grace didn't catch a glimpse of her at all between dawn and dusk.

Often when Grace did see her, Vani was perched precariously high in the rigging of the ship, shading her eyes with a hand, peering into the distance. Once Grace witnessed her balancing on a single foot on the very top of the aft mast, bending and swaying with the motion of the ship almost as if she were dancing. This feat elicited oaths and wide-eyed looks of awe from Magard's crew, and after that the men would stare at Vani whenever she passed. However, the assassin seemed not to notice them.

The rare times Grace found Vani in the cabin, the Mournish woman was usually meditating, legs crossed, hands on knees, gold eyes half-lidded. Despite her relaxed position, Grace knew Vani was aware of everything around her and could leap into action in the space between two heartbeats.

As she did one day when Grace stepped into the cabin. The sea was particularly rough that day, and Grace had decided to give up trying to stay upright on deck. The roaring of the waves must have kept the sound of her stumbling even from Vani's keen ears, for when she stepped through the cabin's portal, Vani did not look up from her position on the floor. Then Grace saw the single *T'hot* card before her. On the card was the picture of a man. He had piercing gray eyes and was surrounded by blue rays of light.

"Vani . . ." Grace said.

In a motion faster than eyes could comprehend, Vani stood. "The weather grows worse?" she said tersely. The card was nowhere to be seen.

Grace nodded. She searched for something to say, but Vani brushed past her.

"I'll keep a lookout for rocks and reefs."

Once again Grace wondered why Vani had come with them on this journey. Was it really her fate, as she said? Or had it simply been her choice?

Whatever the cards say, she wants to find Travis. Just as much as you do, Grace. Just as much as Beltan does.

She couldn't help laughing at the absurdity of it all. For the slightly bumbling owner of a bar in a small Colorado mountain town, Travis certainly had a way of making others interested in him. The Pale King, Duratek, the Seekers, Trifkin Mossberry and the Little People, the dragon Sfithrisir, the Witches, Melia and Falken, Vani, and of course Beltan—all of them had shown a keen interest in Travis at one point or another.

It was the following day when Grace finally understood the reason for Vani's frequent disappearing act ever since they had boarded the *Fate Runner*. After the previous day's choppiness, the sea was unusually calm and glassy—so much so that even Falken and Beltan ventured abovedecks without the lure of ale. Craving fresh air, Grace accompanied them.

They rounded the foremast and nearly ran into Vani. The Mournish woman leaned against the mast, head bent. Grace caught a flash of color in Vani's hands. Then the assassin looked up, and whatever she had been holding was gone.

"There you are, Vani," Falken said. "Grace told us about your little balancing act." He touched the mast. "You weren't planning a repeat performance, were you? I was sorry I missed the display."

Vani's cheeks darkened, and she did not meet the bard's eyes. "It was not a display. One must ever practice to keep one's body and abilities honed. As a musician, I know you do the same. As should others."

Now her gold eyes flickered in Beltan's direction, focusing on his midsection. This time it was the blond knight's face that flushed. Beltan was strongly built, and his health had been restored by the magic of the fairy, but no one would ever describe him as having a perfect physique. His limbs were long and rangy, and his old ale belly had begun to make something of a resurgence during their weeks at the villa outside Tarras.

Failing utterly to make the action in any way surreptitious, Beltan sucked in his gut. "I've had enough practice in my life. I think I'll stick to my instincts."

Vani cocked her head. "And just how good are those instincts of yours?"

Beltan opened his mouth to reply, but Vani was gone. A fraction of a second later, a shadow stepped out of thin air directly behind the knight. Like black serpents, lean arms coiled around his head.

"One twist is all it would take to snap your neck," she said with a sharp smile. "You may be larger and stronger, but if I had wished it, you would be dead."

Beltan grunted. "Maybe so. But then, at least I would have had some company on my way to the grave."

Only then did Grace see the knife in his right hand. The blade was aimed back, its tip less than an inch from Vani's abdomen. Grace calculated the angle of the knife and visualized the anatomy.

He knew what he was doing, Grace. The knife would pierce the descending aorta. She'd be dead in minutes. There'd be nothing you could do.

"All right you two," Falken said with a scowl. "This really isn't the time or place to show each other up."

Vani's eyes narrowed to slits. "No. This isn't."

The air folded in on itself, and Vani was gone.

Beltan rubbed his neck. "Maybe this time she won't bother to reappear again." The knight stalked away.

That was when it struck Grace. *That's why Vani's been staying out of sight. She's been avoiding Beltan. But why come on this journey if she dislikes him so much?*

The answer to that was obvious. Both of them loved Travis. And nothing fueled suspicion like jealousy. The fact that Travis wasn't there—that they might very well never see him again— only seemed to make things worse.

Grace sighed. She didn't have the energy for this. The journey was going to be hard enough without having to worry about keeping Beltan and Vani from one another's throats. And on this cramped ship, it was impossible they wouldn't run into each other again.

Falken must have sensed her thoughts. He took her arm. "Come on, Your Majesty. Let's get our daily ale and head to the aft deck. I've heard there are no Calavaner knights or Mournish assassins allowed there."

Grace gripped the bard's arm. "Sounds wonderful."

13.

Two days later they docked at the port of Galspeth in Perridon.

Galspeth was a small city at the mouth of the River Serpentstail—and, according to Magard, the last navigable harbor until Omberfell far to the north. After more than a week aboard the cramped vessel, Grace was glad to get off the ship and stretch her legs on a surface that didn't move. It would take Magard a full day to unload and sell his cargo of spices. Since the *Fate Runner* wouldn't leave port again until the next day, the four of them would need to find a place where they could stay.

They made their way from the docks into the cramped and crooked streets of the burgh. Galspeth was wedged into a narrow valley; an imposing gray castle perched above it on a crag. The wind rushing down the valley was cold and sliced through her thin gown, designed for gentler, southern climes. Her shivering didn't go unnoticed.

"We'd better find some new clothes," Falken said. "Things are going to get colder the farther we go north."

Beltan slapped his stomach. "Some ale in our bellies would warm us up."

"How interesting," Vani said, raising an eyebrow. "I have heard the seals that swim these northern waters grow thick layers of blubber to insulate themselves from the cold. It looks as if you are well on your way to emulating them."

Beltan's cheerful expression turned into a glower. Grace sighed and interposed herself between the knight and the assassin. Something told her Falken was right—things were going to get much colder indeed.

They made their way farther into the city. After the relative cleanliness of Tarras—a city that had happily known about sewers for centuries—Grace had forgotten just how filthy the medieval towns of the Dominions could be. The half-timbered shops and homes looked sturdy, but they were stained with soot, and lichen splotched their slate roofs. Dark water ran down the cobbled streets—where it didn't freeze into black lumps—and even the cold wind couldn't keep down the stench.

The people looked like those Grace had seen in other towns in the Dominions: small, gnarled, toothless—old before their time. They wore heavy clothes of smoky colors, although some seemed clad in nothing but rags. Grace saw dozens of small children running about barefoot, their shins covered with oozing chilblains. Why didn't their parents buy shoes for them?

Maybe because they don't have parents, Grace.

A band of children approached, eyes and cheeks hollow, holding out their hands. Grace fumbled for the fat leather purse full of coins Emperor Ephesian had given her. However, Beltan was faster. He pressed a small silver piece into each child's hand, and without a word or smile they ran off.

"Galspeth is a bit dirtier than I remember," the blond man said, watching the children go.

Falken nodded. "Of all the Dominions, Perridon was the hardest hit by the Burning Plague. Who knows how many people died?"

Of course—that was why there were so many orphans.

"It will probably take Queen Inara a good while to get the Dominion back in working order," Falken said. "But I'm sure she's up to the task."

Grace would have liked to have seen the young queen again, along with her spy, the Spider Aldeth. Castle Spardis wasn't far from there—no more than twenty leagues upriver according to a map Captain Magard had shown her. However, Grace knew there wasn't time for a visit. It could take some time to find a ship in Omberfell willing to bear them across the Winter Sea. Then, whether or not they found the shards of Fellring in Toringarth—and Grace wasn't entirely certain she hoped they would—they would have to make haste to the Black Tower to reach it by Midwinter.

They found a shop that sold a variety of clothes. The owner

was a jovial man who looked as if he had decided to emulate seals as well—only with far more success than Beltan. He could barely navigate the cramped store as he chose woolen tunics, thick pairs of hose, leather gloves, and winter cloaks for the men.

Vani refused any new garb—she seemed quite attached to her tight-fitting leathers—but she did acquiesce to a supple, finely woven black cloak. For Grace, the shopkeeper chose a wool gown with accompanying undergarments, as well as a hooded cape lined with silver fox fur.

"You men can change over there," the shopkeeper said, gesturing to a wooden screen in the corner. "And you, my lady, may don your new attire in here." He opened the door to a small room. "I'll send Esolda to assist you."

Before Grace could say she didn't really need help, the shopkeeper looked around, then bellowed. "Esolda? Where are you, you wretched girl? Show yourself now!" He glanced at Grace. "If she wasn't the daughter of my beloved sister, who walks this world no more, I would have turned her out into the streets to beg with the other urchins. I don't know what happened to her, my lady. She used to be a good lass, but lately she grows more lazy and surly by the day. Esolda!"

Presently a young woman whom Grace presumed to be Esolda appeared from behind a curtain. Grace didn't think she looked so much surly as she did simple. She wore a drab gray dress, and the dingy bonnet that covered her hair was pulled all the way down to her eyebrows.

"Well don't just stand there, girl. Help the lady on with her things!"

Esolda trudged after Grace into the side room. She held Grace's new clothes, staring blankly, while Grace turned around and shrugged off her Tarrasian gown.

"I'm ready now," Grace said, teeth chattering. There was no fire in this room. "Esolda, my undergarments, please."

No response. Grace turned around.

The young woman didn't move, save to blink dull brown eyes. "That's an ugly necklace," she said in a thickly accented voice. "It's not a jewel at all."

Grace reached up and gripped the cold shard of steel at her

throat. She smiled, hoping that might make the girl more comfortable—and responsive. "No, I suppose it isn't. I'm told it used to be part of a sword."

Esolda chewed her lip, as if trying hard to comprehend what Grace had said. "A sword isn't a jewel," she said at last. "You shouldn't wear that. He doesn't like it when you do odd things. Things no one else does. I'll tell him."

Grace stared, the cold seeping into her bones. "Who will you tell?"

The girl spoke faster, as if excited, although her eyes remained expressionless. "Once I spied in a window and saw a man putting his thing in another man's bum just like it was a woman's locket. I told him about it, and he took the men away and chopped them to bits. I didn't want him to chop them up. But you can't do things others don't do. And the blood . . ." She gasped, and a shudder coursed through her thin body. "I've never seen anything so red in all my life."

If Grace had been in the ED just then, she would have called for a psych consult; the young woman seemed to be suffering from some sort of emotional trauma. The shopkeeper—her uncle—said her parents were dead. Had she watched them die from the Burning Plague? Clearly she was suffering from delusions. But who was the man she was talking about, the one she claimed to have told about what she saw? Was it her uncle?

It was too cold to think. Grace snatched the undergarments from Esolda and hastily shrugged them on. The young woman simply stood there, so Grace took the gown from her and donned that as well. When she had everything adjusted, she stepped through the door into the shop. Falken had just finished counting coins into the shopkeeper's hand.

"What took you so long?" Beltan said.

"Nothing," Grace said. "I was confused by all the straps, that's all."

She glanced over her shoulder. The door was ajar, and through the gap she glimpsed a pair of brown eyes gazing at her. While before they had been dull, now there was a dim spark of light in them.

Grace wrapped the fox fur cloak around herself. "Come on. Let's get out of here."

Newly protected against the bitter chill, they stepped outside and made their way through the streets to an inn the shopkeeper had recommended.

As they approached the door of the inn, Falken hefted his purse. There wasn't much jingle to it. "I should have robbed more from Melia's stash in Tarras. That woman has more gold than she knows what to do with. And our clothes were more expensive than I thought."

Grace pulled out the purse Ephesian had given her. "Here, take this." She plunked the fat purse into Falken's hand. "I believe it's my turn to pay."

Beltan grinned. "The drinks are on Her Majesty tonight."

The next morning, Grace woke in the ghostly light before dawn. Shivering, she rose, crept to the room's fireplace, and stirred up the coals. There was no sign of Vani; her bed appeared untouched.

After Grace dressed, she knocked on the door to Falken and Beltan's room. The bard answered. "Sorry," he whispered, "it's a slow morning. Someone had a bit too much ale last night."

"Quit shouting!" came Beltan's groan from beneath a heap of blankets.

Grace couldn't help smiling. "I think he definitely made some progress on the blubber layer."

"Indeed," Falken said.

"I heard that!" came the wounded reply from beneath the blankets.

Two hours—and many cups of *maddok*—later they reached Galspeth's docks to find the *Fate Runner* nearly ready to depart. There had been no sign of Vani at the inn, but as they approached the ship she stepped from the shadows of an alley.

"Do you really have to do that all the time?" Beltan said with a scowl.

"I don't know what you're talking about," the Mournish woman said crisply.

"Where were you?" Falken said.

Vani glanced back over her shoulder. "Watching. There is something...wrong in this town."

Despite her warm new garb, Grace felt a needle of cold pierce her heart. "What do you mean, Vani?"

"I'm not certain. It's a shadow on the people. A shadow of fear."

Grace wrapped her new cape around herself and thought of the strange words spoken by the clothier's niece. *He doesn't like it when you do odd things.* However, before she could tell the others about her encounter, a rough croak echoed over the street. Grace looked up to see a dark form on a nearby rooftop, perched atop a weathervane. As she watched, the shadow sprang into the sky, spread dark wings, and was gone.

Beltan let out a snort. "The only thing wrong with this town is that we're still in it. Let's get going before Magard sails without us."

Hefting their bags, Beltan started up the gangplank. The others followed, and Grace couldn't say she was sorry to leave the grim town behind.

They left port just as a gray mist poured down the valley. The fog chased them out of the harbor, but soon they outpaced it. The fog seemed to cling close to the shore, and did not extend out into the open sea.

"Anxious to go north, are you?" Magard said to Grace that first evening when he found her at the prow of the ship, gazing into the distance.

Under her cloak, she gripped her necklace. "I'm dreading it."

The captain nodded, his dark eyes serious. "Best to get it over with swiftly then."

Grace could find no reply for that. The captain left her to see to his men. The ship bore only a small crew now that it wasn't laden with cargo. Before, when Grace was abovedecks, she had heard a constant din of bawdy jokes and cheerful, raucous songs. Now all she heard was the wind through the ropes. It made the empty ocean seem even lonelier.

For the next five days, as the *Fate Runner* sailed north, the thick wall of mist was always visible to port, shrouding the land from view. Starting on the third day, Grace sometimes saw flashes of muted light in the mist: yellow, and livid green.

"It's the Barrens," Falken said one evening when the lights were particularly frequent and violent in their intensity. He gripped the rail next to Grace.

Earlier that year, Falken, Durge, and Lirith had ventured into the wasteland of the Barrens to find the Keep of Fire—a fortress raised by the Necromancer Dakarreth to guard the Great Stone Krondisar. Only the keep was abandoned; Dakarreth had come to Castle Spardis, where Grace had dinner with him, not knowing his true nature.

"What happened to the people who lived there?" she said.

Falken shook his head. "No one's ever lived there. At the dawn of the world, the Old Gods and the dragons warred in that place. The gods tried to build up mountains even as the dragons tried to grind them to dust. The land will never heal from the wounds it suffered."

Grace held a hand to her chest and felt the fluttering beat of her heart. She knew about scars that could never heal. But Eldh went on despite its wounds, and so did she.

"The book I found in the library," she said. "Have you learned anything more in it? About the shards of Fellring?"

The wind blew the bard's hair from his brow; it seemed to have a bit more silver in it than Grace remembered. "I've gone through it three times, and while there's much that's fascinating, there isn't a great deal about what happened to the shards. All it says is that, after Malachor fell, one of the last Runelords placed them in an iron box and fled with them to Toringarth. He made it all the way to Ur-Torin, although he was mortally wounded on the way and died soon after."

"People seem to get mortally wounded a lot in your stories," Grace said with a wry smile.

Falken only sighed and gazed at his black-gloved hand. Grace instantly regretted her words.

"Falken," she said, laying her hand on his.

"No, it's all right, Grace. Dakarreth may have thought he was cursing me when he made me immortal. But if I can live to undo what was done long ago, then it won't have been a curse at all, will it?"

Why Falken blamed himself for the fall of the kingdom of Malachor seven centuries earlier, she didn't know. But certainly whatever he had done, he had atoned for it long since. She wanted to tell him that, but the pain in her chest made it too hard to speak, so Grace only smiled.

"No matter," the bard said. "The book has been an enormous help. I had always thought the shards of Fellring were taken west to Eversea. Now I know that didn't happen."

"Eversea?" Hadn't she read that name in the book?

Falken nodded. "Even I'm not sure it's not just a story. But it's a good one. According to legend, Merandon, the second king of Malachor, was something of a brash and proud young man. Many were worried he wouldn't prove to be the king his father was. One day, just after ascending to the throne, he went to an old witch and asked her what would be the greatest deed he would do as king. She told him he should journey to the westernmost end of Falengarth, and there he would find his answer.

"All the king's advisors told him to forget the witch's words, but they burned in Merandon's brain. So a few years later, once he was certain the Wardens could keep things running in his absence, he set out west with a dozen lords. He was gone for seven years, and when he returned, with him were only three of the lords who had set out with him. However, in his company was also a small band of men the likes of which had never been seen in Malachor. They were Maugrim—the first people the Old Gods found in the forests of Falengarth, long ago in the mists of time. The Maugrim where heavier of bone and thicker of brow than the men of Malachor, and they were said to be hairy from head to toe. They wore only the skins of animals and bore weapons made of stone, not iron."

Grace held her breath. *Falken could be describing Neanderthals, Grace. Or some similar protosapien species. How long have Earth and Eldh been in contact? Better yet, on which world did* Homo sapiens *evolve first?*

"Those three Maugrim were the last of their kind ever recorded in Falengarth," Falken went on. "Merandon could speak their queer tongue, but they never learned to speak the language of Malachor, and none took wives, so they died childless. But it wasn't just the Maugrim that Merandon brought back from the West. He also told fantastic tales of his journey. In the end, he claimed, he reached the very western edge of Falengarth, and on the shore of a silver ocean he raised a tower, which he named Eversea.

"It was only thirty years later, on his deathbed, that he whispered to his daughter—who was to become queen after him—the truth of the tower's construction. It was not Maugrim who had helped him build Eversea. Instead, the Maugrim had taken Merandon to a place in the forest where beings of light danced in a circle. The beings reached out to Merandon, drawing him into their dance. They were fairies, and it was they who bid him to raise a tower by the sea. What's more, some accounts say that among the light elfs were a few that were dark and twisted. Nor would it be strange if dark elfs—or dwarfs, as some call them—had helped to raise Merandon's tower, as they were ever cunning at the crafting of stone and metal."

Grace frowned; something was missing from Falken's tale. "The witch said if Merandon journeyed west, he would discover what his greatest deed as king would be. So what was it?"

Falken laughed. "Why, going west, of course. You see, when Merandon returned, he was changed from his journey. He was older and scarred, yes. And wiser, more tempered, and possessed of a gentle strength. It was ever after said that he was the greatest of all of Malachor's kings."

Grace chewed her lip, mulling over Falken's tale. How would this journey change her? Somehow she doubted they would find a band of fairies to help them in the end.

"Falken," she said before she lost her nerve, "even if we do somehow find the shards of Fellring, what good does that do us? What use are a bunch of pieces of broken metal?"

He turned his piercing blue eyes on her. "After all you've seen, you truly think magic is so easily broken as metal?"

She opened her mouth, but the bard turned and moved along the deck, vanishing into the deepening twilight.

14.

The next day, the *Fate Runner* turned west and south as it rounded the northern tip of the Barrens. Almost at once the sea grew gray and choppy, and the ship seemed to lurch from wave to wave as a frigid wind sliced at the sails. The wall of mist that had been in constant view to port was ripped to tatters by the gale. Now Grace could see a rocky shoreline.

"We should reach the port at Omberfell by tomorrow's sunset at the latest," Magard said as he handed Grace and Falken their morning lemons.

Beltan, who had been leaning over the rail of the aft deck, now turned and wiped his mouth, his face as gray as the sea.

"Is it just me and my stomach?" the knight said, taking his piece of lemon. "Or have things gotten considerably bumpier in the last few hours?"

Magard's eyes glittered as he laughed. "We no longer sail the Dawn Sea, my friend. Once we rounded the north horn of the Barrens and set eyes on the shores of Embarr, we entered waters that flow from the Winter Sea. These are cold and treacherous reaches, filled with strange currents and hidden shoals that have been the demise of many a ship."

"That's not exactly reassuring," Grace said, huddling inside her fur cape.

The captain laid a hand on her shoulder. "Don't fear, my girl. I've sailed these waters before, and the *Fate Runner* is nimble enough to dance her way around any trouble we might run into."

Grace gave the captain a grateful smile.

"Where's Vani?" Beltan said, tossing his lemon rind over the rail.

"Your silent friend?" Magard said. "I believe she's up there again." He grinned, pointing upward.

They all looked up to see a slim figure perched atop the ship's foremast.

"She's not my friend," Beltan growled, then turned and made his way along the deck.

Magard gave Grace and Falken a curious look.

"Long story," Grace said, and left it at that.

The wind grew worse as the day wore on, howling from the north, as if it sought to blow the ship onto the jagged Embarran coast and dash it to bits against sharp rocks. Magard and his crewmen worked constantly, barking orders and replies above the roar of the gale, running from foredeck to aft, lashing down ropes and tying off sails. Grace wished there was something she could do to help them, but it was best to stay out of the way. Once one of the sailors lost hold of a rope, and it cracked like a whip mere inches from Grace's head.

She took that as a sign and returned to her cabin. However, things were no less alarming belowdecks. The floor of the cabin rose and dipped as wildly as a carnival ride. At one point Grace checked on Beltan and Falken; the men lay in their cots, eyes clamped shut, so she left them. She wouldn't have minded some company, but no doubt Vani was still high atop the ship's mast. With nothing to do, Grace sat on the floor of her cabin and shut her eyes.

She was only trying to rest; she wasn't trying to reach out with the Touch. However, she wasn't really sleepy, and her mind must have wandered, for suddenly it was there all around her: the shimmering web of the Weirding.

Grace didn't pull back. She could sense all of the lives aboard the tiny ship. Beltan and Falken were in their cabin, Captain Magard and his crew moved abovedecks, and there was Vani, still high atop one of the masts. In addition, countless tiny sparks of light scurried deep in the hold of the ship. Rats. But seen like this, they didn't seem so revolting. Instead they flitted about in Grace's vision like fireflies.

The Weirding flooded Grace with warmth and comfort. She let her mind drift out further. Beneath the ship was a vast, glowing ocean of life. Schools of fish floated beneath the ship's hull like shimmering clouds, and larger creatures flashed by too quickly for Grace to sense what they were. Reveling in the sensation of connectedness, she reached out further yet.

It streaked toward the *Fate Runner* like an angry bolt of lightning.

Grace's eyes flew open. What was it? She didn't know. But it was big, the fire of its life force burning like a star against the web of the Weirding. And it was coming straight for them.

She leaped to her feat, stumbled as the ship lurched, then righted herself and pushed through the cabin door.

"Beltan! Falken!" she shouted, pounding on their cabin door. "Get out here!" Without waiting, she scrambled up the steps to the deck above.

The day had grown darker rather than lighter while she was

below. Iron-colored clouds scudded across the sky, and waves broke all around the ship, crashing together in white explosions. The shore was closer than before—perilously close. Grace could discern the sharp outlines of individual rocks. Just ahead, the land seemed to take a sharp turn to the north. Gripping the rail, she made her way along the deck. She found Magard near the foremast.

"You should get belowdecks!" he shouted above the howl of the gale. "It's too rough up here!"

She clutched the mast to keep from falling as the deck rose and fell beneath her. "Captain Magard! There's something out there. It's coming right for us."

A frown crossed his leathery face. "What's coming right for us?"

"I don't know." She fought to speak against the wind and spray. "It's big. Very big. Almost like it's a . . ."

"It's a ship," Vani said, stepping from between two folds of empty air.

Magard jerked his head around. "A ship? Where?"

"Off to starboard. It's coming toward us quickly."

Grace stared at Vani. A ship? Yes, that made sense. At a distance, all the sparks of its crew would have merged into one, making it look like a single great light. Again she reached out with the Touch. The light was closer. Now she could make out the individual sparks of the lives aboard the vessel.

"There must be a hundred men aboard that ship."

Magard scowled at her. "And how do you know that, my girl?"

Grace opened her mouth, but before she could answer a shout went up from the aft deck.

"Ship ahoy!"

A bell rang wildly. Swearing, Magard moved to the rail. Vani and Grace followed just as Beltan and Falken appeared abovedecks. Off to starboard, a patch of mist clinging to the sea was ripped apart as a massive shape burst through it.

"By the Foamy Mane of Jorus, would you look at that," Magard said, awe written across his face.

The ship was gigantic. It rose from the waves like a fortress made of wood, its decks fully twice as high above the surface of the sea as those of the *Fate Runner*. Grace counted five masts and over a dozen sails, each one as crimson as blood. The mainsail sagged as the wind shifted direction. Countless small, dark forms scurried through the ship's myriad ropes, then all at once the sail filled again with air, billowing outward. Emblazoned on the vast, red field was a symbol: a black crown encircling a silver tower.

Its sails full to the wind once more, the ship surged over the waves.

"Blood and brine," Magard said. "She means to broad-side us."

The captain turned to shout orders at his crew. The men dashed into action, scrambling up the rigging. But there were too few of them; they couldn't possibly turn the ship in time.

Grace clutched the rail and stared at the others, eyes wide. "What do we do?"

"I suggest we move to the port side of the ship," Vani said sharply.

Beltan and Falken returned grim nods. Together, the four fled to the opposite side of the deck and braced themselves against the rail. When Grace turned around, the oncoming ship loomed over the *Fate Runner* like a tower. She could hardly believe something so gigantic could move so swiftly. Decorating the ship's prow was the carving of a woman in a flowing robe, painted in blues and silvers. Except there was something strange about the woman; her eyes were too large and too slanted, her neck too long, her ears delicately pointed.

That's not a woman, Grace.

She glanced at Falken, but the bard only stared at the rapidly growing ship.

"Hold the tiller steady!" Magard shouted, cords standing out on his neck. "Cut the ropes. Give her full sail. Now!"

In the rigging above, several crewmen drew curved knives. Steel flashed, then ropes hissed and whistled through the air like angry serpents. Beltan ducked barely in time to avoid having his head taken off. The sails billowed and snapped, and the *Fate Runner* sprang forward like a rock out of a sling.

The gigantic ship was so close now Grace could see the men lining its deck. They were clad all in black, from horned helms to greaves. Even the swords in their hands were black. Only their shields were different: as crimson as the ship's sails, each marked with the same black crown and silver tower.

"Hold on!" Falken cried, locking his arms around the rail.

Vani snaked a rope around her wrist. Before Grace could move, Beltan wrapped his long arms around her and gripped the rail, pressing Grace tight against it.

"Here she comes!" Magard's shout sounded over the wind.

There was a roar like a jet engine. Grace craned her head around. The gigantic shape of the oncoming ship moved swiftly across her field of vision from left to right; it was falling astern as the *Fate Runner* sped forward.

We're going to make it, Grace. We're going to—

Water sprayed up in a white geyser as a sound like thunder rent the air. The *Fate Runner* groaned like a torture victim as a violent tremor passed through its hull. The deck lurched, and Grace lost her hold on the rail. She would have gone flying save for Beltan's fierce grip. Two crewmen were not so lucky. Grace saw them tumble from the rigging. One struck the deck, landing in a crumpled heap. The other glanced off the railing, then vanished into the sea.

There was a low, grinding sound. Again the planks shuddered beneath Grace. Then the *Fate Runner* shot forward in a cloud of spray. The red-sailed ship fell behind. The men standing at its rail shook black swords.

"Magard's crew moved faster than I thought," Falken said, breathing hard as he stood back up. "We made enough headway that the ship only glanced off our stern."

"Will they not try again?" Vani said, releasing the rope she had gripped.

"They will," Beltan said. "But they're too big. They can't turn as fast as we can. It'll take them a while to come around to starboard."

The blond man was right. The gigantic ship had let its sails go slack to keep from running straight into the rocky coast. It was starting to turn, but only slowly. Every moment the ship fell farther behind them.

Captain Magard was shouting orders again. Grace wriggled free of Beltan's grasp and hurried to the slumped form of the crewman who had fallen from the rigging. Blood oozed from the back of his head. Grace reached out with the Touch, but she already knew what she would find. His thread was dark as ashes, and it fell apart in her hands.

"Hold her steady!" Magard's voice rose on the air. "One notch to port or starboard, and we're all dead."

Grace jerked her head up and gasped. While they had worked to escape the other ship, they had rushed right toward the sharp northward bend in the coast. Cliffs loomed above them. Grace didn't see how they could possibly turn in time. She went rigid, bracing herself for another impact.

Jagged walls of rock rushed by to either side of the ship as the *Fate Runner* sailed forward. Grace counted a dozen heartbeats, then all at once the walls fell away. She turned back to see dark cliffs shrinking behind them. The coast of Embarr was once more safely off to port.

Falken let out a low whistle. He had drawn near to Grace, along with Beltan and Vani.

"I didn't think we were going to make it through that narrows," the bard said.

"You have no faith, Falken Blackhand," Magard said, striding toward them with a broad grin. "I've wriggled this minnow through tighter passages than that."

"The other ship won't be able to make it through that narrows," Beltan said. "Whoever they were."

Vani glanced at the captain. "How long will it take them to sail around?"

"A good half day," Magard said. "Maybe more. That island stretches from the coast far to the north, and the waters are rough around it."

At last Grace understood. Earlier, it had looked like the coast bent north, but that was only because she hadn't been able to see the narrow gap in the rocks. In fact, the landmass before them had been an island, not a promontory. Only now it lay behind them, and the big, red-sailed ship would have to go around. They had lost their pursuers. For the moment. But who were the men on the strange ship? And why had they attacked the *Fate Runner*? Then she pictured their black helms and swords, and she thought maybe she had an idea.

Before Grace could voice her thoughts, Magard's eyes focused on the form lying before her. His grin faded, and he gave her a questioning look.

Grace sighed. "He was dead when he struck the deck."

Magard nodded, his expression hard. "We'll put him to rest in the sea, then, along with his mate who we lost before we entered the straits."

Sickness flooded Grace's stomach. The deck rolled beneath her. It seemed stormier on this side of the narrows. The sky was a swirling iron gray, and the waves leaped high enough that water slopped onto the deck. She struggled to her feet.

A stray barrel, knocked loose in the earlier impact, rolled along the deck. Beltan jumped to get out of its way. The knight frowned as it rolled toward the stern of the ship.

With a cold sensation of dread, Grace understood. "The deck. It's slanting toward the back of the ship."

The angle was visible now, and getting worse by the second.

Magard swore. "She must have clipped us harder than I thought. We're taking on water."

"Captain!" came a shout from one of the crewmen in the rigging. "There are shallows ahead!"

Magard swore again.

Falken gripped his arm. "I thought you said the *Fate Runner* could sail in shallow seas."

"She can," the captain said. "When she isn't riding low in the water. But now that the hold is filling . . ."

Magard didn't bother to say anything more. He dashed forward, barking orders to his remaining crewmen. Grace lost sight of him.

"What do we do?" she said. Her mind raced, but she couldn't think.

Falken gave Beltan a grim look. "Hold on to her, Beltan. Whatever happens, you have to keep her safe."

"On my life," the blond knight said. "I swear it."

No, this was madness. They needed a plan of action, not words of doom. Grace opened her mouth to speak, but a horrible grinding noise filled the air, and once again the deck lurched beneath her. She fell to her knees.

"Prepare yourselves!" Vani called out.

The grinding stopped, but the deck kept moving. It tilted wildly to port. Grace couldn't hold on; she began to slide. Then she felt a strong grip on her arm.

"Swim, my lady," Beltan growled in her ear. "No matter how hard the currents pull at you, swim with all your might."

All at once sky and sea switched places. Screams came from every direction, along with the horrible sounds of snapping ropes and splintering wood. There was one final, rending shriek as the ship broke apart.

Then Grace plunged into cold water, and invisible hands dragged her downward.

PART TWO

THE RAVEN
REBORN

15.

It was strange how quickly time could pass when all you were doing was trying to survive.

Travis knew their only purpose in Castle City was to bide their time until Jack Graystone arrived and helped them find a way back to Eldh, and back to their own time. Grace and the others probably thought they were dead, killed in the collapse of the Etherion. Travis couldn't let them believe that, not when there was still hope. Sometimes he wondered if Beltan had given up on him, or Vani. The thought made his soul ache, but just who the pain was for—fair-haired knight or gold-eyed assassin—he could never say.

Besides, Travis, maybe it's better if you never get back. If the dragon and the Witches are right, you're going to destroy Eldh no matter what you try to do.

Then again, if Vani's grandmother spoke truth, and he was *A'narai*—one of the Fateless—how could it be his destiny to do anything, let alone shatter a world?

It didn't matter. As things stood now, neither Beltan nor Vani had even been born yet. And it seemed anything but likely the four of them would ever get back to Eldh, let alone to their own time. Besides, in the day-to-day work of keeping a roof over their heads, sometimes it was hard to remember he was anything but a bartender in a Colorado saloon in the year 1883.

"Tell me how to concoct a Velvet, Mr. Wilder," Manypenny quizzed him that first evening he reported for work at the Mine Shaft in his new white shirt and black trousers.

Travis rubbed his freshly shaved pate. It had always been a point of pride that he knew the recipe for nearly every cocktail in existence, no matter how odd or obscure. However, his brain was a bit rusty. It had been over a year since he had left the Mine Shaft—in his time line, at least. All the same, he managed to dredge up the knowledge.

"Combine equal parts champagne and porter."

Manypenny gave a satisfied nod. "Now describe the manner for formulating a Flip."

That one was locked in an even dustier corner of Travis's brain, but at last he recalled the Halloween when they had done a Sleepy Hollow theme at the saloon. He had dressed up as Ichabod Crane and had learned to mix drinks that were popular in Colonial times.

"Rum, beer, and sugar," he said, ticking off the ingredients on his hand. "Mix them together in a mug, then plunge in the tip of a hot poker until it foams."

Manypenny stroked his curled mustache, beady eyes glinting. "I see you're not so easily confounded. Inform me, then, of the items that go into a Blue Blazer."

Travis racked his memory, but in the end he was baffled. No doubt it would cost him his new job, but there was nothing to do but admit the truth. He would just have to find work at one of the mines, no matter what Maudie said.

"I'm afraid I don't know," he said, prepared for Manypenny's displeasure.

Instead, the saloonkeeper let out a bellow of laughter. "Well, it appears the Sphinx has won this contest of riddles after all."

Travis could only gape. It seemed Manypenny had been playing with him, determined to best him at the game.

His employer clapped him on the back. "Never fear if you've never heard of a certain beverage, Mr. Wilder. The miner who asks you for a fancy cocktail likely won't know what goes into it any more than you do. No doubt he simply overheard some well-heeled gentleman order such a drink and wishes to try it for himself. However, your typical miner wouldn't know amontillado from mare's piss. So formulate any preposterous concoction, and he'll drink it gladly."

Travis forced a weak smile. He had the feeling working for Manypenny was going to be something of an adventure.

As it turned out, few of the men who walked up to the bar requested cocktails. A good number asked for beer, but the vast majority were there for one thing only: whiskey. Usually it was a shot of Taos Lightning—or Old Towse, as the crustier-looking men termed it. This was a hot and potent liquor distilled in the city in New Mexico from which it took its name.

When Travis tried his first sip, he decided it had all the kick and character of a can of Sterno—after it had been set on fire.

Right away, Travis was struck by the similarity between the men who came into the saloon and many of the men he had seen on Eldh. Trade their muslin shirts and denim jeans for tunics and hose, and any of them could have passed for a peasant in Calavan. Most were short, their faces lined beyond their years, their teeth yellow and rotting, and their hands permanently blackened from labor in the mines.

Many of the men had hard and empty eyes, as if all the life had been leached out of them, just like the silver was leached from carbonate of lead. They drank standing at the bar, downing their whiskey quickly and without relish, then stepping aside to make room for the next man.

Not all of the customers were so cheerless. Just as when Travis owned (would own?) the saloon, many of the men who stopped by each day were regulars and friends of the proprietor. These were townsmen, not miners, and many owned businesses along Elk Street.

Unlike the miners, these men wore suits, with silver watch fobs dangling from their vest pockets. They talked much, laughed more, smoked cigars, and drank bourbon and champagne as often as whiskey and beer. They were men of wealth and success— bankers, merchants, doctors, and lawyers. Travis didn't have the heart to tell them that, in a few more years, once the silver market crashed and the mines closed, they would all be broke.

Whenever Manypenny, in his booming voice, introduced his new bartender to one of these regulars, the customer always bought Travis a drink. In fact, as far as Travis could tell, making the bartender drink seemed to be a popular pastime in the Old West, and almost any occasion called for it.

When a man wandered into the saloon, fresh from the East, full of dreams of striking it rich and still flush with cash, he always insisted on buying Travis a drink. Travis hated to accept the gesture, knowing that a few weeks later, when his claim went bust, the same man would come in again, clothes dirty and torn, and pockets empty. At that point it would be Travis's turn to buy the other a drink while the fellow tried to figure out a way to earn enough for a train ticket home.

Then there was the occasional prospector who managed to find a small pocket of high-grade ore, and who—after paying a visit to the assay office—would swagger in and buy whiskey for the entire saloon. Of course, after a few days of drinking and gambling, his newfound fortune would be gone. Head aching, the miner would return to his claim to start all over.

Even a fair number of the miners—laborers who made three dollars a day—would buy Travis a shot of whiskey along with one for themselves. One look at their haunted and lonely faces, and Travis couldn't turn them down. For all this town's bustle and crowded streets, he had a feeling sharing a drink with a bartender whose name they didn't even know was the closest some of these men came to having a friend. Sometimes Travis would ask the man his name—but only his first, not his last.

"Never ask for anything more than a man's front name," Manypenny admonished him. "As far as I'm concerned, a man who enters here leaves his past at the door."

Travis clenched his right hand into a fist. If only that were true. However, while he could never forget the past, he also knew that it lay behind him—a shadow that followed in his wake, and nothing more. That was what he had learned in the Etherion, when he faced the demon; that was what the ghost of Alice, his little sister, had shown him. So he would raise his glass to the fellow who had bought him the drink, and they'd down their whiskey in silence.

Of course, if Travis were actually to consume all of the drinks that were bought for him, he'd have been lying under the bar by sundown most days. Instead, after filling the customer's glass with the good stuff, he'd pour a shot into his own glass from a bottle he kept behind the bar, which was more water than whiskey—a survival trick practiced by bartenders in any century.

Once the sun slipped behind the mountains, the character of the saloon changed. The somber drinkers who inhabited the bar by day were replaced by a noisier, harder-drinking, and decidedly rowdier crowd. Cigar smoke and laughter filled the air, along with tinny music once the piano player arrived to plink out "My Darling Clementine" and "Sweet Betsy from Pike" on an upright piano so battered it looked like it had been dragged across the Great Plains behind a covered wagon.

It was also after dark that the gambling tables came alive. Each of the tables was rented to a gambler who ran his own game, and who paid Manypenny a share of the table's take. There were plenty of choices for losing one's money, including poker, paigow, and three-card monte. However, by far the most popular game was one called faro.

As far as Travis could tell, there wasn't much to faro. The thirteen card ranks—from ace to king—were painted on the surface of the table. Players placed bets on the various ranks to win or to lose. Then the dealer turned up two cards. The first card was the loser, and the second card was the winner. So if a player bet sevens to lose, and a seven was the first card drawn, the bet paid off. Or, if he bet jacks to win, and a jack was the first card, the dealer took his bet.

After watching a few games, even Travis was smart enough to realize that the odds of winning in faro were pretty much dead even. That was clearly why it was a popular game. The only thing that gave the house a slight edge was the fact that the dealer discarded the first and last cards in the deck—they were neither winners nor losers. That meant, over time, the dealer kept just a thin fraction of all the bets placed. Then again, given the vast amount of money that moved across the faro table, even a few percentage points wasn't a shabby sum, and no doubt accounted for the dealer's silk vest and diamond stud cuff links.

While the atmosphere in the Mine Shaft at night was a bit on the wild side, it was usually good-natured. Men drank, laughed, gambled, and made conversation with the rare woman who entered the saloon—ladies who, while not hurdy-gurdy girls, were certainly not a big step above on Castle City's social ladder. And while many of the town's prominent men could be found at the saloon, their wives were nowhere in sight.

Most men could hold their liquor, and they took their losses at the gambling tables with no more than a sheepish grin. But there were the exceptions. One of the first things Manypenny made a point of showing Travis was the shotgun that hung from a pair of hooks beneath the bar. And, almost every night, at some point the big saloonkeeper brought out the shotgun and cocked it, aiming it square at whatever rowdy had had too much to drink, or had lost too much at poker, or had been jilted by his best girl, and who was determined to fight someone— anyone—over it.

Usually the other was not so drunk or angry he didn't think twice at having a shotgun barrel pointed at his chest, and upon quickly sobering up he hurried out the door. However, one night a young man in grimy clothes shouted that Manypenny was watering down the liquor—an accusation clearly disproved by the man's evident inebriation. The other seemed not to feel the barrel of the shotgun jammed into his stomach as he swung his arms wildly, reaching for Manypenny, who clenched his jaw and slowly squeezed the trigger. Then a pair of men who seemed to be the angry one's friends pulled him off and dragged him out into the street.

Laughter and the sound of music quickly rose on the air again, and Travis suspected he was the only one who saw Manypenny slump against the bar, still holding the shotgun in pudgy hands. The big man's face was red, and sweat stained his shirt in dark patches.

"You wouldn't have pulled the trigger, would you, Mr. Manypenny?" Travis said quietly. "No matter what he did, you wouldn't have shot him."

The saloonkeeper drew in a rasping breath. "Put this away for me, Mr. Wilder." He handed Travis the shotgun. "In the name of God, please put it away."

Travis took the shotgun and placed it on its hooks under the bar, and all the while he wondered—if this was one of the more respectable establishments in town, as Maudie had said—what were the other saloons in Castle City like?

Fortunately, incidents of violence in the Mine Shaft were rarer than Travis might have feared. In fact, for all their drinking, for all their gambling and boisterousness, there was something oddly subdued about the men and women in the saloon. Travis couldn't quite put his finger on what it was. Sometimes he'd see a man stop short in his laughter and look suddenly over his shoulder, or perhaps he'd quickly hush another man who was talking in a loud, slurred voice about something Travis couldn't quite understand.

They lead hard lives, Travis. They're probably tired all the time, that's all.

Except he didn't quite believe that was it.

All the same, in the constant hurry of his work at the saloon, it was easy to forget those peculiar moments. Just like it was easy to forget about Jack Graystone, and how they had to find a way back to Eldh and their own time. In fact, he might have forgotten about everything in his daily labors at the Mine Shaft.

Only then, as he hauled in a fresh cask of whiskey from the back, or swept up the sawdust from the floor, he'd look up and see the yellowed Wanted poster plastered to the wall, staring back at him with his own eyes behind wire-rimmed spectacles.

WANTED DEAD OR ALIVE. TYLER CAINE, THE MAN-KILLER.

And Travis knew he would never forget who he was.

16.

It was about a week after Travis started working at the saloon that he looked up and saw two familiar figures step through the swinging doors and approach the bar.

"Lirith, Durge," he said, surprised. He set down the deck of cards he had been fidgeting with in a slow moment, laying them on the bar. "What are you two doing here? Is something wrong? Is it—?"

"No, Travis, both Sareth and Maudie are fine," Lirith said, her smoky red lips curving in a smile. "If that's what you were going to ask."

It was, as the witch no doubt knew perfectly well.

"I do not believe this was a wise idea, my lady," Durge rumbled under his mustache.

The knight glanced from side to side, and Travis understood his concern. It was afternoon, and the saloon was less than half full. However, the low murmur of conversation had stilled for a moment as the knight and witch stepped through the door, and while the noise had returned, it was impossible not to notice the eyes that kept flickering in their direction.

"I think Durge may be right," Travis said quietly as he polished the bar with a cloth. He remembered what had happened the last time all of them were out in public together—they were accused of being thieves and of nearly burning down the town. "If it isn't an emergency, couldn't it have waited until I got back to the Bluebell?"

Lirith sighed. "Lady Maudie is a dear, Travis. But I'm starting to feel a bit trapped at the Bluebell. And Durge is as well, though he won't say it."

Travis glanced at the stalwart knight. The Embarran only gazed at the floor, and Travis noted that he didn't disagree with the witch's words.

"We can't stay hidden forever," Lirith went on. "But that's not the reason I wanted to come out today. It's good you've been earning money here at this tavern, but your wage only covers what we must pay Lady Maudie for our keep. Yet, if we are to stay here for weeks to come, there are other things we'll require. We each need a change of clothes and new shoes. And there are medicines I would purchase for Sareth to ease his breathing." Lirith placed her hands on the bar, her dark eyes earnest. "Durge and I have decided we both must find—"

"Her kind ain't welcome in here," said a coarse voice.

The three looked up to see a man saunter toward the bar. His face was as battered and dusty as his clothes, and his eyes were dangerous slits. Travis remembered him; he and a companion had come in that morning, had bought a full bottle of whiskey, and had hunkered down at a table in a corner. Now Travis glanced at the corner. The man's friend stood next to his chair. On the table nearby was an empty bottle.

The man stopped a few feet from Lirith and Durge, hands on his hips. He spat on the floor, and a dark line of tobacco juice dribbled down his chin. "Didn't yeh hear me? I said, her kind ain't welcome here."

"On the contrary," came a booming voice, "all kinds are welcome at the Mine Shaft Saloon."

Manypenny stepped through the storeroom door and stood next to Travis, an affable expression on his red face. However, Travis saw the hard gleam in his eyes.

The man spat again. "I didn't know this was no colored saloon. Next thing, you'll be letting in Chinamen. But it ain't no matter, if yeh do. She still don't belong here. Women don't know nothing about likker or cards."

"Is that so?" Lirith said.

Before the others could react, Lirith reached out and swept up the deck of cards from the bar. She shuffled them crisply in midair, fanned them out, tamped them back together, then cut the deck using a single hand, deftly separating it into four parts, each one nestled between two of her dark fingers. Again with one hand she reconstituted the deck and fanned it a second time. She held the cards toward the man.

"Pick one," she said. "And I'll wager a gold coin I can tell you what card it is without looking at it."

This elicited a hoot of laughter from Manypenny. However, Travis knew it had been a mistake. He had worked long enough in the Mine Shaft in two centuries to know the different types of drunks. Some people couldn't stop laughing, others grew maudlin, and some just fell asleep. But for some men, alcohol—like Dr. Jekyll's potion—was a key that opened the door to all their darkest, most dangerous impulses.

"Yeh don't know yer place, miss," the man said through tobacco-stained teeth. "Yeh shouldn't be here. Yeh should be at the hurdy-gurdy, charging a feller two bits for a dance. And two dollars for anything else he wants to do with yeh."

These were the first words the man spoke that really seemed to rattle Lirith. Her face went ashen, and the cards slipped from her hand, scattering across the floor. Grinning, the man reached out to touch the black curls of her hair.

There was a loud *smack*, and his hand flew back. Travis had hardly seen Durge move.

The man shook his hand, and his grin vanished. "You ought not have done that, mister."

"And you ought to know," Durge said, brown eyes stern, "how to properly address a noble lady and your better."

By the time Travis realized what was going to happen, it was too late to do anything but watch. The man reached beneath his coat and drew out a silver six-shooter. He aimed it square at Durge's chest.

Before the man could squeeze the trigger, Durge stepped past the man, braced a leg behind the other's knee, and grabbed the wrist of his gun hand, bringing it up and over his head. The man's knees buckled, and as Durge spun him around, his right arm struck the hard edge of the bar. There was a *crack* as the man's arm broke. The gun flew behind the bar, right into Manypenny's hands. The man sank to the floor, curling around his shattered arm and whimpering. Durge turned around.

There was a click as a gun was cocked.

The wounded man's drinking partner stood an arm's length away from Durge. He pressed the barrel of his revolver against the knight's forehead.

"You just made a big mistake, mister," the man said, baring a scant collection of teeth.

"Then perhaps two wrongs do make a right," Durge said.

The knight didn't smile, but there was a light in his brown eyes Travis could only describe as eager. He batted the man's gun hand aside with a flick of his right hand, then lashed out with his left fist. The man's head flew back, and his eyes rolled up. Without a sound, he toppled backward onto the floor, holding the gun in a limp hand.

Interested gazes lingered on the fallen men and Durge for a few moments, then the saloon's remaining patrons returned their attention to their drinks. However, in response to a nod from Manypenny, one man dashed out the door.

"Are you well, my lady?" Durge said to Lirith.

She smiled and laid a hand on the knight's arm. "Very well, my lord. Thank you. It's not often a lady gets heads cracked in her honor. I'll consider it a rare treat."

Manypenny stepped from behind the bar and retrieved the second man's gun. "That was excellent, sir," he said to Durge with a broad grin. "An incomparable display of skill and prowess. I won many a wrestling match in my day, but even in my prime, I could not have neutralized two men with such Herculean ease. You dealt your blows as deftly as the lovely lady here deals cards."

Manypenny kept the silver six-shooter he had caught aimed at the two men, but neither of them seemed intent on going anywhere, although the second one did wake up. A few minutes later, Sheriff Tanner stepped through the saloon's swinging doors.

"Greeting, Bartholomew," Manypenny said, as Tanner approached the bar.

"Hello, Arthur," Tanner said. He tipped his hat. "And hello again, Miss Lily, Mr. Dirk, and Mr. Wilder. It does seem interesting things happen when you're around."

He must have talked to Maudie. That was the only way he could have known their names.

Travis attempted a grin. "I guess we're just lucky."

"With luck like that, I suggest you avoid the poker tables, Mr. Wilder." The sheriff glanced at Manypenny. "Now tell me what happened here, Arthur."

Fifteen minutes later, Tanner's deputy—a slightly chubby young man by the name of Wilson—led the two men out the door of the saloon. Both seemed considerably less bold than they had before Durge had done his work with them.

"Each of them will need to see a healer," Lirith said.

Tanner nodded. "You're a good woman, Miss Lily, to think kindly of men who didn't act so kindly toward you. But don't worry—I'll have the doctor look after them at the jail."

The sheriff tipped his hat to them all again and started for the door. However, halfway there he stopped and turned.

"Mr. Dirk," he said. "If you could see fit to come visit my office sometime, I'd appreciate it."

Travis and Lirith both shot the knight concerned looks.

Durge gave a stiff nod. "No doubt I broke the laws of this place with my actions. If you wish it, I will surrender myself to you immediately, Sir Tanner."

Tanner grinned behind his sandy mustache. "I'm not going to arrest you, Mr. Dirk. On the contrary, while Deputy Wilson is a good kid, I could use a man like you. It doesn't pay much for the trouble it's worth, but if you come over and get deputized, I'll give you a badge and a gun along with three dollars and fifty cents a day."

There was a flash of sunlight, then Tanner was gone.

Travis could only gaze at Durge in astonishment. Tanner wanted to deputize him? However, as it turned out, the knight was not the only one who received a job offer that day.

"I have need of a new faro dealer," Manypenny said to Lirith as Durge started to lead her to the door. "My last remaining faro dealer has vanished without warning. An old debt caught up with him, I presume. Do you know the game?"

Lirith gave Travis a questioning glance, and he returned what he hoped was a subtle nod. He had figured out the rules of the game quickly enough, and he had no doubt Lirith was smarter than him by a good measure.

"I do," Lirith said.

"Good," Manypenny proclaimed. "It's most felicitous you came in to see Mr. Wilder today. You can rent the table in the corner there. The house keeps half the profits. Be here at sundown if you want the job. And Miss Lily, do find yourself a dress that flatters you a bit more."

Travis couldn't help wondering if it wasn't a bit daring to hire Lirith as a dealer. After all, the man who had approached her couldn't be the only one in Castle City who thought a black woman didn't belong in the saloon. It was 1883; the Civil War had ended less than twenty years earlier. And women possessed only a fraction of the rights men did.

Then again, Manypenny was nothing if not flamboyant, and Travis had a feeling the saloonkeeper enjoyed causing a bit of controversy. It certainly would create talk in the town, which would likely bring in more customers than it turned away.

Manypenny returned to his work, and Travis walked with Lirith and Durge to the door.

"What is a *deputy*?" Durge asked.

Travis tried to think of a way to describe it. "Is there a term for a knight who serves another knight?"

"A vassal knight." Durge stroked his mustaches. "There is honor in such a role, if one serves a good and noble man."

Travis could already see the gears turning in Durge's head. He wondered if he should convince the knight not to go talk to Tanner. The last thing they needed was anything that brought attention to them. However, it could wait for later.

"Lirith," he said, "you never did get a chance to tell me why it was you two left the Bluebell today."

The witch smiled. "I was going to tell you that both Durge and I had decided to try to find jobs."

17.

Lirith's first night as a faro dealer at the Mine Shaft was, by any definition, a rousing success.

"Lord above, you can't deal faro in that dress," Maudie exclaimed when they returned to the Bluebell and told her and Sareth what had happened at the saloon.

"That's what Mr. Manypenny said." Lirith sighed, smoothing her brown-poplin dress. "I suppose this is a rather plain gown. But it will have to do for now. I won't be able to afford a new one until I've earned some money."

"Nonsense," Maudie said in a tone that allowed no room for argument. "This way, Miss Lily."

She took Lirith's elbow in one hand, her cane in the other, and led the stunned witch up the staircase.

"Where are they going?" Durge asked.

Sareth let out a low, chiming laugh. "To work some magic, I would guess."

The Mournish man's guess was correct. A half hour later, Maudie and Lirith descended the staircase into the parlor. At once, the three men rose to their feet.

Durge's brown eyes went wide. "My lady, you look ... you look like ..."

"Like something from a dream," Sareth murmured, his coppery gaze thoughtful.

Maudie let out a throaty laugh. "See there, Lily? I told you that you'd turn men into fools in this dress, if the lot of them weren't fools already."

Lirith's smile was almost shy—and perhaps just a little pleased—as she brushed the jade-taffeta dress she wore, and which flowed and shimmered around her slim form like cool water. Its neckline plunged low to reveal the dark, lustrous skin above her breasts, which were made full and round by the tight bodice. The witch's black hair was woven with red ribbons and fell in shining ringlets about her shoulders. Travis supposed the dress had once been Maudie's.

Sareth reached out and took Lirith's hand. "Be careful tonight, *beshala*."

She touched his cheek. "I will. *Beshala*."

And so entranced were he and Durge that only Travis noticed how Maudie turned away to cough, and how she wiped her lips, leaving a splotch of color on her handkerchief as red as the ribbons in Lirith's hair.

Word about Manypenny's new faro dealer must have spread all over town, for that night the Mine Shaft was more crowded than Travis had ever seen it, and a good part of that crowd was crammed in the corner around Lirith's table.

Travis had explained the rules of the game to the witch—as far as he knew them, anyway—as they walked to the saloon. Travis did his best to keep an eye on her in between pouring drinks and tapping new kegs of beer. However, if Lirith made a single mistake, he didn't notice it—and nor did the dozens of men and handful of women who played at her table that night. Lirith turned the cards with elegant motions and swept in the winnings with a smile so radiant Travis doubted any of the men minded losing. Although there were a few women who appeared less than pleased with the way their beaus stared openly at the dealer.

Lirith is a witch, Travis. You don't suppose she's casting a spell, do you?

She was, he decided. Except it was a spell worked, not with the magic of the Weirding, but rather true and simple beauty and the light of her smile.

Night after night, Lirith's faro table remained every bit as popular as it had on that first—a fact that pleased Manypenny to no end. He had taken to calling her Lady Lily, a title far closer to the truth than the saloonkeeper could ever have guessed. And if Travis noticed the occasional dark glance in Lirith's direction, or a few angry, muttered words from time to time, it was easy enough to forget them in the bustle of his work at the saloon. For with the success of Lirith's faro table, things were busier than ever.

Durge was busier these days as well. The day after their conversation with Tanner at the saloon, he left the Bluebell and walked to the sheriff's office, wearing a brown suit Maudie had pulled from one of her seemingly bottomless closets, and which she said belonged to one of her former husbands. Travis was curious how many husbands Maudie had once had, and what had happened to them. However, Lirith gave him a sharp kick in the shin when he tried to ask.

When Durge returned to the boardinghouse, he wore a silver badge on his vest and a gleaming revolver at his hip.

Maudie pressed her lips into a tight line when she saw him. "That suit is too long for you, Mr. Dirk. Leave it in my sewing room so I can take it up a bit." She hurried away, but not before Travis saw the worry in her eyes.

He felt the same concern she did. "Are you certain you want to do this, Durge?"

The knight's eyes were resolute. "Sir Tanner is a good man. No doubt the job will be perilous, and I'll quite likely perish in the course of it. But I could not refuse him and keep my honor as a knight."

"What about the gun?" Travis said, eyeing the revolver. "Did Tanner teach you how to use it? You don't want to accidentally shoot yourself in the foot."

Durge shook his head. "Sir Tanner said a deputy must wear one of these guns, but I told him I would not use such sorcery, although I did not think less of him that he chose to."

Travis wondered if Durge had used those exact words, and if so what Tanner had made of them. Then again, he was starting to think part of the magic of the silver coin was that it made people hear what they expected to hear.

"This gun doesn't work," Durge went on. "I asked Tanner to remove all of the pieces of metal it throws."

"Bullets," Travis said. "They're called bullets. So the gun's not loaded." He didn't know whether to be relieved or more worried than ever.

Stop it, Travis. Durge can take care of himself. He's the

toughest fighter you've ever met. Even Beltan would have a hard time winning a duel against Durge.

"Well, it seems now I'm the only one who doesn't have work to do," Sareth said that evening as the four of them gathered in the parlor after dinner.

"That's not why we're here," Travis said. "We just needed some money to live on until Jack comes, that's all. And now we'll have more than enough."

"Besides, your work is to stay well," Lirith said firmly.

The Mournish man's health had improved since their first days in Castle City, although not as much as Travis would have liked. Dark circles still clung beneath Sareth's eyes, and he seemed unable to stand up completely straight. Travis wondered what was wrong, but he knew it could be any number of things: the high altitude, the shock to his system from traveling between worlds, or an Earth bacterium alien to Sareth's Eldhish physiology.

Sareth gave Lirith a bitter smile. "Staying well is a job that doesn't pay much gold, *beshala*. And I don't need to read my fate in the cards to know there isn't anyone in this village who would give me work."

"Can you use a hammer?"

They looked up to see Maudie standing in the door of the parlor. Her eyes were on Sareth.

"I can," he said after a moment.

"Then you can start by pounding down the boards on the front porch that are coming loose. I'll pay you two bits for every hour you work." Maudie turned away, then glanced over her shoulder and winked at Sareth. "It looks like you've got a job after all, Mr. Samson."

Sareth gazed down at his hands, but Travis could just make out the smile on his lips.

Days passed. Sareth fixed the loose boards on the front porch of the boardinghouse. Then he painted the porch's peeling railing. And repaired a dozen broken shutters, patched several holes in the roof, cut down the weeds all around, and chased a skunk out from beneath the foundation. He washed all the windows, and fashioned wind chimes from cast-off bits of metal and broken purple bottles and hung them out front, so that the air around the Bluebell was filled with glittering light and bright music. And if sometimes Sareth was forced to pause in his work, placing his hands on his knees while he caught his breath, the next moment he was on to some other task.

Travis and Lirith didn't see a lot of Durge, since they worked at the saloon in the evenings, and Durge assisted the sheriff during the daytime. As far as Travis could tell, Durge's daily work consisted mostly of pitching in when townsfolk needed help: catching a stray horse loose on Elk Street, helping a lady whose wagon had broken a wheel, or putting out a small fire—which seemed to be a regular occurrence in Castle City.

Unfortunately, Durge usually had a darker tale to tell each evening when they gathered at the Bluebell for supper, before Travis and Lirith went to work. Almost every day there was some rowdy or ne'er-do-well—or two or three of them—who had to be ridden out of town.

These stories always made Travis clench his teeth. Durge was skilled with his fists. But his sword was still tucked up in the rafters of their room at the boardinghouse, and most of the men in town carried guns. No matter how strong or fast Durge was, all it would take to stop him was a single bullet. However, Durge and Tanner were always able to prevail. (These days, young Deputy Wilson manned the sheriff's office and the jail.) So far, none of their encounters had ended badly.

At least for Durge and Tanner. On three occasions, a man they had run out of town for breaking the peace showed up again a few days later. They found one floating facedown in Granite Creek, one shoved down an old mine shaft, and one hanging from a cottonwood tree. Every one of them had been shot directly through the heart—even the one that had been strung up.

Who had killed the men, Tanner and Durge didn't know— and nor did anyone the sheriff talked to. Of course, the editors of the *Castle City Clarion* were always happy to render an opinion in the "Morning Mayhem" column.

While our good Sheriff, read the paper one afternoon, *takes the easier (and one might daresay less courageous) road by doing nothing save to ask these ruffians and law-breakers to depart our fair city, it seems Fate is dealing these individuals punishments more suited for those of such violent and shiftless nature. Perhaps the Law will take note, and leave the sentencing of such individuals to Providence no longer, but rather take stronger measures to purge this town of the dregs of society. Then again, when men of questionable history and character are made into Deputies, it is hard to have faith that the Law will see the error of its ways. If that is the case, then it will be up to others to accomplish what the Law refuses. —The Editors.*

"And what would the printers of these words know about courage?" Durge rumbled after Maudie read the article aloud to him and the others. "It is the coward who strikes down the man who is weaker than he."

Lirith laid her hand on the knight's. "I've heard people talk of this newspaper, as they call it, in the saloon. The publishers will print anything if they think it will cause people to buy more papers."

"That's a fact," Maudie said, folding up the paper.

Travis knew Lirith and Maudie were right. Journalistic integrity and ethics were things that hadn't yet made the train ride across the Great Plains to the Old West. All the same, the article troubled him.

. . . when men of questionable history and character are made into Deputies . . . Those words could only refer to Durge. Attention was the one thing Travis hadn't wanted; they needed to keep a low profile until Jack arrived if they didn't want another incident like their encounter with Lionel Gentry and his men.

After supper, it was time for Travis and Lirith to head to the saloon. Travis had to admit, he was starting to look forward to his work at the Mine Shaft. Maybe it was just that, for all the differences, working for Manypenny reminded him of the time when he first came to Castle City and tended bar for Andy Connell. Those were the days when Jack Graystone was just his eccentric old friend—before Travis had ever heard of the Runelords, or the Seekers, or Eldh.

Before long, Travis began to get to know some of the regulars who came into the saloon. There was the town barber, a man almost as big and jovial as Manypenny himself, and all of the clerks who worked at the First Bank of Castle City, and who each evening after the bank closed raised glasses of port in hands stained green with ink. Both of the town's doctors and a good number of its lawyers drank at the Mine Shaft, along with the assayist and the owner of the Castle City Opera House, which was getting ready for its summer production of *The Magic Flute*.

However, of all the regulars who came into the Mine Shaft each day for a drink, Travis's favorites were Ezekial Frost and Niles Barrett.

According to the stories Travis heard, Ezekial Frost had been a mountain man in his younger days. He had trapped beaver in the 1830s, before—in one of history's odd coincidences—the animals nearly went extinct at the exact moment that silk replaced fur as the fashion for top hats worn by gentlemen in the East. In the forties and fifties Frost had worked as a scout, first for the US Army, then as a guide for folk passing through on their way to the gold fields of California.

In 1859, Colorado's own gold rush started, and—at least so the rumors told—shortly thereafter Ezekial Frost vanished. His few friends (former mountain men themselves) had thought him dead, mauled by a grizzly, perhaps, or shot by a claim jumper. Except then, just a few years ago, Frost appeared in Castle City as abruptly as he had vanished before.

Of course, if it hadn't been for the fact that one of Frost's old acquaintances was still alive in Castle City at the time and had recognized him, no one would have known who Frost was or how he had vanished twenty years before.

Certainly Frost seemed more than a little cracked. He had a habit of walking down Elk Street, clad in buckskins as weather-worn and wrinkled as his own skin, talking and laughing to himself, and occasionally breaking out into broken bits of songs that no one could name. He often stopped strangers on the street, grabbing their arms to tell them fragments of stories about lost treasures or secret passes in the mountains. And he was known to pick up the still-burning butts of cigars that had been tossed on the ground and smoke them. As far as Travis knew, he had no home, but slept in a teepee somewhere up in the hills.

While people tended to clear away from the bar when Ezekial Frost approached, Travis always smiled and poured a glass of Taos Lightning.

"Did I tell you about the feller who ate two squaws, an Indian guide, and a Frenchman?" he said one afternoon as Travis poured him his drink.

Frost had a habit of telling bizarre tales, which was one of the reasons Travis liked him. He claimed to have been born in New York in 1811 before heading out West in his twenties—and given his long white beard and a frame as knobby as a wind-twisted pine, that was one story Travis didn't doubt.

"No, I haven't heard that one yet," Travis said, refilling Frost's glass.

"It was back in the fifties, long before this town was even here," Frost said in his rusty voice. "Now, how this feller first got a taste for man meat, I cain't say. But once a feller has that taste in him, he can't be rid of it. Anyways, so he's on his way to Fort Laramie, carrying messages for the general out of Fort Craig, and he and his Arapaho guide get caught in a blizzard, and they sit in a hole in the snow for day after day as their provisions run out. Well, finally the snow lets up, and a while later the feller walks on into Fort Laramie. 'Where's your Indian guide?' the lieutenant at the fort asks him. And the feller reaches into his saddlebag, pulls out a shriveled foot, and tosses it at the soldier. 'Here's what's left of him. You can have it if you want, as I'm shore tired of eatin' him.'"

"That's a most intriguing tale, Mr. Frost," Niles Barrett said, taking a draw on a thin cigar. "But forgive me—it's simply the journalist in me that causes me to call some of your details into question."

Ezekial Frost squinted at the tall, well-dressed man standing at the bar next to him.

People about town whispered that Niles Barrett was the youngest son of a British lord, and that—as a result of some scandal or impropriety—he had been banished by his family to

America. Travis couldn't vouch for these facts, but Barrett did speak with an English accent, and he certainly seemed to have enough money to buy fine clothes, brandy, and cigars, and to stay at the Silver Palace Hotel on a permanent basis, all without having any obvious source of income.

Barrett wasn't a handsome man—his face was too long, and his features too irregular—but his impressive attire and cultured manner of speech lent him an attractive air. Travis liked listening to Barrett talk about anything—although the Englishman's favorite topic was the weekly newspaper he hoped to start soon, which he intended to call the *Castle County Reporter*, and which only awaited a printing press on order from Philadelphia.

"Are you calling me a liar?" Frost said with a snort. "I've traipsed around these mountains for longer than you've been alive, mister, and I've seen things that would make your pretty long hair turn white and fall off your head, I have."

"I have no doubt of it," Barrett said. "However, while some newspapers in this town might print anything they hear without being sure of the facts, that is not how the *Castle County Reporter* will work. If I am to use this tale in my newspaper, I must ask one thing: If this man you spoke of displayed the grisly evidence of his cannibalism—the aforementioned foot— why did the lieutenant at Fort Laramie not arrest him? After all, Mr. Packer was sentenced to jail for eating his companions outside of Lake City some years back."

Frost set down his empty glass and fixed his disconcerting gaze on Barrett. "I'll tell you what, mister. Come on up to my teepee on Signal Ridge, and I'll tell you the reason. Just make sure to fatten yourself up a bit before you do." The old mountain man smacked his lips and rubbed his stomach, then headed out the saloon door.

Barrett cast Travis a startled look. "He isn't serious, is he? He wasn't the man he was telling the story about, the one who ate his Indian guide?"

"Don't forget the two squaws and the Frenchman," Travis said, grinning as he poured another drink.

"Perhaps he wishes to add Englishmen to that list," Barrett said and drained his brandy.

18.

The Fourth of July came to Castle City with a great deal of fanfare and no sign of Jack Graystone.

It was midday when Durge stepped through the doors of the Mine Shaft. The saloon's patrons glanced up, eyes lighting upon the silver badge he wore on his chest, then returned their gazes to their drinks. Durge approached the bar as Travis pushed a glass of whiskey toward a hard-faced miner.

"Travis, there is dark sorcery at work in this town," the knight said in a grim voice.

The miner gave Durge a curious look, and Travis hastily reached across the bar, grabbed the knight's arm, and led him several feet down the length of polished wood. "What are you talking about, Durge?"

The knight's mustache twitched. "It has been going on since dawn. There are foul magics at play in Castle City."

"What do you mean? What's been going on?"

"Smoke that appears with no visible source of fire. Explosions like those at the mines, but here in the midst of town. And lines of flame that streak screaming into the sky. But it's worse than that, for on my way here I saw a small girl touch a match to a rolled up piece of parchment—a spell of some sort, I presume. She tossed it into the street, and it exploded in such a cascade of sparks that horses reared in terror and a man cried out in agony. And the girl laughed." Durge gripped Travis's arm. "Children, Travis. These sorcerers have corrupted children into doing their dark work. We have to stop them!"

The bright sound of firecrackers drifted through the doors of the saloon. Durge whirled around. "There it is again. She must be following me!"

"Calm down, Durge." Travis gripped his shoulder. "It's not dark sorcery at work. It's just fireworks."

"Fireworks?"

Travis poured a few more drinks, then spent several minutes telling Durge everything he knew about fireworks while the knight sipped a sarsaparilla. When Travis finished, Durge stroked his mustaches, now looking more intrigued than alarmed. "So these fireworks are created by means of the same alchemy used to fashion bullets and the blasting explosions in the mines?"

"That's right," Travis said. "It's called gunpowder."

"And these fireworks were brought here by the men from the Dominion you call China?"

"Most likely. They've been making fireworks there for centuries."

"And folk set them off as a way to celebrate the founding day of the Dominion we now dwell in. It's called *Yewessay*. I know that, as Sir Tanner made me place my hand on a book and swear to uphold the laws of *Yewessay*."

Travis grinned. "That's the United States of America. It's the Fourth of July—the day we declared our independence from England. People always set off fireworks."

Durge frowned. "Causing objects to explode seems a peculiar way to celebrate the winning of one's sovereignty."

Lirith approached the bar, jade taffeta swishing.

"Taking a break?" Travis said. Both he and Lirith had come to work early that day because of the holiday. The gambling tables were already alive with action.

The witch nodded. "The house was having an unusually good streak of luck, so I thought it best to let them lick their wounds for a while."

"And you weren't aiding luck, were you, my lady?" Durge said, twitching his fingers.

Lirith looked scandalized. "Durge!"

Travis grinned. "Never mind him. He's got dark magic on the brain today."

Durge crossed his arms, looking sullen. "I still say there is something wicked going on in this town."

"You're not wrong there, my good deputy," said a rich, British voice. "There is indeed evil afoot in this city."

They looked up to see Niles Barrett approach the bar. His usually elegant suit was slightly disheveled, and a black streak marred his crimson vest. Travis poured a glass of the house's best brandy and pushed it across the bar to him. Barrett took a drink and sighed.

"Bloody poor excuse for a holiday in my opinion," the

Englishman said. "Don't these people know the war ended more than a hundred years ago? For God's sake, Queen Victoria and President Arthur just had tea together. Our nations are at peace. But you would hardly know it, given the rowdyism out there. A girl just threw a firecracker at me, and it nearly singed right through to my smallclothes."

Travis refilled Barrett's glass. "So we heard."

Barrett raised a questioning eyebrow.

Travis nodded at Durge. "A report from the deputy here. He's carefully monitoring the nefarious activities of all small girls in town. But don't worry about the firecracker. I doubt there was any malevolent intent behind it."

"Unlike the other violence going on in this town, you mean?" Barrett said, lighting a cigar.

Lirith laid a hand on the bar, her eyes intent. "Is that what you meant before, when you said there was evil at work in Castle City?"

"That I did, Miss Lily." Barrett puffed on his cigar.

Durge glowered at the Englishman. "If you know something about lawbreakers in this village, Lord Barrett, you must tell me at once."

Barrett set down his cigar in a dish. "I'll tell you this, Mr. Dirk. For long months I have awaited the delivery of my new printing press from Philadelphia, for which I paid a handsome sum, and with which I intended to publish my own newspaper, the *Castle County Reporter*, as a weekly tonic of truth to counter the poisonous concoction of lies served up by this city's existing daily publication. At last my new press was set to arrive on today's train from Denver. Only I reached the depot to discover my press was not on the train after all."

"Perhaps it will arrive tomorrow," Lirith said.

Barrett gave her a bitter smile. "No, Miss Lily. I learned from the conductor that my press had indeed been on board. However, some miles outside of Castle City, it was thrown from the train into a deep canyon, where it was shattered to bits."

Durge's expression was one of outrage. "Who did this thing? Did the conductor see these men?"

"He claimed he saw only their backs." Barrett picked up his cigar again and stared at the glowing tip. "And even if that's not the case, I can't blame him for saying it. For I have a good idea who the perpetrators were. There are men in this town who fear the truth even as a creature of the night fears the light of dawn. For surely it would strike them down just as terribly."

"Who are these men you speak of?" Durge rumbled. "We must tell Sheriff Tanner of them at once."

Barrett glanced over his shoulder—just as Travis had seen other men in the saloon do from time to time—then leaned close and spoke in a low voice.

"Sheriff Tanner is a good man, Mr. Dirk, I know that as well as you do. But there is nothing he can do about these men." He pulled a copy of the *Castle City Clarion* out of his coat pocket and tossed it on the bar. "As long as they have the support of the town's most powerful society leaders and institutions, it is they who run Castle City, not Tanner."

Durge shook his head. "I don't understand you."

"Then I'll tell you a story, Mr. Dirk. Some years back, lawlessness ran wild in one of the gold towns down south, past Leadville. The ruffians were too much for the sheriff to control. So a group of the town's men decided to take matters into their own hands, and they started up a vigilance committee."

"A vigilance committee?" Lirith said.

Barrett flicked ash from his cigar. "That's right, Miss Lily. The vigilance committee worked under the cover of dark. They went after the town's thieves and murderers and caught them. But they didn't wait for the circuit court judge to arrive to hold a trial and mete out justice. Instead, the committee acted as judge, jury, and executioner, and any man they caught was hanged before the sun rose."

"It is unpleasant, to be sure," Durge said. "But sometimes harsh measures are required in order to keep the peace, especially in the frontier. And it does not sound as if the men who were executed were innocent."

"No, Mr. Dirk, they weren't. Not at first. For a time the citizens of the town knew peace. But after a while, it wasn't just the thieves and murderers that were found hanging in the morning. It was a miner who had bested one of the town's leading men in a fair hand of poker. Or a hurdy-gurdy girl who had let slip that another of the town's upstanding men was her best customer. Or a preacher who gave a sermon decrying the violence. Soon the people trembled in their houses at night, fearing the sound of guns and horses outside their doors. And when a circuit court judge did arrive to put an end to it all, he was found shot through head, his brains on the floor of his hotel room."

Travis's gaze fell upon the crumpled copy of the *Castle City Clarion*. Wasn't that the pattern he had seen when he went through the stack of papers? Violence decreased for a time, only to return darker and stronger than before.

Durge clenched his hands into fists. "What you describe is wrong. The law must always be respected. They were evil men."

"And yet they acted under the guise of righteousness, Mr. Dirk." Barrett smashed out his cigar in the dish. "But then, perhaps those are the most evil men of all. For how can a man speak out against them without being branded unrighteous?"

Durge crossed his arms. "The three men whom we've found dead these last weeks—the brigands whom Sir Tanner ordered to leave Castle City—it is this vigilance committee who murdered them, is it not?"

"I told you, Mr. Dirk. They take justice into their own hands."

Lirith touched his arm. "You know who these men are, don't you, Lord Barrett?"

"Only a few of them, Miss Lily. And I believe you know who they are as well as I do."

Travis spoke the name without thinking. "Gentry."

"That's right, Mr. Wilder," Barrett said, his voice barely above a whisper. "Lionel Gentry and his cronies, Eugene Ellis and Calvin Murray."

Durge started to pull away from the bar. "I must go tell Sheriff Tanner at once. We must put these men in jail."

"Don't waste your time, Mr. Dirk," Barrett said. "Gentry and his boys are in the pay of the vigilance committee, that much I'm sure of. But they're henchmen, that's all. If you put them in jail, some unknown benefactor would simply post their bail, and they'd be out free. You see, the real members of the vigilance committee are among the town's powerful and wealthy men."

"But who are these powerful men?" Durge said.

Barrett shrugged. "I don't know, Mr. Dirk. I only know that, whoever they are, they'll be among the leading men of this town. Any one of them could be on the vigilance committee."

The knight's voice rumbled with quiet anger. "Where I come from, it is true that lords and men of power can often do as they wish to men beneath them in standing. But Sir Tanner described the laws of this place to me, and they state clearly that all men are equal in the eyes of justice. It does not matter if these men you speak of are wealthy or important. They must be punished all the same."

Until then, Barrett's voice had been soft and weary. Now a sharpness entered it. "I like you, Mr. Dirk. You're a refreshingly honest man. So I'm going to be honest with you in turn. There's nothing you or Sheriff Tanner can do. A star on your chest doesn't give you power over these men. In fact, being on the sheriff's side can only impede you in your efforts. You see, you have to follow to the law; these men don't. The only one who could help us now would be a civilizer like Tyler Caine. And I fear there's not much hope of that."

Travis felt a pain in his chest, but whether it was a pang of fear or a thrill of excitement he didn't know. He glanced at the back of the saloon. The edge of the Wanted poster was just visible, peeking out from behind a column.

"Why do you say that?" Travis licked his lips. "How could Tyler Caine help us?"

Barrett drew a match from the pocket of his vest and lit it with a quick flick of his thumb. "They say one must fight fire with fire, Mr. Wilder. Only a man outside the law can stop those who've taken the law into their own hands. But it's pointless to hope. Tyler Caine was the last great civilizer to walk this part of the West. And all the stories say he's dead." He snuffed out the match between finger and thumb.

19.

Lirith returned to her faro table, and Durge headed out the saloon's swinging doors—probably to make sure no lawless little girls set the town ablaze with firecrackers. Travis left Niles

Barrett to his brandy and went back to pouring drinks. However, as the day wore on, it was hard to concentrate on his work, and often a man had to ask him twice for a glass of beer or whiskey. More than once he found himself gazing at the faded Wanted poster at the back of the saloon.

The saloon grew more crowded by the hour. Travis learned there was to be a parade along Elk Street at sunset, culminating in a fireworks display on the edge of town. This wasn't just a national holiday; it had been exactly seven years since the state of Colorado was admitted to the Union.

Despite the fact that nearly all of the saloon's regulars had shown up for the festivities, Travis never caught sight of Ezekial Frost. The old mountain man usually came in long before nightfall to get his shot of Old Towse. Where was he?

He's probably avoiding the crowds, Travis. Ezekial is pretty much a hermit, and I'm sure he knew today was a holiday.

Besides, there was too much on Travis's mind for him to worry about Ezekial Frost. He couldn't stop thinking about Barrett's earlier words. All day, the Englishman sat at the end of the bar, slowly nursing several brandies in a row, clearly mourning the loss of his printing press. At one point it occurred to Travis that the Englishman might know Jack Graystone, but when he asked, Barrett shook his head.

As afternoon edged into evening, the frequency of the explosions outside increased. Every time he heard the sound of a firecracker, Travis had to clench his jaw and force himself not to jump. The noise was as loud and rapid as gunfire. He couldn't stop thinking about Durge, and he hoped the knight wasn't getting into any trouble out there.

By the time sunset was imminent, the atmosphere in the saloon was sharp with the scent of gunpowder. To Travis, it smelled like fear. The constant din of explosions and talk had set his nerves on edge, and he could hardly hold the whiskey bottle steady as he poured. Often he reached into his pocket to grip the smooth orb of Sinfathisar, and that calmed him somewhat. However, he would be grateful when the night was over—when Durge showed up at the saloon whole and unhurt, and they could return with Lirith to the Bluebell.

Travis was just glad Sareth was safe at the boardinghouse.

Judging by the amount of liquor that was flowing, it wasn't a good time for the Mournish man to be seen in town. The fireworks hadn't even started, and already men staggered into the saloon, drunk before they even bought a drink. Tempers would be flaring before all was said and done. When he was able to sneak a moment, Travis made sure the shotgun behind the bar was loaded. Manypenny noticed his action and gave him an approving nod.

At last the parade began. Travis saw movement outside the saloon's windows. A wagon rolled past, decorated with red, white, and blue buntings. All the employees of the First Bank of Castle City sat in the wagon, grinning and waving, along with the owner of the bank, Aaron Locke. Locke was a bookish but handsome man in his forties, and everyone agreed he was the richest fellow in Castle City, now that Mr. Simon Castle had returned back East following the death of his wife. However, it was also said the fortune of Mortimer Hale, publisher of the *Castle City Clarion*, ran a close second to Aaron Locke's. While it was Simon Castle who had begun the newspaper, it was under Hale's ownership that the paper's circulation and influence had soared.

More wagons passed by, and coaches, and men on horses, all decorated for the occasion. Firecrackers exploded in flashes like lightning. Most of the saloon's patrons headed out the door, drinks in hand, to stand on the boardwalk and whoop and holler as the parade rattled by. Travis leaned on the bar, taking in a deep breath as he enjoyed the sudden calm inside the saloon.

"One sarsaparilla please."

He looked up into Lirith's warm brown eyes and smiled. "Coming right up, ma'am."

Travis poured a glass of the dark, sweet liquid and pushed it toward Lirith; she and Durge seemed to adore the stuff, although Travis couldn't drink it without gagging.

"Aren't you going to watch the parade?" he said.

"I'd rather stay in here," she said with a sigh.

Travis understood. As long as the men were out watching the parade, she could take a break.

"Do you want to go watch the fireworks later?" he asked. "I

imagine the saloon will clear out for that. If it does, I bet Manypenny would let us go."

"No, thank you. I wish to go see a play."

Travis gave her a curious look. She set down her drink and pulled a folded piece of paper from her dress.

"A man at my table gave me this. He called it a playbill, and it says a play is to be performed tonight at the Diamond Theater on Aspen Street."

"A play, you say?" said Niles Barrett from the end of the bar. The Englishman's eyes were slightly blurred, but his voice was as crisp as ever. "That's bloody good news. We could use a deal more culture in this town. Do you know that Oscar Wilde recently visited Leadville? If that collection of hovels can get the likes of Oscar Wilde to come give a lecture, I don't see why we can't in Castle City. I hear from those who saw him that he's a fascinating man."

The miner standing next to Barrett snorted. "And I hear he was more lady than man."

Barrett scowled at the miner, but before he could respond, the next man down the bar spoke—another miner, given his stained hands.

"I was there in Leadville," the man said. "And I saw this Oscar Wilde fellow. He was dressed all in velvet and lace, and he carried a lily everywhere he went. When he visited one of the mines, they served him up whiskey, harsh as snake venom, thinking to make an easy fool of him. But you know what? He outdrank every single one of them miners, for all that he was standing there in white stockings and knickers."

That won a grunt of respect from the first miner.

Barrett rolled his eyes. "I see. So it's for Lord Wilde's drinking prowess that we should admire him, not the subtle skill of his pen."

The two men stared at him.

"Never mind," Barrett said with a pained look. He turned his back to the men and regarded Lirith. "What is the play to be, Miss Lily? Is it Shakespeare? Please let it be Shakespeare. Or better yet, Marlowe. Poor Kit, stabbed in the eye in his prime."

Lirith smiled eagerly. "The man said he thought I'd especially like this play."

She unfolded the playbill and pressed it flat on the bar. Travis's heart sank.

Barrett sniffed. "Ah. American melodrama. What utter rubbish." He turned his attention back to his brandy.

Lirith smoothed the playbill. "Look, Travis. They're like me." She touched the two figures—a man and a woman—drawn on the playbill. Their faces were shaded as darkly as Lirith's own. Above the grotesquely rendered drawing was the play's title.

UNCLE TOM'S CABIN
OR, LIFE AMONG THE LOWLY
A MELODRAMA IN FIVE ACTS

"Lirith..." Travis fought for words. How could he explain it to her? "You don't want to see this play."

Her brow wrinkled. "Why not?"

Travis didn't know where to begin, so he took a deep breath and started by telling Lirith about slavery. He talked about what he remembered from college history, about the slave trade that brought people from Africa to the Americas against their will, about the abolitionists, and the Civil War, and President Lincoln, and how he was assassinated. All the while Lirith listened, her face without expression.

At last Travis ran out of things to say. Lirith was silent for a moment, then she touched the playbill.

"So this Independence Day they are celebrating," she said. "It didn't mean independence for everyone, did it?"

Travis took her hand in hers. "It does now, Lirith. Or at least, someday it will."

She pulled her hand away and picked up the playbill. "If the woman who wrote this was one of these abolitionists, as you called them, then I would still like to see the play. I think it would be good for me to know what it was like for them."

Travis swallowed. He had to make Lirith understand. Yes, Harriet Beecher Stowe had been opposed to slavery, and her novel *Uncle Tom's Cabin* had helped fuel the cause of the abolitionists. However, he also knew that by the time the book became popular as a play, it had more to do with slapstick comedy than commentary against slavery. Lirith wanted to see people who looked like her. But Travis was certain the actors would be as white as he was beneath their thick coating of blackface. However, before he could say these things, a familiar figure stepped through the swinging doors of the saloon and approached the bar, peg leg drumming against the wooden floor.

Travis froze, but Lirith smiled as she looked up. "Sareth. What are you doing here? I thought you were going to help Maudie put up decorations."

The Mournish man scratched his pointed beard. "What do you mean, *beshala*? I came here as fast as I could."

Travis struggled to find his tongue. Something was wrong with this. "Why exactly did you come here, Sareth?"

"In answer to your message," Sareth said, a scowl darkening his coppery visage. "The boy you sent came to the boarding-house. He said you needed to see me at the saloon right away." He glanced from Travis to Lirith, evidently seeing the puzzlement on their faces. "What's going on?"

"I don't know," Travis said. "I—" Confusion gave way to understanding, and dread surged through Travis's chest like a cold gully washer. "Gentry," he said, and the others stared at him.

It had to be. Who else would trick Sareth into leaving the Bluebell? Certainly not Tanner, and no one else in town even knew him. But why do it all?

You saw the way he looked at Sareth that day. Gentry hates him. There's no reason for it, but a man like that doesn't need a reason. Sareth looks different, and that's enough.

But why today? It had been over a month since their encounter with Gentry and his cronies. Why wait until now to do something? Before Travis could think of an answer, the saloon's doors swung open, and three men stepped through, confirming his fears.

"Speak of the Devil," Barrett muttered, gripping his brandy. The saloon had fallen quiet, and despite his soft tone the Englishman's voice echoed loudly.

Lionel Gentry turned his blue eyes toward Barrett. "You don't want to be here, Niles," he said in his easy drawl. "Why don't you go on over to China Alley and buy yourself one of them pigtail boys we all know you like. Wasn't that what they kicked you out of England for? You might as well have yourself a good time. Judgment Day is coming soon for the likes of you. But it's him we've come for tonight." He nodded toward Sareth.

Gentry's words were like a blow to the Englishman. His face blanched, and he backed into a corner, still clutching his drink. Outside, a volley of firecrackers crackled like buckshot against sheet metal. The dozen men left in the saloon all cringed on reflex. Travis forced himself not to glance down at the shotgun beneath the bar. His hands, resting on the polished wood, were only inches from it. He wished Manypenny was there, but the saloonkeeper had stepped outside to watch the parade.

Lirith stepped forward, interposing herself between the men and Sareth.

"You have no claim to him," the witch said.

The long-faced one, Eugene Ellis, took a draw on his thin cigar. "So the stories are true," he said in an exhalation of rank smoke. "Manypenny did hire her. Only I can't quite tell if she's a Negress or a mulatto."

"It don't matter," Calvin Murray said. His downy red beard made him appear more boyish rather than less. "No kind of woman should be dealing cards. It ain't proper."

Ellis let out a sardonic laugh and smoothed his waxed mustache. "Don't be beguiled by her beauty, Mr. Murray. I tell you, without doubt, she's not a proper lady. That's a harlot's dress she wears."

Color darkened Lirith's cheeks, and she turned away. Sareth tried to catch her eyes, but she wouldn't look at him.

Ellis let his gaze flicker up and down the witch's slender figure. "I wonder that hiring her kind for such a public position is even legal."

"Maybe it is," Gentry said, taking a step forward, spurs jingling. "And then again, maybe it shouldn't be. Maybe the law in this town ain't doing what it should. But that's all right. Because there are men who'll do what the law won't." He fixed his cold blue gaze on Travis. "You're friends with that new deputy, aren't you? Mr. Dirk, I believe his name is?"

Travis swallowed but didn't say anything.

"I heard Dirk's a man-killer out of Abilene," Murray said,

his voice high-pitched with emotion. "And I don't doubt it. Not from the look of him. That'd be just like Tanner, to go and deputize an outlaw."

"You're right, Mr. Murray." Gentry kept his focus on Travis. "And there's something shifty about this one, too. Though I can't quite put my finger on it. He doesn't wear a gun, but he's dangerous all the same. I'd keep my eyes on his hands, if I were you."

Outside, a rocket screamed like a mountain lion. Travis let go of the bar. The moist outlines of his splayed fingers lingered on the wood, then evaporated.

"What do you want with Sareth?" Travis said, although he knew the magic of the coin fragment made the name come out *Samson*.

Gentry took another step forward. "We have it on good account that your friend Mr. Samson robbed McKay's General Store earlier today."

Both Lirith and Travis shot astonished glances at Sareth. The Mournish man shook his head in confusion.

"It can't be," Lirith said.

"I talked to one of Mr. McKay's clerks myself," Ellis said, tossing his cigar butt on the floor. "Mr. Samson stole a box from the loading dock. The clerk said it contained a set of silverware intended for young Miss McKay's wedding gift, and that it was worth more than fifty dollars. I suppose this here thief has already melted it down and sold it."

"Is that so, Mr. Ellis?" said a deep, calm voice.

Travis looked up to see two figures standing in the doorway of the saloon. One was slight, with a sandy mustache, the other no taller, but broad and solid. Sheriff Tanner and Durge. Travis felt a surge of relief.

"Sheriff," Gentry said, spitting out the word like bad whiskey.

"I'm sorry it took me so long to get here," Tanner said. "I only just now heard about the robbery at McKay's. And if it hadn't been for one of Mortimer Hale's newsboys, selling the late edition of the *Clarion* fresh off the presses, I might not have heard about it at all. When I saw you all come in here, I thought I'd better stop by. You see, I still can't quite figure out why the folks at the paper heard about this, only I didn't."

"Maybe the clerk at McKay's didn't think you'd do anything about it, Sheriff," Gentry said with a sharp grin. "Maybe he came to people who he knew would help him."

Durge gave Gentry a piercing look. "It is more likely that this clerk you speak of had some compelling reason not to speak to Sheriff Tanner. Perhaps he stole this silver himself and wished to blame another for the deed."

Tanner nodded at the knight. "That's good thinking, Mr. Dirk. We'll be sure to have a talk with him. He might have something more to tell us."

At that, Murray cast a glance at Gentry, his eyes worried. Gentry glared at him.

Ellis's face grew more sallow yet with anger. "Are you calling us liars, Mr. Dirk?"

"Even good men can be made into fools, Eugene Ellis," Tanner said.

"Wait a minute," Travis said, shocked to realize it was he who had spoken. "It doesn't matter if the clerk was lying or not. Sareth couldn't have robbed anyone. He was at the Bluebell Boardinghouse all day. I'm sure Maudie Carlyle can vouch for that."

Tanner raised an eyebrow and glanced at Sareth. The Mournish man chewed his lip.

Travis felt panic rising in his chest. "You *were* at the Bluebell, weren't you, Sareth?"

The Mournish man gave him a sheepish look. "A man came to the boardinghouse while Lady Maudie was resting upstairs. The man said he had a delivery for Maudie, but his arm was in a sling, and he couldn't carry the box, so I said I would carry it for him. He took me to a shop—this McKay's—and pointed to a box on the loading dock. So I took it back to Maudie's."

Travis's right hand itched. It had all been a setup. On Eldh, the Mournish were known to be clever con men. Sareth should have been able to see through what was happening.

Only this isn't his world, Travis. Everything in this place is strange to him. There was no way he could tell that what was happening wasn't right.

The sound of fireworks was reaching a crescendo, mixed with the bright sound of bugles and the stomping of feet.

"Did you hear that, Sheriff?" Gentry said, taking a step toward Sareth. "This thief just confessed to his crime."

"That's not what I heard," Tanner said.

Ellis clenched his hands into fists. "What are you talking about, Tanner? Everyone in this saloon just heard him say he took the box from McKay's."

A few of the onlookers in the saloon nodded.

"That's right," Tanner said. "He took the box this other fellow told him to. And I'm wondering who this man is, the one with the bum arm. Can you describe him, Mr. Samson?"

Sareth opened his mouth to speak, but before he could, Calvin Murray lunged forward and grabbed his shirt.

"You're a thief!" the young man shouted, his face as red as his hair. "And we ain't gonna let you get away with it!"

"Step away from him, Calvin Murray," Tanner said, his voice low with authority, his right hand by his hip.

"Or what, Sheriff?" Gentry said, his lips curving in a sharp smile. "Dropping your gun won't accomplish much."

Next to his hip, Tanner's hand shook violently, moving so quickly the fingers blurred. The sheriff turned away, clutching his right hand with the left, stilling the spasm.

"Let go of me," Sareth said. His eyes glinted with a dangerous light that made Travis think of his sister, Vani.

"You're gonna pay right now for what you done," Murray said through clenched teeth.

Countless flashes of light burned through the saloon's windows as a volley of rockets was launched outside, and in the strobe everything moved with queer, staccato slowness.

Calvin Murray reached into his suit coat and pulled out a silver revolver. The gun glinted in the white-hot light as he pressed it against Sareth's chest. Sareth grabbed for the young man's gun hand. As he did, Murray slugged Sareth across the jaw with his free hand. Then the two men stumbled away from the bar, spinning and grappling, their bodies so close together Travis couldn't see what was happening.

Lirith reached toward Sareth, her mouth open in a cry Travis couldn't hear above the noise of the fireworks. Both Tanner and Durge started forward, but Ellis stepped into their way. Only

Gentry didn't move. Instead he watched, hands on hips, a smile on his face.

You've got to do something, Travis.

But what? The shotgun was in reach, but Sareth and Murray were spinning so fast there was no telling which he'd hit. And using a rune wouldn't be any better.

It didn't matter. He couldn't just stand and watch. Wasn't that what he had learned last Midwinter's Eve? Making the wrong choice was better than making no choice at all. Travis's right hand tingled as he reached out and started to speak a rune.

There was a searing flash of light, and with it came one final report, louder than all the others before it, shattering the air of the saloon, stunning those within. Then the light dimmed, and the noise rolled away like thunder. Outside, on Elk Street, the parade was over.

Travis lowered his hand as a coldness spilled through him. Sareth stood in the center of the saloon, a bruise already forming on his jaw, his expression one of puzzlement. In his hands was Murray's silver gun, and at his feet lay Calvin Murray. The young man stared upward with dull eyes, his cheeks no longer red, but white as ash. Already blood soaked into the sawdust around him, oozing from the hole in his chest.

The silence in the saloon was broken as words of shock and anger rose from the onlookers. It was Lirith who moved first. The witch knelt beside Murray, touched his brow, then looked up at Sareth.

"He's dead," she said, her eyes filled with anguish.

Sareth shook his head, staring at the gun. Travis couldn't quite hear the words he spoke. They might have been, *This cannot be so.*

"Get away from him, Jezebel!" Ellis shouted at Lirith, lifting his hand as if he might strike her. The witch rose and stumbled toward Travis and the bar.

"So the thief's become a murderer," Gentry said. "If he wasn't already." Of all the people in the bar, he was the only one who didn't seem shocked at what had happened. Instead, there was something satisfied about his expression. "What are you going to do, Sheriff? I say we carry out justice right here and now." He rested his hand on the grip of his holstered gun. Murmurs of assent ran around the saloon, along with a few muttered instances of *man-killer* and *hang him high*.

Now all eyes were on the sheriff. Tanner gazed at the dead man with what seemed a thoughtful expression. At last he nodded and looked up at Durge.

"Mr. Dirk," he said, his voice weary. "Arrest Mr. Samson. Take him to the jail. We'll lock him up to wait for trial."

"Lynch him now!" came a shout from the back of the saloon. More shouts echoed this sentiment, but Tanner silenced them all with a stern glare.

"I said take him to the jail, Mr. Dirk. The circuit court judge will be coming in a couple of weeks. Mr. Samson will get his trial then."

Durge let out a heavy sigh, then he stepped forward and took Sareth's arm. "I am sorry. It is my oath to obey Sir Tanner."

The Mournish man nodded. "I understand."

"No!" Lirith gasped. "You can't do this, Durge."

Tanner approached the bar, and he spoke in a quiet voice. "Let Mr. Dirk do his duty, Miss Lily. You'll see it's for the best. We've got plenty of time to sort things out before the circuit court judge comes. And right now, the jail is the only place in town where Mr. Samson will be safe. If I don't put him behind bars, they'll hang him before the sun rises."

Travis knew Tanner was right. More men were coming into the saloon, listening to the words the others whispered, and turning their angry gazes on Sareth.

"I'll be fine, *beshala*," Sareth said, forcing a smile for her sake. "I'm sure Durge will take excellent care of me. Look how good he is with Maudie's cats."

The Embarran knight gave the witch a solemn nod. "You have my word he will not come to harm."

Lirith pressed her lips together but said nothing. Travis moved around the bar and took her trembling hand.

"Will you take Calvin Murray's body to Doc Svensson?" Tanner said to Gentry.

Gentry's blue eyes were as cold as ever. "Don't you worry about him, Sheriff. We'll take care of our boy."

His words sent a chill through Travis. Two men helped Gentry and Ellis pick up Calvin Murray's limp form, and they carried him out the door. Tanner and Durge followed, leading Sareth between them. Once they were gone, Lirith buried her head against Travis's chest, and he held her as tightly as he could as she wept.

20.

A hundred icy hands pulled Grace down into dark, endless depths.

You're drowning, Grace, spoke the clinical doctor's voice in her mind. *You've got to swim. Now.*

It was so hard to move; the shock of the cold paralyzed her. But then, hypothermia could begin to set in almost immediately in water so frigid. The sea roiled around her, and a groaning noise vibrated through her body. The currents spun her around, so that she didn't know which way was up. Her lungs were already starting to burn.

Something warm clamped around her wrist. The brine stung her eyes, but she could just make out a figure silhouetted against wavering gray light. Beltan. The light had to be coming from the surface, and the knight's legs were kicking hard. He was trying to swim upward with her, even as the sinking ship dragged them both down.

Help him, Grace. If you don't help Beltan swim, the ship will take both of you with it.

Her flesh was like clay, but she forced her legs to move. Behind her (below her?) she sensed a hulking shadow. It was the *Fate Runner*. Had everyone gotten off the ship?

She reached out with the Touch, and the sea became a starry sky filled with flecks of light. Most of them were fish, but she saw several brighter sparks as well. Some flickered, descending with the dark bulk of the ship. But not all. She could feel others in the water not far away. To whom did the life sparks belong?

The pain in her lungs grew more urgent, breaking her connection with the Weirding. However, using the Touch had allowed some of the life force to flow into her, warming her, just as it had a year ago in the frozen garden in Castle Calavere, when Lady Kyrene first showed her what it meant to be a witch.

Through his grip on her wrist, Beltan must have gained some of the energy as well. Both of them kicked harder, and the light grew brighter above them. Needles stabbed at Grace's lungs. Instinct to draw a breath screamed at her like a furious child, but she fought it. They were almost there.

Focused as she was on the light, Grace saw it too late to re-act. A ragged chunk of wood as big as a car spun toward them, carried by a violent eddy. It was a fragment of the ship's hull. Beltan tried to twist away from it, but the water slowed his movements. She felt rather than heard a sick crunching sound as the piece of wreckage struck them both.

Grace gasped in pain, and her mouth flooded with water, choking her. Beltan's grip was jerked away from her wrist, and then she was spinning out of control. Light and dark flashed by in dizzying alternation. On one rotation, she thought she saw two murky shapes sinking away from her. One was large and jagged—the piece of the hull—and the other smaller, arms and legs trailing limply. Was that Beltan? Or someone else?

She was descending again, and this time she couldn't resist. Her limbs would no longer respond, and she could feel her consciousness shrinking inward like the aperture of a camera. One more moment, and it would fade to black.

The darkness vanished, replaced by a shimmering light. The light was different than the wavering gray daylight of before. It was brilliant, encapsulating her as if in a glowing sphere. It seemed she heard a faint, chiming music.

You're hallucinating, Doctor, that's all. It's the same thing patients in the Emergency Department see when their hearts stop, just before you jolt them back to life. But no one's here to work the defibrillator in your case.

The visions would only last a few seconds; they were simply part of the dying process. Except the light grew brighter, and it seemed there was a face inside it, gazing at her with large, tilted eyes.

Who are you? she wanted to say. Maybe, somehow, she did.

As if in answer, a profound warmth filled her, making her think of sunlight on ancient stones. The pain vanished from her lungs, and it felt as if she had become marvelously buoyant. She could sense the water rushing around her as the light bore her upward. She was going to make it....

No. I can't abandon them. Despite the warmth, panic filled her. *I can't just leave the others down here.*

The sense of motion slowed. The light hesitated.

Please. Grace felt her consciousness slipping away again. Each word was a terrible effort. *Beltan. And Vani and Falken. They'll drown down here.*

Her last vision was of the eyes in the light gazing at her, and in them was an expression that filled Grace with such wonder that surely she was hallucinating again.

It was a look of love.

Grace felt the water swirl past her once again, in a new direction now. Then darkness at last closed around her, and for a time both thought and light ceased.

21.

Grace opened her eyes.

It was still light all around her. Only this light was the color of ashes, and all traces of the warmth she had felt before were gone. She couldn't see much of anything, and after a time she realized she was lying facedown on wet sand. Every few moments a frigid wave washed over her, chilling her further. Somehow she was alive, but if she didn't get up, if she didn't get moving, she wouldn't be for long.

Sitting up was a lengthy process. For a time she simply thought about moving, and even that was almost too exhausting to bear. When she finally did move, it was only to flop on the sand like a stranded fish. Eventually she made real progress and rose up onto her elbows, eliciting a fierce bout of retching. Spasms racked her body, and water gushed from her mouth.

After that, she felt better.

You've cleared the water from your lungs, Grace. You're getting more oxygen now. You're going to be fine as long as you don't get a secondary infection.

She dragged her body forward until she reached dry sand—it felt soft and amazingly warm, even though she knew it wasn't—then sat up and got her first good look around. She was on one end of a small horseshoe of sand that rimmed a narrow bay. The coast in either direction was made up of black rocks with cruel edges against which the sea broke and foamed. If the waves had washed her up only a hundred yards to her left, she would have been dashed to bits. Hitting this beach had been good luck.

Or had it? Grace remembered the silver light that had surrounded her after the ship went down. It had seemed like there were eyes in the light, and a face. Only that was impossible.

When the brain is deprived of oxygen, neurons begin firing rapidly in a last-ditch effort to stay alive. Visual and auditory hallucinations are the result. You know that, Grace. It had to be a current that carried you ashore.

In which case, it might have carried others besides her.

Grace listened, but all she could hear was the roar of the ocean and the thin lament of the wind over bare rocks. After two attempts, she managed to stand. Her wet clothing clung to her body in a clammy embrace, and she shivered, but that was a good sign. Shivering would generate body heat. So would walking. But which way?

Behind the beach sloped a high bluff of the same black stone that made up the coast, its edges softened here and there by tufts of brown grass. A gray line snaked up the face of the bluff. Was that some sort of trail? Maybe; she could think about it later. The beach itself was littered with driftwood and gelatinous blobs of kelp. Then her eyes picked out a large chunk of wood that was dark and wet. The broken ends of planks stuck out like ragged fingers. At once she knew it was a part of the *Fate Runner*.

Clutching her arms around herself, Grace stumbled along the sand. Pebbles and fragments of shell dug into her bare feet; she must have lost her boots in the ocean. Walking loosened the muscles of her legs, and she quickened her pace. In moments she reached the flotsam—a section of the ship's deck.

Falken was leaning against it.

She knelt beside him. The bard's hair was plastered against his face, and a piece of seaweed was looped over his shoulder like a ceremonial sash. Grace touched his neck and felt for a pulse. It was there, strong and slow. She smoothed his hair away from his face, and his eyes opened.

"Grace...?" he croaked, but he didn't get any further. Instead he leaned over and coughed up water.

Grace held his shoulders. When he finished, she helped him sit back up.

"I thought I had drowned," he said, his voice still hoarse but stronger. "It's not the first mistake I've made."

She picked the seaweed off him. "*Can* you drown, Falken?"

"I'm immortal, Grace, not invincible. I don't age, and I haven't taken ill in seven centuries. But anything else that can kill a man can kill me."

She thought about this. Falken was born in Malachor, and he believed it was his fault that kingdom fell into ruin. She knew that knowledge tortured him. And yet he had endured for more than seven hundred years, when all it would take to end that suffering was a quick thrust of a knife, or a leap from a cliff. Could she have survived so long believing what he did?

But he had hope all those years, Grace. That was what kept him going. Malachor fell, but one of the royal heirs survived— your grandfather twenty times over. Falken made it his purpose to preserve the line of succession until the kingdom could be reborn.

And now he thought that time had come. Wasn't that why he wanted to journey to Toringarth to find the shards of Fellring? He meant to make her a queen in fact, not just in name.

"Can you stand?" she asked.

"I think so, if you would be so kind as to give me a lift." He held out his right hand.

Grace stared, unable to move. Falken gave her a puzzled look, then followed her gaze to his hand. A sadness stole into his faded blue eyes.

Ever since she had known him, Falken had always worn a black glove on his right hand. She had never seen him without it, and surely it was because of the glove that he was called

Falken Blackhand. Only now the glove was gone. It must have been torn away in the currents of the ocean, just like Grace's boots, and the bard's right hand was bare.

Grace clamped her jaw to stifle a gasp. Falken's hand was made out of silver.

He clenched the hand into a fist, and she marveled at the fluid way it moved. The hand was not jointed, like that of some robotic skeleton. Instead it was smooth: a perfectly sculpted mirror image of his left hand, down to the twisting lines of veins on its back. However, Grace was certain the hand was solid metal to its core. She studied it, thinking.

"It would be warm if you touched it." His voice was almost lost in the wind. "Wasn't that what you were wondering?"

"Yes." She knelt again beside him. "May I . . . ?"

He unclenched the silver hand, holding it out. It was warm against her skin, just as he had said, but as hard and unyielding to the touch as ordinary silver. How did he make it function? Through some kind of magic? She tried to see how it was joined to his wrist, but there was only a sharp line where flesh ended and metal began. It looked perfectly healed.

"How . . . ?"

The bard shook his head. "It's a long tale, and one we don't have time for. Suffice it to say that the Necromancer Dakarreth saw fit to cut off my hand as punishment for the dark deed I had wrought with it. And also that a witch took pity on me, and gave me a hand that I might make music again." He sighed. "Only now I've lost my lute in the sea. After all these years, it's gone."

"Lost things have a way of turning back up, Falken Blackhand," said a crisp voice.

They looked up to see Vani standing a few feet away. Her leather clothes were coated with sand, and her usually burnished skin was pale. In her hands was a wooden case.

Vani set the case down on the sand. "Or should I call you Falken Silverhand now?"

The Mournish woman's gaze was curious, but not questioning. Grace supposed she had heard everything Falken said.

Falken moved to the wooden case, wiped it with his cloak,

and opened it. Inside, the bard's lute was dry and undamaged. He carefully shut the case again.

A jolt of panic coursed through Grace. Falken had lost his lute in the sea. What had she lost? However, even as she asked the question, her fingers fumbled at her throat and found the steel necklace. The shard of Fellring was safe.

She let out a breath of relief, but then a new worry filled her. "We have to look for Beltan."

"I already found him," Vani said. "I believe he's fine, although he's moving as slowly as a snail. He should be along any moment."

Indeed, just then Grace saw the tall knight stalking toward them across the beach. His white-blond hair was wet and tangled, and there was blood on his tunic, although not much.

"Beltan," Grace said gratefully as the knight drew close. "Are you all right?"

He touched his shoulder. "It's just a scratch. Nothing to worry about. I'm fine."

"Thanks to my aid," Vani said.

The knight glared at her. "I told you I didn't need your help."

"No," Vani said, hands on hips, "you said something much like *glub, glug, gurgle*. And then I squeezed the water out of your lungs, preventing you from dying."

"No, you crushed my rib cage and just about killed me. I would have coughed up the water just fine on my own."

"More likely you would have coughed up your ghost."

"All right, you two," Falken interrupted. "It's cold enough as it is here. There's no need to make it chillier."

The bard struggled to his feet, and Grace helped him.

"Oh," Beltan said. "You lost your glove, Falken."

Grace glanced at him. "Aren't you, you know . . . shocked?"

"You mean about his silver hand?" Beltan shrugged. "Not particularly. I mean, sure, it's weird and everything. And I've always wondered how it stays on."

Falken gave the knight a piercing look. "You mean you've known about it all this time?"

Beltan grinned at Grace. "It really is convenient when people think you're dumb. They have a tendency to get careless around you and let things slip."

"You're not dumb, Beltan," Grace said seriously.

"I know, but let's keep it a secret."

"We should get off this beach," Vani said.

The assassin was scanning the ocean, and Grace understood. At the moment the rough gray waters were empty. But how long until crimson sails appeared on the horizon? There was no shelter, nowhere to hide.

"What about other survivors?" Falken said.

"There aren't any," Vani said. "I've explored the entire beach. I found some wreckage from the ship, but nothing more." She cocked her head. "Except..."

"Except what?" Beltan said.

"There were footprints in the sand, over at the other end of the beach. They were mostly washed away by the waves. I thought perhaps they belonged to you, Grace, and you, Falken. But now I see that can't be so. You both washed up at this end of the beach."

"Maybe the survivors went up that trail," Falken said. He pointed to the gray line that crisscrossed the face of the bluff.

If it really was a trail, it was the only way off the beach, that much was clear. The bard slung the case with his lute over his shoulder, and together the four started across the sand. Vani led the way, and Grace and Falken leaned on each other for support and warmth while Beltan brought up the rear.

It was a trail, but not much of one. Grace couldn't tell if it had been carved by men or simply worn into the bluff by the hooves of animals. There was only room enough for them to go single file, and the stone was slick with spray and treacherous beneath their feet. For what seemed an eternity they toiled up the bluff. Grace used the tufts of dead grass as handholds to pull herself along. Soon her bare feet were bleeding, but they were so numb with cold she felt no pain. The wind rose to a howl, the sea bellowed in answer, and the clouds churned in circles in the sky.

"Is it always like this in Embarr?" she called out to no one in particular.

"Only on the nice days," Beltan called back.

They kept climbing, back and forth along the steep slope. Then, just as Grace began to think she would rather tumble off the cliff than keep going, and the sky darkened to the color of coal, they reached the top of the bluff.

And there was just enough light left to make out the castle rising up before them.

22.

The lord's name was Elwarrd, and he was the seventh Earl of Seawatch, a fiefdom in northern Embarr of which Grace supposed this castle was the seat.

The rain had finally broken loose from the clouds, pelting them as they made their way from the top of the bluff, over broken heath, to the castle. Or keep, really, for the castle was no more than a single square tower built atop a motte—or manmade hill—and surrounded by a low palisade of soil. The bailey at the foot of the motte was fenced with wood rather than stone, and it housed, not guards, but sheds under which sheep bleated and cows lowed, huddling together for warmth.

They saw no people in the bailey—it was hardly fit for the beasts out there, let alone men—but lights glowed through some of the castle's oiled-vellum windows. They made their way up steps whose edges were rounded by time and wind, and Falken knocked on the keep's great, ironbound door, his silver hand eliciting a ringing *boom*.

It was the castle's steward who answered, and Falken—his right hand now tucked beneath his cloak—bowed low. As soon as the bard finished speaking a formal request for hospitality, the steward hurried them inside and shut the heavy door against the gale. The steward was a young man, little older than Aryn, Grace guessed, but he walked with a stoop that suggested curvature of the spine, probably as a result of malnutrition as a child. His face was homely but kind, and when he beckoned for them to follow they did.

Grace was surprised he didn't ask them questions—who they were, where they were from. From what she had been able to see, the landscape around the castle was bleak and empty; she doubted they got many visitors. Then again, she had learned the laws of hospitality were important, even sacred, in the Dominions. If requested properly, shelter could not be denied to a stranger. However, in turn, leave to depart must be begged from and granted by the lord. Which all reminded Grace of an old rock and roll song, something about checking into a hotel anytime you wanted, only never being allowed to leave. She shuddered, but only because she was soaked from the rain.

Though ancient, the keep was obviously well kept. Tapestries draped the walls, blocking the worst of the drafts, and oil lamps lit the corridors without too much smoke. As castles went, it smelled better than most. Grace knew Durge was an earl, but also that his home was a simple manor house, not a keep like this. Perhaps Elwarrd was high in King Sorrin's favor.

Word of their arrival must have been sent ahead, for the earl was waiting for them when they reached his hall, located on the second floor of the keep. It was much like the great hall of Calavere, but no more than a quarter the size, with soot-stained beams supporting a high ceiling and a wooden gallery overhead. A curtain covered one end of the hall, and Grace knew beyond was the earl's solar, or personal room. To her delight and relief, a fire crackled in a fireplace tall enough for her to stand in, and the hall was deliciously warm and smoky.

Grace was startled when Falken introduced them simply as four travelers in need of shelter. However, the earl didn't ask their names, and instead he introduced himself and his steward, who was named Leweth. There ensued a good deal of bowing and curtsying, and Grace could only hope she approximated the right motions at the right time.

Elwarrd was forty, Grace estimated, but he was still athletic and markedly handsome. He was not tall, even for this world—the top of his head came only to Grace's nose—but he was well proportioned. His eyes were ocean green, his nose was hawkish, and the line of his mouth was strong but not cruel. His auburn hair and beard were both short and curly, and flecked with gray. Grace found herself captivated, and when she finally managed to look away, she saw Beltan's eyes locked on the earl. Vani, in turn, stared at the knight with a look of reproach.

If not for how cold she was, Grace might have laughed. Vani was jealous of Beltan's love for Travis. Yet it was also clear the assassin was outraged that Beltan would look desiringly at another man. Then Grace saw Elwarrd's gaze traveling up and down her body, and she realized there was little chance of Beltan betraying Travis in this castle. Heat washed through her, and not just from the fire. She adjusted her cloak, doing her best to conceal her sodden gown, which no doubt revealed more than she would have preferred. Nor was the cold helping matters any in that regard.

"You must sit by the fire," Elwarrd said, "while Leweth sees to your chambers and finds dry garments for you." His voice suited him perfectly: deep and clear, like the toll of a bell.

Grace was glad for the chair the steward deftly slid beneath her; she wasn't sure her legs would have supported her much longer. They sat as close as they dared to the fire, drinking spiced wine, and their clothes soon began to steam. Despite all that had happened that day, Grace felt curiously awake and alive.

It's the adrenaline, Doctor. It's all that's been keeping you going since the beach. And as soon as your body settles down and stops producing it, you're going to crash. Hard.

She listened as Falken told Elwarrd their story, and it was interesting to see what the bard skillfully left out of the tale. According to Falken, they were from the Free Cities, and they had been bound for Omberfell, where they were to seek out suppliers of precious gems. They all belonged to the gem cutter's guild, except Beltan, who was their hired protector. However, their ship had broken against a shoal, stranding them on the beach.

Falken gave the earl Vani's true name. But the bard named himself Faldirg, and Beltan he called Boreval, and Grace got the name Galinya. Grace supposed that was a prudent idea. No one in the Dominions would know who Vani was. But Beltan was the son of King Boreas, and Grace had made a bit of a splash at the Council of Kings a year earlier. Their names might be familiar, even here in the hinterlands of Embarr. And everyone in Falengarth knew who Falken Blackhand was. It was best to stay under cover, and if Elwarrd was in any way suspicious of them or their story, he didn't show it.

"My lord," Grace said when Falken finished, "did any other survivors of the shipwreck find their way to your keep? We thought we saw footprints other than our own on the beach, but we couldn't be sure."

Elwarrd's green eyes were solemn. "You're the only ones to knock on my door, my lady. And the trail by which you came is the only way off the beach. Surely if there were others, they would have seen the keep and come here. I'm afraid it appears you four are the only survivors."

"Did you see the shipwreck happen?" Vani asked. "If so, you might have seen where others washed ashore."

The lord clasped his hands. "There *is* nowhere else to wash ashore, my lady. Save for the beach below, the coast is nothing but sharp rocks for many leagues in either direction. You're all quite lucky to have turned up there. And at any rate, no one in the keep witnessed your ship's demise."

"Isn't this place called Seawatch?" Beltan said. "How did it get that name if you don't keep a lookout?"

"We have no need to watch the sea anymore," Elwarrd said, then stood. "And here is Leweth to tell us your rooms are ready. Once you've donned dry clothes, please be so kind as to return here and take supper with me."

Leweth led them to a pair of rooms on the third floor of the keep. Falken and Beltan retreated into their chamber, and Grace and Vani into theirs. Leweth said he would return in a half hour's time, then shut the door.

The air was slightly musty, but a fire burned in the fireplace, giving off a sweet fragrance; it must have been laid with fruitwood. The bed—which stood a full five feet off the floor—was covered with fresh linens, and on a stand was a basin of hot water, a bowl of dried lavender flowers, and a bar of fatty soap. Draped over a pair of chairs were two gowns. From what Grace knew of Eldhish fashions (which wasn't much) the style of the garments was long out-of-date, and they were a bit on the small side. All the same, they were clean and not soaked with seawater, and that made them inviting.

The women washed themselves and changed clothes, and soon they were far drier and warmer than before. Grace managed to tug the worst of the snarls from her hair with an ivory comb, and she hung her wet clothes over one of the chairs, positioning it close to the fire. Vani rolled her leathers into a tight ball and placed them in a corner away from the fire.

"I must clean them while they are still damp, then oil them as they dry," the Mournish woman explained. "Otherwise, they'll be ruined."

It was both strange and pleasant seeing Vani in a gown. Grace often forgot how beautiful the *T'gol* was. Her usual garb accentuated the angularity of her features, as did her short hair. But the gown revealed a softer, rounder figure than Grace might have guessed.

Vani scowled. "This garment is both impractical and strange. Did I fasten it incorrectly?"

Grace smiled. "No, it's perfect." She drew closer to the fire, soaking in more of the heat. "What do you think Lord Elwarrd meant?"

Vani started to move across the room, tripped on the hem of her gown, and sat in a chair—quite by accident given the surprise on her face. "What do you mean?" the *T'gol* said.

"He said they don't watch the sea anymore. Which means they *used* to keep watch. So something must have changed. But what?"

Before Vani could answer, a knock came at the door, and faster than Grace could follow with her eyes, Vani left the chair and opened the door. Apparently the gown was no hindrance to the assassin when she wasn't concentrating on it.

It was Leweth. Supper was ready.

Beltan and Falken were already in the hall by the time they arrived. The two men were dressed in borrowed tunics, and the bard's right hand was completely wrapped in bandages; he must have told the earl he had been injured in the shipwreck. It was a good disguise. Elwarrd bowed low as they entered. Grace saw him take in Vani's new attire, but his gaze returned to Grace almost at once. She looked away and pretended counting the columns in the hall was a task of the utmost urgency.

The steward showed them to their seats at the trestle table that had been set up in the center of the hall in their absence. Elwarrd sat at the head of the table, with Grace around the corner to his right. Vani and the steward sat to Grace's right, and

Falken and Beltan sat across the table from them. But that left one empty place at the table, to the earl's left and opposite Grace. The place was set with a cup, a knife, and a trencher, all carefully arranged. Who was to sit there?

Before Grace could wonder more, servants entered the hall bearing steaming platters and bowls, and she soon forgot all other concerns in the act of stuffing food into her face. She was more ravenous than she had ever been in her life. It was the exertion, of course: struggling through the water, dragging herself across the beach, climbing up the bluff. It seemed horrible she should eat when Captain Magard and his crew were most likely drowned. However, she was still alive, and her body craved nourishment. While she couldn't yet say she fully enjoyed medieval cuisine, she had gotten used to it, and an array of meats, puddings, and unidentifiable objects swimming in cream soon found their way into her belly.

In Calavere, Grace had learned that custom dictated that a lord and a lady share a cup at table. When the earl indicated his thirst, it was Grace's duty to pour wine, wipe the rim of the cup with a napkin, and hand it to him. She tried not to notice how his warm hand brushed hers in the exchange. When he handed back the cup, she gulped down several swallows, belatedly realizing she was supposed to wipe the rim again. He seemed to notice this lack, but he only raised an eyebrow, and his expression seemed anything but displeased.

Vani shared a cup with the steward, but since there was no lady to serve them, Beltan and Falken got their own cups. The party ate largely in silence, commenting only on the quality of the food. When the meal was finished, the earl initiated conversation, although they stayed close to polite topics—mostly the weather in Embarr compared to that in the south—and for that Grace was grateful. The earl seemed glad for their company, and he laughed often, a sound Grace found compelling.

"Forgive me if I offend, my lord," Falken said. "But I'm surprised to see so few at your table. Should not a keep of this consequence have a larger household?" The bard's gaze lingered on the empty place setting for a moment.

"Indeed, it should," Elwarrd said, a grimness stealing into his expression. "These days, my court is all but gone."

"Gone where, my lord?" Grace asked without thinking.

"To Barrsunder, my lady, by order of King Sorrin."

"And how is the king?" Falken said. His words were measured and carefully weighted, and Grace understood his intent.

So did Elwarrd. "I see you know something of King Sorrin's condition."

"A little," Falken said. "It's been nearly a year since I last saw him."

The earl sighed. "Then his condition is far more dire than you remember. They say he'll do anything to keep death at bay."

"Why?" Vani said. "Is this king of yours ill?"

Elwarrd met her gaze. "Not in body, my lady."

Grace remembered meeting the King of Embarr at the Council the previous Midwinter. Sorrin had been gaunt and hunched, old before his years. His gaze had usually been keen as a knife, but sometimes a lost and haunted look had stolen into it. Durge had told her that Sorrin had been growing increasingly fearful of his own death, as if it lurked just over his shoulder.

"Sorrin's actions are a mystery to his subjects these days," Elwarrd said. "But he is not mad. Or at least, not mad in all regards, for he's surrounded himself with a loyal faction of powerful men, and any who might question the king are afraid to stand against them."

Beltan refilled his own wine cup. "But for what reason did he call your courtiers to Barrsunder?"

"For protection," Elwarrd said. "By the reports I've heard, he's taken to disguising himself as a common man in an effort to hide from death. He believes that having more people in Castle Barrsunder will somehow help him. It makes no sense."

Grace circled the wine cup with her hands. "No, it's completely logical. He's afraid he's being hunted, so he's hiding himself in a crowd. It's highly adaptive behavior. It's called the selfish herd theory, and biologists on—" Realizing she was about to bring up things she really didn't want to try explaining, she hastily took a sip of wine.

"So you have no one left in your court?" Falken said.

"Just myself, Leweth, and the servants. And there are the serfs who work my lands. You'll not have seen the village coming from the beach. It lies just over the next rise. But no one else is left in Seawatch. All of my knights have gone to Barrsunder, and their wives and children with them."

"Couldn't they have refused?" Vani asked.

Elwarrd gave her a stern look. "To refuse the order of the king is treason, my lady, punishable by death. Sorrin has ordered all of his knights to Embarr. Any who have not yet gone to him have either already been drawn and quartered or will be the next time they set foot in Embarr."

His words sickened Grace, and she wished she hadn't eaten so much.

"But what of you, my lord?" Falken said. "Why have you not traveled to Barrsunder with the other knights?"

For the first time that evening, a crack showed in Elwarrd's demeanor. His right hand twitched into a fist on the table. "I am an earl, my lord. That is my birthright." It seemed his gaze flicked upward, toward the gallery above the hall. Then he looked directly at Falken. "But knighthood is an honor granted by the king, and I am not a knight of Embarr. That is the only reason I am still here in Seawatch. Otherwise, you would have found this keep empty."

They stared at the lord in silence. Slowly, as if only by great will, Elwarrd unclenched his hand.

"You must be weary after your travails," he said, his voice gentler. "Leweth will take you to your chambers now."

And with that, supper was over. The travelers rose, bowed and curtsied, and murmured their thanks to the earl. Leweth bid them to follow him to their rooms.

As they left the hall, Grace stole a glance at the gallery, where it seemed Elwarrd had gazed a moment ago. The gallery was a railed wooden platform above the hall. During feasts, minstrels might sit there to fill the hall with music, but now the gallery was silent, filled only with shadows.

One of those shadows moved.

Grace's heart leaped into her throat. It seemed a figure moved in the dimness of the gallery, a figure draped all in black. She started to reach out with the Touch, to sense if someone—or something—was there. However, Leweth gently touched her elbow, guiding her through the doors of the hall, and the threads of the spell slipped through her hand.

23.

By the next morning, all of them had a fever.

Beltan was the worst. Falken knocked on the door of Grace and Vani's chamber just after dawn. He described the knight's symptoms, and at once Grace marched to the room shared by the men, still clad in her nightgown. Beltan lay in his bed, cheeks flushed, skin dewy with sweat.

"I'm fine," he said, when Grace began to examine him, but the credibility of his protest was significantly damaged by the fit of coughing the words induced.

Grace sat Beltan up, lifted his tunic, and listened against his back while he breathed. She laid him down again, then reached out with the Touch, using the power of the Weirding to gaze deep into the knight's body. What she saw confirmed her diagnosis.

Grace opened her eyes. "You've developed a slight secondary infection in your bronchi—that's the source of your fever—and the inflammation is causing you to cough."

Beltan stared at her without comprehension. Not that this should surprise her. No one on Eldh knew what a bacterium was, and Grace had never had a chance to discuss the finer points of modern medicine with her friends.

"There's a sickness in your lungs," she said, this time trying to use terms the knight would understand. "It's common after inhaling water, like we all did yesterday. And right now it's not a major worry. But if you don't rest, the sickness could grow worse and cause your lungs to fill up with fluid, making it hard to breathe."

Beltan grunted. "You mean wet lung. Why didn't you just say so, Grace? No wonder it feels like a horse is sitting on my chest." He lay back down.

"You're going to have to take it easy," Grace said. "I'll try to see if I can make some medicines. In the meantime, you shouldn't exert yourself. And at no time should you go outside. The cold will aggravate your lungs."

Falken glanced at her. "For how long?"

Grace understood his meaning. The bard was anxious to continue their journey north. However, Grace knew they couldn't rush this. Hurrying to Toringarth wouldn't accomplish much if they all died of pneumonia on the way.

"Until he's better," she said. "I'd say a week at most. As long as he stays quiet."

Falken's look was grim, but he nodded. It was over a month until Midwinter; they had plenty of time to get to Toringarth and then to the Black Tower. Or at least they could hope so.

With the Touch, Grace examined all of them in turn. It turned out Vani was nearly as sick as the knight, and a far worse patient.

"Surely you don't expect me to simply sit here in this room and do nothing," the *T'gol* said, her golden eyes hot with outrage.

Grace gave a tight smile. "Actually, that's exactly what I expect you to do."

"You cannot give me orders. I am a daughter of the blood of the royal house of Morindu."

"Then that makes us both the heirs to monarchies that don't exist anymore," Grace said. "And since you're just the princess of a nonexistent city, and I'm the queen of a nonexistent kingdom, I'm pretty sure I outrank you. Falken?"

The bard rubbed his chin. "I think she's right, Vani."

By her expression, the *T'gol* didn't accept their reasoning, but a fit of coughing prevented any further argument.

Grace turned her attention to herself and Falken. She was sick, but not to the same degree as Beltan and Vani. There was only a slight inflammation in her lungs, and her temp was barely elevated. She would be fine in a day or two, as long as she didn't exert herself.

Grace knew there was really no point in checking Falken—the bard was immortal, after all—but just to be thorough she used the Touch to gaze into his chest.

Her eyes snapped open. "You're sick, Falken."

The bard frowned at her. "That's impossible."

Grace examined him more closely, listening to his chest, touching him lightly as she shut her eyes and examined his silver-blue life thread. At last she opened her eyes again. There was no denying it.

"It's a mild case," she said. "You're certainly not as sick as Beltan or Vani, or even me. But you have a slight infection in your lungs. A fever, I mean."

Beltan propped himself up on his elbow in bed, green eyes curious. "I didn't think you could get sick, Falken."

"Neither did I." The bard gazed down at his right hand. He had removed the bandages, and his silver fingers gleamed in the gray light that filtered through the window. "Then again, this is the first time in seven centuries that I've nearly drowned, so I suppose anything's possible."

Grace returned to her room and changed into her borrowed gown, then helped Vani struggle into her own. Almost fondly Grace remembered the first time she had tried to don a gown like this in Calavere. It had nearly suffocated her before Aryn had come to her rescue.

Just as Grace finished adjusting Vani's gown, a knock came at the chamber door. It was the steward, bearing a tray for their breakfast. Over his shoulder, Grace saw a serving maid delivering a similar tray to Falken and Beltan's room. She invited Leweth in, and he set the tray down. There was oat porridge, dried fruit, cream, and—thank the gods of this world—a pot of blistering hot *maddok*.

Warming her hands around a cup of the rich, slightly bitter drink, Grace asked if she might talk to the earl that morning.

"I'm afraid Lord Elwarrd is not available for an audience today," Leweth said with an expression of sincere regret. "There are matters that demand his attention. However, he asked me to beg your forgiveness for this rudeness, and he requests your presence at table this evening."

"Of course," Grace said. "We would be honored."

Leweth was obviously relieved by her words. Grace wondered where Elwarrd could be; a steady drizzle fell from heavy clouds. Then again, in Embarr, she supposed this passed for a pleasant day.

"If you'll forgive my asking," Leweth said, "what was it you needed to see the lord about, my lady?"

Grace described her need for herbs and a mortar and pestle in order to make medicines.

The steward clasped his hands together, his expression worried. "It's no wonder you've all taken ill. The sea is deathly cold. I'm sure my lord will want all of you to rest here until you're well. I'll do my best to see to your requests, my lady. There is a woman in the kitchens who has some knowledge of herbs and their names. If you describe what you need, she should be able to find the things for me."

Grace described the herbs she needed as clearly as she could. She would rather have written it all down, but Leweth seemed to listen carefully, and he repeated her words back to her verbatim. Besides, she doubted a kitchen wife would be literate enough to read her ingredient list.

To her surprise, Leweth returned not much more than an hour later, bearing a pot of sweet oil—which Vani had requested—and all of the herbs Grace had described. The herbs were old, and had lost some of their potency, but they would do. Grace thanked the steward, and he bowed and hurried away.

Since Grace and Vani's chamber was larger and less prone to drafts, Grace asked Beltan and Falken to spend the day there.

"Is that an order or a request?" Beltan asked.

Grace smiled pleasantly. "It can be either one you like, as long as you do what I say."

"I think this whole queen thing is starting to go to her head," the knight grumbled, as Falken helped him stand.

As the drizzle continued outside, they passed the hours close to the fire. Beltan lay in the bed, and Grace forbade him to leave, save when returning to his room to use the chamberpot became a necessity. With meticulous care, Vani wiped her black garb clean with a damp cloth, then rubbed oil into the leather as it dried in the warmth of the fire, working it with her hands so that it remained supple.

Falken borrowed a bit of Vani's oil for his lute. He rubbed it into the wood with his hand, then tested the instrument. Its case must have been watertight, for the lute was in fine condition, and Falken strummed the strings, filling the chamber with quiet melodies.

Grace spent her time carefully grinding herbs with the pestle in the brass mortar and measuring the resulting powders onto scraps of parchment, which she folded to keep the contents from spilling. After hours of it her arm and back ached from working the pestle, but she had a week's worth of medicine for them all.

At midday, a servingwoman came to the door with a tray of bread, cold meat, and a cheese for their dinner. She was a short, stooped woman with a dirty, fearful face. Grace sighed; she had met few servants on this world who weren't terrified of her.

And why shouldn't they be, Grace? You're royalty. You could have them punished on a whim. Even put to death.

Only she wouldn't. And if somehow, by some strange twist of fate, she ever did find herself a queen with subjects, her first task as a ruler would be to find a way to make sure not one single person in her castle feared her. Maybe it would mean she wouldn't be a very effective monarch, but that seemed by far the better alternative.

Grace asked the servingwoman for a pot of hot water, and this was quickly brought. Grace emptied a packet of the herbal powder into each of four cups and poured hot water, letting the herbs steep to make a tea. She made the others take a cup.

"Is it supposed to taste like horse dung?" Falken said, his expression at once curious and repulsed. "Or is that just a happy coincidence?"

"That's how you know it's working." Grace forced herself not to grimace as she drank her own cup.

"I rather like it," Vani said, taking a sip.

"How can you possibly like it?" Beltan groaned from the bed. "I think this stuff is going to kill me."

The *T'gol*'s eyes flashed. "That's how."

Grace had had quite enough of that. "All of you be quiet and drink," she said in what she hoped was a queenly voice. It must have been, for all of them obeyed.

24.

Grace had remembered her herb lore well, for the medicine seemed to make all of them feel better, which in turn significantly reduced the level of general crabbiness in the room. As the gray afternoon drizzled away outside the window, they spoke in quiet voices.

"I suppose there's no chance they survived," Grace said. "Magard and his crew, I mean."

Falken met her gaze. "I'm afraid not, Grace. You heard what Elwarrd said. Except for the beach where we washed up, the coast around here is nothing but rocks and cliffs. And there's no way off the beach except the trail that leads to this keep. If Magard or any of his sailors survived the shipwreck, they would have found their way here by now."

Grace nodded. She hadn't been looking for false hope, only confirmation. She thought of Captain Magard's rough humor and sly winks, and of his mad plan to sail around the world he believed to be round. Now he'd never get the chance to find out he was right. A tight ball formed in Grace's throat.

"So why us?" Beltan said. "Doesn't it seem awfully lucky that the four of us washed up on the beach and no one else?"

Vani shrugged. "Luck is simply an act of Fate we are not expecting."

Grace took a sip of *maddok*. Despite Vani's invocation of Fate, Beltan's words disturbed her. She thought back to the shipwreck. Everything had happened so quickly. There was the horrible noise of the ship cracking apart, the brutal shock of plunging into frigid water, and the darkness closing in as she sank downward. And then...

"Did anyone else see a light?" Grace said. "In the water, after the ship went down?"

The others looked at her, expressions curious, and Grace explained what she had seen as she sank beneath the waves: the light that had encapsulated her, lifting her to the surface, and the shining face she thought she had glimpsed. Falken and Vani shook their heads; both had lost consciousness in the water, and the next thing they knew had awakened on the beach. However, Beltan seemed to remember something.

"It was just before everything went dark," the knight said, peeling an apple with a dagger. "It wasn't a light, though. It was more like a feeling of suddenly being...safe. And there was a sound. It was beautiful, almost like music. But even I know that's impossible. You can't hear music in the ocean."

"I don't mean to discount your words, Grace," Falken said. "Or yours, Beltan. But the mind can play tricks on you in dire situations like that."

Grace had to agree; no doubt she had been hallucinating. But it was nice to know she wasn't the only one.

After that, conversation turned to their host, with whom none of them could find fault. While the rules of hospitality had required him to take them in, he could have given them a cold room and a loaf of stale bread and have fulfilled his duty. Instead he had treated them with nothing but deference, even though as far as he knew they were only a band of free traders.

Falken strummed a chord on his lute. "Elwarrd seems like a good man."

"And he's very handsome," Grace said, only realizing she had spoken the words aloud when she saw that everyone was staring at her. She fumbled for something else to say, hoping her cheeks weren't as red as they felt. "But what do you think he meant, when he said he wasn't a knight of Embarr? I thought all earls were knights. Like Durge."

"Most are," Falken said. "But what Elwarrd said is true. One is made a noble by birth, but knighthood can only be granted by the king."

Vani looked up from her work on her leathers. "So why would a king deny this honor to a man?"

Beltan leaned on his elbow in bed. "Usually it's because there's some sort of dishonor—a black mark on his name. If the earl did something untrustworthy or cowardly—something that's not exactly a crime, but distasteful all the same—the king might not be inclined to knight him."

Grace chewed on a knuckle. What could Elwarrd have done that cost him a chance at knighthood? It was hard to think of him acting in a cruel or cowardly fashion. Then again, by all accounts, Sorrin was suffering from some form of paranoia. Elwarrd's dishonor might exist entirely in the king's mind. For some reason she couldn't name, Grace found herself hoping that was the case.

"Perhaps I am mistaken," Vani said, folding her leathers—supple and clean now—and setting them aside. "But is not your friend Durge a knight of Embarr?"

A needle of fear pierced Grace's heart. What was the *T'gol* saying?

Falken set down his lute. "You're right, Vani. If we do find Durge, he'll be in great peril if he ever returns to Embarr."

The bard's words brought cold understanding to Grace. Elwarrd told them King Sorrin had commanded all of his knights to journey to Barrsunder. However, Durge had been in Tarras, and now he was somewhere else they couldn't reach him. There was no way he could have responded to Sorrin's command. But Grace knew that wouldn't matter, not to a man as mad as the King of Embarr.

"They'll execute him," she said, her chest tight. "If we find Durge, and he comes back to Embarr, they'll execute him for disobeying the king."

Falken reached out and took her hands. His silver fingers were warm and smooth against her skin. "Don't worry, Grace. Once we find him, we'll make sure Durge doesn't come anywhere near Embarr."

"Embarr is his home," Grace said. "It'll break his heart."

"No, Grace." Falken brought her hands together as if to form a cup. "Durge's home is right here."

Grace couldn't speak, and her heart ached, but in a way it was a welcome feeling. She knew Durge considered himself her loyal servant. But to her, he was the truest friend she could imagine. She would have done anything right then to be able to throw her arms around those stooped shoulders, to kiss those craggy cheeks.

Gradually, the ache in her chest transformed into fierce resolve. They would find Durge. And if King Sorrin so much as laid a finger on him, Grace would take Fellring and put an end once and for all to Sorrin's fear of death.

Wait just a minute, Doctor. You're supposed to preserve life, not take it. Besides, right now all you've got of Fellring is one small piece, and I don't think it would do you much good against a raving king.

Still, the thought heartened her, and she felt better.

"Now I see what's happening here." Beltan sat up in bed, cheeks flushed from fever, but his eyes keen. "King Sorrin has summoned his knights to Barrsunder. That leaves all of the castles and keeps in the entire Dominion deserted. There are serfs, of course. But there are no knights, no guardsmen, no warriors to protect the fortresses. And that means—"

"Embarr is ripe for an invasion," Vani finished for him.

Beltan glared at the assassin, obviously annoyed she had stolen his thunder.

They spoke more as the sullen day waned outside. It was clear Beltan was onto something. With all the keeps and castles abandoned, there was nothing to stop an army from marching across Embarr and laying siege to Barrsunder. And with the capital so overcrowded, food and water wouldn't last very long—and neither would the siege. The Dominion could fall in a matter of days. Just like Eredane and Brelegond before it.

"The Onyx Knights," Grace said, feeling cold despite her proximity to the fire. "Do you think they're the ones behind all this?"

Falken set down his lute. "I don't know, Grace. But I'd give up ale for a month just to know who Sorrin's advisors are. Remember how Elwarrd said the king was surrounded by a circle of powerful men? Men whom everyone fears? Well, maybe Sorrin is getting a little help in his madness."

It made chilling sense. The king's illness rendered him an easy target for manipulation. And once such men got close to him, they could use the king's authority to keep all who opposed them away—or have them put to death for treason. All the signs, here and elsewhere in the Dominions, were clear. Embarr was going to be invaded, and Grace couldn't imagine it was anyone else who planned to take over besides the Onyx Knights.

"First Eredane, then Brelegond," Beltan said, his voice hoarse. "Now it's Embarr. And after that it'll be Perridon, I suppose. Queen Inara is smart, but her Dominion was ravaged by the Burning Plague, and it's still too weak to put up much of a fight. After that, it's only Galt that will stand between these bloody knights and Calavan and Toloria. And since they can attack through Brelegond, Perridon, and Eredane, we'll be fighting on three fronts. There's no way we can win a battle like that, no matter how hard we fight. The Dominions will fall."

"You're right, of course," Grace said, pacing before the fire, trying to burn off some of the nervous energy the *maddok* had given her. "That's exactly what's happening. There's no other possibility that makes sense. But that still doesn't answer one question. Who are these Onyx Knights? Are they servants of the Pale King, or of someone else? And what do they want?"

Falken regarded her with a solemn expression. "Maybe they want you, Grace."

She halted in mid-stride, clutching the necklace at her throat, but before she could respond a knock came at the door. It was Leweth, informing them that supper was nearly ready. The steward had brought them their own clothes, which had vanished wet and filthy while they supped the day before, and which were now as fresh and clean as when they had bought them in the port town of Galspeth in Perridon.

They changed garb, then made their way to the great hall. Grace was glad to have her own clothes back; they were warmer and fit her better. Vani was wearing her leathers, and she looked and moved like a sleek, black cat. However, Elwarrd—who stood by the head of the empty table—seemed not to notice her unusual attire. Instead, his green eyes were fixed on Grace.

As she sat, Grace noticed that, in her haste to dress, she had not given the laces of her bodice the customary final tug to tighten them. As a result, her necklace was in plain view, and for a terrified moment she thought Elwarrd was staring at it, just like Detective Janson, the ironheart, had at the Denver police station over a year ago.

Don't be an idiot, Grace. It's not your jewelry he can't take his eyes off. No doubt you look like some tavern wench, and he's insulted you'd come to his table dressed this way.

However, something told her the earl was anything but offended. She could almost feel his gaze moving over her exposed flesh, and she felt suddenly vulnerable. Oddly, it was not a disturbing feeling.

They took the same places at the table they had the night before. Once again, there was an empty seat to the lord's left: cup, knife, and trencher all placed carefully, as if an important guest would arrive at any moment. As they ate, Elwarrd inquired after their day: how they passed it, and how they were feeling. Grace explained that Leweth had brought her things to make medicines, and that these had helped, and this seemed to please the lord.

"And how did you pass your day, my lord?" Grace asked, not sure if it was polite to question one's host, but Elwarrd seemed not to mind her attention.

"In a most dull fashion, my lady," he said with a smile that was at once pained and self-mocking, and charming for it. "Since I have no vassals left, it's up to me to see to affairs around my fiefdom. I've only just returned to the keep. It was all riding from holding to holding, counting heads of cattle and checking stores of grain against mold."

"It sounds interesting," Grace said.

"And now you're lying, my lady. But duplicity suits you, so you are forgiven."

Grace lifted the wine cup to her lips to hide her smile. She filled the cup again and handed it to Elwarrd. As he leaned close, she noticed he didn't smell of rain and sweat, as she might have expected given his day's activities. Instead he smelled of smoke and soap. Castle smells.

When Elwarrd glanced at a passing servant, she shifted slightly in her chair and looked down so that she could see the lord's boots. They were clean, without any speck of mud. Yet it had rained all day outside. Surely the roads and paths around the keep were a quagmire.

Perhaps you're not the only one being duplicitous, Grace.

But that was foolish. Even if Elwarrd hadn't told her all he'd done that day, it was his right. They were strangers, and it was hardly his duty to tell them his private activities.

As they ate, Grace stole several glances at the gallery above the hall. However, as far as her eyes could tell, the wooden platform was empty of anything but shadows. Then again, Grace knew shadows could trick the eye, and also that she had other ways to look.

While the others were distracted by a joke Beltan was telling, Grace shut her eyes and reached out with the Touch. The life threads of the others glimmered around her, strong and bright, although she could still see the touches of sickness in

Beltan, Vani, and Falken. Leweth's thread was a bit on the dim side. That wasn't a surprise; he was a kind young man, but not particularly vibrant. However, Elwarrd's strand was a blazing green. Grace had to resist the urge to entangle her own thread with it. Instead, she willed her consciousness up toward the gallery.

Coldness filled her, drowning her like the frigid waters of the ocean. The gallery was empty. Not empty like a room in which there were no people or animals, for even there the residual power of the Weirding would linger in air and stone. Instead, the gallery was a void, as if every last thread of life had been excised from that space with a cruel knife.

Then, in the emptiness, something moved.

"My lady, are you well?"

Her eyes opened, and she saw Elwarrd's face close to her own, his eyes concerned. She was dimly aware that the others were gazing at her, and more sharply aware that the lord's hand was resting on her arm, warm and strong. She must have been swaying in her chair while her eyes were closed.

"It's nothing," she said, but her voice quavered.

"On the contrary," the earl said, "you're ill, and I've kept you away from your rest far too long. But I thank you for your company tonight. It would have been lonely otherwise."

The lord stood, and Beltan moved around the table, helping Grace to rise. They bid the earl good night, then followed Leweth out of the hall.

As they walked, Beltan bent down and whispered in her ear. "What happened back there? You were casting a spell, weren't you? I've seen you do it enough to know what it looks like. You go all still, like you're made of stone."

"In the gallery," Grace whispered to the knight. "Did you see anything up there while we ate?"

"No, I didn't. Why?"

Grace moistened her lips. She still felt sickened by the overwhelming feeling of emptiness that had engulfed her when she probed the gallery. The space had been utterly devoid of life. Yet all the same, something had been up there.

"It was Death, Beltan," she murmured. "It was Death, and it was watching us."

25.

Her Highness, the Lady Aryn, Baroness of Elsandry, Countess of the Valley of Indarim, and Mistress of the lands north of the River Goldwine and south of the Greenshield Downs, felt cold, dirty, more than a little nauseous, and anything but noble as she rode her bay mare up the winding road to Castle Calavere, accompanied by Lady Melia and Sir Tarus.

On the journey north from Tarras, there had been many long leagues over which to resign herself to the fact that King Boreas was in all likelihood going to kill her the moment he laid eyes on her. Last summer, she had stolen away from Calavere without his leave to follow after Grace, and she had gone first east and then south without the king's permission. What was more, she had traveled in the company of both witches and the bard Falken Blackhand, and which of these two Boreas disliked and mistrusted the more would be a sore contest to decide.

Don't be a goose, Aryn, she chided herself. *Boreas can't kill you if he's going to marry you off for political gain. The groom will almost certainly notice if you're deceased, thus considerably reducing the value of the alliance.*

Unless, that was, he was marrying her to Duke Calentry. The duke was said to be the oldest man still living in the Dominion of Calavan, and it was whispered there were scarecrows with more flesh and animation. If she met her demise before her wedding, well then, the old duke would simply find her to be all the more companionable.

"Are you well, dear?" Melia said to Aryn, concern in her amber eyes. The lady seemed to float on the back of her white mare.

Aryn managed an expression she hoped could be mistaken for a smile. "I'm fine. Really. Though on the off chance I faint and fall into the muck, I do trust Sir Tarus will be gallant enough to retrieve me."

"Of course, Your Highness," said the red-haired knight, who rode his massive charger to her left. "Right after I've finished having a well-earned laugh."

Aryn glanced at Melia. "You've had a knight protector before. Are they always like this?"

"I'm afraid so," Melia said with a pained sigh. "I believe it's a fundamental flaw in their makeup. It has to do with all that metal they wear. As far as I can tell, it prevents proper functioning of the brain."

"So I've noticed," Aryn said.

Tarus flashed his teeth in a dashing smile and bowed in the saddle. "I am ever at your service, my ladies."

Despite the butterflies in her stomach, Aryn couldn't help laughing. Not for the first time, she found herself wishing her husband-to-be was someone full of cheer like Sir Tarus. Not that Tarus would be particularly glad to have her, of course; she knew he had heard the call of his bull god, just as Sir Beltan had. But no doubt he would do his husbandly duties as custom demanded, and she would not grudge him the time he spent with his fellow soldiers, if in turn he'd leave her to her studies with the Witches. As long as they produced an heir and ruled well in Elsandry, nothing else would be expected of them. It would be an amenable match.

For a moment she amused herself with the fantasy that her husband would indeed be such a man. Then a cart rattled by them, splattering mud onto Aryn's gown, and jerking her back into the gray, early Valdath day.

Your marriage is to serve as an alliance, Aryn, you know that. King Boreas will marry you where he can achieve the most political gain—as he rightly should. A man like Calentry is far more likely for you than one like Tarus.

Sometimes she thought of the stories Grace had told of her world: a place where women could make their own way, where they could choose when and whom to marry, if they married at all. But this was her world, not Grace's.

And whom would you marry anyway, if it could be anyone?

She shut her eyes, trying to imagine someone young, full of charm and grace, and who would not look at her withered right arm as anything other than what it was: a part of her. Lirith had the Sight and could sometimes glimpse the future. Was it possible Aryn possessed some fraction of that same talent? She didn't know, but after a moment a face came to her.

Only it wasn't smooth and handsome. Instead, the man's face was craggy and somber, with deep-set brown eyes that bespoke a lifetime of sorrow, and a boundless loyalty, and above all an abiding gentleness. Aryn gasped as her eyelids fluttered open.

Tarus was gazing at her. "Casting a spell, my lady?" His grin returned. "I'm immune, you know. All that metal. It keeps witch magic out."

Aryn willed her troubled thoughts aside and returned Tarus's grin. "That's what you think, Sir Tarus."

The knight started to laugh, then stopped short, clearly unsure if she was joking or not.

Aryn laughed. Despite the stone walls of the castle that loomed above them, she found her spirits lifting. She didn't know what she would have done without Tarus and Melia on the journey north. Tarus always had a jest or some foolish story to make her groan and take her mind off what awaited her in Calavere. And while Aryn wasn't certain she would ever feel like she truly knew Melia, the lady had been nothing but kind these last three weeks. Aryn had never known her mother; she had died while giving birth to Aryn. It was nice to think she might have been a little bit like Melia.

Aryn knew it wasn't simply out of kindness that Melia had decided to come on this journey. Sir Tarus had spoken of growing troubles in the Dominions, and no doubt Melia wished to observe these for herself. However, they had seen little evidence of strife themselves. The late-autumn weather had been cool and moist, and the villages they had passed through had all been quiet and sleepy now that the last harvest was safely brought in. Then again, Calavan was the southernmost of all the Dominions, and Aryn had learned last Midwinter that it was from the north that ill winds most often blew.

They rode through the castle's main gate as the guards knelt on the cobblestones, having recognized Aryn, but the three travelers didn't stop. They made their way through the lower bailey—thronging with activity—and then through the gate that led to the upper bailey and the main keep.

King Boreas's seneschal, Lord Farvel, was waiting for them at the stables. He was a man well past his seventieth winter, with white hair and a kindly visage—although the expression was marred somewhat by the paralysis that afflicted the left side of his face, a result of a collapse he had suffered some years ago, and which had also weakened his left arm and leg. Boreas had called Farvel away from a comfortable retirement at his manor in western Calavan to serve as seneschal after Lord Alerain's death.

Aryn had kind memories of Lord Farvel. He had served as the king's marshal some years before, and when she was younger he would let her sit upon whatever horse in the stable she wanted, provided it wasn't too wild. The seneschal smiled when he saw her, and he knelt—rather clumsily—as Tarus helped her dismount. She let him kiss her hand, then begged him to rise, letting him lean on her arm as he did. Farvel shouldn't be kneeling on hard stones, no matter what custom dictated.

"Your Highness, it is a joy to see you again," the seneschal said, breathing hard, warmth shining in his eyes. "I thank you, Sir Tarus, for delivering her safely. And your presence is a welcome surprise, Lady Melia. I'm certain the king will appreciate your attending his ward."

"I'll see to it he does," Melia said, smoothing her kirtle, which unlike Aryn's gown and Tarus's tunic was unblemished by dust or grime.

Farvel turned toward Aryn. "King Boreas has been most anxious for your return, Your Highness, and he wishes to see you at once."

"That's nice," Aryn said. "But I don't wish to see him."

Farvel's eyes nearly bulged out of their sockets. "Your Highness, perhaps I did not make myself plain. The king gave strict orders that I bring you to his chamber the moment you arrive."

"That sounds like the king, all right," Aryn said. "But I'm sure he'll find our reunion much more pleasant if I've had a bath and have donned fresher and more proper attire." What was more, that would give her time to compose herself and think. She still hadn't decided exactly what she was going to say to Boreas when she first saw him. Or how much to tell him.

Farvel wrung his hands. "But Your Highness—"

"Has made herself very clear, my lord," Melia said, her voice commanding.

Farvel sputtered, then turned and hobbled into the stable to make arrangements for their horses.

"It's always best to meet others on your own terms," Melia said, her tone approving. "You've learned a great deal since I first met you."

Aryn reached out and took the lady's hand. "I've had good teachers. Boreas may be my king, but a lady still has certain rights, and I'm going to exercise them."

Tarus let out a snort. "You women are determined to take over the world, aren't you?"

Melia gave the knight a pitying smile. "The poor dears. Don't they know that we already have?"

Aryn laughed as Melia took her good arm, and together they entered the castle, Tarus grumbling behind them.

An hour later, Aryn's cheerful spirits were nowhere to be found. She walked through the familiar corridors of Calavere, warm and clean after her bath, clad in a gown the same blue-gray color of the dusk settling outside the windows. One of the king's guards had offered to accompany her to Boreas's chamber, but she had declined. She needed a moment alone to prepare herself for what she was about to do.

No matter how she looked at it, she had been able to come to only one conclusion: She couldn't tell the king about her studies with the Witches. Because if she did, then she would have to tell him what the Witches believed, and what they planned—how they intended to keep watch upon the warriors who worshipped Vathris Bullslayer, and to work against them.

From what little Aryn knew, the Warriors of Vathris believed that a Final Battle was coming. What was more, they believed they were destined to lose this battle, but that in the fighting of it they would gain great glory, and in death they would dwell in the halls of their bull god.

Like the Warriors, the Witches also believed a great conflict was coming—a conflict precipitated by the one they named Runebreaker, and who Aryn was forced to admit was none other than Travis Wilder. The Warriors seemed ready, even eager for this conflict to come. Thus the Witches feared the

Warriors intended to fight on the side of Runebreaker in the Final Battle. So in the weaving of the Pattern, they had decided to work against the men of Vathris.

And it was because of the Pattern that Aryn could tell Boreas nothing of this.

It was only a few weeks ago that she finally understood what it truly meant to be bound to the Pattern. Ivalaine had commanded her to follow Melia and Falken to Tarras, to keep watch, and to send a missive at once if Travis Wilder returned to Eldh. Then Travis did return. Only in the chaos of working against the sorcerers of Scirath and the demon, there had been no time to write a letter to Ivalaine, and then as quickly as he had appeared, Travis was gone again.

At first, in her despair, it had been easy not to think of Ivalaine's command. However, soon enough, thoughts of her duty returned to her. Without even thinking, she would find herself with pen and parchment in hand, and only by great effort could she force herself to let go of them. How could she tell Ivalaine about Travis when she hadn't even talked to Grace? She knew Grace cared deeply for Travis Wilder. And if they ever found him, the Witches intended to imprison him. Grace deserved to know the truth. However, each time she tried to tell Grace about the Pattern, Aryn found herself frozen, utterly unable to form the words.

Perhaps it was part of the Pattern's magic that it could not be revealed to those whose thread was not bound into it. But Aryn's thread *was* bound, and each day she did not pen the missive to Ivalaine, the thoughts in her mind grew louder and more shrill, until they were like a swarm of bats flying out of the mouth of a cave, beating and shrieking at her. It was even worse when she reached out with the Touch. Nor did setting out on the road to Calavere improve things. Melia had begun to cast her frequent concerned looks, and Aryn knew she was muttering to herself and pulling at her own hair.

Finally, there was no resisting it. In a moment of near madness, when they stopped for the night at a hostel outside of Gendarra, Aryn scribbled a letter, explaining how Travis Wilder had briefly appeared, and how he was gone again, and how Lirith had vanished with him. With one of her few jewels, she hired a messenger to take the letter to Queen Ivalaine in Ar-tolor. Almost at once, the shrieking voices in her mind fell silent. She could use the Touch to reach out and grasp the Weirding without being assailed, and she reveled in it. Although the sensation was marred with a slight tinge of guilt.

You should have found a way to tell Grace about the Pattern.

But even if she could have, it was too late. Grace was leagues and leagues away. For all Aryn knew, she and the others were already in Toringarth, finding the shards of Ulther's sword. If only there was a way to speak so far across the web of the Weirding. But there wasn't, and she didn't know when she would see Grace again.

As she turned the corner into the passage that led to the king's chamber, something caught her attention, drawing her out of her thoughts. It was like a soft sound, or a shadow fleeting past the corner of the eye, but it was neither of these things. Aryn halted and quickly reached out with the Touch, probing. There was nothing; she was alone in the corridor.

Except the threads of the Weirding still hummed ever so slightly, as if something had been woven among the strands only a moment ago.

Aryn released the Weirding, reluctantly letting its warmth and light slip through her fingers. Then she moved to the door at the end of the corridor. Inlaid into its surface was the royal crest of Calavere: two swords crossed above a crown with nine points. Aryn lifted her good left hand, but before she could knock, a gruff voice called, "Come in."

26.

The king sat before the fire in a dragon-clawed chair. He did not look up as she entered and shut the door, but instead kept his gaze on the flames. One of the mastiffs sprawled by the hearth lifted its head to growl at Aryn, but a flick of the king's hand silenced the animal.

Aryn found herself thinking of the day years ago when she

first came to Calavere—a girl of ten winters, both parents dead, journeying to meet the king who was to be her new guardian. She would never forget her first sight of Boreas. He had looked like a giant sitting on his throne, and when he spoke, his voice had rumbled like thunder in her body. She had thought him the handsomest man she had ever seen in her life, and it had been all she could do to force her legs to carry her to his throne and curtsy.

So it was again now. For a moment, the fierceness of his profile paralyzed her. If she had fancied he might look haggard from care, then she was disappointed. Despite the touches of gray in his glossy black hair and beard, the king of Calavan appeared as powerful and striking as ever.

Before her hesitation became so great as to be noticeable, Aryn moved halfway to his chair and curtsied. "I have come as you requested, Your Majesty."

He grunted but still did not look up. "You have come, Lady Aryn. But hardly as I requested. I have been waiting for you for over an hour now."

"I felt it was best if I washed away the dirt of traveling before coming to see you."

"Is that so, my lady?" At last he turned his eyes upon her. "And did you know that once Lady Grace answered my summons wearing a gown drenched with the blood of Sir Garfethel? She did not seem to think a bath was more important than my command."

Aryn sighed, only not from the sting of the king's words, but rather at memories of dear, wonderful Garf. Grace had done all she could to save the young knight from the wounds inflicted by the mad bear, but it hadn't been enough.

Boreas seemed to realize his words had not had the desired effect. "Where is Lady Grace?" he said. Did she detect a faint note of disappointment in his voice? "Lord Farvel tells me she did not come with you. Has she remained in the south?"

Aryn stepped toward him and spoke in as direct a manner as she could. "She is on a ship to Toringarth, Your Majesty, where she hopes to find the lost shards of King Ulther's sword."

It was a fault of the king—or a virtue, depending whom one

asked—that he made little if any effort to disguise his emotions. Astonishment registered on his visage, followed a moment later by a look of narrow-eyed caution. He knew as well as she did that the statement had been intended to shock him, and to demonstrate that there were things she knew that he did not. She had not spoken it out of pettiness or anger. He was still her king, and he would always have her respect. But she was no longer a little girl. There was so much she had done, so much she had seen, since the day she dared to venture beyond these castle walls. He needed to understand that before this conversation continued.

Because of his physicality and quickness to action, there were those who believed the king was not particularly intelligent. They were mistaken. Aryn knew Boreas was anything but dull. He leaned forward in his chair, an eager light in his eyes. "Sit down, my lady." He gestured to the chair opposite his.

Yes, he had gotten her message, and he seemed pleased by it rather than angered. But then, Boreas had always preferred dealing with those who dared to stand up to him. Aryn hoped she truly had that strength. She gathered up her gown and sat in the chair. It was hot so close to the fire.

Boreas bared large teeth in a grin. "Tell me everything that's happened to you on your travels, my lady. Leave out nothing. Remember, I am your king."

"Believe me, that's one thing I will never forget, Your Majesty."

She spent the next hour describing what had happened to her since the day she stole away from Calavere the previous summer. Boreas listened without interruption, his eyes at times upon her, at others gazing into the fire. Occasionally he nodded, as if something she said had confirmed some particular belief of his. And more than once he stared at her in amazement.

But then, since leaving Calavere, she had fled beings of fire, had supped with a Necromancer, and had witnessed the birth of a goddess. She had journeyed to the oldest city in Falengarth, had spoken with gods and emperors, and had trembled before a bodiless evil born of blood sorcery. Even she was a bit amazed. Had she really lived these things?

She had. And thinking of what she had survived, she knew that, by comparison, something as small as a royal marriage was not worth her fear.

As she spoke, it was shockingly easy to leave out everything that concerned the Witches. She did it without even really thinking. The High Coven, the decision to keep watch for Travis Runebreaker, the advancement of her own powers—her tongue danced around these things as easily as if they were not there at all. In fact, it was all so simple, she began to wonder if it was not the power of the Pattern that guided her words, making certain nothing of what the Witches planned or believed was revealed to this warrior who sat before her.

After she fell silent, the king continued to gaze into the fire. She wondered what he saw there in the flames.

"A war is coming, my lady," he said in a low voice, and perhaps that answered her question. He rose and began to pace. "I'm certain Sir Tarus has told you of the signs of trouble we've seen. The Onyx Knights—whose purpose and master are both mysteries to us—command Brelegond as well as Eredane now. What's more, King Sorrin of Embarr no longer balances on the brink of madness, but has plunged headlong over the precipice. He has withdrawn his support from the Order of Malachor, and without it the Malachorian Knights are sorely weakened."

Aryn didn't see when he picked it up, but now there was a dagger in Boreas's hand, and he twirled it absently as he spoke. "True, not all of the good that was wrought at the Council of Kings a year ago has come to nothing. Galt still stands with us, though it is the smallest of the Dominions. And it is my belief that our alliance with Ar-tolor will soon be stronger than ever. I count the new queen of Perridon a close ally as well, although from all reports her Dominion was ravaged by last summer's plague, and it will be years before Perridon is restored to its former strength.

"And that's not all, my lady. There is growing unease among the common folk, just as there was last Midwinter. They whisper of creatures that stalk the night and snatch children from their beds, of dark clouds that fly in the night sky against the direction of the wind, and of queer lights that flicker in the depths of the forest where no man lives. What few knights remain in the Order spend all of their time investigating such tales and keeping the folk from descending into panic."

She looked at him, stunned by his words. In the past, the king had never spoken to her so openly of his fears or worries. "And what do you make of it all, Your Majesty?"

"I was wondering what *you* make of it, my lady. After all, there's much you've seen for yourself that I've been able to but guess at. Yet I will tell you what I believe. An evil was averted last Midwinter's Eve, but only narrowly, and not destroyed. And now all the signs point to one thing: This evil stirs anew, stronger than ever."

With a quick motion, he plunged the dagger into the table in the center of the room. The knife sank into the wood as into cheese and quivered there. Aryn couldn't help thinking how easily he had done it. Was he really so hungry for conflict?

Boreas advanced on her. Despite herself, she shrank back into the chair, as she had done as a girl when faced with his wrath. Only he didn't seem angry now, but exultant, and somehow this was every bit as fearsome.

"Now, my lady, just when things are looking their bleakest, you arrive and bring me the King of Lost Malachor. Or the Queen, as it turns out. And what's more, she's our own Lady Grace." He clenched a hand into a fist. "By Vathris, let me have the strength to believe it."

Aryn forced herself to meet his eyes. "Lady Grace is indeed the heir to Malachor, Your Majesty. The royal line was fostered in secret all these centuries by Falken Blackhand and Lady Melia. I have told you the truth."

"Yes, you have. But not all of it, my lady."

A cold sliver of pain cut into her heart. "Your Majesty, I promise I have told you everything."

Boreas heaved his massive shoulders in a sigh. "I always complained you were hopeless at the art of subterfuge, my lady. I feared there must be common blood in your veins for you to have such a dull streak of truthfulness. But I see now I was wrong. You have at last learned how to lie."

Panic flooded Aryn's chest. She was certain she had revealed nothing. How could he possibly know? She rose from her chair and opened her mouth to speak.

Boreas waved a hand, silencing her. "No, my lady. There was no flaw in the fabric of deceit you wove. In fact, I'm impressed by it. I only hope my teachings had some part in the development of your abilities. Regardless, I never would have known you were lying had it not been for this."

On the table, next to the knife, was a piece of parchment. He picked it up.

Aryn tried to moisten her lips with a dry tongue. Would that the king had bid her to pour some wine. "What is that?"

"It's a missive from Queen Ivalaine. I received it last Dursday."

Aryn listened in disbelief as Boreas described what he had learned in the letter from the queen of Toloria: how last winter Ivalaine had determined that both Aryn and Grace possessed talent for witchcraft, how Lirith had been dispatched to Calavere to act as their teacher, and how during her time at Ar-tolor Aryn had continued her studies.

Aryn could hardly breathe. All the while she had studied with Ivalaine and Lirith at Calavere, she had fought to keep the truth from Boreas, knowing how he mistrusted the Witches. And now Ivalaine herself had told him these things. But why?

Boreas set down the parchment. "So now I've had two wards dwelling in that den of mystery and cast under her spell. You can see why I believe Queen Ivalaine owes me a debt of allegiance. But perhaps it will come to good in the end, that I've entrusted the child of my blood and the child of my heart to that witch. By Vathris, I can only hope there was a reason to it all."

Aryn had no idea how to answer those words.

Boreas turned to gaze out the window. Night was coming. "She says you are quite powerful, my lady. She says in her letter that you're the strongest witch in a century."

Aryn thought she detected a slight trembling in the king's voice. Was it fear? Disgust? By the gods, it couldn't be pride, could it?

He turned around. "Is it true, my lady? Can you tell my thoughts even as I speak?"

Horror flooded her, and anguish. She held out her left hand. "No, Your Majesty. By all the Seven, no."

The king held her with his gaze, then spoke, his voice low but hard. "I hope Ivalaine is right. You see, no matter what some might think, the battle is coming, my lady. The greatest battle this world has seen. And it will be fought, no matter how others might try to stop it. I could use power like yours on my side."

Aryn knew things had changed since she left Calavere, that *she* had changed, but only in that moment did she truly realize how much. Here was Boreas, every bit as strong and as fearless as she remembered him. And he was asking for her help.

"You are my king," she finally managed to say. "I am yours to command."

But even as she spoke the words, she wondered if they weren't another lie, and by the sadness in his eyes it seemed he wondered the same. Then, in a flash, the look of sorrow was gone, and she wondered if she had glimpsed it at all.

Boreas clapped his hands together. "That's enough talk of war, my lady. Let us talk of your wedding instead."

He gestured toward a sideboard that held a pitcher and two cups. Aryn hurried over and filled the cups with red wine. She handed one to the king, then greedily drank her own.

"I am thinking it will happen swiftly," the king went on. "I imagine you shall be married by the feast of Quickening."

"If that suits Your Majesty," she murmured. "And am I to know the name of the man who is to be my husband?"

"He is to arrive at Calavere in a few days. I will introduce him to you and the rest of the court then."

She nodded. "As it pleases you, Your Majesty." Aryn didn't mind not knowing who he was. It gave her a few more days to entertain pleasant fancies, like that her husband would have most of his teeth, and that he wouldn't require her assistance in using the chamber pot.

Boreas set down his cup and regarded her. "The castle has been grayer without you in it. I've missed you, Aryn."

Her heart ached so fiercely she thought it would shatter. "And I've missed you, Father."

Before she could think otherwise, she set down her cup and threw herself into his arms, hugging him tightly. He did not push her away, but instead folded his arms around her, and they were as powerful as she remembered, encapsulating her, making her feel like a small girl again. She pressed her cheek against his chest. He smelled of the fire, and of the outdoors. At last, reluctantly, she slipped from his grasp and stepped back.

"You no longer hide it," he said, a smile on his lips. "Your right arm. I'm glad to see it. You have nothing to be ashamed of. Never forget that, my lady."

She wiped her eyes with her good hand and nodded. "I won't, Your Majesty. I promise."

He grinned at her, and she returned the expression. It seemed for the moment all was—if not forgiven—then at least forgotten. All the same, there was a distance between them, a gulf, and Aryn knew it could never fully be bridged again.

He's a warrior, a disciple of the inner circle of Vathris Bullslayer. And you're . . .

But what was she? A witch, yes. What Ivalaine had said in her missive was true; there was no denying it. But what kind of witch was she? Not one like Belira and her cruel friends, who had mocked Aryn simply because she looked different. And not one like Sister Liendra, who had forced the eldest and wisest witches to the edges of the Pattern, and who had called for them to fight openly against the Warriors of Vathris.

Liendra's desires had been softened in the final weaving of the Pattern. Yet they were still there, and the threads that bound all the Witches called for them to keep watch on the Warriors, and to prevent them from fighting their Final Battle. And Aryn was part of the Pattern as surely as Liendra was. She couldn't go against it. Could she?

That question could wait for later. She cracked a great yawn, and Boreas instructed her to return to her chamber and rest. She kissed his bearded cheek, then stepped through the chamber door, leaving the king to his fire, his dogs, and his thoughts of war.

27.

The next few days were curiously pleasant for Aryn.

True, there was much to worry about. She thought often of Grace, as well as Beltan, Vani, and Falken. Where were they now? Had they found someone to carry them across the Winter Sea yet? Perhaps at that very moment, in an ancient keep in Toringarth, Grace was opening the dusty old chest that contained the shards of the magic sword Fellring. Aryn thrilled at the thought, although she couldn't say exactly why. She only knew that she wished to see Grace discover all the secrets of her heritage. Surely, after what she had endured, she deserved that much.

I wish I could be there with you, Grace. At least in spirit, if not in person.

However, Grace was far beyond her reach now, and all Aryn sensed when she reached out with the Touch were the myriad lives in the castle: human, canine, feline, and rodent. If she tried to extend the Touch much beyond the castle walls, she felt an uncomfortable tugging sensation, as if the thread of her life was being pulled too taut. She could reach so far for no more than a few seconds before she was forced to let go, gasping as she felt her life thread snap back into place.

The quartet who journeyed to Toringarth were not the only travelers who weighed on Aryn's mind. She thought often of the four who had vanished from the Etherion. In some ways it was for the better that Travis Wilder was no longer on Eldh. But she missed Lirith achingly, and she feared for her.

At least, wherever Lirith was, Sareth was likely with her. Aryn had begun to sense there was something between those two. However, something seemed to be holding each of them back. Only what was it? Aryn didn't know. There had been no time to ask, and now she wondered if she would ever see Lirith again, or Sareth. Or Durge.

And why was it so important she see Durge again? What was it she would tell him, and why did it matter?

Don't think that way, Aryn. You will see Lirith again, and Durge, and you can worry about it all then. Grace and Falken will find them at the Black Tower this Midwinter. That has to be what Sky's message meant.

Besides, she had more immediate concerns: namely, her impending wedding. Her new husband was to arrive at the castle soon, and Lord Farvel was busy with preparations for a feast to celebrate the occasion. Aryn asked if she might help, but the elderly man looked as confused as if she had just suggested they have a picnic in the garden despite the sleet angling down outside the windows.

"My lady, you're to be one of the guests of honor. I'd sooner ask the king to scrub tables in the scullery."

Aryn would have liked to have seen *that*. However, she didn't want to give Lord Farvel cause for another collapse, so she left him to his work.

As the days passed, she occupied herself with wandering through the castle, visiting all of her favorite spots: the window seat where, as a girl, she had curled up to watch the comings and goings of people in the bailey below, and the gallery above the great hall where the minstrels played during supper, and the cooling room outside the kitchens, where fragrant loaves of bread were placed on stone tables after being pulled from the ovens, awaiting their journey to the king's table.

She did her best to enjoy these places. After all, once she was married, she would be moving back to Castle Elsandry. She would see Calavere again, of course, but only when special occasions warranted travel there. She would have her own house to keep.

Although Calavere's halls were familiar and comforting, they were lonelier than she remembered. The few young women of the court with whom she had spent time in the past were gone now, married to knights and earls. And while she knew many of the servants, they hardly made suitable company for a woman of her rank.

Sometimes she thought of Sir Tarus, but she saw little of the red-haired knight after their arrival at Calavere. He spent much of his time in Boreas's chamber, and it was clear Tarus had risen high in the Order of Malachor. Aryn got the impression he had become one of Boreas's chief advisors in this time of conflict. Of course, in his work for the Order, Tarus had spent much time traveling. He probably knew more about the troubles stirring in the Dominions than anybody else.

The person Aryn saw by far the most was Melia. Much to her surprise, her friendship with the former goddess continued to grow. They often sat in Aryn's chamber, working on pieces of embroidery, and talking as the chill drizzle fell outside the windows. Sometimes Melia told stories of her time in Falengarth, helping Falken keep watch in secret over the line of Malachor. It was thrilling to hear the lengths they had gone to in order to avoid discovery, and over the centuries it seemed they had dwelled almost everywhere in the Dominions: in a remote mountain valley of Galt, in a windswept castle in Embarr, in a cottage on the rocky shore of Perridon, and a small manor on the banks of the Kelduorn, the River Goldwine.

So engrossed did Aryn become in Melia's stories, that once, after Melia finished, she glanced down to see that she had pricked her finger with a needle and had not even noticed it.

"Oh, dear," she said, sighing, "I've gotten blood all over this scarf. And I had nearly finished it."

"You must wrap the embroidery in parchment and put it away," Melia said. "Then you must give it to your husband after you are married."

Aryn looked at the lady, startled. "Why do you say that?"

"There is great power in blood. You've made a sacrifice to the embroidery—a sacrifice of yourself. Now the cloth contains a bit of your power. It will bring your husband luck in battle."

Aryn brushed the embroidery. The bleeding in her finger had stopped, but there was a vivid red stain on the cloth. Was there truly power in her blood? Perhaps there was. Perhaps it had been there all along, just waiting for her to discover it.

"Battle," she murmured, then met Melia's eyes. "You think it's coming, just like he does."

A tiny black puffball leaped into Melia's lap to bat at a ball of string. "Just like who, dear?"

"King Boreas," Aryn said. "And all the Warriors of Vathris." The kitten gave up playing, then yawned and cuddled into the crook of Melia's arm. "Tell me more," the lady said.

And Aryn did. She told Melia everything Boreas had said in their conversation—his belief that a war was inevitable, and that an evil that had been dormant was stirring again, stronger than ever.

When she finished, Melia pressed her cheek to the kitten. It opened eyes as brilliant and golden as the lady's. "So the king sees it, too." Melia sighed. "But I suppose it's plain enough.

Once Tarus told us of the shadows on the rise, Falken and I knew there could be only one answer."

Aryn moistened her lips. "It's the Pale King, isn't it? He's trying to free himself again."

Melia nodded. "Travis bound the Rune Gate a year ago, imprisoning the Pale King in Imbrifale. But he replaced only one of the runes on the Gate—one, where before there had been three. We could not expect it to hold forever, although we might have hoped it would hold for longer."

Aryn shivered, remembering that terrible night last Midwinter's Eve, when forces of the Pale King had harrowed the castle.

Her shivering didn't go unnoticed. Melia released the kitten to scamper on the floor, then rose to pour two cups of wine. She handed one to Aryn. "This will warm you, dear. And try not to worry. The Pale King is still not free yet, and if we are fortunate, he may never be."

Aryn sipped her wine, although she hardly tasted it. "But Travis isn't on Eldh anymore. How could he bind the gate again?" And would the Witches even give him the chance? But she didn't speak those words. "And it's not just the Pale King, is it? His master, the Old God Mohg, is trying to get back to Eldh. He wants the world for himself. Isn't that what Grace learned?"

Melia nodded. "It's true. Mohg does seek a way back to Eldh. But that doesn't mean he'll ever find one. After all, the Pale King's servants sought out the Scirathi in the belief the sorcerers could find a way to open a gate and allow Mohg to return to Eldh. But Xemeth betrayed them, and the demon consumed them before Travis destroyed it."

Aryn chewed her lip. Yes, Travis had destroyed the demon. Just as he had wrested the Stone of Fire from the Necromancer Dakarreth. And just as he had sealed the Pale King behind the Rune Gate. There was no denying Travis's power. He had to be the Runebreaker; the prophecies couldn't be wrong in that. Yet everything she had seen him do had been to help Eldh, not to harm it. It was Mohg who wanted to break the world, not Travis. It didn't make any sense.

Her confusion must have been evident on her face. Melia raised an eyebrow. "What are you thinking, dear?"

"I don't know." That was truthful enough. "I just wish I knew what to do."

"We must live our lives," Melia said firmly. "What is the point of fighting darkness if we forget to stand in the light and feel its warmth? We must prepare for your wedding and celebrate the occasion."

Aryn brushed the bloodstained embroidery on her lap. "And what of war? Should we prepare ourselves for that as well?"

Melia pressed her lips into a thin line. "Don't forget," she said. "Save that cloth for your husband." Then she bent her head over her own embroidery and began to sew.

Aryn did the same, and they worked that way in silence until the light failed outside the window.

The next morning, she wandered through the castle alone, wondering if she had told Melia too much. Had she betrayed the king's confidence? But Aryn didn't see how it harmed things that Melia knew Boreas's thoughts. After all, the king had been glad to learn the truth of Grace's heritage, and it was Melia, along with Falken, who had guarded the line of Malachor in secret all these years.

Aryn turned her thoughts to another, more troubling question: Travis Wilder. He was the Runebreaker the prophecies foretold, but she couldn't believe he was evil—not after everything she had seen. Should she send another missive to Ivalaine, one telling the Witch Queen what she thought? Or would the Witches cast her out for having such doubts? The idea sent a shudder through her.

So engrossed was Aryn in her thoughts that she didn't see the servingman as she rounded a corner, and she ran full into him. He stumbled back, dropping the bundle of kindling he had been carrying. The pale sticks clattered to the floor; for some odd reason, they looked like a pile of bones to Aryn.

She steadied herself. "Are you all right?"

The man simply stood there, his brown eyes as dull as his brown tunic and hose. He didn't look particularly old—his face was smooth except for a few pox scars—but he carried himself in a hunched position, like an old man. He made no motion to pick up the fallen kindling.

Aryn frowned. "Excuse me, are you well?"

Still the man didn't move. She started to reach a hand for him, but at that moment a young woman in the dove gray dress of a serving maid rushed toward them.

"Alfin. Alfin, there you are." She came to a breathless halt, clutching the man's arm. "My lady, do forgive him. Please. Don't let him be beaten again. My brother didn't mean it. I beg you, my lady." Her eyes shone with tears.

These words took Aryn aback. "What on Eldh are you talking about? Of course I won't have him beaten. This was my fault. But there seems to be something wrong with him."

The young woman picked up the scattered kindling. "It's all right. You just have to know how to talk to him now, that's all." She pushed the bundle of kindling against his chest, and his arms closed automatically around it. She took his face in both her hands and spoke in a slow voice. "The kitchens, Alfin. Take the wood to the kitchens." She gave him a gentle nudge, and he started shuffling down the corridor.

As he passed her, Aryn saw it: the dent in the back of his head, made visible because of the scar where no hair grew. But that wasn't the only thing that troubled her; something about the young man seemed familiar.

She cast a shocked look at the young woman. "What happened to him?"

The serving maid wrung her hands. "Please, my lady. It was an accident. The guard was giving him his beating as commanded, and he wasn't being too harsh with the rod, really. But Alfin slipped on the stones, and the last blow caught him on the head. It weren't the guard's fault. We aren't angry."

Aryn tried to comprehend these words. It seemed like she should know what they meant. "His mind," she said. "It was addled by the blow."

"He's all right, my lady. Truly. I'll see it that he makes it to the kitchens." She curtsied low, then hurried down the passage after her brother.

Aryn took a hesitant step after her. Something was wrong.

There was something she was supposed to remember, she was sure of it. She took another step.

And heard the high, chiming music of bells.

28.

Aryn turned on a heel. The sound of bells had come from behind her. But from where exactly? And why did the sound cause her heart to flutter up into her throat?

Even as she thought this, she heard it again. The sound seemed to float through a nearby archway. For some reason she found herself thinking of Trifkin Mossberry and his queer troupe of actors who had come to the castle the winter before. Before Aryn even considered what she was doing, she stepped through the archway.

Three more times she heard the bells, always just ahead and around a bend. Aryn followed, and soon she found herself in a cold and dusty part of the castle. Just ahead, she saw a flicker of orange light playing on the wall. It spilled through an opening that led to an old guardroom. Someone had lit a fire there. But who would be in this deserted part of the castle?

There was only one way to find out. Picking up the hem of her gown, Aryn moved as quietly as she could and peered through the opening. Except for the fire burning on the grate, the small chamber was empty.

Or was it? Once again, as on her first night in the castle, she glimpsed something just beyond the edge of vision. Quickly, she reached out with the Touch.

A cry escaped her. The brilliant threads of the Weirding wove around him, making his form as evident as if she had thrown a silver mesh over a glass sculpture. The man stood no more than three paces away.

She opened her eyes and took a step back. "I know you're there. Show yourself."

The man pushed back the hood of his gray cloak and tossed the garment over his shoulders, revealing himself as suddenly as if he had stepped out of thin air. The cloak looked just like the one that belonged to Travis Wilder, although it was in far better condition. It shimmered with a faint iridescence as the man moved, like a skim of oil on water.

"It seems I'm caught," the man said in a mocking tenor. He was not tall, and he was slender of build, with wavy yellow hair. A closely trimmed beard adorned his pointed chin, and beneath his cloak he wore tight-fitting black garb.

Recognition flashed in Aryn's mind. "I know you. You're that spy we met in Perridon. Your name is Aldeth, and you're one of Queen Inara's Spiders."

The man let out a pained sigh. "You know, I'm bound by my oath as a Spider to kill those who discover me." He gave his hand a swift flick, and a slim dagger appeared in it. "But I suppose it might cause something of a political incident if I murdered the king's ward and a baroness. So you're fortunate in that, Lady Aryn."

So he remembered her as well. "And what makes you think it's not you who's the fortunate one?" she said, feeling indignation at his words. She lifted her withered arm and spun the swift threads of a spell. Aldeth's right hand gave a jerk, and the knife fell clattering to the floor.

He raised a single eyebrow. "How did you do that, my lady?"

Her lips curved in a smile. "If I told you . . ."

"Yes, yes, I know—then you'd have to kill me." He scowled, but the effect was more comical than alarming. "I thought that was my line."

Aryn answered with what she knew was a noxiously sweet smile. She'd forgotten that she rather liked the Spider. "What are you doing in the castle?"

He retrieved his knife and tucked it away somewhere beneath his cloak. "I could ask the same question of you, my lady. Here I go to all this trouble to pick an out-of-the-way place to get a little rest, and then you insist on barging in here completely uninvited."

Aryn shrugged. "If you wanted to avoid discovery, you might have considered not building a fire. Nothing says, *Look, I'm over here*, quite like a cheery blaze."

Aldeth's blue-gray eyes narrowed. "Now you're simply

being cruel, my lady. I was cold. And I hardly thought there would be eyes about to see the fire. You know perfectly well you have no right to be wandering this part of the castle. By Jorus, I think even the rats have forgotten about this particular wing. What are you doing here?"

"Ruining the days of spies, evidently."

Aldeth gave a grunt of assent.

"So why are you in Calavere, really?" Aryn said, feeling bold enough to take two steps farther in, nearer the fire.

The young man spread his hands and grinned, displaying rotten teeth. "I'm a spy, my lady. What do you think I'm doing? I'm watching the king, of course."

"But why? Aren't Perridon and Calavan allies?"

"And now you've just told me you don't know the first thing about politics, my lady. Spying on your enemies is useful. But spying on your friends is absolutely essential. Queen Inara knows there are dark times ahead, and she wants to learn what Boreas intends to do about it."

"Then why doesn't she just ask him herself?"

"Because she wants to know what he's really going to do, not what he wants her to think he's going to do. And very rarely are those two the same thing, my lady."

Aryn frowned. "That really doesn't sound like how friends should act."

"Nonsense, my lady. All the best friendships are built upon a solid foundation of lying and deceit. It's the friends who are utterly truthful who end up killing one another."

"Now you're being preposterous."

"Really?" Aldeth smoothed his beard. "And what would you tell one of your lady friends if she was wearing the most hideous-looking gown you had ever seen?"

Aryn thought about it. "I'd find a way to spill a glass of wine on her and make it look like an accident. Then she'd have to change gowns, and she'd never have to know how awful the first was, and—oh!"

Aldeth grinned again and bowed. "I'll take that as an admission of defeat, my lady."

Aryn let out an exasperated breath. "So now what do we do?"

"Don't toy with me, my lady. You know perfectly well this is the point at which you extort some unspeakable favor out of me in exchange for not revealing my presence to the king."

Aryn mused over these words. "Well, I hadn't thought of that. But I must admit, it's a good idea. So let's do that. The extortion thing."

Aldeth glared at her. "I think you're enjoying this."

"Maybe a little. Is that wrong?"

"Just tell me what it is," he said. "What favor do you want in exchange for keeping our little meeting a secret?"

She tapped her cheek with a finger. "I'm not certain yet. But I'm sure I'll think of something. I'll let you know as soon as I do."

"And what makes you think you'll find me again?"

Aryn thought of the sound of bells that had led her here. Melia and Boreas believed the Pale King stirred again, just like a year ago. But he wasn't the only ancient power that had appeared again last Midwinter. She had a feeling someone—something—had wanted her to find Aldeth. Perhaps it would help her again.

"I'm certain I'll find a way," she said with what she hoped was a mysterious smile. She moved to leave, but as she stepped through the archway she glanced over her shoulder. "We were all glad, Aldeth. When we learned you had recovered from your injury. I'm sure you're a credit to your queen."

He nodded. "Only the gods know how I try, my lady."

Aryn left the Spider to his fire, then traversed the corridors back to more populated regions of the castle. She wondered if it had been the right thing to promise Aldeth she would not reveal him to the king. However, this way the Spider was beholden to her, and it gave her a way to keep an eye on him. Surely that was better than ousting him from the castle—an act that would no doubt cause an incident between Perridon and Calavan—something the two allies couldn't afford right now. Besides, Aryn had a feeling Aldeth's favor would come in handy at some point, although she still didn't know what she would ask him to do. Satisfied she had done the best thing for her Dominion, she turned down the corridor that led to her chamber.

And found Lord Farvel standing outside the door.

"My lady!" the seneschal said, a light of relief in his rheumy eyes. "There you are. The king's guards have been scouring the castle for you."

"Not very thoroughly then," Aryn said. "As you can see, my lord, I'm right here."

"You must come with me at once."

Without asking her permission, he took her arm and started leading her down the corridor. Aryn was too surprised to resist.

"What is it, Lord Farvel?"

"He's here, my lady. And a day early, by all the Seven! Things aren't ready, they aren't ready at all, but somehow they'll simply have to do."

Aryn shook her head, trying to grasp what Farvel was saying. "What do you mean, my lord? Who's here?"

"Why, your husband, of course."

His words struck Aryn like a blow. Her entire being went numb, and she allowed the seneschal to pull her along like she was a simple child. Her husband was there? So soon?

They reached the entrance of the great hall. A pair of guards bowed, then pushed the gigantic oak doors open, and the breeze they generated seemed to propel Aryn through as much as the urging of Lord Farvel.

Fresh rushes strewed the floor of the great hall, and torches had been lit against the faltering daylight. The king sat on his wooden throne on the dais. Two figures stood before the dais. Their backs were turned, and both wore heavy traveling cloaks, so that Aryn couldn't tell if they were men or women, although both seemed slender of build.

A third figure—this one without doubt a woman—sat in a chair that had been placed on the first step of the dais and was angled toward the king's throne. This sight shocked Aryn. Only the most noble of guests were allowed to sit when in audience with the king. Aryn couldn't see the woman's face, for it was turned toward Boreas, but her hair was the color of flax, and her cloak was thrown back over her shoulders, revealing a gown as pale and green as the rushes covering the floor.

The doors shut with a *boom*. Boreas looked up, and the woman in the chair turned her head, her eyes—as clear and colorless as ice—gazing upon Aryn.

It was Queen Ivalaine.

Aryn faltered and might have stumbled if not for the tenacious grip of Lord Farvel. She steadied herself, thrust her chin up, and kept moving toward the dais, her mind racing all the while. What was the queen doing in Calavere? Had she received the missive Aryn had sent, and journeyed to Calavere to speak of it?

She's come to punish you for taking so long to write to her, Aryn thought with rising panic. *She's come to pluck your thread from the Pattern. By Sia, it will be agony, won't it?*

But that was absurd. The messenger would have reached Artolor the same day Aryn arrived at Calavere. That was just three days ago. There was no way the queen could have traveled here so swiftly. She must have left her castle a week ago.

Which meant she didn't get your letter, Aryn. She doesn't know about Travis, or what happened in Tarras.

"I'm so pleased you decided to join us, Lady Aryn," Boreas rumbled on his throne, sounding anything but pleased.

Queen Ivalaine rose from her chair. "Lady Aryn, it's so good to see you again."

Aryn hastily curtsied, averting her eyes, not so much out of deference but dread. "Your Majesty," she said, her head still down. "I didn't . . . I didn't know you were coming."

"Is that so?" Ivalaine said in her cool voice. "And who else did you believe would bring him to you, Lady Aryn?"

These words jerked Aryn upright. There was a queer light in the queen's eyes. Like sorrow, but emptier, more haunted. However, Aryn's attention alighted on the queen for only a heartbeat, for the two figures on either side of her had turned around.

To the queen's left was a woman of later middle years. A single streak of white marked her jet hair, and her almond-shaped eyes shone with gentle wisdom. Sister Mirda.

Shock flooded Aryn, followed by joy. It was Mirda whose calm presence had cooled the fever of hatred ignited by Sister Liendra, and which had ameliorated the Pattern, changing the weaving so that the Witches would not kill Runebreaker, but merely seek him out and prevent him from doing harm.

Before Aryn could wonder more, a soft, sarcastic voice spoke.

"Hello, cousin."

The voice was deeper than the last time she had heard it, but she recognized it at once.

"Prince Teravian!" she gasped, turning toward the young man who stood to the queen's left. After a moment she remembered herself and curtsied. When she rose, a smirk was coiled about his lips. She was not surprised; Teravian always seemed to enjoy seeing others get flustered.

King Boreas's son had grown since she had seen him last at Ar-tolor. He was taller than she, and his shoulders were quite broad, although he was still slender. He must be eighteen now, but even as he grew older, he would never be heavy of build like his father. He was shaped like a dancer, not a warrior. All the same, he was handsome in the same dark, scowling way as the king, a fact that clearly marked him as Boreas's son. Then again, there was a fineness to his visage that the king lacked. It must have come from his mother, although Aryn couldn't say for certain, as she had never seen Queen Narenya herself. King Boreas's wife had died before Aryn came to Calavere.

"Well, aren't you going to greet me?" Teravian said. He looked at once both bored and amused.

Aryn managed to draw a breath. "Forgive me, Your Majesty. It is good to see you, of course. But tell me, why have you returned to Calavere? Is your stay in Ar-tolor at an end?"

Teravian stared at her like she was a complete idiot. And indeed, Boreas and Ivalaine were gazing at her as well, along with Farvel and Mirda. Although Mirda's gaze was far more kindly than the stares of the others.

Aryn looked from each one to the next, desperately trying to understand what was happening. Then, as if heard from down a long corridor, her conversation with Lord Farvel echoed in her mind.

What do you mean, my lord? Who's here?

Why, your husband, of course.

"You," she said, staring at the slender young man clad all in black. "It's you that I'm to marry."

"You don't have to sound so disgusted," the prince said, his thick eyebrows descending in a scowl. "Believe me, I'm not happy about it any more than you." And without begging leave of either king or queen, he stamped away from the dais and vanished through a side door.

"Well," Sister Mirda said, gently breaking the silence, "we can simply believe the marriage will improve from here."

29.

Their third day in Seawatch dawned even more gloomy than the first two. No wonder Embarrans had a reputation for somberness; this place made Seattle look like Palm Beach. If it hadn't been for the serving maid who brought them breakfast, Grace would have had absolutely no idea the sun was up.

"Thank you, Mirdrid," Grace said sleepily, rising on an elbow in bed as the serving maid set down the tray.

Grace had spoken a little with the young woman the previous day—part of her new effort to not terrify servants. Surprisingly, it had seemed to work, as the young woman curtsied and gave a shy smile. She was pretty, like a flower bud only just beginning to open. One of her brown eyes was lazy, but the other focused on Grace.

"Let me know if you need anything else, my lady."

"Of course, Mirdrid. And do bring me the embroidery you've been working on—the piece you told me about yesterday. I'd love to see it."

The serving maid smiled again, then hurried from the room. Grace pushed back the bedcovers, only then realizing that Vani wasn't there. She touched the place where the assassin had lain, but the sheets were cool. Grace climbed down from the bed using the wooden step, poured herself a cup of *maddok*, and sat by the fire.

The others appeared a half hour later. First Falken and Beltan showed up at the chamber door—the bard to talk, the knight to see what he could scrounge from Grace's breakfast tray, having evidently vanquished the contents of his and Falken's own. Grace was still in her nightgown, but she had wrapped a blanket around herself, and she hoped it rendered her sufficiently queenly. Then Vani was there, and it was testament to her poor state of health that all of them saw the assassin enter the room.

"Where were you last night?" Grace asked.

"I was searching the keep."

None of them needed to ask what she had been searching for. After supper last night, Grace had told them what she had seen in the gallery: the presence. Watching, but not alive.

Falken glanced at the *T'gol*. "Did you find anything?"

"No. As Lord Elwarrd said, there are few left in his keep, so it was easy to move about. And I found no trace of one such as Grace described. There was only..." A frown crossed Vani's face.

"There was only what?" Grace said.

"Nothing." Vani reached her hands out toward the fire. "I saw no trace of anything such as you described, Grace."

Beltan gave her a skeptical look. "What makes you so certain this person wasn't just hiding from you?"

Vani treated the knight to a withering glance. The message was plain: If there was something to find, the *T'gol* believed she would have found it. However, now that she had gotten a night's sleep, Grace wasn't so certain what she had sensed with the Touch last night. It had been so fleeting, and she was still running a slight fever. Maybe there hadn't been anything there at all.

Then why can you still feel it, Grace? Death. The feeling was so strong it almost stopped your heart.

"You shouldn't have been out last night," Grace said to Vani. "You're still not well. You need to rest."

"I will rest now." The *T'gol* sat cross-legged by the fire.

Beltan swabbed a porridge bowl with the last scrap of bread. "So, does what you saw change our plans?"

Grace considered the options. The medicine was beginning to work; a quick check of all of their threads showed she and Falken were greatly improved. And Vani and Beltan were better as well, but not so much that Grace felt they were out of danger. If they left the keep and marched through this wretched weather, their condition could easily deteriorate.

So regardless, they couldn't leave Seawatch yet. Should she tell Lord Elwarrd what she had seen, in case there was a danger to the keep? No, she decided. If there had been any sort of mundane intruder, surely Vani would have found it. And Grace didn't care to explain to the lord just how she had sensed what she did. They would simply have to keep their eyes open while they rested for a few more days.

With no other options for entertainment, they spent the day in their chambers again. Falken played his lute to help pass the hours, and sometimes he would sing in a low voice, and Grace would find herself drifting through visions of ancient halls and secret towers.

Leweth came just after midday to make sure all was well. Grace asked after Lord Elwarrd—not out of a desire to see him, but simply out of curiosity.

"I'm afraid the earl is engaged again today," the steward said, bowing in apology. "But if we are fortunate, he will be available for supper. In which case I know he would be most pleased if you would join him again."

"Of course," Grace said.

"It seems Lord Elwarrd is a busy fellow," Falken said after the steward left.

"With all his knights gone, he probably has a lot to take care of by himself," Beltan said.

Vani and Beltan both slept the entire afternoon, which pleased the doctor in Grace. And if their repose was aided by the powder she had slipped into their cups when they weren't looking, well, they could be angry with her when they woke. Grace herself was beginning to feel a bit restless—a sure sign she was getting better—but she was content enough to pass the time talking with Falken. However, sometimes the light shining in his eyes when he spoke of their plan to find the shards of Fellring troubled her. Even if they did somehow find Ulther's sword—and then somehow managed to make it whole again—it still didn't mean Malachor was anything but a memory. And what good would that do them?

The truth was, despite Falken's obvious faith, Grace didn't see how any of it was going to help them against the Old God Mohg. Or his servant, the Pale King. Or the Onyx Knights, whoever they were and whatever they wanted. In the end, she would just be one skinny woman with a rusty old sword she didn't know how to use. But when she tried to tell Falken of her concerns, she saw the unguarded hope in his expression and the way he clenched his silver hand into an excited fist, and the words died on her tongue. Instead, Grace asked if she could examine his silver hand again. The thing fascinated her, especially since Falken said a witch had made it for him.

Though made of metal, the hand was alive, just like Falken was; she could see the hand's outline shimmering when she used the Touch. So that seemed like something a witch might do. But forging metal into such a fine shape, and enchanting it so that it could move in such a complex manner—from what little she knew, that seemed more like the magic of runes to her. And sure enough, when she turned it over, on the palm were three small runes—so faint she saw them barely as a glimmer—arranged in a circle. But how could Falken's hand be a result of both witch magic and rune magic? Her examinations failed to reveal an answer.

Outside, the sky turned from slate to pitch as the sun set. Leweth came to their door again, this time to regretfully inform them Elwarrd's duties would not allow him to take supper with them as he had hoped, and that trays would be delivered to their rooms. Grace was just as glad; she had no desire to return to the great hall and gaze again into the shadows of the gallery. Although she did feel a momentary pang of disappointment that she would not see Elwarrd.

Vani and Beltan had awakened by then, and both were better for the rest, although Grace was worried about the blond knight's cough. She made him spit in a napkin, and traces of rust showed against the white cloth. Grace prepared a brew for both of them, and while they eyed their cups suspiciously, they drank the tea after she gave each of them a stern look. They ate their supper and, with little else to do, went to bed.

The next day passed in much the same way, as did the next. The weather remained oppressive, and their host remained curiously absent, leaving them to take meals in their rooms.

"It's going to be impossible to beg our leave if Lord Elwarrd never shows up," Falken said in frustration the afternoon of their fifth day in Seawatch.

Grace was cutting shapes from a stiff piece of parchment

using the knife she usually kept tucked in her boot. "I don't know what's keeping Elwarrd away. But couldn't we go if we had to? Surely the lord would understand."

Falken gave a grim shake of his head. "To break the rules of hospitality is a crime worse than stealing. And it's a mortal insult. If we left, Elwarrd would have every right to hunt us down and clap us in irons."

"Not that he has any knights to send after us," Beltan said, lacing his fingers behind his head. "Besides, didn't you once leave Kelcior without begging permission from King Kel?"

The bard looked every bit as indignant as a wet rooster. "That was different. Kel had already decided to put me to death, so it wasn't as if leaving could have made things any worse."

Grace didn't see how the knight could argue with the logic of that. She kept cutting with the knife.

Vani sat at the table beside her. "What are they, Grace?"

"I don't know. I was bored and felt like making something, and this is what I came up with." Grace picked up one of the shapes she had cut from the parchment. It was vaguely human-looking, only lopsided, and the proportions were wrong. Evidently she was better at putting people back together than making them from scratch. "I suppose they must be paper dolls."

Beltan picked up one of the shapes, turning it this way and that, clearly trying to decide which way was up. "So what are you supposed to do with it?"

"I'm not really sure. I never had a doll." Grace brushed the parchment figure in her hand. She found herself thinking of Tira: the mute, burnt, red-haired girl who had become a goddess before her eyes.

Falken gave her a piercing look. "You mean you've never had a doll since you were a girl."

Grace shook her head. "They didn't allow toys in the..." She swallowed the words. "I mean, no, I never did."

Vani took up the knife and a piece of parchment. "I'll show you a better way to make them. My al-Mama taught me, just as her al-Mama taught her. It was when I was a girl, before I went to the fortress of Golgoru for my training as a *T'gol*."

The men quickly lost interest in this activity, but Grace and Vani spent the rest of the day folding dolls from the stiff parchment and cutting out clothes for them. Grace made paints from some of the herbs Leweth had brought and from dried berries stolen from the supper tray, and they used bits of charcoal from the hearth as pencils. Soon they had a king, a queen, and a dozen courtiers to attend them.

Last of all, Grace made a tiny doll—a child—with long, berry-red hair. When she was done, she stroked the child doll. She might even have whispered a song to it. Then, when no one was looking, she tossed it into the fire. Bright flames curled around the doll, and in a puff of gold it was gone. Grace pressed a hand to her stomach, and she shut her eyes to hide the tears. Like the doll, even Tira's star was gone now.

By the next morning they still hadn't seen Lord Elwarrd, and Falken was determined to go in search of the lord.

"I'll accompany you," Vani said, uncoiling her lean frame from a chair and stretching, as if she were simply bored and this sounded like a diversion.

Falken nodded, and Grace gave the *T'gol* a grateful look. They were all beginning to feel uneasy, no doubt just a result of being ill and confined these last days. All the same, she was glad the assassin was going with the bard.

Beltan made noise as if he wanted to go look for the earl as well, but Grace forbade it with a sharp glance. Beltan's cough was subsiding, and the last time she checked, his phlegm had been clear. He was nearly well—and she wanted to make sure he stayed that way.

"One more day, Beltan," she said, laying a hand on his arm. "That's all I'm asking. Falken and Vani will find Elwarrd and get his permission, and we'll go tomorrow."

Beltan sighed. "As you wish, my lady. One more day, but no more. I'm getting tired of this gloomy place. If we stay any longer, we'll all end up talking like Durge." Thunder crashed outside, punctuating his words.

Grace couldn't disagree with the knight's sentiments. She hoped Falken succeeded in finding the lord, and that Elwarrd would let them purchase horses. Without horses, it would be a long walk to Omberfell.

It was Beltan who came up with a way to pass the time until the others returned. "I don't know much about dolls, Grace. But I do know about fighting. And since we're going to Toringarth to get you a sword, you should probably learn how to wield one."

Grace wasn't certain she liked this idea. Beltan had once showed her how to use her knife to defend herself, but a knife wasn't all that much bigger than a scalpel. "You lost your sword in the shipwreck," she said. "It went down with your armor. There's nothing to practice with."

"How about this?" Beltan picked up the iron poker that leaned next to the hearth. He hefted it, testing its weight, then gave it a few swings. "This feels about right. The balance is better than some blades I've wielded. It'll do until we can get the real thing."

Grace stared at the poker. A year earlier, she had used a similar instrument to beat back the *feydrim* that attacked her and Travis in her chamber in Calavere. The gangly monster had nearly killed them, but together she and Travis had defeated it.

Grace swallowed. *Maybe learning to defend yourself isn't such a bad idea after all, Your Majesty.*

She took the poker. "Teach me."

They started slowly. Beltan showed her a series of positions, standing behind her and moving her arms so she held the poker just so, and using his own feet to push hers into place. Then he stood back and watched as he called the names of the positions, and she assumed each one as quickly as possible. She was pathetic at first; she couldn't even hold the poker steady. But after an hour, she showed a few faint glimmers of improvement.

Panting, arms and shoulders aching, she sat in a chair and let the poker clatter to the hearth.

"Not bad, Your Majesty," Beltan said, his face lighting up with a grin. "You're better than most beginners I've seen. It comes naturally to you."

Grace gave a weak smile. "I suppose it's in my blood."

Beltan's grin faded, and he looked away.

Despite her aches, Grace stood and moved to the knight. "What is it, Beltan? If something's wrong, you can tell me."

He shrugged. "It's nothing, Grace. It's just that what you said made me think about what's in my own blood these days."

Grace understood. In Denver, Duratek had given Beltan a transfusion of the fairy's blood. It had healed him. And maybe it had changed him as well.

She took his big, rough hands in hers. "You're still you, Beltan. No matter what they did to you."

There was sadness in his green eyes, and wonder as well. "I'm not so sure that's true. I remember what I used to feel like, Grace. And it wasn't like this." He moved to the window, gazing at rain outside. "Do you remember how Falken says it's impossible to tell when the sun sets here for all the clouds?" He turned around. "Well, it's not impossible for me. I get a sort of tingling feeling up my back, and I know the sun's just set, no matter how cloudy it is. And I know when it's risen, and when the moon is showing, and when it's not."

Grace stared at him, words eluding her.

"I feel things like that, Grace. And I hear things that I shouldn't possibly be able to hear. Like the sound of the stars. They have a sound, did you know that? It's like bits of crystal all clinking together. Only a thousand times that, and so far away I can only hear it if I hold my breath. And the wind—it has a voice, I can hear it, too. But I never know what it's saying, except that sometimes it's sleepy, and sometimes it's sad. And when a storm is coming, it's excited and maybe even angry." He passed a hand before his eyes. "And I see things."

Grace moved a step closer to him. "What sort of things?"

"I'm not sure." He seemed to be looking past her. "Sometimes, in bright daylight, I'll glimpse a shadow out of the corner of my eye, only when I turn it's gone. And then at night, I'll see a flicker of light, but only for a moment, never long enough for me to be sure it's really there." He ran a hand through his thinning hair, and now his eyes did meet hers. "Am I going mad, Grace? Like King Sorrin?"

"No," she said softly, firmly. "You're not going mad."

"But I'm different, aren't I? The fairy's blood changed me."

Grace hesitated, then nodded. "You should tell Falken. He might have an idea what it is you're seeing."

"I know. But not just yet. I don't mind your knowing, Grace. I'm glad for it, really. But I don't think I'm ready for Falken to start poking and prodding me. Not until I get a little more used to feeling like this."

"I won't tell anyone. You have my word."

A hint of the knight's grin returned. "Thank you, Your Majesty."

She groaned. "If you want to thank me, then don't call me *Your Majesty*."

"Yes, Your Majesty."

And then she was hugging him, fiercely, and she was surprised to feel him trembling despite his strength. And she was trembling as well. But then, he wasn't the only one who had changed.

"We'll get through this, Beltan. We'll get through it together. I promise."

The knight didn't reply, but she felt the solid beating of his heart, and that was answer enough.

30.

Falken and Vani didn't return until well after midday.

"Did you find the earl?" Grace said, rising from her seat by the fire. She grimaced as she stood, holding her hip just as she had seen old ladies do when descending a staircase.

Falken cocked his head. "What's wrong?"

"Nothing, really." Grace stretched herself tall, forcing the kinks in her legs and back to loosen. "Beltan decided to teach me how to wield a sword, that's all."

The bard let out a soft whistle. "You're letting Beltan teach you how to fight? That's not a good idea, Grace. That is, not unless you *want* to end up getting horribly maimed."

"I'm right here, you know," Beltan said, glaring down from the bed.

Falken paid the knight no attention. "We didn't find Elwarrd—I suppose he's out seeing to his lands again. But we did find the steward, Leweth, and he promised us the earl would be at supper this evening. So it looks like we'll finally get a chance to beg our leave. And none too soon. I think this rain will be turning to snow before long."

"Did the steward seem distressed to you?" Vani said, her leather garb creaking faintly as she moved nearer the fire. Grace knew that the Mournish woman—raised in the balmy south—found these northern lands harsh and frigid.

Falken rubbed his chin. "Now that you mention it, he did seem just a bit on the frantic side. I suppose he was just working hard to make sure the lord's supper would be a fine one. I'm sure the earl and the steward both know we'll be requesting our leave tonight, and it's not as if they get many guests to entertain here."

Vani nodded, but she didn't say whether she agreed with the bard's explanation or not.

"Anyway, that wasn't why we were gone so long," Falken said, unwrapping the bandages from his silver hand. "We found something interesting. Or Vani found it, anyway."

The *T'gol* rested her hands on her hips. "It would have meant nothing were it not for you, Falken."

Beltan climbed from the bed, and Grace sat down again as the bard and the assassin described what they had seen. The two had gone over every inch of the keep, telling the occasional servant they ran into they were looking for the steward. They would nod and listen as the servant offered directions, then would promptly pretend to get lost again so they could keep exploring. They even peeked into the earl's solar, behind the great hall, although they had found nothing special within: his bed, a chest for clothes and bedding, that was all.

They were about to give up and return when Falken realized they hadn't yet been to the mystery shrine. Every keep and castle in the Dominions had a shrine to the lord's favored mystery cult—even in Embarr, where the mysteries were not so popular as in other Dominions. Vani knew where the shrine was, for she had passed by it during her explorations several nights before. The shrine was a square stone structure that jutted from the back of the keep. It contained little more than an altar along with a trapdoor that led to a small family crypt.

"The altar was bare of anything but dust," Falken said.

"There were no figurines, no candles, no cups for wine— nothing that would indicate any of the seven mysteries have been followed here in years. But many Embarrans aren't religious these days, so that's not unusual. On the other hand, the secret door opposite the altar most definitely was."

Grace shot a startled glance at Vani. "But I thought you didn't see anything unusual the night you went wandering."

"I didn't. Though I did have a feeling there was something I was missing. I told Falken about it, and so he took a closer look around the shrine."

"And it's no wonder Vani missed the door," Falken said. He looked at Grace and Beltan. "You see, the door is bound with *Alth,* the rune of shadow."

Despite her proximity to the fire, a shiver coursed through Grace. She leaned forward in her chair as the bard spoke in a low voice.

"The art of runebinding was lost centuries ago—at least until Travis Wilder showed up on Eldh—so the door's obviously ancient. It's likely no one in the keep even knows it's there— not even Elwarrd. The rune of shadow makes it completely invisible to the eye. Keen as her senses are, Vani couldn't see it, although she had the feeling she should see something."

Beltan gave the bard a critical look. "So how come you could see it, Falken?"

"Because of this." He raised his silver hand. "It grants me some degree of sensitivity to rune magic. Enough that I felt the presence of the rune of shadow once I stood close to the door. And by concentrating, I was able to glimpse through the veil of shadow and see the door beyond."

Grace folded her arms, trying to keep warm. "So what do you suppose is beyond the door?"

"It could be almost anything. My guess is that long ago a runebinder dwelled in this keep. Maybe he kept his secret books there. The door is sealed, but only with what looks to be a mundane lock. The rune of shadow conceals its presence, nothing more. If we had the key, we could open the door. But I imagine the key was lost centuries ago."

The bard's story fascinated Grace—there was so much

history in this world, her knowledge barely scratched the surface—but she knew this was no more than an intriguing aside. The scientist in her longed to open the door and catalog all of the ancient artifacts within. But they had other purposes, and it was time to leave Seawatch.

The afternoon waxed and waned. Grace was just lighting candles against the falling dark when a knock came at the door. Falken and Beltan had returned to their chamber to rest an hour before, and Vani had ventured to the keep's kitchen in search of more oil for her leathers, which were not quite as supple as the *T'gol* wished. Grace opened the door, supposing it was a servant come to summon them to dinner.

It was the serving maid, Mirdrid.

"Forgive me, my lady. Is this an ill time?"

Grace had been staring. After all she had been through, sometimes the simplest human actions could still shock her. "Of course not, Mirdrid. Come in. Please."

The young woman curtsied, then entered. Grace sat by the fire and indicated Mirdrid should do the same.

"Oh! No, my lady, I mustn't sit. It isn't proper. I only came to show you this. You said you might wish to see it." She held out a folded piece of cloth. "It's the embroidery I've been working on."

Grace smiled, glad the young woman had felt comfortable enough to return. Evidently Grace was good at this whole not-being-terrifying thing. She took the cloth—it was surprisingly large—carefully unfolding it and spreading it on her lap.

The fire on the hearth went dim; her heart froze between beats.

"I made it for my father," Mirdrid said, her voice seeming to come from down a long corridor. "He's gone now, you see. It was just three days before you came to the keep. He had been getting sicker and sicker ever since Fallowing. So I started this for him a month ago. I wanted . . ." She smudged the tears from her eyes with the corner of her dirty apron. "I wanted him to be able to see it. Only I haven't had enough time, and it's not finished yet."

Grace hesitated, loath to touch the thing, then as if compelled by some dark force ran her fingers over the embroidered fabric. The pictures upon it were crude but expressive, rendered in uneven stitches of colored thread.

There were several images, arranged in a circle. Most depicted scenes of domestic life: men harvesting grain, women baking bread, children herding cows with switches. In many of the scenes there was a man with hair as yellow as Mirdrid's, watching over the task at hand. However, it was the scene in the center of the embroidery to which Grace's eyes were drawn. It showed the same man with yellow hair, only lying on a bier. Next to the bier was a tree, and perched in the tree was a shape stitched with black thread, like a dark stain on the fabric.

It was a bird.

Grace fought for words. "What is this?"

"It's a shroud for my father." Mirdrid knelt, smoothing the wrinkles from the embroidery with gentle motions. "Lord Elwarrd is so kind. He saw to everything himself. He put my father in the crypt, that's what he told me, right alongside all the lords and ladies of old. Wasn't that so wonderfully kind? And he said that when I've finished this embroidery, I can go there myself and lay it upon him. It's to help him remember what he did when he was alive. And see? My father's not alone. He'll always be watched."

Grace felt sick. "What do you mean, he'll be watched?"

Mirdrid touched the shape of the bird. "We're all being watched, all the time. Isn't that the safest feeling, my lady? I used to be afraid of so many things, of the dark, of dying, but I'm not anymore. The eye watches us, and it makes sure we always do the right things, that we don't stray from the path before the end comes and—"

"Mirdrid, what are you doing?"

Both Grace and the serving maid started at the sound of the stern voice. They looked up. Leweth stood in the doorway.

Mirdrid rose, snatching the cloth from Grace and wadding it into a tight ball. "I was doing nothing ill. I was just talking to my lady, that's all."

"You should be seeing to your chores."

Mirdrid gave a wordless nod and hurried from the room, not so much as glancing at Grace.

"I'm sorry, my lady," Leweth said, his voice gentle now. "Was my sister bothering you?"

Sister? So Leweth was Mirdrid's brother. Which meant Mirdrid's father must have been the old steward. That was why Leweth seemed so young to hold the position; he had inherited it from his father just days before they came to Seawatch.

Grace took a deep breath to make sure her voice would be calm. "No, she was no bother."

Leweth nodded. "Supper will on the board soon. The lord requests your presence in the great hall immediately." Then he turned and was gone.

Grace hurried to tell Falken and Beltan it was time for supper, and when they started downstairs Vani was there. Grace wanted to tell them of her odd encounter with Mirdrid, but there was no time. And she wasn't certain what it meant—if it meant anything at all.

As they entered the great hall, Grace couldn't help a glance up at the gallery, but it was dark and empty, and she knew if she were to reach out with the Touch she would sense nothing there. Whatever it was she had glimpsed before, it had felt her attention, and now it was wary. If it even existed at all.

It's probably your nerves, Grace. They're just frayed after the shipwreck, and then being cooped up in a gloomy castle. No wonder you're seeing shadows.

All the same, it was hard not to think of the dark bird on Mirdrid's embroidery, and the words the young woman had spoken.

We're all being watched, all the time. . . .

"Are you all right, Grace?" Beltan whispered in her ear.

She squeezed his hand. *I'll tell you about it later,* she spun the words across the Weirding, and by his surprised grunt she knew he had heard her.

As promised, the earl was present, and he stood as they approached the table. Grace felt some of her dread evaporating under the force of his smile. In the days since she had seen him, she had forgotten how handsome he was. He wore a sort of long vest over a loose shirt, breeches that clung tightly to strong legs, and leather boots.

"My lords, my lady," Elwarrd said, "you must forgive my absence these last days. There has been much to see to. Orders have come from Barrsunder requesting additional tithes of food. It's been hard to fulfill our duty to our king, and yet make certain we have stores enough for winter."

Grace saw Beltan and Falken exchange knowing glances. Grace thought she understood. Why would Barrsunder request more food if someone there didn't know a siege was coming? And depleting the resources of Embarr's keeps and castles would make them all that much easier to defeat. It seemed the king's advisors indeed prepared for war—against Embarr itself.

"You needn't worry, my lord," Falken said. "We've been well attended to, and the rest has done us good. But now that the threat of illness has past, it's time for us to—"

The earl held up a hand, smiling. "No, my lord, save your requests until supper is finished. These may be the hinterlands of the Dominions, but we do things properly here."

Falken pressed a hand to his chest and bowed. Grace wondered what the bard was thinking, but if the Touch could be used to read minds, it was a skill she had yet to develop.

They took their places at the table. Once again an empty setting had been arranged to the earl's left, although this time there was no place at the table for Leweth.

"I'm afraid the steward has duties that cannot wait," Elwarrd said, "so he's unable to join us tonight."

Vani took the place beside Falken, leaving Beltan to serve himself. Once again, it was Grace's duty to serve the lord. She poured wine and handed him the cup, and when his hand brushed hers it was like an electric charge, shocking her.

As before, they made idle conversation as they ate, but Grace hardly heard it. She could not stop thinking of the lord's presence; she could feel the heat of his body as if from a fire. Nervousness caused her to gulp wine, and soon she felt her fear subside, and a strange boldness came over her.

"My lord, I have a question for you."

Elwarrd raised an eyebrow. Before she could think better of

it, she went on. "The empty place that's always set so carefully to your left. Who is it for?"

The others gaped at her, and Grace knew she had made a grave error. The wine-induced giddiness fled, leaving only a dull throb in her head. However, the lord didn't rebuke her for her rudeness. Instead, after a moment, he smiled.

"I'm surprised it took you so long to ask, my lady." Elwarrd's voice was jovial, but there was a hardness in his eyes. "Indeed, it does seem passing strange, does it not? That chair is for my mother. Every night, I bid the servants set a place for her. And every night she refuses to sit there. It is how she punishes me, you see."

Grace licked her lips. "Punishes you?"

"Yes, my lady. For my disobedience." He lifted the wine cup and took a reckless draught. His voice rose as he spoke. "You see, I haven't always lived my life precisely as she's wished. I have, on occasion, dared to disobey her. For these crimes, as a young man, she punished me by telling lies to the king, claiming I had a frail constitution, and begging him not to make me a knight, claiming it would be the death of me. And so I was passed over for knighthood." He drained the wine cup and wiped crimson fluid from his beard with the back of his hand. "And now that my father is three years gone, and I am earl in his stead, she punishes me still by refusing to acknowledge me as the rightful lord. Isn't that so, Mother?"

These last words became a shout. He shoved his chair back and stood. "Don't you think it's time you showed yourself to our guests?"

His body went rigid, the cords on his neck standing out as his voice echoed throughout the hall. Grace stared, unable to speak. She saw Vani rise and stalk fluidly toward the curtain that hung over the end of the great hall. A second later Grace saw it: The heavy curtain moved, as if someone—something—stood behind it. Vani reached out and snatched the curtain aside.

Nothing was there; the earl's solar was empty.

Elwarrd passed a hand in front of his face. "You must forgive me." His voice was low now. "I am weary from my recent labors, that's all. There are things I…that is, I must take my leave. Please forgive me."

And before they could say anything, the earl of Seawatch strode from the hall.

31.

"Well," Falken said, "that was a bit on the awkward side." They had gathered again in Grace and Vani's chamber, not knowing where else to go.

Beltan spun a knife in his hand; he must have taken it from the dinner table. "I don't know where his mother has been hiding all this time, but it looks like we've gotten ourselves stuck in the middle of a family argument."

"A topic you know something about, is that not so?" Vani said, arms crossed.

Beltan thrust the knife into the mantel above the fireplace and glared at the *T'gol*. "Just what is that supposed to mean?"

Grace held a hand to her head. She didn't need Vani and Beltan's animosity right now. There was something going on, something she needed to remember.

"What is it, Grace?" Falken said, touching her shoulder.

"Something happened to me just before dinner. I didn't have the chance to tell you about it, but it was very odd."

She related her encounter with Mirdrid: the shroud the young woman had made for her dead father, and the bird that watched over him, embroidered in black thread. Then, as she repeated Mirdrid's words, Grace finally remembered why they had seemed so familiar at the time. She had heard words like them before, in the port town of Galspeth in Perridon, spoken by the clothier's daughter when she saw Grace's necklace.

You shouldn't wear that. He doesn't like it when you do odd things. Things no one else does….

"Something is wrong in this keep," Grace said after she told the others what she had remembered. "Just like it was in Galspeth. I think we should get out of this place. We're all well enough to travel now."

However, the earl had left the hall before granting them leave to go, and Falken still seemed reluctant to depart without permission. Grace supposed it was akin to Falken telling her to rob a bank just because she was a little short on cash.

"Elwarrd favors you, Grace," Beltan said gently. "We've all seen it. Maybe you could talk to him alone and ask permission to leave. I don't think he would deny you anything."

Grace felt their expectant gazes, and she knew she couldn't let them down, even though going to see Elwarrd was the last thing she wanted to do right then.

And is that true, Grace? Don't you want to see him after all?

Her body was trembling beneath her gown, but whether out of fear or anticipation, she didn't know.

"I'll do it," she said.

Finding the earl was easier than she had guessed it would be. She stopped a servant who was lighting lamps; an hour had passed since supper, and it was full dark. The servant had just seen Elwarrd minutes before, returning to his solar at the end of the great hall.

Grace pushed through the hall's massive doors. They dwarfed her, making her feel like a small girl doing something forbidden. The only light was from the fire that still burned in the cavernous fireplace. Grace walked across the hall, conscious of her echoing footsteps, to the heavy curtain drawn over the vast room's far end.

She cleared her throat. "My lord?"

The only answer was the *snap* of a burning log.

Perhaps she had not spoken loud enough. "Lord Elwarrd, are you there?"

Grace lifted a shaking hand, touching the rough fabric of the curtain. Then, steeling her will, she pushed the curtain aside and stepped through.

Lord Elwarrd, Earl of Seawatch, turned around.

She had caught him just in the act of taking his shirt off. The garment slipped from his fingers, falling to the floor in a heap. He wore only boots and breeches, and the bare skin of his chest gleamed in the light of a dozen candles.

A gasp escaped Grace. "My lord, forgive me." She began to turn away.

"And what should I forgive you for, my lady?" His voice was deep, soft: for her only. "For making manifest what I had been dreaming of moments ago? When I saw you there, I thought you were only a phantom, conjured by the fever that has burned in my brain since I first laid eyes upon you. But you're here, aren't you? You're real."

Despite herself, his words drew her back around and led her farther into the dim space of the solar. Her eyes adjusted to the candlelight, and she saw him more clearly. His chest was smooth, damp with sweat, and his stomach was so taut she could see shadows flicker across it in time to the beating of his heart. Dimly, she wondered where he had gone after supper, and where he had just come from.

She realized it was her turn to say something, and she grasped for something, anything to say. "It was very kind of you, my lord, to take care of Mirdrid's father as you did."

"What?"

"Mirdrid. The old steward's daughter. She told me of your generosity—how you laid him in the family crypt."

"My lady, I won't believe you came here to talk of serving maids." He made a dismissive gesture with his hand. As he did, several dark droplets scattered across the floor.

Grace's instincts as a doctor leaped to the fore. "Your hand, my lord. It's bleeding."

He stared at his hand, as if he had not noticed it himself until just then. Grace took his hand in hers, turning it over, examining it. Blood oozed from two sets of puncture wounds, one on the back of his hand, one on the palm. She pulled a handkerchief from her gown and wiped away the blood so she could examine him more clearly. She had seen wounds similar to this in the Emergency Department. It looked almost like a dog bite.

"It's nothing, my lady. I can't even feel it. Not with you here."

"Hold still." She wrapped the handkerchief around his hand and bound it in a makeshift bandage. Immediately, spots of crimson began to soak through, but it would do for the time being. All at once she was conscious of how close she was to him. She took a step back.

"Thank you for your care, my lady. But now you must tell why you really came to see me."

Grace drew in a breath, gathering strength. "I have come to

beg your permission to leave Seawatch, my lord. My companions want to depart in the morning."

"Then why not let them go?" His gaze ran over her face, her throat, her breasts. "But look at me. Look at me, and then tell me you really wish to leave."

He was a lord, and his words a command, and she could not resist them. She did look at him, touching him with her gaze, her thoughts. His face was fine, his lips surprisingly full for a man, his arms sculpted with muscle. Against the tight cloth of his breeches, the shape of his desire was plain: hard and compact like the rest of him.

A shudder coursed through her. For so long she had been unable to touch another, to allow another to touch her. But she had put that shadow behind her in Tarras. This time it would be her choice, an act of passion not violence. A heat rose within her, so fierce it must surely burn her gown to ashes.

In a single step he closed the distance between them. He coiled his unbandaged hand around her neck and bent her head down with irresistible strength, for she was taller than he. Her lips brushed against his nose, his beard, then found the hot, hard moistness of his mouth.

And from the shadows around them, a voice spoke, at once shrill and croaking, like the call of a crow.

"Heretic! Trespasser! I see what you do."

Grace froze. A moan ripped itself from Elwarrd—fear or rage?—and he jerked away from her. The taste of metal flooded Grace's mouth. She touched a finger to her lips, and it came away dark with blood. Blood that was not her own.

"I know what she is," the voice croaked. "A harlot. A witch. And far more. She is not for you!"

Elwarrd spun around, searching for the source of the voice. Motion caught Grace's eye. There, in the darkest corner of the room, where the light of the candles did not reach, something moved. Grace started to reach out with the Touch.

As if struck a cruel blow, her mind was slapped back, her concentration shattering.

"Keep your foul magics to yourself, witch! I have labored too long to let you poison him now with your spells!"

By the time Grace saw it coming, it was too late to move.

Candlelight glinted off steel as the dagger flew through the air. She braced herself for its deadly bite.

The dusky air before her rippled, folded. A hand lashed out and clamped around the dagger, stopping it before it could strike. Grace found herself staring into golden eyes.

Vani threw down the knife and lunged in the direction from which the weapon had come. She snatched a tapestry from the wall, and the resulting puff of air caused the candles to gutter, flare. Their light reached the far corner, revealing a wooden door. It stood ajar.

"Whoever it was went this way," Vani said.

Laughter bubbled out of Elwarrd. "You won't find her. I can never find her. I don't know where in this godsforsaken keep she finds to hide." He pressed his wounded hand to his temple; the bandage was soaked with crimson. "Everything I want, she denies me. Everything I try to do, she mocks." He threw his head back, chest heaving as he shouted. "I won't do it, Mother! Do you hear me? I won't be what you want me to be. You'll have to kill me first, just like you did my father!"

Vani watched this spectacle in silence, hands on hips. Grace reached out a trembling hand. "My lord, we have to go. Please. We have to leave Seawatch."

He batted her hand away. "No one is leaving until I say so. I am the earl, and this is my fiefdom. If you leave, you will all be outlaws in Embarr. I will send word of your crime to every corner of the Dominion. You'll be caught and beheaded before you can reach the borders." He clenched his wounded hand, and blood ran down his arm. "Return to your chamber. Now!"

Grace couldn't move—shock paralyzed her—but Vani pulled her, guiding her back into the great hall and the corridor beyond. Cooler air struck Grace's cheeks, and she returned to her senses. What had she done? And what had Vani seen? She felt again the lord's lips on her own.

"Vani, I didn't . . . what happened in there, I . . ."

The *T'gol's* strong hand on her arm propelled her forward. "Do not think of it now, Grace. We must go tell the others what has happened."

Minutes later they gathered in Falken and Beltan's chamber. Grace was still shaking, so Vani told the two men what had taken place. However, the *T'gol* did not speak of Grace and Elwarrd's kiss, and for that Grace gave her a grateful look. Falken poured wine for all of them, and Grace gulped hers down, feeling her nerves grow a bit steadier.

Beltan set down his empty cup. "It sounds like Elwarrd's mother is completely mad. I can't believe she tried to harm you, Grace." His expression was hard with anger.

"It was not Grace his mother was trying to kill," Vani said, her voice cool, almost clinical. "The dagger was aimed at Elwarrd. Had I not stopped it, the blade would have pierced his heart."

Falken flexed his silver hand. "But that doesn't make any sense. Why would she kill her own son? Grace is right—something strange is going on in this keep. And I bet the earl's mother is the only one who knows what it is. Vani, did you see which way she ran?"

"No, she moved with a strange swiftness. The only trace I found was this, caught on a nail in the door." The *T'gol* set a small scrap of black cloth on the table.

"It doesn't matter where she is," Beltan said. "We're getting out of here."

Falken glanced at Grace. "Did he grant us leave to go?"

It was Vani who answered. "No, he did not. And he threatened that if we go, we will be branded as outlaws and hunted down."

"I imagine he means it," Falken said with a sigh.

Beltan jerked the knife from the mantelpiece. "We can take care of anyone who follows us."

Grace stared into her empty wine cup. Something about her conversation with Elwarrd nagged at her. Then she had it: When she mentioned Mirdrid and the old steward, he hardly seemed to know what she was talking about.

She looked up. "Vani, the other day when you searched the keep, did you go into the family crypt?"

"I did. There was nothing in there save old bones."

A chill coursed through Grace. "Are you sure? You didn't

see the body of a man? Elwarrd told Mirdrid he put her father in the crypt just a few days before we arrived."

Vani crossed her arms. "The only bodies in the crypt had been there for years."

"Maybe it's somewhere else in the keep," Beltan offered.

Falken shook his head. "Vani and I went through the entire keep, and we didn't see any bodies. The only place we couldn't go was behind the door marked with the rune of shadow."

With an electric surge, two pieces of knowledge connected in Grace's mind. "That's it—it has to be. Elwarrd said he didn't know where in the keep his mother hid from him. He doesn't know about the door, but she's found a way to open it."

The bard rubbed his chin. "I suppose you're right, Grace. But I don't see how that helps us. It's Elwarrd who has to grant us leave to go, not his mother. Besides, there's no way we can see beyond the door."

But there was, and Grace knew it. She stood, forcing her legs to stop shaking, and picked up the scrap of black cloth from the table. Yes, it would be enough. She turned around to regard the others.

"I'm going to do a spell. But it's dangerous. Once before when I did it, I was…" It had been the time she had used the half-coin to see Travis being hauled to his execution at the Gray Tower. She had nearly been lost, her spirit permanently severed from her body. "I need you all to keep watch over me."

Falken's expression was grave. "Are you sure you want to do this, Grace?"

"We have to know what's happening here," she said, although she could feel the dread rising in her chest.

In minutes she was ready.

"I still don't like this," Beltan said, pacing. "How can we defend you when you're not in your body?"

Grace sat in a chair, the scrap of black cloth in her lap. "You'll see it on my face if I'm in trouble. And the potion will wake me." She had given Falken a bitter concoction of herbs. The smell should shock her out of her trance.

Falken knelt beside her chair. "I'll watch you closely, Grace. I'm not going to lose you a second time. And Beltan and Vani will make sure no one bothers us."

Grace held his gaze a moment, grateful for the bard's calm. Then it was time. She shut her eyes and reached out with her mind to Touch the scrap of cloth.

Instantly she was flying through the keep.

Bodiless, she floated through stone corridors, down winding staircases, and past an old servingman who couldn't see her, but who shivered as she went by. A pair of huge wooden doors loomed before her; she slipped through them like they were an illusion, only it was she who was without substance.

Both times before when she had cast this spell, Grace had glimpsed events that had not yet taken place. This time she was seeing the present, she was sure of it.

With a note of faint panic—she was so cold, so hollow, it was hard to feel anything at all—Grace realized she was being drawn to the curtain at the far end of the great hall. Before she could fear more, she fluttered through the fabric like a delicate breeze. The earl was no longer in his solar. The blood on the floor was the only trace of him. Grace flew onward, through the half-open door in the corner, down a winding flight of steps, and then through an archway into a small room.

It was the shrine. There was a bare altar, and shelves where stone gods might once have stood. But the gods had forsaken this place long ago. Or had they been cast out? Grace was moving faster. She floated to the shrine's corner and saw a darkness so pure, so perfect, she would have cried out if she had possessed lungs. The darkness was hungry, conscious, but not alive. Surely it would consume the feeble wisp of her spirit. Drawn by the power of her own spell, she hurtled directly toward it.

She would have thought the darkness to be cold, but instead it was horribly hot, suffocating her like a black blanket. There was terrible resistance, as if she was being pushed through tar. She could feel it eating at the very substance of her being. Then, all at once, she was through.

Once again she was flying down a set of stone steps. She glanced back and saw an ironbound door, tightly shut. Set into the surface of the door was a small circle of iron marked with an angular symbol which she knew Falken would tell her was *Alth*, the rune of shadow. Then the door was lost to sight as the staircase led her deeper down. Three times it circled around, and she knew she was far beneath the keep. There was an opening ahead; crimson light spilled through. Grace floated forward, then her motion ceased. This was it, this was where the spell had led her. She peered through the opening.

And somewhere, far above and away in the keep, she knew her living heart faltered in her chest.

She didn't doubt Falken's belief that at one time this place had been used by a wizard who had bound the rune of shadow into the door. But it was clear that, when it was first built, this had been the keep's dungeon. There was a central room ringed by a series of alcoves, each one walled with rusting iron bars. Things sinuous and gray prowled back and forth inside some of the cells. Whuffles and snarls echoed off stone.

Along one of the dungeon's walls, set into the stone, was a row of iron manacles. The remains of three men hung there, although there was not much left of them besides bones. At first Grace thought perhaps they had been mauled to death, but then she saw it had been more careful than that. She understood the crisscrossed pattern of cut marks on the bones. These men had been butchered, the flesh systematically carved from their bodies. Somehow she knew they had not yet been dead when the process had begun. Sickness washed over her, and an overwhelming desire to vomit, but of course she could not.

There was another body lying on a bench, carved up like the others. Atop its head remained a shock of yellow hair shot with gray. Why did that seem important to Grace?

Before she could think, her attention was drawn to the two figures in the center of the room. One had his back mostly to her, but Grace recognized him as the steward, Leweth. The other was a woman clad in a severe black gown. From a chain around her neck hung an iron key. She was old, that was clear, but she stood straight and stiff, her bearing proud. Her iron-gray hair was pulled back so tightly it stretched her expression into something that was at once smile and grimace. White makeup plastered her face, and her cheeks and lips were colored red, done up in a garish facsimile of life.

The illusion failed; it was quite clear the woman was dead. In her present form, Grace could see the threads of the

Weirding as clearly as the torchlight. None of them spun around the other. The old woman was dead.

And she was speaking.

"How does the Gift suit you?" It was the same croaking sound Grace had heard in the earl's solar. It was she, Elwarrd's mother.

"It suits me well, Lady Ursaled. I feel strong. Stronger than I have in all my life. I thank you." There was something queer about Leweth's voice. It was harder than Grace remembered.

"You were wise to accept it," the earl's mother said. "Your father would be alive had he not been such a fool as to refuse it."

Laughter rose from Leweth. "But he has made himself a service in other ways, has he not?" He gestured to the body on the bench, the one with the shock of yellow-gray hair. Wet snarls emanated from the cells. Iron rang like broken chimes as hard talons were dragged across the bars.

"They are hungry, my lady," the steward said. "And there is nothing left to pick from these corpses. Not from my father, or from these three I found on the beach. We'll have to let them gnaw on the bones, but I doubt that will keep them long. Would that I had had time to go back and find the others on the beach before they woke."

The woman moved to a table in the dungeon's center. "It is just as well you did not. What fate brought her here, I know not, but she is the key to all we desire. Elwarrd will present her to our Master, and so my son shall rise high in the Master's favor just as I have planned all these years."

"So the Master truly does seek her?"

"Yes," Ursaled hissed. "And He wishes her alive of all things! Do not the stories say that only one of her blood has the power to harm Him? But it is not for us to question His ways. Our only task is to please Him, so that my son may rise high in His favor."

Leweth took a hesitant step forward. "And why must it be the earl, my lady? Why can you not deliver her to the Master?"

"You show your ignorance. I am but a woman, and of common birth—a countess by marriage only. What standing could I expect in the Master's dark court? No, it must be my son. He is a noble by blood. The Master will be sure to reward him. And Elwarrd in turn will reward us."

Gray bodies flung themselves forward; iron bars groaned.

"Did Elwarrd catch the one that escaped?" Leweth said. "Did you not send him after it?"

Ursaled sniffed. "It was the least he could do, after all I have done for him. But he failed in the task."

"Should I look for it, my lady?"

"No, it matters no longer. The time has come to free my pets. The Master's magic has shaped them well; they will not harm the pale-haired harlot, the witch. And they can feed on the others to gain strength."

"And what of Elwarrd? Do you truly think the earl will do as you wish? I believe that he fancies her, my lady."

The old countess pounded a gnarled fist on the table. "Of course he will do as I wish! All these years, I have made every sacrifice for him. I protected him from the attention of the king in order to save him for greater opportunities. I kept him from becoming entangled in a woman's snare. And all this time he has been ungrateful. But soon, all that will change. Soon he will understand everything, just as you do, Leweth!"

Ursaled took an object from the table and thrust it above her in triumph. It was a fist-sized lump of iron.

Fear permeated Grace's being. It was impossible she could scream, yet somehow it seemed she did make a sound, for both the countess and the steward turned in her direction. The front of the steward's shirt hung open, and the torn cloth was soaked with blood. In the center of his chest was a jagged wound, the raw flaps of meat held together with crude stitches. Yes, Grace saw it clearly now that she looked: the lump of iron in his chest where his heart should have been. He was every bit as dead as the countess.

The steward peered forward with dull eyes. On his forehead, burned right through the skin and into his skull, was a brand. The brand might have been a raven's wing. Or a staring eye. Grace looked again at the countess, and beneath the thick layer of makeup she glimpsed the same mark.

The countess moved forward, turning her head back and forth. "There is something here, something watching us." Then, impossibly, her eyes locked on Grace. "You!"

Grace's entire being moaned in horror. The old woman reached a hand toward her, her face a white mask of murder—

—and Grace opened her eyes, slumping in the chair by the fireplace in her chamber. Falken lowered the vial with the bitter potion. Beltan and Vani stared at her.

"It's the Raven Cult," Grace said.

32.

It was no longer a question of begging their leave. Any obligation they might have had to the earl had been erased by what Grace had witnessed. Now it was just a question of getting out of the keep. Grace could only hope that she was wrong, that what she had seen had taken place in the future after all, and that they still had time to escape.

"They had imprisoned three crewmen from the *Fate Runner* down there," Grace said. She felt weak, horribly weak, and so empty. "Leweth must have found them on the beach, he must have led them to the keep. I'm not sure, but I think one of them was Captain Magard. And the other body, it was the old steward. They were using the corpses to feed them. *Feydrim.* They had *feydrim* in the dungeon. They . . ."

Beltan laid a hand on her shoulder. "Don't think about it, Grace. We're getting out of here. Now."

Falken slung his lute case over his shoulder. "I just wonder why Magard and his crewmen didn't see us there on the beach, and why they went to the keep with Leweth without looking for other survivors. I suppose it's a mystery we'll never know the answer to."

But maybe she did know. Grace thought again of the light that had buoyed her in the water, and the face she had glimpsed: ancient, beautiful. Maybe something had hidden them, protecting them. If so, it was gone now.

"Come," Vani said, peering through the crack she had opened in the door. "The way is clear."

The keep was silent. Grace was acutely aware of every sound as they moved: the scrape of their shoes on the wooden floor, the whisper of her fur-lined cloak as she pulled it more tightly around her. Surely their going would be noticed. Vani led the way, and Beltan brought up the rear. They saw no one as they made their way past several doors to the head of the stairs.

As they started to descend, Grace heard the pounding of footsteps. Someone was running up the staircase. Beltan pushed past Grace and Falken, knife in hand. Vani crouched, ready to spring. Grace saw a shadow lurch across the wall, followed by a figure that came hurtling up the stairs. The runner tripped on the last step and fell sprawling to the floor.

It was Mirdrid, the serving maid. Leweth's sister. Beltan knelt and helped her up. Her gray dress was tangled and torn, and she was weeping, tears making streaks on her dirty face. Beneath the grime, a bruise was clearly forming on her cheek.

Concern dulled the edge of Grace's fear. "Mirdrid, what is it? What's happened to you?" She smoothed the young woman's snarled hair from her face.

"Oh, my lady!" Mirdrid sobbed, clutching at Grace. "I saw them, and they're horrible, and they're going to eat me. They're going to eat all of us!"

"What did you see, Mirdrid?" Grace made her voice sharp, knowing it was the only way to cut through the other's hysteria. "And who hit you?"

The young woman shook violently. "It was the earl. I saw him in the great hall, and he was in a terrible rage. He was talking about death, my lady, about how we all must die, and it was the most frightful thing. I've never seen him so. He struck me, and I fear he might have made ill with me, but I managed to get away. I ran, I wanted to go the village to see my mother, but . . ." Sobs racked her body.

Grace gripped her shoulders, hard. "What, Mirdrid? You have to tell us."

The young woman's brown eyes were wide. "Monsters, my lady. By the front door of the keep. I saw them in the shadows.

They had teeth like knives. Two of them. Perhaps three. I don't know. I ran, but now they're going to eat me!"

"No one's going to eat you, I promise," Grace said, holding the young woman.

Beltan shot a look at Vani. "Is there another way out of the keep?"

"The kitchens!" Mirdrid said before the *T'gol* could speak. She pushed away from Grace and wiped the tears from her face. "That's where we have to go. It's the only other way out."

Beltan raised an eyebrow. Vani nodded.

Mirdrid started unsteadily down the corridor. "This way. There's a back staircase only the servants use."

They exchanged glances, then hurried after the serving maid. Mirdrid was right; at the far end of the corridor, hidden behind a tapestry, was an opening that led to a narrow staircase.

"Mirdrid!" Grace hissed, but the girl had already started down, vanishing into shadow.

"The girl is right," Vani said. "These steps lead down to the kitchens below the great hall. There is a small side door there that opens to the outside. Hopefully it will not be guarded as the main door."

They started down the stairs single file. Darkness closed around Grace like a fist. She thought she saw a shadow darting below her. Mirdrid?

They turned a corner, and a square of ruddy light appeared below them. A few more steps, and the four tumbled into the kitchens. Wooden posts supported soot-stained beams; a fire roared in the fireplace, and it was unbearably hot.

Grace pushed her damp hair from her face. "Mirdrid?"

Beltan moved toward the door of iron-banded wood on the far wall, but Vani was faster. She pushed against it.

The door didn't budge.

Now the blond knight had reached the *T'gol*. He threw his weight against the door along with hers. There was a groan, but the door remained shut.

Falken frowned at Beltan. "What's wrong?"

"I'm not sure. Something's blocking it."

Laughter sounded behind them; they turned around. Mirdrid

stepped from the shadows behind a cupboard and sauntered toward them, flouncing her dirty dress.

"Mirdrid," Grace said. "Is there a way to open the door?"

The young woman smiled, displaying rotten teeth. "Oh, no, my lady. It's barred with iron from the other side. You'll never open it in time."

Grace shook her head, trying to comprehend these words. The young woman only laughed again. In three swift strides, Beltan covered the distance to Mirdrid. He grabbed her wrist and, before she could resist, turned her arm over and pushed up the sleeve of her dress.

On the underside of her forearm was a puckered brand. The rune of the Raven. The Eye of Mohg.

Mirdrid snatched her hand back. "They're coming for her now." She pointed at Grace. "The Master has sent for her. And the rest of you will be meat for the Master's pets."

Grace reached out toward Mirdrid with the Touch, but the heart in her chest was alive, a thing of flesh, not iron. So she was just a Raven cultist, not an ironheart. "Why, Mirdrid?" Grace said, voice shaking.

The young woman only continued to point at Grace, her face solemn now. Then she turned and ran from the kitchens.

"By the Blood of the Seven," Falken said through clenched teeth. "She's led us into a trap. We have to find a way to open that door."

It was too late. Grace heard the echo of grunts, the scraping of talons on stone. Misshapen forms slunk into the kitchens, five, six, seven of them. Their backs were humped, their gray fur matted, their yellow eyes filled with pain and hunger.

The *feydrim* arranged themselves in a half circle on the far side of the room, looking like nothing so much as spider monkeys crossbred with wolves: feral, intelligent, tortured. What were they waiting for? Beltan had only the small knife, and even Vani could not fight so many in such a small space. Then the half circle parted, and two figures stepped through, one slightly in front of the other, and Grace understood. The *feydrim* had been waiting for their mistress.

"You cannot escape," the old countess said.

She looked just as she had in Grace's vision: clad in a dusty gown of funereal black, her face a white death's mask, her lips and cheeks smeared with crimson. Just behind her stood the steward, Leweth, a leer on his homely face, blood still oozing from the wound in his chest. Beltan started to move forward, knife ready, but at a sharp look from the countess he stopped. Even Vani stood frozen. The *feydrim* crouched, ready to spring.

"What do you want from us?" Falken said.

"I want nothing from you, save the flesh from your bones to feed my minions." She ran white-stick fingers over the head of one of the *feydrim*; it whimpered as if she had struck it a blow. The countess nodded toward Grace. "It is only she that matters. The Master has made it clear He wishes her for His own. I have received the missives, carried by the Master's own ravens, instructing all of His servants to keep watch for a fair-haired woman with a necklace marked by runes. When I saw her from the shadows of the gallery, I could not believe our good fortune. For so long I have sought a way to ensure that my son rises high in the Master's favor. And here she comes to our keep, the very thing He desires."

"Berash, you mean," Falken spat. "The Pale King."

The thick paint on the countess's face cracked. "You are not worthy to speak His name! You will die tonight, just as all who dare to stand against Him shall soon perish. The forces of the Raven will march across the Dominions, and they will purge His foes from the face of the land like dark fire!" She turned toward Leweth. "Take her now. I want her out of the way before I release the *feydrim* upon the others. They are hungry, and the Master's desire is clear: She must not come to harm."

"Yes, Lady Ursaled." The steward moved forward, his dead gaze paralyzing Grace. "Come, wench. It will be easier for you if you do not resist. The Master wants you alive. I imagine he will care nothing if you are . . . damaged."

A bellow of rage erupted from Beltan. "Get away from her!"

He lunged forward, driving his knife deep into Leweth's gut. The steward stared dully at the hilt protruding from his stomach as black blood oozed around it. Then, in a mechanical motion, he plucked out the knife and turned it back on Beltan, sticking it into the knight's shoulder.

Beltan moaned and staggered back, his hand curled

around the hilt of the knife, blood streaming between his fingers. A howl rose from the *feydrim*; the scent of blood excited them.

Falken pulled Grace toward the barred door. At the same moment, moving in a blur, Vani gripped Leweth's arm, bent it backwards, and twisted it around. There was a *snap*, and a ragged white stump pierced the skin of his forearm, jutting outward at a horrible angle.

No, Vani, Grace wanted to say. *It's no use. They don't feel pain, not like we do.*

There was no time. Leweth lashed out with his other arm, moving with an impossible speed that surpassed even Vani's own. His hand contacted her square in the chest, and she flew backward, striking the stone wall with brutal force. She slumped to her knees.

Leweth clutched the collar of Grace's cloak, pulling her away from Falken. "Now, my lady, you will——"

His words ended in a gush of dark fluid that poured out of his mouth. The steward stood rigid, eyes staring. Then his head toppled from his neck, striking the floor with a *thud* as his body came tumbling after.

Grace struggled to comprehend what had happened. Then she saw the figure step away from the shadowed mouth of the staircase down which they had come. It was Elwarrd. He gripped a sword in his hand, its edge slick with blood. On his face was a peculiar expression: solemn, thoughtful.

"You idiot!" the countess shrieked, her scarlet lips smearing in rage. "What are you doing?"

"Saving you, Mother." He moved toward her, sword raised before him. "Saving all of us."

The *feydrim* watched him with yellow eyes, but they didn't attack. Elwarrd bared his own teeth in a sharp grin. He let his free hand run over their humped backs, tangling his fingers in their lank fur. They licked his hand with black tongues, whining and pissing on the floor.

"You trained them well, Mother. They serve you, but they won't attack me if I don't hurt them, will they? They know I'm important. You taught them that much."

The countess stepped forward, reached past the sword, and slapped his face with a withered hand. "Listen to me, insolent boy. Everything I have ever done, I have done for you. The Final Battle comes, and it is the Master who will be victorious. I saw it when your father could not."

Elwarrd pressed his hand to his cheek. "So you killed him."

"He was weak. He did not survive the transformation wrought by the Gift. So I took the Gift upon myself. I did it for you, my son. And when I survived the change, I knew I could dedicate myself to make sure you rose high in the Master's favor when the dark times came." She clutched his shirt with bony fingers. "And now that time has come at last! All we must do is give this harlot, this witch, to Him, and He will surely reward us. There is no need for you to give up your heart. I did that for you, my son. I am your mother, and I have made every sacrifice for you. Now I ask only that you do this one thing for me!"

Elwarrd hung his head, shoulders slumped, and the sword slipped from his hand, clattering to the floor. The old countess clasped her hands, her expression exultant. Grace glanced at the others. Vani had regained her feet, and Beltan had pulled the knife from his shoulder. The wound was bleeding freely, but a swift glimpse with the Touch told Grace it was not serious. Falken gave them all a sharp look. If there was a time to act, it was then.

Before they could move, Elwarrd lifted his head. His green eyes shone with sorrow, but his expression was hard. "Mother," he whispered tenderly. "Beloved mother. You have done so much for me. But now there is only one thing I can do for you."

And with a gentle motion, he pushed her backward into the fireplace.

The old countess gaped in surprise. Then, like a piece of magician's flash paper, her black gown went up in a puff of flame. The fire licked at her, melting the white paint that masked her face and bubbling it away, withering and cracking her flesh.

"My son!" came a piteous cry. Two shriveled arms reached outward from the roaring fire, and the countess stumbled out of the fireplace, groping for Elwarrd. She collided with one of the posts, and flames streaked up the wood. "Help me, my son!"

"Yes, Mother."

Elwarrd retrieved the sword, and with one clean swing he lopped off her head. The grisly orb rolled into a corner, still smoking, and her body fell against another post, setting it ablaze like the first. Grace jerked her head up. Flames ran along the wooden ceiling.

"Go!" Elwarrd said to Grace, his voice hoarse as he shouted over the roar. "All of you. You have my leave."

Fear stabbed at Grace's heart. She moved to the earl. "What about you, my lord?"

"I will see to it these creatures do not follow you. But there may be others at the front door. Take this." He held the sword out toward Beltan, and the knight accepted it.

Panic blossomed in Grace's chest like the fire. The heat was already almost unbearable. "But you can't stay here. The castle is going to burn."

It almost seemed he smiled. "Please, my lady. If you truly do care for me somewhere in your heart, let me do this. Let me do this one noble thing in my life." He gazed at the charred husk of the old countess. "She denied me my chance to be a knight, and my chance to be a man." His sea-green eyes locked on Grace. "Don't you deny me this, my lady."

Anguish filled Grace—as well as understanding. She hesitated, then leaned toward him and kissed his brow. Without waiting to see his reaction, she turned away. In the ED, she had always known when to let a patient go.

"Come on, Grace," Falken said, taking her arm, pulling her toward a doorway. Flames filled half the kitchens now, turning the place into an inferno. "We have to go."

Numb, Grace let the bard pull her forward. They ran down a long corridor as flames raced behind them and hot cinders rained from above. They dashed up a smoke-filled stairwell, then came to the front door of the keep. They glanced around, but if there were any *feydrim* lurking, they were invisible for the smoke. Grace could feel a great wind as air was sucked into the keep through the doors, feeding the greedy fire. Everything within the keep's stone walls was made of wood. The whole structure was going to burn.

Clutching one another, they stumbled through the doors into the night. They raced down the steps, away from the inferno, to the bailey below. Only when they came to a halt did Grace look back. The keep burned atop its hill like a great torch, sparks rising to the stars.

"Thank you, Sir Elwarrd," Grace whispered.

Beltan let out a grunt. "I think we just found the rest of the countess's *feydrim*."

Grace turned around. They were clearly visible in the firelight: a dozen lanky forms scattered around the bare ground of the bailey, their maws open in frozen snarls, their fur matted with dark blood.

Vani knelt beside one of the creatures. "It was a sword that slew this creature."

"This one, too," Beltan said, standing back up.

Falken raised a hand. "Listen."

After a second Grace heard it: the pounding of hooves against hard ground. There was no point in running; they could never move fast enough on foot, and the barren moor offered no cover. Moments later, the black horses came pounding into the bailey, forming a circle around the four.

Grace craned her neck to look up at the massive horses. The beasts wore black armor on their breasts, just like their riders. Black helmets covered the faces of the knights, and in their hands were black swords. Their shields were crimson, emblazoned with the symbol of a black crown encircling a silver tower.

Beltan held the sword before him, but his shoulder still bled, and the sword wavered in his grip. Vani's hands were raised, ready, but she couldn't stand entirely straight. Leweth's blow had bruised her ribs badly.

Falken moved in front of Grace. "What do you want?"

One of the knights spurred his horse forward. Grace knew if he stood on the ground, the man would tower over even Beltan. He seemed almost to burst out of his armor. His jet breastplate was marked with three silver crowns. She supposed he was their leader. With his sword, he pointed past Falken, toward Grace. She could see blood on the tip of the blade.

"She's the one we want." His voice was deep, echoing inside his helm. "You know what to do, brothers."

And Grace could only watch as the circle of dark knights closed in.

PART THREE

THE WHITE

SHIP

33.

Travis sat in a rickety chair on the front porch of the Bluebell, Miss Guenivere curled up on his lap, and watched dark clouds roll in from the west.

Summer laid claim to the mountains now. The Fourth of July had come and gone, and just about every afternoon thunderheads built up on the shoulders of Castle Peak, filling the valley with the distant booming of Indian war drums. Most days the clouds kept close to the old mountain, but sometimes, as the afternoon wore on, the clouds would reach out over the valley and—with a crack like a dynamite blast—down would come a torrent of raindrops so big and so cold, each one made you think of snowmelt lakes under lonely skies.

For ten minutes the rain would pound against the tin roofs of Castle City, loud as a herd of mule deer, turning gritty avenues into red, rushing creeks. Then, as suddenly as it started, the rain would cease. The clouds would roll down the valley; the sun's rays would reach through thin mountain air, lapping at the puddles. And both earth and sky were left as green and vivid blue as the flowers that grew in the shade next to the boardinghouse, and from which the establishment took its name.

Sometimes, as he sat there on the porch, Travis wished the rain could wash away all of his worries, just like it washed the dust from Grant Street, and give him a clean beginning.

And what would you do with a new start, Travis? Stay here in Castle City, in this century?

In a way it was tempting. He liked living at Maudie's, and he had his job at the Mine Shaft. What was more, Jack Graystone would be arriving in town soon. He imagined Jack coming to see him as he worked at the saloon, wanting help carrying brass lamps or moth-eaten chairs or whatever unwieldy load of antiques he had just bought. It would be like old times.

Too old, Travis. You don't belong here. You don't own the

Mine Shaft. You can't stay at Maudie's because she's going to die soon. And they're going to hang Sareth.

He waited all afternoon, but the rain never came that day. Just the clouds and the thunder, filling the air with a buzzing energy, like lightning about to strike.

At five o'clock, the smell of frying fish drifted out the front door of the Bluebell. Guenivere yawned and hopped down from Travis's lap, no doubt in search of Maudie and a few morsels of rainbow trout. Travis reached into his pocket and pulled out the scarab.

The spider jewel crawled across his palm, probing with delicate gold legs. The ruby set into its abdomen glistened, as red as the single drop of blood he knew remained inside the scarab. That blood could transport them back to Eldh using the gate artifact safely hidden in the rafters up in their room. But what other wonders might be worked with it? Sareth said a single drop of blood from the god-king Orú was as powerful as the blood of a thousand sorcerers. And Travis had witnessed the transformation that consuming the blood of the scarab had wrought upon the Mournish man, Xemeth.

But what good had that power done him? The demon had drawn Xemeth in, consuming him. Orú himself was shackled by his own priests. Despite his power—or perhaps because of it—Orú had fallen into an endless slumber, and his priests had preyed upon him, drinking his blood to gain magic, storing the crimson fluid in scarabs like this one. Maybe, in the end, power was simply a prison. Or a death sentence.

His right hand tingled as the scarab crawled across it; he could feel the symbol embedded in his skin. It was invisible now, but the moment he spoke a rune it would glow bright silver.

And what about your power, Travis? Will it be your own undoing in the end? Or a world's?

Before he could answer that question, a stoop-shouldered figure approached along Grant Street and walked up the steps of the front porch. It was Durge, and he was bleeding.

Travis jumped to his feet and slipped the scarab into his pocket. "Durge, are you all right?"

There were small cuts on the left side of Durge's craggy face, and a bruise was forming along his cheekbone.

"It's nothing," the knight said in his somber voice. "A bottle thrown by some troublemaker, that's all. It struck me as I was returning to the jail with food for Sareth, and it was my own fault I was not quick enough to duck. I told Sir Tanner there was no reason I could not continue my day's work, but he ordered me to return here, and I am bound by my oath to obey him."

Travis knew the stoic knight would never admit he was hurt, and no doubt Tanner had known the same. "The sheriff was right," Travis said, taking Durge's arm and steering him toward the door. "We'd better have Lirith look at you."

They found the witch with Maudie in the kitchen.

"Lord above!" Maudie cried when she caught sight of Durge. "Mr. Dirk, what's happened to you?"

Lirith moved swiftly to the knight. She reached her hands toward him, then hesitated. Durge gave a stiff nod, and Lirith touched his cheek, examining him with gentle fingers.

The witch opened her eyes. "No bones are broken, so that is well. But there is glass in some of the cuts. We must get it out, or the wounds will not heal."

They seated Durge at the kitchen table. Maudie boiled a pair of tweezers, and once they cooled, Lirith used them to pluck slivers of glass out of Durge's cuts. Her motions were deft, and it was not in the knight's character to complain, but all the same he flinched each time she drew out a sliver.

"There are going to be scars," Lirith said, dabbing at the wounds with a cloth, cleaning them.

Durge winced. "Perhaps it will result in some improvement in the character of my countenance."

"Forgive my language," Maudie said, "but that's a bunch of bull droppings, Mr. Dirk. You have a fine face. It's strong and thoughtful. Why, I'd even daresay it's noble. And that's a long sight better than handsome any day. I bet you have a sweet woman waiting for you somewhere—don't tell me you don't. And you'll be a damn fool if you keep her waiting much longer just because you think she deserves someone better-looking."

Durge turned away, but not before crimson colored his cheeks along with the deepening bruise.

After that, Travis and Lirith helped Maudie set supper on the table while Durge went upstairs to change out of his blood-stained shirt. They talked little during the meal; Travis was keenly aware of the trio of miners who sat at the table. But once the men were gone—off to the saloons—Maudie made it clear she wanted to hear the full story of what had happened to Durge.

There wasn't much more to tell. Durge hadn't seen who threw the bottle, and if anyone else had glimpsed the perpetrator, they hadn't volunteered the information. Not that this surprised Travis. The furor over what had happened in the Mine Shaft on the Fourth of July had quieted in the week since, like a pond after a rock is thrown in, but a current of anger still flowed beneath the surface. The people of Castle City had been denied a lynching, and that didn't sit well with them. Even so, it might all have been forgotten if it hadn't been for those who kept dredging it back up, making sure the people remembered their outrage.

"Have you seen the *Castle City Clarion* today?" Travis said to Durge. The knight shook his head.

Maudie banged a hand on the table. "I've told you, I won't tolerate that dirt in my house!"

A few days ago, Maudie had collected all of the newspapers in the Bluebell and burned them out back. However, one of the miners had left that day's paper in the parlor, and Travis had found it before Maudie. He ran up to their room, retrieved the newspaper, and returned, unfolding it on the table. Maudie turned away, refusing even to look at it, but the others leaned close, reading the top story.

SHERIFF CONTINUES TO HARBOR MURDERER

Further proving Justice has no provenance in this town—at least not within the office of the Law—our own Sheriff, bound by an oath to serve and protect us, instead serves and protects a known fugitive within the very jailhouse the citizens of this town built with gold from their own pockets. This fugitive—one Mr. Samson of unknown and dubious extraction—was seen by many on the Fourth of July murdering one of our town's finest young men, Mr. Calvin Murray, in cold blood.

Even if the laws of Colorado require that this murderer be held until the arrival of the circuit judge two weeks hence—and by no means is it clear the laws do indeed demand this in such an extraordinary and egregious working of malice—certainly the laws do not require that the prisoner be kept in such a grand state, as would better befit a mining baron in the Silver Palace Hotel than a drifter and a man-killer.

Yet witnesses of the highest reliability report the prisoner sleeps on a soft bed, drinks fine whiskey, and has only to snap his fingers to be brought expensive meals of steak and potatoes by the town's own Deputies. Tell us, citizens, if you are eating so well yourself these days. —The Editors.

Travis sighed. "I think we know now why someone threw a bottle at you, Durge. Didn't you say you were taking Sareth his supper when it happened?"

"A man must eat," Durge said. "There is no kitchen at the jail, so we buy his meals from Mrs. Vickery's restaurant, as she gives us a good price. But by any estimation, Mrs. Vickery is not a skilled cook. I don't believe she knows how to prepare aught save beef and potatoes."

Travis glanced at Maudie. "And didn't you send a feather bed to the jail?"

"It's old, and it's lost half its feathers," Maudie said. "But I was worried about Mr. Samson sleeping on those bare wooden benches. He isn't well."

"And you gave Durge whiskey for him, didn't you, Lirith?"

The witch's brown eyes flashed. "It was not for Sareth's amusement. It is a distillation of herbs to ease his breathing. The alcohol provides a base for the elixir, nothing more."

"So it's all true, then." Travis folded the paper, hiding the article. "And it's all right here."

Lirith clenched her hands into fists. "How can they make the truth sound so . . . so horrible?"

"They're good at their job," Travis said. "And their job is selling papers."

Durge stroked his mustaches. "What I wonder is how the writer of these words learned all of these things. I believe I should like to talk to the owner of this newspaper."

"No, Mr. Dirk!" Maudie said, eyes going wide. "Mortimer Hale owns nearly half this town. He's the most powerful man in Castle City, and he's one of the hardest. I know that firsthand. Don't you go near him. Promise me you won't."

But Durge stayed silent and did not meet her eyes. Maudie clamped a hand to her mouth, stifling a gasp, and hurried into the kitchen.

"I want to go see him," Lirith said, rising from the table. "I want to go see Sareth. Now."

Durge shook his head. "Perhaps tomorrow, if there isn't another newspaper story. It isn't safe right now, my lady."

"And what about Sareth?" Lirith was trembling. "Is it safe for him?"

"Sir Tanner is watching him. And Deputy Wilson is at the jail as well. Sareth is safer there than anywhere else, my lady."

Lirith let out a shuddering breath. "I know, Durge." Her voice was low now. "I know he is. Thank you."

The knight nodded, then picked up a load of dishes and carried them into the kitchen after Maudie.

Travis stood and touched Lirith's shoulder. "We should be getting to the Mine Shaft now."

"Let me just wash my face."

While he waited, Travis sat again at the table and flipped through the newspaper. Besides the story about Sareth, there was little else of interest. "Morning Mayhem" reported that there must be wolves in the vicinity, as two head of cattle had been found mauled at a ranch just south of town. However, it wasn't the predators outside of Castle City Travis was worried about.

Lirith returned, face freshly scrubbed and wearing a brave expression. Travis took her arm, and together they headed out, cutting over to Elk Street, then walking along the boardwalk to the saloon.

Travis was aware of the occasional glance in their direction. But that was hardly unusual; both he and Lirith had a tendency to stand out in a crowd. As far as he knew, it still wasn't widely known that Sareth was their friend.

Or more than a friend to some, Travis.

"You love him, don't you?" he said as they walked. "Sareth."

Lirith missed a step, then kept walking, her gaze fixed forward. "It doesn't matter whether or not I love him. We can never be together. It is forbidden for a man of the Mournish to marry outside of his clan."

Travis felt a hot spark of anger. He hated things like that: arbitrary rules prescribed by a society, forcing you to live your life a particular way for no reason at all, save that that was how others wanted you to live it.

"Why doesn't he leave his clan, then?"

"And if he was not Mournish, would he still be Sareth?" She shook her head. "It's possible he might give that up for me. And if he did, I would never forgive myself. I would never be able to look at him without seeing in his eyes that I made him sacrifice everything he was, everything that was in his blood, just to be with me."

"Maybe that's what he wants."

"I suppose he might even believe that. For a time, at least. But in the end it would eat at his heart like a serpent." She let out a heavy breath. "No, I love him too much to be the one who destroys him."

"But his clan is a world away, Lirith."

"And does that change what he is? Better still, does it change what I am? It is more than his clan that keeps us apart. There are—"

She pressed her lips shut and held a hand to her stomach. What had she been about to say? Travis couldn't bring himself to ask. He tightened his grip on her arm, and she leaned against him as they kept walking.

The boardwalk was crowded with people, as was typical for a Friday evening, but the throng seemed quieter than usual, faces longer and more subdued. Maybe it was anger that had stolen the life out of the air—anger over Sareth and Sheriff Tanner.

Or maybe it was fear.

At first all Travis saw was a tight knot of people on the boardwalk. A buzz of conversation rose on the air, along with a number of jeers. There was a stifled scream, and a man hastily led a woman away, her hand clamped to her mouth.

"What's going on up there?" Lirith said.

Travis felt dread trickle into his stomach. "I don't know. I'm going to go look."

He released Lirith's arm and pressed forward, aware that the witch followed after him. The crowd was gathered around the mouth of an alley. Something was there in the space between buildings. It dangled like a bunch of rags caught on a fence.

"Serves him right!" a man called out.

"Sinner!" hissed the woman next to him, her expression exultant.

The pair turned and moved away. Travis and Lirith jostled their way forward, then saw what the crowd was gawking at. In the alley, draped on a pair of crossed timbers that had been planted in the dirt, was Niles Barrett.

The Englishman's arms were spread wide, lashed to the crosspiece with rope, and he was slumped forward, so that Travis couldn't fully see his face. He wasn't moving. Blood stained his forehead, and several of his fingers splayed out at crooked angles, broken.

"Who did this?" Travis said, choking on the words. The man next to him pointed at Barrett's suit coat. On it was pinned a piece of paper bearing neatly lettered words.

> THY SHALT HONOR THY FATHER
> AND THY MOTHER.

And below that, in smaller lettering.

> THERE IS A NEW LAW IN THIS TOWN. THIS IS
> WHAT HAPPENS TO THOSE WHO DEFY
> THE CRUSADE FOR PURITY.

"Travis!" Lirith clutched his arm. "He's still alive."

Barrett's head shifted to one side. A moan escaped his bloodied lips. The man next to Travis let out a laugh. Travis turned and glared at him.

"Get Sheriff Tanner," he growled. "Now!"

There must have been some authority in Travis's tone, for the man's laughter fell short. He stared for a moment, then turned and ran down the boardwalk, calling for the sheriff.

"All of you, get out of here," Travis said, his voice rising. "I said get out!"

A crack of thunder shook the air, and Travis wasn't so certain it was from the clouds in the sky. He could feel his right hand tingling. Startled, the people hurried away. Although some didn't go far, and they stood on the boardwalk, watching with hard eyes. Energy sizzled inside Travis, straining to leap out. All he had to do was speak a rune.

No, he wouldn't hurt others; he wasn't like them. He clenched his jaw, and together he and Lirith began to untie Barrett.

34.

Lirith shut the bedroom door—softly, even though Lord Barrett could not have heard it—and headed downstairs. Would that she possessed Grace's abilities as a healer, or even Aryn's untamed but depthless strength. It was in the art of the Sight where Lirith's greatest talents lay. However, even she could not see whether he would live or die. She had done all she could; now they could only wait.

She found the others in the parlor of the Bluebell.

"How is he?" Travis said, setting down a chipped porcelain coffee cup.

Lirith opened her mouth to speak and yawned instead. It was just after dawn; she hadn't slept all night. "His wounds are no longer bleeding, and I've set the fingers that were broken. I believe he comes close to waking at times. He'll mutter a few words, as if in a dream, before sinking again into slumber. I caught one word. I think it was *gold*."

Durge gave a grim nod. "Likely the men who did this to him took his gold."

Travis glanced at the knight. "Do you really think they were just common thieves, Durge?"

The knight blew a breath through his mustaches.

Lirith sat and accepted the cup of coffee Travis poured for her. Coffee wasn't *maddok*—it was more bitter, and it lacked the other drink's characteristic hint of spice—but she couldn't deny its power was considerable. After a few sips she felt a welcome tingling in her chest.

"How was your work at the saloon last night?" she asked Travis.

After they had brought Niles Barrett back to the boarding-house with the help of the sheriff and Deputy Wilson—Durge had been keeping watch over Sareth at the jail—Travis had headed for the Mine Shaft to tell Manypenny what had happened and that Lirith wouldn't be in that night.

Travis sighed, running a hand over his shaved head. "I probably shouldn't have bothered staying. The place was almost empty. Not even old Ezekial Frost came by."

"Perhaps people decided it was a good night to stay in," Durge said, holding his littlest finger out as he lifted one of the fragile coffee cups with exaggerated care.

Lirith imagined Durge was right. Once word of what had happened to Lord Barrett spread through town, people had quickly gone back to their homes. Travis had told her the message pinned to Barrett was from a list of ten such commandments made long ago by a god of this world. And who in this town had not broken at least one of those commandments?

Lirith set down her cup. "I am not certain I have done everything for Lord Barrett that can be done. Do you think we should send for the town's doctor?"

"No, Miss Lily," Maudie said from the door of the parlor. She moved to the table and set down a fresh pot of coffee. "Better that you see to Mr. Barrett than Dr. Svensson."

Durge gave her a sharp look. "Why should we not send for the doctor, Lady Maudie?"

"This is why, Mr. Dirk." She tossed down a copy of the *Castle City Clarion* next to the coffeepot. "Dr. Svensson is married to Bertha Hale Svensson. Mortimer Hale's sister."

Lirith understood Maudie's meaning. Mortimer Hale was the publisher of the *Clarion*, and Travis believed it might be

Hale who was behind the vigilance committee—or the Crusade for Purity, as it had named itself last night. Of course, what had happened to Lord Barrett bore the violent mark of Lionel Gentry. But Gentry could be working for Hale. And, given his connection by marriage, so could Dr. Svensson.

Travis gazed at the paper. "I thought you had forbidden the *Clarion* in your house, Maudie."

"That I did. I cleaned this out of one of the boarder's rooms upstairs. And it's going right to the incinerator."

She swept up the paper before they could read the story on the front page, but Lirith caught the headline:

AT LAST, JUSTICE IS COME.

Durge stood and put on his hat. It was time for him to head over to the jail to relieve Sheriff Tanner. Travis yawned—evidently he hadn't slept the previous night either—and went up to their rooms to rest. Lirith supposed she should do the same; she was exhausted. However, the coffee had done its work, and she felt abuzz with energy. Better to put it to use. She picked up the empty cups and headed to the kitchen to help Maudie with the breakfast dishes.

Maudie greeted her with a smile as Lirith put on an apron, and the two women worked in that busy, pleasant sort of silence that comes from simple work and comfortable companionship. When everything was clean, Maudie toasted slices of bread on the top of the stove and set them on the table with a jar of wild strawberry jam.

"Early mornings need two breakfasts," she said.

Lirith's stomach was growling, and she didn't disagree.

"It's a shame what they did to poor Mr. Barrett," Maudie said with a sigh. "And after all he's suffered in his life."

Lirith raised an eyebrow. "What do you mean?"

"He was banished to America, you know." Maudie turned her gaze toward Lirith. "His father is an English earl, and Niles is the eldest son. But some years ago, his father stripped away all of Niles's right to his inheritance and put him on a ship to New York, telling him never to come back."

Lirith thought of the notice that had been pinned to Barrett's coat. *Thou shalt honor thy father and thy mother.* "Why did his father banish him?"

"I suppose there aren't many in town who know the whole story. Of course, most everyone knows Barrett isn't a ladies' man. He used to come into the Bluebell, but just to have a drink and talk, never to engage one of my girls." Maudie let out a fond laugh. "He said he liked the ambiance."

Lirith smiled. She reached across the table and took Maudie's hand.

"He told me about it late one night," Maudie went on. "We were swapping sad stories after drinking too much gin. I told him the tale of every one of my husbands. And then..." She lifted her shoulders in a sigh. "He was a lieutenant in the Royal Navy. Niles showed me a picture, and he was the handsomest young man you could imagine. Eyes as deep and calm as the sea. Only then the elder Lord Barrett found the letters they had exchanged. Niles's officer was stripped of his rank and sent to a post in Australia. And Niles was sent here."

"I don't understand," Lirith said. "Why were Niles Barrett and his lieutenant made to part?"

Maudie let out a gasp. "You must come from another world, Miss Lily, if you don't know. Society is hard to those who live outside the borders drawn by those within. I suppose I know it as well as Mr. Barrett does. I've given up inviting the town's best ladies over to dinner. I suppose they think you can take the woman out of the brothel, but you can't take the brothel out of the woman."

Lirith went stiff, and Maudie regarded her with a gentle understanding. But how could Maudie know about those years Lirith had spent dancing in Gulthas's house? No one knew. Only somehow she did.

Lirith started to pull away, but Maudie held her hand tight. "Don't you believe them who say such things, Miss Lily. You're a good woman through and through. I can see it. Mr. Samson is lucky to have you."

"Is he?"

Maudie let her hand go. Lirith pressed it to her stomach. She could feel it: the dark space inside her that would never be filled with life. What did she have to give Sareth besides what she had given all the men who came to Gulthas's house?

But maybe that was the answer. Sareth could not take a wife outside his clan. But what about a mistress? As Maudie had said, there were those who lived their lives outside the circle drawn by proper men and woman. Did not Lirith already dwell beyond those boundaries?

She stood up, flushed with an energy that came not only from the coffee. "I have to go see Sareth now."

Concern filled Maudie's eyes. "Are you sure that's a good idea, Miss Lily? Mr. Dirk says it isn't safe for you to go to the jail. You know folk are still calling for Mr. Samson's hanging. You don't want to make matters worse by drawing attention."

But Lirith hardly heard her. She untied the apron and threw it down. "Good-bye, Lady Maudie," she said, then without waiting for a reply she rushed out the kitchen door.

Lirith hurried down Grant Street. The jail lay at the far end of town, a mile away. She ran until her lungs burned, walked until she caught her breath, than ran again. She felt eyes watching her in curiosity, but she didn't care. Grant Street dead-ended at the livery. She turned down a narrow side street to cut over to Elk Street.

And collided with Ezekial Frost.

"Whoa there, missy. Where are yeh going in such a hurry?"

Bony but strong hands caught her, keeping her from falling. She found herself face-to-face with the old mountain man. Scraps of white hair jutted out from beneath a cap of mangy animal fur. Tobacco had stained his beard and teeth, and his eyes were yellow with jaundice—no doubt caused by too much drink.

"Well, now, so it's purdy Miss Lily from the Mine Shaft who's run into me."

"Excuse me," she said, extricating herself from his tenacious grasp. "I have to be going."

A canny look stole into his eyes. "I'm going to be going, too, Miss Lily. Going back."

Some of her urgency was replaced by puzzlement. The old man's words seemed important somehow. "What do you mean?"

He let out a cackle of laughter and slapped his thigh. "Yeh be a smart one, Miss Lily, to play dumb like that. But I know yeh know all about them Seven Cities just like I do."

"What Seven Cities?"

"Why, the Cities of Cibóla. Them cities of gold that men have hunted fer five hundred years, first the Spaniards, then them who came after. Only it weren't them who found the way, it were me. I been there once, and I never should have left." His eyes locked on hers. "I know yeh've been there, too, Miss Lily. I seen yeh come on through, just like the gold man. I got to know the likes of him there. He'll be looking for a way back. Only when he opens it up, I'm gonna scamper on through before he does, quick as a jackrabbit." The old man reached for her arm. "I'll take yeh with me, Miss Lily, if that's what yeh want."

Frost's breath reeked of corn liquor and decay. She pulled away from him. "I have to go," she said, and this time she ran down the street before the mountain man could say anything more.

When she reached the sheriff's office, she expected to find Durge or young Deputy Wilson sitting behind the battered desk, but instead it was Sheriff Tanner himself. His eyebrows rose as he took her in.

Lirith supposed she was a mess. She did her best to straighten her dress. "I've come to see Sareth."

"All right, Miss Lily," the sheriff said in his calm drawl. "He's allowed a visitor. But just for ten minutes, and you're not to reach through the bars or give him anything. That's the law, and I know as a good woman you'll respect it."

She gave a curt nod. Anything to see Sareth.

Tanner rose and moved to a door at the back of the room. It was wood with an iron-barred square that provided a view into the jail. Tanner took a ring of keys from his belt and chose one. Lirith noticed that it took him a long moment to fit the key in the lock. He opened the door.

"I'll come get you when your time's up."

She stepped through. Tanner shut the door behind her, and she heard the lock turn.

"*Beshala,*" said a soft voice.

Her eyes adjusted to the dimness, and she made out three cells, each one fitted with a door made of iron bars. Two of the cells were empty, but in one stood a shadowy figure. Wasn't this how she had first glimpsed him—standing in the gloom in the grove beneath Ar-tolor?

Lirith moved to the row of bars. She had not seen him since the night of Calvin Murray's death, and she knew it was not just the dimness of the jail that caused the darkness to gather beneath his eyes and in the hollow of his cheeks.

Her chest grew tight. "Sareth, you're not well."

"I am now that I see you." He stepped closer to the bars, but as he did he winced.

"Your leg," she said. "It's hurting you, isn't it?"

"I had thought that wound healed. But I've noticed it more and more since we came through the gate to this world. Yet it's nothing, *beshala*. A memory of pain, that's all. And I am not capable of any feeling but joy right now."

She started to reach for him through the bars, then pulled her hand back. "The sheriff says I am not to touch you."

"And my people say I am not to touch you."

Lirith folded her arms over her chest, as if to hide her heart. The laws of his people were like the iron bars, designed to keep them apart. But Lirith knew now there was another way.

She couldn't meet his eyes. "I cannot give you marriage, Sareth. And I cannot give you a child, for no life will ever take root inside my body again, that I know. But there is one thing yet I can give you."

She felt his confusion. "What are you talking about, *beshala*?"

She held her chin up, forcing herself to look at him. "I would be your whore, Sareth. I cannot give you love or life. But I can give you my body, for it is all I have left to me. And I give it freely, that you may do anything with it you wish. Even your clan's laws cannot deny that gift."

He clutched the bars, and a moan escaped him as he shook his head. Pain pierced her chest. Was he refusing this, the only gift she could give to him?

"Oh, *beshala*." His deep voice thrummed with anguish. "Your heart I would take gladly, if only the ways of my clan allowed it. Your love I would cherish as if it were the greatest of gems. Only I would not lock it away. I would wear it about my throat, letting it rest against my chest where it could burn bright for all to see. But your body is a treasure I cannot make my own."

No, she wouldn't accept this. "But surely the laws of your clan allow you to take a mistress."

"They do."

"Then I would follow the Mournish like a ghost, always hovering in the darkness and cold just beyond the bright circle of their fires. I care not. I would wait only for those times when you could steal away, into the shadows, to fill me with your warmth."

"And that is the one thing I cannot do, *beshala*."

She stared, beyond words.

He leaned his head against the bars. "It was the demon, *beshala*. It stole not just my leg from me. It stole my power as a man as well."

"You mean—?"

A bitter smile touched his lips. "No, *beshala*. All of my body is intact, save for my leg. But it might as well not be. No passion, no matter how strongly I feel it, can cause me to stir as a man should. It has been thus ever since that day Xemeth and I first found the demon, and I knew its touch."

It was too cruel. Lirith tried to laugh, but the sound came out as a sob. "So the one gift I can give you is the one that means nothing to you."

His coppery gaze found hers, held it. "No, *beshala*. You have given me the greatest gift I could ever have asked for. What man ever truly knows his fate? Yet here is my own fate, made manifest as you stand before me. So what if it is bitter? At least I know it, and it is mine."

She pressed her own face to the bars, so close to his she could feel the heat radiating from his cheek, touching her skin like the most intimate caress.

"I will love you forever, Sareth."

"And I love you this moment," he said.

They stayed that way until a knock sounded at the door.

"It's time, Miss Lily," came Tanner's voice through the bars.

The lock turned; the door opened. Without a word, Lirith turned and left her heart in the shadows behind her.

35.

Durge knelt amid the sagebrush, leaning close to examine the dead lamb. The sun jabbed through the thin mountain air like a hot knife, and horseflies lurched around in drunken circles. Vermin had only just begun to discover the little white corpse. A few more hours in this heat, and Durge knew that would change.

"Do you think it was wolves or coyotes, Señor Dirk?" asked the man who squatted beside him. He was wiry and compact, his hair black and his skin a wind-worn brown. His name was Manuel Dominguez, and Durge guessed he came from the Dominion of *Meksako*, which Sir Tanner said lay to the south of *Yewessay*.

Durge studied the pattern of wounds that penetrated the lamb's woolly skin, exposing flesh and bone. There were long gashes on the creature's back and deeper punctures in its right side. The throat was the worst; it had been savaged so brutally the creature's head twisted backward, attached to its body by only a grisly cord of bone and sinew. The other two lambs had shown similar patterns of mutilation.

"This looks to me like the work of wolves," Durge said, pointing to the lamb's shredded neck. In Embarr, there were huge gray wolves that came out of the mountains to prowl the moors in winter, and he had seen the damage they could wreak upon sheep or kine. "But the wounds upon its back look more like those made by a great cat."

Dominguez looked up. "Would a mountain lion come so far into the valley?"

Durge rocked back on his heels and shaded his eyes. Dominguez's small sheep ranch was in the middle of the sage-covered plain that blanketed the floor of the valley; the mountains were two leagues away, perhaps three.

"One might come so far, if it were hungry," Durge said. "But it makes little sense that a lion and a wolf should work together. And I do not think these marks were made by an animal at all." He pointed to the deep wounds on the creature's side. "These look as if they were made by a knife. Did one of the men who work for you begin to butcher the creature?"

Dominguez shook his head. "I have no men who work for me, only my sons. And I was the first to find the lambs."

What he saw confounded Durge. This creature had been slain by talon, tooth, and knife—each weapon wielded seemingly by a different creature. Even stranger, why had the predator not fed upon the lamb after killing it? He brushed his fingers over the dirt around the lamb. It was hard and dry; there was no trace of blood. Perhaps the slayer had fed after all. But what creature killed only to drink blood? No animal Durge knew of behaved in such a manner.

"I will tell the sheriff what has happened here," Durge said to the rancher as they stood. "I imagine he will send men out to hunt for the animal that did this."

Dominguez nodded, his brown eyes filled with gratitude. "I thank you, Señor Dirk. My ranch is small, and so is my herd. A man offered not long ago to buy my land from me. If I lose many more sheep, I will have to take his offer."

Durge felt sympathy for the rancher. In Embarr, there was no greater shame than to be a freeman without land, save to be a serf or a beggar. "Who is this man who offered to purchase your land from you?"

"I do not know his name. He came from over there."

Dominguez pointed to the east. Durge squinted and could just see it in the distance: a split-rail fence stretching for league after league, and beyond it the shapes of barns, stables, and a gigantic house with many wings and pointed spires that made Durge think of the finer manor houses of Eldh. A local lord must live there. That made sense. It was cruel but not unusual for a nobleman to buy the land of a freeman who was in debt to him, and then allow the man to keep working the land he had once owned, thus turning him into a serf in all but name.

Durge bid the rancher farewell, then mounted the horse he had ridden from town and urged it into a canter. Sir Tanner kept three horses at the livery, and while they were fine animals, none had a fraction of the strength or heart of his own charger, Blackalock. He supposed Blackalock was still in the stables at Ar-tolor where Durge had left him. Would Durge ever return to Eldh to claim him again?

I imagine Blackalock will grow old and die waiting for you to come back, Durge.

The gloomy thought occurred to him out of habit. It was his nature always to assume the worst; that way disappointment could never be a fact. Only, for some reason, today this thought annoyed Durge. What use was it to imagine Blackalock pining in his stall? Why should Durge not get back to Eldh? From what Travis said—and Durge had never known Travis to be anything but trustworthy—his friend Jack Graystone was a runelord, and little as Durge cared for magic, it was magic that had gotten them there, and surely such a powerful wizard could help them.

You will get back to Eldh, Durge tried telling himself, and the thought felt strangely good. *You will find a way back, and you will see your old friend Blackalock again.*

Durge found himself grinning as he rode, although the expression felt oddly tight, as if the muscles of his face had all but forgotten how to work this way. Then an image flashed in his mind, and it wasn't of a big warhorse. It was of a regal young woman with dark hair and sapphire blue eyes.

Durge's grin shattered like glass.

You are a fool, old man. You are a doddering fool if you hope one so young and fresh can love you.

Yet he did hope, didn't he? Much as he wished he could deny it, the old Mournish woman who had read his fate was right. He loved Lady Aryn, foolish as it was, and he could sooner stop autumn from turning to winter than stop himself from feeling such tenderness for her.

Then maybe it is better if you do not return to Eldh.

And even though he knew that was a lie, he held on to that idea, letting it armor his heart. Because never seeing his home or his horse again was better than seeing the horror in her blue eyes when she discovered the truth of what he felt for her.

It was early afternoon by the time Durge rode back into

Castle City. Elk Street bustled with people and animals like the bailey of a great castle, but for all its activity there was a pall that hung over the town like smoke. By now everyone in town knew of Lord Barrett's beating. And while few seemed to care for the Englishman, many feared who this so-called Crusade for Purity might see fit to punish next.

Durge returned the horse to the livery, then walked to the sheriff's office. He entered to find the front room empty; neither Sir Tanner nor young Deputy Wilson sat behind the desk. Perhaps one of them was in the jail?

As Durge started toward the back, a glint of light caught his eyes. He knelt. On the floor next to the desk lay a small glass bottle. It was empty, save for a few drops of some dark residue at the bottom. Durge picked up the bottle, then moved to the door to the jail and peered through the bars.

In one of the cells, on a wooden cot overlain with Maudie's feather bed, lay Sareth. The Mournish man seemed to sleep more each passing day. Durge was no healer, not like his noble mistress Lady Grace, but he knew Sareth's sickness was growing worse. If he stayed in jail much longer, Durge feared he might die.

Then again, if Sareth left the jail, his death was all but certain. The vigilance committee would hang Sareth by the neck the moment he was freed. Nor would any of Castle City's folk stop them. Many of the town's people had come to Sir Tanner these last days, asking him to release Sareth. Folk whispered that it was because Sir Tanner kept Sareth locked up that the Crusade had made its presence known by harming Lord Barrett. They believed things would only get worse until the Crusade lynched Sareth for the murder of Calvin Murray. Durge knew they were right on one count: Things were indeed going to get worse.

Other than Sareth, the jail was empty. There were no lawbreakers to imprison these days—no thieves, no swindlers, no drifters. The Crusade had run them all out of town. Or, Durge supposed, had shot them and pushed their bodies into ravines or off cliffs, even if their crimes were as simple as public drunkenness or petty theft. Durge believed men should be punished for their crimes. However, the Crusade for Purity seemed to offer but one penalty for any transgression, no matter how slight—or how imaginary.

Where was Sir Tanner? Surely the sheriff would not leave Sareth alone. Then Durge heard a faint sound: the clink of glass against metal. It had come from the shed tacked onto the side of the jail, where coal for the stove would be kept if it were winter. Durge moved to the narrow door; it was open a crack, and he peered through.

Sir Tanner stood in the shed, his back mostly to Durge. He bent forward, his narrow shoulders hunched as if in pain. Durge could just see two objects in his hands: a tin cup and a small glass bottle like the one Durge had found on the floor, only this one was full of the dark fluid. Tanner was trying to pour some of the liquid into the cup, but his right hand shook violently, and the bottle rattled against the rim. At last he managed to hold the bottle steady, and he poured several drops into the cup. Tanner lifted the cup, draining it. He stood perfectly still for a moment, then—his hands finally steady—he stoppered the bottle.

Durge knew he had just seen something he shouldn't. He slipped the empty bottle into his pocket and stole quietly to the front door of the office. Duplicity ran counter to his nature, but all the same he opened the front door, then shut it again loudly. He walked toward the desk, making certain his boots stamped on the floor.

Tanner stepped from the side door. "Hello, Mr. Dirk," the sheriff said in his calm drawl. "I didn't think you'd be back so soon from the Dominguez place."

"I believe I saw all there was to see," Durge said, and he described the three mauled lambs the rancher had shown him.

Tanner's eyes were sharp as he listened, although his face bore the shadow of weariness that was always present. It seemed he had grown thinner these last days; his suit hung on him as upon a tailor's rack.

You should talk to Lady Lirith about it later, Durge told himself. *If there is something wrong with Sir Tanner, no doubt she will have seen it.*

The afternoon was long and troubling.

Not long after Durge returned to the jail, Deputy Wilson

arrived, his round cheeks flushed from running. There was some sort of commotion over on Aspen Street.

Leaving Wilson at the jail, Durge and Tanner jogged several blocks. They saw the crowd first, then pushed their way through to find a disconcerting sight. One of the storefronts that lined the street was completely gone. Only the rear of the building remained; broken planks and shards of glass littered the ground. Smoke drifted on the air, and Durge caught a sharp tinge of sulfur that reminded him of his alchemical experiments.

After questioning people in the crowd, Durge and Tanner managed to piece together what had happened. The building housed a gambling establishment run by a family from the Dominion of China, offering a game of chance called paigow. The building had been torn apart by an explosion—no doubt worked with the same volatile black powder that was used to make fireworks and break apart rocks in the mines.

Astonishingly, no one had been seriously injured in the blast. A few people passing on the street had suffered scratches from flying glass, but none of the members of the family that ran the establishment had been inside. Durge spoke to the head of the household, a tiny old man with a long white braid and eyes that were all but lost amid wrinkled skin.

According to the old man, a pair of men wearing black masks had entered the gambling parlor, which was closed at the time, brandishing guns. One of the men had forced the frightened family out back. After a few minutes, the second man had come running out, and the two strangers rode away, laughing and discharging their pistols into the air. Before the family could enter the building again, the explosion had ripped it apart.

"My daughter found this just before the men came," the old man said, handing a paper to Durge. "It was nailed to the door, but I cannot read it."

Durge looked at the paper. It read simply: *Thou shalt not steal.* So it was another one of their commandments. But had not the Crusade just stolen everything from this family? It seemed the crusaders wished only for others to follow these commandments; they felt no need to follow the rules themselves.

"What does it say?" the old man said.

Durge crumpled up the paper. "It says these were evil men who did this."

The old man nodded, eyes sad, and returned to his family.

Tanner gave Durge a curious look as they headed back to the jail. "I didn't know you spoke Chinese, Mr. Dirk."

Startled, Durge realized the old man must have been speaking in a different tongue than the one spoken here. However, with the fragment of the silver coin in his pocket, it seemed to Durge that everyone spoke the tongue of the Dominions, even though he knew they weren't.

Unsure what to say, Durge settled for saying nothing. Once at the jail, Tanner sent Deputy Wilson off on a number of errands, making sure the Chinese family had a place to stay, and arranging for workmen to clean up the debris left by the explosion. Durge wondered what Tanner intended to do. Surely the sheriff could work against this Crusade now that they had acted in such an open manner. However, Tanner said nothing, except to tell Durge to go home.

"I believe I would like to keep watch at the jail tonight," Durge replied, eyeing Tanner's weary face. "You can relieve me in the morning."

"What about your supper, Mr. Dirk? And sleep?"

"Mrs. Vickery always makes food enough for two." That wasn't entirely true, but Durge knew Sareth would eat little. "And I feel I have no sleep in me tonight."

Tanner looked like he wanted to protest, then he sighed, and it seemed weariness won out. "All right, Mr. Dirk. I'll stop by the Bluebell on my way home and let Maudie know not to expect you. She'll fret otherwise."

Just as the shadow of Castle Peak fell across the town, Mrs. Vickery's husband brought a tray to the door. (After the bottle was thrown at Durge, Tanner had begun paying Mrs. Vickery extra to have meals delivered.) Durge took it back into the jailhouse, woke Sareth up, and uncovered the tray.

As usual, it was beef and potatoes—the former every bit as

overdone as the latter were undercooked. Durge dragged a bench forward so they could sit close and share food, and it might have been like a meal at the boardinghouse save for the bars between them. Sareth picked at one of the potatoes but ate none of the beef. Durge ate what Sareth did not—although his jaw ached by the time he finished chewing the beef—then rose to take away the tray.

"I'm not going to make it, am I, Durge?" Sareth said.

Durge stopped in the doorway, turning around. Sareth sat on the edge of the cot, hands clasped. His face was lost in shadow, although Durge could see the glint of his coppery eyes.

"Lady Lirith is a capable healer," Durge said. "I am certain you will not perish under her care."

Durge had meant the words to comfort. However, Sareth winced as if he had been stung.

"That's not what I meant." The Mournish man's voice was low and hoarse. "They're going to come for me soon. Gentry and Ellis and their gang. Promise me you won't let yourself get hurt trying to protect me. Lirith needs you, and so does Travis." Sareth stood, gripping the bars of the cell. "Don't fight for my sake. Promise me."

Durge's voice was stern. "I will promise you no such thing. I am a knight and lord of Embarr. It is not your place to say how I shall employ my sword."

Without further words, Durge left the jail, locking the door behind him.

The horned moon rose outside the window. Midnight came and went like a ghost. Durge sat at the desk, back rigid, eyes forward. It was no burden for him to keep watch all night; he had done it countless times over the years. Sometimes younger knights would ask him what his trick was, how he stayed awake as the hours passed. It was simple, Durge told them. The will to do one's duty had to be stronger than the desire to sleep. Durge's will always was.

Or always had been.

There came the crystalline sound of shattering glass. Durge snapped his head up, and only as he did this did he realize it had been resting against the desk.

You are getting old, Durge of Stonebreak. Old and feeble. It is time to spend your years wrapped in a blanket by the fire, drinking soup from a wooden bowl held in trembling hands. If you don't get killed first.

Despite his lapse, he was up and moving before the shards of glass finished tinkling to the floor. He made out the scene in the lamplight. One of the panes of glass in the front windows was broken. Lying on the floor was the stone that had done the deed, and tied to the stone was a small piece of paper.

Durge moved to the window and peered outside, but the street was deserted. He bent, knees creaking, and retrieved the stone. The message on the paper was printed in a neat hand: *Release the gypsy or prepare for all Hell to break loose.*

Durge set the paper on the desk, then opened the front door and stepped outside. He knew he would be silhouetted against the light inside, making him an easy target. However, he also knew he would not be harmed. Not tonight. They wanted to send a message, that was all.

The sound of far-off laughter and the tinny music of a piano floated on the air. And there was something else. A low whuffling sound. Then, out of the corner of his eye, Durge caught motion. He turned his head in time to see a shadow dart toward the mouth of an alley. At first he thought it was some kind of large animal, for it seemed to run on all fours. Only then the shadow rose onto hind legs, moving with a loping cadence, and he realized that the figure was a man's.

Or mostly that of a man.

Just before the shadow reached the mouth of the alley, it passed through a stray square of light that fell from a second-floor window. The man wore ragged, filthy clothes, and his feet were bare. Encircling his left wrist was a bloody line, and below the wound, instead of a hand, his arm ended in a large paw, its curved talons extended.

Durge let out a low oath. The figure turned its head, and for a heartbeat Durge glimpsed its face. Green eyes gazed at him beneath a shock of red hair, but where a human mouth should have been, instead there jutted a long snout filled with sharp teeth. Black lips pulled back in a rictus. Then the thing moved out of the light, vanishing into the alley.

Durge staggered back, his blood cold water in his veins.

Only it wasn't because of the figure's claws and teeth that he gripped the rail of the boardwalk for support. It was because, despite the horrible deformities, he had recognized the man behind the face of a wolf.

And that man was Calvin Murray.

36.

Travis lay in bed, letting the sunlight that fell through the attic window warm his face. As long as he stayed there, as long as he kept his eyes shut, he could pretend he was still dreaming.

It had been a wonderful dream. In it, Jack Graystone had finally come to town, gray-haired and professorial just as Travis remembered him. Travis had shaken Jack's hand, and with a sound like the crackle of lightning, all the power in Travis had coursed out of him, streaming back into Jack. When Travis lifted his right hand, there was no trace of the silvery rune embedded in his palm. He was just Travis again. Harmless.

The bedsprings squeaked, and Travis felt a weight on his chest. He opened his eyes and found himself gazing at a delicate, feline face.

"I suppose you're trying to tell me that it's time to stop dreaming and wake up?"

Miss Guenivere only licked a paw. Travis sighed and sat up. He cradled the little cat against his chest and rolled out of bed, then set her back down in the square of sunlight. She curled up next to his pillow and promptly went to sleep.

"So that was your plan all along, you charlatan."

Travis dressed in his daytime clothes—denim jeans and a calico shirt—and splashed some of last night's wash water from the basin on his face. As he moved to the door, he noticed that Durge's bed was still neatly made; the Embarran hadn't come back to the Bluebell last night. Travis swallowed the lump of worry in his throat and headed downstairs.

He was too late for breakfast. The miners who stayed at the Bluebell had all headed off to the silver fields. He could hear Maudie humming in the kitchen as she washed dishes, and

Lirith was just folding up the tablecloth. To Travis's relief, Durge sat at the table, hands gripping a cup of coffee.

"Good morning," Travis said.

Durge looked up. The knight's face was haggard and care-worn. Travis's relief evaporated. He glanced at Lirith; the witch wore a tight-lipped expression.

"What's happened?" he said.

"You'd better sit down," Durge said in his somber voice.

Travis did so. He listened as Durge told what had happened at the sheriff's office last night. A wave of sickness crashed through him, so strong he feared he would vomit, and he was glad he had been too late to get anything to eat.

"You're sure it was really Calvin Murray?" Travis said when the knight finished. He didn't doubt Durge's words; they were just so hard to comprehend.

"It was." Travis had seldom seen the knight shaken, but there was a haunted look on his face as he spoke. "I recognized him despite . . . what had been done to him."

Travis shook his head. "But Calvin Murray died at the Mine Shaft. You checked, Lirith. You said he was dead."

"He was," the witch said. "And I would warrant, despite what Durge saw, that he still is."

Travis shuddered. How could a dead man throw a rock through a window? Better yet, how could that dead man have the paw of a mountain lion and the jaws of a wolf? One thing was certain at least: Now they knew what—or who—had been mauling livestock around town.

The kitchen door swung open, and Maudie came through, leaning on her cane, spurs jingling. "There you are, you layabout," she said to Travis. "I saved back a couple of biscuits for you. I'll bring them out with some gooseberry jam. Was it a long night at the saloon?"

Travis nodded, even though it hadn't been. The Mine Shaft had been nearly deserted. After what had happened at the pai-gow parlor on Aspen Street, folk seemed reluctant to visit any business establishment. Travis couldn't blame them. There was no telling who the Crusade's next target would be.

Maudie brought the biscuits and jam, then returned to the kitchen. Through the door, they heard a long fit of coughing.

Travis asked Durge more questions about what he had seen the night before, but there was nothing that explained what had been done to Calvin Murray. Or how. The only thing they did know was that, in death, young Mr. Murray was still working for the vigilance committee.

"Can I see the message that was on the rock?" Travis said.

Durge pulled a scrap of paper from his pocket and handed it to Travis. Travis smoothed it out on the table and sorted the letters out. *Release the gypsy or prepare for all Hell to break loose.*

"My lady," Durge said to Lirith, "there was something I wished to show you, but after what happened last night it escaped my mind until just now."

Along with the piece of paper, the knight had drawn a small glass bottle out of his pocket. He handed it to Lirith.

"What is it?" the witch said.

"I'm not certain. Some kind of medicine, I think. There is a drop or two left at the bottom. I thought you might be able to tell me what it was."

Lirith unstopped the bottle and held it beneath her nose. She ran her finger around the mouth of the bottle, then touched it to the tip of her tongue. Her eyebrows rose.

"This is a powerful and dangerous potion," Lirith said, setting the bottle on the table. "A small amount can dull pain and bring pleasant dreams. Too much can bring dark visions, or even death. And the more one takes of this drug, the more one's body will crave it."

"What is it?" Travis said.

"It's a tincture of poppy."

Durge's brow furrowed. "Tincture of poppy?"

"Laudanum," said Maudie from the kitchen doorway. "You mean laudanum."

They looked up as Maudie stepped into the dining room. Next to her was Sheriff Tanner, his expression thoughtful behind his handlebar mustache.

"That's a devil's brew," Maudie said, her voice hard. "It did in too many of my girls. A customer would give them their first drop, and once they had a taste for it they couldn't stop. At least not until they set aside the camellia for the lily and were laid in the cold ground. Where did you get it?"

Tanner stepped forward and picked up the bottle. "I believe Mr. Dirk found it in my office."

The others stared at Tanner, all except Lirith, who nodded. She rose and moved to the sheriff, her dark eyes intent.

"How long have you been taking it?" the witch said.

Tanner stared past them at the wall. Then his watery blue eyes focused on Lirith, and he sighed.

"Five years. I've been taking laudanum for five years now, Miss Lily. Every day I wake up and tell myself I'm going to stop. Sometimes I even try. But by noon I'm wet and shaking like a newborn foal, and it feels like there's blasting going on in my head, digging a mine deep into my brain. And then it's all I can do to get the cork out."

All of them stared at the sheriff. He sat at the table, placing the bottle before him. Lirith hesitated, then rested a hand on his shoulder.

"How?" she said simply.

"It was in San Francisco. I was a deputy US Marshal then. A doctor prescribed the laudanum when my old shoulder wound got to troubling me, the wound I took in the war."

"What war was this?"

"Why, the war to free the slaves, Miss Lily," he said, looking up at her, and she nodded. "I never should have fought, I suppose. I wasn't of age—I was just sixteen when I ran off and joined the Union Army. But I saw my share of battles before taking a bayonet on the field of Gettysburg. The wound never bothered me much, not until I got older. That's when I saw the doctor, and he gave me the laudanum. Only long after the pain was gone, I kept on taking it. It was the only thing that kept me from remembering the...that is to say, it was the only thing that kept my gun hand steady. But soon it took more and more to stop the shakes, and I knew it was only a matter of time before the Marshals found out and took my badge. So I gave it back to them before they could, and I took a train here, to Castle City, when I heard they needed a sheriff." He hung his head. "Only it looks like I'll be turning in this badge, too."

Maudie's eyes were bright with tears. She sat at the table. "Oh, Bart, why didn't you tell me?"

He didn't look at her. "And what would you have thought of me, Maude?"

"I would have thought, Maudie, here's someone who needs your help. So you'd better see to it you take care of him. Because there isn't a finer man you could find, not for all the gold in the ground from here to California." She took his hand in hers, holding it tightly so it couldn't possibly tremble. "That's what I think, Bart."

He looked up and met her eyes, and only in that moment did Travis realize that Tanner and Maudie loved one another. He wondered why it had taken him so long to see. But then, no doubt they had made an effort to keep it hidden, even from each other. After all, he was the sheriff, and until only recently she had been the madam of a brothel. What would Castle City's society ladies whisper to their husbands if Tanner married Maudie? Travis doubted Tanner would have stayed sheriff long.

"Mr. Dirk," Tanner said, standing, "I've got to turn in my badge and gun to you now. You'll be sheriff in Castle City until the county board can hire a new one. And when they do, I hope they have the sense to give you the job."

The knight shook his head. "I swore an oath to serve you, Sir Tanner, and I do not break my word. Yet it is more than that. If ever this village needed you, it is now. Like me, you are a man of war, and that means you can feel it in the air even as I do. There is a battle coming."

For a moment, Travis was struck by how much Tanner looked like a knight of Embarr, with his drooping mustache and somber eyes. No wonder Durge called him *Sir*.

"If you're right, Mr. Dirk, and if there's a battle coming, then I'm not going to be any use in fighting it." Tanner lifted his right hand; his fingers vibrated like the wings of a hummingbird. "If I take the laudanum, or if I don't, either way I'm no use with a gun anymore."

"There are other ways to fight."

"Not men like these. Even you'd be hard-pressed to stop them, Mr. Dirk, and not just because you won't put bullets in that revolver you wear. I don't think there's anything a sheriff can do."

"But you're the law in this town," Maudie said, indignant now. "You can throw the lot of them in jail!"

"And then more men would come and break them out." Tanner shook his head wearily. "Laws only matter when they're the strongest authority around, Maudie. But there's another authority in Castle City, and that's the Crusade. People might respect the law, but they fear the vigilance committee more. Only someone outside the law himself can stop men like these."

Maudie glanced over her shoulder, then looked back. "You mean like the stories I've been hearing about town? They say he's going to come. The civilizer, Tyler Caine."

A jolt of energy coursed through Travis. Was it fear? Or something else?

"I've heard those stories, too," Tanner said. "And I wish I could believe they were true. He's wanted for killing men in five states and territories. All the same, I'd welcome the sight of him. But they say Tyler Caine is dead."

Travis wanted to ask why everyone seemed to believe this Tyler Caine had the power to stop men like Lionel Gentry. Only before he could speak, a strangled sound escaped Lirith. The witch went rigid, her spine arching. She clutched the back of a chair and threw her head back, her eyes shut.

Maudie rushed to her. "Miss Lily, are you well? What's the matter?"

Lirith went limp, and Durge rushed forward before Travis could move, gripping her shoulders, holding her upright. Her eyes fluttered open.

"I saw it," she whispered. "It was so clear."

Maudie wrung her hands. "What are you talking about, sweetheart? Are you ill?"

Travis moved closer. Lirith wasn't ill. He knew the witch had the power to sometimes glimpse the future. She had just done it—she had seen something with the Sight.

"What is it, Lirith?" Travis said. "What did you see?"

"It was him. He will come."

Tanner shook his head. "Who do you mean, Miss Lily? Who's coming?"

"Tyler Caine." She looked not at Tanner, but at Travis. "He's going to come and fight the men of the Crusade. And there's someone else he's going to fight, but I couldn't see who."

Travis clenched his right hand into a fist. Tyler Caine was dead; all the stories said he was. There was no way he could come there to Castle City, and even if he did, what could he really do? Lirith had once said the power of her Sight was far from perfect; her vision had to be mistaken.

Travis didn't want to talk about laudanum or Tyler Caine or the Crusade for Purity anymore. He glanced at Tanner. "Sheriff, was there a reason you came by?"

Tanner nodded. "I wanted to give you the news before you heard it somewhere else. I know you were a sort of friend of his, Mr. Wilder. As good a friend as he had, at least."

Travis shook his head, confused. "What are you talking about?"

"He was found by Edward Strange Owl this morning, in his teepee up on Signal Ridge," Tanner said. "Ezekial Frost. From the looks of it, he was mauled to death."

37.

Lirith drew Travis and Durge into the lace-filtered light of the parlor. Travis could hear Maudie and Tanner talking in the dining room in low tones. From the sound of her voice, it seemed she was unhappy with something he was saying. A pair of cats lay on a balding velvet chaise, dozing in a stray sunbeam.

"What is it?" Travis said to the witch, keeping his voice quiet, although he wasn't certain why. There was something about Lirith's expression. Was it fear in her eyes?

"I ran into him. Yesterday, on my way to the jail to see Sareth. He said such strange things. I should have listened to him, I should have known something was wrong. But I was so worried about Sareth, and I just hurried on without thinking."

"Who is this you speak of, my lady?" Durge said.

She met the knight's questioning gaze. "Ezekial Frost."

Travis and Lirith sat on a horsehair sofa, and Durge paced

back and forth as the witch described her encounter with the old mountain man. She shut her eyes, doing her best to repeat Frost's words exactly. Travis listened, at first in confusion, then in growing dread.

I know yeh know all about them Seven Cities...them cities of gold that men have hunted fer five hundred years...I seen yeh come on through, just like the gold man. I got to know the likes of him there. He'll be looking for a way back....

"Are you sure?" Travis said when Lirith finished, his mouth dry. "You're certain that was what Ezekial said?"

She nodded. "What is it, Travis? What are these Seven Cities he spoke of?"

"A legend. A myth, that's all. Centuries ago, when explorers first came here from across the ocean, the native people who lived here told them stories about seven cities filled with riches, cities where the streets were paved with gold. The explorers were greedy men, and for centuries they searched for the Seven Cities of Cibóla. Only they never found them."

Understanding flickered across Lirith's face. "I have never been to Al-Amún—the land that lies south across the Summer Sea. But it is famous for its cities, which are the most ancient still standing in all of Eldh. I have heard the greatest of the cities are seven in number, and that they are built of white stone." She drew in a deep breath. "Stone that is painted the color of gold by the light of the sun. At least so the stories say."

Travis had no doubt those stories were true. How it had happened he didn't know, but he could picture it: Ezekial Frost falling into a ravine, or wandering into a forgotten cave in the lonely desert of southwestern Colorado, and finding it hanging on the air: a window rimmed with blue fire. Somehow in his wanderings, the mountain man must have come upon a way that was still open.

Where the gate was, or how it had come to be there, he supposed they would never know. But after the sorcerers of Al-Amún created the gate artifacts, would they not have used them to explore worlds beyond the void, just as the conquistadors explored the lands of the New World? Sorcerers could have found their way here. And perhaps people had gone through the other direction as well. Five hundred years before the Spanish explorers first came to Colorado, an entire people—the Anasazi—vanished without a trace.

Travis rose. "We have to go to the jail. We have to tell Sareth."

Durge stopped pacing. "Tell him what?"

"That a sorcerer followed us through the gate."

A quarter of an hour later, Travis, Lirith, and Durge burst through the door of the sheriff's office. One of the front windows was boarded up. Deputy Wilson sat behind the desk, a dime novel open before him. On one of the pages was a pen-and-ink illustration of a gunfighter clutching his chest, taking a fatal wound. Wilson looked up, confusion on his pink, pudgy face.

"What's going on, Mr. Dirk?" he said, hands still gripping the pulp novel.

Durge wiped sweat from his brow. "Give me the keys to the jail, Deputy. Now."

Wilson stared a moment, then jumped up, fumbling with the ring of keys at his belt. At last he got the ring unhooked and handed it to Durge. Durge unlocked the door to the jail. Wilson's jaw was agape as he watched the three of them enter. Durge shut the door behind them.

Sareth stood up in his cell as they entered. He and Lirith exchanged a long look, then glanced away. What had the two spoken about the previous day? It seemed to Travis that sorrow registered in his eyes as well as in hers.

He could wonder about it later. They were in danger, and Sareth needed to know about it; the Mournish man knew more about the Scirathi than any of them. In quick words, Travis explained what they had learned.

Sareth leaned against the bars of his cell, his expression grim. "One of the Scirathi must have remained in the Etherion after you destroyed the demon, Travis. We must not have seen him amid all the rubble. And after we passed through the gate, the sorcerer must have followed."

"But would we not have seen him if he followed us?" Durge said, glowering.

Sareth gripped the bars. "His kind are used to the magic of

sorcery. We were all dazed for a short time after passing through the gate. The sorcerer would have recovered more quickly. That would have given him time to escape."

"I felt him," Lirith said, hugging her arms around herself, her dress whispering as she paced. "That first night we stayed in the cabin."

Travis remembered. Lirith had sensed a presence outside the cabin, only when they opened the door nothing was there.

"I imagine the sorcerer heard us speaking that night," Durge said, a grim light in his eyes. "We must assume he knows all that we discussed."

Travis swallowed, but he couldn't get rid of the metallic taste of fear in his mouth. If the sorcerer had heard them, that meant he knew about the gate and the scarab.

"I should have known it was one of the Scirathi." Sareth spat out the word like poison. "Only a sorcerer could make a monster of a dead man. They have performed their foul work on animals for thousands of years, combining different beasts into one. I should not wonder that they would do the same to a man. Although I did not know they could work with dead flesh."

Travis's stomach cramped into a sick ball. "Maybe Murray was still . . . fresh enough when the sorcerer got him. Do you remember what Gentry said that night? 'We'll take care of our boy.' I suppose he and Ellis took Murray right to the sorcerer."

Shock played across Durge's craggy face. "Are you saying you believe this sorcerer is in league with Gentry?"

"No, I'm saying he's in league with Gentry's employers." It was the only possible conclusion. "Look, the sorcerer made Calvin Murray into a . . . into whatever he is. And it was Murray who threw the rock through the window. There's no doubt that the message on that rock was from the vigilance committee. Somehow, the sorcerer and the Crusade are working together."

"But why?" Durge said, glowering. "Does not the sorcerer simply desire the gate artifact and the scarab for himself?"

Sareth nodded. "He would want them, yes. Badly."

"Then why would he ally himself with these other men? I can see how the vigilance committee might benefit from the sorcerer's abilities. But what does the sorcerer stand to gain?"

Sareth's lip curled in disgust. "The Scirathi dislike doing

their own dirty work. Once he learned of the Crusade, I imagine he thought it would be easy to bend it to his own purposes."

But what were those purposes? If all the Scirathi wanted were the gate artifact and the scarab, he could simply have attacked them that first night in the cabin. So there had to be a reason he didn't. Travis voiced these thoughts to the others.

"Perhaps the sorcerer was weak when he came through the gate," Sareth said. "He may have been wounded in the Etherion and has only now regained his strength. After all, we have been here a month, and the Scirathi has only now made himself known."

Lirith coiled a hand under her chin. "Perhaps. Or perhaps he's simply in the same bind we are. If he heard us speaking, then he knows we have found ourselves adrift on the sea of time. If he uses the gate artifact to return to Eldh, it will be over a century before he left. I doubt he desires that any more than we do."

Understanding jolted through Travis. "Of course. He heard everything. And that means he's waiting for the same thing we are—Jack Graystone."

"And while he waits for the wizard Graystone to arrive, he is using the vigilance committee to gain power," Durge rumbled. "That way, he can be sure to get what he wants when the time comes."

Lirith heaved her shoulders in a sigh. "Ezekial must have seen us all come through the gate. I suppose he went looking for the sorcerer, hoping to find a way back to Al-Amún and to his seven cities."

"And Frost must have found him," Sareth said.

"There is still one thing I don't understand," Durge said. "Why does the sorcerer wish for us to release Sareth?"

Travis rubbed his shaved head. "That message might not have come from the sorcerer. He may just be letting them use Murray for their own purposes. It might just be Gentry and the Crusade who want Sareth."

"No, it's him."

The others looked at Sareth. The circles beneath his eyes were as dark as bruises. "My people and his are ancient enemies. Even as magic runs in his blood, so does hatred for me. He would see me dead before he goes."

"Then I shall see him dead first!" Lirith said, voice rising, hands clenched into fists.

The three men stared at the witch; her eyes glittered like black opals. Travis had never seen her like this. Always in his experience Lirith had shown a profound and abiding reverence for life. He had never believed she had the will or power to bring death. Until now.

"*Beshala.*"

Sareth's word was soft. A plea. Or a prayer. Lirith drew in a ragged breath, then leaned against the bars.

"I won't lose you, Sareth," she said in a fierce whisper. "I will *not.*"

He reached up to touch a dark ringlet of her hair that had slipped between the bars. "You could never lose me, *beshala.*"

There was nothing more they could do now. Sareth was still safest at the jail—if he was safe anywhere. Durge opened the jail door, and they stepped into the front office. Deputy Wilson was still reading his dime novel. The young man must have been a slow reader, given that the book was still open to the page with the picture of the dying gunfighter. For some reason the illustration bothered Travis.

"I will not be at the boardinghouse for supper," Durge said. "But I will try to come to the saloon this evening and see if you are well."

Travis and Lirith returned to the Bluebell and spent the afternoon sitting in the torpid air of the parlor. For a time they spoke in low voices, but soon they ran out of words, and after that they were quiet, each lost in their own thoughts. The silence was punctuated only by the intermittent rattle of a wagon outside or, from somewhere upstairs, the sound of Maudie's coughing.

"She's getting worse, isn't she?" Travis said, scratching Miss Guenivere between the ears. "It won't be long now."

"No," Lirith said. "It won't."

"I wonder if Tanner knows."

"He knows."

Travis nodded. The little calico cat purred, rubbing her head against his hand.

The heat broke about five o'clock, and an hour later Liza came to the parlor to tell them supper was ready. They did their best to put on cheerful faces for Maudie. However, Maudie's green eyes were hazy and distant, and more than once she nearly dropped a dish off the table as she served supper, and Travis knew she was thinking about Bartholomew Tanner.

After supper they went upstairs to change clothes before going to the saloon. Lirith stopped to check on Niles Barrett, but there was little for her to do. Liza had been caring for him, keeping him clean and changing the dressings on his wounds. The Englishman was still unconscious. He no longer tried to speak, and only lay very still. Travis wondered if he would ever wake again.

"Give him time," Lirith said when Travis voiced his fears. "Lord Barrett is stronger than you think."

At seven o'clock, Travis and the witch headed to the saloon. The dusty swath of Elk Street was already beginning to clear out. No doubt word of what had happened to Ezekial Frost had already spread across town; after this, few would wish to be caught out after dark anymore. Only those who cared for whiskey more than their own skins.

As they approached the door of the Mine Shaft, they saw a piece of paper tacked next to the door. Travis's heart caught in his throat as he read the notice:

Thou shalt not bear false witness.

He tore down the paper and wadded it inside his fist, then pushed through the swinging doors, Lirith close behind him.

A half dozen men were scattered throughout the saloon, hunkered over their glasses. Manypenny stood behind the bar, absently wiping the glossy wood with a rag. His usually jovial face was sober, and his ruddy cheeks uncharacteristically pale. Sweat stained his crisp white shirt.

"What is this, Mr. Manypenny?" Travis said, spreading the crumpled paper out on the bar.

Manypenny glanced down at the paper, but his eyes seemed

distracted, and he looked up again. "I should have told them what they wanted. But I'm a good man, or by Jove I try to be. It's not my nature to deceive, no matter what they might say."

Lirith laid a hand on his. "Who, Mr. Manypenny? Who did you talk to?"

The saloonkeeper blinked, as if only now seeing the two of them standing there. "It was them, Lady Lily. They were wearing masks, but I recognized them, and I don't think they cared that I did. Lionel Gentry and Eugene Ellis. They came in a few hours ago. They asked me what I planned to tell the circuit judge when he comes to town."

"What you plan to tell the judge about what?" Travis said, feeling cold despite the sweat running down his sides.

"About the night Mr. Murray met his end. I told them I intended to speak the truth, as I always do, and that I didn't see who shot Mr. Murray. Only then Gentry said that wasn't the truth at all, that the truth was I saw Mr. Samson shoot Mr. Murray dead. And that if I . . . if I didn't . . ."

Manypenny slumped forward, leaning on the bar, his massive shoulders shaking.

Lirith tightened her grip on his hand. "What did he tell you?"

The saloonkeeper's voice was a hoarse whisper. "I always thought I was a strong man. In my day, I could wrestle any man to the ground with one arm tied. But I can't wrestle men like these. They said lightning would strike my saloon, that it would burn the place down if I didn't say what they wanted. That it would be God's punishment." He drew his hand from hers and held it to his face. "It's all I have, Lily. My strength is gone, if ever I had it. I can't lose the saloon."

"You won't," Lirith said, her voice resolute. "Those men are cowards, and it is they who shall be struck down."

Travis wadded the notice back up, anger giving way to weariness. He moved away to don his apron and wash glasses while Lirith spoke quiet words to Manypenny. Whatever she said must have comforted the saloonkeeper, for after a time he laughed, and his cheeks were ruddy again. Travis shot her a look of thanks as she headed over to the faro table.

Dusk came, bringing welcome coolness if not many

customers. As Travis had suspected, only the hardest drinkers and gamblers stepped through the saloon's swinging doors. However, Aaron Locke and his clerks from the First Bank of Castle City came through at nine o'clock, right on schedule.

Travis was glad to see them. They were always polite and cheerful, and their presence brightened both the saloon and Manypenny's mood. Aaron Locke himself came up to the bar, a smile on his boyish face, and bought a round of whiskey for the entire saloon.

"I think we could all use a drink tonight," Locke said, eyes twinkling behind his gold-rimmed glasses, and this elicited a good deal of vigorous whooping. A number of people were drawn in from the neighboring saloons by the noise, and soon the Mine Shaft was, if not crowded, at least far from empty. Travis let himself think that maybe things would be all right after all. He smiled at Locke, and the bank owner tipped his hat in Travis's direction.

"She's so purdy she almost makes losing easy," said one grizzled miner to another, as they left Lirith's table and headed to the bar.

"Almost," the other said, peering into his nearly empty billfold.

Travis poured two glasses of whiskey. "Don't worry, gentlemen. Mr. Locke is buying the whiskey tonight."

"Well bless him!" said one of the men.

"Now that's how a man with money should behave," said the other, setting down his glass. "Not like that Mortimer Hale. He owns half this town, but he never has two bits in his pocket for an old woman or a man down on his luck."

"Well, I heard old Hale got his comeuppance the other night."

"How's that?"

Travis had moved away to pour more drinks, but he kept an ear tilted in the direction of the two miners. They were speaking in lower voices now.

"I heard Hale lost at paigow the other night. Lost big, fair and square. Ten thousand dollars."

"Ten thousand? Lord Almighty, the whiskey that could buy a man."

"I heard Hale was in a royal fit. Only I say it serves him right. Half the land he owns, he's swindled out of folk. He got Abraham Jesco to sell him the livery by threatening to foreclose on Jesco's brother's farm. And I heard he got Miss Ladyspur to deed over the Bluebell to him by promising to make her a society lady. He's a liar and a thief."

"Whoa now, watch what yeh say about Hale," said the first miner, glancing over his shoulder. "He's got ears everywhere in this town. And yeh know what happens to folk as cross him."

The men headed back to the faro table. Travis watched them go. So Mortimer Hale had swindled Maudie out of her home. But why did it surprise him Hale would do such a cruel thing? The signs were clear; Hale was the man behind the Crusade. And in league with the sorcerer. Why else would the *Castle City Clarion* print the stories it did?

"Travis."

It was Lirith; he had been so lost in his thoughts he hadn't even seen the witch approach. Her dark eyes were wide.

"What is it?" he said, his heart skipping in his chest.

She pressed her hands against the bar. "He's coming. I think he's taking a stagecoach from the train depot. His thread is so bright, Travis, even brighter than yours. I could see it like lightning in a clear sky."

Wonder filled him. "Whose thread, Lirith?" But even as he spoke the words, he knew.

"It's your friend," the witch said. "The wizard, Jack Graystone."

Five minutes later, Travis stood in front of the Silver Palace Hotel. He had told Manypenny he needed to step out for a moment and get some air, and the saloonkeeper's mood had lifted so much he simply waved Travis away with a smile.

Travis peered into the night. Elk Street was empty, save for the slinking shadow of a dog and the occasional miner staggering between saloons. Then he heard it: the thunder of hooves, the rattle of wheels.

He saw the coach's lantern as it hurtled around a corner. The driver pulled on the reins, and the horses clattered to a stop. Dust swirled around Travis. By the time it cleared, the driver had climbed down to open the door of the stagecoach.

"This is it, sir," the driver said. "Castle City."

"By the winged feet of Mercury, couldn't you have hit fewer ruts along the way?" said a fussy, gentle, and familiar voice. Travis's heart soared at the sound of it.

"Sorry, sir," said the driver in a disinterested tone.

A figure climbed out of the coach and started down the steps. The satchel he carried got caught in the door, and he tugged at it to no avail. The driver helped him turn the bag sideways, and it came free so suddenly the man nearly tumbled down the steps. Only a fortuitously placed hitching post kept him from falling to the street. The driver shut the door, climbed back into the bench, and the coach rattled away.

"Blessed Isis, I thought I'd never make it here," said the man, steadying himself and futilely trying to brush the wrinkles from his wool suit. He was an elderly gentleman, perhaps sixty years old in appearance, strikingly handsome, with vivid blue eyes. His white hair fluttered wildly about his head. "Zeus help me, what an utterly barbarous country this is!"

Gripping his lumpy satchel, he climbed up the steps to the boardwalk and promptly ran into Travis. The man stepped back, muttering more curses to long-forgotten gods. Joy filled Travis. It was Jack Graystone. His old friend, right there, looking just as Travis remembered him.

The white-haired gentleman frowned up at Travis. "Excuse me, my good fellow, but I've had a terribly long journey, and I—" He cocked his head, his blue eyes glittering. "Pardon me, but do I know you?"

Travis couldn't help the grin that spread across his face. "No," he said. "But you will."

38.

The metallic odor of hot steel hung on the air, cauterizing Grace's lungs. Atop its hill, the keep of Seawatch blazed like an alchemist's cauldron full of naphtha. However, there was no time to think of Lord Elwarrd, who remained within the keep, or to wonder if the serving girl Mirdrid had escaped. In the bloody light of the fire, Grace could see her own desperate eyes reflected in the polished surfaces of ten onyx breastplates. Black swords naked in their hands, the knights urged their horses, closing the circle.

Grace started to reach down, to fumble with the knife tucked inside her boot. But that was ridiculous. What would she do with it? Cut through their armor as if it were cheese? She abandoned the knife and reached out with her thoughts, indiscriminately clutching the glowing life threads around her: those of men, horses, the wind-twisted plants that eked out an existence in the hard soil of the moors. She didn't know what she would do with the strands, only that she had mere moments to weave them into a spell.

She was dimly aware of the others forming a triangle around her. Beltan gripped the sword Elwarrd had given him. Vani's gold eyes shone in the darkness, and her hands were poised, ready to strike. Falken held only a slim dagger in his silver hand. He might as well have been holding his lute for all the good the blade would do him.

The enormous knight—the one with the three crowns of leadership emblazoned on his breastplate—was the nearest, and three others were close behind him. The remaining six knights were moving in as well, but the leader raised his free hand and they held back. No doubt the massive knight wanted to leave some room for him and the other three to swing their swords. Even with Vani and Beltan at her side, Grace knew four knights were more than enough. After all, it required only one to lop off her head. And that was what they wanted, wasn't it? Not the others, but her—the heir to Malachor. They had been trying since she was an infant to kill her. And now they would.

"Get ready," Beltan growled beside her.

Grace clutched the necklace at her throat and frantically wove the threads of the Weirding. A mist was starting to rise off the damp ground. Yes, she could weave a spell around the fog. She had done it once before, on the common green of the village of Falanor. She used the power of the Weirding to gather the mist in on itself, making it denser, pulling it toward her. Unseen by the knights, a gray wall rose up behind them. If she could get it closer, engulfing the knights, blinding them, it might give them the chance to get away.

The leader of the knights brought his charger to a halt before her, looking more machine than man in his black armor. His three closest companions joined him, the other six maintaining the larger circle, from which there was no escape.

"You know what to do, brothers!" the enormous man shouted. "It's time for death to come to those who deserve it. Now!"

Beltan raised his sword. Vani started to move, her dark form melding with the gloom. In unison, the four armored men raised their swords—

—and whirled their horses around to face their six brethren. The gigantic knight let out an earsplitting roar as he spurred his charger forward, sword raised before him. The three knights closest to him did the same.

Grace stared, the spell unraveling as her shocked mind tried to grasp what was happening. Clearly the six more distant knights hadn't expected this turn of events any more than Grace. Before any of them could move, the gigantic knight swung his sword. There was a bright *clang*! A visored helm fell tumbling to the ground, a head still in it, and a lifeless body followed after, armor clattering like a heap of junk.

Now the five remaining knights reacted. Swearing and shouting, they turned their swords on their attackers. However, they could not move fast enough. Another toppled from his horse, crumpling to the ground where he lay motionless.

It was chaos. Riderless horses screamed. The mist Grace had gathered broke apart into swirling eddies, obscuring what was happening. The sound of steel on steel rang out again and again.

"What's going on?" Falken shouted.

"I can't see," Beltan called back.

A patch of fog broke apart, and a horse came charging through, pounding straight for Grace. The rider pulled his sword back, then swung it around to strike her down. She could only watch as the blade sped toward her neck.

There was a chiming sound. Sparks flew as the sword contacted Falken's silver hand, which he had thrust into the path of the blade. Falken tumbled to the ground, and the sword went wide—just barely. Grace watched as a lock of her hair drifted down into her outstretched hands. The knight recovered, pulling his sword back for another blow.

The darkness above him unfurled, like a black rose. Vani fell upon the knight, knocking him from the saddle. The knight spilled to the ground, landing on his back with a grunt. Before he could move, Beltan was there. He planted a boot on the man's breastplate, then threaded the tip of his sword through the slit in the knight's visor. Beltan clenched his jaw and leaned on the sword, driving it down. There was a crunching sound. The knight flopped once, like a fish on dry land, then lay still.

The night fell silent, save for the roar of flames from the keep. Beltan jerked his sword free; the tip was dark with blood. Vani peered into the fog. Falken had recovered his feet, and he moved close to Grace, taking her arm. Then they heard it: hooves against hard ground. A bank of mist broke apart, and four knights rode through.

One of them was the gigantic knight with the crowns on his breastplate. The others seemed to be the three that had followed him in the attack. Grace felt the others tense beside her. What did these four want? Did they have some terrible purpose the others would have opposed? As the fog dissipated, Grace saw six black forms on the ground scattered among the twisted bodies of the *feydrim*. Behind her, the keep consumed itself. Cinders fell gently all around like black snow.

The four knights came to a halt a few paces away. Falken stepped in front of Grace.

"What do you want from us?" the bard said.

The knights said nothing. Then, suddenly, the enormous one began to laugh. The sound echoed from inside his visor: booming and ferocious. When the big knight spoke, it was in a voice every bit as loud and deep as his laughter.

"By the foamy mane of Jorus, I never thought I'd see the day when I'd be saving the Grim Bard's neck. I always thought I'd be wringing it instead."

Beltan lowered his sword. Falken stared, mouth agape. Vani gave him a puzzled look.

"What, Falken Blackhand?" the enormous knight thundered. "Don't you recognize your protector?"

With that, the man reached up and plucked the helm from his head. So much shaggy red hair spilled forth that Grace wondered how it could ever have been contained within. The man's beard looked as if it could have housed several robins' nests; only his nose and eyes were visible above it.

Falken took a staggering step back. "King Kel!"

The gigantic man grinned. "So you recognize me at last. I suppose that means I won't have to kill you after all."

He sounded slightly disappointed. The three men beside him had removed their helms as well, and while none was so prodigious or shaggy as the man Falken called King Kel, they were wild-looking all the same.

Falken sank to his knees, and Grace had no idea if this was a sign of obeisance or if the bard was simply collapsing in shock. Regardless, she followed suit, and Beltan and Vani did the same, although the *T'gol*'s eyes remained suspicious.

This display seemed to please the gigantic man to no end, for he threw his head back and laughed again, and the sound rose above the crackling of flames, filling the night with his mirth.

39.

It was in the dead of the night when they finally reached King Kel's camp.

For hours, Grace clung to the back of a charger that had belonged to one of the slain Onyx Knights. The horse was so huge she couldn't sit astride it, but instead simply bounced atop the saddle, and its gait was rough and yawing, heaving up and down like the deck of the *Fate Runner*. After a time she slipped into a half dream in which she was running across an empty plain, trying to get to Travis. Only the land buckled and cracked beneath her feet, tossing her about like a pebble on a drum.

A lonely howl rose on the air, the call of a wolf, startling Grace awake.

"That's one of my wildmen," said a deep voice. "This will be the place where my people made camp."

At first Grace thought she had fallen off the charger into dry grass, only then she realized her face was mashed down in the beast's mane. She spat out horsehair and sat up, and for a moment she wondered if her dream hadn't been true. The gibbous moon sailed low in the western sky, illuminating a jumbled rockscape marred by crevices and softened only slightly by wind-stunted bushes.

"You can come down now, lass."

One of Kel's warriors, still clad in black armor, reached a hand toward her. She started to swing herself down from the saddle. Only there was no way to control her descent from the massive horse. She started slipping, then falling. The warrior caught her in strong arms, and he bared crooked teeth in a grin as he repositioned his hands, moving them to new locations which were not, she suspected, chosen out of a simple desire to better support her weight.

"Let her go," Beltan growled, sliding from his charger and marching toward them. Blood crusted his right shoulder. "I said let her go, man. You aren't worthy to lay your hands upon a queen."

The warrior started to curl his lip back, but King Kel made a sharp motion with his hand. At once the man released Grace, and she barely got her legs beneath her in time to keep from sprawling to the ground. The warrior stalked off, throwing down pieces of his armor as he went.

"Are you all right?" Beltan said, steadying her.

Grace lifted a hand to her throat. "I'm fine, really. I think he was just being . . . friendly."

"A little too friendly I would say."

"Well, they did just save our lives. How's your shoulder?"

Beltan touched the wound Leweth had given him and winced. "I'll live."

Vani and Falken climbed down from their horses with more skill than Grace. Kel and the other men stripped off their black armor, throwing it clattering to the ground as if they found its touch distasteful. Beneath they wore rough tunics. Grace caught the flickering light of a fire not far off.

"This way," Kel said, gesturing for them to follow. "My men will take care of the horses. Let's go get warm. Some *melindis* berry spirits should help us in that regard."

Vani frowned at the shaggy king. "You mean for us to drink hard liquor? But it is nearly dawn."

"Very well, wench, we'll hurry then," Kel said, slapping Vani on the back with a gigantic hand.

The assassin stumbled, and her eyes bulged, although whether this was due to the king's friendly bludgeoning of her bruised ribs or the fact that he had just called her *wench*, Grace couldn't say. Beltan started to laugh, but Vani shot him a molten look, and he quickly clamped his mouth shut.

"Where are we?" Grace murmured, as they walked.

"Near the edges of the Barrens, I think," Falken said. "I can see why King Kel told his people to hide here. In the entire history of Falengarth, no one has ever lived in this place."

They reached the campfire, which was nestled in a hollow out of the worst of the wind. A dozen or so forms lay huddled in blankets around the fire, and they stirred groggily as the king stamped among them. He gave an affable kick to what looked like a bundle of rags. The bundle let out a yelp, then scurried on all fours at the king's heels.

"It's not right to kick a dog," Grace said.

Falken let out a low chuckle. "Trust me, Kel would never kick one of his hounds. He loves them more than anything. Except maybe ale."

"But then—?" Grace's question faltered as the ragged dog looked up at her, and she saw that it wasn't a dog at all, but a man. His hair was caked with mud, and he smiled at her, baring teeth that had been filed into points. Beneath the grime, she could make out the swirling tattoos that covered his arms, his neck, even his face.

"That's one of Kel's wildmen," Falken said in answer to her unfinished question. "They live in the remote highlands of the

Fal Erenn. Mostly they avoid civilization and keep to themselves, but Kel has a way with them."

The king pulled a gristled scrap of dried meat from a pocket. He tossed it down, and the wildman caught it in his jaws before scurrying off to gnaw at it.

"So I see," Grace said dryly.

All the members of Kel's motley band had awakened and were staggering to their feet. Most were rough-looking warriors like the ones who had helped defeat the Onyx Knights, but there was another wildman, as well as several buxom women with frowsy hair, saucy smiles, and rosy cheeks. Grace had a feeling none of them would object to being called *wench*. On the contrary, given the way not one of them had bothered to lace the bodice of her dirty gown, that seemed to be precisely the look they were going for.

The atmosphere around the fire was lively and boisterous, like that of a revel. Cheers and laughter went up as Kel ordered the aforementioned spirits to be brought out. Hands pulled at Grace, seating her near the fire, and someone pressed a wooden cup into her hand. She drank, then nearly coughed the liquid back up; it tasted a good deal like extraordinarily bad gin. However, someone gave her a hearty slap on the back, and she choked it down.

Instantly, warmth spread through her. Beltan and Falken accepted cups of the crude but effective liquor, and even Vani did not resist the offering of their host. After giving her cup a suspicious sniff, the *T'gol* downed the liquid in a single gulp without so much as batting an eyelash, eliciting whoops of approval from all around the fire.

Grace stared into the flames, watching as wood was turned to ash. Had everything in Seawatch been similarly consumed? She thought of the touch of Elwarrd's lips on her own. Part of her wanted desperately to believe the earl was still alive; all the same, she knew he wasn't. He had stayed behind so they could escape—the first and final noble deed in his life.

And what did it gain him, Grace? His mother was mad, but in her way she was trying to help him, to protect him. Instead you killed him.

Except that wasn't true. Grace didn't know if she had loved

Elwarrd—she wasn't certain that was something she was even capable of. But he had brought to life feelings she had thought long ago dead and buried. And in return she had given him a way out of shadow where there had been none before. No matter what happened, she would not let herself regret meeting Lord Elwarrd of Seawatch.

Nestled between Falken and Beltan, Grace listened as Kel told his people—in a bold and bawdy fashion—what had happened in the time since he last saw them. In deference to the newcomers, he also spoke of how he had come to be in that part of the world, for the king and his people were far from their home.

Grace vaguely remembered Kel's name from the Council of Kings a year earlier. As far as she knew, he didn't rule a Dominion, which was why he hadn't been invited to the council. The other rulers had referred to him as a petty king, which meant he wasn't a true noble at all, but rather a self-styled monarch ruling over a small band of people. More like a chieftain, really. Except looking at the gigantic bear of a man now, it was hard for Grace to think of him as *petty*.

Kel had ruled over Kelcior, which Grace gathered was an old keep north of Eredane, on the western slopes of the Fal Erenn. It seemed that about two months before, a troop of men in black armor had ridden into Kelcior. They carried a standard no one had ever seen before—a black crown encircling a silver tower against a crimson field. Kel's wildmen saw them coming, and at once the king knew there was no hope of fighting them. The knights were two hundred in number, clad in tempered armor, riding heavy warhorses. Kel's warriors were only half that in number, with no armor and only stout ponies (better suited for the rocky terrain). Kel was bold, but he wasn't stupid. Quickly, he gave the orders. His people gathered what things they could, then hurried into the mountains, following hidden trails the black knights and their horses would never be able to traverse.

Periodically over those next weeks, Kel and some of his men would creep down from the mountains and watch the dark knights who inhabited the fortress, trying to determine their purposes. Kel particularly seemed to relish describing the various surprise raids and midnight sorties he and his people launched against the knights. They caught mice and let them loose in the granary, poured salt in the well, or banged their swords together just out of arrow shot and shouted insults. The wildmen would steal among the horses and tie their tails together. And once they used makeshift catapults to launch flaming, liquor-soaked heaps of horse dung over the walls of the keep.

Their actions infuriated the knights, but by the time they rode forth on their horses, swords drawn, Kel and his people had vanished once more into the maze of the mountains. No matter how the knights searched, they could never find the hiding place of their enemies.

"Did you ever learn anything?" Grace asked, when Kel paused in his telling. "Did you ever find out what they wanted?"

The merriment drained from Kel's visage. He looked serious, and menacing. "That we did. From time to time, when they rode out from the keep, my wildmen would hide in the bushes and catch some of their words. For one thing we learned they come from the far west, from a place called—"

"Eversea," she murmured.

Kel raised a bushy eyebrow. "How did you know that, lass?"

"A lucky guess," she said, gritting her teeth.

Beltan set down his empty cup. "Do you have any idea why they've come to the Dominions?"

"As a matter of fact, I do," Kel said. "Their general—they call him Gorandon—wants to restore the kingdom of Malachor."

Falken let out an oath, then recovered his composure. "I suppose in a way it makes sense. If they're truly from Eversea, then they're descended from people of Malachor. They might see it as their right—even their destiny—to restore the kingdom. And Kelcior was once part of Malachor."

Vani's eyes shone in the firelight. "But what of the other Dominions? If what I have learned is true, they were never part of this Malachor, but instead came after. So why do the Onyx Knights seek to conquer them?"

Beltan grunted. "That's easy. There's nothing left of Malachor but ruins and rubble. Even the better part of Kelcior has fallen down. That doesn't leave much to build a kingdom out of. But in a way the Dominions *are* descended from Malachor. At least, most people can trace at least one branch of their lineages back to the kingdom. So the knights will just take over the Dominions, raise their standard over all seven of them, and call it Malachor reborn."

"Except the standard they carry isn't the standard of Malachor," Falken said. "With that tower, I suppose it must be the flag of Eversea. Although I suppose the crown tells us something: This Gorandon means to rule."

Vani shook her head. "But that makes little sense. If these knights truly wish to restore Malachor, then why is it they seek to slay the last remaining heir?" She glanced at Grace.

King Kel let out a low whistle. "So that's why they want your hide, lass. I thought Sir Beltan was just being a gentleman when he said you were a queen. So you truly are the heir to the throne of Malachor?"

Grace reached up and touched her necklace, a bitter smile on her lips. "That's what they tell me."

Kel continued his tale, his voice gruff. "It was about five days ago that we saw one of them come pounding hard to Kelcior. His horse was ragged, and my guess was he had been riding long leagues without a rest. Well, almost at once a band of eight knights rode out from the keep, spurring their chargers at a gallop. From what we overheard, they were supposed to meet four knights waiting for them on the banks of the River Fellgrim, and then be off on some important mission. I figured this was a good chance to get closer and learn what they were about, so I took a band of my folk, and we hurried to get ahead of them."

Beltan frowned. "They were on chargers. How could you get ahead of them?"

"Good question, lad," Kel said with a grin. "We knew the knights would have to ride north around the tip of the mountains. So we went through."

"That's impossible," Falken said. "There isn't a pass through the Fal Erenn. Folk have looked for centuries, but they've never found any. Because there isn't one."

"Actually, there is," Kel said. "We learned about it from the Maugrim."

Falken was openly incredulous. "The Goblin People? I'm sorry, Kel, but I haven't drunk nearly enough to believe that. The Maugrim vanished a thousand years ago, when the Old Gods and the Little People retreated into the Twilight Realm."

The king shrugged monumental shoulders. "I don't care one mouse turd whether or not you believe me, Falken. We've never seen the Maugrim, but we know they're still there in the deepest reaches of the mountains. Sometimes we leave food for them, and it's always gone when we go back. And we know it's not animals that take the food, as the Maugrim leave things they've fashioned in its place."

From beneath his tunic, Kel drew out a stone knife hanging from a leather cord. The knife was crudely made from a piece of flint. One edge had been left rough to provide a handhold, and the other appeared to have been shaped by using another stone to knock off large flakes. Grace had seen arrowheads in museums that were far more delicately made.

"So we called out to them," Kel said, "and let them know what we needed, and before long we started seeing the signs— a knotted branch here, or a pile of pinecones there, and we followed them, all through the mountains to the headwaters of the Fellgrim."

Falken still looked skeptical, but he didn't disagree.

"What happened then?" Grace said, entranced.

"We built a raft and floated down the Fellgrim," Kel said. "We were nearly to Omberfell when we spied the four knights who were waiting for their brothers from the keep. We waited until they took their armor off to clean it. Without that armor, it was easy enough to jump them, stick swords in them, and dump them in the river. Then I picked my three best men, and we put on their armor while I told the rest of my folk to head in this direction and find a good hiding spot."

"One of the knights was truly as large as you?" Vani said, openly incredulous.

"Close but not quite, lass." Kel snorted. "Lucky for me. But still . . . It was a bit of a tight squeeze. I'm not sure I'll be siring any more whelps in the near future, if you know what I mean."

He adjusted his breeches with a grimace, and Vani studiously looked away.

Beltan rolled his empty wooden cup in his hands. "So when did the other knights, the ones from Kelcior, finally show up at the meeting place?"

"Only this morning," Kel said. "They were in a great hurry, so it was easy enough to trick them into thinking we were their brothers, and that I was the leader of the band. We learned quick enough what they were up to. It seems there was this woman they were bent on finding and killing at any cost, and they had reason to believe she might have washed ashore not far from there. If she wasn't already dead, they wanted to finish the job."

Vani nodded. "It was a week ago their ship spied us. They might have guessed that we sank, but there was no way they could land to see if you survived, Grace."

"So they landed in Omberfell and sent a runner to Kelcior for reinforcements to help search for Grace," Beltan said.

Falken rubbed his chin. "But there were at least a hundred knights on that ship. Why not just dispatch a band of them to go after us?"

Vani shrugged. "Perhaps the ship and its men were needed elsewhere right away."

It was possible, but Grace knew there was some part of the story they were missing. If the Onyx Knights really wanted her so badly, why not send all the men on the ship after her?

The question would have to wait for later. The horizon was turning to gray, and Grace felt her head drooping.

Falken let out a breath. "Regardless of why the knights acted as they did, we owe you our lives as well as our thanks, King Kel."

The big man grinned, clearly pleased to hear these words. "And I won't let you forget your debt. I should have known you'd be tangled up in all of this somehow. Darkness follows you like a cloud follows lightning, Falken Blackhand." He scratched at the thicket of his beard. "Although your hand is black no more. Or never was, I suppose."

Falken flexed his silver fingers. His hand was undamaged despite the sword he had deflected with it.

"No, it isn't." The bard sighed and looked up. "So what are you going to do now, Kel?"

The king scowled. "I hadn't thought that far. Wait!" He snapped his fingers. "I know—I'll ask my witch."

Falken's eyes went wide, but before the bard could sputter anything, Kel stood up and bellowed. "Where is Grisla? Somebody bring me my witch!"

A scraggly-looking bush gave itself a shake, and only after a moment did Grace realize it wasn't a bush at all, but a woman clad in drab tatters.

"I'm right here, Your Obstreperousness," the witch said in a complaining croak. She looked ancient beyond years. Her back was a gnarled hump, her gray hair lank as wet cobwebs, and her one bulbous eye looked ready to pop right out of her skull.

Falken groaned. "Not you again. What are you doing here?"

The witch hobbled forward and made a mocking bow. "I'm just like a rash, Lord Catastrophe."

"How so?"

"I'm everywhere you don't want me to be."

Falken muttered angry words under his breath, and the crone clucked her tongue.

"Such language, Lord Expletive. You are unkind to an old witch. And after one of my own sisters made that pretty silver hand for you."

Falken glared at her. "The witch who made this for me was kind and beautiful."

The crone brushed her withered face. "The young grow old, kind hearts harden, beauty withers. How do you know I'm not she? Perhaps I am."

"I don't think so."

The bard crossed his arms and turned his back. However, Grace could only stare. The crone reminded her strongly of Vayla, the old wisewoman she had met in the village beneath Calavere, and whom she had last seen a year before in the castle's council chamber. But it was impossible this was the same woman. Calavere was far away. And Vayla had never been quite so...impertinent as this. Besides, Kel had called her Grisla, and it seemed the crone had served the petty king for some time. After all, Falken recognized her. The resemblance had to be a coincidence.

"And what are you staring at, Lady Broken Sword?"

"Nothing," Grace blurted out of shock. "I was just... that is I..."

The witch snorted and glanced at Falken. "If you don't mind my saying, she's a bit dim for a queen. Then again, I suppose wits never were a prerequisite for royalty." She cast her one eye in a pointed look at Kel.

The king seemed not to notice. "Read your bones for me, witch."

Grisla squatted and drew a handful of thin, yellowed objects from a leather bag. Grace supposed they were metacarpals—finger bones. Each one was incised with an angular symbol. The crone held the bones between her hands and mumbled some words, then threw them on the ground.

She blew out a breath, lips flapping.

Kel bent close, expression curious. "What is it?"

"A great mess."

Kel's visage darkened. "Well, cast them again if the magic's gone afoul."

"It's your brain that's gone foul, like a joint of meat in the summer sun." The witch fluttered crooked fingers over the bones. "A mess is what you've gotten yourself into. If you go back to Kelcior, you'll be in terrible danger, and you'll almost certainly die in a horrible and embarrassing manner."

The king crossed his arms. "Well, that doesn't sound promising. What if I stay here in Embarr?"

"Even worse."

Kel ran a hand through his hair. "Well if I can't go back, and I can't stay here, then I suppose I'll have to go somewhere else."

The witch rolled her eye. "What a brilliant conclusion, Your Utter Obviousness."

"Do your bones say where I should go?"

Grisla let out a disgusted snort. "I'm a witch, not a holiday planner. You'll have to decide for yourself." She gathered up her bones.

As the others spoke with the king, Grace moved closer to

the witch. "They're runes, aren't they? The symbols on your bones. You gave one to Travis once, the rune of hope."

"And does he still have it?"

"The rune, you mean?"

"No, hope."

Grace thought about that. "I suppose I have hope for him."

"As do we all," Grisla muttered, stuffing the bones back in their bag. "As do we all."

"I never knew it was possible." Grace gestured to the bag. "I didn't know witches could use runes. I thought that women can't wield them."

Grisla gave her a piercing look. "Can't wield them? Or aren't allowed to wield them?"

It was a good point. How many professions had women on Earth been kept from pursuing over the centuries, not because they were incapable of doing them, but simply because men refused to allow them to? Maybe the Runespeakers simply wished to keep their order exclusively male. But what about the reverse?

"It's true I've never seen a woman runespeaker," she said. "But I've never seen a male witch, either."

Grisla displayed a haphazard collection of teeth in a grin. "Haven't you, lass? I think you have, though it's true he couldn't see you. Not with mortal eyes, at least."

Grace shivered. "You mean Daynen, don't you?" She knew the blind boy they had found in the village of Falanor had seen a vision of his own death, a vision that had later come true.

"Another one, you'll see," Grisla said, her voice softer now, and again Grace was reminded of the old wisewoman Vayla. "Not a boy this time, but a man freshly made. His talent is strong—as strong as your own. But then, a hammer must be every bit as strong as the anvil it strikes against, no?"

Grace wasn't sure what that meant. She hugged her knees to her chest, wondering if it could all really be true. "So men can be witches," she murmured. "And witches can wield runes. But I don't understand it. They seem so different. Rune magic and the Weirding, I mean."

Grisla shrugged knobby shoulders. "Sometimes two things that seem different turn out to be the very same thing."

Grace couldn't think of a case where that could be true. Or could she? She stared at the witch. "Vayla?" she whispered.

The old crone laughed softly. "Farewell, daughter." Then she turned and hobbled away, disappearing into the gray light of dawn.

40.

It was late morning of the following day when they reached the port city of Omberfell. They brought their four stolen black chargers to a halt on a scrub-covered ridge south of the city. Below them stretched a colorless patchwork of fields that ended in the rough line of the shore. Beyond that was only ocean, dull and flat as a sheet of crudely forged iron.

The wildman who had guided them grunted and pointed toward the city. Then, without a word, he gathered his mangy furs around himself, dropped to all fours, and scurried away into the underbrush.

"Talkative fellow, wasn't he?" Beltan said, gazing at the bushes where the wildman had vanished. "I think the only thing he said in the last day was his name. Ghromm."

Falken glanced at the knight. "Are you sure that was really his name? I thought he was just clearing the feathers out of his throat after swallowing that sparrow in one bite."

"Good point," Beltan conceded.

Vani turned her golden eyes on the knight. "Reticence is an admirable quality others would do well to emulate."

Beltan started to sputter some hot reply, but Grace nudged the flanks of her charger and managed to interpose the beast between the knight and the *T'gol*. "I wish we could have given Ghromm something," she said to Falken. "As a reward for leading us here."

The bard shook beads of dew from his blue cloak. "Gold doesn't mean anything to one like him. King Kel will know how to reward him."

No doubt with scraps of meat, Grace imagined. The day before, when they took their leave of the petty king, Kel had thrown bits of rancid venison to the wildman and had instructed him to guide them to Omberfell by unseen ways.

"There could be more of these dark knights around," Kel said in his gruff voice. "And there are other dangers that lurk about these moors."

Grace thought of the *feydrim* they had encountered in Seawatch, and she didn't doubt the king.

"What are you going to do now, Your Majesty?" she asked Kel, as they were about to depart.

The king scratched his bushy red beard. "My witch says I can't stay here, and that I can't go back to Kelcior, either. So I suppose I'll just have to go somewhere else."

"And where will that be?" Falken asked.

Kel let out a booming laugh and slapped him on the back. "You think I'd tell you, my good Grim Bard? Trouble follows you as closely as dingleberries follow a bull."

Falken winced at the analogy, but Grace found herself smiling. She liked the big, boisterous king, and she hoped she would see him again someday. And not just him. However, even though she looked around as they mounted the black chargers, she saw no sign of the hag Grisla anywhere.

Kel's wildman had shunned roads, instead leading them along winding game paths and directly over heath and down, avoiding all signs of habitation as they went. Grace didn't know if it was due to the wildman's skill or to luck, but they encountered no people as they went, and no creatures larger than the few birds the wildman occasionally caught and killed with his bare hands and ate raw.

Now the wildman had left to hurry after King Kel. And Grace knew there was only one direction she and the others could go. To the city, and north across the sea.

"Let's get going," Beltan said. "There's no use hanging out here in the cold, not when there's ale so close at hand."

"How do you know that?" Grace asked him, curious.

The blond knight shrugged. "Cities have taverns. Taverns have ale. It's a pattern I've noticed over the years."

Falken adjusted the rags that concealed his silver hand. "Be on your guard, everyone. After what happened in Seawatch, I think we've learned we can't trust anybody in Embarr."

It was hard to get a good view of Omberfell until they were close. A haze obscured the air, muting all colors to shades of gray, although whether it was from fog or smoke Grace couldn't tell. The city stood on the banks of an estuary, where the River Fellgrim oozed into the Winter Sea. Beyond, Grace could just glimpse rows of docks and the tall masts of ships, rising like a leafless forest in the fog.

As they drew near the city's walls, they merged with a steady stream of people moving toward the gates, no doubt coming for reasons of trade. To Grace's relief, the people didn't appear any more grimy or somber than common folk in Calavan or Toloria. She wasn't certain what she had been expecting—perhaps the same faces of despair she had seen in Galspeth.

Though the main road leading to the gate was crowded, things moved with surprising efficiency. Of course, this was Embarr. Even the average peasant here was likely to be as much an engineer as a farmer. Logic and order were revered, and the dreary landscape certainly wasn't likely to inspire flights of fancy in the general populace.

They took their place in the line of people waiting to have their goods examined before passing through the archway. However, a stern-looking guard gestured at them, and for a moment panic clutched Grace's heart. Their warhorses towered over the wooden carts and shaggy ponies, making the guard suspicious of them; they should have abandoned the chargers outside the city.

There was nothing to do but obey the guardsman. They guided their mounts toward him.

"There is no need for you and your retainers to wait in that queue, my lady," the guard said. "You may enter here at once." He gestured to a smaller side gate.

Grace could only stare. However, Falken smoothly interposed himself.

"The countess thanks you. She is weary from her journey and looks forward to her rest."

"Are you guests of the duke?"

"Not yet," Falken said. "My lady comes of her own accord to seek an audience."

"You'll be wanting to find the Sign of the Silver Grail, then," the guard said.

Falken nodded. "It's the finest lodging in the city, is it not?"

"That it is, my lord. All nobles who journey to Omberfell stay there until the duke summons them to the keep."

The guard told Falken where they would find the Silver Grail, and Falken thanked him with a coin. As they rode through the side gate, Grace let out the breath she had been holding. Now that she thought about it, it wasn't a great mystery that the guard had mistaken them for nobles. In the Dominions, only the nobility could afford to keep horses like the chargers they rode.

The Silver Grail was situated near the center of the city, not far from the stone fortress that rose on a hill above Omberfell. No doubt that was the duke's keep. To Grace's relief, the banners that flew from the towers of the fortress were purple, not crimson.

Slate-roofed houses crowded along either side of the narrow cobblestone streets down which they guided their horses. The city looked much like others Grace had seen in the Dominions. However, as she looked closer, she noticed that everything appeared to be remarkably clean and ordered. The streets were free of debris, and frequent iron grates—as well as the general lack of streams of raw sewage—indicated some sort of sewer system had been installed. Although drab in color, the houses were all neatly kept, their doors painted brown or a deep moss green. The people who passed by seemed generally sober, but not furtive or fearful, and they neither dawdled nor hurried as they moved about their tasks.

Falken guided his horse close to Vani's. "Are there any signs of the Onyx Knights around?"

"I see no indication of their presence," the *T'gol* said, scanning the streets. "If the knights had laid siege to this city, I would expect signs of strife. However, all seems to be in good order."

Beltan let out a snort. "Everything seems boring, you mean. No offense to Durge, but I had forgotten how dull and predictable Embarrans can be."

"At least the trains probably run on time," Grace said with a smile.

They reached the street the guard had described and saw a sign painted with a cup that was not so much silver as putty gray. However, the three-storied edifice was built solidly of stone, and despite the lateness of the year pansies bloomed in the flower boxes mounted beneath each of the building's windows.

As they entered the inn, a white-haired man hurried toward them and bowed low. Once Falken told their story, the proprietor, whose name was Farrand, was more than happy to accommodate the traveling countess—who for delicate political circumstances could not reveal her name until she was able to see the duke.

Again Grace was struck by the fact that common folk didn't ask questions of nobles. Farrand accepted the bard's fantastical tale without so much as an eye blink. He instructed a boy to see to their horses, then led them to their rooms on the third floor. These were spacious and clean, if spare in their appointments. Grace was beginning to think Beltan was right about the dull nature of Embarrans. Didn't these people know how to have fun? Then again, despite his serious nature, Durge was anything but boring.

Maybe Durge is an exception, Grace. It could be he was the flighty one in his family.

This thought made her laugh aloud, but when the others stared at her, she only responded with a smile. It made her feel good to think of the stolid Embarran knight.

After they stowed their few things and washed the grime of travel from their hands and faces, they headed down to the inn's common room to find food. And some ale for Beltan.

The midday meal was long over, and the common room was all but empty at that hour. However, Farrand was happy to see to their needs. They sat at a table in a private corner and ate a rich meal of pheasant pie, hare stewed with herbs, and dried apricots in cream. Grace wondered how much gold this would cost, and if it would leave them enough to buy passage on a ship. However, she was supposed to be a countess, and no doubt it would draw suspicion if she didn't eat like one.

After servants cleared away the dishes, they drank the warm, gritty cups of ale Beltan ordered for all of them.

"It tastes like boar's vomit," Vani said after taking a sip.

She pushed the mug aside. Beltan quickly drew it toward him; his own was already empty.

"So what do we do now?" Grace said to Falken.

The bard picked at the bandages that concealed his silver hand. "I suppose I should go down to the docks and start looking for a ship to take us across the Winter Sea. I had hoped to get to Omberfell before the first of Valdath, but we've missed that by a week now."

Grace hadn't realized so much time had already passed. Midwinter's Day was less than a month away. "Is that a problem?"

"It might be. The farther we are into Valdath, the more ice there will be floating down on the currents from the north. If there's too much, no captain will be willing to risk taking us across the sea."

"What if we can get a ship to take us across the sea, Falken?" Grace said. The closest servants were on the other side of the common room, and she kept her voice low. "How do we know the Onyx Knights won't just follow us again?"

"They can't know we're here," Beltan said, wiping foam from his mustache. "There's no way they could follow us."

Vani gave him a sharp look. "They followed us on the *Fate Runner.*"

"That's right," Falken said. "And I still wonder how it was they knew we were on that ship."

Grace reached up, feeling her necklace beneath the bodice of her gown. "It was the girl in Galspeth, the one at the tailor's shop. She was a member of the Raven Cult—I'm sure of it, after what we saw in Seawatch. And she saw my necklace. The knights must have questioned her. Or maybe they're in league with the Pale King, just like the Raven Cult is. Maybe the knights are like holy warriors for the cult."

"Maybe," Falken said, his tone skeptical. "But if the Onyx Knights serve the Pale King, why did they kill the *feydrim* at Seawatch? That doesn't make sense."

Beltan set down the empty ale cup. "That's not the only thing that doesn't make sense. We know the Onyx Knights want to kill you, Grace. But you heard that old countess at

Seawatch. She said the Pale King wants you alive for some reason. So how can the knights and the Pale King be on the same side?"

A shudder ran through Grace. What could the Pale King want with her? She was Ulther's sole heir. Didn't that make her Berash's mortal enemy? That was what the legends said.

"I'm not sure what it all means," Falken said. "But I think it's more important than ever that we find the shards of Fellring. And that means we've got to find a ship to—"

Soft, musical laughter rose on the air. The sound came from a dim alcove Grace hadn't noticed before. She strained her eyes and thought she saw a shadowy figure sitting within.

Beltan reached for the knife at his belt. Vani was already on her feet.

"Show yourself," the *T'gol* said.

"As you wish, my lady," said a voice as clear as the laughter. "But I beg you not to snap my neck, at least not before you've heard my excuse for eavesdropping."

A man stepped from the alcove. He was beautiful.

Tall and slender, the stranger was clad all in soft shades of gray, and he moved lithely, like a dancer. His shoulder-length hair was pure silver, but the color had to be premature, for by the smoothness of his face he was no older than Grace. His features were fine, even delicate, and his eyes were a vivid green flecked with gold, like emeralds in sunlight.

"Who are you?" Beltan growled. "And why were you listening to us?"

"I suppose I can't claim to be a friend, now can I?" the man said. "But I believe I can help you all the same. I'll tell you right off that you'll never be able to hire a ship to take you across the Winter Sea. And as for why I was listening..." He shrugged. "That was quite by accident. I had simply retired to this quiet alcove to doze after dinner. Then I woke to the sound of your voices. And I hope you'll forgive me that I didn't make myself known at once. But you were all saying such fascinating things..."

Grace cast a startled look at Falken. The man had heard everything they said. All the same, for some reason she didn't feel afraid. There was something about the other—his voice, or perhaps his striking eyes—that seemed almost familiar to her. Had she seen him somewhere before?

That's impossible, Grace. He's the prettiest man you've ever seen. Surely you'd remember him.

"Don't fear, my lady," the man said, nodding to Grace. "I know how to keep a secret. I won't reveal what I've heard. So I'd appreciate it if you could rein in your companions."

Grace glanced at Beltan and Vani, then shook her head. Grudgingly, the *T'gol* stepped back, and the knight let go of his knife. Grace gestured for the man to sit.

"What's your name?" she said.

"You can call me Sindar. It's as good a name as any."

His words should have troubled her, but they didn't. "Why don't you think we'll be able to book a ship?"

"The port has been closed," Sindar said. "By order of the duke, no ship is allowed to sail in or out of the harbor."

Grace chewed her lip; that might explain why the Onyx Knights hadn't landed in Omberfell. At best they had been able to sneak a rowboat ashore with a single knight, who had then ridden to Kelcior for reinforcements.

"I haven't heard of any such order," Falken said.

Sindar gestured to the door with a long hand. "Go to the docks yourself and ask. But don't waste too much time. For I must sail away on my own ship before sundown."

Falken grinned, and it was not an expression of humor. "You speak smoothly, Sindar. But now I see your true intention. I'm a bard by trade, so let me tell your tale. First you lurk about an inn known to be frequented by nobles. Then you eavesdrop on a group of newcomers and learn of their intention to hire a ship. So you tell them no ship can leave port, except, conveniently, for your own. Next you offer to bear the strangers to their destination for a modest fee, then you lead them to your ship. Only you have no ship, and when the hapless strangers reach the docks, the miscreants you work with jump out and rob them. Well, I'm sorry to inform you, but we're not such simple travelers."

Sindar appeared nonplussed by these words. "No, I don't believe you are." He stood up. "And you're right about one aspect of my tale. I do have a ship, and it can leave the harbor—unlike any other ship you'll find in Omberfell. However, I have no need to rob you in secret, for I can do it openly. My fee for bearing you to Toringarth is anything but modest. And my ship leaves at sundown tonight. Be here an hour before if you truly wish to go."

With that, Sindar gave an elegant bow, then turned and left the inn for the street outside.

Beltan let out a whistle. "That was a peculiar fellow. You don't think he was serious about the duke's order, do you?"

"I can't believe he was," Falken said. "All the same, I'm going to go to the docks and find out."

"I'll come with you," Vani said. "I wish to see if this thief follows us."

Grace gazed at the door where Sindar had vanished. "Did he look familiar to any of you?"

"No," Beltan said, scratching his chin. "Though I will say his eyes are almost the exact same color as yours, Grace."

41.

It was midafternoon, and a mist of rain had begun to fall over Omberfell as Grace and Beltan made their way through clean, ordered streets to the city's market.

Vani had gone to the dockyards with Falken to help the bard see about hiring a ship, and Grace had asked Beltan to accompany her on a mission to buy supplies. If they were going on a long voyage, it would be good to have some extra foodstuffs with them. More importantly, this seemed like a prime opportunity to give the knight and the assassin some time apart.

They found the city's market in a broad plaza, and it was as efficiently run as everything else in Omberfell. The stalls were organized according to what each was selling, prices were fair, and people waited in patient lines to pay their coins and take away their goods. Soon Grace and Beltan carried several packages wrapped in cloth, containing hard cheeses, nuts, and dried figs.

"That was the worst market I've ever seen," Beltan grumbled, as they walked.

Grace glanced at him, puzzled. "Really? And here I was thinking I haven't had that much luck shopping since my last trip to Safeway."

"Oh, sure," Beltan said, glowering. "If you like excellent goods at cheap prices, I suppose it was just fine. But did you notice? Nobody was selling ale."

"You just had ale at the inn, Beltan."

"What's your point?"

She shifted the packages in her arms. "I'm not really sure."

"I tell you, Grace. There's something wrong in this town. I don't care how tidy or pleasant-smelling it is, there should have been ale in the market. It's like they don't want people to have any fun. There are dark forces at work here."

Grace couldn't say she shared the same feeling. As far as she could tell, for all the prevalence of gray, Omberfell was one of the nicest cities she had seen in the Dominions. She almost hoped it took Falken and Vani a few days to find them a ship. The journey had been long and exhausting, and she knew it was far from over. It would be good to pause and rest, if for just a little while. Besides, while she still wasn't the best judge of human nature, she had a feeling Beltan's dark mood didn't really have to do with ale.

"Why do you hate her?" she asked before she could consider the wisdom of it. "Vani's saved all of our lives more than once."

Beltan looked away. "I don't hate her."

"You have a tendency to act like it."

"You're mistaken, Your Majesty."

Grace winced at the sharpness in his voice, but she wasn't going to let go that easily. "It's Travis, isn't it? He loves you—you know he does. Only maybe you're afraid he might love Vani, too. That's why you can't stand her."

Beltan came to a sudden halt, and Grace nearly collided with his shoulder. He looked at her, and she swallowed. It had been a long time since she had seen the knight really angry, and now she wished she hadn't so casually invoked his ire. His face was hard; in that moment she remembered he was a man of war.

"It could be easy to hate her, you know," Beltan said, his voice rough. "If she was wicked, if she was foolish, if she led us time and again into danger with her actions, then I would despise her. But she's not those things, is she?" He sighed, his anger fading. "She's beautiful, and strong, and, as you've reminded me, she's risked herself to save our lives—my life— with her deeds. How could I possibly hate her? And how could I possibly blame Travis for loving her instead of me? After all, she's a princess of an ancient people. And I'm just a bastard who murdered his own father."

Grace's heart crumpled in her chest. She wanted to say, *You're one of the finest men I have ever met, Beltan of Calavan, and Travis does love you.* But before she could, the deep toll of a bell rang out.

The sound of the bell came again, closer this time, echoing off slate roofs. The crowd that had filled the avenue parted as people pressed themselves close to the houses on either side, leaving the center of the broad street empty.

"What's going on?" Grace said.

Beltan glanced around. "It looks like they're making room for some sort of procession. Whatever's coming, I don't think we want to get in its way."

They hurried to one side of the avenue, but since the crowd was already densely packed, they found themselves in the front row facing the street.

"Be careful, my lady," said the man standing next to Grace. He was a merchant by his well-made but plain garb. "You must be sure not to stand any farther into the street than those around you when he comes. Our line must be even."

She shook her head. "When who comes?"

"Why, the duke, my lady."

So Beltan was right—a procession was coming, one led by the Duke of Omberfell.

The merchant craned his neck, as if eager to catch sight of the coming parade. "The duke has been preparing himself for great trials, my lady. They say he will soon ride to war."

"War?" She clutched the packages to her chest as she

was jostled from behind. Beltan held out an arm, trying to keep the crowd from pressing too close to her. "War against whom?"

The merchant seemed puzzled by her words. "Against the enemies of the Master, of course."

"The master? You mean the duke?"

"Nay, my lady. The duke serves the Master even as we do. Surely you know that." A hint of suspicion crept into his gaze. "You do know, don't you?"

"I'm new to town," she said, hoping that was a good enough excuse for any ignorance.

The bell tolled again. This time, she saw the source of the sound. Four men carried a wooden frame from which the bell hung. Another man trailed behind, striking the bell at intervals with a hammer. The men were filthy, their backs bowed. Blood crusted their ragged tunics, and chains clinked around their ankles as they trudged along.

"Who are they?" Grace whispered to herself. However the merchant heard and answered her question.

"They are transgressors."

She looked at the man. "Transgressors?"

"Ones who have gone against the Edicts." His eyes narrowed. "You do know the Edicts, don't you?"

Her chest felt suddenly tight; she struggled for breath. "I'm not...that is, I..."

Despite the press of the throng, the merchant took a step back from her, his eyes growing wide. "Everyone knows the Edicts, my lady. Even a little child." He began to murmur quickly, as if speaking the words of a litany, pressing his hands together. "One cannot resist the will of the Master. One cannot do things which the many do not. One must give one's heart should the Raven ask for it..."

Grace clasped a hand to her mouth, but she couldn't stifle her gasp of fear. Beltan glanced at her, concern in his eyes. Before she could speak, the merchant raised his arm and pointed a trembling finger at her.

"You're a heretic," he whispered. "You disobey the Edicts, just like those transgressors. But I won't be tainted by you." His voice rose into a shrill cry. "Heretic!"

Until that moment, people had been watching the street, but now several turned their heads in Grace's direction.

Beltan leaned close to her. "We'd better get out of here."

However, at that moment the full body of the procession rounded a corner and marched down the avenue. A man on a gray horse rode at the fore, and there was no doubt he was the duke. He wore elegant black clothes, with a long cloak trailing behind, and his expression was proud and fierce. An ornate scabbard was slung at his side, and gems glittered on his fingers. However, it was not his finery Grace stared at. It was the symbol drawn in ashes on his forehead. It was the wing of a Raven. Or a blind, staring eye.

They marched behind him four abreast, and Grace could see no end to their procession: a line of figures in black. Their robes had heavy hoods, but some had pushed the hoods back, and their foreheads bore the same symbol as the duke's. Except some were marked, not with ashes, but with a puckered brand.

From the midst of the procession rose a series of wooden poles, their bases gripped by the black-robed ones. Atop the poles, swinging like leather skins filled with water, were lashed limp figures. It took Grace a long second to realize they were people. Or had been, at any rate, before their hands and feet were cut off, and their eyes plucked out. Bile rose in her throat.

So that's why things are so ordered and efficient in this city, Grace. If you dare to go against the rules, if you dare to be different somehow, this is what happens to you.

More of the figures in black robes marched around the corner, and more. A chant rose on the air.

> *drink the ice*
> *breathe the fire*
> *Shadow be your lover*
>
> *chain the mind*
> *still the heart*
> *Darkness rules forever*

Most people watched the procession, but a few more had noticed the merchant's accusing finger. He was silent now, his face a mask of revulsion, still pointing at her. Others gestured in Grace's direction. Angry murmurs of *heretic* and *witch* ran through the crowd.

Beltan shifted the parcel he held and grabbed Grace, propelling her through the crowd, snarling at people to get out of their way. Most did, shrinking in fear before the big knight, but some resisted. The packages were knocked out of Grace's hands. She tripped over them and would have fallen but for Beltan's grip on her arm.

Now others picked up the merchant's cry.

"She's broken the Edicts!"

"Heretic! You befoul the name of the Raven!"

"Get the witch!"

Beltan was no longer just pushing. He swung the package of food, knocking several people aside, then let it drop. A man clutched at Grace, and Beltan punched him in the face. Blood and teeth flew. Someone screamed.

Grace gathered her will. If they were going to accuse her of being a witch, she might as well do the crime. But there was no mist to weave into a wall as she had done before. What else might she be able to use? Then she felt the life strands vibrating with fear and anger around her, and she knew. She reached out with her mind, grasping the threads of the people around her, then with a thought, she tied them all into a tangled knot.

At once, people began tripping over one another, flailing as they stumbled and fell to the street. The ordered line of the crowd became a churning sea of chaos. Shouts of pain and confusion rose on the air. In the street, some of the Raven cultists paused, staring.

"Now, Beltan," Grace said, clutching the knight's hand.

He roared, using his free arm to toss a man out of their way, then pulled Grace toward the mouth of an alley. It was cool and dark inside. They ran, and the noise of the crowd echoed after them. After a dozen yards they came to an intersecting alley. Which direction should they go? In moments, the mob would see where they had gone and would follow.

"This way," said a musical voice.

Grace turned and saw him standing in the mouth of a shadowed archway. He was barely visible in his dark cloak, but she caught a flash of silver hair, a glint of vivid, green-gold eyes. Beltan sucked in a breath.

The other motioned, urging them toward the archway. "Quickly. They're already coming."

Then he was gone.

Grace felt Beltan's hesitation. However, shouts rang out behind them. There was nowhere else to go. She tightened her grip on the big knight's hand, and together they ran through the archway, following Sindar.

42.

More than once, Grace thought they had lost their mysterious rescuer in the maze of alleys they traversed. Sindar moved swiftly, and often Grace caught only a flash of silver before he vanished around a corner or through an opening, leaving her and Beltan to run after or become hopelessly lost.

And they did not want to get lost. Omberfell had seemed cleaner and more orderly than any city she had seen in the Dominions, but now Grace knew that had only been on the surface. All the grime, all the poverty, all the suffering, had simply been swept out of sight—into this tangled web of back alleys where she and Beltan often couldn't walk side by side.

Rats scuttled over their feet, racing between heaps of rotting garbage. Sewage formed rank puddles through which they splashed. Eyes peered out of windows that had never opened on sunlight or a blue sky, and dirty hands reached from doorways, plucking at Grace's cloak as voices moaned for alms and mercy. Beltan batted the hands away and pulled Grace onward. Only after a while did she realize that many of the heaps she had taken for garbage were people. She couldn't tell whether they were alive or dead. The rats didn't seem to care.

At last they passed through an archway and found themselves on a clean, wide street not far from the Sign of the Silver Grail. There was no trace of Sindar.

"Come on," Beltan said, tugging at Grace's arm. "We need to get inside before we're seen."

As they approached the inn, Grace expected to see a line of figures in black robes pointing at her with accusing fingers. Instead, the street was empty. They looked both ways, then stole inside the inn and hurried up to their rooms.

Falken and Vani were already there.

"What happened?" Falken said, eyeing their clothes. "You look like you you've been rolling in a pigsty. And where's the food you were going to buy? Not that it matters. Our mysterious friend was right—the docks have been shut down. No ship can enter or leave the port, by order of the duke."

"Just as I told you."

They looked up to see Sindar shutting the door behind him; Grace hadn't heard it open. Nor, by the angry look on her face, had Vani. She started moving toward the slender man.

Grace held out a hand. "Vani, no—he just saved our lives."

Falken cast Grace a curious glance. She drew in a deep breath, then explained what had happened. When she finished, Vani moved to the window, gazing outside.

Sorrow shone in Falken's faded blue eyes. "It seems things are darker than I feared. A year ago, the Raven Cult operated in secret. The Pale King must grow bold to let his cult work so openly now. No wonder the men we spoke to on the docks were so fearful when I even mentioned the idea of booking passage on a ship. I suppose just talking about breaking the duke's order could get them executed."

Grace took a step toward Sindar. "Where were you?"

"My question exactly," Beltan growled. "You were certainly in a hurry back in those alleys. I almost think you were trying to lose us."

Sindar laughed. "I promise, you of all people would have found me." He turned toward Grace. "As for where I was just now, I was making certain you weren't followed."

Vani turned from the window. "Were they?"

"No, but you can't stay here long. The duke won't allow troublemakers to go uncaptured in his city. There will be a search."

"They'll know what we look like," Beltan said, pacing. "Lots of people saw our faces. It won't take long before the duke's men knock on the door of the inn. And they'll be watching the city gate as well."

Grace held a hand to her throbbing head. "If we can't leave by the gate, and no ship captain will disobey the duke's orders, how do we get out of the city?"

They all looked at Sindar. The handsome man spread his hands and smiled. "My offer still stands."

"I don't like it," Beltan said, as if Sindar weren't even there. "We don't know anything about him. And it seems awfully convenient that he just happened to overhear our conversation, and that he just happens to have a way around the blockade. I'm sure of it when I say he's lying about something."

"I agree," Vani said, glaring at Sindar.

Falken moved close to Grace. "What do you think?"

Now everyone was looking at her, and she hated the attention. "I don't think we have any choice. Even if he's lying to us, I'd rather deal with a swindler than the Raven Cult. And he did help Beltan and me escape that mob." She gave Sindar a weak smile. "I suppose we'll just have to trust you."

In minutes they had gathered their things and were ready. Vani reported that the street outside the inn was still clear.

Falken swung his lute case over his shoulder. "It would be good if we could leave without Farrand or any of his workers seeing us."

Grace nodded. "I can arrange that."

Sindar opened the door and gestured to Grace. "After you, Your Majesty."

A jolt of shock coursed through her. "How do you know about that?" She studied Sindar's face, once again struck by the queer feeling of familiarity. "How long have you been following us really?"

"We must go," Sindar said, and moved through the door.

It was shockingly easy to escape the inn without being seen. Grace wove the threads of the Weirding like a cloak around the five of them, concealing them from any eyes that might look their way. They walked down the stairs, into the common room, and through the front door. Neither Farrand nor any of his servants so much as glanced up from their work.

They left the inn on foot—they would have no need of the horses—and Grace maintained the illusion as they made their way through the city. At one point fear stabbed at her chest when they rounded a corner and saw a trio of men in black robes moving toward them. They froze, but the robed ones simply walked by them swiftly. Grace forced herself to concentrate, keeping her grip on the spell.

They reached the docks. There were many men about—no doubt from the crews of the dozens of ships locked in port—but they seemed to be doing little besides playing at cards or dice. Here and there, guards kept watch on the proceedings with hard eyes. Sindar moved to a narrow space behind a stack of wooden crates, and the rest of them followed.

Once they were all behind the crates, Grace released her grip on the Weirding. Never had she held on to a spell for so long. Although, now that she had released it, she didn't feel exhausted. Rather she felt alive, even exhilarated.

Vani peered around the edge of a crate. "I wonder why the duke has ordered the port closed. Could it be they spotted the ship of the Onyx Knights? We know now that the knights are the enemies of the Pale King."

"I believe you're right in that," Sindar said.

Falken raised an eyebrow. "You know about the Onyx Knights?"

"Every ship's captain who sails these waters knows about those pirates. If you don't pay them a third of the value of your cargo in gold, they broadside your ship and send you to sleep at the bottom of the ocean."

Beltan ran a hand through his thinning hair. "I suppose it all makes sense. The Onyx Knights think they're going to restore Malachor, so naturally they consider the Pale King their enemy. But the Raven Cult is in charge of Omberfell, and the cult serves the Pale King. Even the hundred knights on that ship wouldn't be enough to take over a hostile city this size. They'd need at least double that number."

"It might be even more than that," Sindar said. "From what I've heard, the Onyx Knights despise the Cult of the Raven. I've seen that firsthand. Only they've gone out of their way to avoid conflict with them. It's almost as if the knights are using the cult for their own purposes."

Falken nodded. "I see it now. The knights are letting the Raven Cult sow chaos and strife in Embarr, weakening it, making it ready for invasion. And to get rid of any witches, runespeakers, or anyone else who might be able to stand against them. Then the knights will stamp out the cult once they take over the Dominion. That's what they did in Eredane, and in Brelegond, too, I suppose."

"You can speak more of this later," Sindar said, glancing at the overcast sky. "The sun will be setting soon. We must be on my ship by then."

Vani gazed out over the docks. "Which of these ships is yours?"

"None of them," Sindar said with a laugh. He moved from the crates to the mouth of a large storm drain. It was covered with an iron grille, bolted in place. The grille looked new.

"That was not there when I last came in this way," Sindar said, pointing at the grille. He glanced at Beltan and Vani. "Could you do the honors?"

The knight and the *T'gol* gripped the iron grille. Beltan clenched his teeth, and Vani shut her eyes. To Grace, it seemed the grille warped and rippled under Vani's hands. With a grunt, Beltan pulled it free of its moorings.

"This way," Sindar said, leading the way into the storm drain.

They followed after, hunching over, as the drain was no more than five feet high. Beltan came last, pulling the grille into place behind them.

The tunnel was dank and slippery and sloped gently downward. They moved for what seemed to Grace like hours, although she supposed it was only minutes. The tiled walls pressed close, making it hard to breathe. However, she supposed that was good, as otherwise she would have screamed.

After a hundred yards it should have been pitch-dark in the tunnel, but for some reason there was just enough light to make out the forms of the others before and behind her. At last, just when Grace was ready to turn and scrabble her way back out of the tunnel, she saw a gray circle ahead. They quickened their pace, and she breathed in relief as they reached the end. The five gathered on a small lip of stone. The roar of the sea thrummed on the air, and salty spray splashed against Grace's face, moistening her cheeks like tears.

"Now what?" Beltan said, glaring at Sindar.

Grace blinked the water from her eyelashes, then understood. The tunnel ended in a cliff. To either side of them were vertical walls of rough stone. Water spilled from the tunnel, over the ledge, and into cold waves that lapped ten feet below.

"Our transport already comes for us," Sindar said.

He pointed, and at first Grace was confused. It looked like a gigantic bird floating on the ocean, its neck curving down over its breast, its white wings tucked against its side. Only after a moment did she realize it was a ship.

Falken swore a soft oath.

"I have never seen a vessel like that before," Vani said.

Sindar smiled. "No, you haven't."

The ship was coming toward them. It was not so large as the *Fate Runner*, but it was infinitely more graceful. The ship was not painted white; rather, its color came from the pale silver wood of which it was built. The vessel came closer.

"The sea is too rough," Beltan said. "It's going to be dashed against the cliffs."

Only it wasn't. The ship sailed smoothly, as if it didn't feel the force of the waves. It drifted close to the cliff, until it was no more than a dozen feet away, then halted. Only then did Grace realize that there were neither masts nor sails nor oars. How was the ship propelled?

In the failing light, she saw figures scurrying on the deck of the ship. Some were small and twisted, and others tall and slender as willow saplings. It seemed some bore antlers upon their brows, and others flowers in their hair. Grace shivered. She had seen forms like these once before. It was the previous Midwinter's Eve, when Trifkin Mossberry's troupe of actors had performed their play in the great hall of Calavere.

A plank extended from the ship, reaching to the stone ledge. Grace felt strangely light, her nerves tingling. She looked at Sindar. His eyes glittered in the ghostly light.

"Who are you?" she whispered. "Who are you really?"

"I think . . . I think that I'm a friend."

Sindar stepped onto the plank and moved lightly to the ship. Grace glanced at the others, searching their faces, but there was nothing for them to do but follow. One by one, they stepped over to the deck. The queer figures hurried into action, the plank was pulled back. And the graceful ship moved away from the cliff, into the open sea and the coming night.

43.

The doors of Calavere's great hall shut with a thunderous *boom*. Aryn felt as if she had just been struck by lightning. She had finally learned the name of the man who was to be her husband, and it was none other than King Boreas's son, Prince Teravian.

She was alone with the king. The servants had withdrawn, leading Queen Ivalaine and Sister Mirda to their chambers. Aryn wished they had remained; she had so many questions for the two witches.

Later, sister, Mirda's gentle voice had sounded over the threads of the Weirding as the women left the hall. *Come to our chamber when the moon has risen and her light shines over the castle wall. We shall speak then.*

Aryn's heart beat against her rib cage like a frightened bird. She was painfully aware of the king's gaze. There was no way she could disobey his order; she had to marry as the king commanded. But Teravian? Couldn't it have been anyone else? Even ancient Duke Calentry didn't sound so horrible now.

"Tell me, my lady," the king growled before she could gather her wits. He descended the steps of the dais, moving with the murderous grace of an animal stalking its prey. "What do you think of my choice of husband?"

Aryn knew his words were a challenge; Boreas was daring her to defy him. That was not a trap she would fall for. "I think, Your Majesty," she said, forcing her chin up, commanding her eyes to meet his, "that once I marry the prince, you will be my father not only in my heart, but in fact as well, and this gladdens me beyond all my abilities to express."

The words rang with the power of truth. Because they *were* true. Whatever she thought of Prince Teravian's character—or the lack thereof—and no matter how she feared the king, she loved Boreas as the only father she had ever known.

Boreas blinked as if she had slapped him, then a broad grin crossed his face. If this were a battle, and she a general, the tactical victory would be hers—even if there was no hope she could win the war against such a vastly stronger force.

The king lifted a hand to her cheek, and when he spoke his usually booming voice was gruff. "Do not think I'm unaware of my son's failings, my lady. If I had forgotten them in his absence, then they were made painfully clear to me once more the moment he set foot in this hall. Yet it is not such a bad lot to marry a prince, even one so peevish. And it is my hope, with a companion of strength and temperance by his side, that he might one day even learn to be a man and a king."

Aryn could find no words with which to reply.

"You'll need to speak with Lord Farvel soon. You must tell him how you wish your wedding to be. Now go." He bent down and kissed her forehead. "Daughter."

He withdrew, and she curtsied low, bowing her head so that he would not see the tears she knew were welling forth in her eyes; generals did not cry. Without words, Aryn turned and hurried from the great hall.

She wandered through the castle, as there was nothing else for her to do. Mirda had told her to come at moonrise, but that was hours away. And resigned as she was to her noble duty, she was far from ready to talk to Lord Farvel about wedding plans.

You should consider yourself lucky, Aryn of Elsandry, she chided herself as she sat on a window bench. Beyond the rippled glass, the land marched away in rows of gray-green downs. *You were afraid the king would marry you off to someone thrice your age and with a face like a turnip. Well, Teravian certainly isn't old. He's your younger by two winters, and he's actually rather handsome. When he isn't scowling.*

She sighed. *All right, so he's always scowling. But maybe Boreas is right—maybe there's hope he can change.*

"What's wrong, my lady?" said a bright tenor voice. "Did you get a bad bit of cheese in your breakfast?"

Aryn turned from the window and looked up. Sir Tarus stood above her. The knight wore leather riding garb. Mud spattered his boots, and rain darkened his red hair.

She shook her head. "Cheese?"

"Or maybe a rotten nut? You were sighing and holding your stomach. I though perhaps you had eaten something that didn't sit well with you."

She sighed again. "It's not something I ate."

The knight raised an eyebrow.

Aryn supposed there was no point in keeping it from him. "The king just told me who my husband is to be."

Tarus let out a low whistle. "And you're not happy about him, I take it?"

"I suspect it's rather the other way around."

Tarus said nothing. Aryn supposed it was hard for him to understand. An unhappy marriage was little burden to a man of noble birth; he had other activities to occupy him—politics, hunting, war—and he could always take a mistress. But for a noblewoman, a wife was all she was allowed to be.

And is that true, Aryn? Do you honestly think Teravian can stop you from being a witch?

Besides, she supposed things were not the same for Tarus as for other men. She gazed again out the window.

"Tell me something, Sir Tarus," she said. "Do the Warriors of Vathris . . . do you ever marry? Or do you just . . . that is, with each other . . . ?"

He let out a chuckle, and she heard him move closer. He smelled of mist and horses. "We're men of war, my lady. We don't spend all of our time romping about a fire in loincloths and spanking one another. Really."

Aryn couldn't help a gasp of laughter. She turned around and looked at him. "But I thought all of you . . . I mean, that women were . . ."

"Tell me, do all of your sister witches spurn the favors of men in their beds?"

Aryn chewed her lip. "I know that some of them do. They say the touch of a man weakens their magic, although I can't see how this would be. And there are some who will lie with any whom they love. But I believe most witches are like most women, and that they desire the touch of a man in bed."

Her cheeks flushed with warmth. She had hardly ever spoken so frankly to another woman about such matters, let alone a man. Then again, she supposed she was quite secure with Sir

Tarus. And, she realized, that was one reason why she liked the knight. She felt safe with him in a way she felt with no other man. Or woman, for that matter. He was strong, as men were; yet he would never harm her.

She gestured for him to sit on the bench, and he did so, although he was careful to keep his muddy clothes away from the folds of her gown. It occurred to her she had not seen Tarus in the last day or two; he must have ridden off somewhere on an errand for the king.

"The Warriors are not so different than your Witches," he said. "I can't tell you about our secret ways, but I can say there are certain initiations which all young men undergo when they seek to follow the Mysteries of Vathris, rituals in which they are paired with one who is older and wiser and who acts as their mentor. But it's also true that the great majority of the men of Vathris go on to take wives and father children. Only a few of them ever hear the Call of the Bull."

"Like you have. And Sir Beltan."

The knight looked away, and Aryn winced. She knew Tarus had cared for Beltan, just as she knew Beltan's heart beat for another. Perhaps she should leave the topic. However, she found it all too fascinating to let go.

"Are you and Beltan to be priests of Vathris, then?"

Tarus looked at her again, his face uncharacteristically solemn. "It's usually those who've heard the Call who go to the inner circle, as it's forbidden for a priest to marry. Maybe, when I'm older and wiser, I'll choose to become a priest. But I don't imagine Beltan ever will. Speaking prayers isn't for him—he'd rather be fighting. Only I think I might get tired of it someday. Of fighting."

Aryn considered these words. She knew Tarus was giving her a rare gift: a glimpse into the smoke-shrouded labyrinth where the Cult of Vathris Bullslayer worked its mysteries. Rarer all the more because he knew she was a witch.

"I've heard King Boreas has reached the innermost circle," she said, more to herself than to Tarus.

Now the knight laughed. "The king's wife passed away, my lady, and he elected not to marry again out of deference to her memory. So he is free to enter the innermost circle. But I think if you were to spy upon the king at night, it would be a pretty woman you'd find sharing his bed, not a handsome man. Then again, when I . . ."

The knight's gaze seemed suddenly distant, as if he was remembering. "What is it?" Aryn said.

"I can't know for certain." Tarus shrugged. "They throw pine boughs on the fire, so the air is thick with smoke, and they give you strong wine to drink. And the one who has been chosen for you wears a mask shaped like a bull's head."

Aryn suddenly felt she was hearing something she shouldn't. It was too secret; too private. "Should you be telling me this, my lord?"

"Most likely not. But . . ." He shook his head. "But, my lady, I like you, and I like Lady Lirith. No matter what you are. Or what I am. No matter that they say we are enemies."

So the Warriors talked of the Witches, just as Aryn and her sisters spoke of the men of Vathris. They all knew a conflict was coming. The Final Battle, as the Warriors called it.

"Are we?" she said quietly. "Enemies, I mean."

"What do your sisters say?"

"Much the same as your brothers, I suppose."

They were silent for a long minute. Outside the window, a hawk sped by in pursuit of a dove.

"Let us forge a pact, my, lady," Tarus said suddenly. "If in the future we find ourselves on opposite sides, we'll still be friends. And we'll be honest with one another. As honest as we can possibly be, at least, without breaking any other vows we have made." He stood up and held out his hand. "Will you make this pact with me?"

Aryn didn't hesitate. She stood up and took his hand in her one good one. "I accept your word, my lord, and you have mine in turn. I swear it in the name of Sia."

"And I swear it in the name of Vathris."

Warmth flooded Aryn, and new hope. Only at that moment did she realize how deep was the well of her despair, now that a new glimmer of light shone into it. If there were men like Tarus and Beltan among the Warriors, then why did the Witches have to be their foes?

However, Aryn knew the answer to that. Just as Liendra and her faction craved only conflict, Aryn supposed most of the followers of Vathris wanted the same. But as long as there were witches like Mirda, and Lirith, and herself, and warriors like Tarus and Beltan, maybe all was not lost.

"Well," Tarus said, withdrawing his hand, "that's that, then."

Aryn nodded. "You'd better go to the king. I'm certain he's waiting for your report."

Tarus opened his mouth, then shook his head and walked away. Aryn smiled. Just because they were friends didn't mean she had to give up all of her air of mystery. She had only assumed he had been on an errand for the king based on the visible evidence; and in that case, of course he would have a report to give. But let him think she had the power of the Sight. That way he'd be sure to keep their pact.

And will you, Aryn? Will you keep your promise to tell the truth no matter what? Even if it goes against the Pattern?

Yes. Whatever it took, she would keep her vow. For she was not just a witch; she was a baroness, and soon to be a queen. She would not break her word.

44.

The day passed slowly, and with no sign of Prince Teravian. Aryn was thankful for that, although this reaction made her feel guilty. She supposed she should apologize to him for her words in the great hall. No matter that he was the one who had stamped off; if they were going to be married, they had at least better learn to act civil.

However, the prince was nowhere to be seen. Although once she glimpsed Lord Farvel at a distance, speaking to a manservant, and she distinctly heard the sound of her own name echo down the corridor. The servant turned and pointed, but before the old seneschal could start moving in her direction, Aryn scampered away.

There was no avoiding supper in the great hall that night. Aryn found herself seated at the opposite side of the high table from Ivalaine and Mirda. The queen sat to the king's left and Teravian to his right, next to Lord Farvel. Fortunately, there were two visiting earls between Aryn and the seneschal, and the few times Farvel tried to speak across the noblemen to ask her something about her upcoming wedding, she feigned deafness and merely smiled, raising her goblet to his health.

Boreas seemed unusually subdued, and Aryn wondered what Sir Tarus had told him. The red-haired knight was not at table, although there was an empty space for him at the far end, next to where Melia sat, looking elegantly bored. Boreas leaned often toward Ivalaine to speak something in a voice too low to overhear. However, Ivalaine never responded to the king. She simply gazed over the hall, her eyes glittering like the opals woven into her flaxen hair. Only once did Aryn risk a glance at Teravian, but the prince didn't meet her gaze. He was scowling at no one in particular, his eyebrows drawn into a single brooding line.

Aryn slipped away from supper at the earliest possible moment and was out of the great hall before Lord Farvel could rise from his chair. She considered going to look for the Spider, Aldeth. However, she didn't know exactly what she would say to the spy. And she couldn't go to her chamber; that was the first place Farvel would look for her. Without really thinking about it, she found herself at the door to Melia's room.

"Come in," said a clear voice from beyond before Aryn lifted a hand to knock.

She entered to find Melia just sitting down to her embroidery. The black kitten played on the rug before the fire, pouncing and batting at a ball of string.

Aryn cleared her throat. "I was wondering . . ."

"Of course dear," Melia said. "I'm certain no one will find you here."

Aryn was too grateful to ask just how the lady could be so sure of that. She sat in a chair near the fire, then promptly regretted it as she began to sweat.

"Are you happy, dear?" Melia said, eyes on her embroidery.

Aryn nearly jumped from the chair. What did Melia mean by that? Of course—she was referring to the news of Aryn's husband-to-be.

"I'm lucky the king considers me worthy to wed his son," Aryn said.

Melia looked up from her work. "That wasn't what I asked."

Aryn rose from the chair and moved to the window. "Do you mind? It's a bit warm in here."

"Of course, dear."

Aryn pushed back the curtain and opened the window a crack. The cool autumn air felt good against her face, but she was more interested in being able to see past the curtain.

They passed the time in silence. Melia continued to work on her embroidery, and Aryn wound thread on to spools in an attempt to be useful, although the kitten quickly undid most of her work. At last the fire burned low, and the kitten collapsed in a heap of fur and tangled thread, nose to tail, fast asleep.

"Isn't it about time for you to be going, dear?" Melia said. "You don't want to be late."

Aryn started at the sound of the lady's voice. She must have been dozing. Quickly, she glanced out the window. A sliver of pale silver was just edging over the castle's eastern rampart.

Aryn turned to see the lady's amber eyes upon her. So Melia had known all along why Aryn had really opened the window.

"Be careful, dear," Melia said. "There is great joy in wielding magic. But there is danger as well. As I'm certain Queen Ivalaine knows well."

What did she mean? Aryn was too startled to ask, so instead she merely murmured good night and hastily departed. She hurried down empty corridors and found herself at the door of Ivalaine's chamber. She knocked softly, and a young maidservant in a green dress, barely more than a girl, opened the door. The maidservant led Aryn to a comfortable room draped with tapestries.

"You may go now, Adeline," Mirda said to the maidservant. "I shall call if the queen has further need of you or your sisters this evening."

The girl curtsied, then departed through a side door. For a moment, through the open doorway, Aryn caught a glimpse of a half dozen curious faces peering out. The queen's attendants. No doubt the young women had entered Ivalaine's service hoping they might get the chance to learn something about magic. If so, their hopes were dashed for that night. The door shut, leaving Mirda and Aryn alone.

"Where is the queen?" Aryn said, glancing around.

"And am I not a fine enough teacher for you, sister?"

Aryn winced. That wasn't what she had meant. Then she saw the smile on Mirda's lips, and the warm light shining in her almond-shaped eyes, and she knew the elder witch was not angry.

Emotion welled up in Aryn's heart. "Sister Mirda, what you did that night—when we were weaving the Pattern—it was..." She shook her head, at a loss for words to describe what she felt. So she spoke over the Weirding instead, for that way her feelings could come across as clearly as her thoughts.

It was wonderful. More than wonderful. It was like a candle shining in the middle of the darkest night. If it hadn't been for you, Sister Liendra would have—

Mirda gripped her hands. *Let us not speak of what is done. I only did what I must. And so shall you.*

"But you have been too long from your studies with Sister Lirith," Mirda said aloud. "That's why the queen asked me to accompany her when she brought her ward to Calavere. We know what happened in Tarras—King Boreas told the queen at supper. It is a dark tale, to be sure, and we can only pray to Sia for our Sister Lirith's safe return. However, in the meantime, I will be your teacher. You are to be a queen by marriage, but you are a witch by birth, and that is something you must never forget."

Aryn nodded, but something in Mirda's words didn't quite add up, only she couldn't grasp what it was.

"Did you bring a cloak?" Mirda asked.

Aryn shook her head. It was perfectly warm in here. What on Eldh would she need a cloak for?

"Some things are best learned by moonlight," Mirda said in answer to Aryn's unspoken question. "But don't fear, you won't freeze. I have an extra you may borrow."

She opened a wardrobe and rummaged through the clothes within. Once again Aryn found herself wondering how old Mirda was. Fine lines accentuated her eyes and mouth, and a single lock of white made a striking contrast with her jet hair. Yet surely Mirda couldn't be any older than five-and-thirty winters. Then again, there was a depth to her gaze, a wisdom, that reminded Aryn of Melia. And Melia had been born over two thousand years ago.

Before Aryn could wonder more, Mirda pulled a woolen cloak from the wardrobe and helped Aryn wrap it around her shoulders. Then she took up her own cloak. As she donned the garment, a low sound emanated from one of the chamber's side doors. Not the door behind which the maidservants slept, but another.

Aryn cast a startled look at Mirda. "What was that?"

Again came the sound, clearer this time. It was a woman's voice, moaning as if in pain. Understanding pierced Aryn's brain.

"It's the queen!" She started toward the door.

Mirda's touch was as light as a hummingbird on Aryn's arm, but it stopped her all the same. "The queen is weary, that is all. Her sleep has been troubled of late, for there is much that weighs upon her mind. But she prepared a draught for herself this evening, and so her slumber must not be interrupted."

The sound did not come again; Ivalaine must have settled into sleep again.

"Is she ill?" Aryn said.

"No, sister. Not in any way you might think."

What could it be then? A dark thought occurred to Aryn. "Is it safe for her to have left Ar-tolor?"

"Come," Mirda said, moving to the door. "The moon has risen. It is time for your studies to begin."

Mirda walked swiftly through the castle, her cloak fluttering like blue wings, and Aryn had to half run just to keep up; there was no chance for further questions. Still, Aryn couldn't help thinking she had struck a nerve.

Boreas had summoned Teravian back to court, and protocol required that the one who had fostered the prince these last years present him upon his return. Calavan was Toloria's oldest ally; for Ivalaine to deny tradition would have been a grave insult. So the queen had been forced to leave Ar-tolor. But whom had she left behind? Certainly Tressa, her advisor, for the red-haired witch had not come to Calavere. Was there anyone else? Most of the witches at the High Coven had returned to their homelands immediately after the weaving of the Pattern. But not all. And Aryn had a feeling that if any had stayed behind, Sister Liendra would be among them. After all, Brelegond had fallen to the dark knights, so she couldn't have returned home.

What is she up to, Aryn? What is Liendra doing in Ar-tolor while the queen is away? She can't possibly be up to good. Is that why Ivalaine is so worried?

There was something important here, something to do with what she had been thinking about earlier. What was it Mirda had said? Before Aryn could remember, Mirda opened a door into the upper bailey. She led the way to the arched entrance of the castle's garden. Despite the lateness of the year, the scent of green, living things rose on the air.

Aryn followed Mirda down a stone path. Calavere's garden was a dense tangle: a place not so much planted as left to its own devices. There was a wildness to the garden that made her think of Gloaming Wood, the forest to the north of the castle, which most folk in Calavan avoided as a place of shadow and rumor. The garden was neither so deep nor so ancient, of course. All the same, she had a feeling that Trifkin Mossberry and his troupe of actors would be at home in it.

They were nearly to the entrance of the hedge maze when Mirda came to a halt. The two women stood in a grotto surrounded by slender *valsindar* trees. The bark of the trees shone white in the moonlight, as did the statue in the center of the grotto. Aryn had seen the statue many times before, but never—she realized as she gazed upon it now—in the light of an almost-full moon. In the eerie glow the statue seemed almost alive.

It was made up of two figures. One was a fierce and beautiful man. Muscles seemed to ripple beneath stone skin; his hair and beard flowed back in intricate curls, as if he faced a roaring wind. The other figure was a bull, a beast as strong as the man that fought it. One of his hands gripped its horns, pulling its head back as the beast opened its mouth in a silent bellow. In his other hand was a sword that pierced the bull's throat. From the wound poured a stream of dark fluid: not blood, but water.

Aryn glanced at Mirda. Why had the witch led her there, of all places—to a statue of Vathris Bullslayer, god of the mystery cult of the Warriors?

"What do you think when you look upon him?" Mirda said.

Aryn gathered the cloak about herself and studied the statue. Somehow she knew Mirda did not want a glib answer, but the truth.

"I think he's beautiful. And perilous. Beautiful, because I believe there is no one, neither woman nor man, who could deny him anything were he to ask for it. Not their loyalty, not their body, and not their blood. And he is perilous, because he would take it, take it with joy, even if what was offered were a life."

Mirda moved closer. "Yes, he is dangerous that way. See how he smiles as he slays the bull, a living creature."

"But the stories say he saved a dying kingdom with its sacrifice." A wisp of cloud scudded before the moon, casting shadows, and Aryn could almost imagine the statue moved in the ghostly light. "They say the bull's blood became a great river that returned life to a parched land."

"Yes, so the stories tell us." Mirda circled slowly around the statue, as if wary. "But do they say why the land became a desert in the first place? Was it not because of the wars he waged that his kingdom became a wasteland?"

Aryn shook her head. "I don't know. But even if that were so, slaying the bull still brought back life."

"Really?" Mirda came to a halt, her eyes catching the starlight. "Do you truly believe death can bring life?"

It was so cold. Aryn's head ached with the chill; it was hard to think. "I'm not sure. No. Maybe. Certainly death doesn't bring life to that which dies. That was the lie the Raven Cult told its followers—that death is a release, a reward, and somehow better than life itself. But that's perverse. Life is everything. It is blessed. But it is also true that some things must die that others might live. The roe consumes the grass, and the wolf consumes the roe. So it has always been."

"But roe and wolves are animals," Mirda said. "They have no choice but to live by their natures. Is it not the gift of Sia that a woman may choose her own nature? There are many witches who eat not the flesh of animals, only plants."

Aryn shook her head. "Plants are alive. I can feel it, even now as winter draws near. The trees sleep, but life flows inside them, like water under the ice of a frozen river. I think no matter what we do, we can't escape it. Death is a part of life, the other side of the coin." She paced now, feeling warmer and strangely excited. "Yes, of course. A tree dies. It rots, and mushrooms grow from it for a time. Then they perish as well, and enrich the soil with their bodies. And then a new tree grows, nourished by the loam where others died before it. It's a circle, just like the moon. Light to dark to light once more. It never ends. As long as there's a seed in the soil, a hope, then life will always come again."

Aryn stopped, suddenly conscious that Mirda was gazing at her. She felt her cheeks flush. Who on Eldh was she to prattle on like this, as if she knew anything at all? She was not the teacher here; Mirda was. "Forgive me, sister. I did not mean to presume so much. Please, would you tell me what is to be my lesson this night?"

"That was your lesson, sister," Mirda said, her voice soft. "And you have learned it well." She drew closer, cloak rustling. Somewhere in the night above bats winged past. "And now I think you are ready to know."

Aryn could only stare. "Ready to know what?"

"A truth few of your sisters know. It is a truth few of them are ready to know, as you are, or even capable of understanding, as you can."

Somehow Aryn knew what she was about to hear would change her forever.

"You know the prophecies," Mirda went on, "the ones spoken at the High Coven. The prophecies tell how the Warriors of Vathris will fight the Final Battle, and how they will lose that battle. Because of their actions, the one called Runebreaker will succeed in shattering Eldh."

Aryn could only nod.

"The prophecies are true. They were spoken long ago by the wisest and most powerful of those witches who possessed the Sight, and they will come to pass. However, there are other prophecies they made, prophecies that were silenced even as the wise ones uttered them, and in the centuries since only a scant few have ever heard them."

Aryn found her voice. "But why? Why would their prophecies be ignored, even concealed?"

"Because the Witches did not care for them. And people have a powerful ability to deny or ignore that which does not fit their existing views. But these second prophecies are every bit as true as the first. And they tell us that the Runebreaker will save Eldh."

Aryn felt dizzy; the stars seemed to spin overhead. How could this be? This went against everything she had learned since her initiation into the Witches. Runebreaker was going to shatter Eldh. Mirda herself said the prophecies were true.

"I don't understand," Aryn said, choking out the words. "How can the Runebreaker destroy Eldh and save it at the same time? How can both prophecies be true?"

Mirda spread her hands. "Those of us who know of both prophecies would give much to understand the answer to that question. We only know that each of these things is true. Runebreaker will be the end of Eldh. And he is its only hope."

"But that's impossible!"

"Is it?" Mirda glanced at the statue of Vathris. "And what did you tell me just moments ago, sister?"

And in a beam of understanding as clear and brilliant as the moonlight, Aryn understood. She reached out, touching the frigid water that poured out of the bull's neck like blood.

"From death comes life," she whispered.

45.

Aryn woke with the crimson fires of dawn and knew that everything in her world was different.

Her teeth chattered as she dressed quickly in a woolen gown; the servants had not yet come in to stir up the fire. Normally she would have stayed in bed until they did, but she couldn't sleep any longer, not that day, not knowing what she did.

Runebreaker will be the end of Eldh. And he is its only hope....

Mirda's words seemed impossible; they defied everything Aryn had learned in the last year. All the same, Aryn could feel the truth of it in her heart. Travis Wilder was the Runebreaker foretold by prophecy, and three times she had seen him do everything in his power to save Eldh. She would not believe, could not believe, that he would harm the world.

But he will destroy Eldh, Aryn. You don't possess the Sight, not like Lirith, but the prophecies can't be wrong. And even the dragon said it would come to pass.

Last night, lying in her bed and far too excited to sleep, she had gone back over all of their journeys in her mind. And it was only then she realized she had heard words similar to Mirda's once before.

Go. Runebreaker! Go destroy the world by saving it!

The ancient dragon Sfithrisir had spoken those words to Travis in the forgotten valley in the Dawning Fells. The dragon's words made it sound like Travis might try to save Eldh only to destroy it despite good intent. However, according to Falken, while dragons always told the truth, that truth was carefully honed to cut like a knife.

So what was the real truth in the dragon's words? Aryn knew it had to be there, but she couldn't quite grasp it. Despite her talk with Mirda the night before, it was all so hard to comprehend. How could shattering the world save it?

She didn't know, not yet. But she was going to find out. And when she saw Travis Wilder again, if she saw him again, she was going to tell him everything.

But won't that go against the Pattern?

She had addressed the question to Mirda as they walked from the garden, back into the castle.

On the surface it might seem so. The threads that aligned themselves with the call to destroy Runebreaker were many, and they were woven tightly together. But remember, the Pattern was changed at the last moment, and you were part of what changed it. Your thread, your voice, is part of what now binds the Witches. Look deep inside yourself, sister, and you'll find the answer to your question there.

Aryn wasn't certain it was so easy. She had tried looking inside herself, and she hadn't seen anything at all, except maybe what she had had for supper and a whole bucketful of worries and questions wriggling like eels. All the same, considering the idea of talking to Travis didn't fill her with the same nausea that avoiding writing the missive to Ivalaine had caused.

Aryn dashed out the door of her chamber just as a startled

serving maid was opening the door. The woman dropped the bundle of sticks she had brought to build up the fire.

"Sorry!" Aryn called back over her shoulder. "But I won't be needing a fire this morning anyway."

Before the serving maid could so much as sputter, "Yes, my lady!" Aryn was racing down the corridor. It was still early. However, she couldn't wait any longer. There was so much she wanted to ask Mirda; she had to hope the elder witch was already awake.

She was nearly to Queen Ivalaine's chamber when she heard a voice echoing from up ahead. The sound drifted through an open archway that led to a small antechamber. Something about the voice brought Aryn up short. It belonged to a woman, and it sounded as if she was having an argument. Yet whoever it was she was arguing with must have been speaking in a hushed whisper, for Aryn could only hear the woman herself. Aryn knew she should keep moving; it was wrong to eavesdrop. All the same, she found herself drawn toward the archway.

"You have no choice. No matter how cruel that truth may be, you must bear it. You must. Are you not a queen above all? Your duty is to your Dominion first and all other things second."

Shock and fear melded together in a cold amalgam in Aryn's chest. She froze just outside the archway, one wide, blue eye spying the figure who paced in the antechamber beyond.

It was Ivalaine. She wore only a loose nightgown, and she was barefoot despite the cold stone floor. Her hair was snarled, and her skin was pale and shadowed, so that Aryn couldn't help wondering again if the queen was sick. Then the previous day's conversation with Mirda came back to her.

Is she ill?

No, sister. Not in any way you might think.

She caught a fleeting glimpse of the queen's eyes; they were bright, as if with a fever.

"The Pattern does not bind you in matters of state." She twisted a lock of her hair with quick motions of her fingers. "It can't; it never could. And even so, what you did was right. He had to know, man of the Bull or no." Laughter tumbled from her lips, cracked and bitter. "And is that the only reason? Or is it more? Perhaps you are neither queen nor witch. For is not your first duty as a mother? Would you truly sacrifice him so easily for the needs of your Dominion, and for the desires of your sisters? Would you?"

She was no longer twisting her hair. She was pulling at it, tearing it. Gold strands came away in her fingers, and she stared at them, as if not understanding what they were or where they had come from. Aryn clamped a hand to her mouth; this couldn't be happening. She backed away from the arch, then turned around.

Sister Mirda stood before her.

"Go," the witch said, her voice gentle but commanding. "Wait for me in your chamber."

Aryn swallowed a gasp and nodded. Picking up the hem of her gown, she ran down the hallway, not looking back.

A minute later she burst through the door of her chamber and shut it behind her. She leaned against the door, heart pounding, then pushed herself forward and slumped in a chair by the fire. The serving maid had stirred up the coals, and now it was too hot in the room, but Aryn didn't care. Her mind raced; what had just happened?

She still had no answer a half hour later when a soft knock came at her door. It was Sister Mirda. Her dark hair was drawn into a sleek knot at the nape of her neck and held in place with crossed wooden skewers. The witch gestured for Aryn to sit, then took the chair next to her.

They were silent for a long moment, until Aryn could bear it no longer. "Is the queen mad?" she said, gazing at the fire.

"No, she is not mad," Mirda said. "If she were, I think it would be easier to bear. But she is quite sane, and that is why it is so burdensome. I believe she paced there much of the night, thinking. I suppose she left our chamber so as not to disturb me or her attendants. Even in her distress, she thinks of others."

Aryn knew it was not her place to ask about Ivalaine's private matters, but all the same she couldn't help herself. "But what is it? What troubles the queen so?"

"The moon wears three faces, does it not? And so does Ivalaine, even though she is but one woman."

Aryn chewed a knuckle. It did seem as if that was what

Ivalaine had been saying to herself: something about how she was a queen before she was a witch, and how maybe she should be a mother above all. But that didn't make sense. The queen wasn't married, and she had no children. Perhaps she was referring to her subjects. Were they not like children to a queen? That had to be what she meant.

"It must be very hard for her," Aryn said.

"Sometimes we are forced to make unbearable choices." Mirda reached out and took Aryn's left hand. "Even as you yourself have a choice to make."

Aryn felt a surge of warmth that was not from the fire. Mirda had not spoken in her mind with the Touch, but all the same Aryn understood.

"Yes," Mirda said, her almond-shaped eyes serious. "A dangerous path lies before you. I have given you knowledge some in the Witches have sought to keep secret for long years—knowledge they yet try to hide, or even destroy. It is up to you what you will do with it. But before you decide, let me tell you this: There are those among the Witches who have never forgotten the prophecies of the wise ones. We are the same who were saddened to see the crones shunted to the very edges of the Pattern. And while we are few, there are yet things we can accomplish, as you saw in the weaving of the Pattern. For many years we have met and worked together in secret."

The heat of the fire went thin; it felt as if a cold draft had blown through the room.

"You're part of a shadow coven!" Aryn gasped.

Mirda gave a tight smile. "I suppose that's what others might call us."

Lirith had told Aryn of the shadow covens during one of their lessons: small groups of women who met apart and in secret from the Witches, working their own spells, weaving their own patterns. Many of the shadow covens of old had been dark in nature, seeking ways in which to use the Weirding for the purpose of controlling and manipulating others. It was the discovery of this by common folk that had, a century ago, led to the burning and drowning of many witches.

Aryn pulled her hand back from Mirda. "But all of the

shadow covens were disbanded. That's why we come together in a single High Coven now, so that we all work as one."

"And would you work with Sister Liendra and her faction?"

Mirda's words were spoken in her usual even tone, but all the same they were like a slap.

"So one shadow coven survived."

"One that I know of, at least," Mirda said. "But if we persisted, who is to say there might not be others? Regardless, now you come to your choice. You can join with us, and in so doing become a renegade, a heretic—crimes punishable by having your thread plucked from the greater Pattern of the Witches. And believe me, it is a terrible punishment, worse even than you imagine. For once the spell is worked, if enough Witches join in its weaving, you can never Touch the Weirding again."

Aryn shuddered; the very thought made her ill. It would be like death, only worse. For she would know every minute of every day exactly what she was missing.

"Or you can reveal our presence to our sisters in the Witches," Mirda said. "You can send a missive to Sister Liendra. Be assured this will cause you to rise high in her favor. And you can watch as my sisters and I are discovered and, one by one, cut from the Pattern and the Weirding forever."

"And what if I do nothing?"

"That is the one thing you cannot do."

"Then I—"

Mirda held up a hand. "No, sister. Such a decision should not be made in a moment. Think on it until the moon is full, three days hence, and tell me your decision then. Unless, of course, it is your desire to go to Liendra at this moment."

"No!" Aryn blurted out, horrified.

"Then in the meantime let us continue your lessons."

It was nearly impossible to concentrate after what she had seen, after what Mirda had told her. All the same, Aryn commanded herself to focus on the task at hand. Her goal that day was to learn her first spell in the art of illusion, and soon Aryn lost herself in the lesson.

"By reshaping the threads of the Weirding," Mirda said, "you can convince the eye that it sees something that isn't truly there."

Mirda handed Aryn a silver hand mirror. Aryn's task was to alter the appearance of her own face in the mirror. It was *hard*. Aryn stared into the mirror for what seemed an eternity, but the only alterations to her visage were in the way it twisted into horrible grimaces as she concentrated, and the slight blue tinge it took on when she held her breath too long.

She couldn't do it. How could she ever deceive another if she couldn't even deceive herself?

But that's not true, Aryn. There was another once whom you deceived, wasn't there?

Even as she thought this, the mirror seemed to ripple like the surface of a smooth pond after a pebble is thrown in. A woman gazed at Aryn out of the mirror, her hair a burnished red-gold, her eyes sharp and scheming. Aryn gasped, and in a heartbeat the image of the strange woman was gone; now it was her own startled face that stared out from the mirror.

"Very good," Mirda said, taking the mirror. "That was a difficult spell. Few master it their first time. But you'll need much more practice to be able to maintain it."

Aryn hardly heard these words. What had she been thinking just before the image in the mirror changed? She was certain it was important, only now she couldn't recall what it was. Just that for some reason it made her think of Lirith and Grace.

"Sister?"

Mirda's voice was soft with concern. Aryn shook her head. "It's nothing. I was just thinking of Sister Lirith and Lady Grace, that's all." A sigh escaped her. "I wish I could speak to them."

"Then why don't you?"

Aryn stared at the elder witch. What was she talking about?

"You know the spell of speaking across the Weirding," Mirda said. "I've heard your voice."

"But I don't know where in the world Lirith is. And Grace is leagues and leagues away from here. I can't possibly talk to someone so far away."

"And why not?"

Aryn didn't have an answer to that, other than that it seemed impossible. Once she had tried to speak to Lirith over the Weirding when the witch was in another part of the castle, and she had failed.

Mirda moved to the window; sunlight bathed her face. "The Weirding is a vast web. It spans the entire world, weaving among all things and connecting them together no matter how far apart they are. Wherever your friends are, if they are on Eldh, then at this very moment you are connected to them. All you have to do is follow the right threads, and you'll find them."

It was madness. Aryn's power couldn't possibly reach so far. All the same, she found herself saying, "I want to try it."

Mirda studied her for a moment, and Aryn didn't know what she saw, but at last the witch nodded.

"Sit down," Mirda said. "Shut your eyes and form a clear picture of your friend in your mind."

Aryn did as instructed. She closed her eyes and felt the warmth of the sun against her cheeks. In her mind she pictured Grace—for of the two Grace seemed somehow a little closer right then.

"Start with your own thread," Mirda said, her voice a low chant. "Follow it outward until it crosses another strand. Test that strand, ask it if it will lead you closer to your friend. If so, follow it, if not, stay on your original path. At each crossing, test the strands again."

"But how do I know that what the strands tell me will be true?" Aryn said, eyes still shut. "What about the illusion I just wrought with the Weirding?"

"You are the worker of the spell. Just as you knew what you saw in the mirror was illusion, so you will know what is a lie and what isn't in the Weirding. Life cannot deceive you if your heart is true." Aryn felt a gentle touch against each of her temples. "Now go, find your friend."

Aryn gathered her will, then reached out with the Touch. Her own blue strand shimmered before her. She followed it outward and saw other threads: Mirda's brilliant pearl-white strand, the threads of servants passing by outside the room, and the delicate gossamer of other creatures that lived in the castle—spiders and mice and doves. Then she was in the garden, a vibrant green tapestry of life.

She came to a crossing of threads. Which way? She tested one of the threads as Mirda said, probing it gently, showing it the picture of Grace in her mind. *This way,* the thread seemed to say to her.

Eagerly, Aryn followed the strand. Soon she came to another crossing of threads. She tested one of the threads, and words seemed to resonate in her mind. *Yes, this is the way.* Again she tested threads, and again. Each time they led her onward. Exhilaration filled her.

And then confusion. Why was she still in the garden? Shouldn't she be outside the castle already? And why was it that at each crossing she was always lucky enough to test the right thread the first time?

She came to an intersection of many threads. She tested one. *Come this way,* it seemed to whisper to her. However, this time she didn't follow the strand. Instead, she tested another thread, and another.

This way. Yes, this is right. Follow me!

They couldn't all be the right strand to follow, but each one claimed it was. Only how could that be? Mirda had said life couldn't lie.

No, that wasn't exactly what she had said.

Life cannot deceive you if your heart is true. . . .

The spell unraveled in Aryn's hands, and her eyes fluttered open.

"Oh," she said.

Sister Mirda gazed at her with sad eyes. Then the witch turned away. The door opened and shut, and Aryn was alone.

46.

That afternoon, Aryn went hunting for spiders.

She walked through empty parts of the castle, down dusty corridors, searching with both her eyes and her mind. No bells drew her onward this time, but she didn't need them. Once she got close to her quarry, she would know he was there. For it was not an arachnid she wanted to find, but a man with a pointed blond beard and a gray cloak.

As she walked, thoughts crowded her mind. Never would she have guessed, of all witches, that Sister Mirda belonged to a shadow coven. Nor would Aryn have ever thought she would be deciding whether or not to join herself. Was Mirda leading her down a path to darkness? Perhaps. To danger? Most certainly. The shadow covens had all been banned by the Witches a century ago, and seemingly for good reason, for many of them had practiced evil magic, using their talents to bind and control others. Only it was difficult to believe Mirda could be leading her astray.

Was Ivalaine a member of this shadow coven as well? Aryn didn't see how that could be; after all, the queen had joined her thread with Liendra's faction in the weaving of the Pattern. Ivalaine had had no choice, not if she wished to remain Matron.

Then again, it seemed likely Ivalaine was aware of Mirda's shadow coven, and if she believed the same as they believed, it might explain why she had told Boreas so much about Aryn and the Witches. Liendra and her cronies believed the Warriors were the enemy because they were destined to somehow aid Runebreaker in the Final Battle. But if Runebreaker wasn't their foe, then neither were the men of Vathris. That might be why Ivalaine confided in Boreas, especially since Calavan and Toloria were historically close allies.

Aryn turned her mind to other matters. After returning to her chamber the previous night, she had finally realized what it was that had been bothering her since her first conversation with Mirda. It had to do with the missive she had sent to Ivalaine, the one she had written in Gendarra describing what had taken place in Tarras. Ivalaine couldn't have gotten the missive; she had to have left Ar-tolor before it arrived there. So how had she and Mirda known about Lirith's absence?

Maybe there really is a way to speak so far across the Weirding, even though you couldn't do it. Maybe someone in Ar-tolor contacted Mirda or the queen.

But who was it? Who in Ar-tolor would have received the missive in Ivalaine's absence?

With a sudden surge of dread, Aryn realized she knew the answer.

"Liendra," she whispered aloud.

Yes, it made perfect sense. Liendra had a way of usurping power that didn't belong to her. In the queen's absence, surely she would have elevated herself above any other witches in Ar-tolor. Likely even Tressa, the queen's advisor. Although Aryn guessed it was probably Tressa who had somehow contacted the queen over the leagues, letting her know about the missive.

However, there could be no doubt Liendra had seen Aryn's letter, perhaps had even seen it first. And that meant she knew everything about Travis.

But Travis is lost, along with the others, I know you want to see them all desperately, but maybe he won't come back. That way Liendra and her witches can't capture him.

But that wouldn't do, would it? Travis had to come back to Eldh because somehow he was going to save the world in the Final Battle. And if he didn't come back, then neither would Lirith and Sareth. Or Durge.

Thoughts flitted about in Aryn's mind like agitated bees. It was all so confusing, and in just three days she was supposed to make a decision that would at the very least change her life, and which could even cause her thread to be cut off from the Weirding forever. If only there was a way she could discover more before she had to decide, something that would help her know what to do.

But there was a way she could learn more, and that was why she had come there. At that moment she felt it: a ripple in the threads of the Weirding. Something—someone—was near.

"Spider!" she hissed on the dusty air. "Spider, I know you're there. Show yourself!"

The solid stone to her left seemed to melt, and suddenly the slender blond man stood beside her.

"Why were you hiding from me? I'm certain you knew I was looking for you."

Aldeth smoothed his gray cloak. "Just as I'd know if there were a herd of cattle walking down the corridor. But I'm a spy, my lady. Hiding is in my blood."

Aryn was quite certain she hadn't been *that* loud, but in the spirit of goodwill she opted to ignore the insult. "So, have you found out anything spying on the king?"

"If I did, I would have to be a drooling half-wit to tell his ward and soon to be daughter-in-law."

"Interesting," Aryn said, tapping her jaw. "You know I'm to marry Prince Teravian. So that's one thing you've learned so far. Is there anything else?"

He scowled. "Don't ask me, my lady. Go talk to that Witch Queen of yours. She's the one who's been meeting with Boreas every night in the council chamber. I'm certain she can tell you everything you want to know about this little war they're planning."

"So they're making plans for a war?" Aryn chewed her lip. "But of course, it makes sense. All the signs point to the Final Battle. They must believe it's coming soon. You're full of all sorts of interesting facts, Spider."

Aldeth shook a fist at her. "Stop it!"

"Stop what?"

"You know very well what. You're reading my mind with some sort of spell, aren't you?"

"No, but we could try it if you'd like. It could be fun. You see, I've never done that sort of spell on a human before, just mice. And all they ever seemed to think about was cheese. Until their brains oozed out of their ears, that is. And after that, they were no fun at all."

The Spider backed away from her, mouth open.

She rolled her eyes. "I'm kidding."

"Well, it's not funny," he said in a wounded voice. "Some of us are rather attached to our brains. They provide us with hours of joy and entertainment, and we'd really prefer to keep them inside our skulls."

"Fine. No mind reading. I promise."

"Good. I'm glad we've got that settled. Now maybe you'll tell me why you've come here. Unless it was just to bother me, in which case you can consider the mission a rousing success."

Aryn took a step forward. "It's about our conversation the other day."

"And here comes the extortion part."

"Well, it was *your* suggestion."

The Spider gave her a sour look. "Get on with it. You're cutting into my valuable skulking time. What onerous favor do you want in exchange for not revealing my presence to the king and having my head put on a pike?"

Aryn could hardly believe she was really going to say the words. "I want you to spy on Queen Ivalaine."

Annoyance left the Spider's expression, and he raised a

single eyebrow. "It seems you've taken to heart my lesson about the importance of spying on one's friends. What do you want to know about the queen?"

Aryn drew in a deep breath. "Everything."

Minutes later, feeling less than good about herself, Aryn walked back toward more frequented parts of the castle. It was wrong to ask Aldeth to spy on Ivalaine, but it seemed like the only choice. Ivalaine knew something that was causing her grave distress. It had to do with the shadow coven, and what they believed about Runebreaker, Aryn was certain of it. If she could learn what Ivalaine thought, it might help her to make the right decision. Still, she felt vaguely ill. Despite Aldeth's admonition, she was fairly sure that true friends didn't spy on one another.

"Well," said a sneering voice, "did you have fun talking to your little spy?"

Aryn's heart skipped a beat in surprise. He had no mistcloak to hide him from her eyes, but his black attire served almost as well in this dim corridor. She had been walking briskly, head down, lost in thought, and so hadn't seen him until he spoke.

"Prince Teravian!" she gasped.

A smile cut across his face. Clearly he enjoyed having startled her. "You aren't going to fall over from fright, are you? Not that it wouldn't be funny . . ."

Her cheeks grew warm. "Is that so, my lord? No doubt you'd laugh even harder if I was so lucky as to crack my head open and bleed. Well, when you are my husband, you may order me about as you wish. I can perform a pratfall for you anytime you like. Perhaps the prince would prefer it if I wore not a gown at our wedding but a jester's motleys."

He crossed his arms and leaned against the wall. "Gods, I was only joking, Aryn. Don't you have any sense of humor at all? You witches really are a grotty boring lot, aren't you? I don't know how Lirith can be one of you. She knew how to laugh once in a while."

Aryn felt her anger cool. Maybe Teravian was right. It wouldn't harm her to laugh a bit more. "Maybe it would help if you made better jokes."

He snorted at that but said nothing.

Now that Aryn had caught her breath, the prince's first words registered on her. A needle of fear pierced her heart. "What do you know about a spy?"

"Don't try to act all coy. I saw you talking to him. The spy from Perridon."

"How—?"

"It was easy. I knew you were going to come to this part of the castle. So I just waited in an alcove until you passed by. It was simple to sneak after you without being noticed. You made more than enough noise for both of us, so the spy never knew I was there."

Aryn felt rising indignation. "I am not loud," she said, then winced as her voice echoed all around.

"Suit yourself," he said with a smirk.

Aryn turned away, her mind racing. This was very bad. The prince enjoyed nothing more than to make trouble for her. What if he told Boreas about her meeting with Aldeth? How would she explain to the king that she had discovered a spy in his castle but had not seen fit to tell him about it? Even worse, what if he told Ivalaine about Aryn's request to have Aldeth spy on the queen? Ivalaine had fostered Teravian for years. And while Aryn wasn't certain the two were close, surely he felt some degree of loyalty to her.

She could feel Teravian's gaze on her. Aryn turned around, searching for something, anything to say that would convince him not to give her away.

It was too late. Footsteps echoed down the corridor. Aryn swung her gaze around, searching for a place to hide, but before she could move, her worst fears were realized, and Lord Farvel ambled around a corner.

"Lady Aryn, there you are!" the old seneschal said. "And Prince Teravian, you're here as well. This is a glad sight. It's good to see the two of you getting along."

Teravian grimaced. "Oh, we're getting along all right. Just like a weasel and a—"

Aryn quickly moved forward before the prince could complete his analogy. "Good day, Lord Farvel. Is there something I can aid you with?"

"My lady, it's quite the other way around." The seneschal

clasped his hands together. "I haven't had an opportunity to speak with you since the happy occasion of Prince Teravian's arrival. Now that he's here in Calavere, I'm certain you're anxious to start planning your wedding. The Feast of Quickening will come sooner than you think, and I'd like to begin making preparations. I was wondering if there is anything you've decided upon that you'd like to tell me."

Teravian stepped away from the wall, a sharp smile on his face. "Oh, I have something I'd like to tell you. You see, Lady Aryn has definitely been scheming something of late, and I think everyone in the castle will want to hear it."

Farvel tilted his head, directing his good ear toward the prince. Panic surged through Aryn. She fought for breath, grasping for something to say, but she was too slow. Teravian spoke first.

"It seems Lady Aryn wishes to—" The young man hesitated, then cast a furtive glance at Aryn. "It seems Lady Aryn wishes for orange to be the primary color for her wedding. Is that clear, my lord? Everything is to be in orange."

The seneschal bobbed his head, white hair fluttering. "Yes, Your Highness. If Her Highness desires it, orange it shall be. I shall get the dyers working at once. We shall have yards and yards of orange. Thank you, Your Highness."

Seemingly greatly relieved to have something to do at last, Farvel bowed stiffly to each of them in turn, then hobbled down the corridor and out of sight.

Aryn stared after the steward, hardly believing what had just happened.

"Well, aren't you going to thank me?"

She forced her gaze to focus on the prince. "Why?" she managed to say.

He glared at her. "Isn't it customary to thank the person who just did you a favor? Or are witches conveniently exempt from courtesies like that?"

"No, Your Highness. I mean, *yes*. Of course, I thank you, from the depths of my heart. What you did, it . . ." She drew in a breath, forcing herself to stop babbling. "It's just that I don't understand why you did it. I didn't know that you could do something—"

"That I could do something nice?" He turned away, gazing out a window. "I'm not evil, you know. I don't know why everyone thinks I am."

"Maybe you should try wearing something other than black on occasion."

He glanced at her in surprise. "That's exactly what she said."

"Who?"

"Lirith." He crossed his arms. "We spoke that last night you were in Ar-tolor. Talking to her was fun, the most fun I'd had in ages. She's the only one I've ever met who didn't treat me like an object or some kind of monster. She said she'd talk to me again. Only I knew she wouldn't. I knew she would be leaving, and she did."

His words stunned Aryn for two reasons. First, a warm light shone in Teravian's eyes as he spoke, and a tenderness she had never heard before stole into his voice. His countenance relaxed as he spoke, and a faint smile touched his lips, not mocking, but longing.

By Sia, he has a crush on her. On Lirith. You've never heard him talk about another person like that. That's why he keeps bringing her up.

It might have been sweet and amusing. After all, Lirith was beautiful in body and spirit; that a young man might fall madly in love with her was hardly a surprise. And that Teravian could feel such feelings for anyone was reassuring. Aryn had feared he was incapable of caring for another. However, something else about his words had struck a dissonant chord in her.

I knew she would be leaving . . .

It was impossible. A boy might have some shard of the talent, but not a man. And while he was just now eighteen, by the shadow on his chin and the deepness of his voice, Teravian had left boyhood behind. She had to be mistaken. All the same, she found herself speaking.

"How did you know, my lord? You said you knew you'd find me in this part of the castle. Only I told no one where I was going, and I don't believe anyone saw me come this direction. So how did you know I was here?"

His eyebrows drew down in a scowl. "I don't know. I just did. Why are you all always asking me things like that? Ivalaine.

Tressa. Even Lirith. Well, I'm tired of it, all right? I'm not some insect you can pin to a board to examine as you please."

Aryn found this response telling. First, it meant others, including the queen, had noticed similar instances. So this was not the first time Teravian had known something he shouldn't have. And second, by his defensive tone, it was clear he knew they were onto something, and it frightened him.

And why shouldn't it, Aryn? If it's true, if he really does have some shard of the Sight, then he is unlike almost all other men. And who wishes to be different from everyone else? Even you hid your right arm most of your life.

Perhaps she could find a way to bring it up with Mirda; the elder witch might be willing to discuss it with her.

"I'm sorry, my lord," she said. "It was not my place to pry. Again, I thank you for what you've done for me today. I won't . . . I won't forget it when we're married."

He crossed his arms. "When we're married. It sounds so ridiculous. I'd think it a bad joke. Gods know that's the only kind my father knows how to make. But it's real, isn't it?"

Once again, Aryn decided to let the insult pass. After the way she had reacted to seeing him in the great hall the previous day, she deserved a jab or two. "We should probably get going," she said. "Supper will be on the board soon, and you know your father hates it when members of his court are late."

She held out her left arm. He stared, uncomprehending, but after she gave him a pointed look, he clumsily took her arm in his, leading her down the corridor.

"By the way," she said as they walked, "I positively hate orange."

His smirk returned. "I know. That's why I suggested it to Lord Farvel."

47.

They sailed across a black ocean under the light of cold northern stars.

Beltan knew he should be freezing. Chunks of ice drifted

past the hull of the ship; his breath fogged on the air, and frost clung to his mustaches. All the same, he was warm inside his woolen cloak; his skin tingled as if he had rolled in a snow-bank after spending hours in the smoky heat of a sweat lodge. It was the same tingling he had first felt in the prison in Travis's world, after his captors had done their experiments on him, had infused his veins with strange blood. The sensation grew a little stronger each time one of the shadowy figures passed nearby.

It was difficult to get a good look at the ship's crew in the starry light. They never seemed to stand still, and their motions were fluid and unpredictable, like shadows that caught the corner of his eye only to vanish by the time he turned his head to gaze at them full on.

"What are they?" Vani said beside him, her black leathers merging with the dark.

As usual, he hadn't seen the assassin approach. Couldn't she just walk up to him like a normal person?

Of course not. Popping out of thin air is far more mysterious, and she just can't help showing off.

Except, much as he wanted to believe that, he knew it wasn't the case. She moved the way she did because it had been in-grained in her by decades of training. Just as for the rest of his life he would always walk like there was the weight of a sword at his hip, whether a blade was buckled there or not.

He swallowed the angry words he had been going to say. "They're Little People. At least, I think that's what they are. A troupe of them came to Calavere last Midwinter and helped us uncover a conspiracy in the castle."

Vani crossed her arms. "Little People? You mean like the fairy we saw in Tarras?"

"Sort of." Beltan scratched his scruffy chin. "I'm pretty sure fairies are a kind of Little People. From what I know, there are different types—fairies, dwarfs, greenmen, and the like. Of course, I always thought they were all just stories for children until they showed up in the castle last year. But you should be asking Falken about this, not me. I'm no expert on fairies."

"Truly?" Vani said, raising an eyebrow.

Again Beltan felt the tingling sensation coursing up his

arms and down his back. "Come on," he said. "Let's go see what they're saying to Sindar."

Grace and Falken stood near the stern of the ship, speaking with the silver-haired man. He seemed to be answering a question the bard had asked.

"... only that it's impossible for me to say where I found them. You see, it was they who found me."

Even in the dim light, Falken's shocked expression was clear. "What do you mean they found you?"

Sindar passed a hand before his eyes. "I don't remember much. I was stranded on a rocky shore, alone and lost—that's all I know. What events led me there, I can't say. I think I had been traveling to someplace important. Or rather, to some*thing* important. I believe I had been injured, and also that I had been healed, but that I was still far weaker than I once had been. I know I was weary, that somehow I had exerted myself beyond all limits, and that I didn't have the strength to do anything save sit there on the beach and stare at the sea until the waves washed me away like the foam."

These words didn't quite make sense to Beltan. It sounded almost like Sindar had been in some sort of shipwreck, just like they had. Had he been injured in the wreck and lost his memory?

"I'm not certain how long I was there," Sindar said. "Only that it was twilight when I saw the white ship come. Impossible as it seems, I knew it had come for me, that the ship was going to take me where I had been going, and that I had something I was supposed to do there, something important. So I splashed out into the sea as far as I could go, and a rope was cast out from the ship. I took it, and *they* pulled me in."

Grace gazed at the shadows that flitted around them. "Did they tell you what it was you were supposed to do?"

"In a way. They didn't speak to me. Not with words, at least. All the same, I knew we were going to Omberfell, that there was someone there I was supposed to meet, someone who needed to come with us. Then, when I overheard your story, I knew it had to be you."

"But how did you know to find us at the Silver Grail?" Falken said, frowning.

Sindar laughed. "I didn't. I simply asked people in the city where I was most likely to find important travelers, and they directed me to the inn."

"And what about the story you told us?" Falken said, arms crossed. "I thought you were a ship's captain who cared only for gold. Why did you lie to us?"

Sindar gestured to the ship around them. "Would you have believed me if I had told you the truth? When I first reached Omberfell, I spent some time at the docks, listening to the sailors there. That was how I learned about the duke's edict, and the dark men whom you call the Onyx Knights. I decided to pose as one of those captains, thinking it would make it easier for you to believe and follow me. And it worked, didn't it?"

Falken said nothing, but he appeared unsatisfied by this answer. Beltan couldn't blame him. Sindar's story begged more questions than it answered. A shipwreck might explain how he was stranded on a beach with no memory. But why had this mysterious ship come to him? Beltan could imagine the Little People had decided to help Grace get to Toringarth, just like they had helped in Calavere the previous Midwinter's Eve. But what was Sindar's part in all this? Beltan shivered and was startled to realize Sindar was gazing at him.

"I have to admit," the silver-haired man said, "even if I hadn't overheard your tale at the inn, I think I would have known it was you I was searching for. You look familiar to me somehow." He nodded at Beltan, then glanced at Grace. "And especially you. But I suppose that's impossible. Even if I did know you before I lost my memories, it seems you don't know me."

Grace lifted a hand to her chest. Beltan remembered she had said the very same thing about Sindar.

"Do you know who Trifkin Mossberry is?" Grace asked softly.

"No. But that name . . . it sounds like someone they would know." Sindar gestured to a pair of dim forms that scurried by, one with an antlered brow, the other trailing hair tangled with leaves.

A thought occurred to Beltan. "Speaking of names, how is it you know your own? I thought you lost your memories."

"I have. And I don't know my name. Not my real name, at least." His eyes followed after the shadows. "Sindar is simply what they called me."

"Of course," Falken said. "*Sindar* means silver in the tongue of creation."

After that, they asked no more questions of Sindar. Not because they didn't have questions, but rather because the silver-haired man seemed to wish to be alone with his thoughts. He moved to the prow of the ship and gazed into the night, as if he could see where they were headed in the gloom.

Despite searching the length of the deck, neither Beltan nor Vani could find any way belowdecks, so the four of them simply sat near the center of the ship. With a spell, Grace conjured a small globe of witchlight to give them illumination, if not warmth. Not that that they needed the latter; despite the frosty air, none of them felt cold.

Beltan stared at the ball of green light dancing in the center of their circle. It reminded him of the magics his mother used to work late at night when she thought he wasn't awake. Only he was. He would sit at the edge of the loft where he slept, quiet as a mouse, watching as she worked by the fey light, grinding herbs and making simples with deft hands.

They didn't sleep that night. Nor did it seem they remained entirely awake. Speaking became too great an effort, so they sat in silence as the stars wheeled overhead. Only gradually did Beltan realize that it was dawn, and that a thick mist had risen off the water, cloaking the ship as if in a silver cloud. By the goose bumps on his arms, he knew the sun had risen.

The others blinked, and frost fell from their eyelids like white dust. More frost powdered their faces, their hair, their clothes. However, as they stood it turned to beads of dew, then was gone. Beltan was a little stiff, but that was all.

It was no easier to get a glimpse of the ship's crew by day than it had been by night. The fog clung to them, muting their twisted forms. All the same, from time to time, Beltan caught the glimmer of jewel-like eyes watching him.

"Where's Sindar?" Grace said.

The mist swirled, and they saw the silver-haired man standing at the prow of the ship, staring into the fog.

"It looks like someone left us a present," Falken said.

A small table had appeared on the deck of the ship where none had been before. On it was a clay jug and five wooden cups. Falken filled the cups and handed one to each, leaving the last for Sindar.

Beltan eyed the cup in his hand. "Isn't it dangerous to swallow fairy drink?"

"Almost certainly," Falken said with a grin, then took a long drink from his cup.

Grace gave a hesitant smile and took a sip, and Vani took a long draught, staring at Beltan as she did. He felt a prickling that he knew had nothing to do with magic and raised his own cup to his lips.

At first he thought it was water. Then he decided it was a kind of clear wine. By the time he finished his cup, he knew it had been neither. But whatever the nature of the liquid was, he felt suddenly alive and awake. Before, his stomach had been growling. Now his hunger was gone, although he felt light rather than full.

After Falken called to him, Sindar approached and took one of the cups. He bid them good morrow before he drank. Beltan noticed that his green-gold eyes seemed to move often toward Grace. Then, without a word of explanation, Sindar returned to his place at the front of the ship.

"Do you think he's all right?" Grace said.

Falken set down his cup. "I'm not sure. I think maybe he's wondering who he really is, and why it is the Little People chose him for their purposes."

"He's not the only one," Beltan said with a snort.

Vani prowled back and forth on the deck. "Falken, do you know how long it will take us to get to Toringarth?"

"With this haze, it's impossible to tell where we are. But it seems to me we're traveling swiftly. More swiftly than any usual ship. My guess is it won't be long. A day or two, that's all. In the meantime, it seems we're safe enough here."

"Really?" Grace said, folding her arms over her chest. "And I was just thinking that we've never been in more danger."

Beltan knew Grace was right. He had never believed in the

Little People until a year earlier. And while he could no longer deny their existence, he wasn't about to let himself get used to them. They were strange and terribly old. What they did, they did for their own reasons. And while he supposed they bore no particular enmity for men, they bore humankind no love either. For most of history, Falengarth had belonged to them. Then, when men marched across the continent over a thousand years before, the Little People were forced to retreat to the Twilight Realm, from which they were only now, in these dark times, returning.

"They want you to find Fellring, don't they, Grace?" Beltan said. "That's why they're helping us."

Grace gripped the steel pendant at her throat, and Falken nodded.

"We knew the seal Travis put on the Rune Gate couldn't hold forever," the bard said. "All the signs point to the gate weakening again. If the Pale King rides forth, the only thing that can stop him is Ulther's sword. And the only one who can wield it is you, Grace."

She shook her head, but she didn't protest. Beltan understood her fear. Last year, he had stood with Travis before the Rune Gate, and he had felt the dread, the power, the majesty pouring through those iron doors. He loved Grace; he would do anything to protect her. And he knew she was strong. Perhaps, in her way, stronger than any of them. But she was just one woman. How could she fight the ancient king of a vast army? Sometimes he wondered if Falken put too much stock in his own stories.

"He wants to open a door for Mohg, doesn't he?" Grace said softly, to no one in particular. "The Pale King. Berash hasn't forgotten his master, the one who made him. He wants to open a gate so the Lord of Nightfall can get back to Eldh and reforge the world in his own image."

Vani glowered at these words. "I know nothing of Old Gods. But I do know something of gates. And the only two that I know to exist are now lost. One was surely consumed in the destruction of the Etherion. And the other is lost with . . ."

Her words faltered so briefly Beltan was sure the others didn't notice.

". . . with our companions. I don't see how the Pale King can open a door for his master without one of the gate artifacts."

"He can," Falken said. "All he needs are the three Great Stones. He already has Gelthisar. And there's already a crack between our world and Travis Wilder's. That's how Melia and the New Gods sent Grace there thirty-odd years ago, and that's how the Pale King sent his own ironhearts there as well, probably around the same time. If Berash fits the iron necklace Imsaridur with the other two Imsari, he'll have all the power he needs to rip the crack wide open. Mohg will step through, and he'll take the Great Stones from the Pale King and use their power to break the First Rune."

"Eldh," Grace murmured, face gray as the mist. "He'll break the rune Eldh and shatter the world."

Falken gave a grim nod. "And then Mohg will remake Eldh in his own image. He'll be the new Worldsmith, and all of Eldh will fall under his shadow forever."

"And Earth, too," Grace said. "They're like two sides of a coin—just like the coin Brother Cy gave me and Travis. Earth and Eldh. What happens on one happens to the other."

Falken didn't disagree.

Even though his mother had been a witch, Beltan had never been comfortable with magic. Elire's spells hadn't been powerful enough to save her in the end. All of this talk of gods and runes left a queasy feeling in his stomach.

"Mohg can really do that?" he said. "Remake Eldh?"

Falken nodded. "The Imsari hold the power to break runes as well as to bind them. We've seen that firsthand with Travis. Whoever holds all three will have everything he needs to destroy Eldh, and then forge it anew."

Vani rested her hands on her hips. "Wait a moment. As you said, we've seen Travis Wilder work great deeds with the Stone in his possession. What did you name it? The Stone of Twilight?"

"It's called Sinfathisar," Falken said.

"But Travis is lost."

A cold hand seemed to grip Beltan's heart. He understood what Vani was getting at. "That's right. Travis has the Stone of

Twilight. As long as he stays lost, there's no way Mohg can get it." Which meant it was better if Travis never came back to Eldh. He saw pain flicker across Vani's face, and he knew she had come to the same realization.

"How do you know?" Grace said, her eyes haunted. "How do you know Mohg can't get to Travis where he is? Maybe Mohg has already gotten Sinfathisar. And Krondisar, too. Maybe that's why Tira's star has vanished."

Falken laid a hand on her arm. "No, Grace. Whatever's happened, that's not it. Because if it had, we'd have already lost. Remember the words in the book—somehow Travis wrote that message. We know he didn't do that before he was lost, so somehow it had to be after. And you still have the iron key Sky gave you. We're going to get the shards of Fellring, and then we're going to the Black Tower. We'll find Travis there." He tightened his grip on her arm. "I promise you."

Grace pressed her lips into a thin line and said nothing.

And what about you, Beltan? Do you think Falken's right?

He didn't know. On the one hand, it seemed a grave peril for Travis to return to Eldh with Sinfathisar. They had to do everything they could to keep the Stone out of the Pale King's hands. Then again, Beltan knew that he would risk any danger, no matter how dire, to see Travis again, to tell him how he felt.

Really, Beltan? Even if it meant hearing him tell you that it's another he wants, not you?

Feelings rose in him: a muddied torrent of fear, need, and anger. He glanced at Vani. She was looking at him. He could feel his lip curling back from his teeth and couldn't stop it. Her eyes narrowed, then she stalked away into the mist.

They spent the rest of the day pacing, restless. Time slipped past silently, like the white ship as it ghosted through the Winter Sea. For a time Beltan leaned over the rail, watching chunks of ice go by. As the day wore on, the pieces of ice grew larger and more frequent. However, none of them so much as grazed the hull.

The mist cleared with the coming of night, and once again stars glinted in the sky like chips of crystal. The pitcher on the table was refilled with the clear liquid, of which they again partook—although Sindar continued to remain apart. It seemed to Beltan that the man's green-gold eyes were troubled, and occasionally a spasm would pass across his face, usually when he was gazing at Grace. Were his fragmented memories coming back to him?

Once again the clear, sweet liquid lifted Beltan's spirits, although it couldn't entirely calm the pain in his chest. It felt like a splinter of ice had lodged in his heart, and it was working its way deeper. He was glad when, after setting down her cup, Vani stalked away, vanishing like one of the shadowy figures that slunk about the boat, working at tasks Beltan could neither name nor imagine.

After that, Beltan again stood at the rail, looking for dark silhouettes reaching up from the horizon to blot out the stars— a sign that land was close at hand. According to Falken, no one had been to Toringarth in centuries. What would they find there? However, despite straining his eyes, Beltan saw nothing but the dim shapes of icebergs drifting like ghostly islands.

"What do you think happened to her?" Grace said.

Beltan nearly jumped. He had been concentrating so hard he hadn't seen her approach. She was gazing at the sky. Not the north, but the south. He understood. She was gazing at the place where the red star had shone.

"I don't know."

Grace shivered, although it couldn't be from cold, not there on the ship. "Do you think Tira's all right?"

"She's a goddess, Grace. I'm sure she's fine."

Except they knew now that gods weren't invulnerable, that they could be killed. The demon had taught them that.

Grace sighed and looked down. There was something in her hand. Beltan moved closer; it was the iron key Sky had given her in Tarras, the key to the Black Tower of the Runebreakers. She must have heard Beltan's sharp intake of breath, because she looked up at him.

"We'll find him, Beltan." Her words were quiet but strong. "We'll find him for the world. And for you."

He clenched his jaw; the splinter of ice dug a fraction deeper into his heart. "I'm not so certain it's for me that he wants to be found."

"He loves you," Grace said simply.

"What's love against fate?"

Grace closed her hand over the key. "If the Mournish are right, he doesn't have a fate."

In the night, two glints of gold shone for a moment, then were gone.

"No," Beltan said, voice gruff. "But she does have a fate. And maybe I do, too."

One of the queer shadows passed nearby, and he shuddered.

Grace touched his shoulder. "You can feel them, can't you?"

"I've been feeling them ever since Omberfell. But the feeling is stronger here. It's like snow." He shook his head. "No, it's like cold fire. I can feel it in my blood."

Grace touched her necklace. "Maybe we all have something in our blood. Like a mystery waiting to be discovered. Something we can't escape no matter how hard we try." She lowered her gaze, and her words seemed for herself rather than him. "No, I won't believe that. I won't believe everything is planned out, that there's no way to avoid destiny. All of this, all we've done—it can't be for nothing."

"Grace?"

"Promise me, Beltan." She looked at him. "Don't let fate decide what happens to you. Or to Travis. Promise me you'll be the one to decide in the end."

Beltan wasn't sure he understood. How could he decide something if it wasn't in his power? However, there was an urgency in her eyes, so he nodded and promised he would do his best. This seemed to satisfy her, and she left him to go look for Falken.

Beltan had no wish for more conversation himself. Some said misery favored companionship, but Beltan knew it flourished best in solitude. Sindar was at the prow of the ship again, and Grace and Falken would likely be at its center, so Beltan headed toward the ship's stern.

He tripped over something that made a bright *clang*. Beltan let out a curse, then bent down to see what it was that had caught his boot.

It was an iron ring fitted into the deck. In the dim light he saw the outline of a square—a trapdoor. He knew it hadn't been there before; he had gone over every inch of the ship.

"You should go fetch Falken," Beltan whispered. He knew the bard would want to see this. However, even as he thought this, Beltan gripped the ring and pulled. The hatch lifted easily, making no sound. Beyond was darkness. Beltan reached into the opening and felt the first rung of a wooden ladder. He held his breath a moment, then swung himself through the opening and climbed down the ladder.

He wasn't certain when he first became aware of the light. It was soft at first but grew stronger as he descended. The light was not the smoky red of a torch, but rather a gentle green-gold that made him think of Grace's eyes. A scent rose on the air, fresh as water, and he realized that he had been climbing for some time, that he must have gone several fathoms down, impossible since no ship had so deep a hold. He glanced up, and he could see the ladder leading up to the black square of the trapdoor, and beyond that the faint pinpricks of stars. Somewhat reassured, he continued his descent.

The ladder ended. His boots landed on, not hard wood, but spongy turf. Beltan turned around, and wonder filled him.

He was in a garden. Slender trees grew in a circle all around, their arching branches entwining into a canopy overhead, their leaves fluttering in a warm breeze. Drops of sunlight dappled the mossy ground like scattered coins. Daisies gazed at him with moist eyes; somewhere birds sang.

"This is impossible," Beltan said, but the words were merely a habit, like blinking. Everything about this ship and this journey was impossible; all the same, here he was. He drew in a breath, and a feeling of peace filled him. Whatever this place was, surely no evil could come here.

He walked deeper into the garden, brushing flowers with his fingertips. There was a path, leading off through a grove of trees; he followed it, and the sound of water grew louder. A curtain of ferns draped over the path. Beltan parted the fronds. Beyond was a grotto where a brook tumbled over stones into a pool. Lilies floated on the water. A thirst rose in him, and he knelt to drink from the pool.

Just as he brought his cupped hands to his mouth, there

came a soft sound behind him: footsteps against the mossy ground. He froze. Perhaps there was danger in this garden after all. Beltan waited, ready to spring into action. The footsteps stopped. In the mirror of the pool, a face appeared over his shoulder, next to the reflection of his own.

His heart ceased to beat. Water poured between his fingers, and ripples spread out over the pool, obscuring the image. Beltan rose and turned around.

He looked just as he had in Tarras, that night they met beyond the circle of the Mournish campfire: all in black, his head smooth-shaven, wearing a reddish goatee and silver earrings. Different than he looked when they first met—paler, older— but still *him*. His gray eyes were solemn, only then he smiled, and with a sharp jolt Beltan's heart started beating again, faster than before.

"Travis?" The word was barely a whisper. He swallowed. "By the Blood of Vathris, is that really you?"

Travis kept smiling as he moved closer. He smelled clean, alive, like the forest. A wave of dizziness crashed over Beltan, and he staggered. Travis gripped his arm with a steadying hand. His touch was warm and solid.

Beltan was trembling, trying to comprehend. "We thought we had lost you in the Etherion—I thought I had lost you. Only you weren't there. We learned that when they cleared away the rubble, and we've been searching ever since, for you and the others. But we didn't know where you'd gone. And now you're here. Except how can that be? How can you—?"

Travis lifted a finger to his lips and shook his head. He was right; there was no point trying to understand. Wasn't this ship impossible, this garden? Why shouldn't Travis be there? How he had come to be in that place, where the others were—those were questions that could wait. At that moment Beltan had to tell him what he had been wanting to say for the past year, and this time no one could possibly interrupt them.

Beltan's voice grew fiercer. "I didn't give up looking for you. I would never give up, no matter how far away you were, no matter how many worlds were between us. I knew the day I met you in Kelcior that I was going to love you, that I would never be able to stop myself. You're the one thing in my life that makes me feel like a better man." Beltan dared to press a hand to his cheek, stroking the roughness of his beard with a thumb. Still Travis did not speak.

"It's all right. You don't have to say anything. I know you're as far above me as the stars above the stones. You're a runelord, after all, and I'm just a bastard. And I know..." The words were bitter, but Beltan forced himself to speak them. "...I know that you love Vani, and that she loves you. I haven't been very kind to her on this journey, but she's strong and brave and good. You deserve someone like her. And I'll keep away from you both, if that's what you wish. I just wanted to tell you what's been in my heart all these months, and now I have." Beltan felt a strange resolve; it was sorrowful, yes, but comforting as well. He knew what he had to do. "So if you want me to go away, I will. Just tell me what you want me to do."

Travis smiled again, then kissed him.

Beltan was stunned for only a moment, then he returned the embrace. It felt easy, natural, for Travis was nearly as tall as he. They pressed against one another, as if making up for the distance that had separated them before. A tingling welled up in Beltan, warmer and more urgent than what he felt when the fairies passed nearby. This was not the answer he had expected, but by all the gods he would accept it.

A soft sound of dismay escaped him as Travis stepped back, but delight returned as Travis pulled his shirt over his head and tossed it down. He was leaner than that day when they had bathed together in a frigid stream in Eredane, talking about scars; his body had been hardened by his travails on two worlds. Dark red hair traced a line down his stomach. Beltan shrugged off his tunic and they stood close again, chest to chest.

So many times Beltan had imagined this moment, but his foolish fantasies were nothing to this. It was neither awkward nor overpowering. Instead it felt simple, true. Not as if they were meant for one another, as if it were fate. Instead it was like stumbling upon a key lying in the road and finding that, against all odds, it fit the lock to his heart. Whether he would turn the key was up to him. Grace was right—it wasn't destiny. It was his choice. Their choice.

"I love you, Travis Wilder." Beltan said the words like a vow, circling his arms around Travis, meeting his gray eyes. "No matter what may be, no matter where we are, I will always love you."

Travis laughed, then sank to the mossy ground, pulling Beltan down after him.

48.

Vani woke to gold light filtering through her lashes.

She lay on the mossy ground, naked, but she was not cold. His arms still encircled her, holding her close against the hard warmth of his body. She opened her eyes a fraction more and saw the lilies floating in the pool beside which she had found him. She must have dozed off. How long had she been asleep? It seemed as if they had lain here together for hours, but the angle of the light had not changed.

You should return to the ship above. You should find the others and tell them of this place, of what you've found.

No, not yet. She wanted this moment to last just a little longer. After all, she had been waiting all her life for it.

Vani still remembered the first time her al-Mama had read her fate. She had been five summers old—there was no use reading the *T'hot* cards for one who was younger, for an infant's Fate was not yet fully formed—and they sat together in the cramped, cozy space of their family wagon. Her al-Mama shuffled the cards, then made Vani cut them—a difficult task, for her hands were small. Then she had watched as al-Mama laid the cards out one by one, clucking and humming under her breath.

"Does it say whom I'm to marry?" Vani had asked, for one of her older cousins had just wed, and ever since her mind had been consumed with fantasies of marriage.

"It is as I suspected, and as your father and mother fear," al-Mama said, tapping two cards: a citadel crossed by a woman holding a sword. "You are to be wed to steel, married to knives." She pointed to three cards arranged beneath the two:

One showed a pair of lovers, one the moon, and one a grinning skull. "No man will have you for a lover. Death will be your only consort in the fortress of Golgoru."

That was the first time Vani heard the name Golgoru, the Silent Fortress where she would spend nine years of her life training to become *T'gol*. But that day, when she was five, she thought nothing of the name.

"But I have to marry someone, al-Mama," she had said, frowning.

"It is not the fate of those who enter Golgoru to wed," her al-Mama replied. "Their destiny is to—what's this?" The old woman's fingers fluttered to another trio of cards, lying above the crossed two. "The Empress, the City, the Magician. But no, it cannot be. Or can it?" She had looked up, her gold eyes thoughtful.

Her al-Mama had not told her what the cards meant, not that day. However, she had spoken to Vani's mother and father, and Vani had crept into the shadows—skilled at keeping silent even as a child—and had listened as they spoke.

"She is our only daughter," her father had said, his face ruddy with anger. "I will not send her away to the vultures of the Silent Fortress."

"You have no choice," al-Mama snapped at him. "It is her fate."

"What of the other cards, Mother?" Vani's own mother asked, her eyes shadowed.

The older woman passed a hand before her eyes. "It is a mystery, yet the cards cannot lie. One day she will bear a child to him."

"To whom?" her father demanded.

"To the sorcerer who will raise Morindu the Dark from the sands of time," al-Mama said. And neither of Vani's parents had had an answer to that.

Her father had resisted and delayed for many years, but in the end—tired and gray and broken—he had relented to the will of the Mournish elders and sent Vani to Golgoru in the autumn of her twelfth year. Vani had not wanted to leave her mother and brother. And she had known, if she left, she would never see her father alive again. But she had had as little choice as he, and she had ridden on a pony alone into the Mountains of the Shroud without looking back. She had cursed fate all the way.

However, as the years passed, she grew to like her training, then to love it. There was a joy to giving in to fate, to being what one was destined to be, and she excelled at her studies. Many entered the Silent Fortress; few left as *T'gol*, or in so few years as Vani. Many took thirteen or more. She passed the ordeals in nine.

Joyous, she had returned to her people, only to find that in her absence her mother had followed her father to the grave. But she still had Sareth and her al-Mama. And she still had her other fate, which had not changed. The cards were the same on her twenty-first birthday as on her fifth. The Empress. The City. The Magician. *One day she will bear a child to him.*

The cards could not lie, that much Vani had learned. She would be wed after all—to the one who would restore all of the secrets lost to her people two eons ago. Ten more years had passed. And then...

Vani shifted, pressing her back against his naked chest, and he sighed in his sleep. She had dared to use the gate artifact to cross the Void between worlds and find him on his Earth. Often over the years, she had wondered what he would be like. He was a powerful sorcerer, that much she had known. Would he be old and cruel, his face disfigured by scars? If so, she would still have given herself to him; such was destiny. Then she found him, and he was gentle and kind and pleasing of aspect, and that only made her fate seem more true than ever. Everything had seemed exactly as it should be—

—then they had rescued the blond knight Beltan from the prisons of Duratek.

You should have known, Vani. You've read the cards for others often enough. Fate is always true, yet it is often cruel as well.

She had believed they would fall in love as soon as they met. And they had; the cards had not lied about that. The moment she saw Travis Wilder, she had felt a weakness in her such as she had never experienced in all her years in Golgoru, but it had not been a troubling sensation; rather, she had reveled in it, as if she had craved it all her life. She wanted to give herself to him. And in his eyes, she could see he felt the same. What the cards had not told her was that he already loved another.

Whatever Beltan might think of her, it had never been her desire to steal Travis from him, to cause him hurt.

And is that not what you do? Did not your training make you skilled in the art of inflicting pain and death?

Yes, but Beltan was every bit as skilled in that craft as she was. If he had been weak, or foolish, or selfish, it would have been easy to disregard him; she would have felt no shame in taking Travis from him. But he was courageous, full of laughter, and possessed of boundless loyalty, and it was precisely for those reasons that she had been so vicious to him on the journey. Beltan had earned Travis Wilder's love; she had simply been granted it by the shuffle of the cards. If someone had asked her a year earlier if love was more important than fate, she would have laughed at the idea. But now . . .

He stirred again; he was waking up. His lips nuzzled against the nape of her neck, soft, tender. She smiled, placing her hand atop his, pressing it against her stomach. Perhaps it wasn't just fate. Maybe she had earned his love as well.

How he came to be in this garden, she didn't know. She wasn't certain herself how she had gotten there. It had grown cramped and stifling on the ship; she had been wishing she could get away from the others somehow, to get away from Beltan. Then she had seen the trapdoor in the deck—a trapdoor she was certain had not been there before. Strange as it was, she had opened it, and had followed it down to the garden.

She supposed some magic of the Little People had created this place within the ship, although the garden was certainly too large to be contained within the ship's hold. It didn't matter; it was not her nature to question the workings of magic. Some believed the craft of the *T'gol* was worked with sorcery, but all of it—even the skill of making matter phase in and out of being—was worked by focusing the mind.

For a time she had wandered, enjoying the peace and solitude of the garden. Then she had seen him, kneeling next to the pool of water. Whatever magic had created her surrounding, somehow it must have brought him there as well. She had gone to him, and he had stood, smiling at her. He did not speak, and in her shock the truth had bubbled out of her. She told him that it was not simply due to fate that she loved him; she loved him for who he was as a man, and would have even if he were not the one who would someday raise Morindu the Dark from the desert.

He had only smiled at her, stroking her hair with gentle fingers, and words that were more bitter—but still true—spilled from her.

"I do not care what the cards say, what fate demands," she had said. "I will not cause love to be broken. I know you love the knight Beltan, and that he loves you, that the bond between you is strong and deep. I would not come between you. If you wish me to leave you alone, I will do so. Forever."

The words were like knives in her heart, but she meant them, and she had stood proud and straight. However, he had touched her cheek, wiping away the moistness there, and without words he had leaned down to kiss her.

In that moment, fear and uncertainty melted. The green scent of the garden intoxicated her like wine. Their clothes had fallen away, and they had sunk together to the soft ground.

Vani had never known the full touch of a man before. She had been sent to Golgoru as a girl, and in those walls men and women were kept in seclusion from one another. In her nine years there, she saw men but once, at her final testing. In the time since, she had known the caresses of admirers, but always she had forced them away before they could have their will with her. They were not her fated. One was forever bound to one's first lover—whether one wed that lover or not—and it was to him, to the Magician, she wished to be tied.

Now there was no need to resist. After a lifetime of waiting, she wanted him as much as he wanted her; more, even. When first he entered her, she felt a tearing, and there was pain and some blood. However, he was gentle, and he took her from behind, which made the pain less. Soon the pain ceased altogether, and there had been only joy, and finally a sensation she had never experienced before, passing through her in shuddering waves. She heard his cry—the first sound he had made—and felt his warmth coursing deep inside of her.

After that they had lain together, spent, damp with the dew of sweat, content with small caresses. She whispered some things to him—of fate and love and pleasure—and he answered with kisses. Then, at last, naked on the ground in the impossible garden, they had slept.

Behind her, a soft groan escaped him. He released her, straightening his arms as he stretched. So her fated was finally awake. Smiling, she rolled over to face him.

He stared back at her with green eyes, not gray.

For a moment, both of them were too stunned to move. He was naked, as she was. Leaves were tangled in his blond hair, and bits of moss clung to his lean, rangy body. She could see the red marks on his neck where she had nibbled his flesh. Then, as one, they were moving.

It took a moment to untangle her legs from his, then she leaped to her feet, clutching the bundle of her leathers in front of her. He rolled away, snatched up his breeches, then stood with his back to her, hastily tugging them on. By the time he turned around, she had swiftly managed to don her leathers, although there had not been time to fasten the straps and buckles.

"What are you doing here?" Beltan growled. He brushed the moss from his bare chest and arms.

Vani eyed him, wary. "I might ask the same of you."

"You have to ruin every good thing I have, don't you? You can't help yourself." He advanced on her, his cheeks bright with anger. "Where is he now? I was here with him, then we fell asleep. What have you done with him?"

Indignation rose within her. Why was he always accusing her of wrongdoing? "I have done nothing with him. And it was I who was here with Travis Wilder. I don't know how or when you got to this place."

He shook his head, his green eyes clouded with confusion. "What are you talking about? I came down the ladder. I found him here in the garden, and we—"

"No, *I* came down the ladder." Vani held a hand to her throbbing head. There was moss in her own hair. "It was I who found him here, and together we..."

Despite the balmy air of the garden, a coldness swept over her. Both she and Beltan gazed at the hollowed place on the ground between them, then at one another.

His eyes went wide, and he took a step back, holding up a hand. "By all the Seven..."

A spasm passed through her, and she knew her eyes were every bit as wide as his own. "No, it cannot be."

Except it was.

"It wasn't Travis," he said in a choking voice. "It wasn't Travis I . . . it was you. It was you who I . . ."

She clamped her arms tight over her stomach, fighting an urge to be sick. "It was I to whom you made love. And I to you." She should have been furious, she should have flown at him in a rage, striking him for what he had done to her, for this disgrace, this humiliation. But she felt only a gray emptiness inside, and a dull ache between her legs. She had thought it was he, her fated, her Magician. And instead it had been Beltan. She had been betrayed. But by whom?

"Blast them," Beltan snarled, circling around, shaking his fists at the trees. "It was them—the Little People. They did this to us. They tricked us with their enchantments."

"Yes, but why?"

"I don't know. But they'll pay for this. Do you hear me? You'll be sorry!" He lashed out at one of the trees, striking it. The slender trunk bent under his wrath, then gracefully straightened, unharmed. Leaves shook with a sound like soft, smug laughter.

Vani's words were weary, resigned. "It's no use. We can do nothing against their magic. And for whatever reason they wished it, the trick is done."

Beltan turned on her. "How can you be like this? How can you be so calm? Aren't you angry at what they did to us, what they did to you?"

"I am well aware of what has been done to me," she said, feeling the heat rising in her cheeks, but she kept her chin up. "More than you can possibly know. All my life, I have saved myself for him."

The color drained from his cheeks. He stood still, his hands limp at his side. "Blood and ashes, Vani. I'm sorry. By the gods, I truly am. I shouldn't have been the one to take that from you, to take your . . ."

She turned away. "No, you shouldn't have. But you had no choice in the matter, and neither did I. It was their will." She gestured to the trees.

Silence descended over the garden. A long minute passed,

then she heard his footsteps behind her. He laid a hand on her shoulder. The gesture was tentative, awkward. She started to flinch away, then stopped. What was the use?

"Are you all right?" he said, the words gruff.

She shut her eyes. No, she was not all right. She would never be all right again. Her fate had just been taken from her. Instead she said, "We are bound now, you and I. A woman's fate is forever entwined with the man who first makes love to her."

He was quiet for a time. "And what of a man?" he said finally. "Is his fate entwined with his first woman?"

She opened her eyes and turned around. There was a look of anguish on his face, but there was a resolve in his gaze.

"You have never been with a woman before this?"

He shook his head.

She sighed. "Then you are bound as I am."

"But what does it mean?" He was gazing at the lilies floating on the pond.

She answered with the truth. "I don't know."

"I still love him, Vani." He looked up at her. "I can't stop loving him. I won't."

"Then you must vow never to tell him this happened." It was their only choice; this was how their fates would be forever entwined, by this vow, this secret.

Beltan nodded and held out his hand. "I swear it, by the Blood of Vathris. I will not tell another of this."

She took his hand in a tight grip. "And I swear it as well, on the blood of my ancestors."

They released their hands and stepped back.

"Now what?" Beltan said, his broad shoulders slumped.

Vani drew in a breath. "Now we live a lie," she said, and started back for the ladder.

49.

Dawn came again, blue and bright silver, and this time no mist shrouded Grace's view of the world. She stood at the prow of the ship, gazing at the white mountains that jutted out of the ocean.

A being perched on the rail near her elbow—the first time she had seen one of the Little People that inhabited the ship close at hand. It was a withered thing, with a face like a root and a cap of mossy hair. The being pointed a finger toward the peaks, as if it were possible Grace didn't know her future lay there.

She had thought them icebergs at first. Then they had grown larger, reaching into the sky. Now she could make out the rough gray lowlands at the base of the mountains, and white dots floated before her eyes. Gulls.

Grace gripped the cold piece of steel at her throat. The creature patted her other hand—its touch soft and dry as year-old leaves—then hopped down and loped away.

Boots sounded on the deck, then Falken stopped at the rail beside her. "It's Toringarth," the bard said, the wonder in his voice as tangible as his breath fogging on the air.

For the first time since stepping onto the ship, Grace felt cold. She shivered inside her cloak and pressed her cheek against the fox fur collar. "I'm not sure I can do this, Falken."

"You can, Grace. You're Ulther's heir. Even broken, his sword will know you."

"How?"

"By your blood."

She thought maybe she understood. After all, wasn't that what she had done countless times at the hospital? She would draw a vial of a person's blood and send it to the lab to be analyzed. So much could be learned just from those few drops of fluid—if a man was drunk, if he had had a heart attack, if his kidneys were failing. Fellring would test her just the same.

Grace glanced around. The Little People were nowhere to be seen, as if they shunned the brilliant northern light. All the same, the ship raced toward land with smooth purpose. She caught sight of Sindar at the ship's stern. His face was turned out to sea—not where they were going, but from where they had come. What was he thinking, now that they were near their destination? Did he wonder what would become of him once his task, given him by the Little People, was done?

Grace felt a sudden urge to go to him, perhaps even to try to comfort him. However, the shore was close now; the mountains bit into the sky like white teeth. She could see the mouth of a bay—deep and narrow, like a fjord—and cliffs spattered with the droppings of the gulls.

"Have you seen Beltan and Vani?" Grace asked Falken instead.

She hadn't seen either for some time; she had assumed they were merely off somewhere in the dark, except it had been light for a while now. However, even as she said this, she saw Beltan halfway down the length of the ship, leaning over the starboard rail. And there was Vani on the opposite side of the ship, sitting cross-legged, hands on knees, eyes closed and face tilted toward the sun.

"I'll go get them," Falken said. "Something tells me we all ought to be ready."

When the three returned to the prow, the doctor in Grace rose to the fore. "Beltan, Vani, what's wrong? Are you sick?"

Beltan was pale, his forehead beaded with sweat. His face had a greenish cast. Vani looked little better. The *T'gol*'s jaw muscles bulged—she was clenching her teeth—and she hunched over her stomach.

"I'm fine," Beltan said in a growl.

Vani's words were equally terse. "There is nothing wrong."

It was quick, but all the same Grace caught it: The knight and the assassin each cast a furtive glance at the other, then quickly looked away. Grace's heart skipped a beat. Something had happened between the two, she was sure of it. Something terrible. Only what?

Like a gull skimming the surface of the waves, the ship sailed between knife-edged ridges of stone into the fjord. Falken let out an oath, and Grace turned around. That was when she saw the frozen city.

It stood on a prominence above the bay, its parapets and spires reflected in the jade mirror of the water. Except, Grace realized as the ship sped closer, the city didn't stand on the crag; rather, it had been carved out of it. The smooth walls merged with rough gray bedrock at their bases. Streets angled along natural faults and fissures. Horned towers rose like sentinels, joined without seam to the rest of the city.

Once before Grace had seen a spire like them. The Gray

Tower of the Runespeakers had been hewn in the same manner, from a natural finger of stone. Maybe it was from the folk of Toringarth that the Runespeakers had learned the art.

The ship skated across the glassy surface of the fjord, closing in on the shore. Gulls dipped and wheeled above, and the snow-covered mountains reached up, closing out all but a narrow strip of the sky. In the preternatural gloom, the city seemed to glow.

"It's beautiful," Grace said.

Beltan's mustache pulled down in a frown. "Where are all the people?"

"And ships," Vani added. "Should there not be ships besides our own?"

Falken rubbed his chin with his silver hand. "I don't know. I always believed Ur-Torin would be a populous city. And it looks impressive enough. But I can't see anyone."

The white ship drifted to a stop alongside a stone pier that jutted out into the bay. The rush of wind and waves ceased, and there was no sound except the murmur of water lapping at stone, echoing and reechoing off the high cliffs of the fjord, like a chorus for the dead.

"Look," Vani said.

They turned in time to see several twisted forms slink through a trapdoor and vanish into the hold of the ship. The trapdoor closed, and Grace could see no trace of it. Looking up, she saw that the plank of grayish wood had been extended from the deck of the ship to the pier. Sindar stood at the near end of the plank, waiting. Grace moved to him, and the others followed.

"I thought maybe they wanted me to stay," the silver-haired man said when she drew close to him. "I thought maybe I was to be part of their crew. But I suppose that's impossible. I'm not like them. Even though sometimes I..." He shook his head. "But it doesn't matter anyway. They said I wasn't done yet, that I was to go with you."

Grace reached out and took his hand in her own, squeezing it. "I'm glad."

Surprise registered in his eyes. Then he smiled, and the expression was like an incandescence upon his face. Grace let out a gasp. His features were fine, even delicate, but she hadn't noticed before how sharp they were, how proud, how strong. Without doubt, Sindar was the most beautiful human being she had ever seen in her life.

He bent down and kissed her brow. Somewhere—echoing from the city, perhaps—she heard the faint music of bells. Then the others were there. Grace turned and did her best to give them a brave smile.

"Come on, everyone," she said. "Let's go find my sword."

The moment they stepped from the plank onto the pier, the bitter air struck them. Grace felt the skin of her face tighten, and her nostrils pinched in with each breath. Almost at once, ice formed on Beltan's mustache. They huddled inside their cloaks, raising hoods and donning caps. There was no wind, but, all the same, frigid tendrils seemed to find the gaps in their clothes and slip inside to caress bare skin.

"This cold air rolls down from the Icewold," Falken said, pointing toward the snow-covered peaks that loomed above the city. "I've heard it said it's so bitter in those mountains that nothing can live there save for trolls."

Grace shivered. "Trolls?"

"Don't worry, Grace." The bard grinned. "I'm sure they're only a legend."

"Like magic swords, you mean?"

Beltan stamped his boots. "Can we please get moving before we freeze completely solid?"

Now that they were off the ship and had a purpose, the big knight seemed more his usual self. Vani, too, seemed to have largely recovered from whatever it was that had troubled her.

"I will lead the way," the *T'gol* said. "Beltan, you keep guard at the rear."

Grace expected an argument, but to her amazement the blond man nodded.

In a tight knot, they walked from the pier toward the walls of the city: Vani at the fore, Sindar, Falken, and Grace in the center, and Beltan keeping watch behind them. However, as far as Grace could tell, there was nothing to keep watch for. There seemed to be no living things in the place, save for themselves and the gulls, winging above like ghosts.

The city gates stood open, but even if they had been shut, Grace wasn't certain that would have been much of a barrier. The thick iron bars were rough and red, corroded from countless years of salt and water. Beltan grasped an iron point, and the brittle metal snapped off in his hand. He cast it to the ground, then they moved through the gate into the city.

They found themselves on an empty avenue. Square houses lined the street, each carved from a single piece of stone, their walls thick, and their windows narrow and doors low, designed to let in a minimum of cold air. However, all that remained of the wooden shutters and doors that had once covered the openings were piles of splinters. Beltan peered into some of the houses and came away shaking his head. Empty.

They moved on, past more empty houses, silent towers, and barren squares. Grace glanced through a few of the windows, and she saw iron pots still hanging from chains in fireplaces, and tarnished silver cups sitting on stone shelves, like heirlooms set carefully away. Wherever the denizens of the city had gone, they hadn't stopped to take their most precious items with them.

They came to a well from which water had bubbled up and frozen, forming a fantastical sculpture of ice. Still they saw no signs of people or animals, not even bones. The city was more than dead; it seemed it had never even been alive.

"What happened to this place?" Grace said, daring to break the silence. "Was it a war?"

Beltan shook his head. "It wasn't war. Even if it had happened long ago, there would still be signs. Things would be burned, broken. There would be bones, if not bodies."

"But everything is solid stone," Falken said. "It couldn't burn. And animals might have taken the bones away over the years. I can't imagine this city fell without a battle. It was said once there were a thousand Wulgrim here, and surely no fighters in history have been as strong or as fierce as the wolf-warriors of Toringarth."

Vani crossed her arms. "No. Beltan is right. Whatever happened here, it happened without blood, without fire. This city did not die a violent death."

Grace clenched her teeth to keep them from chattering.

Somehow Vani's words were even more troubling than the idea of war. A city could be conquered, its people slain; Grace could imagine that. But how could an entire city full of people vanish without a trace?

They came to a crossing of streets. Grace glanced at Sindar. "Which way should we go?"

The silver-haired man shrugged. "The Little People said only that I was to follow you."

"I was afraid of that," Grace said with a sigh. "Falken, do you have any idea where we'll find the sword?"

"I looked through the book again yesterday." From inside his cloak, the bard pulled out the small volume Grace had found in the library at the University of Tarras—the one entitled *Pagan Magics of the North*. Falken flipped through it, past the page with the impossible message that could only have been written by Travis, to a passage near the end. He read aloud. "'And so this pilgrim came to the tower of Ur-Torin, and he was filled with much joy to find the shards of fabled Fellring were not hidden away, but instead were made plain for all the people to see, that they might remember Lord Ulther, who last wielded that fabled blade, and who was their greatest of kings.'"

Grace chewed her lip, trying to fathom these words. "What does it mean, Falken?"

"I'm not entirely sure." He spirited the book away beneath his cloak. "But the author, whoever he was, mentions that he went to the *tower* of Ur-Torin, not the city. I think he was referring to the main keep." The bard pointed to the great, blocky tower that crowned the summit of the crag from which Ur-Torin had been hewn.

"Could the shards have been moved since then?" Beltan said. "Maybe the people took them when they left."

"If they left," Grace said softly. She hadn't meant to speak the words aloud. They didn't make any sense; if the people hadn't left, then where were they?

Vani started up the street that led toward the center of the city. As they went, Grace felt a scream rising inside her. It started as a queasiness in her gut, then became a choking feeling in her throat. Now it hovered right behind her lips, and only by gritting her teeth together did she hold it in. The silence, the emptiness, was maddening.

More abandoned buildings slipped by, their windows staring like dead eyes. They ascended a wide staircase of a hundred or more steps. By the time they reached the top, Grace gasped for breath, and the frigid air knifed at her lungs. She coughed, and the taste of iron filled her mouth.

In many ways, Ur-Torin's main keep reminded her of the central tower of Calavere. It was tall, but broad as well, almost a square, wrought of the same gray stone as the rest of the city, with countless slits for windows. However, while Calavere was crowned with blue banners, the keep of Ur-Torin was surmounted by four horns of stone, like those that topped all of the spires in the city. Only these were larger, wickedly curved like talons.

"Dragons," Sindar said beside her. "The horns would keep dragons from landing on the towers." He must have noticed the direction of her gaze and the question in her eyes.

Falken gave the silver-haired man a sharp look. "I thought you couldn't remember anything."

Sindar only smiled. "I can't say who I am or where I'm from. But I know the sky is blue, that fire is hot and ice cold. And I know that those tusks were meant to ward off dragons."

"I suppose it's possible," Falken said, although he didn't look entirely convinced by Sindar's words. "Ur-Torin is an old city—nearly as ancient as Tarras. I imagine a fair number of dragons still lurked about the north in those days."

Beltan shaded his eyes with a hand. "I can't see anything following us."

"Then let's go in," Vani said, "and get out of this wretched cold."

Like the main gates of the city, the doors of the keep were made of brittle iron, and working together Falken and Beltan wrenched them open far enough to slip through, although Sindar seemed loath to do so. Only after Grace coaxed him did the slender man dart through the gap, careful not to touch the iron gates as he did.

Unfortunately for Vani and her thin southern blood—as well as for the rest of them—it was colder inside the keep. The thick stone walls held in the chill. Despite the cold, a foul scent hung on the air. Grace found herself thinking of her days in medical school, and of the steel cold room next to the Gross Anatomy Lab where cadavers waited before they were infused with formalin to preserve them.

Like the city, the keep was empty. Bits of rotted furniture scattered the floor, and the remnants of tapestries—gray and feathery as cobwebs—hung from above, rippling as the five walked past. They followed a broad passage toward the center of the keep, then came to a pair of large iron doors. The doors were shut.

These were not so corroded—or so easily opened—as the outside gates. Grace and Beltan gripped the iron handle of one door, Falken and Vani took the other, and after some tugging they managed to wrench the doors open with a *boom*. A puff of frosty air rushed out. The sound rolled away through the keep like thunder.

Grace led the way into the vast space beyond. It occurred to her she should have let Vani go first, to make sure the way was clear, but somehow she knew her leading was right. After all, it was her heritage, wasn't it?

Two rows of columns, carved like trees, marched in twin colonnades, their stone branches weaving high overhead to form the arch of the ceiling. Sunlight shafted through narrow windows, and tiny crystals of ice danced and glittered in the sunbeams, disturbed by the opening of the doors. Frost covered the floor, as thick and feathery as white moss. It crunched to dust under their boots as they entered.

At the far end of the hall, on a dais, was a chair of stone. It was carved in massive proportions, as if the ones who had sat upon it had been giants. But Grace supposed they had been men and women, mortals just like her. Slowly, the five approached the throne. Like everything in the hall, the chair was covered with ice. Several large, jagged crystals rose from its back like the points on a white crown.

Grace looked around, but she saw nothing save for the columns and the throne. "Are you sure the shards would be here, Falken? Couldn't they be somewhere else in the keep?" Flecks of ice snowed down, jarred loose by the sound of her voice.

"No," the bard said quietly. "This was the heart of the kingdom. If they were on display for all to see, they would be here."

However, though they looked all over the hall, they saw no sign of a broken sword. Vani found a bit of corroded iron in the fireplace, but it looked like the tip of an old poker, and Beltan found some hinges from a side door long since rotted away. They brushed patches of frost from the floor and the columns, revealing only stone. Nor were there alcoves or niches where such precious objects as the shards might be displayed.

"Maybe they're in a secret room," Beltan said.

Falken let out a cloudy breath. "That would hardly qualify as 'plain for all the people to see.' "

"Might the shards have rusted away?" Vani said, weighing the scrap of iron in her hands.

"No," Falken said. "Even broken, there is deep magic in Fellring, imparted to it by the blood of the three fairies who threw themselves upon it."

Sindar turned around and stared at the bard. "What did you just say?"

The bard cocked his head. "Do you know the story of Fellring?"

Sindar shook his head, and briefly Falken related the tale Grace had heard before: how a thousand years ago King Ulther had stood alone before the Rune Gate, waiting for the Pale King to ride forth and strike him down. Then three fairies had drifted toward him across the field where his army lay scattered. The radiant beings had thrown themselves upon Fellring, and their blood had entered the sword, enchanting it. Thus, when Ulther smote the Pale King, the sword pierced his breast and clove his iron heart in two, defeating him—if not quite slaying him. At the same time, the sword shattered. Ulther fell to his knees, and the Pale King's Necromancers drew near. However, at that moment the armies of Tarras, led by the Empress Elsara, entered Shadowsdeep. The forces of the Pale King, quailing at the sight of their fallen master, fell before them. Most of the Necromancers were slain, and a few fled back to Imbrifale with their fallen master. And Elsara came to Ulther, recovering both the king and his broken sword.

As Falken finished, a visible shudder ran through Sindar. He passed a hand before his eyes.

"What is it?" Grace said, touching his shoulder.

"I don't know. Nothing." He lowered his hand and met her eyes. "The bard's tale sounds familiar somehow, that's all."

"Maybe you've heard the story before," she said. "Maybe you're remembering it."

"Maybe."

Vani rested her hands on her hips. "What do we do now?"

"I say we search the keep," Beltan said.

The assassin and the knight started to discuss plans with Falken, while Sindar seemed lost in his thoughts. Grace was too cold to just stand there; she had to keep moving. Without thinking about it, she approached the throne. She started to take a step up the dais, then hesitated.

And why shouldn't you ascend, Grace? If Falken's right, then you're the only person in the world who can claim to be descended from Ulther. That means you're the Queen of Toringarth as well as Malachor.

Marvelous. Chalk up two dead kingdoms under her name. Careful not to slip, she walked up the steps. Perhaps having a different view of the hall would help give her an idea of where the shards might be.

The hope was futile. The hall looked no different from atop the dais. Falken, Vani, and Beltan were still talking in low voices. Sindar had wandered off a bit from them, and he gazed down at his clasped hands. Grace sighed and turned her attention to the throne.

She considered trying out the massive chair, but it was covered with frost, which would make sitting in it a chilly proposition. The white crystals that fanned out from the back of the chair were particularly large. Curious, she reached out to touch one.

A small cry escaped her. Red oozed from her fingertip. She snatched off her glove. The gash was clean and deep, as if made by the sharpest scalpel.

"Are you all right, Grace?" someone said. Beltan maybe. Grace hardly heard him. Instead, she frowned, staring at her bleeding digit, forgetting her pain.

Maybe it was a scientific hunch, or maybe it was the

Weirding that told her something was other than it appeared. Regardless, Grace leaned forward and breathed on the crystal that had cut her.

The frost melted under her warm breath, beading up on a smooth surface engraved with angular symbols. She blinked, and for a brief moment—before the water turned to frost once again—she saw her own startled eyes reflected in polished steel.

Despite the cold, a warmth filled her. She grabbed the corner of her cloak and rubbed at one of the crystals, and another, and another, wiping away the rime of frost. Then she stood back.

They weren't crystals of ice at all. They were jagged pieces of steel whose ends had been set into the back of the chair. If she were to sit in the chair, they would hover just above her head like a crown, where anyone standing in the hall could see them. Hand trembling, Grace took the steel pendant at her throat, pulled it to the end of its chain, and held it against one of the pieces of metal protruding from the chair.

The rough edges fit perfectly, the angular runes flowing unbroken from one piece to the other. In her mind, she thought she heard a high, singing tone, like that of a tuning fork. She looked up at the crunch of footsteps and saw the others standing at the foot of the dais. Tears rolled from Falken's bright eyes, freezing on his cheeks, only somehow the bard was smiling.

"You found Fellring, Grace."

50.

Grace removed the shards from the back of the throne. They came free easily, with just a tug, as if they had been fitted loosely into the stone, although she was certain that wasn't the case. It was just as Falken said: The shards knew her blood. They hummed beneath her touch, until she could hear a dozen tones in her mind. But the chord was dissonant, meaningless; the voice of the sword had been broken long ago.

As Grace freed the shards, she arranged them on the seat of the throne like the pieces of a puzzle, using the runes engraved along the flat as a guide. Each piece fit against the next with an audible *snick*, and it seemed the shards gripped one another as if they were magnetized. Grace could pick up two pieces, and they would not come apart on their own, although she could pull them loose with some effort.

When Grace finished, the sword was complete. The last gap was filled when she removed her necklace, freed the pendant from the wire that fastened it to the chain, and fitted the final piece in place. The sword was surprisingly delicate. Its flat was about the width of two of her fingers, tapering to a slender point at the end. It was hard to believe this was the weapon Ulther had used to defeat the Pale King. All the same, even broken, there was a deadly beauty to it.

Attached to one of the end pieces was a steel hilt, but the wood and leather that had formed the grip had rotted away centuries before, so Grace wrapped a handkerchief around the hilt instead. She picked up the sword. Despite the cracks that marred its surface, the blade remained in one piece. She moved it back and forth gently; yes, the sword would hold together if she were careful with it. However, one good blow, and she knew the blade would fly apart. Whatever magic held the shards to one another, it was not enough to repair the blade all on its own.

Grace turned around, holding the sword, and looked at Falken. "Now what?"

The bard ascended the steps of the dais, his blue eyes brighter than Grace had ever seen them. "We have to find a way to reforge the blade."

"I don't think we're going to find any smiths around here," Beltan said. "Not that I'd mind standing next to a forge full of hot coals right now." He rubbed his mustache, trying to remove some of the icicles.

"No," Falken said, studying the sword, but careful not to touch it. "Fellring was forged by the art of dwarfs and imbued with the blood of fairies. No mundane smith will be able to re-work this blade. He might join the pieces, but he could never make its magic whole."

"If the blade cannot be repaired," Vani said, hands on hips, "why did we journey all this way to retrieve it?"

Falken opened his mouth, but Sindar—who had been quiet

all this time, hunched inside his cloak—interrupted. "We need to get back to the ship."

Grace lowered the sword. "What is it?"

The silver-haired man shook his head. "I heard ... I'm not sure." He clasped and unclasped his hands. "I simply think we should be getting back, that's all."

"There's nothing more for us here," Falken said. "It'll be warmer on the ship, and we can decide what to do from there."

Grace tore a shred from one of the rotten tapestries and wrapped it around the sword. Beltan offered to carry the blade, but Falken shook his head, and Grace knew the bard was right. Fellring *wanted* her to carry it. Besides, the sword was shockingly light. She carried it easily, using both hands, as they left the hall.

"Please," Sindar said. "We have to hurry."

Grace squinted against white light as they stepped out of the keep. She had thought it would still be morning—everything seemed frozen in this city, even time itself—but the pale eye of the sun stared down from the zenith. Hours had passed since they had left the ship.

Speaking of the ship, where was it? From the top of the steps outside the keep they had a clear view of the fjord, but the bay was empty; even the gulls seemed to have fled. *You can't see the pier from up here, that's all, Grace. It's too close to the city.*

There was no time to keep looking; Sindar was already moving down the steps of the keep. The others hastened after him. They made their way through Ur-Torin, not speaking or pausing, concentrating on keeping up with Sindar's long strides. As they turned onto the avenue that led to the city gate, a harsh call rang out. Grace looked up. At first it was only a silhouette against the sky, perched atop a slate roof. Then it spread dark wings and opened its beak to let out another raucous call. Black eyes bored into Grace. The raven launched itself upward and winged away over the city.

"I don't like this," Falken said. "I think Sindar's right. We should hurry."

"I saw nothing guarding the gates," Vani said, stepping from a rippling patch of air, and only at that moment did Grace realize the assassin had been gone at all.

Beltan gripped his sword. "Let's go, then."

Sindar was walking through the gates. Grace adjusted her hold on Fellring as they hastened after him. The stone arch slipped past, then they were beyond the walls. Grace caught sight of Sindar just ahead. He was no longer moving, and instead stood at the point where the road began to slope down to the edge of the bay.

They reached him, and Grace could finally see the pier jutting out from the rocky shore not far below. A ship was moored against the pier, just as she had expected. Only the vessel wasn't small and white. Instead it was massive, its hull fashioned of wood dark like iron, its deck surmounted by three masts bearing crimson sails. On the mainsail was a symbol: a black crown encircling a silver tower. There was no sign of the white ship anywhere.

Bitter air filled Grace's chest, freezing her heart. "No," she whispered, cradling Fellring in her arms. "Not after we've come all this way."

Falken let out an oath in a flowing tongue. Dully, Grace supposed it was ancient Malachorian, but the magic of the half-coin allowed her to understand. *May the Light protect us.* Vani circled around, hands ready, gold eyes searching.

"Get back into the city," Beltan growled. "Now! We have to find a place we can hold against them."

Sindar shook his head. "No. We're already too late."

Beltan glared at Sindar. The blond man started to reach for Grace, to grab her arm and pull her toward the gate. Then a deep voice spoke a word.

"Reth."

Like a mirror struck by a stone, the air in front of them shattered. Fragments of sky, water, and stone flew in all directions, then vanished, revealing a new vista in their place. Grace could still see the shore, the bay, and the dark ship. But now she could see the man who stood not a dozen feet before them, as well as the men in black armor arranged in precise rows on the pier. There were at least a hundred of them.

The man took a step toward them. He was clad like the knights below, although his armor was more ornate than theirs. Spikes curved upward from his shoulders, and twin horns crested his black helm. A cloak fluttered behind him, like a shadow the wind was trying in vain to tear free. On his breastplate were emblazoned five silver crowns.

With a roar, Beltan drew his sword and lunged forward. However, the black knight was ready. He twitched a finger and spoke another word.

"Hadeth."

Grace saw the frost crystals snake their way up Beltan's sword a heartbeat before the blade contacted the dark knight's breastplate. The sword shattered like a rose dipped in liquid nitrogen, and she clamped her eyes shut against the spray of metal splinters. When she opened her eyes again, she saw Vani stepping from thin air next to the knight.

"Gelth," his voice echoed from inside the visor.

This time it was ice, not frost. The substance seemed to condense out of empty air, encapsulating Vani's boots like a thick sheath of crystal, climbing her legs up to her knees. A cry escaped the *T'gol*. She struggled, but the ice held her fast. The knight stepped to the side, moving out of her reach. Snarling, she reached inside her leather jacket, then flicked her wrist. Three metal triangles sped toward the knight.

"Dur," he said, and the triangles stopped in midair, turned, then hissed back toward Vani. The assassin was pinned in place by the ice; she couldn't leap away. Instead she bent over, ducking to avoid the three projectiles—which Grace was certain were poisoned.

Beltan bared his teeth, ready to launch himself bodily at the dark knight, but Falken grabbed the blond man's arm.

"Hold, Beltan. I don't know how he's doing it—from everything we've learned, I believed the Onyx Knights despised magic—but he's speaking runes. And he's doing it better than anyone I've ever heard in my life, even Travis Wilder. He'll strike you down before you can so much as touch him."

Beltan's body was rigid, but he didn't shake off Falken's grip. "He'll kill us anyway."

Falken shook his head. "I imagine he has some plan for us, or we'd already be dead. All it would take to kill us is a single word."

Laughter emanated from inside the black helm. "Well-spoken, Falken of Malachor. Then again, you of all people know how deadly mere words can be."

Sindar still wasn't moving. He seemed to stare at the sea rather than the black knight. Grace was shivering; she couldn't stop. She wanted to move to Vani, to help her. The *T'gol*'s face was ashen with pain. How long would it be until frostbite set in, until the sheath of magical ice caused irreparable damage to her feet, her legs? But all Grace could do was gaze at the black knight, and whisper, "Who are you?"

"I know who he is," Beltan spat. "Look at his armor—five crowns. I know a war general when I see one, and I'd bet my sword this is Gorandon himself, the man who leads this bastard order of knights." He glared at the armored figure. "Aren't you?"

The other gave a curt nod. "I believe it's you who is the bastard, Sir Beltan. But otherwise you're correct. Which is fortunate for you, as you have no sword with which to settle the wager had you lost. Gorandon is the name my people call me. Then again, I believe Falken would know me by another name."

The bard's face was red with cold and anger. "What are you talking about? I don't know you."

"Really, Falken? Has your memory failed you after so many centuries? Or did Dakarreth's spell simply addle your already deluded brain? Let me remind you, then." The knight reached up, gripped his helm, and lifted it from his head.

He was older than Grace would have guessed from his powerful voice; his white hair fluttered in the wind, and his face was deeply creased. All the same, he was handsome, and obviously still hale; the width of his shoulders was due not just to his armor. Above a hawklike nose, his eyes were the color of ice at dusk. His expression was not stern, but rather mocking, intelligent. Cruel.

More shocking than the man's age was Falken's reaction. The bard pressed his silver hand to his chest and staggered. His face was white as frost.

"It can't be," Falken whispered, and the man in black armor

smiled, a wolfish expression not unlike the bard's own grin. In fact, given their similar looks, the man might have been Falken's uncle or cousin. Except Falken was over seven hundred years old; his family had all turned to dust long ago. "Kelephon," the bard murmured.

"So, you remember me after all," the dark knight said.

Falken opened his mouth, but words—always his power and his pride—seemed to have fled him.

Beltan shot a hard look at the bard. "Kelephon? I don't know that name."

Grace did. She remembered the story Falken had told them once, of the trio of runelords who had fled the destruction of Malachor with the three Imsari, the Great Stones. Jakabar took the Stone of Twilight and fled across the void between worlds to Earth, where he became Travis's friend Jack Graystone. Mindroth followed centuries later, after the Necromancer Dakarreth stole the Stone of Fire from him. But the third runelord, the one who took the Stone of Ice, vanished. No one knew what became of him. And his name was—

"Kelephon," Grace said. "You're the last of the three runelords who escaped the fall of Malachor with the Great Stones."

The man bowed to her. "You know your history well, Your Majesty. But I suppose that's only natural." He eyed the sword in her hand. The shred of cloth had slipped from the blade, and to Grace it seemed—just for a moment—that a light flickered in his eyes. A light like fear.

"So that's the legendary Fellring," he sneered. "I must say, it doesn't look like much."

Despite his scoffing tone, Grace noticed Kelephon made no effort to take the sword from her. It was utterly foolish—it was clear this man had the power to destroy them with a word—but the scientist in her couldn't resist an experiment. She moved the point of the sword a few inches closer to Kelephon. He took an unconscious step back, then shot her a withering look, as if realizing what she was doing.

Falken was crumpled over, like someone had punched him in the stomach. "I don't understand, Kelephon. I thought you were lost. I know the Pale King has Gelthisar, the Stone of Ice, that he's had it for centuries. But how did you survive his wresting the

Stone away from you? What have you been doing all these years? And why are you dressed as the leader of these knights?"

"He *is* their leader, Falken," Beltan said, gripping Falken's shoulders, supporting the bard. "And the reason he's still alive is because he gave the Stone of Ice to the Pale King in exchange for his life. Make that his immortal life. There's no other answer—even I can see that."

Grace knew Beltan was right. Kelephon had fled with Gelthisar after the fall of Malachor, and not long after that the Stone came into the Pale King's possession. Now, seven centuries later, here was the runelord, alive and well before them.

But is he really alive, Grace?

She hesitated, then reached out with the Touch, probing for his life thread. There—it was hot and bright as a thread of tungsten in a lightbulb. There was no dark lump of metal in his chest, but rather a warm, beating heart. He was alive, just like Falken was.

Maybe he didn't give the Stone of Ice directly to the Pale King, Grace. Maybe he gave it to Dakarreth. After all, the Necromancer cursed Falken with immortality so Falken could always remember how he helped destroy Malachor. Dakarreth could have worked the same magic on Kelephon as a reward in exchange for the Stone. And then the Necromancer could have presented the Stone to the Pale King.

She let go of his thread. Then, with a start, she realized he was watching her.

"Satisfied, Your Majesty? I'm every bit as alive as you and your friends are. But if you touch me again with your witch magic—" He twitched a finger, whispering a word, and Vani moaned as the ice crept a few inches farther up her legs. "—the *T'gol* will find out what it's like to try to breathe through solid ice."

"Let her go," Beltan said.

"Or what?" Kelephon said, gazing down his nose in disdain. "You'll leave a damp stain on my armor?"

Beltan clenched his fists. Vani was trapped, Sindar still wasn't moving, and Falken seemed stunned. Grace knew she had to do something. She laid a hand on Beltan's shoulder, touching his life thread, speaking calming words in his mind.

Don't, Beltan. He's a runelord. I don't know what that

means, not entirely. But I do know he can bind and break runes as well as speak them. You've seen what Travis can do, and Kelephon has seven hundred years more experience. We can't stop him with force. We have to talk to him, to find out what it is he really wants with us. It's our only hope.

Grace wasn't certain those last words were true; she wasn't certain they had any hope at all. But Falken was right—Kelephon must want something; otherwise, they would already be dead. She released Beltan, and he let out a grunt of assent.

Kelephon's eyes narrowed. "What did you just say to him, witch?"

Despite her fear, Grace felt a small note of satisfaction. So Kelephon couldn't listen to words spoken across the Weirding. Perhaps that was something that could work to their advantage. She affected what she could only hope was a royal air and moved between Beltan and the runelord. "It's chilly standing out here, Lord Kelephon. Are you going to tell us what you want with us or not?"

"Do you mean to say you don't already know, Your Majesty?"

Some of Grace's fear transmuted into frustration. "No, I don't. It doesn't make any sense. We learned in Embarr that the Pale King wants to capture me alive for some reason. But it's clear your Onyx Knights want me dead. Then there's the fact that your men obviously have no love for the Pale King's *feydrim*; they killed a band of the creatures in Seawatch. It all makes it look like the Onyx Knights are the enemies of the Pale King. Only now we learn you're in league with him."

Kelephon's eyes flickered up and down her figure. "You of all people should know that appearances can deceive, Your Majesty. After all, one would hardly think just by looking at you that you are the true heir to Malachor."

Maybe it was something in the way he said these words, or something in his eyes. Or maybe it was some feeling communicated unintentionally to her over the vibrating threads of the Weirding. Either way, at that moment, Grace understood.

"It's all a lie," she said, breathless. With a shaking hand, she pointed to the men lined up on the pier below. "You've been lying to them for centuries. They think they're fighting the Pale

King, don't they? That they're fighting evil. They think they're going to restore the kingdom of Malachor, that the light of its glory will shine again. But you're just using them. That's why you're up here alone. You didn't want your men to see you speak runes. They think only heretics work magic, but their own leader is a runelord."

Falken, Vani, and Beltan all stared. Kelephon laughed.

"Very good, Your Majesty. I don't think the bard would have gotten that even if he had another seven centuries. Which he doesn't, by the way." His boots ground against stone as he moved closer to her. "You're clever, Ralena. The members of the royal house of Malachor always were, blast them all. That cleverness nearly cost me everything. But I won't make that mistake again."

Renewed fear flooded through Grace. The man before her was ancient, powerful, and cruel beyond imagining. There was nothing he couldn't do. To her. To anyone.

"Why?" she croaked. "Why have you done all this?"

At last Falken spoke, his voice weary, haggard. "He wants your sword, Grace. That way he can set himself up as the new king of Malachor."

"Once again the bard misspeaks. I don't want just your sword, Your Majesty." Kelephon lifted a gauntlet and gently caressed Grace's cheek. "I want your blood as well."

A roar ripped itself from Beltan. "Don't touch her, you dog!"

The blond man lunged for the runelord. Grace tried to shout, to tell him to stop, but it was no use.

"Shen," Kelephon whispered, and the silver half-coin in Grace's pocket worked its magic, so that she heard not just the rune, but its meaning as well.

Sleep.

As if through a gray veil, she saw Beltan slump to his knees, then fall to the ground next to Falken. Vani wavered, held up by the ice that gripped her legs. Of them all, only Sindar remained standing. However, before Grace could wonder about it, the sky fell over, and the ground leaped up to strike her.

PART FOUR

SHOWDOWN

51.

It was verging on midnight, and Castle City was dark and silent by the time Travis guided Jack up the front steps of the Bluebell.

Travis let out a relieved sigh when he saw the warm light shining though the parlor window. Nothing had accosted them on the walk from the Silver Palace Hotel, but that fact could only be attributed to luck, for Jack had chattered loudly and constantly as they went, mostly complaining about the train trip and the coach ride from the depot into town.

"Denver isn't a city, I tell you," Jack said, waving his arms, "it's a barbarian encampment. When I disembarked the train from Kansas City, I was forced to carry my own bag all the way across the platform. And when I asked a porter if he might be so kind as to help, he ignored me. Can you imagine the rudeness?"

"I think I've got an inkling," Travis said, gritting his teeth and shifting the lumpy satchel in his arms to get a better grip. He wasn't entirely certain how it happened, but somewhere along the way he had found himself carrying Jack's luggage. Travis didn't know what the bag contained, but right then he was guessing lead ingots. Lots of them.

"And the coachman did nothing to raise my opinion of the general character of the populace in this state," Jack went on blithely. "He couldn't speak two words without stopping to spit tobacco juice between. I fairly had to dance a jig to keep my boots clean. Prometheus grant me perseverance, but I don't know how I'm going to manage in a land where people have such little regard for their fellowman." He stood next to the front door, waiting for Travis to open it.

Travis reached for the doorknob, but the satchel started to slip through his arms. He cocked a knee, catching the bag, then pressed it between his body and the door to hold it up. He fumbled with blind fingers, found the knob, and managed to twist it. The door opened, immediately removing the support for the satchel. Travis stumbled forward, barely catching himself from falling facefirst atop the bag.

"For shame, Mr. Wilder," Jack scolded, strolling into the front hall after him. "Don't you know it's proper manners to let your elders go first? I do hope the coarseness of the American West isn't rubbing off on you."

The only thing rubbing off was the skin on Travis's palms from trying to hold on to the satchel. He set it down, letting it fall to the floor with a *thud*.

"Do be careful with that," Jack said, glowering. "Its contents are quite delicate."

Evidently not so delicate as Travis's back, which made a crunching noise as he straightened. A path of lamplight spilled into the hall. They followed it to the parlor and found Maudie sipping a cup of tea, Miss Guenivere on her lap.

"Maudie, I'm glad you're still up. This is Jack Graystone. He's going to need a place to stay for a while."

Maudie looked up. "Is this the old friend you've been waiting for, Mr. Wilder?"

How had she known that? Maudie must have heard more than he thought in their time there.

"No, madam, Mr. Wilder and I have only just met. At least, I think that's the case." Jack cast a curious glance at Travis.

"Well, you're welcome all the same." Maudie's eyes twinkled. "As long as you can pay a dollar a day, that is. I hope you don't mind if I don't get up to say hello." She gestured to the kitten asleep on her lap. However, Travis saw the handkerchief she had wadded in her hand; a corner stuck out, stained crimson.

She's getting weaker. Liza is doing most of the work around the boardinghouse these days.

Travis's heart ached, but he couldn't think of that at the moment. Jack was finally there. He should head back to the saloon to get Lirith; it wasn't safe for her to walk to the boardinghouse alone at night. However, even as he had the thought, the witch walked through the front door, her arm coiled around Durge's.

Maudie smiled. "Miss Lily, Mr. Dirk, I'm so glad you're back, along with Mr. Wilder. I hate to think of any of you being out after dark these days."

"Is there something amiss in this town?" Jack said, shaggy eyebrows rising.

"I'll let these three fill you in. I'm too tired for talk about such things tonight. Miss Lily, could do me the favor of showing Mr. Graystone to his room? I think we'll put him in the blue room, on the second floor."

"Of course," Lirith said.

Maudie started to rise from the couch, and Durge hurried to help her. She gave his arm a grateful pat, then shuffled from the parlor, leaning on her cane. A few days ago, she had taken a room on the first floor near the back of the house; Travis and Durge had moved her things down from the second floor. They heard the sound of coughing, muffled as a door shut.

After making introductions, they sat, and Lirith and Durge fetched tea for them all from the kitchen.

"I must thank you for bringing me here, Mr. Wilder," Jack said, blowing on his tea. "This establishment seems a good deal more convivial than a standard hotel. And, I confess, the rate will be easier for my much-reduced wallet to bear. You see, a mishap befell my business in London, where I had made my home for quite some time. I fear I lost so much."

"You mean in the fire," Travis said.

Jack set down his teacup, his blue eyes sharp. "How did you know it was a fire that took my shop?"

There was no use waiting. Travis reached into his pocket and pulled out Sinfathisar. The Stone shimmered gray-green in the lamplight.

"Oh," Jack said in a surprised voice. And then again, this time in a deeper and far more knowing way, "Oh."

Jack reached into the pocket of his green waistcoat and pulled out a small iron box covered with runes. Travis recognized it; once he had used the very same box to keep Sinfathisar safe. Jack opened the lid. Inside the box glimmered a Stone that was the mirror image of the one on Travis's palm.

They don't just look the same, Travis. They are the same. They're both Sinfathisar. Only mine is from the future.

He remembered late-night movies about time travel he had seen as a kid. If the hero met himself, all sorts of terrible things happened, mostly involving accidentally killing his father so he'd never be born. However, the two Stones were quiescent, dull. Curious, Travis leaned forward, bringing his Sinfathisar close to the one in the box. They touched.

He felt it rather than heard it, like the vibration of a dynamite blast from a mine deep beneath the earth.

Jack snatched the iron box back and clamped the lid down. "Oh dear. This isn't good at all."

"What is it?" Travis said, throat dry.

Jack shook his head. "Something just...changed. I'm not certain what, but I don't think we should let the Stones come in contact again. Or the Stone, I suppose, in the singular. For they're both one and the same." He cast a piercing look at Travis, Durge, and Lirith. "You're from the future, aren't you?"

"We are," Travis said, fighting to keep his voice steady. "Our time is more than a hundred years from now."

"And where will you get that Stone?"

"From you."

"And I suppose you'll knock me over the head when I'm not looking and steal it from me," Jack said, scowling. "Of course, now I'll be on my guard. Come a hundred years from now, I'll be watching for you. You won't find me so easily duped this time, young man!"

Travis clenched his fingers around the Stone. "No, you don't understand. You gave it me. Or *will* give it to me."

"Nonsense," Jack huffed. "I shouldn't think I'd be handing out Great Stones to any Tom, Dick, or Harry."

Travis had forgotten how frustrating talking to Jack could be. "I'm not Tom, Dick, or Harry. I'm Travis, and we're best friends. Or we will be, anyway. And you had a very good reason to give me the Stone."

"Yes," Jack said, his voice quiet now. "It seems I did."

His eyes were on Travis's hand, the one which clutched the Stone. Travis looked down. Silvery light welled from between his fingers. Hastily, he shoved Sinfathisar back into his pocket. He rubbed his right hand, and the rune on his palm faded.

Jack leaned back in the sofa. He looked haggard, and older than Travis remembered. But Jack was a century younger now than the last time Travis had seen him.

Lirith touched Jack's hand. "Are you well, my lord?"

He gave a weak smile. "I am when I look at you, my dear lady. You're from Eldh, aren't you? From the south, no? And you, good sir, are surely a knight."

Durge nodded. "I am the twelfth earl of Stonebreak."

Jack smiled. "Then I find myself in far better company than I could ever have imagined encountering in these barbarian lands. A daughter of Sia, a knight, and"—his eyes locked on Travis—"a runelord."

Travis's throat grew tight. "I've missed you, Jack. There were so many times I wanted to talk to you, times when I didn't know what to do."

Except he *had* talked to Jack. In his mind, at least, for Jack had given part of himself to Travis that terrible night beneath the antique shop. *And maybe that's why Jack is so weak. He's just like the hero in those time-travel movies. If part of Jack is in me, then he's existing in this time in two different forms.*

Jack patted his shoulder. "There, there, young man... Travis, did you say? We're all here now, so it seems everything has turned out fine."

Except you're dead in my time, Travis wanted to say. However, he only nodded.

"Now," Jack said briskly, "it's late, but with the aches imparted by my rough journey, I imagine there's no sleep for me tonight, and I have the feeling from your grim looks there's much you wish to tell me. So if one of you would be kind enough to fill my teacup again, we can begin."

Lirith started to get up, but Durge bid her sit and volunteered to fetch more tea himself.

"And perhaps a scone or biscuit to nibble on, good sir," Jack called after him.

It was one of the stranger sights Travis had witnessed over the course of the past year: Durge walking gingerly into the parlor, carrying a tray laden with a steaming teapot, milk, lemon, honey, and a plate of shortbread cookies arranged in regimented formation. The knight set down the tray, and Travis imagined he wasn't supposed to notice as Durge surreptitiously placed a saucer of milk on the floor for Miss Guenivere.

"I confess," Jack said over his tea, "things are already becoming clearer to me. I thought it mere whimsy that caused me to settle on the frontier of Colorado as my destination, but I can see now it wasn't chance at all that brought me here. It was you and your Stone that pulled me, Travis, whether I knew it or not."

"There's more you need to know, Jack." Travis glanced at Durge and Lirith. "Much more. About how we got here, to Castle City. And about what else—who else—came with us."

Jack set down his cup, his face solemn. "I think it's time you told me your story."

Travis drew in a deep breath. He wasn't certain what he should and shouldn't tell Jack. After all, couldn't giving Jack too much knowledge change the future? However, once Travis began, the words gushed out of him. He told Jack everything, starting with that late-October night when Brother Cy blew into Castle City, and everything changed. Finally, he told about what had happened to them since arriving in Castle City, and how they now knew that one of the Scirathi had followed them through the gate.

Jack sat bolt upright, eyes wide, and his teacup—which had been balanced on his knee—would have gone flying if Lirith hadn't deftly snatched it away.

"By Hades Himself!" Jack pounded a fist on the arm of his chair. "So that's who attacked my shop—a sorcerer. I wasn't able to catch a glimpse of him—I only had time to flee—but I should have known the noisome odor of his blood magic. Only I never expected I would encounter one of his kind, not here, so far from Eldh."

Travis leaned forward. "Tell us, Jack. Tell us what happened to you in London."

"I fear it caught me—he caught me—by surprise." Jack slumped back into the chair, his eyes haunted. "But I had been ill, you see. Not that I've been ill in seven centuries, mind you, not since taking up the burden of the Stone. All the same, perhaps a month and a half ago, I felt a terrible weakness come upon me, as if half my life had suddenly drained away."

Lirith's dark eyes were concerned as she glanced at Travis. "That would have been the same time we arrived here."

"I think it's me, Jack," Travis said. "I think I'm the reason you feel so weak. You gave me so much of what you were, and now—"

"And now here you are," Jack said softly. "Of course—my magic can't be in two places at once."

Durge cleared his throat. "How did the Scirathi make his attack, Lord Graystone?"

"It was a fortnight ago," Jack said. "I was in my bookshop. It was the dead of the night, and I was working on a small volume I've been writing on and off for centuries. It's a treatise concerning the magics of Falengarth. I've got it in my satchel—it's one of the few things I managed to save from the shop. Would you like to see it, Lord Stonebreak?"

Durge nodded. "But not now. You were saying . . ."

"Ah, yes. The attack. It was quite sudden, completely out of nowhere." Jack's eyes grew bright, and he sat back up, as if now that it was all over it seemed more like an adventure. "The windows shattered, and glass went everywhere. Then a swarm of bats flew in, swirling all around me, and by their odor I knew they were quite dead for all their fluttering and scratching. That should have been my first clue that it was a sorcerer. But really, there was no time to think. Usually I would have spoken a rune and"—he gestured with his fists—"those creatures would have been nothing but dust. Only then I felt . . ." The light in his eyes faded, his hands fell into his lap.

Lirith touched his arm. "What did you feel?"

"Death." He sighed. "I felt a presence—dark and full of hate—and it was as if a hand gripped my heart, squeezing it, forcing it to cease beating. I was too feeble—I couldn't fight. It was all I could do to whisper the rune of fire. That was enough to break the spell of my attacker for a moment. I managed to flee into the night as my bookshop went up in flames. After that, I knew I couldn't stay in London, that my attacker would only find me again. So I boarded a ship, then a train, and now I find myself here. No doubt exactly where the sorcerer intended for me to come."

Travis hadn't thought of that. The sorcerer must have left Castle City not long after overhearing their conversation in the old cabin. He must have traveled to London, where he tracked

Jack down. But why go to so much trouble to find Jack and attack him? The sorcerer could have just waited like they did for Jack to come to Castle City.

Don't you see, Travis. This is how Jack came to Castle City in 1883. It was all because of you. And the sorcerer. And it's because Jack came here that, over a hundred years from now, you'll go to Eldh.

The thought made his head spin. However, he could wonder about it later. Jack was in town, but so was the sorcerer, and he was planning something. What it was, Travis wasn't certain, only that the Scirathi no doubt wanted to use Jack to find a way to return to the future. And that the sorcerer intended to kill Sareth before he left.

"May I see it, Travis?" Jack said, his expression eager. "The scarab you spoke of? I've heard of such artifacts, but I've never witnessed one with my own eyes."

Travis reached into his pocket and drew out the golden spider. The drop of blood that lay within was their key back to Eldh, along with the gate artifact hidden in the rafters up in their room.

"Hold out your hand," Travis said. He let the spider crawl to his fingertip, then over onto Jack's hand.

"Why, it tickles!" Jack said, laughing.

Lirith smiled. "I think it likes you."

"Yes, I suppose it does." He lifted his hand, studying the scarab. "How marvelous, to think that in my hand I hold the blood of a god."

Durge glowered at this. "King Orú was not a true god. We heard the tale from the Mournish, who are descendants of his people. Orú was a sorcerer into whose veins entered thirteen spirits. He was powerful, yes, but he was only a man, not a god like Jorus or Yrsaia or Vathris."

"My good man," Jack said, looking up, "it was from the blood of Orú that Jorus, Yrsaia, and Vathris arose. They and all of the New Gods of the mystery cults."

Durge's mustaches pulled down. "But that's impossible."

"And have you made a particular study of the origins of gods, Lord Stonebreak? Do tell me more of your studies concerning gods."

Durge clamped his mouth shut.

Lirith reached out and stroked the scarab with a finger. "How can it be, Lord Graystone? How can Orú have been the father of the New Gods?"

Jack smiled at the witch. "I'm afraid I don't have all the answers, my dear. It was all very long ago, and well before my time. And it wasn't just Orú—it was all the sorcerers. Do you know of the cities of Amún, which were raised in the far south eons ago?"

She nodded. "They were home to sorcerers and ruled by the god-kings. One of the most powerful cities was Morindu the Dark, which was ruled by Orú. But after the thirteen *morndari* entered his body, Orú fell into an endless slumber, and his priests ruled in his name. And then there was a great conflict, in which the sorcerers rose up against the god-kings, and the god-kings tried to smite them, and all of Amún was laid waste."

"Yes, that's right," Jack said. "And in the destruction of Amún, the blood of countless sorcerers was spilled, so that the great river Emyr ran red with it, and the land was stained dark. In the end, the course of the Emyr was changed, so that it flowed north, not south, and Amún became a desert, and those who survived fled. But the blood of power remained in the soil. And the soil became dust. And the dust blew out over the world, and people breathed it, and ate it, and took it inside them grain by grain over the centuries."

Lirith's eyes were wide with wonder. "But what did it do to them, to the people?"

"I think it gave them the power to believe." Jack let the scarab crawl into his other hand. "Of course, one person alone could never have breathed enough dust to amount to anything much. Nor a dozen people, or even a hundred. But when thousands came together and believed in the same thing . . . well, my dear, that was when magic happened."

Understanding sizzled in Travis's brain. "So when enough people believed in a god, that god became real."

"In a way," Jack said. "Although I think it's a bit more complicated than that. You see, the mystery of each cult tells how one man or woman was transformed into a god. I think those people must have been different somehow. Perhaps they were more sensitive to the ancient dust, or consumed more of it. People like King Vathris, and the young huntress Yrsaia."

And Melia, Travis thought, *who escaped betrothal to a tyrant by marrying the moon.*

The gold spider perched on the tip of Jack's finger. "The blood of the mysteries is right here in my hand," he said softly. "And it's in every one of us, just waiting to become something wonderful, if only we believe."

Travis felt a tingling course through him. He glanced at Lirith and Durge, but the witch seemed lost in thought, a hand to her breast, and the knight gazed down at his gnarled hands. Travis reached out, and the scarab crawled back onto his palm.

"Jack, there's something we need to know—is there a way we can get back to our own time?"

"Why, don't you like this one?"

Travis bit his lip. "It's fine. It's just not ours, that's all. There are people who will miss us." In his mind he pictured a tall blond man with a brilliant smile. However, the image kept wavering, becoming a woman with golden eyes before flickering back. "Please."

"Well, it's simple enough. You're a runelord, Travis. And a good one, I might add, since it's my ability you've got in you. All you have to do is break the rune of time."

"And where could I find the rune of time?"

"You don't have one?"

"I'm fresh out," Travis said through clenched teeth.

"Oh, dear," Jack said. "That was always a tricky one to make. It took a good number of us to bind, so we never had many of them. Let me think." He tapped his brow. "It was all so long ago—things can get a bit foggy after seven centuries. And it was not long after we all fled Malachor that I used the Stone to come here, to Earth. But I did manage to speak with a band of apprentices, those who favored the art of runebreaking. They told me they were going to raise a tower at the western tip of the Fal Sinfath. They had a good number of artifacts in their possession. I'm quite certain a bound rune of time was among them. You could go to their tower."

"To the Black Tower of the Runebreakers?" Travis said, and Lirith shot him a startled look.

"Weren't they evil?" the witch said. "The Runebreakers. Didn't they destroy things?"

Jack gave her a sharp look. "Really, my dear, I would think a daughter of Sia of all people would know there can be no sowing without reaping, and no creation without destruction."

Lirith said nothing, but Travis could still feel her eyes boring into him.

"Is it not dangerous to break runes?" Durge said.

"Oh, yes," Jack said excitedly. "Quite dangerous. Why, the apprentices I met, the ones who were going to raise the tower and study runebreaking, had some artifacts of terrible power and peril. It's a wonder, really, that they didn't do something horrible."

Durge scowled. "Like what?"

"Like breaking the rune of sky and opening a crack in the world. Trust me, my good man, that's something you don't want to do. All sorts of horrible and nameless things lurk just beyond the boundaries of the world. They've been there for eons, only waiting for a chance to get in."

Travis looked at Durge and Lirith. "We have to go to the Black Tower of the Runebreakers. If the rune of time is anywhere, that's where it'll—"

Crash!

The muffled noise of splintering glass came from above. All of them looked up. There was a thudding sound, followed by another crash.

"By Vesta, that doesn't sound good," Jack said.

Durge was already on his feet and moving toward the stairs. Travis hurried after him.

"Lirith," he said over his shoulder. "Watch Jack."

The witch nodded. Jack nervously petted Miss Guenivere, for the little cat had leaped into his lap at the noise.

Travis followed Durge up the stairs. The boardinghouse was quiet now. Travis wished he had his Malachorian stiletto, but it was up in their room. All Durge had was his empty gun.

They reached the third-floor hallway. All of the doors were shut. Durge opened the door to Lirith's room, but there was nothing inside. Then the knight opened the door to the room he and Travis shared.

Night air rushed out, cool against their faces. Glass crunched under their boots; the window had been smashed in. The beds were overturned, and the drawers of the bureau had been ripped open.

Durge peered out the window. "It seems the thief is gone."

Travis moved farther into the room. Nothing seemed to be missing. The sack of money they had saved was still in the bureau. So what had the thief taken?

Durge must have had the same thought. As one, the two men looked up at the rafters. Then they were moving. Durge got a chair, and Travis scrambled onto it, reaching up a hand and feeling along the top of the rafter.

His fingers met nothing. He searched a few moments more, but in his heart he already knew the truth, and by the look on his face so did Durge. A wave of dizziness crashed through Travis, so strong he would have fallen if Durge hadn't helped him down.

"The gate artifact is gone," Travis said.

52.

Morning brought light but little comfort. Travis, Lirith, Durge, and Jack sat around the dining table in grim silence. The other boarders had headed off to the mines for the day, and by the clatter of dishes and the sound of coughing that drifted through the door, both Liza and Maudie were in the kitchen.

They had finally gone to bed as the grandfather clock in the parlor struck three, after Durge and Travis cleaned up the broken glass in their room and boarded the window. Lirith had cast a spell around the Bluebell, one that would alert her if anyone tried to enter, but not even Durge had believed the sorcerer would return that night. The Scirathi had gotten everything he had come for.

Or had he? Travis slipped a hand into his pocket, and he felt the touch of the scarab. Without the blood contained in the jewel, the gate was worthless. *Which means he's coming back.*

The sorcerer isn't going to stop until he has both the gate and the scarab.

Lirith raised an eyebrow. "Is the coffee too strong, Travis?"

He must have been grimacing. "I don't think it could possibly be too strong today."

Lirith nodded as she took a sip from her own cup. Travis doubted any of them had gotten a wink of sleep during the fractured remnants of the night. There were dark circles under Lirith's eyes, and Durge's face was even more careworn than usual.

Of them all, only Jack seemed to be of good cheer. The gray pallor of the previous night was gone, and his cheeks were rosy and eyes bright. Which made sense. Jack had been feeling ill and weak ever since Travis entered the year 1883; his power as a runelord had been stretched thousands of miles across an ocean. But now Travis was sitting just a few feet away.

"I must say, Travis," Jack said, munching on a piece of toast slathered with marmalade, "I didn't have the foggiest notion of what I was going to do with myself here in Castle City. But I rather like your suggestion of an antique store. This town is far too new—it could do with a bit of history."

Travis rubbed his stubbly head. "It wasn't a suggestion, Jack. You *will* open an antique store. I know because that's how I met you. Or will meet you. You'll come by the Mine Shaft one day and ask if you can look for antiques in the—oh." He clamped his mouth shut. Had he said too much?

Maybe you're supposed to affect the future, Travis. Maybe nothing that's supposed to happen then would take place if you weren't here now. After all, if Jack didn't meet you here in 1883, he probably never would have come by the Mine Shaft that day, and you never would have become friends, and that means you would never have gotten Sinfathisar or gone to Eldh.

Travis felt queasy. There was something there, something important, just out of reach. It had to do with affecting the future. Before he could grasp it, Durge spoke.

"I suppose the sorcerer heard everything we said last night. Only I don't understand how he could get so close without my detecting him. Or you, my lady." The knight glanced at Lirith.

Jack drizzled honey into his tea. "The sorcerer didn't need to get close. I don't know a great deal about the magic of the far south, but I suspect a spell that allows him to hear others at a distance is well within his capabilities."

"Then that means he could be listening to us right now," Durge said, glowering.

Jack nodded. "Almost certainly."

"No," Lirith said, setting down her cup. "If he listens, he will hear talk, but it will not be ours. I've seen to that."

Jack smiled at Lirith. "That's clever, my dear—clever indeed. We can't prevent him from listening to us, but thanks to you we can choose what he will hear when he does. You're very skilled at the craft of illusion."

Durge cast a startled look at Lirith. However, before the knight could speak, Maudie stepped through the kitchen door. Durge rose and pulled out a chair for her.

"How's your tea, Mr. Graystone?" she asked as she sat down. "I bought it at McKay's, but I don't know what it's called. Is it as good as that tea you said you liked—your Prince Green?"

"Earl Grey," Jack gently corrected. "And I believe that's exactly what this is. So it's quite good, thank you."

Maudie looked a little better that morning. She had slept all night, thanks to one of Lirith's potions. And that meant she hadn't heard about the break-in. Travis knew they had to tell her, only Durge was faster.

"Lord above!" Maudie said, pressing a hand to her chest, when Durge finished speaking. "The hoodlums in this town get bolder by the day. Was anything stolen?"

Jack started to open his mouth, and Travis gave him a hard look.

"No," Travis said.

Maudie leaned back in her chair, looking relieved. "Well, then it sounds like they weren't thieves at all. Just vandals—young men who had drunk more whiskey than they could hold. I suppose they threw a rock through the window."

"How is Lord Barrett this morning?" Lirith said, deftly changing the subject.

Maudie's smile was both fond and sad. "Liza said he's still

sleeping. His cuts are starting to heal up, so that's good. Some are going to scar, but he never was much of a looker anyway. His charms were all in his manner of speaking."

Lirith took Maudie's hand in her own. "He does have a beautiful voice."

"Only I wonder if we'll ever hear it again." Maudie shook her head. "Poor Niles. He never hurt anyone in his life. It's not right that such a kind man should have to suffer so, and for no reason at all. Just because the Good Lord chose to mold him from different clay than other men."

A fit of coughing gripped Maudie, and Lirith helped her up and into the kitchen to get some water. Lirith returned a minute later with a fresh pot of coffee.

Travis gazed at his hands on the table. "I suppose he'll be coming for the scarab soon." He knew he sounded a bit like Durge right then, but he couldn't help it. Niles Barrett wasn't waking up, Maudie was dying, and the sorcerer was in league with the Crusade for Purity. "It's the only thing he still needs to return to the future."

"You're not thinking, Travis," Jack said, shaggy eyebrows drawing together in a glower. "Our enemy is a sorcerer, not a runelord. There's simply no way he can use the rune of time to return to his own century. And he knows it."

Travis hadn't thought of that. And by their surprised looks, neither had Lirith or Durge.

"I don't know what the sorcerer wants," Jack said. "However, whatever it is, I imagine it's the same thing he came to London for. Our enemy is up to something, and I'm quite certain it can't be good."

That was surely an understatement. "Can't you do something, Jack? Can't you stop him?"

A bit of weariness stole once more across Jack's face. "I don't think I can. Even if my powers were great enough to do so, as long as you're here, they're not at my command. I'm afraid you're the runelord now, Travis, not me."

Travis's heart sank. So far he hadn't shown himself to be much of a runelord. He was as likely to harm with his power as help. However, he felt Lirith and Durge watching him.

"I'll just have to find a way to get the gate back from the

sorcerer," he said, although he didn't sound very convincing even to himself.

Jack took another piece of toast. "Why go to all the bother with that old thing? Why don't you simply use the Stone to return to Eldh?"

Travis's blood ran cold. "What?"

"You needn't act so surprised," Jack said, scowling. "After all, how do you think I got here in the first place? The three Great Stones fell *to* Eldh, but they're not *of* it. In a way, I think they belong to all of the worlds. And with a Stone, travel among the worlds is possible. Or at least between this world and Eldh, for they seem to be rather close together. And getting closer all the time."

Travis was sorry he had drunk so much coffee. It seemed to burn a hole in his stomach.

"Can you do it, Travis?" Durge said. "Can you use the Stone to return us to Eldh?"

Jack waved a butter knife at the knight. "Didn't you hear a word I said? By the gods of this world and that, he's a runelord. And a good one, since I made him. It's in his blood. The Stone will heed his command."

"Please, Travis," Lirith said. "We have to go back. We have to take Sareth home. I think I know now why he's been getting sicker. It's his leg. It was the demon that took his leg from him. The demon was forged from the *morndari*, and the *morndari* inhabit the Void between the worlds. I think passing through the Void inflamed his wound somehow. I think it's consuming him, and it won't stop ..." She took a shuddering breath. "It won't stop until he's gone."

She reached across the table and touched his hand. "Please, Travis. If we get him back to Eldh, I think I can heal him. But I can't do it here. The Weirding is too weak, and I have none of my sisters to lend me their power."

She didn't know what she was asking. He wasn't Jack. And he wasn't a runelord, despite everything that had been done to him. He hadn't asked for this power, and he had done everything he could to hide it away. Because it seemed like every time he let it out, people died.

*That's not true, Travis. You've done good with your power.
You sealed the Rune Gate.*

And he had set people on fire.

He pulled his hand away. If there had been no other choice,
maybe he would consider using the Stone. However, he still
had the scarab. All they had to do was get the gate back from
the Scirathi. And the idea of facing the sorcerer was far less terrifying than the idea of acting like a runelord. Because the moment he believed he really did have control over his power was
the moment he was lost.

Before Travis could explain this to her, Lirith let out a gasp.
She stood, body rigid, eyes wide.

"Sareth!" she cried out.

Durge rose from his chair. "What is it, my lady?"

"Something's happened," she said, breathless. "Something's
wrong."

Durge frowned. "No, my lady, I'm certain he is well. Sheriff
Tanner was keeping watch at the jail last night, and young
Wilson was going to stay to help. I imagine Sareth was safer
last night than we were."

"No, you're wrong," Lirith said, her voice anguished.

By the way she stared into space, Travis knew she had seen
something the rest of them couldn't—something with the
Sight. "What is it?"

Lirith was already moving. "I have to go to the jail."

Travis knew there wouldn't be any stopping her. "Durge,
don't let her out of sight. Jack, you stay here with Maudie.
Don't leave the Bluebell, do you understand?"

Maybe Travis had better control of his power than he
thought, because Jack only nodded, gripping his teacup. Lirith
and Durge were already out the door, and Travis grabbed his
hat and dashed after them.

The sun had just crested Signal Ridge, and Travis started
sweating instantly. He caught up to Lirith and Durge, and they
ran down the dirt street without speaking. When they reached
the jail, nothing looked out of the ordinary; the street was quiet.
Durge led the way, pounding up the steps, and together they
burst through the door.

Sheriff Tanner slumped in the desk chair, arms dangling, his face pressed against the desktop in a pool of yellow bile. He wasn't moving.

"Sareth!" Lirith cried, flinging herself forward. The door to the jail stood ajar, and she threw it wide. Travis didn't need to look beyond to know that Sareth's cell was empty. A moan escaped Lirith, and she fell to her knees.

Durge was already next to Tanner, two fingers pressed to the sheriff's throat. "He's alive, but his heart beats weakly."

Travis forced his legs to carry him forward. What was wrong with Tanner? Next to his hand was a half-drunk cup of coffee. Durge leaned the sheriff back; Tanner's head lolled to one side.

"Lirith," Durge said. "You must see to Tanner."

The witch rocked back and forth, hands clenched over her stomach, weeping.

Something caught Travis's eye. The door to the back shed was open. He moved to it, stepped inside. There wasn't much to see. Just the small stove on which Tanner and the deputies brewed coffee in a tin pot. Both stove and pot were cold. Then Travis caught a glint of light.

He knelt. On the floor were two small glass bottles. One still had a small amount of syrupy residue in the bottom. He picked up the bottles, and as he stood he saw that the front door of the stove was ajar. Inside were wadded up pieces of paper. Most were burned, but a few were only charred around the edges. Travis pulled one of the papers out. He set the bottles on the stove, then unwadded the paper, spreading it flat. It was a pen-and-ink illustration, depicting a man in a black hat shooting a man with a star pinned to his chest.

Travis's sweat turned to a clammy chill. He grabbed the bottles and paper and returned to the main room. Lirith seemed to have recovered her composure, although her face was ashen. She was examining Tanner as Durge watched. Lirith lifted one of his eyelids; his eye was dilated wide. She picked up the coffee cup and sniffed it, then looked up.

"This coffee is thick with tincture of poppy," she said. "Far more than a usual dose."

Durge glowered at her. "What are you saying?"

"I think . . . I think Sir Tanner did this to himself."

"No," Travis said before Durge could protest. "It was done to him." He set the laudanum bottles on the desk, along with the piece of paper. He had recognized the picture at once; it was from the dime novel he had seen Deputy Wilson reading.

"Treachery!" the knight hissed, clenching a fist.

"Look," Lirith said, leaning over Tanner. "There's something in his pocket."

The witch pulled out a small piece of paper and unfolded it. She scanned it with darting eyes, then a sigh escaped her. "Oh, Sareth. Forgive me for not coming sooner."

The slip of paper fell from her fingers to the desk. Travis glanced at it, wishing for the first time in his life that he wouldn't be able to read something, that his dyslexia would prevent him. Only it didn't, and he could. The neatly written letters all fell into place.

Bring the gold spider to the Bar L Ranch at sundown on Friday if you want to see the gypsy alive.

53.

Travis and Durge carried Tanner back to the Bluebell, using a board as a makeshift stretcher, and Lirith covered Tanner's unconscious form with a blanket to keep him out of view. At first Travis was afraid it would be too far to bear the load. However, the sheriff hardly seemed to weigh anything—a fact that caused Travis far more worry than relief—and he and Durge were able to jog most of the way.

Telling Maudie what had happened was a far greater burden. She didn't gasp or cry out. Instead, her face went as white as the fresh handkerchief clutched in her hand, and she sank to the sofa in the parlor, staring with blank eyes.

"I don't want to see him. I don't want to see him like that, lying on a stretcher. Not Bart." A hard fit of coughing took her, and Liza held her shoulders and rubbed her back while Travis and Durge started to carry Tanner upstairs.

"No, not up there!" Maudie managed to call between spasms. "You put him on my bed."

They laid Tanner in Maudie's room while Lirith ran upstairs. The witch returned moments later with a bag of compounds she had bought at the apothecary. She turned Tanner on his side, tilted his head back, and cleared his mouth and throat with her fingers. After that his breathing sounded easier, although it was still shallow and rapid. Lirith unfolded a scrap of paper and measured powder into a cup, then filled the cup with warm water.

"Help me," she said, cradling an arm beneath Tanner's head.

Durge helped her sit the sheriff up, and the witch slowly poured the liquid into his mouth.

"What is it?" Travis said.

"The apothecary called it foxglove, but I know this herb as heartwort."

"What does it do?"

Lirith kept tilting the cup. "I believe Sir Tanner vomited much of the laudanum. That is well, for if he did not I fear he would already be dead. All the same, too much of it has entered his blood. The poppy has quickened the rhythm of his heart. If it goes any faster, his heart will give out. This simple will make his heart beat more slowly and strongly."

"That sounds good," Travis said, daring to hope.

"It would be. Except I don't know how much of the laudanum is flowing in his veins. If the dosage is too small, it won't be enough to help him."

Durge cleared his throat. "And if it's too large?"

"His heart will slow so much it will stop beating."

Lirith set down the empty cup; she had gotten most of the liquid into the sheriff. Durge helped her lay him back down.

"Now what?" Travis said.

She looked up. "Now we wait."

Travis bit his lip. Why was it, in all his studies of rune magic, he had never learned the rune for healing? But maybe there wasn't one. And maybe that's why Eldh needed witches as well as runelords—to heal the world after the wizards broke it apart.

What about Sinfathisar, Travis? You know the Stone has the power to choose between states. Life or death, light or dark.

That's its magic. It made the demon just a rock. And it turned the feydrim *back into fairies.*

But what would it do to a man? As far as Travis knew, the runelords were the only human beings who had ever learned to touch the Great Stones and live to tell the tale.

They left the bedroom and returned to the parlor.

Maudie didn't look up. "How is he?"

Lirith sighed. "We'll know by sundown."

"Well, there's no use sitting here then, not when there's work to do." Maudie leaned on her cane and rose. "Come on, Liza. I'll help you get dinner started."

Travis felt his stomach twist into a knot. Sundown—that would be Tanner's reckoning hour. And in two more days, it would be Sareth's. Only why was the sorcerer making them wait three days? Why not make them bring the scarab today?

"He's scheming something, that's why," Jack said, popping into the parlor from the hallway.

Travis nearly jumped out of his boots. "Can you read my mind?"

"It's not my fault you think so loudly," Jack said in a huffy tone. There was something tucked under his arm. "If you ask me, you have an unwelcome propensity for being maudlin."

"So what is the sorcerer planning?"

Jack scowled. "I'm connected to you, Travis, not him. I haven't the foggiest notion what he's up to. However, one thing's certain—he fears you."

"Fears me?" Travis said, incredulous.

"As well he should. You're a runelord, after all. If you weren't, most likely he would have stolen the scarab long ago. The Scirathi is afraid of confronting you directly, so he's planning this exchange for the scarab quite carefully."

Jack's words made sense. But what was the sorcerer intending to do? Travis would have given anything to know. If they could prepare, they might have a chance of rescuing Sareth. Because there was one thing Travis did know: Sareth's only value to the Scirathi was as a bargaining chip. Once the sorcerer had the scarab, Sareth would die.

Jack sat on the sofa, took the object that had been tucked

under his arm, and unfolded it. It was a copy of the *Castle City Clarion.*

Travis eyed the paper. "Where did you get that?"

"From a boy passing by on the street." Jack's voice grew testy. "And you needn't worry—I didn't disobey your rather rude command and leave the boardinghouse. He came to the front porch, and I leaned over the rail. So I don't believe that counts as a violation. I thought I'd catch up on the news." He flipped through the pages. "Only there doesn't seem to be a single story about London in this wretched publication."

Travis hardly heard Jack's words. He could only stare at the headline boldly printed on the front page:

MURDERER BREAKS FREE FROM JAIL

In two steps, Travis crossed the room and snatched the paper from Jack's hands.

"Gods, man, have you no manners at all?" Jack exclaimed, but Travis wasn't listening. The paper bore that day's date. Travis scanned the story beneath the headline as Lirith and Durge moved close, reading over his shoulder. Travis only made out a few fragments before his vision began to swim.

. . . a cold-blooded killer . . . to be considered armed and dangerous . . . and no man will be blamed for shooting on sight, as it would be a matter of self-defense . . .

Travis tossed down the paper. "Jack, when did you buy this?"

"Not long after you all left in such a rush," Jack said. "Why do you ask?"

Travis looked at Durge and Lirith. "These newspapers must have been printed hours ago. That means they already knew what had happened at the jail. It's got to be Mortimer Hale—he's the publisher of the paper. He has to be behind the Crusade. And in league with the sorcerer."

Durge hesitated, then placed a hand on Lirith's shoulder. "We'll get Sareth back, my lady."

She raised her chin, and her voice was as hard as the expression in her eyes. "Yes. We will."

But how? A thought occurred to Travis. "Durge, do you know where the Bar L Ranch is? And if it's owned by Mortimer Hale?"

The knight crossed his arms. "I cannot say on either account. But I can find out."

Travis nodded; there was nothing more to do just then. Lirith headed to the back bedroom to keep watch over Tanner, and Jack went upstairs, saying there was something he wanted to get for Travis.

"It's going to be a trap, you know," Durge said once he and Travis were alone. "There is no telling how many men the sorcerer will have waiting for us at this ranch—Gentry, Ellis, Hale, and Wilson at the least."

Travis swallowed. "It's not men I'm most worried about."

By his grim look, Durge caught Travis's meaning. Had the sorcerer had time to work more experiments like those he had on Calvin Murray?

"I must go to the sheriff's office now," Durge said, starting for the door.

Travis grabbed his arm, stopping him. "You don't have to do this, Durge. You're not the sheriff of this town."

"I am until Tanner awakens," Durge started to pull away, then paused. "I will be careful, Goodman Travis."

Travis couldn't find words. He squeezed Durge's arm, then let the knight go.

Jack reappeared a minute later. In his hands was a leather-bound journal. He held it out.

"What is it?" Travis said.

"It's the book I mentioned. The one I've been working on. It's a slight volume, really, something I undertook for my own amusement. There's a bit of history here and there, but mostly it's about magic. I thought you might find it inspiring." Jack gave him an eager grin. "You know, as you get ready to do battle with the sorcerer."

Travis pressed his lips in a tight line in an effort to keep from vomiting, only Jack must have mistaken the expression for a smile. He pressed the book into Travis's hands.

"Do take good care of it, Travis. It's the only copy I've got."

Jack headed upstairs to rest. Travis checked in on Lirith, but she was bent over Tanner, her fingers on his wrist, and didn't even notice him. Maudie and Liza were busy in the kitchen, and Travis knew he would only be in their way, so he went to the dining room. Not sure what else to do, he opened Jack's book and began to read.

He wasn't certain what language the book was written in, but he had the sense that it was both ancient and formal. However, with the help of the coin fragment in his pocket—along with a stray pencil, which he laid across the page to help focus his eyes on each line—he was able to wade through the flowing script.

The book was fascinating. And horrifying. There were passages about the first War of the Stones and the history of Malachor, but it was the tales of the Runelords that claimed Travis's attention. Last night, when Jack told them about the rune of time, Travis had thought binding such a thing—let alone breaking it—must have ranked as one of the greatest feats of the Runelords. Now he knew that wasn't so.

According to the book, the Ironfang Mountains—the peaks that bordered Imbrifale to the south—had once been little more than a line of hills. However, after Ulther defeated the Pale King, a hundred runelords spoke the rune *Fal* as one, and the mountains soared toward the sky, becoming an impenetrable wall, transforming Imbrifale into a prison.

But that was only one of the wonders wrought by the runelords. They raised castles simply by speaking the rune *Sar*, then bound the rune of stone so that the fortresses were far stronger than any wrought by human hands. They caught the light of the stars and bound it into the stones of Malachor's highest tower, so that it shone like a beacon in the night. And they worked magics upon themselves, so that even the shortest-lived among them endured long into his second century.

"Can I do those things?" Travis whispered.

It seemed a chorus of voices whispered in his mind. *Yes, we can . . .*

Travis continued reading about all of the wonders wrought by the runelords. He turned another page—

—and excitement drained from him, leaving the cavity of his chest hollow. The words on the page burned his eyes.

It is well known to the Runelords that gods, dragons, and witches of the Sight have all foretold his coming. The one named Runebreaker will shatter the rune Eldh, which was the First Rune spoken by the Worldsmith, who bound it in the Dawning Stone at the very beginning of the world. And so the First Rune shall also be the Last Rune, for when it breaks, the world shall end, and in that instant all things will cease to be.

None of it mattered. The wonders, the beautiful things created by the rune magic. Nothing mattered if in the end he was doomed to destroy it all.

Was there no escaping it? Even here, in Castle City, he couldn't avoid reminders of what it was his destiny to do. Vani and Sareth's al-Mama had said he was one of the Fateless, but how could that be right? Wasn't it fate that was driving everything? He clutched the pencil and stabbed it at the open book, as if to strike out the words. Instead he scribbled furiously in the margin next to the passage. Then he flung down the pencil and shut the book.

He pushed away from the table and rose. It was hot in there; he couldn't breathe. He needed to get out. Travis started to turn away, hesitated, then grabbed the book and shoved it into his back pocket. He headed out the front door, down the steps, then strode down Grant Street as fast as his legs would carry him.

You shouldn't be doing this. There's no telling whom you might run into—Gentry, Ellis, maybe even Hale himself. The sorcerer probably has them all keeping watch on you.

Only they wouldn't attack, would they? The Scirathi was laying a trap for him at the Bar L Ranch, and he was far too smart to let any of his minions jeopardize that by striking too soon. Feeling bold, even reckless, Travis turned two corners, then strode down the dusty swath of Elk Street.

The main avenue was largely deserted. It seemed everyone in town knew something was coming, something terrible, and they were lying low until the storm blew over. The usually bustling shops were empty, and many of the storefronts—mostly saloons—were boarded up. The Crusade for Purity had done its work well. They had stamped out the sin in this town. And just about every spark of life along with it.

A paper nailed to a post caught his eyes. Was it one of their commandments? However, as he drew closer, he saw it was a battered Wanted poster, the same as the one he had found in the back of the saloon. WANTED DEAD OR ALIVE. TYLER CAINE, THE MAN-KILLER.

Travis tore the poster off the nail, folded it up, and tucked it into his shirt pocket. He considered swinging by the jail to make sure Durge was all right. Then again, Travis doubted there was much lawbreaking for the knight to take care of. He was starting to think there was nobody left in Castle City.

Then he saw the small gathering of people and the black wagon.

Travis found himself moving closer. The wagon had halted to one side of Elk Street at the mouth of an alley. It was a rectangular vehicle with one small round window in its side; its black-lacquered panels were dusty and blistered. At first Travis thought it must be a stagecoach. Then he considered the shape, the color, the smallness of the window, and he knew the vehicle had been designed to carry passengers, not in a seat, but in a coffin.

Two swaybacked horses were hitched to the vehicle, heads bowed, looking like they didn't have enough life between the two of them to pull the hearse ten feet, let alone over a mountain pass. The crowd of about twenty gathered in a half-moon around the wagon didn't look much better. By their shabby clothes they were miners and washwomen. They gazed up with grimy faces that were too haggard for hope, too weary for despair.

Just as Travis reached the edge of the crowd, the wind turned, and that was when he heard the voice. It crashed and rolled like thunder out of a clear sky. Recognition flashed through Travis. He circled around the throng until the speaker came into view.

The door at the back of the wagon had been thrown wide,

and the man stood in the opening, at the top of a set of wooden steps. He looked exactly as Travis remembered him. His skin was like yellow parchment stretched over his bony frame, and the black suit he wore looked as if it had been freshly stolen from a grave. The man held on to his broad-brimmed pastor's hat with one long hand, while the other was balled into a fist and shook in time to the cadence of his speech.

"...and there's no point in hoping things will get better," Brother Cy was saying in his booming voice. "Hope caught the last train to Denver, and she didn't look back. You're all on your own now, and there's no one who can help you." A sly look crept into the preacher's black-marble eyes. "That is, unless you all decide to help yourselves."

"But what can we do?" one of the miners shouted. "I can't swing a pick anymore. My lungs—it's like they're on fire all the time. Only if I don't work in the mines, my wife and children are going to starve."

"What can you do?" Brother Cy roared, drawing himself up to his full, terrible height, and the crowd fell back a step. "Why, you can spit in the face of Death, that's what you can do. You can pick out the plot for your own grave, then dance upon it. You can laugh as long as you've got a breath, and when your breath is gone, then you'll know at least you put every bit you had to good use."

A woman raised her hands. "Well, that sounds fine, but how will it put bread in our bellies?"

Brother Cy laughed. "It won't, madam. It can't. Nothing I can possibly say will heal you, or feed you, or make you wealthy, or give you something you don't already have."

"Then why should we be listening to you at all?" a man shouted, shaking his fist.

"Because," said a soft, lisping voice, "he tells the truth that most people in this town fear. Only you have dared to come forth and listen to it."

The murmurs of the crowd fell silent. Brother Cy descended the steps to the ground, and a girl and a woman appeared in the back of the hearse. The girl's hair was as black as her dress, her face was a cherub's cameo, and her eyes were purple. The woman wore a dress like the girl's, high-necked and severe, but her hair was wild and red, flying like fire about the oval of her face. She stared with stricken eyes.

The girl folded her small hands together. "Only a deceiver offers hope when there is no hope to be had. Only a devil takes your hand to guide you down the path to joy, when the only path from this world is barred with thorns."

"Child Samanda speaks wisely," Brother Cy said, his voice a low rasp, but commanding no less attention. "All I'm saying is that you'll all have plenty of time to be dead soon enough. So don't start acting like you're dead before you are. That's not why you were granted this life. I can't take away your sickness. I can't give you money. But I can help you find the truth, and in these days that's more precious than gold, and more welcome than water in the desert."

Brother Cy fell silent.

"But what is it?" the man who had shouted before said, lowering his fist.

"What is what?" the preacher snorted.

"The truth you're going to give us."

Again Brother Cy grinned his cadaverous grin. "I didn't say I was going to give you the truth. I said I was going to help you find it. And so I have, if you've been listening. Everything you can ever possibly have is already inside of you—be it love or fear, laughter or sorrow, madness or peace. No one else can give you those things, not man, woman, child, or god. They're in your blood. They were born with you, and they'll die with you. No matter what life dishes out, no one can take those possibilities from you." Brother Cy's grin vanished, and with a start Travis realized the preacher was gazing at him. "And that's the truth."

"The wind!" Sister Mirrim called out, her eyes wide and empty. "The wind is changing. I can see it!"

At that moment, a gust raced down Elk Street. Dust devils sprang to gritty life. The people turned their backs and hurried away, hanging on to hats and hands, and then—as if the wind had blown them all away—they were gone. The air grew still; the dust settled. Travis stood alone in front of the wagon.

He blinked his stinging eyes to clear them. Child Samanda

and Sister Mirrim were gone; they must have retreated into the wagon. Brother Cy stood like a crooked post, watching.

"Who are you?" Travis said. But didn't he already know the answer to that? He took a step closer. "You're Old Gods, aren't you? The ones who helped trap Mohg beyond the circle of Eldh. Only you got trapped there with him."

Sadness filled the preacher's black eyes, but he smiled. "It doesn't matter who we are, son. All that matters is what you're going to be."

Travis didn't let go. "But how did you get here?"

"A way beyond has been opened. The world has been cracked."

"What are you talking about?"

Brother Cy brought his spidery hands together. "Two things can't be in the same place, son, you know that. It was the only way it knew how to fix things, to make an opening, to give one of the two a direction to retreat. The Stones are powerful, but they're not really all that clever, if you know what I mean."

Travis reached into his pocket, feeling the smooth shape of Sinfathisar. He had felt it, like far-off thunder, when his Sinfathisar had touched Jack's Stone. Hadn't Melia and Falken talked about a rift? One that had allowed the New Gods to transport Grace to Eldh—and had allowed the Pale King to send his minions after her. It was his fault; he was the one who had caused the rift.

"All I ever do is break things," Travis said, anguished.

The preacher shrugged. "Some things ought to be broken."

"Not an entire world. I can't do it. I won't. I won't break Eldh."

"What if it's your fate?"

He met the preacher's hard eyes. "I don't have a fate."

"Everyone has a fate, son."

"Not me." Travis held up his hand. "See? It's smooth. No lines, so no fate."

The preacher sighed. "All that means is you don't know what your fate is. And don't you see what a gift that is? It means your fate can be anything you choose it to be."

That first time they spoke, that night in the revival tent, Brother Cy had talked about choices. And at the Rune Gate,

Travis had learned that it was better to choose the wrong thing than to choose nothing at all. Still, dread filled him.

"I didn't want this. I don't want to break the world."

"That's good, son. Because if you did, you wouldn't be any different than he."

Somehow Travis knew whom Brother Cy meant. "You said a rift has been opened. That's how you got here, to Earth. And that means Mohg is here as well, isn't he? And from Earth, all he has to do is find an open gate to get back to Eldh. That's his plan. Or it will be."

Brother Cy nodded. "My brother must be what he must be. It is his nature. And what will you be, son?"

Suddenly it was so clear. Determination replaced dread. Brother Cy was right; there was no use hoping, so he might as well do something, anything, while he still had a breath to breathe. He pulled the poster from his shirt pocket and unfolded it. His own face stared back at him from behind wire-rimmed spectacles.

"I'm going to be an outlaw," Travis said.

And Brother Cy's booming laughter rose to the sky.

54.

Aryn was far more relaxed at supper than the previous night. Her plans with Aldeth had narrowly avoided discovery by the king—thanks to the unlikely help of Teravian. She tried smiling at the prince on a few occasions, but he was back to scowling now. He gazed at the shadows in the corners of the hall, almost as if he was searching for something there.

She spent most of the meal chatting with the visiting earls who sat around her; they were a universally dour lot. Not that she could fault them for it. All spoke of the rumors of war in the Dominions, and one—whose lands were not far from the borders of Brelegond—claimed to have seen a troop of men in black armor riding black horses.

Melia's seat at the high table was empty, and no one seemed

to know where the lady was. Aryn supposed she was working toward purposes unknown. Or maybe she just felt like staying in her chamber and working on her embroidery. Even Melia enjoyed simple things. After all, if one had to do something mysterious and important every day for two thousand years, it could get a trifle exhausting.

Unlike the previous night, Boreas hardly spoke to Ivalaine at all. Instead, he glared at no one in particular, eyes stormy, while the queen often bent her head to murmur something to Mirda. Aryn wondered what it was the queen said; she even fancied trying a spell to find out, but even as she thought this she felt Mirda's calm gaze upon her. She hastily raised her wine goblet and discarded the idea.

After supper, she ventured to Melia's room to check on the lady. Aryn didn't bother to knock on the door, but instead waited for the clear voice to call out, "Come in."

"How do you always know when I'm at the door?" Aryn said, sitting in one of the two chairs near the fire.

Melia smiled. "I'm not a witch like you, dear, but I do have my talents."

That was an understatement. Just as Aryn had supposed, Melia's embroidery lay on her lap. However, it didn't appear she'd made much progress on it. Dark circles clung beneath the lady's amber eyes, and her face seemed uncharacteristically pinched.

Aryn spoke before she thought better of it. "Are you ill, Melia?"

The question was absurd, of course. Melia was a former goddess. It wasn't as if she could fall prey to a head cold. Then again, she *could* fall ill. They had seen that in Spardis, after Melia touched the marble bust of the Necromancer Dakarreth, which had contained a grain of the Stone of Fire. Aryn knew that certain kinds of magic—like runes, and the Great Stones—caused the lady distress.

Melia sat up straight. "Thank you for your concern, dear. I'm quite well, really. It's just . . ."

"What is it?" A tiny black fluffball pounced into Aryn's lap, demanding attention with a *mew*. Absently, Aryn stroked its soft fur. "Please, I wish you would tell me."

Melia gazed at Aryn, as if studying her, then she nodded. "It's hard for me to describe in words. In a way, it's a feeling like being watched. Only when you turn around and peer into the shadows, you can't see anything there."

"Do you think it might be the Little People?"

"And why do you say that?"

Aryn considered it a moment, then told Melia everything—about hearing the sound of bells, and finding Aldeth, and even how she had asked the Spider to keep watch on Ivalaine. If she had expected the lady to be shocked, then she was disappointed. However, curiosity shone in Melia's eyes.

"I wonder if I shouldn't have a conversation with Ivalaine," she mused, hand beneath her chin. "The queen and I haven't always been the best of friends, but there is a certain . . . understanding between us. Perhaps Ivalaine senses the same disturbance I do, and that is part of the cause for her distress."

It was a good theory. Certainly Ivalaine's behavior seemed unusual, no matter how torn she was between her duties as witch and queen. But if Melia were to tell Ivalaine . . .

The panic in her eyes must have been evident, for Melia gave her a reassuring look. "Don't worry, dear. I won't reveal the presence of our little friend the Spider to her. If there's a spy in the castle, it's far preferable to have him working for us, so you certainly did well in that regard."

Aryn's cheeks flushed, and she bowed her head, although not before she could conceal a smile. However, after a moment, the smile faded. Something about Melia's words troubled her. Why was it they seemed so familiar?

Then she had it. Tharkis, the mad fool—and former king of Toloria—had whispered something similar to her just before they found him hanged by the neck, something about how the eyes in the shadows had watched him. And there had been something else. The fractured, singsong words echoed again in her mind.

Fear the one alive and dead, for you cannot escape her web . . .

But what did it mean? She told Melia everything she could remember about her conversation with Tharkis.

"That is rather strange," Melia said. "Then again, Tharkis was mad. There's no reason to believe what he thought he saw has anything to do with what I'm sensing now. After all, Ar-tolor is nearly fifty leagues from here."

Aryn gazed at the fire. No doubt Melia was right. Tharkis's ramblings couldn't mean anything. Unless—

She looked up. "When did you start feeling as if you were being watched, Melia?"

The lady frowned. "Let me think. It was yesterday, I believe. In the morning. Yes, I remember it—I was taking my breakfast, and it came upon me so suddenly that I spilled my cup of *maddok*. Why do you ask?"

Aryn's mouth had gone dry. "Because yesterday morning is when Ivalaine arrived at Calavere. From Ar-tolor."

"Ah," Melia said, eyes gleaming.

They spoke more as the fire burned low, but they came up with no more ideas about what it might be Melia was sensing. All the same, it felt good to be talking like this. Not like equals; they certainly weren't that. But rather like friends.

"Perhaps your little spy could help us," Melia said.

The same thought had occurred to Aryn. "I'll tell him about it. But Aldeth's only working here inside the castle, and Tharkis saw the shadow when he was out riding. So I think we need someone to keep watch outside the castle as well."

"And who did you have in mind, dear?"

"A friend," Aryn said with a smile.

She found him the next morning in the upper bailey, in front of the stables, checking the saddle of his charger. Tarus looked up and grinned as she approached. He was dressed in riding gear of leather and wool. The day was gray and blustery, and shards of ice blew on the wind. However, she had spied him from a window, and she had dashed out with only a shawl thrown over her gown. Already her teeth were chattering.

"Is it your particular intention to freeze yourself this morning, my lady?" he said cheerfully.

She clutched her arm about herself, shivering. "No, that's just a happy accident of coming out here to see you. But at least it will keep me from having to suffer the agony and humiliation of donning an orange wedding gown."

He scratched his red beard. "Is that supposed to make any sort of sense?"

"Not really. Can I talk to you? Alone, I mean."

She glanced at the other men who saddled their horses nearby. They were members of Boreas's guard. Tarus hesitated, then nodded and drew her aside, into the shelter of the stables. The scent of horses hung thickly on the air.

The knight's expression was curious. "Is something wrong, my lady? Or have you decided to try another spell on me?"

"Yes," she said. "I mean no. To the second one, that is. But yes to the first."

"I think the cold's addled your wits."

"More than likely," she conceded. "Where on Eldh are you going in this weather?"

"Out."

"That's conveniently vague."

"My lady—"

"Never mind, Sir Tarus. I honestly don't care what errand the king is sending you on. But there's something you have to know, something about me. About us, the Witches." She paced back and forth on the straw, speaking fast, but it was the only way to get it all out. "You see, we aren't enemies. We're not on different sides at all. I can't tell you exactly why just now. The fact is, I don't understand everything myself. But it's true."

His expression was alternately stunned, then wary, then relieved. "I'm glad to hear it, my lady. I never wished for the Witches to be our foes."

"But they are," Aryn said. "I mean most of them are. They'll do anything they can to hinder you and the Warriors of Vathris. You see, they think—"

He waved a hand. "Yes, yes, we know what they say about us. They think we're going to help destroy Eldh in the Final Battle."

"Then you know about Runebreaker?" she said, shocked.

He frowned. "I've never heard of a *Runebreaker*. Our stories tell of the Hammer and the Anvil."

Aryn gave a wry smile. "You'd think all of these prophecies could actually specify someone by name once in a while."

Tarus snorted. "That would be a help, wouldn't it?" He took a step closer to her. "But I'm puzzled, my lady. First you tell me we're not enemies, but then you say your sisters will work against my brothers."

"Not all of us." Aryn forced her chin up.

He held her gaze, then nodded. "So you're betraying the Witches."

She winced, and she recalled the words spoken by the dragon Sfithrisir. *And here are two Daughters of Sia, both doomed to betray their sisters and their mistress. . . .*

"No, I'm not betraying the Witches," she said, forcing her voice to hold steady. "It is others who have done that for many years now by ignoring the truth."

His gaze was sad and knowing. "I think I understand you, my lady. There are those in the Cult of Vathris who seem to spend so much time praying and chanting around the fire that I think all the smoke has gotten to them. They've forgotten what it means to be a warrior—not to make war for the sake of war alone, but to protect, to preserve."

She found herself smiling. Yes, he did understand.

He stamped his boots. "I have to be going now. Off on my errand, as you call it. So what is it you came out here to ask me? And don't pretend you don't want something. We swore a pact to be as honest as we can with one another, remember?"

"I need you to keep your eyes open for me."

"That's easy enough, my lady. I find I fall down far less often that way."

She did not try to disguise her pained expression. "That's not what I meant." She explained how she wanted him to keep a lookout for anything unusual around the castle. Anything in the shadows, watching.

"And who is this person who you fear is watching us?"

"I'm not certain. In fact, I'm not certain it's a person at all. Or even if it's alive."

The knight groaned. "Well that's all good and fine. I'm supposed to be looking for a not-human, not-living thing that's spying in the shadows. Next you'll be telling me the Little People exist."

She snapped her fingers. "That's right—I almost forgot. Could you keep your eyes open for them as well? Especially near Gloaming Wood. I think they're stirring again, and that can only mean there's danger close at hand, just like last Midwinter's Eve."

Tarus looked nauseous. "You're serious, aren't you?"

"Perfectly."

He sighed, then bowed low. "Very well, my lady. For you, I'll chase after fairies and shadows. And after my brethren cast me onto the fire for being a heretic, I'm sure I'll feel a sense of great peace and comfort knowing that everything I did was not foolishness, but utterly worthwhile."

"I'm sure you will," Aryn said, and with a smile she left the young knight to his mission.

The remainder of the day passed quickly, as did the day after that. Farvel asked her an endless array of questions about her wedding (How many attending maids did she wish? What were her favorite flowers? Did she prefer mead or wine to be served at table?) and Aryn did her best to answer them. One happy stroke of luck was that the king's dyers were having trouble making large quantities of orange cloth, as the best dyes of that hue came from Eredane, with which there had been no trade in a year. Feigning disappointment as best she could, Aryn informed Farvel that they would just have to make do using orange as an accent color, and that she would somehow manage if the primary color for the wedding was blue.

After one of her conversations with the seneschal, the shadows behind a statue uncoiled, and Aldeth stepped out, causing Aryn to clutch her chest.

"You like startling people, don't you?"

"Is that so wrong?" the Spider said.

She glared at him, and his smile quickly vanished.

Unfortunately, the spy had discovered very little since their last meeting. Ivalaine spent most of her time in her chamber, where it was difficult to get close to her.

"Your sisters have a way of seeing things others can't, if they choose to look," he said with disgust. "All of those years spent practicing my hiding skills are useless when all you have to do is wriggle your fingers and I start glowing."

"It's hardly that easy," Aryn said, but she knew the Spider

was right. If he lurked too long around Mirda and Ivalaine's chamber, one of them was bound to feel his presence.

Despite those limitations, Aldeth had discovered a few interesting items. First of all, King Boreas and the queen had spoken once again in the council chamber, and the meeting had ended in some sort of argument.

"I couldn't get close enough to hear properly," Aldeth said, annoyance flashing in his gray eyes. "There were guards at the entrance, which I expected, of course, but there were also men posted at the secret door that leads to the council chamber. And I ask you, my lady, what good is a secret door if you're going to place guards at it? It's an insult to spies everywhere. Why I ought to give King Boreas a—"

"Aldeth," Aryn said, prompting the Spider. "The meeting."

The spy regained enough composure to tell her what he had heard from his perch outside one of the chamber's high windows. The king and queen had talked of war, but that was hardly a surprise, with Brelegond under the control of the Onyx Knights.

"That's all you heard?" Aryn said.

"Doves nest on the ledges of those windows. The blasted birds kept cooing in my ear. But there was one more thing. The king mentioned his son, Teravian. Isn't that your husband-to-be? Well, I don't know what he said about the prince, but that was when the show began. Ivalaine slapped Boreas."

Aryn gaped. "She *slapped* him?"

"Right across the face. His cheek turned crimson, and not just from the blow, mind you. He was shaking, and he looked ready to throttle her right there and then. She spoke several things I couldn't catch. But then she said one thing that echoed clearly in the chamber. After that, she turned and left."

"And what did she say?"

"She said, 'I won't let you sacrifice him like one of your bloody bulls.'"

Aryn paced, thinking. Had the queen still been speaking of Teravian, or someone else? "Didn't you say there was something else you found out?"

The spy nodded. "The queen has been writing daily missives to Ar-tolor. I think they're for her advisor, Lady Tressa."

"That's odd. I wonder why she doesn't just speak to Tressa over the—" Aryn clamped her mouth shut, but it was too late.

"So you witches can speak to each other with a spell, even when you're leagues away."

Aryn sighed. "Not all of us." Despite trying again several times over the last two days, she still hadn't been able to reach any farther along the Weirding than the castle garden. The threads always tricked her into going in circles.

Except they can't be deceiving you, Aryn. Mirda said the magic of the Weirding can't lie.

Which meant the deception lay within herself.

Footsteps echoed down the corridor. Aryn recognized the uneven cadence of Lord Farvel.

"Until next time, my lady," Aldeth said, and before she could say anything the Spider coiled his shimmering cloak around himself and was gone.

Once she extricated herself from Farvel's questions—this time he wondered about her preference for swans or doves, and she didn't know if he meant as decoration or as something to eat, so she said she liked both—she headed for Mirda's and Ivalaine's chamber. It was time for another lesson.

On the way she caught a glimpse of Teravian, but only at a distance, and he was quickly gone. He seemed to be avoiding her since their last conversation. No doubt he was enjoying his last few days of freedom. The next day, on the night of the full moon—the same night Aryn was to tell Sister Mirda her decision—a feast was to be held at which the prince and Aryn's engagement would be presented to the entire court.

Aryn still wondered how Teravian had known to follow her the other day. Could the prince really possess the Sight? If Ivalaine believed so, it might explain why she had been arguing with Boreas. Perhaps the two had differing plans for the prince. But if so, what were they?

Aryn didn't know. However, she imagined those missives Ivalaine was writing to Tressa would tell her. There could be only one reason the queen was committing her words to paper: She feared they would be overheard if she used the Weirding. Which meant Liendra was indeed still in Ar-tolor.

Maybe the missives contain something about the shadow coven, Aryn thought with growing excitement. Except what did any of that have to do with Teravian? Nothing Aryn could imagine. But she still wished she could see one of those missives; it might help her with the decision that lay before her— whether or not to join the shadow coven herself.

There was no sign of Ivalaine when Aryn reached the queen's chamber, but Mirda was waiting for her. However, once again the lesson ended in frustration, as Aryn tried to reach far across the Weirding but only ended up getting lost somewhere in the sheep pen in the lower bailey.

"I don't understand, Mirda. What's wrong with me? I know you're right, that the Weirding can't possibly lie. But how is it that I'm deceiving myself into going astray?"

"No one has more power to deceive us than ourselves," the elder witch said, pouring a cup of rose hip tea. "How often do we tell ourselves it is fine for us to do something when deep down we know it is not? Listening to the truth of the Weirding means listening to the truth inside yourself. I'm afraid that's something it seems you're not yet willing to do."

Aryn shook her head, frustrated. "But I *am* willing. I know I'm far from perfect, Mirda. I know others stare at my arm, and that they think it's horrible, but I don't care anymore. It's part of who I am, and I accept that. That's why I don't hide it anymore. Isn't that being honest?"

"It is. And I'm proud of you for it." Mirda sipped her tea. "But there must be something else, something you're hiding even from yourself. Something you have forgotten."

Outside the window, the sun dipped below the horizon, and a shadow stole into the room. The darkness brought words to Aryn—words first spoken to her in the cramped space of one of the Mournish wagons below Ar-tolor.

See how the woman rides so proudly? All love her beauty even as they fear her sword. Yet there is always a price to wielding power. For see? She does not notice the poor man in the grass who is trampled beneath the hooves of her horse.

Yes, Aryn remembered the card: a proud queen in blue, a

sword in her arm, riding from a castle with seven towers. It had been like the vision she had once seen in the ewer, revealed by Queen Ivalaine. Except for the man lying in the grass, eyes shut.

Again the old Mournish woman's voice rasped in her ear. *You have forgotten about one who bore pain for you....*

All at once, in a terrible flood, it came gushing back to Aryn. The sweltering day the previous summer, stealing away from Calavere to ride eastward after Grace, convincing Lirith to go along with the plan. But their absence would be quickly discovered. They needed to find a way to throw the king's knights off their trail. With her growing power, it had been so simple. Talk to a young servingman and sow in his mind a small seed, so that when he was questioned later he would say he had seen the Lady Aryn riding away from the castle. Riding westward.

A sickness gripped her, one so strong she feared she would vomit. That was why he had looked so familiar to her, despite the vacant stare in his eyes, despite the dent in his skull.

Please. Don't let him be beaten again. My brother didn't mean it. I beg you, my lady...

And in that moment Aryn knew what she had been hiding from herself, from the world. It wasn't the ugliness of her arm. It was the ugliness inside herself.

She sank to her knees, chest aching, and a sob ripped itself out of her. "Oh, Mirda, what have I done?"

The witch's eyes were filled with sorrow, but her touch on Aryn's brow was warm and gentle.

"You've just told yourself the truth, sister."

55.

Aryn sat beside the window as darkness settled over the world outside.

"I thought they were the cruel ones, Mirda. Those young witches—Belira and her friends, the ones who mocked me at High Coven. When I stood up to them, I felt like I was so much better than they were. But I'm not, am I? They only used words to harm. But I used my magic to hurt them when they were laughing at me. Just as I used it to hurt the servingman."

"You don't have the Sight as your sister Lirith does," Mirda said, standing by the fire, her face serene as always. "You couldn't have known he would come to such harm. Did not his sister say the blow to his head was an accident?"

Aryn clenched her left hand into a fist. "No—that doesn't make it any better. If I'd thought it through, I would have known he would get a beating for misleading the king's men. But all I cared about was running after Grace."

"And did not your following eastward after your sister Grace result in much good? Did you not aid the Runebreaker in ending the plague of fire by your actions?"

"It doesn't matter. Whatever happened after doesn't change what I did at the time. I did this thing, and I won't deny it. Because that would be crueler still."

Mirda nodded, and while her expression was serious, there was a faint smile on her lips. At last Aryn realized what Mirda had been doing. With each of her questions, the elder witch had offered her a way out of her predicament, a way to explain away her actions. But Aryn hadn't taken the lure, as tempting as it was. She wanted more than anything to dull the pain in her chest. But that pain was nothing compared to what she had caused others. If Mirda's actions had been some sort of test, Aryn supposed she had passed it, but that didn't matter now.

"You have found the deception in yourself, sister." Mirda rested a hand on Aryn's shoulder. "And now it can no longer deceive you. You should try once more to reach out across the Weirding. Nothing can hold back your power now."

Aryn trembled at these words. No, there was nothing to hold back her power. But shouldn't there be? She had known since Midwinter's Eve that she had the power to harm; with a thought she had murdered Lord Leothan. Yet he had been an ironheart, and he had attacked her, provoking her. Just like Belira and her cronies had done with their taunting. But what had the servingman—Alfin, he had a name—what had Alfin ever done to her to deserve her cruelty? And what good was power if all she ever used it for was to hurt others? Maybe Belira and the rest were right. They weren't the monsters; she was.

"No, do not think such thoughts." Mirda moved in front of Aryn's chair, her face stern. "You have many choices before you. But one thing you cannot choose is to deny the talent within you. You are strong, sister—stronger than any witch in a century."

Aryn looked out the window, into the night. "But I didn't ask for this power. And I don't want it."

"And you can no more change it than you can the shape of your right arm. Power is in your blood. And the more you try to deny it, the less control you will have over it, and the more control it will have over you."

"But what's the point of it?" Aryn caught a glimpse of her reflection in the window: pale and lost as a ghost. "What good is all this power anyway?"

"That," Mirda said, her voice crisp, "is up to you."

In that moment, Aryn knew Mirda was right. Power was neither good nor evil in and of itself. It was only what the wielder chose to do with it that made it one or the other. She felt a sharp pain in her chest, only it was a good feeling. It was like something breaking, like some small piece of her falling away. Aryn knew what it was; it was her pride in believing that she was better than others, that she was kinder and more virtuous than they were. However, from that moment on, she would use her power as wisely as she could. And not just her power as a witch, but her power as a baroness—and soon as a queen—as well.

Aryn rose from her chair and met Mirda's steady gaze. "I must talk to the king at once."

Mirda only nodded.

A quarter hour later, Aryn stepped into Boreas's chamber. She was not nervous, as she had been every other time she had set foot in this room; she knew what she had to do. The king sat at the table, poring over sheaves of parchment; at last he looked up, squinting at her with tired eyes.

"I'm busy, my lady."

"Forgive me for disturbing you, Your Majesty. I have something I must tell you. Something that can't wait."

The king cocked his head and set down the parchments. "What is it, my lady?"

"Your Majesty, there are others who must hear this as well. May they enter?"

The king was clearly puzzled by her words, but he nodded, and she moved to the door, gesturing for the two waiting outside to come in. They did so, one tentatively, her eyes wide as she gazed around, the other with shuffling footsteps.

The serving maid gasped when she saw the king and hastily dropped into a curtsy.

"Alfin!" she whispered, tugging on the young man's sleeve. "Alfin, you must bow to the king!"

She tugged again, and he slowly bent forward.

"Rise," the king rumbled.

The young woman leaped up and tugged again at her brother's tunic, causing him to straighten. He gazed forward, expression placid. The dent in the side of his head was plain to see.

Boreas frowned, although not unkindly. "What is all this about, Aryn?"

She drew in a breath, expecting it would be difficult to form the words, only it wasn't. "I have done a grave wrong to this man. And to his family."

The young woman—her name was Alfa, Aryn had learned when she went to find the pair working in the kitchens— clasped a hand to her cheek. "My lady, nay, it—"

The king raised a finger, silencing her. He looked at Aryn. "Explain yourself, my lady."

She spoke in precise words, leaving nothing out, in no way trying to disguise the lowness of her act or the suffering it had caused. The king listened, his visage unreadable. At last she finished, and she stood, shoulders straight, waiting for him to mete out his justice.

"What you tell me is regrettable, my lady," he said, moving toward the fire. "But you are a baroness. It is your right to order servants as you wish. There is no crime in what you did that I can punish."

Shock jolted Aryn. But there was a crime—a horrible one, and it was done by her hand. Then she felt his piercing blue eyes upon her, and she understood his meaning. There was no crime *he* could punish.

"Then I will make amends for my own deeds, Your Majesty."

"What do you wish to do, my lady?"

She thought about it. "Alfin and his family will be paid one thousand pieces of gold in reparations. However, the money shall come not from the Dominion's treasury, but from my own dowry. In addition, he shall have a house, and a servant to attend him at all times. The servant shall be one of my own, and I shall always have one less than I would otherwise. In addition, he and his sister will eat in the great hall at all feasts, and on the Feast of Fallowing each year, he shall be served meat before me, that I never forget how I wronged him."

Alfa was beyond fear now. The young woman only stared, quite as slack-jawed as her brother.

"It shall be as you say, my lady," Boreas said.

"Thank you, Your Majesty." Aryn turned toward the other young woman. "You may take your brother home now, Alfa. I will come to you tomorrow, to discuss arrangements for your house and the payment of your reparations."

Alfa was still too stunned to do more than whisper a hoarse, "Yes, my lady."

Aryn hesitated, then lifted a hand and touched it to Alfin's cheek. His flesh was warm and slack beneath her touch. "Forgive me," she said.

The young man only stared forward, his eyes peaceful and empty.

Aryn lowered her hand. Alfa took her brother's arm and pulled him from the chamber. Aryn could hear Alfa whispering excitedly to him as she led him away.

"That was well-done, my lady," Boreas said behind her, his voice gruff. "One day you will be a good queen."

She drew in a deep breath. "I will try first to be a good daughter, Your Majesty."

Then she excused herself and returned to her own chamber. To her surprise, she found Sir Tarus waiting at her door. He wore riding clothes, and his red hair was wild from wind.

"What is it, Tarus?" she asked once they had entered her room.

"My lady, remember how you told me to keep my eyes open. Well, I was riding back from—"

A sound interrupted the knight: someone clearing his throat. Tarus turned toward the sound, his hand moving to the hilt of the sword at his hip. Aryn turned as well, then gasped. They were not alone in the room. A slender figure clad all in black sat in a chair by the fire.

"Hello," Teravian said, a smirk on his lips.

Tarus quickly let go of his sword and bowed.

"Your Majesty!" Aryn said, shock renewed. "What are you doing in my room?"

"I told him to meet us here," said a cool voice.

Aryn was beyond surprise now. She glanced around to see Melia glide through the door in her snowy kirtle.

"Melia," Aryn said, "what on Eldh is going on?"

The lady shut the door. "I believe our good Sir Tarus has something to tell us. Something I think we all need to hear."

The knight scowled. "But I only just came back to the castle. How did you—?"

Aryn touched his arm. "Tarus, what is it you have to tell us?"

He sighed, evidently seeing the futility of resisting. "It happened a short while ago, about dusk. I was coming back to the castle after doing some work for the king, and my course took me not far from the old circle of standing stones. You know the one, near the eaves of Gloaming Wood?"

He began to pace, shaking his head. "It was strange. I thought perhaps I was tired, that my eyes were playing tricks on me, only I knew that wasn't the case. It looked like there was a shadow inside the circle—a patch of air darker than the twilight around it. I remembered what you had said about shadows, so I started to ride closer. Only then I saw lights."

"Lights?" Aryn said, puzzled.

Tarus's gaze went distant. "It's hard to describe them. They were like sparks from a fire. Only brighter, and far more beautiful. They seemed to come from the forest, and they danced toward the circle of stones, surrounding it, and moved inward. And then—my lady, it seems impossible!"

"If it only seems impossible, then it actually *is* possible, isn't it?" Melia said. "Tell us, Sir Tarus."

He swallowed and nodded. "The sparks of light moved in toward the center of the circle, and as they did it seemed a cry rose on the air. It was so high I could hardly be sure I heard it, but around me birds that had been nesting for the night flew into the air, and my horse reared back, and I knew the beasts had heard it even as I had."

Melia folded her arms. "And then what happened?"

"I'm not certain. It was over so quickly, and I was trying to calm my horse. But it seemed to me the lights streamed back into Gloaming Wood and vanished, and after that the darkness that gathered inside the circle of stones was only the same as that which settled over all the land. Still, I rode toward the circle of stones. As I suspected, it was empty. Except . . ." The knight shivered visibly. "All the plants that grew within the circle were dead."

Teravian snorted. "That's because it's Valdath. Everything is dead."

"No, that's not true," Aryn said, moving to the fire. It felt suddenly cold in here. "The *melindis* bushes that grow in the circle are evergreen."

Tarus drew a twig from his cloak and handed it to Aryn. It was blackened and withered. "I plucked this from one of the *melindis* bushes."

Melia reached out and took the twig from Aryn. "I'm not surprised. Death ever followed in her wake." She threw the twig into the fireplace. It flared, then was gone.

Startled, Aryn looked at the lady. "Who are you talking about?"

Melia gazed at Teravian. However, the young man only stared into the fire. At last she sighed. "I know now who has been watching the castle these last days. She had been cloaking herself from me, but at dusk I felt her go. It is just as Sir Tarus described. She was attacked by the forces of Gloaming Wood, and in that moment her guard was down, and I was able to sense her presence before she fled."

Aryn grasped for comprehension but failed utterly. "I don't understand, Melia. Who fled?"

"Oh, don't be such a thicky," Teravian said, rolling his eyes. "She means the Necromancer, of course."

56.

Aryn found herself in the chair opposite Teravian, even though she couldn't remember sitting down. Someone pushed a cup into her hand. Sir Tarus.

"Try this, my lady. It will calm you."

Aryn gulped the spiced wine, choked, and drank some more. How could it be true? How could there be a Necromancer there in Calavere?

"I don't understand, Melia," she managed to croak, lowering the cup. "Dakarreth was destroyed in the fires of Krondisar. We all saw it happen. How can he be here now?"

"He isn't, dear." Melia smoothed her white kirtle as she paced. "For many years now Falken and I have suspected that Dakarreth was not the only one of Berash's Death Wizards who survived the War of the Stones. And now I finally know that to be true."

Tarus crossed his arms. "I'm not even going to pretend I understand what you're talking about. But I think I'd like to know who this Necromancer person is."

Melia smiled, but it was a bitter expression. "She's not a person, Sir Tarus. And she never was. The Necromancers were all gods once—thirteen gods of the south—but the Pale King seduced and corrupted them with the aid of the Old God Mohg. The Necromancers took bodily form to walk the world and do the Pale King's bidding. I believe Shemal is now the last of her kind. But even one Necromancer is a peril beyond imagining."

Tarus opened his mouth, but no words came out. Aryn knew the knight would have been even more astounded if Melia had told the other part of the story: how nine other gods of the south had forsaken their celestial dwellings to walk the face of

Eldh and work against the Necromancers. And of those nine, only Melia and the golden-eyed old man Tome remained.

"Shemal," Aryn murmured the name. Just the sound of it gave her chills. "What does this Necromancer want, Melia? Why was she here in Calavere?"

"That's something I would give much to know, and would that Falken were here so I could ask his opinion. Shemal was ever among the most subtle and scheming of her kind. It might be that she was simply watching me. If so, perhaps there is no great cause for worry. But then, it might also be that she was up to something else."

Once again the lady's gaze moved toward Teravian. The prince slouched in his chair, eyes on the fire.

Something occurred to Aryn. "Teravian, how did you know there was a Necromancer here in Calavere?"

Without taking his eyes from the fire, he waved a hand toward Melia. "She told me about it. Earlier today."

Both Aryn and Tarus cast questioning gazes at Melia.

"I thought perhaps the prince might have seen or heard something," Melia said. "Something that could help confirm my suspicions. I know he has a habit of . . . observing others unnoticed."

He looked up, a vicious grin on his face. "It's all right. You can say *lurking*. I don't mind."

Melia raised an eyebrow. "Very well. What I mean to say is that I know the prince has a habit of lurking about the castle like a fox all in black, just as curious and with ears every bit as large."

Teravian clapped his hands. "I love it when someone tells it like it really is."

"Is that so, my lord?" Aryn said. "Then perhaps you'll tell us what you've seen in the course of all your lurking?"

The prince gave an exaggerated yawn, as if bored by the whole topic. "Why don't you ask your little spy? He's right over there in the corner."

They all turned their heads, and a harsh string of oaths emanated from the dim corner they stared at. With a flick of his shimmering cloak, Aldeth appeared.

Tarus drew his sword and lunged forward, holding the tip of

the blade an inch from the spy's throat. "I can kill you in an instant."

"And you'd be dead before you could move."

Aldeth's silvery eyes flicked downward, and Tarus followed his gaze. The spy held a long needle in his gloved hand, its point resting lightly against Tarus's thigh. A green residue stained the needle.

"That's enough, you two," Melia said, her gaze bright with ire. "We're all very impressed with how fast each of you might kill the other. But would you please put your little toys away? We have important matters to discuss."

Tarus snorted and took a step back, sheathing his sword. The Spider spirited the needle inside his cloak.

"Who is he?" Tarus said, glaring at the Spider.

Aryn rose from her chair. "A friend. From Perridon."

The Spider bowed low.

"From Perridon?" Tarus's eyes narrowed. "He's a spy then, my lady. We must tell the king at once."

Aryn laid a hand on the young knight's arm. It would be so easy to cast a spell; she could feel the hum of his life thread. All she had to do was entangle it with her own strand for a moment, and she could prevent him from telling the king.

No. Just because she had the power didn't make it right. That was what Alfin had paid so dearly to teach her. She would have to use words, not magic, to convince him.

It took some time, but eventually she succeeded. She told Tarus how she had come upon the Spider, as well as why she had determined it best not to tell the king in order to avoid an incident between Perridon and Calavan. Tarus didn't look happy, but in the end he acquiesced.

"I won't tell the king of his presence," he said, glaring again at Aldeth. "For now."

Aryn let out a breath of relief. With that settled, she turned once more to ask Teravian whether he had seen anything or not, but the prince's chair was empty.

"Where is he?" Aryn gasped.

Melia smiled. "Off lurking again. He must have left while all of us were distracted by you, Sir Tarus."

The knight's cheeks went red.

"Not bad," Aldeth said admiringly. "Not bad at all. That boy has the making of a Spider."

Melia gave the spy a sharp look. "Don't get any ideas. I believe his career has already been decided for him."

The next day Aryn was a jumble of nerves. She tried to brush her hair after she woke up but only succeeded in snarling it so badly it took one of her maidens an hour to undo the damage. At breakfast she spilled *maddok* on herself and had to change her gown. And she fidgeted in her chair, unable to concentrate, while Lord Farvel discussed various, excruciatingly detailed plans for her wedding and made her choose among them.

"Don't fret, my lady," the old seneschal said. "It will be a lovely wedding."

Aryn forced herself to smile. Lord Farvel was a kind man, and he deserved her attention and respect. But he was wrong about the source of her apprehension. It didn't have to do with the wedding, or even the feast that night, at which her engagement would be announced. Her gaze moved to the window. When the moon finally rose, it would be full. And it would be time to give Mirda an answer. Aryn wanted to trust the mysterious witch, but all of her instincts warned there was grave peril there.

By afternoon she still hadn't made a decision, and it was time to prepare for the feast. She stood for hours while her maidens whirled around her, bathing her, perfuming her with flower petals, arranging her hair into an intricate tower of curls and ringlets and helping her into an elaborate gown of sky blue. By the time she stepped into the great hall for the feast, she felt less a person than she did an oversize doll.

"You look radiant, my lady," a gruff voice said in her ear.

It was the king. Aryn gratefully leaned on his strong arm—with the heavy gown and the towering coif on her head, she felt ready to topple over—and let him lead her toward the high table. Teravian stood at the foot of the dais, clad all in black as usual. However, his garb was finer than what he normally wore, and the silver brooch pinned at his throat made a striking contrast. His expression was solemn, and he looked older than he had the night before.

Aryn curtsied to the prince, and he bowed low, but they

didn't touch. The hall quieted as King Boreas made a speech—
one that was overly long, Aryn thought as she stood there, legs
aching to sit—concerning the joy of the coming marriage and
the great felicity of the match. All the while, Aryn was aware
of Queen Ivalaine sitting at the high table, her icy eyes
locked—not on Boreas or herself—but on Teravian.

At last Boreas finished speaking, and the hall erupted in
applause. Then the king led Teravian and Aryn to the high
table, seating them in the center on either side of himself, and
ordered the feast to begin. At once loud talk, laughter, and music filled the hall.

Aryn was numb to it. She hardly tasted the food that was put
before her, and while she knew Boreas asked her questions,
and that she responded to them, she could not for the life of
her recall what either of them had said. Again and again her
eyes moved to the windows above the hall. She could not see it,
but she knew it sailed against the night sky: the full moon.
Mirda was not sitting by Ivalaine, nor was she anywhere in the
hall.

"My lady," said a sibilant voice next to her. "This is for you."

A servant bent down beside her, holding out a silver tray
covered with a napkin. She waved a hand without looking at
him. "No, thank you. I'm far too full already."

"Trust me, my lady. You'll be hungry for this."

She glanced at the servant, only he was bent over low, so she
couldn't see his face. He was clad like all the other serving-
men—although his tunic seemed a bit too large for him. Then
he looked up. She saw the pointed blond beard on his chin, then
met his gray eyes.

Her mouth opened in an exclamation, but he gave his head a
slight shake, and she clamped her jaw shut. She was painfully
aware of King Boreas on the other side of her. However, he
seemed to be engaged in discussion with his son.

"We have only a moment, my lady," Aldeth said. "I am at
dire risk of discovery here. However, I knew this could not
wait." He held the tray toward her. "Under the napkin is a
parchment. Take it."

She did as he told her, taking the folded piece of parchment
and hiding it under the table.

"What is it?" she dared to whisper.

"A copy of a missive written a short while ago by Queen Ivalaine. I managed to pilfer it from the courier's bag while he readied his horse. Forgive my poor script, but I had only minutes to copy the missive before replacing it."

Aryn opened her mouth to ask the Spider what the missive contained, but he had already bowed and hurried away, disappearing through a side door. Boreas was still speaking to Teravian, and the earl next to Aryn was far into his cups and lolled in his chair. She angled her back to the king and dared to unfold the parchment in her lap. Quickly, her eyes scanned the hastily written words. By the time she reached the last lines, her heart was no longer racing but was still and cold in her chest. She folded the paper once more.

"My lady, are you ill?"

It was the king. He was looking at her, as was Teravian. She clamped her hand around the parchment, wadding it up inside her fist. She was dizzy, and she knew her cheeks were flushed. But perhaps that could work to her advantage. "I'm tired, Your Majesty, that's all. Would it speak ill of me if I were to retire for the evening?"

Boreas snorted. "On the contrary, my lady, it would show an amiable restraint and delicacy on your part to leave before the members of my court get any drunker."

Aryn smiled at him and stood. "I believe I'll go then. Good night, Your Majesty." She nodded to Teravian. "Your Highness."

The prince's eyes were curious—he knew she was up to something—but before he could speak she hastily made her way from the high table and departed the hall.

She turned a corner and, once she was sure she was out of sight, she began running, the copied missive still tight in her hand. The words on the paper changed everything; she knew what she had to do. Beams of moonlight spilled through narrow windows as she raced down the hall toward Ivalaine's chamber. She knocked on the door. It opened.

"Come in, sister," Mirda said.

Aryn glanced in either direction, then hurried into the chamber as Mirda shut the door.

"What's going on?" Aryn said, shocked anew. A dozen

wooden trunks stood neatly in a line; all of the queen's things had been packed.

"Ivalaine has fulfilled her duty," Mirda said. "She has returned the king's son to him after his fostering at her court and has heard his engagement announced. She will return to Artolor on the morrow."

"And what about you, Mirda? Will you be going as well?"

The witch's gaze was as serene as ever, yet there was a questioning light in her almond-shaped eyes. "That depends upon what you have to tell me."

Aryn struggled for words. But there was an easier way than explaining it herself. She opened her hand and unfolded the crumpled parchment.

"Read this," she said in a hoarse voice.

Mirda took the parchment in careful hands. She read the words, her eyes at first curious, then darting rapidly across the page. Aryn saw the words again herself, as if they were burned into her brain.

> *My dearest T,*
>
> *I commence my return to Ar-tolor at dawn tomorrow, and I am glad for it. I fear I have been too long away already, and I grow anxious to learn what has occurred in my absence. I wish to know most specifically what Sister L has been doing.*
>
> *That she is in league with someone unknown to us or to our sisters, I grow more certain each day. But who is this person L speaks to? That I would give much to discover, and I hope you have made progress in this regard.*
>
> *I confess, I have become more fearful each day I reside in Calavere. What it is, I cannot say. A darkness has seemed to oppress my mind like a cloud ever since beginning my journey here. Although today it is suddenly far less than it was before. All the same, I know my fears are not unfounded. How Sister L discovered that there was not just the one Runebreaker we know of, but a second of his kind, I still cannot imagine. But even more disturbing is that*

she seems to be using this one, controlling him, to some end we cannot foresee.

The prophecies say there will be a Runebreaker at the end of all things, and the prophecies cannot be wrong. So perhaps Sister L works to a greater good, and she believes that if she can command this second Runebreaker, then she can be sure that things will go as the Witches desire in the end and Eldh will not be shattered. I will try to believe this good of her, no matter what she has done to me.

But what if her power over this second Runebreaker is not so perfect as she believes? Even now, if our secret sources are correct, she has sent him on an errand to the Black Tower that was once the dwelling of all the Runebreakers. Do not fell magics yet remain in that spire which might aid him if his intent were to cause strife? I fear for us, dear sister. I fear for all the world.

I must close this hasty note now. It is time to discharge my final duty to the king by presenting his son to be married. Yet I suppose it is not truly my final duty after all, is it? Perhaps to the father, but not to the son.

I loathe speaking to you this way, dear T, but it is the only way to be certain our words will not be overheard. If all goes well, and I travel as swiftly as my courier does, then I will see you but a day after you read these lines.

Your Sister,
I

Mirda lifted her gaze and folded the paper. In three strides she moved to the fireplace and tossed in the parchment. In a puff of flame it was gone.

"This is grave news," the elder witch said, turning around. "Do you know who it is the queen spoke of in this missive?"

Aryn gulped, then nodded. The queen had signed herself I, and Sister T was no doubt Tressa. Which meant Sister L could only be . . .

"Liendra," she whispered. "Somehow Liendra has found a second Runebreaker. I didn't know there could be more than one, but there is, and she's trying to control him. Only he's going to betray her and get something in the Black Tower, something he could use to harm Eldh."

Mirda nodded, her expression grim. "I fear it is as you say. It seems that I and my sisters in secret have much work before us." She tilted her head, her brown eyes locked on Aryn. "That is, unless you have decided to reveal the presence of our shadow coven."

Aryn no longer needed to think about what to do. Liendra was authoring a perilous scheme, and even though she was not Matron, it was she—not Ivalaine—who controlled the threads of most of the Witches. Aryn felt a jolt of fear, replaced by determination, as well as a thrill of excitement.

"I want to join you," she said, stepping forward. "I want to be part of what you're doing."

"This is no small thing you do, sister. Are you certain?"

Aryn had never been more certain of anything in her life. "Yes."

Mirda's gaze remained solemn, but it seemed a smile briefly touched her lips. "Then when the queen leaves on the morrow, I will remain in Calavere as your teacher. There are others in Artolor who can do my work there."

Aryn's heart soared at the news—she could imagine no better teacher than Mirda—then descended again as a new fear filled her. "The Black Tower!" she gasped as two thoughts connected in her mind.

Mirda gave her a questioning look, and Aryn hastily explained how Grace and the others had set out for the Black Tower in the hopes of finding Travis Wilder.

Aryn was trembling now. "But this other Runebreaker, the one loyal to Liendra, he could be at the Black Tower as well. Maybe he's already there."

"Then I fear your sister Grace and her friends are in terrible danger," Mirda said.

"I have to warn them." Aryn paced back and forth. "Only that's impossible, isn't it? The Black Tower is in the wilderness leagues and leagues from here. I could never get a courier to go that far."

"Then why not go there yourself, sister?"

She gaped at the witch. "I can't travel to the Black Tower."

"Not in body, perhaps. But in mind?"

At last Aryn realized what Mirda was saying. Trepidation welled up within her, but she had to try, for Grace's sake. For Eldh's.

Use your power, Aryn. Use it for good.

"Help me," she said aloud.

Mirda pointed to a chair by the fire. "Sit down. Now shut your eyes."

Aryn did as she was told. She felt Mirda's light touch on both of her temples.

"Now reach out to the Weirding. Follow the threads, and at each crossing ask them which is the way to your friend. Remember, life cannot lie to you. Not when you are true to yourself."

Aryn hesitated, holding her breath. Then she reached out with the Touch, seeing the shimmering web of life all around her. She followed her strand outward and quickly came to a crossing of threads. She tested it. *This way,* one of the threads hummed. She hurried on, then came to another crossing. *Follow me.*

Again and again she tested the threads, following them onward, and only dimly did she realize that she was not stuck in the garden, that the castle was far behind her, and that her mind seemed to fly through deep forests and over lonely, starlit mountains.

I'm coming, Grace! she called out with all her being.

And Aryn followed the glowing strands as the leagues spun away behind her.

57.

A voice was calling to her.

Grace strained, trying to listen. She felt she should recognize the voice, but it was so faint, so distant, she couldn't be certain she heard it at all. The world was dark and empty, and she was all alone. Except that wasn't true, was it? Somehow she wasn't alone.

Grace . . . the voice said, and she woke up.

The first thing she knew was that she was still clutching Fellring, holding the fragile sword against her chest. The second thing was that the ground was heaving up and down beneath her. Was it an earthquake? Then cold spray moistened her face, and she knew it wasn't.

Grace sat up. The gray spires of Ur-Torin were already shrinking in the distance as the black ship sped out of the bay, crimson sails billowing in the force of a bitter wind. Grace's heart leaped as she caught a glimmer of white—the fey ship?—but no, it was only an iceberg, far off to starboard.

She and the others were near the front of the ship. Beltan and Vani had been lashed to the foremast, their backs toward one another. Their arms and legs were clamped down by thick coils of rope, and their heads nodded forward; they were still asleep. Falken sprawled on the deck nearby, eyes shut.

Grace swiped her tangled hair from her face. Why had she awakened when the others were still caught under the magic of the rune spell? Then she thought of the voice she had heard. Maybe she hadn't been dreaming; maybe the voice really had spoken to her and had helped her wake up. But who was it?

Before she could think of an answer, she realized she wasn't the only one who was awake. A few paces away, Sindar sat on the deck, knees to his chest, arms wrapped around his legs, gazing at the sea with green-gold eyes.

Grace cast a furtive look around. Three of the dark knights stood in a triangle formation around the mast. Their backs were toward the prisoners, but Grace didn't think for a moment that the guards were unaware of what she was doing. More knights scattered the deck of the ship. Some barked orders at ragged slaves who worked the ropes and climbed into the rigging to attend to the sails. There was no sign of Kelephon.

Cradling Fellring against her chest, Grace crept toward the silver-haired man. "Sindar." He didn't move. *"Sindar."*

He turned, his eyes meeting hers, and smiled, only it was one of the saddest expressions Grace had ever seen.

"Something's happening to me, Grace."

"What do you mean? Are you hurt?" He did seem paler than before. Had the dark knights done something to him?

He shook his head, still smiling. "I think . . . I think I'm starting to remember, that's all. I first noticed it in the throne room, in Ur-Torin. Things have been coming back to me. Just flashes, that's all. Like shards. But they're coming faster now."

Grace pressed her lips together. She had worked with amnesiacs at the hospital; she knew the havoc a head injury could cause to the brain, and how desperate the injured could be to recover his or her identity. She lifted her free hand to his cheek; it was cool to the touch.

He laid his hand over hers. "I do know you, Grace. I don't know how, but I was certain of it right from the start. That has to be the reason why the Little People chose me to help find you. It's our eyes. They're the same. That's how I knew. Maybe we share the same blood."

Grace found herself smiling. "Maybe we do."

Before she realized what was happening, Sindar bent close to her, and his lips brushed against hers. He smelled like sunwarmed grass.

A groan sounded behind her; it was Beltan. Grace leaned back, feeling amazement rather than shock. "I have to wake the others." Sindar only nodded.

She shut her eyes and reached out with the Touch. The threads of the others were clear to her immediately, glowing with familiar light. She could see the threads of the Onyx Knights and the slaves as well, and one brilliant strand near the stern of the ship: Kelephon.

Grace worked quickly, touching Beltan's, Vani's, and Falken's threads in turn, whispering to each of them. *Wake up.* It was hard. The lingering rune magic seemed to pull at her hands, making it almost impossible to grasp the threads of the Weirding, but she clenched her jaw, concentrating.

It worked. Falken sat up. Beltan gave his head a groggy shake, and Vani blinked gold eyes. In moments they were all fully awake.

"I didn't know witchcraft could counteract rune magic," Beltan said after Grace explained what she had done.

"Neither did I," Grace admitted. She was conscious of

Falken's curious gaze upon her. "So where do you think they're taking us?"

Falken flexed his silver hand. "I'm not sure. To one of their fortresses, I suppose. He needs a safe place where he can work the rune of blood on you."

"Is that what he meant? When he said he wanted my blood?"

"I'm sure of it," Falken said, his face grim. "Kelephon is a powerful wizard. He can speak the rune of blood to steal your very essence from your veins, then he can bind it into something, some object—say a gauntlet. With that gauntlet, he'll be able to wield Fellring, and the sword won't resist his touch."

Bile rose in Grace's throat. "And what will happen to me after he steals my blood?"

"You'll die."

She tightened her hand around the hilt of the sword. So that was why she still had Fellring. Kelephon didn't dare touch it; he couldn't take it from her until he worked the rune of blood. But he couldn't just work rune magic in plain sight of all of his men. Grace looked up and saw Sindar gazing at her. No, not at *her.* He was gazing at the sword in her hands.

"We need to break free," Beltan said, straining against the ropes.

"Stop it!" Vani hissed. "Unless it is your particular wish to crush me."

The ropes were tied in such a way that when one of the warriors pulled, it tightened the bonds on the other.

"Can't you just do your little vanishing act?" Beltan snapped.

Vani's gold eyes were molten. "If you could suck in your girth, I might have a little room to work, but you seem unwilling. Or unable. Besides, aren't you supposed to be the strong one, warrior? Why don't you simply break the bonds?"

"Maybe I could if you didn't whine about getting bruised every time I tug on the ropes. I didn't know assassins were so delicate."

"Stop it," Grace said. She stood up, wobbled a moment while she got her sea legs underneath her, then moved to the mast. She gave Beltan and Vani the same icy glare she gave to patients who weren't cooperating. "I don't know what happened between you two back on the white ship. But whatever it is, it will have to wait. Right now I need you both."

The knight and the assassin gazed at her a moment, then hung their heads.

"It doesn't matter if we get free anyway," Beltan said, his voice gruff. "There have to be a hundred knights on this ship."

"And do not forget the magic of the wizard," Vani said. "He defeated us easily all on his own."

Her cheeks glowed, and Grace realized the *T'gol* was ashamed; Beltan, too. Grace hadn't wanted to chastise the warriors for their failure, only to say that they all needed to stand together, now more than ever. She opened her mouth to try to explain these things, but words failed to come out.

What does it matter, Grace? They're right. Kelephon will take us somewhere, he'll work the rune of blood on you, and he'll kill the others. There's nothing we can do.

Except she didn't believe that. She didn't know exactly what it was; perhaps it was that same pride that kept her from giving up on a patient when any other sane doctor would have called time of death. She wasn't just going to sit there and let Kelephon have his way with her, not without a fight.

Grace's legs were steadier now. Before Falken could stop her, she approached one of the three knights that were guarding them.

"I want to talk to Kelephon," she said, trying to ignore how huge the man looked inside his black armor.

His voice rumbled out of his helm. "There is no one on this ship by that name, prisoner."

"Gorandon," she said. "That's the name you call him. I want to talk to him. Now."

"Sit down. You have no right to make such demands."

Anger shot through her, like a jolt from the charged paddles of a defibrillator. "What do you mean I have no right to make demands? I'm the bloody queen of Malachor, you tin can full of dung. That means you serve *me*."

She heard the sharp intake of breath behind his visor. "I would strike you down for those words, usurper. However, the general is far more merciful than I. He says that before you are executed, you will be allowed to beg forgiveness for the terrible deeds committed by you and your ancestors. And then, when the blessed sword of Lord Ulther is freed from the curse your forebears placed upon it, Gorandon will take up the blade, as is his holy birthright, and the Light of Malachor will shine forth once more."

Grace could hear the mindless fervor in his voice. So that was what Kelephon had told the knights. No wonder they had tried to wipe out her family. Even the fact that she wielded the sword was not enough to convince them of the truth. Kelephon had accounted for everything with his lies.

The knight snapped around, clamping a fist to his breastplate in salute. Kelephon strode toward them, head still bare, his white hair and black cloak fluttering in the wind.

"Leave us," Kelephon said to the knight.

Without a word, the guard and his two companions marched away. No doubt Kelephon didn't want his men to overhear anything that might undermine his authority with them. Then again, given the fanaticism with which the knight had spoken, Grace wasn't sure that was possible. He could have worn pajamas embroidered with runes, and his men would not have questioned the action.

Only maybe that's not true, Grace. You heard what happened in Eredane—how the Onyx Knights killed all of the runespeakers and witches. Kelephon has taught the knights to hate anyone who works magic. And with good reason, as they're the only ones who might have stood against the knights. But Kelephon might have taught his men too well. If they learned about his true nature, they would strike him down. No doubt they would think it was the only way to save him from heresy.

Fear crept into Grace's throat, but she swallowed it down. She was already a prisoner; she had nothing to lose by taking the offensive. "Have you come to steal my blood with your magic now?" she said, raising her voice. However, not even the closest knights reacted to her words.

Kelephon let out a chuckle. "Shout all you want, Your Majesty. They won't hear you."

"The rune of silence," Falken said, gaining his feet and moving close to Grace. "He's bound it here somewhere."

"Indeed," the runelord said to the bard. He glanced at Grace.

"Not that it was truly necessary. Even if my men could hear you, they would hardly be inclined to believe you. After all, you're a heretic and a usurper—hardly the most trustworthy sort. Even worse, you traffic with workers of magic."

Grace crossed her arms, hoping to hide her trembling. "You seem to know an awful lot about me."

"Oh, I do, Your Majesty. You see, I've been watching you ever since you were an infant."

"So you could kill me?"

"On the contrary, so I could take you and raise you as my own daughter."

Grace had been prepared for any words but these. "What?"

Kelephon leaned close to her; his breath smelled of stones. "Yes, Ralena. Your parents were beyond hope—I would have killed them no matter what that day. But I would have taken you. I would have nurtured you as my own child."

"You would have poisoned her, you mean," Falken spat. "You would have stolen Ralena, fed her lies to make her your slave, and when she was older you would have bid her retrieve Fellring. Then you would have commanded her to give up her blood for you, and she would have done so willingly."

Kelephon shrugged. "You have to admit, it was rather elegant. Only you ruined it all with your interference, Falken, you and that tart Melindora. Granting you immortality was yet another example of Dakarreth's idiocy. You hid Ralena somewhere beyond my reach. Only now she's back. And while things have been more difficult than if my initial plan had succeeded, it's of no great matter." He turned his cold eyes on Grace. "Whether you are my willing slave or not, Ralena, your blood—and your sword—will be mine."

He's come to gloat, Grace realized. *He didn't come here to tell us anything in particular—he just wants to show us how much power he has over us. That's why we're out here in plain view instead of in a cell belowdecks.* A hard feeling rose within Grace, and it took her a moment to understand that it was disdain.

"How did you find us, Kelephon?" Falken said. "As far as you knew, Grace wasn't even on Eldh anymore."

The bard's voice was gruff, his posture dejected, but Grace

caught a gleam in his eyes, and she was certain Falken had come to the same conclusion about Kelephon she had. This was their chance to get information out of the runelord.

"It was a stroke of good fortune," Kelephon said, his voice edging into a croon. "You see, I happened upon an old friend of yours and Melindora's. What was his name? It was something about a book. Yes, that was it—his name was Tome."

Falken's eyes went wide. "No!"

"Your friend was most helpful." Kelephon's thin lips pulled back in a smile. "Before I met him, I had begun to despair that I would ever make Fellring my own, that I would have to find a way to work my plans without the sword. Then I came upon your friend Tome in the Winter Wood. Don't you think it was reckless for a frail old man to be walking there alone? And do you know, I think he was looking for you, Falken? After a bit of encouragement, Tome revealed that Ralena was once again on Eldh. After that, it was trivial. The Pale King has spies everywhere, and they were given a description of what to look for. Soon, I learned that Ralena had been seen in the town of Galspeth."

Grace pressed a hand to her forehead; she felt feverish. "Esolda," she said. "The tailor's daughter. She saw my necklace. She must have reported it to a local leader of the Raven Cult. That's how the Onyx Knights knew to pursue us."

"Tome," Falken said, his voice a croak. "What did you do to him?"

Kelephon let out a dramatic sigh. "It was foolish of him to resist my runes. What he might have given to me freely, I was forced to take from him instead. By the end, there was no more substance to him than an old rag. And even as I watched, he melted into the air, and the wind blew him away."

Falken bowed his head, and Beltan leaned back against the post and let out a roar. However, Vani looked puzzled; the *T'gol* hadn't met the gentle, golden-eyed man. Tome had been one of the nine lesser New Gods who had forsaken their celestial homes, who had taken human guise to walk the face of Eldh and work against the Necromancers. Now he was gone, and Melia was the last of her kind. A pang of sorrow passed through Grace, but a moment later it was subsumed by anger.

Who did Kelephon think he was to destroy a being so mild, so beautiful?

Then again, what was a single person—former god or not—to the runelord? Hadn't he corrupted an entire nation?

"How did you do it?" she said, knowing he would be only too happy to tell her. "How did you make the Onyx Knights believe you're the heir to Malachor?"

Kelephon let out a laugh of pure delight. "It was easier than I could ever have imagined. For centuries they dwelled in Eversea, pining for their precious lost kingdom, feeling sorry for themselves. They thought it was their fault Malachor fell. They thought they should have been able to save it. So they fled to Eversea, and there they spun stories and forged plans for the day when they could return to Malachor and restore the kingdom. It was all quite pathetic, really. For no matter how they schemed, there was one thing they were missing: a royal heir."

Falken roughtly wiped his eyes. "So you gave them one. Yourself."

"Precisely," Kelephon said. "And they were all too willing to believe my tale. I told them I could show them the way back to Malachor. I gave them new armor and new purpose. And I told them it was the Runespeakers and Witches who had caused the downfall of Malachor, that they had thrown their lots in with the Pale King and betrayed the shining kingdom. So the crusade to reclaim the blessed land began. We took Eredane first, then Brelegond. Embarr will soon be ours as well, and then the rest of the Dominions will fall before us."

Grace couldn't suppress a shudder. The Onyx Knights believed they were working against the Pale King, and all the while they were clearing the way for Berash to ride again.

"But you still needed Fellring," Falken said. "Without it, the Onyx Knights would only follow you for so long."

Kelephon's gaze flicked to the cracked blade in Grace's hands. "I tried to get it once before, three hundred years ago, and that was when I learned that only one of Ulther's blood could touch it. A score of my knights were burned to bits trying to pry it from the throne in Ur-Torin. It was quite remarkable."

"I don't understand," Falken said, sorrow replaced by confusion. "How could you have set foot in the throne room? I don't know what befell Toringarth in the years since, but surely three centuries ago Ur-Torin was still a living city. The king's wolf-warriors would have stopped you."

A smirk crossed Kelephon's face. "What wolf-warriors?" He made a breaking motion with his hands.

The blood drained from Falken's face. "No," he whispered. "You monster. You broke the rune of life, didn't you?"

Grace struggled for comprehension. "What are you talking about, Falken?"

The bard's voice was hoarse. "It took all of the Runelords working together to bind so powerful a rune as the rune of life. Only a few such disks were ever made. Then the Runelords realized the folly of their deed, and all of the runes were undone." He looked at Kelephon. "Only you must have kept one in secret."

"I don't understand, Falken," Vani said, her voice breathless from the tightness of her bonds. "Why does it matter if he broke this rune of life?"

"Breaking a rune negates its power. So by breaking the rune of life..." Falken staggered.

Amazement filled Grace, and dread. "It destroyed every living thing in the city. All of the animals, all of the people—everything alive simply vanished."

"And likely for ten leagues all around," Falken said, his face ashen. "A rune so powerful would have a long reach."

"So that's why we didn't see any signs of a war," Beltan said softly.

"But the magic was wasted," Kelephon said, his tone annoyed. "No one could touch the shards." He glanced at Falken. "Only then I learned from one of my spies that you and Melia had managed to preserve the royal line of Malachor in secret all these centuries. Clever bard. I honestly didn't think you had such strength in you. I suppose you must have cut the infant from Queen Agdela's corpse. As if preserving her child really made up for murdering her."

Falken opened his mouth, but only a strangled sound came out. The bard's face was stricken.

Beltan glowered at the runelord. "What's he talking about, Falken?"

"What's this?" Kelephon pressed a gauntlet to his chest, feigning a look of surprise. "I thought you were a teller of tales, Falken. How could you neglect to tell your dear friends such an important story—you know, the one in which you kill the king and queen of Malachor with a song? Well, if you haven't told them the tale, then I will."

Grace willed herself to turn away. She didn't want to hear. However, she stood frozen, unable to do anything but listen to the runelord's mocking words.

"When I first met Falken, he was a lowly traveling bard who performed in any tavern or inn that would take him. Of course, his name wasn't Falken then. It was Tythus Mandalor. He was the son of Madrus Mandalor, who had been banished twenty years prior for high treason. You see, Madrus Mandalor had sold himself for gold to spies of the Pale King, who even then was beginning to stir once more. However, Madrus was discovered, and only the king's mercy saved his neck—although he met his end not long after, in the wilds south of Malachor."

A moan escaped Falken. Grace's throat tightened so that she couldn't swallow.

Kelephon circled around the bard. "I suppose Falken never told you he was the son of a traitor. Treachery was in his blood—I could see it that day I met him, in a tavern in the city below Castle Malachor, even though he didn't know it himself. He told me he wanted more than anything to become a royal bard, to play for King Hurthan and Queen Agdala. Since he knew I was a runelord of great power, he asked me what he should do. I told him he needed a new name—one not tainted by treason—as well as a new lute if he was going to achieve his desire.

"The name came easily enough, and he took to calling himself Falken Fleethand. The lute was another matter. He didn't have the gold to buy an instrument worthy of a king's ear. So I told him a tale, one about an enchanted lute that was said to lie in a cave deep in the Winter Wood, left there by a bard of the first days of Malachor. I warned him that there was danger in magic, that there was likely a good reason the ancient bard had hidden the lute there, but I knew by the light in Falken's eyes that he hardly heard my warnings.

"Falken found the lute, of course, returning in triumph to Malachor. Again I warned him of the perils of magic, but he wouldn't hear me. He made straight for the castle and begged an audience with the king and queen. He was granted it. There, in the throne room, Falken Fleethand played for their majesties, and the music that rose from the instrument in his hands was like nothing the listeners had ever heard before. It was beautiful: as fine, as bright, as quavering as strands of spider's gossamer beaded with dew.

"The queen, who was heavy with her first child and weary from the burden, was especially delighted with this entertainment, and she bid the bard to play on. And on. And on. As day turned to night and day again, the courtiers yawned and slumped in their chairs, and Falken's fingers began to bleed. Still the queen begged for more songs, each request growing more urgent and demanding, her voice growing more shrill, her eyes wide and staring. The king became concerned, and at last he laid a hand on her arm and begged her to let the bard stop. However, when he did, she flew at King Hurthan, the man she loved more than life itself, in a rage. Queen Agdala plucked a long needle from her hair and—as all in the throne room looked on—she plunged it into the king's eye, driving it deep into his brain."

Despite the icy air, Grace felt hot and sick. Falken stood still now, as if carved of stone. Beltan's expression was anguished, but Vani gazed at the bard with curious gold eyes. Kelephon was grinning.

"The queen stared at the king's body and the needle in her hand, as if not comprehending what had happened. The courtiers stared, dumbfounded. I was the first to act. I strode forward and snatched the lute from Falken's hands. I broke it open, then I showed all in the throne room the rune that had been inscribed, in small and secret fashion, inside the lute. It was the rune of madness. As Falken played the lute, it had worked its magic on the one who listened closest—Queen Agdala. The bard's music had driven her mad, and in her madness she had killed the king. But once the music ceased, she returned to her senses. A terrible cry rose from her, and she ran from the castle before anyone could stop her. It wasn't until the next day her body was found in the woods, her throat torn out by the fangs of what all supposed had been wolves." Kelephon spread his hands. "And that's how Falken murdered the king and queen of Malachor."

Silence descended, broken only by the snap of the sails and the whistle of the chill wind through the ropes. At last Falken looked up, his expression shattered. "I had examined the lute when I found it in the old cave, but I had never thought to look inside. I should... I should have..." He hung his head; the wind tangled his black-and-silver hair.

It had all been so long ago. The horror Grace felt was hollow and distant, but it was no less terrible for it. The queen had loved the king, and she had killed him. True madness must have come when she realized what she had done. "What happened after that?" she said, but she was fairly certain she knew the rest of the story.

Kelephon stalked around her. "Falken was thrown in the dungeon, but before his fate could be decided by the king's Warden, an army surrounded the castle—an army of *feydrim* and wraithlings, led by the Necromancer Dakarreth. Without its king, Malachor was in chaos. The blessed kingdom of light, which had guarded the Rune Gate and the vale of Shadowsdeep for three centuries, fell to the invaders in a single day. Except for a few hundred who escaped to the west, all the people were slain." The runelord's breath was hot and moist against Grace's neck. "So much for the glory of your kingdom, Your Majesty."

Beltan let out a snarl. "Get away from her."

Kelephon gave the blond knight a dismissive look, then returned his attention to Grace. "As for what happened next, Falken will have to tell you. All I know is that, in a rash act quite in fitting with his flawed character, Dakarreth freed Falken from the dungeon. As both punishment and reward, Dakarreth cut off Falken's hand—the one with which he had played the cursed lute—and granted him immortality. After that I can only imagine that Falken somehow came upon the body of the queen and cut the babe from her womb before it died."

They looked at Falken, but the bard only shook his head, his shoulders hunched. "It was my fault. By my hand Malachor fell. It was all my fault."

Sorrow filled Grace's heart. And then anger. It was time to put an end to this charade. Seven centuries was far too long to believe in such a cruel lie. She placed a hand on the bard's shoulder.

"No, Falken," she said, her voice low and certain. "You didn't cause the fall of Malachor."

Falken looked up, his eyes hazed with pain and confusion. "You heard the story, Grace. It's all true. I played the cursed lute, I drove the queen mad. It was my fault."

Kelephon let out a snort of disgust. "Come now, Falken. Do you honestly believe the fall of Malachor was really about you? What arrogance. Has the truth never dawned on you in seven hundred years? Even Ralena can see it plainly."

Falken gaped as the runelord moved closer to him.

"Did it never occur to you," Kelephon said, words honed like knives, "how Dakarreth was ready with his army just at the moment the king and queen perished? And how do you think you found the lute in the first place? Well, if you're too dull, let me be the one to tell you. It was I who put the lute in the cave. It was I who bound it with the rune of madness. And it was I who told Dakarreth to be ready. You, Falken, were nothing more than an instrument in my hands."

Falken staggered. "What—?"

The runelord jabbed a finger at the bard's chest. "You didn't cause the fall of Malachor, Falken. I did."

58.

For a minute, Grace feared that Kelephon's words had acted like the rune of madness upon Falken. He slumped to his knees, and his face seemed oddly slack, like that of a stroke victim.

"It seems the bard has come undone," Kelephon said, smirking.

Grace knelt beside Falken and laid a hand on his brow. He was feverish.

Beltan glared at the runelord, his green eyes filled with murder. "What have you done to him?"

"I did nothing to him. Everything Falken did was of his own free will."

Grace clenched her teeth. What use was free will when everything you were told was a lie? She gripped the bard's shoulders. "Falken, please."

"Let . . . let me try."

Sindar had moved close, his face lined from thought. Was he still remembering things? Before Grace could ask what he meant to do, Sindar placed his hands at both of Falken's temples and shut his eyes. For several moments the two men were motionless, then Falken drew in a shuddering breath.

"By the Seven," he rasped. "What have I done, Grace?"

Grace was more curious what Sindar had done to the bard, but the slender man lowered his hands and moved away without offering an explanation.

"It's all right, Falken." Grace knew there was nothing to forgive, that he had been a victim along with everyone else. All the same, she knew he needed absolution, and that she was the only one in the world who could give it to him. "I forgive you. Do you understand? In the name of Malachor, if I am truly its queen, I forgive you for all of your deeds."

The agony in Falken's eyes gradually transmuted to wonder. Then he pulled her close and hugged her fiercely. "I owe my life to you, Ralena."

Grace couldn't help laughing at the absurdity of it. "No, Falken, I'm quite certain that it's I who owe my life to you. And to Melia."

Together they gained their feet, and somehow—whether it was the Touch or her doctor's instinct—Grace knew that, despite the depth of his wounds, Falken was going to survive.

As long as any of them were going to survive, that was.

"How sad," the runelord sneered, "to see a man so utterly broken and defeated."

Despite her fear, Grace felt a spark of defiance blaze to life within her. She held her chin high and cast a stern look at the runelord. In that moment—for the first time in her life—Grace felt like a queen.

"You will never defeat me," she said.

Kelephon took a step back, as if she had slapped him. His

voice grew shrill. "Silence, witch! I've already defeated you. You're as full of pride as your wretched ancestors. So high, they believed themselves, so far above everything and everyone. The Runelords were the greatest wizards in the world, and I stood first among them, and yet Queen Agdala and King Hurthan thought they could order me about like a servant. But I showed them, just as I'll show everyone, that I am not to be commanded."

As he spoke these words, Grace understood everything. She had known attending physicians at the hospital who had so doubted their own worth that they could only feel secure ordering others. They were no different from schoolyard bullies. And Kelephon was no different from them. Only this was a bully who possessed far more power than she could comprehend.

"You're going to betray him, aren't you?" Grace said, her voice clinical. "The Pale King. It's been your plan from the start. You wanted to rule Malachor, but the only way you could think to do it was to destroy it first. You gave the Stone of Ice to the Pale King in exchange for immortal life. Then you took control of the knights of Eversea, knowing you could use them to get Fellring. And once you have Ulther's sword, you'll have everything you need to slay the Pale King and take his place."

She held the cracked blade out before her. On reflex, Kelephon started to reach for it, then snatched his hand back.

"That's right, Your Majesty. And once I kill Berash, I'll take my Stone back from him. As well as the other Great Stones, for I'll wait until he's gained them all before I strike. Then I'll take the iron necklace Imsaridur from his dead body, and I will rule not just Malachor reborn, but all of Falengarth."

"You can't," Falken said, voice hoarse.

"Why not?" Kelephon snapped. "What difference does it make which master you serve, the Pale King or me? Either way, you will be slaves. Except that's not entirely true. For while Berash fancies making both you and Ralena willing servants with hearts of iron, I prefer to see all of you dead. And soon enough, you will be. None of you will be able to see the glory of my eternal rule, but you can take satisfaction in knowing that, without your help, my ascendance could never have come to pass."

The runelord turned on his heel and strode away across the deck. Beltan let out a cry of fury, straining at the ropes, but at a hiss from Vani he stopped.

"So he really means to betray the Pale King?" Beltan said when he had regained some of his composure.

Vani grimaced. "No, I'm certain he was merely making a jest to amuse us."

Falken's wolfish face was haggard, but he was standing up straight now. "I suppose that's why Kelephon couldn't land in Omberfell. His knights would have slain the Raven Cultists, and that would have alerted the Pale King to his treachery."

Grace moved to Vani and Beltan and picked at the ropes, seeing if she could loosen them, but the bonds were too tight, and they had taken her knife from her boot. Perhaps she could use a piece of the sword, but what good would it do anyway? There were a hundred knights on the ship, and if they jumped into the water, they would die of hypothermia in minutes. Kelephon was right; there was no hope. Either the Pale King would rise again, or Kelephon would murder him and take his place. Either way, Eldh would fall under shadow. Forever.

"It's no use," she said, and she wasn't certain if she meant the ropes or everything. All anger, all fear, all feeling poured out of her. She leaned against Beltan, laying her head against his chest.

Grace . . .

"What is it, Vani?"

The *T'gol* craned her head around. "I didn't say anything."

Grace looked up. She had heard a voice. And it couldn't have been Beltan or Falken. It had been a woman's voice. She opened her mouth, but then the voice spoke again. It was the same voice she had heard in the darkness before she woke, only this time she knew it was real. And she knew to whom the voice belonged.

Grace, please, you have to hear me.

She was almost too astonished to think. Then, tentatively, she reached out with the Touch. *Aryn?*

There was darkness, then the bright energy of connection.

Yes, Grace. It's me. By Sia, I can hear you as if you were in the room with me!

Oh, Aryn. Sorrow filled Grace, and wonder, and joy.

Grace, what's wrong? Are you well? What's happening to you? We've been so worried.

She didn't know how to reply to that one. *Where are you, Aryn?*

I'm in Calavere. I've been searching and searching for you, all last night and all today. I'd almost given up hope I could do it, but now I've found you at last.

What? But how can—?

I understand it now, how to speak across the Weirding no matter the distance. But there's something I need to tell you first. You have to know it before you get to the Black Tower. You see, I've learned that there's a second—

"Grace!"

This time the voice really was Vani's. Grace opened her eyes, and her heart froze. Kelephon strode toward them with swift purpose. There was something in his hand: a small disk of creamy stone. None of the dark knights were in view anymore, only the slaves who manned the sails.

"By the tower and the light," Falken murmured. "No."

Beltan was facing the wrong direction. He tried to twist his head around. "What is it? What's happening?"

Grace couldn't take her eyes off the object in Kelephon's hand.

What's happening, Grace? I can feel it—something's terribly wrong.

She forced her mind to piece together the words, to send them over the humming strands of the Weirding. *Aryn, we're in trouble. We—* But there was no time for words. Instead, she gathered all that had happened since leaving Tarras, all that was happening now, into a single thought and sent it hurtling along the threads. She felt shock come back to her, then understanding.

Oh, Grace . . .

Kelephon had come closer. She could see some sort of angular symbol incised on the disk in his hand.

"Don't look now," Beltan said gruffly. "He'll see you if you do. But it's just visible off to starboard."

"What is?" Falken whispered, inching toward the blond knight.

"The white ship," Beltan said. "It's coming toward us. Fast."

Vani went stiff. "We must find a way to get free."

Grace's mind raced. It was coming for them, the white ship that had borne them over the Winter Sea. But even if it drew near, how could they get to it? Kelephon could stop them with a single rune.

Or could he? Hadn't her magic been able to free the others from the rune of sleep? Runes were the magic of creation, of permanence, and of destruction. But witchcraft was the magic of life. Surely it was just as strong in its own way. And this time, she would have help.

Aryn, listen to me—I need you. Words were too slow; again she sent an entire thought across the Weirding. Aryn seemed to withdraw, and for a terrible moment Grace feared the connection had been broken. Then, to her relief, she sensed the familiar sapphire brilliance of her friend. Only there was another presence with her this time, subtle and deep.

We're here, Grace.

Kelephon came to a stop before her. Grace forced herself to meet his gaze. The runelord couldn't overhear words spoken over the Weirding; as long as she kept her eyes open and her focus on him, he couldn't know she was casting a spell.

"Why have you sent your men below, Kelephon?" she said.

A smile sliced across his hawkish face. "I think you know, Your Majesty. I've decided there's no point in waiting. I can work the magic just as well here as at one of our fortresses." He tightened his hand around the rune of blood.

"Get away from her!" Falken shouted.

Kelephon spoke the word in a bored tone. *"Meleq."* A dozen planks snapped up from the deck, forming a wooden prison around the bard, halting him. Vani and Beltan both strained at the ropes, but it was no use. Sindar stood apart, his back to them all.

"It's time, Your Majesty." Kelephon drew close to her. The air seemed to grow colder yet. "Now your blood—and your sword—will be mine."

Grace forced herself to stand still, both her hands wrapped around the hilt of the sword. Kelephon raised the disk before her. She could see the rune clearly: five short lines arranged in parallel, like dark drops falling. Then the runelord pressed the disk against her brow. It was smooth and cool. The light of triumph glinted in his eyes, and he opened his mouth to speak one final word.

Now! Grace called out in her mind, and she felt two other strands bind with her own.

Energy surged through her, more than she had ever felt in her life. It was so much that it almost washed her away like a leaf caught in flood, but somehow she held on to the energy, shaped it, and flung it all at the man before her.

It struck him like a blow. The word Kelephon had been speaking turned into a cry of pain and shock. He staggered back, arms going wide, and the rune flew from his splayed fingers. All of them watched as it traced an arc, white and shimmering, through the air. Then the rune descended, past the rail of the ship. Grace heard a faint *plop* as the sea swallowed it.

"No!" Kelephon cried. "Blood is the key to everything!" He lurched away from Grace, toward the ship's rail, and stretched out both hands. *"Sharn!"*

The sea frothed and boiled. A column rose up like a jet from a fountain. Spinning atop it was a disk of white stone. But the ship had already moved far beyond the column of water.

"Bring the ship around!" Kelephon screamed. "Bring it around!"

Slaves scurried, lines groaned, sails snapped. The ship began to turn, but it was a ponderous movement.

Grace moved to Vani and Beltan. *Aryn, help me.* Again she felt the surge of bright energy. She touched the bonds, and they fell into loose coils around the base of the mast. Beltan and Vani sprang free. Grace turned and brushed her hand over the wooden planks that imprisoned Falken; they fell clattering to the deck. Rope and wood were dead now, but they yet remembered life.

Kelephon whirled around, his expression livid. *"Gelth!"*

Grace felt a sensation of cold, like a gust of icy wind, but it quickly passed, driven off by the warmth of the life energy that spilled into her from the Weirding, and from Aryn. However, Vani, Beltan, and Falken all ceased to move. Each one was encased from head to toe in ice. Panic shredded Grace's heart.

No, sister, spoke a calm voice in her mind—not Aryn's voice. *If you would help them, you must let fear go.*

Grace didn't know to whom the voice belonged, but it was right. Kelephon had turned around again. He hadn't bothered to wait to see if his rune had worked on her; in his pride, he had simply believed it would. Now he leaned over the rail, muttering the rune of water over and over, keeping the white disk dancing on the waterspout. The ship had come around. It was heading toward the frothing column.

She had to do something. But what? Perhaps she could knock him into the ocean, but what good would that do when water was at his command? Grace took an uncertain step forward, Fellring in her hands.

Sindar stepped before her.

"No, don't stop me," she said. Shouldn't he have been frozen by the runelord's spell? "I have to do something."

"I know."

His words were quiet, but there was something to them—a clarity, a power—that made her tear her gaze from the runelord and look at the slender man. A gasp escaped her.

"Sindar—you're shining."

He smiled. Light danced around him like a silver corona. "I've finally remembered, Grace. Who I am, and what I'm supposed to do. I was so tired. What I did in the water, it was too much. It made me forget everything. But I'm stronger now, and it was the runelord's own words that helped me."

Grace shook her head. "What do you mean? What words?"

"Blood is the key to everything."

"I don't understand."

"You will. You saved me once, Grace. And for that, I loved you. Now it's my turn to save you."

Fellring twitched in Grace's hands. As if it had a life of its own, the sword rose, until it was pointed directly before her. Sindar shut his eyes—green-gold, just like Grace's own—and stepped forward.

The point of the sword slid easily into his body. The fragile blade didn't shatter.

"No!" Grace choked, but she couldn't move, couldn't pull the sword back. Agony flickered across Sindar's face, then rapture. The corona grew brighter, like diamondfire, and the silver-haired man was gone. In his place was a willowy being of light.

Horror became wonder. "You," Grace said, gazing into large, ancient eyes. "You're the one we found on Earth. And it was you who saved us in the sea after the shipwreck, wasn't it? But why? Why are you doing this?"

The voice was more like the music of crystal chimes, but all the same she understood the fairy's words.

It was not the bard Falken who took the infant from the dead queen long ago. It was one of my kin. The baby was too small to live, so the fairy bore it within herself until the infant was strong enough. Then the infant was left on a stone where the bard came upon it. But some memory of the light of the fairy dwelled yet in the child's blood, and it was passed from father to daughter, from mother to son, and dwells in you still.

After you saved me from the cruel prison of iron, how could I not love you when I saw the light of my own kind shining in your eyes? It is bright within you, even as my own blood is bright within your friend, the knight. And yes, my kind can love, though to us the word does not mean what I believe it does to your kind. To us, to love another is to know you are but two beams from the same source of light.

So I followed you, and when your ship descended into the sea, I saved you. But the effort was too great, and I was yet weakened by what had been done to me on the gray world across the Void, and I was nearly lost. My light would have dimmed forever, but at the last I cast myself into mortal form, that my spark might have a shell in which to heal. But that form was so limiting, I could not remember my purpose. Only now I have.

The words came to Grace in the space of an instant, along with an emotion so deep, so vast, she couldn't possibly have expressed what it was, except to say that maybe it was like being a star: so tiny in the night sky, but so bright and pure, like all that was perfect reduced to a single, shimmering point.

"But what is it?" Grace whispered, tears streaming down her cheeks. "What is your purpose?"

Only this, Ralena. By the blood of my kind was it forged. By my own blood it is remade anew. Keep this sword close, for if you do, then we will always be together.

The form of the fairy grew brighter yet, so that Grace thought she must go blind if she didn't turn her head. Only she couldn't look away, and the light didn't burn her eyes. Instead it shrank down, collapsing into a blazing line. Then she realized that the line was the sword in her hand.

The light vanished. Grace raised Fellring before her. All traces of the cracks that had marred it were gone. The sword was gleaming and whole, the runes tracing it from hilt to tip in an unbroken line.

There was so much to think about, so much to comprehend, but there was no time. The dark ship had drawn close to the waterspout. The column of water coiled forward like a crystal serpent. Kelephon reached out and snatched the rune of blood. He turned around, holding it in his hands.

His eyes went wide, locked on the sword in Grace's hand. She stood three paces before him.

"But that's impossible," he said, his voice soft with puzzlement.

A strength welled up in Grace, not that of a witch, or a queen, or even a doctor, but simply that of a woman who knew one who loved her had given everything for her. She would not let that gift be for nothing.

"I *will* keep you close, Sindar," she murmured. "I promise." She stepped forward and thrust with the sword.

Perhaps her body recalled some of her training with Beltan, or perhaps Fellring understood her wishes and obeyed them without hesitation, for the point of the blade slipped through a narrow gap in Kelephon's armor and sank easily into his right shoulder. Blood sprang forth. It fell on the bound rune in his hand, and the white stone drank the fluid, turning crimson as the ship's sails. More blood flowed into the rune, and more, as if the fluid were being pulled into it.

Kelephon stared at the rune, horror blossoming in his eyes. *"Reth!"* he said in strangled voice. The stone disk shattered in his hand, and the broken pieces fell to the deck.

Grace withdrew the sword from his body, and Kelephon cried out again. She poised the tip at his throat. "Release them," she said. "Now."

The runelord twitched a finger. *"Reth,"* he said again, and the ice crumbled away from Beltan, Vani, and Falken. The three staggered, falling to their knees, but they were alive.

"Look," Vani said, pointing with a shaking hand.

Grace glanced to one side and saw the white ship draw close, sleek and graceful as a swan. Goat-men and tree-women scurried about on the deck. A plank of silvery wood reached up toward the deck of the crimson-sailed ship. She turned her gaze back to Kelephon.

"What are you going to do with him?" Beltan said.

Falken's expression was hard. "You should kill him, Grace. Now, while you have the chance."

"No," she said, amazed at her own words. "No, I want him to live. I want him to crawl back to Imbrifale, to tell the Pale King that I have Fellring, and that nothing he can do will stop me from cutting out his iron heart and melting it down." She flicked the sword, tracing a thin red line on Kelephon's throat. "Do you understand?"

The runelord's cold eyes were filled with hatred. "I understand perfectly."

Grace waited for the others to move onto the silvery plank, then she backed toward them, keeping Fellring poised before her. Kelephon didn't move. He simply watched as the four of them made their way down the plank, onto the white ship. Grace still felt the presence of Aryn in her mind. How Aryn had managed to speak so far across the Weirding, Grace didn't know. However, Aryn's news would have to wait just a little longer, until they were safely away.

Figures moved to and fro on the deck around them. The plank was drawn in. Powered by neither sail nor oar, the white ship began to speed away. Kelephon's ship shrank to a dark blot, then both it and the runelord were lost to sight.

"I think that was a mistake, Grace," Falken said softly. The bard's lips were still tinged blue from the ice, but it was warm on the fairy ship. He would be all right, as would Vani and Beltan. The knight placed an arm around the assassin's shoulders, as if to help her stand; it was a strangely tender gesture.

Grace turned her gaze back to Falken. "So you think Kelephon still has the power to harm us?"

"I know he does."

A sigh escaped her. She felt bone tired. "I suppose you're right. But I had to do it. I want the Pale King to know Fellring is whole once more."

Falken searched her face with his faded blue eyes. "Why, Grace?"

"Because I want him to feel every bit as afraid as I do right now."

They said nothing more as the white ship carried them south, away from the ice and the dead lands of the north.

59.

By the time Travis got back to the boardinghouse, Sheriff Tanner was awake.

"He opened his eyes not long after you left," Lirith said, meeting him in the hallway. She was on her way from the kitchen with a pot of hot water.

Travis drew in a breath. "Is he . . . ?"

"He's fine," Lirith said, taking his hand. "Or he will be, anyway. Right now he's still weak. It will be some days until he fully recovers."

"But the laudanum . . ."

Lirith sighed. "Yes, even after this, his body will still crave it. But there are herbs I can give him that will lessen the need. With them, in time, I believe he can leave the laudanum behind. His is a strong spirit."

And even a strong man needed help sometimes. Travis thought of the words Niles Barrett once spoke to him at the saloon. *Only a man outside the law can stop those who've taken the law into their own hands. But it's pointless to hope. Tyler Caine was the last great civilizer to walk this part of the West. And all the stories say he's dead. . . .*

That was exactly what Brother Cy had said. *There's no point in hoping.* So you might as well do something.

"What is it, Travis?" Lirith touched his arm. "Your face looks strange. Did something happen out there?"

Travis thought of his meeting with Brother Cy, and how

when it was over the preacher had shut the back door of the hearse and climbed up into the driver's seat.

I guess I'll be seeing you, Travis had said.

Brother Cy had gazed at him with those black-marble eyes. *So you will, son. So you will.* Then the preacher flicked the reins, and the wagon rattled away, vanishing into an eddy of dust.

"I need to talk to the sheriff. Can I see him?"

Lirith led the way to the back bedroom. Tanner was sitting up in the bed. His skin was pallid, and his chest was sunken beneath his white undershirt, but his blue eyes were clear, if a bit too bright. Travis had never seen Tanner without his hat before; the sheriff possessed a thick shock of sandy hair, which, at present, stood out in all directions. Maudie sat next to the bed, her hand on the covers, not quite touching Tanner's wrist. Durge stood at the foot of the bed.

"Afternoon, Mr. Wilder," Tanner said. His voice was a bit thinner than usual, but his drawl was still slow and calm. "I understand you carried me all the way here, along with Mr. Dirk. I suppose that means I owe my life to both of you."

Travis couldn't suppress a grin. "No, you owe your life to Lirith. All you owe me and Durge is a drink."

"I'm so glad you're back," Maudie said, looking up at Travis. "I can't imagine it's safe to be out there. Not with the Crusade in charge of this town. Why, they went so far as to board up the sheriff's office. As if they owned Castle City!"

Only they probably do, Travis thought. So that was why Durge had returned to the Bluebell.

"They cannot keep me from my duty," the knight said, crossing his arms. "I only returned to fetch a crowbar so I can pry off the boards and reopen the sheriff's office."

"I'll lend you a hand, Mr. Dirk," Tanner said, and started to push himself up from the bed.

Lirith crossed the room in two strides and pushed him back down. "I will not have all my work undone by pride and foolishness."

Astonishment registered in Tanner's watery eyes. "I'm the sheriff, Miss Lily."

"Not in this room," she said, hands on hips. "In here, you're my patient and nothing more. And you don't leave until I tell you it's time."

"But Miss Lily, aren't you worried about Mr. Samson? He's trapped there in the jailhouse. We've got to go get to him."

Travis looked at Durge. "He doesn't know yet?"

"I know it was Wilson who played this trick on me," Tanner said. "He was the one who brought me that coffee. I should have known something was up. Wilson couldn't boil water to save his life, let alone brew a pot of coffee. He must have brought it from Mrs. Vickery's. Only where did he get the laudanum? The Crusade has shut down China Alley."

"Dr. Svensson," Maudie said, her voice hard. "That's where." She took Tanner's hand in her own. "Oh, Bart, I think they wanted to make it look as if you did it on purpose. What if Miss Lily and the others hadn't found you in time?"

He squeezed her hand. "They did find me, Maude." He looked up at Travis. "So what is it I don't know, Mr. Wilder?"

Travis took a deep breath, wondering just how much he could say. "Sareth isn't at the jail. He's been kidnapped by the Crusade for Purity, and the note they left says they're holding him hostage. You see, there's someone with whom the Crusade is in league, and he wants something— something that I've got. And they're using Sareth to get it from me."

Tanner's mustache drooped. "You think there's someone behind the Crusade?"

"I know there is."

"But what on Earth could he want from you?" Maudie said.

Travis hesitated, then slipped his hand into his pocket and drew it out. "He wants this."

Travis opened his hand. The scarab crawled slowly across his palm, probing with slender gold legs.

"Lord above!" Maudie clasped a hand to her cheek. "What is that?"

Tanner's expression was sharp, curious. "Is it mechanical?"

Travis stroked the spider with a finger, then slipped it back into his pocket. "I can't explain what it is. Not just yet, anyway. But I can tell you that it's important, and that no matter what happens, I can't let him have it."

Tanner stroked his mustache—a gesture that reminded Travis of Durge. "I don't pretend to understand everything you're saying, Mr. Wilder. Then again, it doesn't matter. None of it changes the fact that Mr. Samson is in danger. I failed in my duty to protect him, and now I've got to find a way to get him back. Can I see that note you talked about?"

Lirith had it. She unfolded it and handed it to Tanner.

A grunt of surprise escaped him. "They want you to come to the Bar L Ranch?"

Travis nodded. "Do you know where it is?"

"It's south of town," Tanner said, "next to the Dominguez place."

Durge swore, then glanced at Travis. "I should have known our foe was lurking nearby. It was there I saw the mauled lambs. But we didn't know then he had followed us here. The great manor I saw must belong to his ally, the leader of the Crusade. This Lord Hale."

"You're right on one count, Mr. Dirk. The men of the Crusade will want to meet you in their own territory. And I suppose the Bar L does belong to the man who leads them." Tanner lowered the note. "But it sure doesn't belong to Mortimer Hale. Even Hale doesn't have that much money."

Travis tried to swallow, but his throat was clogged with dust. "Then who does own the ranch?" However, even as he asked the question, he knew the answer. The Ranch was called the Bar L. And the L could only stand for . . .

"Aaron Locke," Tanner said. "Owner of the First Bank of Castle City. And the richest man in town. All Mortimer Hale owned were the clothes on his back before Locke took him in and gave him the newspaper to run."

And in return, Hale used the *Clarion* to help Locke take over the town—and look clean the entire time. Travis thought of all the occasions Aaron Locke and his clerks from the bank had come into the saloon. Travis had been glad to see them, had served them drinks. Locke had seemed so cheerful, always a smile on his boyish face.

"Why now?" Lirith said. "If Lord Locke has gone to such trouble to deceive us, why has he now revealed in this note that he is the leader of the Crusade?"

"Pride," Durge said. "A man who builds something of which he is proud cannot resist claiming it as his own."

Tanner nodded. "I think you're right in that, Mr. Dirk."

"At least now we know whom we're fighting," Travis said.

Maudie wrung her hands. "But you can't fight them, Mr. Wilder. Not all of them. Aaron Locke is a powerful man. Who knows how many men he has working for him?"

Travis made a list in his mind. Gentry. Ellis. Hale. Wilson. The thing that had once been Calvin Murray. Maudie was right, he couldn't fight all of them. But maybe he didn't need to. Wasn't that the idea Brother Cy had helped give him?

"What if we don't fight all of them, Maudie?" Travis said. "What if we fight just one of them?"

The others looked confused, all except Tanner. "You're talking about challenging Aaron Locke to a duel."

"He's a prideful man, we know that. Do you think he'd accept?"

"He'd have to," Tanner said. "The kind of men he's got working for him only respect power. If a man challenged Locke, they'd expect him to take the challenge. But that doesn't mean it would be a fair duel. Locke's men wouldn't mind a bit of low dealing. And what's more, I've heard Locke is a crack shot."

Travis was less worried about Locke's skill with a gun than he was about the sorcerer. But Sareth had said the Scirathi wouldn't want to dirty his hands, that he would leave the crude work to his henchman. And that meant they might have a chance, even if Locke and his men cheated.

"So it might work," Travis said.

"No, Mr. Wilder. It won't." Tanner lifted his right hand. It vibrated, outline blurring. "I can't fight a duel."

"No, but I can." Travis reached into his shirt pocket and pulled out the folded poster. He also pulled out his wire-rimmed spectacles and slipped them onto his face. At once everything in the room looked strange and wavering, as if viewed underwater. Coronas of light danced around everyone, but this wasn't the time to study them. Travis unfolded the poster and held it where all could see.

Maudie stood—forgetting her cane in her surprise—and

pressed both hands to her chest, her mouth wide-open. "I knew there was something curious about you, Mr. Wilder, something you were hiding. Only a man's business is his own, so I never asked. But I knew it!"

Tanner's expression was thoughtful. "No matter what Miss Lily says, I'm still the sheriff in this town. And last I knew, you were a wanted man in five states, Mr. Caine."

Travis carefully folded the poster. "So are you going to arrest me, Sheriff?"

Tanner only grinned.

60.

They began spreading the rumor at the Mine Shaft that night.

When Travis and Lirith first got to the saloon, it was emptier than they had ever seen it. A lone miner stood at the bar, and a pair of ranch hands were hunkered down at a table in the corner, but that was all. Travis doubted there were enough people in the place to transmit an especially virulent strain of the flu around town, let alone a story.

Lirith sighed. "I suppose people aren't coming for fear of the Crusade."

"That didn't stop us," Travis said with a grim smile.

As the daylight outside burned from fire red to ash gray, more people drifted into the saloon. They were a hard-looking lot, their hands dirty, their faces haggard. They drank their whiskey without a smile and played at Lirith's faro table without uttering a laugh or curse. These were people who had nothing left to lose.

By dark the saloon was, if not crowded, at least no longer desolate. Behind the bar, Manypenny flipped through the pages of the ledger. "By Jason's Golden Fleece, even if this blasted Crusade doesn't burn down my establishment, they'll still put me out of business."

Travis looked over the saloonkeeper's shoulder at the ledger. According to the figures in the last column, the daily take for the saloon was a third of what it had been just a month ago.

Manypenny slammed the ledger shut. "Those hoodlums have chased away all of my regular customers. Why, even Mr. Locke and his boys from the bank didn't come in tonight."

A fact for which Travis was glad. He supposed the sorcerer had promised Locke all kinds of rewards in return for gaining the scarab. Once Locke delivered the jewel, the Scirathi would give Locke whatever he needed to take over the town once and for all. Travis wasn't certain what that might be. However, a picture of the thing that had been Calvin Murray flashed through his mind, and he shuddered.

Durge stepped through the swinging doors at nine o'clock— right on schedule. The knight paused near the entrance, surveying the room, his deputy's badge gleaming. After a minute he headed for the bar.

"Did I do it properly?" Durge said in a low voice, as Travis poured him a sarsaparilla.

Travis pretended to wipe down the bar. "You were perfect. Everyone saw you come in, and from the way you looked around, they'll all think you're looking for someone."

Travis moved to the other end of the bar, and Durge sipped his drink. Then, a minute later, Lirith called a break at her faro table and sauntered up to the bar next to Durge. The knight caught the attention of Manypenny, who brought a second sarsaparilla, this one for Lirith. She laughed and thanked Durge with a kiss on his craggy cheek. That drew the notice of more than one pair of eyes in the saloon. Travis knew many of the saloon's patrons would have fancied a kiss themselves from the pretty Miss Lily, and no doubt they wondered how the deputy had gotten so lucky.

"You've hardly touched your drink, Deputy." She draped her arm around Durge's shoulders. More eyes followed this action. "Is something wrong?"

"I'm afraid so," Durge said, his voice just loud enough for those nearby to hear. "You know the sheriff has taken ill? It seems others have heard the news as well and have decided to take advantage of the situation."

Durge was a better actor than Travis would have guessed. His words were suitably grim, but there was also a private note in them, as if they were meant only for Lirith. However, Travis noticed a number of ears cocked in the knight's direction. He kept wiping down the bar.

Lirith took a sip of her drink. "What do you mean?"

"I've been hearing stories," Durge said. "Stories that tell a gunslinger is coming to town, and that he plans on challenging the leader of the Crusade for Purity to a duel."

Lirith lifted a hand to her throat. The witch was also not without dramatic skills. "A gunslinger?"

"That's right. I've got to be on the lookout. They say he'll be coming into town at sunset the day after next—a man by the name of Tyler Caine."

The saloon was so quiet Lirith's next words rang out almost like a shout.

"Tyler Caine the man-killer? He's coming here to Castle City?"

The echo of Lirith's words faded. She and Durge both cast suspicious glances around—a nice touch, Travis thought.

"I'd better go now," Durge said. "I've got to keep a lookout for Caine. I don't know who the leader of the Crusade is, but it doesn't matter. I can't let this Caine challenge him to a duel. No matter what a man's honor might require, gunfights are against the law."

Lirith touched his hand. "Be careful."

Durge tipped his hat, then headed out the doors. A moment later conversation erupted, far louder than before.

"Did you hear that?" Manypenny said in a stage whisper that could have been heard a mile away.

"Hear what?" Travis said innocently, gathering up empty shot glasses.

Manypenny glowered at him. "Come now, Mr. Wilder, surely you heard the deputy just as well as I did. He's coming here, to Castle City—Tyler Caine!"

"You can't put stock in rumors," Travis said, although it was quite clear Manypenny did.

The saloonkeeper smoothed his waxed mustache, eyes eager. "Whoever heads up this blasted Crusade for Purity, there's no way he can win a duel against a gunslinger like Tyler Caine. By Jove, Caine is a bona fide hero."

"I thought he was a murderer," Travis said, only it didn't

seem that Manypenny heard him over the clamor for whiskey that rose from the saloon's patrons.

An hour later, Travis finally got a chance to talk to Lirith. The whiskey had done its work, and the men in the saloon, dour and silent before, were whooping it up. No one overheard Travis and Lirith's words.

"It's working, isn't it?" she said.

Travis nodded. "Right now I imagine rumors are flying all over town. I think people have gotten desperate. They'll grab at any scrap of hope they can. It looks like your vision was right. Tyler Caine will come to Castle City."

She laid a hand on his arm and met his gaze. "Will he really?"

"What do you mean?"

"I mean Tyler Caine is a warrior skilled at wielding these guns which men of this world use for weapons. And you——"

Travis gave a weak grin. "And I've got two days to learn how to shoot."

Travis got up early the next morning. He washed his face in the basin, picked up the straight razor Maudie had lent Durge, and looked in the mirror. He had kept his head and cheeks shaved over the last weeks by visiting the barbershop near the saloon, but he still had his goatee, and this was a job he needed to do himself. Concentrating on keeping his hand steady, he lifted the razor and scraped the whiskers from his chin.

When he was done—and the bleeding had stopped—all that remained of his goatee was a red-gold handlebar mustache. He took the wire-rimmed spectacles from the bureau, unfolded them, and put them on. Finally, from the bedpost, he took the black-felt hat Maudie had found in her closet the previous day, shaped the brim, and put it on his head. He turned around, and Tyler Caine gazed back at him from the mirror.

Except you're not Tyler Caine. You look like the drawing on the poster, but who knows how true that likeness is? It's certainly not a very good sketch. In life, Tyler Caine probably looks nothing like you.

Except Tyler Caine probably didn't look like anything in life anymore. The stories were true; he was dead. Only Travis wasn't, at least for the moment. He headed downstairs.

He wasn't the only early riser. Lirith and Maudie were in the kitchen making breakfast. Durge and Jack sat at the kitchen table drinking tea. When she saw him, Maudie let out a cry and dropped the iron skillet of eggs onto the stove. She started coughing, then recovered and laughed.

"Why, Mr. Caine, you give me shivers just to look at you." She winked at him. "Or should I say, Mr. Wilder."

Travis cringed. "Let's stick with the second one for now."

Travis had thought Maudie would be upset after he showed them the Wanted poster. Instead, she had been more excited than he had ever seen her.

"Why, it was the Lord Himself who sent you to us, Mr. Caine!" she had said, beaming. "You'll set things right, I know it. First you'll rescue Mr. Samson, and then you'll blast that Crusade right out of town." She made her hands into guns, cocked her thumbs, and shot her fingers in all directions.

Travis didn't have the heart to tell Maudie he had never fired a gun in his life. But insane as it seemed, it was the only way out. They couldn't possibly fight the whole Crusade at once. Travis had to hope that Locke would take the bait and accept the duel.

And what if somehow you do manage to win the duel? What then? You'll still have to deal with the sorcerer.

At least with the Crusade out of the way, the Scirathi wouldn't have servants to do his dirty work anymore. Nor would he have the scarab. Maybe that would give them a chance to get the gate back. Of course, they didn't really need the gate, not if what Jack had said was true. All he had to do was use Sinfathisar.

No. He didn't dare use the Stone; there was no telling what would happen if he unleashed its magic. And it was more than that. He couldn't just leave this town, these people. It was his fault things were so bad; he was the one who had brought the sorcerer through the gate. And that meant he had to set things right, just like Maudie said. If he couldn't, then what was the point in having all this power anyway?

Travis accepted a cup of coffee from Lirith and sat down at the table.

Jack let out a snort as he shook the newspaper in his hand. "I don't see how they can call this news. I haven't read a single story concerning London since coming to this town. Is no one here even remotely civilized?" He folded the paper and tossed it onto the table.

Travis stared. On the front page of the *Clarion* was a picture of a man: the same sketch as on the Wanted poster. BE ON THE LOOKOUT FOR THIS MAN, ALIAS TYLER CAINE, read the caption. HE IS CONSIDERED ARMED AND DANGEROUS. IT IS ADVISED THAT ANYONE WHO ENCOUNTERS HIM SHOOT ON—

Durge picked up the paper, crossed to the stove, and tossed it inside. "Perhaps you should remove your hat and spectacles for the time being, Travis."

Travis did.

Lirith set a plate of toast on the table, then on her way back to the stove she stumbled.

Maudie moved to her, spurs jingling. "How are you holding up, sweetheart?"

Lirith managed a brave smile. "I'm fine, really."

Except she didn't look fine. She looked like she hadn't slept in two days.

"I must say," Jack announced in a loud voice as he dunked a piece of toast in his tea, "this town is quite barbaric, what with these dirt streets, the ruffians and hoodlums, that terrible disgrace for a newspaper, and sorcerers running hither and thither." He waved a hand at Travis. "You're a runelord. You really should do something about it, you know."

"I'm working on it," Travis said, gritting his teeth. He glanced at Lirith. "How is Sheriff Tanner this morning?"

"He's alive, if that's what you mean," drawled a slow voice.

They looked up to see Tanner standing in the doorway. He was dressed, his cheeks and chin freshly shaved.

"And I suppose it's Mr. Tanner," he said, stepping into the kitchen. "Seeing as how according to Miss Lily I'm no longer the sheriff until I get her say-so."

"That's right," the witch said briskly. She moved to Tanner, laid a hand on his brow, and shut her eyes. "You're better!"

"Maybe I've got a spark of life left in me after all, Miss Lily."

She smiled. "I imagine you do. But today you're still *Mister* rather than *Sheriff*. You're doing well, but you're far from fully recovered."

"I think I knew that already." Tanner lifted a hand to the back of his head and winced. "It feels like I've been trying to waltz with an ornery mule."

"Can I get you some coffee, Bart?" Maudie said.

"Thank you, Maude. That would be good." He moved stiffly to the table and sank into a chair.

Liza came downstairs then. She had been seeing to Niles Barrett—the Englishman was still unconscious—and now she helped Maudie put out breakfast in the dining room for the boarders. However, the rest of them ate at the small table in the kitchen, where they could talk.

"I'll need a gun, I suppose," Travis said.

Maudie gave him a sharp look. "Why, surely you have a gun, Mr. Cai . . . I mean, Mr. Wilder."

Travis opened his mouth, but Lirith was faster. "He lost it. Isn't that right?"

"Well, you can use my gun, seeing as it does me no good." With a shaking hand, Tanner pulled a revolver from the gun belt at his hip and set it on the table. It gleamed bright silver; the grip was carved of smooth ivory. "It's a .45 caliber Colt Single Action Army. A Peacemaker. Although, back when I was with the US Marshals, some of the men liked to call it a Thumb Buster."

Travis peered at the gun but didn't touch it. It was big, the barrel as long as his hand, but sleek all the same. It looked powerful. And dangerous.

"I've never shot one of these before," Travis said.

Tanner gave him a curious look. "A Peacemaker, you mean? It's not so different than any other six-shooter you'll have fired. It's heavy, and the action's stiff, but that's about it. Though I suppose it would be good for you to practice some to get the feel of it."

"That would be good," Travis said, letting out a breath. "I'm a little . . . rusty."

Tanner nodded. "I know a place we can go shoot. That is, if the doctor will allow me outside."

Lirith crossed her arms, her expression stern. "As long as you ride instead of walk."

"Yes, ma'am," Tanner said.

However, it seemed Lirith didn't entirely trust Tanner, as she decided to go along, as did Durge. The Embarran fetched a pair of horses from the livery, and Lirith and Tanner rode while Travis and Durge walked. Travis was worried someone might see them leave town, but the streets were deserted, and no one accosted them as they rode toward Granite Creek.

They stopped in a small gulch. On one side, scattered on the dirt slope, were mutilated tin cans and the shattered remains of glass bottles. So they weren't the only ones to use the place as a shooting range.

Durge set up several of the less hole-ridden cans in a row, then returned to the others. Tanner handed Travis the six-shooter.

"Go ahead and give it a try," Tanner said. "It's loaded."

Travis tried to recall what he knew of guns. There wasn't much. He took it in his hands, trying not to fumble. "Is the safety off?"

Tanner frowned. "Safety? What's that?"

"Nothing," Travis muttered. He raised the gun, aware of Tanner's eyes on him. Clenching his jaw, he pulled the trigger. Nothing happened.

"You really are rusty," Tanner said, letting out a low whistle. "You forgot to cock it. Go ahead—it's easier if you do it all in one quick motion with your thumb. That's right. Now keep your arm straight. Don't tense up your shoulder. And squeeze the trigger, don't pull."

Travis tried to keep all of this clear in his mind. He aimed, fired. Thunder rent the air of the gulch. Lirith and Durge winced. The cans, however, appeared unaffected. Travis fired again and again, until the gun clicked when he pulled the trigger.

"Don't forget to count your shots," Tanner said as Travis lowered the gun. "You've only got six before you have to re-load." He gave Travis a handful of bullets.

Travis stared at them; they felt hot in his hand. Tanner gave him a sharp look, then took both bullets and gun and showed

Travis how to slip them into the chambers. He handed the gun back to Travis. "Ready to try again, Mr. Caine?"

Travis made a decision. "I'm not Tyler Caine."

"I know," Tanner said.

"My shooting gave me away?"

"It's not that." Tanner seemed to reconsider his words. "Well, it *is* that. You're a terrible shot. But I knew it even before you picked up the gun. You look like him all right. But you don't walk like a gunslinger."

"How does a gunslinger walk?"

"Like he's got death riding at his hip." Tanner glanced at Durge. "Like our Mr. Dirk here walks."

Durge gave him a surprised look.

Tanner grinned. "You don't know any more about guns than Mr. Wilder does, Mr. Dirk, but I'd bet my life you're no stranger to carrying a weapon. Only I can't think what on Earth it would be."

"A sword," Durge said in his deep voice.

Tanner raised his eyebrows.

"Can you teach me?" Travis said. "To shoot?"

Tanner nodded. "You've got a steady hand. And there's something about you, Mr. Wilder, something I can't put my finger on. You don't walk like a gunslinger, but you know something about power, and something about keeping it in check. That should serve you well. A man's got to wield his gun, and not the other way around."

"So you can teach me."

"I can. But not in two days. It would take two months for you to get any good. And two years before you could face someone who's as quick on the draw as Aaron Locke."

Travis's hope crumbled. "So I have a steady hand but no skill."

"And I've got the skill and a hand that shakes like a scared jackrabbit," Tanner said. "Between us we make one gunslinger, Mr. Wilder. Too bad there's no way to put us together."

"Isn't there?" Durge said.

They all looked at the knight. He shifted his feet and glanced at Lirith. "Can you not do something, my lady? Something like what you did to . . . what you did in the Barrens?" There was a queer expression in the knight's eyes. At first Travis thought it was fear. Then he realized it was awe.

Lirith met Durge's gaze. "It might work."

"What are you talking about?" Travis said, confused.

Lirith moved to him. "There's a way for me to grant some of Sir Tanner's knowledge to you. If he's willing." She glanced at the sheriff.

He shrugged. "I don't pretend to know what you're talking about, Miss Lily, but if there's a way to help Travis learn more quickly, I'll be happy to see what it is."

"Very well," Lirith said, and she took Tanner's wrist in one hand and Travis's in the other.

Travis started to ask Lirith what she was planning, but before he could she shut her eyes and murmured something he couldn't quite catch. Travis heard—no, *felt*—a rushing noise, and images flashed before his eyes. Only they weren't just images, because he could hear and feel and smell.

He stood in a valley between two forested ridges, his too-big boots squelching in thick mud. The hot air thudded with the noise of cannons, and ragged clouds of smoke drifted by like mist. Then a bugle called out, and he was running alongside men dressed in blue uniforms.

He threw himself down on his stomach behind a fallen log, then raised himself up on his elbows, rifle cradled in his arms. A line of men in gray trampled a bean field, running toward him and the others. Shots rang out. The men in gray uniforms fell like wheat before a scythe. Travis fired, reloaded, and fired again until the rifle grew hot in his hands.

More shots rang out, behind him now, along with the screams of men. A shadow fell over him, and he looked up into a pair of frightened eyes. The soldier didn't look more than seventeen, his dirty gray uniform sagging from bony shoulders. Travis started to reload, but the soldier thrust down with his bayonet. Pain sank deep into Travis's shoulder, but his scream was drowned out by the bellow of a gun. The young soldier's head dissolved in a spray of red and gray, and his body toppled on top of Travis.

The image blurred, refocused. Now Travis was on a sidewalk in a busy city. Brick buildings rose several stories above him. Horses clattered down steep cobbled streets. He caught the glint of a bay in the distance.

A shout. There was a man running toward him. Travis saw his hand rise in front of him. Only it wasn't his hand. It was smaller, knobbier, stronger. In it was a silver six-shooter with an ivory grip. The man running toward him pulled out a gun, aimed. Travis knew what to do. His gun fired, the man fell dead.

More images flashed before Travis. He shot two men riding away from him on horses. A sack tumbled to the sage-covered ground; green bricks of paper money spilled out. Another man, a kerchief hiding his face, ran out of a bank, gun blazing. Travis felled him with a single shot between the eyes. He turned, and for a second, in a store's plate-glass window, he caught the reflection of a man: He was slight of build, handsome in a sober way, with a sandy brown mustache and watery blue eyes.

Sun glinted off the window, so bright Travis was forced to look away. When his vision cleared, he found himself staring at the same face, only older, wearier. Tanner stood before him. Lirith released his wrist. The sheriff took a staggering step back. He stared at her, then at Travis.

"Who are you?" he said.

Travis glanced down at the gun in his hand and ran a thumb over it. A minute ago it had felt heavy and alien. Now it seemed to fit snugly in his grip, and he could feel the expert way its weight had been balanced. In an easy motion, he raised the gun, cocked it, and fired. A tin can flew toward the sky, then clattered back to earth. He fired again, and again. Four, five, six. Each time, one of the tin cans skittered away. He lowered the gun and met Tanner's stunned eyes.

"We're not who you think we are," he said.

They told him everything: how Durge and Lirith were from another world, and Travis from the future of this one, and how the sorcerer had followed them through. When they finished, Tanner was silent. He stared at the twisted metal cans. Finally, he nodded.

"Maybe Maudie's right. Maybe you really are Tyler Caine."

Travis tightened his grip on the gun.

Lirith cast a worried look at Tanner. The sheriff's face was gray. "We should be getting back."

"I'll get the horses," Durge said.

They rode back to the town in silence and reached the Bluebell around noon. Tanner and Lirith dismounted, and Durge took the reins of the horses to lead them back to the livery. However, before he could go, the front door burst open, and Maudie rushed onto the porch, leaning on her cane. "Thank the Lord above you're back!"

Tanner seemed to forget his own weariness. He bounded up the steps and took her arm. "Maude, what is it?"

"It's—" A fit of coughing took her. He gripped her shoulders until it passed. "It's Mr. Barrett."

The rest of them were on the porch now.

"What is it?" Lirith said. "Has Lord Barrett finally awakened?"

"No," Maudie said, gasping. "He's dead."

61.

They buried Niles Barrett the next day.

It was late morning when Durge fetched a wagon from the livery and drove them up the hill outside town to Castle Heights Cemetery. As Durge brought the wagon to a halt, a tall man in a black suit approached. For a moment Travis wondered if it might be Brother Cy.

It wasn't. The undertaker was about Travis's age, his face as dusty as his suit. Tanner spoke to him, and he pointed across the cemetery. Durge helped Maudie down from the wagon and guided her across the rough ground. Tanner offered his arm to Lirith in a polite gesture. However, Travis could see the way the sheriff leaned on her as they walked. Travis came last, along with Jack, holding on to the small bunch of wildflowers Lirith had picked that morning. Travis, Durge, and Tanner had donned their best shirts, and Lirith her gray dress, which matched Jack's suit. Maudie was dressed all in black.

"He doesn't have a wife to mourn him," she had said back at the Bluebell. "So I guess it's up to me."

They found his grave on the far side of the cemetery, a

hastily dug pit. Lying within was a pine coffin. The only marker was a plain wooden cross.

"Oh, Niles," Maudie said, wiping the tears from her cheek. "I'll sure miss your voice."

Tanner laid a hand on her shoulder, and she leaned back against his chest.

"What happened?" Travis had asked Lirith the previous afternoon, after she examined Barrett's body.

Lirith's face was tightly drawn. "His injuries were too great. I wish Grace was here—I can't be as certain as she could be—but I believe there was bleeding in his head."

An aneurism. Brought about by the blows to his skull, Travis supposed. "But I thought you said he was waking up."

"No, I said he was trying, and that he was strong. But sometimes..." Lirith's voice caught in her throat. "Sometimes, no matter how strong you are, it isn't enough."

Those words echoed in Travis's mind now. What about him? Would he be strong enough to do what he had to that day? Last night, at the Mine Shaft, he had overheard a number of whispers that let him know their plan had worked. Word was all over town that Tyler Caine had challenged the leader of the Crusade for Purity to a gunfight, and that the showdown would happen tonight at the Bar L Ranch.

There was no way Locke couldn't have heard the rumors. But did he know their source? More than once Travis had looked up as the saloon's doors swung open, expecting to see Lionel Gentry and Eugene Ellis, or even Aaron Locke himself, step through. But he never did. They were waiting, just like he was. Waiting for sundown tonight.

"Where's the preacher?" Maudie said, looking around the cemetery.

Good question, Travis thought. Where was Brother Cy? He wasn't sure. Only that he had a feeling he wouldn't see Cy again, at least not in this century. "I don't think there is a preacher," Travis said.

"Then we'll have to speak prayers for him ourselves," Lirith said.

Each of them talked in turn about how they had met Niles Barrett, and some memory of him: his sardonic laughter, his intelligent gaze, how he had wanted to start a newspaper to rival the *Clarion*.

"I wish I had gotten the chance to meet this fellow," Jack said wistfully. "It sounds as if he was the only civilized man in Castle City."

When they were done, Travis set the flowers on top of the coffin. Maudie smiled, tears shining on her cheeks. "He's gone to meet his lieutenant. I don't think I told you, Miss Lily. Niles found out last fall, more than a year after his ship went down off the coast of Australia. But they're sailing away together now, aren't they?" Her smile faded, and she looked at Tanner. "Aren't they, Bart?"

Tanner took her hand in his. "Forever, Maude." He put his arm around her shoulder, and slowly the two made their way back to the wagon as the rest of them followed.

The afternoon was long and hot. None of them felt like eating when they got back to the Bluebell, but Liza made lemonade with the last bit of ice in the cellar, and that provided a bit of relief. Tanner went upstairs to rest, but Maudie seemed unable to sit still. She bustled from room to room dusting and straightening, until finally a fit of coughing seized her.

"Please, madam," Jack said when her spasm subsided, "will you keep me company in the parlor?"

Maudie daubed at her lips with her handkerchief. "I can't imagine I'll be very good company, Mr. Graystone. But I'll sit with you, if you like."

Travis shot Jack a grateful look. He spent the rest of the afternoon sitting on the front porch with Lirith and Durge. They didn't speak much, but Travis knew they were all thinking the same thing. Would they get Sareth back alive? Then, just as the shadows stretched down the length of Grant Street, the front door squeaked open. Tanner stepped onto the porch.

"It's time," he said.

Travis went upstairs, looped the gun belt around his hips, and put on the black hat. Last of all, he slipped the wire-rimmed spectacles onto his face. As usual, everything looked strange. Not blurry or distorted, but instead too clear. Travis met his eyes in the mirror, then he went downstairs to say good-bye.

"We're coming with you," Durge said.

The knight had strapped his sword to his back, although it was still wrapped in a blanket. In Tanner's hands was a sawed-off shotgun, and while Lirith carried nothing, by the set of her jaw Travis knew she meant to come as well.

"I'm supposed to do this alone," Travis said.

Tanner shook his head. "In every duel, a man has to have his seconds."

Travis's heart ached, and he didn't know if it was from joy or dread. "But Durge, your gun is never loaded. And Sheriff, your hand—"

"—doesn't need to be steady to shoot this," Tanner said, hefting the shotgun. "I just need to be close."

Travis shook his head. "And Lirith—"

"Is coming." She laid a hand on his arm, and her expression softened. "I love him, Travis. I cannot stay here."

Despite the fear pooling in his stomach, Travis felt a sense of relief. No matter what happened, at least he wouldn't be alone.

Maudie was still in the parlor, and she refused to come out and see them.

"I won't say good-bye," she called through the door. "I won't say it because you're coming right back, do you understand me? You're coming right back!"

"Yes, ma'am," Tanner, Durge, and Travis all said.

Thankfully, Jack hadn't gotten the notion that he was going to the Bar L with the rest of them. "I intend to stay here, put my feet up, and drink tea," he said. "I find, after what happened in London, I've quite lost my appetite for adventure."

Travis swallowed hard. "What do you think the sorcerer will do, Jack?"

"I don't know, Travis." For the first time, worry crept into Jack's blue eyes. "But be ready for trickery. His kind are skilled at deception. Nothing will be as you think. And remember the runes. They're all inside of you—all you have to do is listen."

"I have to go now," Travis said.

"You *will* be careful, won't you? I find I rather like you, and I'm looking forward to our future friendship. I'd hate very much if that didn't come to pass as you said it will."

Despite the heat, a shiver coursed through Travis. There was something about Jack's words that struck him, something important. But what was it?

"Travis," Durge said. "Sundown comes."

Whatever it was, Travis couldn't quite grasp it. He headed out the door. They still had the wagon, and Durge drove the four of them in silence. They met no one on the road south of town.

The sun was still a handspan above the shoulder of Castle Peak when the gables of the opulent Victorian ranch house came into view, so Durge halted the wagon and they walked the rest of the way on foot. Travis was just as glad. It was hard to sit still. Energy buzzed through his nerves, making him twitch like a dead frog hooked to a battery.

They reached the gate to the ranch. It was open.

Tanner gazed around. "Be on the lookout."

"For what?" Durge rumbled.

"Everything."

Durge reached up and removed the bundle from his back. He unwrapped the blanket, and the ruddy light flickered up and down the length of his greatsword like blood.

Tanner's eyes went wide. "Sweet Jesus, Mr. Dirk. You weren't joking, were you?"

"Durge doesn't make jokes," Lirith said, and she gave the knight a fond smile.

Handling it as if it weighed nothing, Durge slipped the massive sword into the scabbard strapped to his back.

"Let's go," Travis said, and together they stepped through the gate.

Keep your guard up. This isn't going to be a fair fight. Locke will do anything to get the jump on you.

Where had that thought come from? Then Travis understood; the thought wasn't his, it was Tanner's. It was part of the sheriff's knowledge Lirith had granted him with her spell.

Don't forget your blind spot. And keep your hand close to your gun.

It already was.

The four followed the dusty road as the western sky caught fire. The only sound was the hiss of the wind through sunburnt grass. Halfway to the ranch house, the road widened. On the right was a corral bounded by a split-rail fence, empty save for a scattering of troughs and barrels. On the left was a long row of stalls; the gates on all of the stalls were closed.

"It looks like they're going to make us run a gauntlet."

For a second, Travis thought he was hearing Tanner's thoughts again in his head; then he realized the sheriff had spoken the words aloud. Slowly, they passed several of the stalls, then came to a halt. A tumbleweed lurched by, but nothing else moved.

Lirith shut her eyes, and her fingers circled in a weaving motion. "We're being watched."

Travis moved closer to the witch. "How many, Lirith?"

"I don't know. I..." She opened her eyes. "Something's wrong. The threads of the Weirding keep pulling away every time I try to weave them. It's as if there's something they're recoiling from."

"The sorcerer?"

"I don't think so. For all his power, the Scirathi is a living man like any other. He would show up clearly to me. But this is different. It's as if it's both alive and—"

Twenty yards away, the gate of the last stall swung open, and Calvin Murray stepped out. Or what remained of Calvin Murray, for even from a distance Travis could see the dark blotches of decay. Black spittle drooled from the lupine jaws that had been grafted onto Murray's face; the cougar's paw dangled loosely at the end of his arm. With lurching motions, Murray used his human arm to reach into the stall behind him and pull something out.

Lirith held out a trembling hand. "Sareth!"

The Mournish man was gagged, his hands bound behind his back; a crusted scab marred his forehead. They had taken his peg leg away from him, so he was forced to hop on one foot. His eyes went wide as they locked on Lirith.

The witch started to rush forward, but Durge grabbed her arm. "You'll be killed if you try to go near him."

"You're right on that account, Mr. Dirk," drawled a voice behind them. "And I'd hate to see a pretty woman get killed, no matter the color of her skin."

They must have come from one of the first stalls, Travis thought as he and the others turned around. Lionel Gentry ambled toward them. Flanking him were Eugene Ellis and Deputy Wilson. Guns glinted at their hips. A scent rose on the air: sweet, cloying.

Travis tried to pretend he felt more anger than fear. "I didn't come here to fight you."

Ellis took a drag on a thin cigar; the smoke poured back out of his mouth. "You don't have to fight anybody, Mr. Caine. You look quite well for a man who's supposed to be dead. I'm sure you don't want to do anything to alter that. All you have to do is give us what we want."

Travis had to force his left hand to stay away from his pocket; he could feel the steady warmth of the scarab against his leg.

Durge cast a stern look at Wilson. "Deputy, why have you cast your lot with these evil men?"

The young man only stared, his pudgy face pallid. Gentry laughed and tousled his hair. "Go ahead and tell them, Mr. Wilson. You wanted to lead a life of adventure, didn't you? Just like you read about in those dime novels. Well, here you are. Ain't it grand?"

"Where is Locke?" Travis said loudly. "Is he too much of a coward to defend his honor? Or doesn't he have any?"

"Honor is overrated, Mr. Caine," answered a voice from behind. "As I'm sure you'll agree."

Travis turned. Aaron Locke stood a few paces in front of Sareth and Calvin Murray. He was clad in a stylish brown suit topped off by a smart hat. His boyish face was freshly shaved. He looked ready for a night at the opera house. The only thing dispelling the image was the six-shooter belted at his side.

"However," Locke said, "I will not be called a coward. You may be a cold-blooded man-killer, but I've seen things that would make even your blood curdle."

I bet you have, Travis thought, gazing past Locke toward Murray, who still held on to Sareth. The Mournish man's eyes were hazed with pain. Instinct that was not Travis's own stirred inside him. He knew, just like Tanner would have, that he had to buy more time so he could take proper measure of the situation.

"Where's your servant, Mortimer Hale?" Travis called out, taking several steps toward Locke.

Locke matched them, striding closer. "Hale? He truly was a coward, Mr. Caine. He liked to write about violence, but he didn't have the guts to perform it himself. He grew uncomfortable with some of the things my new . . . associate was doing. As did some of my other men."

"So you killed them," Travis said, moving closer.

Locke matched him stride for stride. "No, I didn't. Mr. Gentry, Mr. Ellis, and Mr. Wilson did the deed. That's how I knew they weren't cowards themselves. And for that they've been rewarded." He smiled, a charming expression. "Oh yes, and good Mr. Murray helped as well."

The creature behind him grunted, as if it recognized what had once been its name. It was a horrible, pitiful sound. The thing pressed its rotting muzzle against Sareth's cheek, licking him. A moan escaped the Mournish man.

Only a dozen paces separated Travis and Locke now. Travis adjusted his spectacles. It seemed a shadow clung to Locke, cloaking him. The sun had touched the shoulder of Castle Peak; the daylight was staring to fade, that was all.

Travis started to take another step, then halted as Locke's hand moved to his gun. So this was it, then. Travis was aware of Durge, Lirith, and Tanner behind him. He would have to hope they could keep Gentry and his men from interfering. As for Murray, the creature's orders seemed to be to keep hold of Sareth. That meant all Travis had to worry about was Locke.

Remember, Locke is fast. You probably can't beat him on the draw. You're going to have to hope his shot goes wide, and then make sure yours doesn't.

He didn't know if the thoughts were his own or Tanner's. It didn't matter; he knew they were right. He brushed his fingers against the grip of the Peacemaker at his hip and kept his eyes on Locke.

You can't do this, Travis.

Those were his own thoughts. But they weren't true. He *could* do this because Tanner could, and Travis had the sheriff's skill, his knowledge. Only it was more than that. Travis had stood before the gates of Imbrifale. He had faced a

Necromancer. He had stared into the empty heart of a demon and had survived. What was facing one man to that?

Now he was getting cocky, and that was a sure way to die. He forced all thoughts from his mind. The only thing that mattered was the gun at his side.

"Are you ready, Mr. Caine?" Locke said, his voice calm, even pleasant. The shadow seemed to thicken about him. "I assure you, this time the rumors of your death will not be in error."

"I'm ready," Travis said. "But not to die."

Time shuddered to a halt. The last sliver of the sun hovered just above the ridge of the mountain, casting a bloody sheen over the world. A low peal of thunder rolled across the land, and Travis knew it was a single beat of his heart.

Then he saw it: a glint of red as Locke's hand reached for his six-shooter and drew it from its holster. Travis knew he had to start moving, then realized his gun was already in his hand, his arm was already rising.

It should have been hard, but it wasn't. In an easy motion, Travis thumbed back the hammer, aimed, and squeezed the trigger. New thunder rolled, far louder than before, and Travis felt heat and pressure as the bullet was released from the gun.

Locke was still cocking his own six-shooter. Somehow Travis had gotten his shot off first. His aim was true; the bullet flew straight toward Locke's chest.

With a sharp *ping*! it ricocheted away.

Time resumed its normal cadence. Travis heard an oath sworn behind him—Tanner?—as well as laughter. Locke's smile widened, and with an easy motion he took aim.

That's why you beat him on the draw, Travis. He was taking his time. He knew your bullet couldn't hit him.

That was impossible. This was 1883. There were no such things as Kevlar vests.

Only maybe there was something better than Kevlar. Travis squinted. Yes, he could see it more clearly now that the sun was gone. The shadow surrounded Locke like black gauze. But what was it really? Travis bent his head, peering over the rims of his spectacles. When he did, the shadow vanished.

A spell. The sorcerer had cast a spell on Locke, one that protected him from harm. Jack was right; he should have been expecting a trick.

"Travis!" a voice shouted. Lirith.

There was a roar of fury, followed by the bright ringing of metal, and Travis was certain that if he turned around he would see that Durge had drawn his sword. What else would he see? Sareth's eyes were wide, but whatever he was shouting was muffled by the gag.

"Get back!" came Tanner's stern voice.

Metal clanged against metal. Then came the sound of gunfire. Travis wanted to turn, to do something, anything, but he couldn't take his eyes off the six-shooter in Locke's hand.

"Good-bye, Mr. Caine," Locke said amiably. And fired.

62.

It must have been some magic of the spectacles. Travis watched the bullet leap free of the cloud of smoke that erupted from the barrel of Locke's six-shooter. The bullet flew toward him, spinning on its axis as it ripped through the air. It was headed straight for his chest. No matter how long this second lasted, when it was done, so was Travis.

Speak a rune, Travis, said Jack's voice in his head.

But that was impossible. Jack wasn't here. He was safe at the Bluebell with Maudie.

Did you hear me? There's no time to waste. Dur *should do the trick nicely, I think.*

No, this was a gunfight. It was the fastest draw and the best shot that won, not magic.

By the Lost Eye of Olrig, you're not a gunfighter, Travis. You're a runelord! Now speak the rune of iron before it's too late.

It was impossible. There shouldn't have been time; he should already be dead. All the same, Travis opened his mouth and spoke the word.

"Dur."

Time sped up. Travis groped at his chest with his left hand, expecting to feel a bloody pit. He didn't; he was whole. The high-pitched *zing*! of the bullet still echoed on the air. It had gone wide and struck a fence post.

Travis heard another shot behind him, followed by a grunt of pain. "No, do not touch him!" a woman cried. Lirith. However, there was no time to turn around. Locke frowned at his gun, then stretched his arm out and fired again.

"Dur," Travis said again, flicking his hand to the left. The bullet whizzed by his head, then was gone.

Travis moved forward. Locke swore, cocked his six-shooter, fired. Again Travis spoke the rune of iron, again the bullet obeyed his command. He kept closing in on Locke, speaking the rune each time the other fired.

Finally, Travis was so close he could have reached out and put a finger in the barrel of Locke's six-shooter. Sweat beaded Locke's boyish face; his carefully shaved upper lip was trembling. He adjusted his grip on the gun, thumbed back the hammer, pulled the trigger.

This time Travis didn't bother to speak a rune.

Click.

"You forgot to count, Mr. Locke," Travis said, a grin spreading across his face, only he didn't feel like laughing. "You're out of bullets."

"But not out of guns," Locke snarled. He threw down the six-shooter, reached into the breast pocket of his coat, and pulled out a small derringer. Before Travis could move or speak, Locke pulled the trigger.

It felt like someone had clapped Travis on the ears. Fire ignited in his right hand; the Peacemaker flew from his grip and skittered to the dirt a dozen feet away. Travis prepared himself for the next shot, ready to speak *Dur* this time, but Locke had already turned and was running.

"Kill them, Murray!" Locke shouted over his shoulder. "Kill them all now!"

The creature that had been Calvin Murray opened its wolf jaws, emitting a wet growl. Sareth jerked, twisting away from the monster, but he lost his balance and tumbled to the ground. The thing bent over him, raising its lion paw.

With practiced motions he had never used before in his life, Travis lunged for his six-shooter, rolled on the ground, and came up firing. *Two more bullets,* Travis thought, keeping count. Both struck what was Calvin Murray square in the chest. The beast toppled backward, thudding to the ground.

Travis looked down. Blood streamed from an angry red line on the back of his right hand, but it was only a graze. He tightened his fingers around the grip of the Peacemaker and ignored the pain.

Sareth lay on his side, struggling with his bonds, trying to get his leg through the circle of his arms. Travis glanced over his shoulder. Dusk was falling, and there was too much smoke; he couldn't see what was happening. Someone was on the ground. But who? Tanner was trying to take aim with his rifle, but he couldn't get a clear shot. Lirith's eyes were shut, her fingers weaving.

Travis wanted to go help them; they needed him, and so did Sareth. Then he clenched his jaw, turned, and ran the other direction, after Locke.

He's going to fetch the sorcerer. No matter what happens, you can't let him do that.

Locke had vanished around the end of the line of stalls. Panting, Travis reached the last stall, then edged around the corner. A gunshot sounded, the wood next to Travis's cheek splintered. He ducked back around the corner. Locke must have a supply of bullets.

But the derringer only holds one bullet in its chamber. He'll have to reload between every shot.

How did he know that? But he didn't; Tanner did. Lirith's spell was still working. He dashed around the corner. Ahead was a scattering of tack sheds and outbuildings. He lowered his head and ran.

Gunfire sounded again just as Travis made it to the first of the buildings and pressed himself against the clapboard wall. It seemed Locke was a quick reloader.

Travis peered around the corner. There—a shadow in the

dim space between two sheds. The grip of the revolver was slick with blood, but Travis tightened his fingers around it, cocked the hammer, and fired. The bullet sped straight toward its target—

—and once again ricocheted off with a bright *ping*. The shadow turned and fled.

Travis ran toward the two buildings where he had seen the shadow. By the time he reached the sheds, the path between them was empty. He started around the corner and nearly got a bullet in the face, but this time he was quick enough to speak *Dur*, and the metal slug slammed into a wall instead. He adjusted his spectacles, then saw the shadow he knew was Locke dart from the cover of an overturned trough toward a tall windmill. Travis led the figure slightly with his aim—Tanner's instinct again—then fired.

Another *ping* let Travis know the sorcerer's enchantment was still working. Maybe if he was close enough, a bullet would be able to pierce the shadowy cloak. But he had been counting, and he knew five of the chambers in his revolver were empty. He had one chance left.

Travis raced forward and dived behind the trough. A second later a bullet dug deep into the weathered wood. He had his chance, while Locke was reloading the derringer. Travis sprang up and ran.

He didn't head straight toward the windmill, but instead ran to the right, then turned to approach from the side. It was hard to see in the gloom, but he could make out the wooden shed that housed the mechanism of the windmill, as well as a large cistern that held the water the windmill pumped from the ground.

"Sirith," Travis murmured as he drew closer. Silence folded in around him. Careful to keep out of sight, Travis circled around the back of the windmill's shed.

A dim shape huddled between shed and tub, fumbling with something. Locke was reloading the derringer. He darted upward, fired the gun over the cistern—in the opposite direction from Travis—then ducked back down.

The rune of silence had worked. Locke hadn't heard him coming; he still thought Travis was hiding behind the old trough. Locke started to fumbled again with the derringer, reloading it. Then he halted at the sound of a gun being cocked. Travis felt a fierce grin slice across his face. He had dismissed the rune of silence; he wanted Locke to hear death coming.

Locke scrambled to his feet and turned around. The whites of his eyes showed in the twilight. Travis pointed the Peacemaker at Locke's chest. The empty derringer slipped from Locke's fingers and fell to the dust.

"You can't kill me," Locke said.

Travis tightened his grip on the bloody gun. "How do you know that?"

"Because you're just a man, and he's..." Locke shuddered, but then his teeth showed in the half-light like a crescent moon. "He's strong. Like nothing you've ever seen. Strong, and clever, and just. After he showed up, taking over this town was as easy as winning at poker with all the aces in your hand. Once we're done with you, we'll take over another town, and then another. And the next thing you know, I'll be governor of Colorado. Then I can purge the sin from this whole state just like I did from this town."

Travis felt neither pity nor sorrow. "He's only using you, Locke. All he wants is the scarab. Once he has it, he'll dispose of you like you disposed of Hale."

"You don't know what you're talking about," Locke said. However, even in the dimness, Travis could see fear flicker in his eyes. "He needs me to make his way in this world."

"He doesn't care about this world," Travis said. "It's not his own. All he wants is to escape it."

Somewhere an owl hooted, beginning its nightly hunt. Locke's eyes narrowed. "Go ahead, Mr. Caine. You're a man-killer. Shoot me. Then you'll see how strong he really is." He spread his arms wide. "Go on. He's cast a cloak over me, a cloak stronger than any armor. A cloak of righteousness. No bullet alone is enough to pierce it."

Travis knew Locke was right. No bullet alone could break through the sorcerer's spell. But Jack had been right as well. Travis wasn't a gunfighter. He was a runelord.

He leveled the revolver at Locke's chest.

"Reth," Travis said.

And fired.

A hot strobe of light cauterized the gloom. In the flash, Travis saw the shadow that surrounded Locke rip to tatters like cheap cloth. Then dusk closed back in.

Travis blinked, trying to clear his vision, then he sucked in a breath. Locke still stood before him. Faint sparks of light seemed to dance in front of Locke. Afterimages from the flash of gunpowder? Travis blinked again, but the sparks of light didn't go away.

They were stars. The sparks of light he was seeing were stars just appearing in the sky low to the horizon. They weren't dancing on the air before Travis's eyes. He was seeing them through the hole in Locke's chest.

Travis reached out and touched the other man's shoulder. Aaron Locke toppled backward, falling to the ground with a *thud*. It had worked. The rune of breaking had destroyed the shield created by the sorcerer. The empty gun slipped from Travis's wet fingers. He stepped back from the body and turned around.

With a roar, the creature that had been Calvin Murray lashed out with its human fist, striking Travis in the cheek.

Travis heard a sound like breaking glass. Blood spilled into his mouth. He staggered, then sat down hard on the ground. The beast reared above him in the gloom, baring wolf teeth, extending lion claws. Black fluid oozed from the two holes in its chest. Travis tried to speak a rune, but there was too much blood in his mouth, along with sharp pieces of something hard.

It's going to tear your throat out, Travis.

Light and sound rent the night like lightning. Illuminated by the flash, Calvin Murray's head vaporized in a wet cloud of blood, bone, and brains. The creature fell to the ground in front of Travis, jerked once, then lay still.

Travis looked up. Another figure was visible in the starlight: a slightly built man with a drooping mustache and a shotgun in his hands.

"Are you all right, Mr. Wilder?" Tanner said.

Travis glanced at the two fallen forms, one on either side of him, then cradled his hand against his chest. It stung a little, that was all. "I think so."

"Then you'd better come. It's Mr. Samson. Miss Lily and Mr. Dirk are with him."

Alarm coursed through Travis, clearing his head. He gained his feet and started moving. Tanner retrieved the fallen Peacemaker and followed.

Travis reached the row of stalls and saw Durge standing above Lirith, who knelt on the ground beside Sareth. Travis hurried closer. Three forms sprawled on the dirt not far away, and he was dimly aware of the fact that none of them seemed to have heads. Then he turned his attention on Lirith.

"What is it?" It was hard to talk. His jaw wasn't working right. "Is something wrong with Sareth?"

The Mournish man shook his head. "I'm fine. Weak, that's all. They didn't hurt me."

"What of Lord Locke?" Durge said.

"He's dead," Tanner said, limping toward them. "Travis got him with a clean shot."

Travis winced at these words. How could a shot be clean? It was anything but. He had killed a man. That was a terrible deed, no matter how evil Locke had been.

"And the beast?" Lirith said. "We saw it run that way, pursuing Travis."

Tanner hefted his shotgun. "This took care of it."

Travis leaned back on his heels, looking over his shoulder at the three bodies. "Gentry?"

Durge nodded. "And Ellis and Wilson. It would not have been so difficult to deal with them, save that I had to take their heads off."

"They were not alive," Lirith said in answer to Travis's confused look. "The sorcerer had slain them and had remade them with his magic."

Travis felt sick. So that was their reward for their loyalty. "Like Murray, you mean?"

"In a way. He did not alter their bodies. But their blood was . . . wrong. They were tainted. I knew it was not wise to come in contact with them."

"I had a hard time getting in a shot," Tanner said. "Luckily, Mr. Dirk is pretty handy with that big knife of his."

Travis's gaze moved to the sword Durge gripped before him, tip resting on the ground. The blade was dark with blood.

"So the Crusade for Purity is gone," he said. "It's all over."

"No, Travis, it's not," Sareth said. A shudder passed through him. He said they hadn't harmed him, but Travis doubted that. It wasn't just the darkness that caused shadows to gather beneath his eyes and in the hollows of his cheeks. By the grim line of her mouth, Lirith saw it, too. She gripped Sareth's hand as if she never meant to let go.

"What do you mean?" Travis said.

Sareth licked his lips. "The sorcerer. I heard him talking to Lord Locke earlier. I didn't see him, but . . . that voice. Like the hiss of a snake. It had to be him. I didn't hear much, but I heard him mention something about the Bluebell. And then he spoke a name I recognized."

Travis felt cold, his sweat-soaked shirt clammy against his skin. "What name?"

"Jack Graystone."

Travis sprang to his feet. He felt like vomiting. Instead he spat out a mouthful of blood and the remains of a tooth.

"Travis, you're hurt," Lirith said. "Your jaw. And your hand . . ."

"It's nothing. We've got to get to the Bluebell. Now."

Durge knelt, circled his arms around Sareth, and picked up the Mournish man as easily as if he were a child. It was testament to Sareth's state that he did not protest. Lirith gave Tanner her arm to lean on, and Travis led the way as they hurried back down the road to the wagon.

It seemed to take forever. By the time they reached the wagon it was full dark. They laid Sareth in the back, and Lirith cradled his head in her lap. Tanner sat beside her, shoulders slumped, face gaunt.

They were a mess, Travis realized. All of them. Even Durge. He was bleeding from a shallow wound in his side; a bullet must have grazed him. A few inches farther in and it would have hit his heart.

"Why, Travis?" Durge said as he climbed into the driver's bench. "Why would the sorcerer care about Lord Graystone?"

Travis clambered up next to him. "I don't know, Durge, I—"

The metallic taste of blood filled his mouth, trickled down his throat, filled his stomach with dread.

"What is it, Travis?"

He was wrong; he did know what the sorcerer wanted with Jack. Jack himself had said it earlier when they were leaving the Bluebell; that was why his words had bothered Travis.

I find I rather like you, and I'm looking forward to our future friendship. I'd hate very much if that didn't come to pass. . . .

"Oh, God," Travis said softly. He was shivering. "That's what he's wanted all along. The sorcerer. Not to go back, but to keep from coming in the first place."

"You're not making sense, Travis."

But he was. "Don't you see, Durge? He's going to try to stop it from happening."

The knight shook his head. "To stop what from happening?"

"The future."

63.

Durge gripped the reins in tight fists as the wagon hurtled through the night. Travis knew it was reckless to go so fast in the dark. If they hit a deep rut, an axle could break, sending the wagon careening down a slope or into a gully. All the same, he only adjusted his grip on the bench as Durge slapped the reins, urging the horses to gallop faster.

A moan of pain emanated from the back of the wagon as they rattled over a section of road that had been turned to washboard by the passage of countless wheels. Travis looked back over his shoulder. The moon had just eked its way over Signal Ridge, and in the wan light he saw Lirith bending over Sareth's head, her hands on his temples.

"How is he?" Travis asked above the rattle of the wheels.

"He drifts in and out from moment to moment," Lirith said. "He's weak from thirst and hunger. But that's not what concerns me. It's his illness. It grows . . . worse."

Travis understood. It was as if the demon was continuing the work it had begun two years earlier when it took his leg, and was now consuming him bit by bit.

Lirith looked up, her eyes dark as the night. "We must return to Eldh. The Weirding is far stronger there than it is here. I believe I can sustain his thread while he heals. But not in this world."

Travis couldn't find words to answer her. He glanced at Tanner. "Are you—?"

"I'm fine," the sheriff said, although he looked anything but. He leaned against the wall of the wagon, his face sharply lined in the moonlight. "Don't you worry about me, Mr. Wilder. Just go and help your friend, Mr. Graystone."

Travis turned around on the bench. Gold sparks danced in the distance. Castle City. "How much longer?"

"Not long." The knight glanced at him. "You believe the sorcerer is going to try to kill Lord Graystone."

"I know he is. That's why the Scirathi went to London. We were wrong—he's not interested in returning to the future. He wants to stop it from happening. Or at least from happening the way it did."

"And how would killing Lord Graystone achieve this?"

"If he kills Jack in 1883, then more than a century from now Jack won't be here in Castle City to give me Sinfathisar. And if I didn't have the Great Stone, there's no way I would have been able to defeat the demon in the Etherion. The Scirathi would have won."

Durge let out a snort. "But they would not have won regardless. Xemeth betrayed the sorcerers. The only reason this sorcerer survived to follow us was because you destroyed the demon Xemeth unleashed."

"That's true." Travis put the pieces together in his mind. "But there's no way the sorcerer could know about Xemeth's betrayal. In the Etherion, he was under the spell of the demon. And we never talked about Xemeth those times he was listening to us."

Durge tugged on the reins, and the wagon veered around a bend. "I see it now. The sorcerer believes you are the reason things went wrong with his brethren in the Etherion. He thinks it was because of you and the Great Stone that he and the other Scirathi were defeated."

"But now he wants to change that," Travis said, "by making sure it never happens at all."

They had reached the outskirts of town; the streets were deserted. The wagon clattered around a corner onto Grant Street, and Durge pulled hard on the reins. The wagon lurched to a stop.

"It looks quiet," Travis said. No lights shone in the windows of the boardinghouse. The front door was shut.

"I would prefer noise," Durge said, as they climbed down from the bench.

"I need to stay with him," Lirith said, her hands still pressed to Sareth's temples, her face haunted in the moonlight. The Mournish man's eyes were closed.

Travis glanced at Tanner. "Sheriff, can you keep watch over them?"

Tanner patted the shotgun resting across his knees. "I'll make sure no one comes near the wagon. Here, you'd better take this. I've reloaded it." He held out the Peacemaker.

The gun shone like liquid silver in the moonlight. He started to reach out, then pulled his hand back. This duel wouldn't be won with a six-shooter.

"Take care, Sheriff," Travis said, and started toward the boardinghouse. Durge jogged up beside him, his greatsword in his hands. Travis knew better than to tell the knight to stay in the wagon.

"Durge, I want you to find Maudie and Liza and make sure they're safe. And all of the boarders, too."

"What about you?"

"I'm going to find Jack."

"And will not the sorcerer be with him?"

Travis took a deep breath. "That's what I'm counting on."

Together, they walked up the steps to the front porch. Travis was keenly aware of every squeak of the boards beneath his boots. Did the sorcerer know he was there?

No, he thinks you're still at the Bar L Ranch. That was his plan all along. The sorcerer probably didn't believe for a minute that Locke and the Crusade could get the scarab from you. He was just using them to distract you, to get you away from Jack so he could make his move. Getting the scarab doesn't matter to him. He only stole the gate to make sure we didn't leave. Once he kills Jack, the future will change, and none of you will even be here anymore.

Travis moved his hand to his pocket, feeling the warmth of the living jewel within. Then he opened the door. There was only darkness beyond. He met Durge's eyes, then he and the knight moved into the hallway.

Something white shot through the dark like a ghost, hurtling toward Durge's chest. Durge swore, transferring his sword to one hand, using the other to fend off the attacker.

The ghost let out a *meow* of protest. Travis's heart started beating again. Durge let out a sigh and coiled his arm around the little calico cat. She must have jumped from the landing of the stairs above.

"You stay here, Miss Guenivere," Durge whispered, setting the cat on the floor. She purred, rubbing against his leg.

They stood in the hallway for a minute. Travis could see clearly in the gloom, but he knew Durge's eyes would need to adjust to the dim light of the moon spilling through the windows. Durge nodded, and they moved through the parlor door, then into the dining room, the kitchen, and Maudie's bedroom. All were empty. In moments they were back at the foot of the stairs. Miss Guenivere had vanished.

Durge gestured with his sword. Up. Travis started up the stairs, Durge right behind him. His hand started to move to his pocket—not the left where he kept the scarab, but the right, which contained Sinfathisar. By force of will he pulled his hand back; it was still bleeding from the shallow gunshot wound.

They met only shadows as they ascended the stairs. When they reached the second-floor landing, they halted. Silence. They moved down the hallway, opening doors, peering into the bedrooms on either side. All were empty. They reached the last door. Durge tried the knob. It was locked.

Durge knelt to peer through the keyhole. The knight sucked in a breath. "Lady Maudie!"

"What do you see?" Travis whispered. *Is she all right?* he started to ask, but then he heard a small, frightened sound come through the door.

"Lady Maudie," Durge called softly through the keyhole.

There was a scrabbling sound, then a weak cough. "Mr. Dirk? Is that really you?"

"It is. And Travis is with me."

A sobbing noise. "Oh, Mr. Caine. You have to stop him. He's going to do something horrible to Mr. Graystone."

"Who, Maudie?" Travis whispered, but he already knew.

"The man in the gold mask," Maudie's voice came wavering through the keyhole. "Is he a member of the Crusade for Purity?"

Travis didn't know how to answer that one. "Maudie, can you unlock the door?"

"It won't open," said her muffled voice. "I think he did something to it, something that keeps it from budging."

A spell. The sorcerer had bound it with magic.

"Maudie," Durge said, "what happened? And where are the others?"

"Liza and I were in the kitchen, cleaning up after supper. The boarders had all headed out to the saloons. Then we heard the front door bang open. I thought maybe it was the wind. Only when I went into the hallway, I saw him instead. He spoke in the most terrible voice—just like a snake—and he said, 'Where is Graystone?' I shouted for Liza to run out the back, then I turned and headed upstairs, thinking he'd follow me and stay away from Liza, and he did."

Another fit of coughing sounded through the door, harsher this time. She shouldn't have been climbing stairs.

"I ran into this room and shut the door," Maudie said. "I thought for sure the door would burst to splinters, but it didn't. The place got real quiet after that, and I decided to try to come out, only I couldn't open the door. Nor the window."

Travis swallowed. "Maudie, do you know where Jack is?"

"He went to his room after supper. That was the last I saw him."

Jack's room was there on the second floor, and all of the rooms were empty except the one Maudie was hiding in. There was only one more floor of the boardinghouse: the attic floor.

Another sob drifted through the keyhole. "Oh, Mr. Caine, Mr. Dirk, he was so horrible. That mask—it looked like the face of death. I thought he had come for me, that my time was up. I feel so weak. My heart is beating all wrong. And I haven't gotten to tell Bart...and I'm so frightened I won't—" Her words were lost in another fit of coughing.

Travis put a hand on Durge's shoulder. "Get this door open, Durge. Be with her."

"What of you?" the knight said.

"I'm going up."

Travis couldn't get out any more words, so he turned and headed for the stairs. Behind him, he heard Durge say, "Move away from the door, Lady Maudie." Then Travis was climbing the stairs.

He reached the landing. The third floor was as quiet as the rest of the boardinghouse. *Maybe you're too late. Maybe the sorcerer has finished his work and Jack is already dead.*

Except if Jack were dead, then Travis couldn't still be here because the path of the future would have changed. Somehow there must still be time.

Travis started down the hallway. He looked in the first door: an empty storeroom. Next was the door to Lirith's room, but there was nothing inside. Another empty room, and then there was only one more door, to the room Travis had shared with Durge these past weeks. Travis gripped the knob, supposing it would be locked by a spell.

It wasn't. He turned the knob, the door opened. Travis stepped inside, and terror gripped him.

"Jack!" he shouted.

Jack was on his knees on the floor, his left hand clutched to his chest. His skin was gray, his hair tangled, his face lined with anguish. Above him stood the sorcerer. The Scirathi's gold mask was wrought into the serene smile of death; his black robe sucked in the moonlight. The sorcerer's hand—the skin covered with a webwork of scars—stretched toward Jack's chest. Travis had felt the terrible effects of that spell once before. The sorcerer was stopping Jack's heart.

"No," Travis cried out. He didn't know what to do, only that he had to distract the sorcerer, that he had to break his spell. "Get away! It's me you want, not him!"

The sorcerer didn't move. His body was rigid, his arm stiff, as if his whole body—and not just the gold mask—were wrought of metal. Jack wasn't moving either. His eyes stared without blinking, his mouth hung open in a silent cry of pain.

"I said get away from him!" Travis lunged, grabbing for the sorcerer.

It was a queer sensation, like moving through thick syrup. The closer Travis's hand got to the sorcerer, the harder it was to move. He clenched his teeth, struggling, but when his right hand was an inch from the Scirathi's robe, he could move it no farther. At last, with a grunt, Travis pulled his hand back. It tingled fiercely, and for a moment the rune of runes shone on his palm.

Still neither Jack nor the sorcerer moved. Something was wrong. The Scirathi's black robe seemed to billow out behind him, as it would if he were in the act of striding swiftly across the room. Only he was standing still. And Jack was in a precarious position. There was no way he should be able to remain on his knees, not leaning back at the angle he was. He should have been falling.

Then Travis understood. Jack *was* falling. The sorcerer *was* striding across the room, hand outstretched, killing Jack. Only somehow the two of them had been frozen in the act.

Fresh fear replaced old. Travis circled around the two motionless figures, gazing at them from all angles. He tried to touch Jack, but it was just as impossible as trying to lay a hand on the sorcerer. Whatever had caused them to cease moving, it affected Travis if he got too close. Only what was it? Some spell cast by the Scirathi?

A spell, yes. But not one of blood sorcery.

On the bed lay an open book. Travis recognized it; it was the book Jack had given him to read. Travis picked up the book, careful not to turn the page. He scanned the lines in the dim light, forcing the words to arrange themselves in an order that made sense.

Only they didn't make sense. It was something about a runelord, and how he had fought a dragon alone in the Barrens. In the end, the runelord had realized it was impossible, that there was no way he could win the battle.

This wasn't helping; Travis needed to know how he *could* win an impossible battle. He started to put down the book—then halted as the last few lines on the page caught his eye.

> ... *and knowing he could not win, Handerul spoke the rune of time, and time was his to command, and he told it, 'Cease!' And it is said, if one could but discover the secret vale in which the two struggled long ago, he would discover the wizard Handerul and the dragon Grash still locked in mortal combat, just as they were a thousand—*

Travis dropped the book on the bed and turned around. Jack and the sorcerer still hadn't moved, as if they were caught in a moment of time.

And that was the message Jack had left for him. Jack was weak; he had known he couldn't win a battle, that the sorcerer was going to kill him. But he must have had just enough strength left to speak the rune of time, and he had left the book for Travis as a clue. That gave Travis a chance.

But how much of a chance? Once time started to move again, how long did he have before the sorcerer finished his spell and killed Jack? A second? Less? Travis had to find a way to get the sorcerer's attention, to draw it away from Jack. But what could do that?

Yes, of course.

Travis positioned himself next to Jack where the sorcerer would be sure to see him. He reached into his pocket, then lifted his hand, opening his fingers. The scarab crawled across his palm on slender gold legs. Even if the sorcerer had not intended to gain the jewel, he would not be able to resist its allure, not with it right here before him.

Now, Travis. Speak the rune of time.

Only what was it? He didn't know that rune.

Yes, you do. Jack was right—the knowledge is already in you. You just have to listen.

He heard the voices speaking in chorus: all of the runelords who had gone before Jack. As they spoke, he saw it burning against his brain as if outlined in blue fire: two triangles, one inverted above the other.

"Tel," Travis said.

And time flowed like a river undammed.

The sorcerer completed his step, coming to a halt before Jack. His black robe settled into place around him. Jack let out a strangled sound as he fell back onto the floor. The sorcerer's splayed fingers began to close into a fist.

Fear evaporated under the heat of anger. "Get away from him," Travis said in a hard voice.

The sorcerer's head snapped up. The serene expression of the gold mask didn't change, yet all the same Travis could sense confusion. There was no way the Scirathi could have known Jack's rune had stopped time. To the sorcerer, it would seem as if Travis had appeared out of thin air.

The scarab crept onto Travis's fingertips, and the sorcerer's mask tilted, his hand lowered. Yes, he had seen it.

Jack drew in a gasping breath. He rolled over, then crawled toward the corner of the room. "Travis!" he called hoarsely. "The mask..."

Jack's words were lost in a fit of coughing, but Travis understood. The mask was the key to the sorcerer's power; he had learned that much in Denver. The Scirathi glanced at Jack and hesitated. Travis could feel him making a decision. Then the sorcerer turned his gold visage toward Travis

Travis knew he had only a second. He opened his mouth to speak *Kel*, the rune of gold, knowing he could use it to fling the mask from the sorcerer's face.

He was too slow. The sorcerer raised a hand, and Travis's heart lurched in his chest. A pounding drummed in his head, and sparks swam in front of his eyes. He staggered.

The rune, Travis. Speak the rune. Now.

But he had no breath with which to make a sound. He could feel his heart slowing, each beat a labor more terrible than the last. He couldn't take his eyes off the smiling gold face before him.

Jack was shouting something. Something about blood. Or was it the chorus of voices in his mind that was speaking? It didn't matter. Travis couldn't hear anything over the noise in his ears. *Thud.* An eternity seemed to pass between each beat. *Thud.*

The scarab, Travis. You don't need to speak, just use the blood. It's your only hope.

The thunder of his heart was fading; he could hear the words now. But how could he use the scarab? It was so hard to think; he felt his mind shrinking inward.

Travis forced his eyes from the gold mask of the sorcerer. He gazed at his hand. The scarab was dipping its slender legs into a smear of blood on his palm. It seemed excited by the fluid and began moving quickly. Maybe he didn't have to know what to do; maybe the scarab did. Maybe that was its mystery.

Thud.

Movement was agony; all the same Travis turned over his hand. The scarab scuttled from his palm to the back of his hand. A line of blood still oozed from the cut just below his knuckles. The gold spider followed it eagerly until it reached the open wound.

Thud...

The sorcerer closed his fist, and the thudding of Travis's heart ceased. His vision dimmed, and he watched as if through a veil as the scarab extended a pair of gold chelicerae toward the wound on the back of his hand. Like a tiny ruby, a single drop of crimson fluid appeared between the spider's chelicerae.

The sorcerer hissed, and the invisible hand that gripped Travis's heart let go. He reeled back as the organ shuddered painfully into motion again. With a cry, the Scirathi snaked out a hand and snatched the scarab from him. In a single motion, the sorcerer tilted his head back, poised the jewel above the mouth slit of his mask, and crushed it.

Nothing came out.

Travis lifted his hand and stared. There had been one drop of blood left in the scarab; he had seen it. Where had the drop of blood gone?

Gold fire surged through his veins, and he knew the answer.

Travis's spine arched. He threw back his head and screamed. When the fires of Krondisar consumed him, he had known a pain more terrible than any he had ever endured in his life. However, this was worse than pain. He could feel it as a chain reaction in his blood. As one cell changed, it caused those next to it to undergo the same metamorphosis. It was like a cancer, only faster than wildfire, and it blazed through arms, his chest, his legs. Then the fire burned up into his brain. The world became a cauldron of molten gold. He fell to his knees, his hands twisted into claws before him.

The fire ceased. There was no fuel left to burn; the change was complete. Slowly, Travis unclenched his hands. Faint but visible, gold sparks swam just beneath his skin. Then they were gone.

What's happened to you, Travis?

But he knew. He had seen Xemeth undergo the same transformation in the Etherion. Only Xemeth's change had not been accompanied by agony; it had been nearly instantaneous. Then again, Xemeth had consumed three drops of the blood of Orú, and there was only one in Travis's veins.

"Now, Travis!" Jack shouted. "Stop him before he completes his spell!"

Travis jerked his head up. The sorcerer had retreated and cast down the crumpled remains of the empty scarab. He drew out a small knife and made a gash across his left arm. Dark blood oozed out. A chant emanated from behind the gold mask. The stream of blood on the Scirathi's arm vanished, as if evaporating. A spasm passed through him, but he kept mumbling dissonant words.

Now Travis saw it, forming on the air like a blob of shadow. The shadow twisted in upon itself, gaining strength and substance as it drank the sorcerer's blood. With a cry, the sorcerer thrust his hand out, and the shadow struck like a viper, uncoiling itself, heading straight toward Travis's throat.

A fierce smile sliced across Travis's face. If it was blood the shadow wanted, then he would give it some—blood far more powerful than the sorcerer's could ever be. He held up his wounded hand.

The shadow halted in mid-strike. It rippled, slithering through the air, and coiled itself around Travis's arm. A sick sensation filled him as he felt the shadow suckling at his wound. It pulsed along its length, growing larger, sleeker, and far stronger than it had been.

"Yes, that's it," Travis whispered. "Drink."

The sorcerer froze, staring with empty gold eyes—

—then turned to flee the room.

With a flick of his hand, Travis sent the shadow to do its task. The viper shot out and struck the sorcerer in the back like a black spear. Something gold went flying and clattered to the floor. The Scirathi screamed, arms flung wide, back arching, as the shadow passed through him. Then it was gone.

The sorcerer fell to the floor. There was no hole in his black robe where the shadow had struck him. All the same, he did not move.

"Well," said a hoarse but shockingly cheerful voice, "that was a remarkable display."

Jack crawled across the floor, retrieved something, then used the bureau to pull himself to his feet. His face was ashen, his blue eyes were bright.

"Jack," Travis croaked. Every joint and muscle in his body ached, as if he was recovering from a severe fever. "Jack, are you all right?"

"I was going to ask the same of you. You look as white as a sheet. I'm quite well now, thank you. Though if I hadn't managed to stop things with the rune of time, I wouldn't have been well at all. My heart felt ready to leap right out of my chest. That's quite a spell this fellow was able to cast."

Jack raised the object in his hands. It was the sorcerer's gold mask. He spun it around, then started to lift it. "I wonder if I might be able to—"

"Don't even try," Travis said.

Jack sighed, then tossed the mask back to the floor. "I suppose you're right. One brand of wizardry is quite enough for me." He raised an eyebrow. "Although I don't think you'll be able to say the same anymore."

Travis lifted his hand. The wound was closed now; only a faint white scar remained. All traces of blood were gone. Fear filled him. But there was another sensation as well, one even more disturbing. It was exhilaration.

Travis moved across the room to the crumpled black heap. With his boot, he flipped it over. A ruin of a face stared up at him, so covered with scar tissue it was barely recognizable as human. Only the eyes revealed that this had once been a man; they stared upward in empty supplication. Travis knelt, reached into the sorcerer's robe, and pulled out the gate artifact. He rose.

Jack stood next to him. "I suppose this means you'll be going soon." His voice was sad but resigned.

Travis smiled at his old friend. "Don't worry, Jack. I'll see you again."

"No, I'll see you again. In a century or so. But not the other way around, I fear."

Travis reached up and slipped off his wire-rimmed spectacles. He held them out. Both of the lenses were cracked; in all the chaos, he hadn't noticed. "I think I'd better give these to you. For safekeeping."

Jack took the spectacles, folded them up, and slipped them into the pocket of his waistcoat. "I'll give them to you when I see you again."

Travis shivered. How could you say good-bye to someone knowing you would never see him alive again? But sometimes you had to. "Thanks, Jack." He gripped Jack's right hand between both of his own and squeezed. "For everything."

Jack's smile was slightly befuddled, yet full of cheer all the same. "By the love of Isis and Osiris, of course, my boy. You're quite welcome. Now, don't you think we should go find the others and see how they're doing? I imagine they've all had quite a fright. We should fetch them and have a cup of tea before you go."

PART FIVE
THE BLACK TOWER

64.

Travis had always heard it said that time was like a river: a great flood flowing inexorably to its destination and atop whose currents one could only drift. But to Travis, time was more like a hall with many rooms—chambers in which one dwelled for a while, either short or long, before opening the door and stepping through to see what was next.

They passed through many such doors and rooms—many such times—on the road to the Black Tower.

There was their time in Castle City, their last few hours there. It seemed odd that they should have to hurry. After all, if Jack was right about what they would find at the Tower of the Runebreakers, then they had all the time in the world. There was no reason they couldn't stay at the boardinghouse with Maudie and Tanner, at least for a little while. No reason except the dark circles beneath Sareth's eyes, the shadows in the hollows of his cheeks, the rasping cadence of his breathing.

"We have to go now," Lirith said, pulling Travis into the dining room, her face drawn, exhausted. The others were gathered in the parlor where Sareth lay unconscious on the sofa. "I can't hold on to his thread much longer."

"But traveling through the Void again—won't it make him worse?"

She shook her head. "The damage has already been done. On Eldh, I believe I can bind his thread. But not here."

It didn't take long to get ready. They gathered their scant possessions, and Travis set the gate artifact in the center of the parlor floor. The onyx tetrahedron absorbed the light, but Travis knew what it really wanted. Blood.

"What is all this?" Maudie said, her voice edging into panic. "What's going on?"

Tanner gripped her hand. "I'll try to explain it later, Maude."

"I believe I can help you in that regard," Jack said.

Maudie shook her head; she was calmer now. "No, I think

I understand." She looked at Travis, Lirith, and Durge. "You're going somewhere, aren't you?"

Travis nodded. "To another world."

Her green eyes were startled for only a moment. Then she pressed her hand to her chest. "I suppose I'll be traveling soon, too. To another world."

They made their farewells swiftly, as if that somehow made the pain less. Travis shook Tanner's hand. What could he possibly say to express what he felt? He settled for saying, "Thank you, Sheriff, for everything."

"You're welcome, Mr. Wilder. But Miss Lily is right. It's Mr. Tanner now." He cast a glance at Maudie, who was giving Lirith a fierce hug. "I sent to the governor for a new sheriff over a week ago. When he comes in a few days, I'll turn in my badge."

"But what will you do?"

Tanner shrugged. "Mr. Manypenny's always said he has a job waiting for me, so I suppose I'll take him up on that. And I need some time to follow Miss Lily's instructions and get myself off the laudanum. But mostly, I want to spend it with Maude. The time she has left."

Travis glanced at Maudie. She was hugging Durge now, holding on as if for dear life, but the stoic knight didn't resist. "I'm glad," Travis said.

It was midnight. Durge and Travis laid Sareth on the carpet next to the gate, and Lirith knelt beside him. Travis removed the triangular top of the artifact, exposing the reservoir within. Travis took the Malachorian stiletto and made a small cut on his left arm. A red line of blood flowed, dripping into the artifact, filling the reservoir.

Travis replaced the onyx triangle atop the artifact. For a second he feared nothing would happen. After all, only a single drop of blood from the god-king Orú had entered his veins. Then the gate crackled into being: a dark oval rimmed by blue fire. The last thing Travis heard was Jack's voice saying, "By Jove, what a grand adventure this will be!"

And it was like a door opening and shutting, taking them from one room to the next.

After that came their time in Tarras. It was a slow, quiet

time, warmed by a gentle southern sun, redolent with the scents of spices, oranges, and the sea. A healing time.

For a month, they rented a small white house in the bustling fourth circle of Tarras. It had been both Durge's and Lirith's idea to come to the city. Durge had reasoned Tarras would have changed less in a hundred years compared to the Dominions, and thus the four had a better chance of reaching their destination intact if they visualized the ancient city when they stepped through the gate. Lirith's reason was different but no less compelling: In Tarras, of all places, she knew she could find the herbs and medicines she needed.

The first three days were the worst. Sareth drifted in and out of consciousness, his body shaking and drenched with sweat, as Lirith worked over him without rest. She sent Durge and Travis on many errands to fetch herbs, spices, and oils. Her medicines had an effect, reducing his fever and the severity of his spasms. All the same, it seemed her work would be for nothing. The shadows in his cheeks deepened; dark lines snaked up from the stump of his leg, spreading across his body.

Then, on the third night, as a full moon rose over the sea, a knock came at the door. Durge opened it, and three women in green robes drifted in. Travis knew at once they were witches. Hadn't Lirith once said she had found a coven in Tarras? But they were strange and secret, not like the witches of the north. All the same, they were there.

The three women said nothing. Or at least, nothing that Travis or Durge could hear. However, Lirith stood quickly, her dark eyes locked on the witches. The three women joined hands with Lirith, forming a circle around Sareth. They shut their eyes, and it seemed nothing happened as, for an hour, they stood without moving.

Then Sareth sat up, his eyes open and clear.

Without spoken words, the three women in green turned and moved through the door, into the night. Lirith was on her knees, her arms around Sareth, sobbing.

"Beshala," he said softly, resting his head on hers. "I'm here, *beshala*. I'll never leave you again."

She pulled away, gazing at him with frightened eyes. "And won't you, Sareth?"

"No," he said. And again, "No."

A gasp escaped her. The moment was too private, too sharp with fresh pain. Travis and Durge retreated into the other room, shutting the door behind them.

After that, Sareth's strength returned a little more each day. In a week he was making music on a reed flute he had fashioned for himself. In two weeks he was moving about the house on the new wooden leg Durge had carved for him, and in three he took his first steps outside. Color returned to his coppery cheeks. He laughed often, especially when Lirith was in view.

Their love was clear, in his smile, in her eyes. All the same, Travis sensed something holding them back from one another. Their touches were tender, but tentative, fleeting. Travis didn't know the reason, and nor was it his place to ask.

Sareth was not the only one who recovered as the weeks went past. All of them had been weak and exhausted after their ordeal in Castle City. However, the wound in Durge's side healed under Lirith's ministrations, and Lirith herself seemed to bloom like a flower under the warm Tarrasian sun.

Travis's own wounds, received in the gunfight, had been healed when he turned the spell of blood magic against the sorcerer—although he couldn't stop using his tongue to probe the empty socket of his missing molar. As for the cut he had made on his arm, it had closed after passing through the gate. Sometimes he ran a finger over the pale scar. How many more would mark his body in the coming years? Would he one day be forced to use a mask to hide the ruin of his face?

Troubling as those thoughts were, he didn't dwell on them. The fact was, despite the alien blood running in his veins, he felt good. Not powerful or strange or terrible. Just good. The voices of the runelords in his mind were quiet, and even Tanner's knowledge of gunfighting—which Lirith had granted him—had faded away as the spell unraveled. He was Travis: nothing more and nothing less.

Their only real worry was money. There was the rent to pay, and food, and soon they would need to buy horses and supplies for a long journey. They had some gold dollars from Castle City they were able to spend. Lirith made simples and potions and sold them to the neighbors, and both Durge and Travis hired themselves out for day labor. In the end, however, Travis was forced to sell some of his things. He couldn't bear to part with the Malachorian stiletto. However, he sold the mistcloak Falken had given him to a merchant, and he sold Jack's hand-written book to a curious scholar at the University of Tarras.

"My research is specialized in pagan mythology of the north," the scholar said, eyes eager. "It's quite fascinating in its crudeness and barbarism, wouldn't you agree?"

Travis only gave a tight smile. He hated selling the book. That last night in Castle City, Jack had told him to keep it as a memento, and it was the only copy Jack had made. However, the scholar had offered a huge sum of gold for it, and he had promised to donate the book to the university library when he was finished with it, which made Travis feel a bit better.

Finally, when the moon was full again, it was time to pass through another door; it was time to journey north.

Traveling was easy at first. They followed the Queen's Way north, staying at the clean, if austere, Tarrasian hostels that were spaced precisely a day's ride apart. Things grew rougher when they reached Gendarra and the other Free Cities, and rougher yet as they traveled into the Dominions.

"Calavan and the other Dominions are going to get considerably more civilized over the next century or so, aren't they?" Travis said, as they rode past the umpteenth band of ragged peasants laboring outside a cluster of daub-and-wattle huts.

"Fortunately," Durge said, his nose wrinkling at the stench.

"Of course, some Dominions will always remain a step ahead of others," Lirith said brightly.

Durge cast her a sharp look, and Sareth laughed. "Be careful, *beshala*. You meant to number Embarr among the more civilized Dominions, didn't you?"

"But of course," she said.

In the Dominions there were no hostels, and inns were few and far between. Occasionally they stayed in the manor of some local lord, but increasingly they found themselves camping out. Travis didn't mind. It was late summer, and while the days were gold and warm, the nights were cool and bright with stars. He would watch them wheel slowly in the heavens until sleep came.

Days passed, and weeks, as they rode across the rolling terrain of Calavan and Brelegond. Then, on the first day of Revendath, in a year none of them could number, they reached the edge of the Dominions. To the north was the rocky line of the Fal Sinfath, the Gloaming Fells. Travis knew the Black Tower lay at the western tip of that range.

"We'll be riding through wild and empty lands from now on," Durge said. "I believe we should hire guides who know this corner of the world."

However, they were in a dirty village on the far western marches of Brelegond, and the only scouts they found for hire were two sons of a freeman farmer. They were stocky men with rough hands and dull eyes. Travis didn't miss the look the father gave the sons when he accepted a handful of gold from Durge and told the two young men to guide the travelers where they wished.

The brothers did seem to know the wilderness well. They led the riders through dense forests and over moors, avoiding bogs and deep gorges, always picking out a navigable path, always keeping the mountains to the right.

The murder attempt came on the fifth night. By the stars it was well after midnight when Travis woke to see a shadow above him. Moonlight glinted off the pale edge of a knife.

Speak a rune, Travis, he told himself. But did he dare? What would it be like to work rune magic with the blood of sorcery running in his veins?

"Step away from him," Durge rumbled.

The young man scrambled to his feet. Durge stood five paces away, legs apart, his greatsword—which he had kept concealed in a blanket these last days—naked in his hands, all four feet of its blade gleaming in the silver light. The knight's eyes were merciless pits of shadow.

"Now begone with you, lest you suffer my wrath."

The farmer's son stared as if he had seen some fabled monster emerge from the depths of the woods. He dropped his knife and ran, his wail rising in the air. His brother, who had been bending over Sareth, did the same. After a minute, their cries faded into silence.

"Do you think they'll come back?" Sareth asked.

Durge snorted as he sheathed his sword. "Would you?"

"Now that you mention it," Sareth said, "no."

Just to be safe, they kept watch all night, but they saw no trace of their two scouts. At last dawn drew near.

"I don't blame you for chasing away our guides, Durge," Lirith said as she stirred the coals of the campfire and nestled the *maddok* pot among them. "But do you think we'll be able to find our way?"

Just then the sun lifted above the low downs that were the last remnants of the Fal Sinfath, and Travis saw the black finger of stone jutting into the sky.

"We already have," he said.

Another door, another room. Their journey was over. A new time had begun.

Unlike the Gray Tower of the Runespeakers, the Black Tower was not carved from the hill it stood on. Rather, it was built of a stone that seemed alien to this region. It was nothing like the gray rock of the Fal Erenn, but was greenish black and had an oily feel to it. The spire rose over a hundred feet to a horned summit, its walls without windows.

A single door was set into the base of the tower. Though made of iron, the door was untouched by rust. To Travis's surprise, there were no runes carved on the door. It was featureless, save for a small keyhole in the center.

"I suppose we've journeyed all this way for nothing," Durge said. "Unless Lord Graystone happened to give you a key?"

Travis shook his head. But it didn't matter; somehow he didn't think he'd need one, that this place would know him. He pressed his hand against the door.

There was a deep, grinding sound. The door swung open. A puff of dry air struck their faces.

"Let's go in," Travis said.

In the time that came after, Travis was never certain how long they spent in the tower. Certainly days. Perhaps weeks. He was lost most of the time in study of the runestone.

They found it on their first day of exploration, floating in the topmost chamber of the tower: a three-sided pillar of black stone, its surface carved all over with runes. Travis had learned his lesson at the Gray Tower, and he never touched more than one or two runes at once, and always let the shimmer of magic fade before he touched another rune and listened to its name spoken in his mind.

While Travis spent most of his time in the highest chamber, the others preferred the lowest chamber, and they made their camp there. It was a vast space, no doubt used long ago for gatherings of all the Runebreakers. A staircase circled around the wall, rising without railing to the levels above. The lower perimeter of the chamber was lined with a colonnade that provided many alcoves and nooks, and it was in these where they stowed their supplies and made their beds.

With Durge's help in moving stones, Lirith set up a kitchen just outside the door of the tower, and Sareth fashioned clever chairs from willow switches so they could sit around the fire as they ate their supper. They had replenished their supplies in Brelegond, and Durge was able to snare several rabbits. All the same, although no one spoke of it, they all knew their food would not hold out forever.

However, although they scoured the tower, they found little in its many chambers besides the runestone itself. Travis didn't know how long ago the Runebreakers had vanished, but certainly by the dust and cobwebs the tower had been abandoned for more than a century. Only where had they gone? The Runebinders had destroyed themselves with the folly of their pride, but that didn't seem the case there. The tower was bare, as if the Runebreakers had taken everything with them when they left. That didn't suggest a hasty or violent departure.

The runestone itself held no answer to that mystery; it had been forged long before, in the time of Malachor. All the same, Travis learned much by studying it, and the knowledge he gained thrilled him as much as it terrified him. No wonder the Witches feared the one called Runebreaker. Without doubt, from what Travis read, the Runebreakers were by far the most powerful of the three orders of runic magic.

Yet they didn't use that power to gain command of the Dominions, Travis. They could have brought down a castle with a single rune. They could have broken apart all of the water molecules in a lake, turning it to hydrogen and oxygen, and set-

*ting off a devastating explosion with a single spark. It's just like
Jack said. They could have broken the sky itself.*

Only they didn't find the rune of sky. Or any other bound
runes anywhere in the tower, including the rune of time. They
searched every chamber again and again. Durge and Sareth ran
their hands over every wall, searching for secret niches. Lirith
tried to use the power of the Weirding to search with her mind.
And Travis dared to whisper the rune *Sar*, calling on the very
stones of the tower itself to help him.

It was no use. "It's not here," Travis said, as they gathered
around the campfire, eating the very last of their food. He
gazed at Durge, Lirith, and Sareth, meeting their grim eyes.
"We have to face it, we're not going to find it."

"Well," Lirith said briskly, "it was worth a try. Perhaps this
century won't be so terrible to live in."

Sareth squeezed her hand. "It won't be as long as you're in
it, *beshala*."

"But we do not all have to stay here, do we?" Durge said, his
voice low, his brown eyes thoughtful. There was something in
his hands; startled, Travis realized it was his silver deputy's
badge. "Did not Sir Tanner say Castle City was in need of a
new sheriff? And did not Lord Graystone say Sinfathisar could
send one across worlds?" He looked up and met Travis's gaze.

Fear gripped Travis's heart, and it wasn't just the thought of
Durge being a world away. The knight didn't know what he was
asking. Travis opened his mouth to explain that he couldn't do
it, that he didn't dare use the Stone. Not now, after the blood of
the scarab had entered his veins.

However, before he could speak, the sharp sound of a stick
breaking echoed off the wall of the tower, and they all turned to
see a man walking toward their fire. So shocked were they all to
see another human being in those wilds that they simply stared
as he drew near.

He was short and muscular of build, and for a moment
Travis thought it might be one of the two farmer's sons, come
back to try to rob them again. Then the other drew closer. He
was a young man with a homely, cheerful face, his nose broad
and crooked, his lips rubbery. He wore a simple brown robe,

and there was something in his hands. It was hard to see what it was in the failing light.

Travis rose to his feet as the young man halted a few feet away. *This was impossible; there was no way he could be here. The last time Travis had seen him had been at the Gray Tower, over a hundred leagues and a hundred years from this place, this time. All the same, here he was.*

"Sky?" Travis said.

The young man smiled, a grin that revealed the dark stump of his missing tongue. He held out the object he had been carrying. It was a disk of creamy white stone, and on it was engraved a symbol: two triangles, one inverted over the other.

65.

They spoke late into the night—although *speaking* wasn't exactly the word for it. Eloquent as they were, it seemed impossible Sky's gestures could carry so much meaning as they did. But that wasn't the only thing that seemed impossible about Sky. The young man looked just the same as when Travis had encountered him—would encounter him?—at the Gray Tower of the Runespeakers more than a hundred years later.

"Who are you, Sky?" Travis said as darkness closed around the circle of their campfire.

Sky made a motion as if striking an object with a hammer. *I am a servant, a tool, that's all.*

Durge glowered at him. "A servant? For whom? An enemy of ours, I suppose."

Sky shook his head fiercely. With a stick, he drew a pair of symbols in the dirt next to the fire.

"Do you know what those mean?" Sareth said, glancing at Travis.

Travis studied the two symbols, then pointed to the one on the left. "I know that one. I learned it from Rin and Jemis. It's the rune for Olrig One-Eye. He was one of the Old Gods, the most loyal to the Worldsmith. But I'm not sure what the other symbol means. It—"

Voices spoke in his mind. He knew the rune after all; he had only to listen.

"It's the rune for Sia."

Lirith gasped. "A rune for Sia? But that's impossible."

However, Sky was nodding and smiling.

"So you serve both of them?" Durge said with a skeptical look.

Sky held a finger to his chest. *I serve but one.*

They talked until a horned moon rose behind the tower, but all of Sky's answers were similarly frustrating.

"But how did you find us?" Travis said for what must have been the dozenth time. "And why?"

However, Sky only yawned and laid his cheek against his hands. *It is time to lie down.*

It was long before sleep came to Travis. He lay in the dark, tracing his fingers over the smooth white disk. With this, they had all the time in the world. So why did it feel like time was running out?

The next morning, after they drank a cup of *maddok*, Sky led them to the topmost chamber of the tower. Sunlight fell through a small window just below the high, domed ceiling.

"What is it, Sky?" Travis said. "Are we supposed to do something with the runestone?" It was the only thing they had ever found in that room.

The young man shook his head. He pointed to the rune of time in Travis's hands, pointed up, then made a breaking motion.

"What's he saying?" Sareth asked.

Travis was completely bewildered. "I don't know."

"I think I do," Lirith said. She touched Sky's shoulder. "You want us to go atop the tower, don't you? That's where Travis should break the rune."

"But there's no way we can get up there, my lady," Durge said, craning his neck. "It must be three fathoms to that opening. And there are no stairs."

A jolt passed through Travis. It felt like . . . possibility. "Let me work on that."

He pressed a hand against the wall and closed his eyes. *"Sar,"* he whispered. The stones obeyed. There was a rumbling, followed by a grating noise. As the sound faded, Travis heard gasps. He opened his eyes.

Blocks of stone jutted out from the walls of the tower, forming a rough staircase that spiraled up the walls, leading to the small window.

Travis smiled at Durge and gestured to the stairs. "After you, my lord."

The knight's brown eyes were startled. However, he took a deep breath and started up the stone steps. The others followed. The window was just large enough for them to pass through, and beyond was a narrow ledge that led to an even narrower staircase which clung precariously to the side of the tower; so they were not the first to come that way.

They made their way to the top of the stairs and found themselves on the edge of a broad circle of stone. Ringing the circle were four tapered onyx pillars: the horns they had seen from below. A larger pillar, shaped like an obelisk, stood in the center of the circle. Above was only blue sky.

They fanned out across the circle, exploring. The stone beneath their feet was carved with shapes and symbols. Large concentric rings spread out from the central pillar, and lines radiated toward the four outer pillars. Travis found it curious that the pillars were not spaced evenly around the perimeter of the circle. Two stood closer together on the east, while two stood to the west. He stopped by the central obelisk, arms crossed, thinking. Why did he have the feeling that the place was familiar?

"It's a clock!" Durge said excitedly.

So that was why it had seemed familiar. *It's like Stonehenge, Travis, or other stone circles. Remember that show you and Max saw on the Wonder Channel? Didn't shadows from some of the stones reach the center of the circle on certain days of the year?*

Yes, and as they examined the circle atop the tower more closely, that was certainly its purpose.

"Durge," Lirith said, touching the knight's arm, "you have studied the motions of the heavens, haven't you?"

The knight nodded. "Certain alchemical procedures can only be performed when the alignments of the sun, moon, and stars are auspicious." He paced around the circle. "If I have gotten my bearings correctly, at sunset on Midsummer's Day, this stone will cast a shadow that touches the central obelisk." He pointed to the northwestern pillar. "And this stone"—he pointed to the next closest pillar—"will cast its shadow toward the center at sunset on the Feast of Fallowing."

"I see now," Sareth said. He stood between the two eastern pillars. "These stones will cast their shadows toward the center at dawn, one on Quickening, the other on Midwinter's Day."

Fallowing, Quickening—those were the autumn and spring equinoxes, Travis knew. And Midsummer and Midwinter were the solstices. A thrill ran through him as he realized what this meant, but Lirith spoke the words first.

"We can use this to count, can't we?" She turned toward Travis. "We can count the passing years to make sure we return to our proper time."

Sky was nodding and smiling. Again he made the breaking motion with his hands.

There was no point waiting. They gathered on the north edge of the circle, standing close together. From there, Travis could see all four pillars, as well as the central stone. He gripped the rune of time in sweating hands. It was 1883 in the reckoning of Earth. All he had to do was count up to the year it was when he last left home. But how to get to the right day?

It was Durge, as usual, who had the solution. "It was late Revendath when we defeated the demon. Count to the next Fallowing, which would be a week later. That would prevent any chance of us . . ." The knight looked queasy.

"Of us overlapping," Lirith finished, and Durge nodded.

Sareth grinned. "You do count better than you read, don't you, Travis?"

Travis swallowed hard. "Yes. And thank you for your utter lack of confidence."

Sky grinned and made a gesture. *Good luck, Master Wilder.* Then he started to move away.

"Wait!" Travis said, his voice tight with panic. "Aren't you coming with us, Sky?"

The young man made another series of motions. *I have many things to do in the meantime. Do not worry—I'll be waiting for you when you return.*

Fear turned to wonder. Of course Sky couldn't go with them. There was the time he would spend at the Gray Tower. And who knew what else he had to do? The young man waved, then disappeared down the staircase, leaving the four alone atop the tower. Travis drew in a breath, then held the stone disk out before him.

Durge gave him a sharp look. "You do know what you're doing, don't you?"

"Not really," Travis said, and broke the rune.

It was easy. Terribly easy. He didn't even speak *Reth*, the rune of breaking, he simply thought it, and a crack shot through the stone disk in his hand, dividing it into two pieces with the sound of thunder. Light flickered around him like a strobe, alternating gold and black.

Count, Travis! By Olrig's Eye, you have to count!

The sound of Jack's voice snapped him out of his daze. Travis watched as the sun raced across the sky chased by the moon. Shadows reached out, fell back, then reached again. Stars spun in wild circles, faded to pale blue, then reappeared. The days flew by faster, and faster yet, one with every beating of his heart, until all he saw was the image of one day's sunset superimposed by that of the next day's. It was like a series of photographs, each taken a day apart just as the sun died in the west, and placed in order in a stack so that he could flip through them with a thumb.

Long shadows moved across the circle from north to south. Then it happened, so swift he almost missed it. The shadow of the westernmost pillar brushed the central stone. Fallowing. Then the shadows moved on.

Don't watch the other pillars, Travis. Keep your eyes on the western one. Each time its shadow touches the center, add another year to the count.

It was harder than he would have thought. The pace continued to increase. At first it seemed to take a minute for the shadow to swing into position again. Then half a minute. Then mere seconds.

Sometimes things went gray; there must have been clouds obscuring the sun as it set some days. However, Travis became familiar with the pattern and cadence of the motion; he could still tell when the equinox had passed, for the shadow of the western pillar swung north and south like a dark pendulum.

He was dimly aware of the others beside him. However, he couldn't turn to look at them. Were they being rained and snowed on? If someone ventured to the top of the tower, would they see four people standing there like pillars of stone themselves? He wasn't sure; somehow he didn't think so.

Travis kept counting. He was past ninety, and still the years came faster. One hundred. One hundred twenty. He kept his eyes wide; he didn't dare blink.

Now!

The shadow touched the central stone. In his hands, Travis shoved the halves of the disk together. Only he fumbled, almost dropping one, then recovered. The shadow started to swing past the central stone...

Be whole! Travis shouted in his mind.

The two halves of the rune united with a blue flash. The whirling dance of shadows ceased. Travis staggered and would have fallen but for Durge's strong grip on his shoulders.

Sareth took a step forward, his peg leg beating a staccato rhythm against the stone. "Did it work?"

It was nighttime. But what day? What year?

Durge gazed up at the starry sky, studying them. "From the position of the constellations, I would guess it is at least a month past Fallowing."

Travis brushed the rune in his hand; it was whole again. "I had a little trouble stopping things."

"I hope not too much," Sareth said. "What year do you suppose it is? Did we go far enough forward?"

"Yes," Lirith said, pointing. "Look."

They followed her gaze, then saw it. The star pulsed low to the southern horizon like a brilliant ruby.

"It's Tira's star," the witch said. "It appeared the summer before we left. So we must be in the right year."

Unless we went too far, Travis wanted to say, *and we're years beyond the time we left.* However, before he could speak, a gasp escaped them all.

The red star winked out of being.

"What happened?" Sareth said, rubbing his eyes. "We

weren't just imagining it, were we? Maybe it was wishful thinking. After all, we wanted to see something that would let us know this was the right year."

Durge gave the Mournish man a sour look. "I do not engage in wishful thinking. It was there."

"He's right," Travis said. "We did see Tira's star."

But only for a moment. Where had it gone? Before they could consider it further, they heard the sound of footsteps They turned and saw a figure approaching across the circle.

"Sky!" Travis said, filled with sudden relief.

The young man pushed back the hood of his brown robe and grinned. Sky looked just as he had before Travis broke the rune of time. More than a hundred years earlier.

Sky made a series of motions. *I've been waiting.*

Travis gave a sheepish smile. "Sorry. It's my fault we're a little late."

Sky's grin faded. He cast a worried glance over his shoulder, then looked back at Travis. *Perhaps you should have been later yet. Danger draws near.*

There was so much Travis wanted to ask. What had Sky been doing for the past century? However, it seemed that would have to wait. "What kind of danger?"

Sky made his hands into claws, a gesture that spoke more clearly than any words.

"I see shadows approaching," Durge said. The knight had moved to the edge of the circle and was peering into the darkness below. The others hurried beside him. "I cannot be sure in the gloom, but I think they are *feydrim*."

Travis's eyes worked just fine in the dark. "You're right. They are *feydrim*. There must be a hundred of them, and they're coming fast. By why are they here?"

A tap on Travis's shoulder. It was Sky. The young man made an intricate series of gestures.

I should have expected this. He knew you would be here, and now it seems the Pale King does as well.

"Who knew I would be here?"

Sky only kept gesturing. *I will take a message to Lady Grace. I can reach her ... swiftly. However, it will take her many weeks to journey to this place. It is best if you move forward to Midwinter's Day and meet her then.*

Travis struggled to comprehend these words. Why was Grace coming here?

"They're closing in on the tower," Durge said. Metal rang out as he drew his greatsword.

Lirith cast a frightened look at Sareth. "The tower door. Did we leave it open?"

The Mournish man met her eyes, then nodded.

Do not fear, Sky spoke with his hands. *I will lock the door as I go.*

"But you can't fight them yourself," Durge said.

I do not think I will need to. Once you leave, I believe they will as well. It is the Stone of Twilight they seek. Sky made a breaking motion with his hands. *Go now, Master Wilder. To Midwinter's Day.*

Then he turned and disappeared down the stairs. As he did, a shadow passed over them. They looked up to see a raven winging away into the gloom.

Lirith gazed at Travis with frightened eyes. "What do we do?"

"Exactly what Sky says." And once again Travis broke the rune of time.

He was ready this time. He kept his eyes on the pillar to the south and east, willing himself to see, not the succession of sunsets, but the succession of dawnings. He watched the shadow of the pillar stretch toward the center stone, growing closer with each flashing of light and dark.

Time. Travis shoved the two halves of the rune together, commanding them with his will to be whole. There was odd resistance this time, but he squeezed harder. Blue light welled through his fingers; two halves became one. The sun ceased its frantic race across the sky. Now it hung just above the western horizon, sinking slowly.

Durge stepped forward, gauging the position of the sun. "I believe you were a bit hasty this time, Travis. It is Midwinter's Eve. Tomorrow will be Midwinter's Day."

The knight's breath fogged on the air. Lirith was shivering, and Sareth wrapped his arms around her. It was clear and bitterly cold. They were dressed for autumn, not the depths of winter.

"I didn't want to overshoot the day this time," Travis said. "I might have stopped even earlier, except I had some trouble with the rune this time. Somehow it was hard to—"

The stone disk crumbled. White dust sifted from his cupped hands like snow.

Sareth let out a hot oath in the Mournish tongue. "What did you do to it?"

"I'm . . . I'm not sure." The frigid wind blew the last of the dust from Travis's hands. "I think maybe being bound and broken again was too much for it."

Lirith shook her head. "It doesn't matter. We won't need the rune of time again. Sky said this is where—this is *when*—we need to be."

Speaking of Sky, where was he? Travis expected to see the young man striding toward them, but there was no sign of him anywhere.

"Travis," Durge called out, "you had better come look at this."

The knight was peering over the outer wall at the edge of the circle. They moved to him. Far below, the trees were bare, and the ground was covered with snow. It was easy to see the dark shapes slinking toward the tower from all directions.

Sareth looked up. "I thought Sky said they would leave."

"Maybe they're back." Travis thought of the shadow of the raven that had flown over the tower just before he broke the rune of time again. "Maybe they knew again to expect us. To expect me." He felt the hardness of the Stone in his pocket.

The sun sank lower. Red light stained the snow like blood.

"The door," Lirith said. "Do you think Sky locked it as he said?"

The four stared at each other. Then they were running for the stairs.

They reached the narrow window and slipped through. The steps Travis had conjured with the rune of stone were still there. They picked their way down, reaching the chamber that held the runestone, and ran to the top of the tower's main staircase. Durge held up a hand; they needed to be cautious.

They descended the staircase slowly. Halfway down, they heard the sounds of fighting drifting up from below. There was a crash. Something let out a shrill, animal cry. Then came another cry of pain, only this one was human. A man.

"Sky," Travis said, casting a startled look at the others.

They quickened their pace. Durge went first, followed by Travis, then Sareth and Lirith. They passed through an archway and stepped onto a landing. Below was the large chamber at the base of the tower.

Sky stood at the foot of the stairs, using his bare hands to fend off at least five *feydrim*. The creatures paced before him, spitting and snarling, talons scraping against the stone floor. Sky managed to keep just out of their reach. However, he was limping. There was a rip in his robe, the ragged edges dark with blood.

Two more *feydrim* scuttled toward the young man. Where were they coming from? The iron door of the tower was shut. It seemed the creatures had emerged from the shadow of one of the alcoves that lined the chamber. The two *feydrim* loped toward Sky from the left. He couldn't see them coming.

"Sky!" Travis shouted, his voice echoing.

The young man turned, saw the creatures, and thrust out with both hands. The *feydrim* flew backward, squealing. One of them sprawled to the floor and did not get up. The other shook its head, then started forward again, but more slowly.

"We must help him," Durge said. He gripped his sword and started down the stairs. After a stunned second Travis followed. However, as they began their descent, another figure stepped from the shadow of one of the alcoves.

It was not a *feydrim*, but a man clad from head to toe in a black robe. He walked straight toward Sky, swiftly, with purpose. In his hand was a slender dagger. The *feydrim* saw the man and fell back whimpering. Sky turned just as the man in black raised the dagger.

"Sky!" Travis shouted again.

The young man looked up at Travis. It almost seemed he was smiling.

The dagger descended, its blade piercing Sky's robe and sinking deep into the center of his chest. The young man's eyes went wide. His hands fluttered to the hilt of the dagger, then fell to his sides.

Travis crashed into Durge's shoulder; the knight had stopped on the staircase.

"No!" Travis screamed.

The five remaining *feydrim* were already bounding up the stairs. Below, the man in the black robe pulled the dagger from Sky's chest. There was a burst of blue light. When it faded, Sky was gone. Something clanged, stone on stone, and Sky's empty robe fluttered to the floor. The man in black knelt, groping at the heap of brown cloth with his hands.

"Travis, Durge!" Lirith shouted behind them.

Travis jerked his gaze away from the man in the black robe. The *feydrim* raced up the stairs. Ten steps away. Five.

"Be ready!" Durge gritted between his teeth, holding his greatsword before him.

Travis pulled the Malachorian stiletto from his belt. The ruby in the hilt blazed wildly. The *feydrim* bared curving fangs; hunger and pain shone in their yellow eyes.

And with a sound like a cannon, the iron door burst open below, and light poured into the tower in a silver flood.

66.

To Grace, the journey was like a dream.

Time moved strangely, for one thing, just as it did when she was dreaming. One moment she might be standing at the prow of the white ship, watching the sun rise. Then, in the space between two blinks of an eye, the sun was gone, and a horned moon sailed in the black ocean of the sky. At times the stars wheeled dizzily around the invisible axis of the heavens, and at others the sun hung just above the horizon for what seemed hours and hours, turning the sea to molten copper.

Certainly the Little People who piloted the ship were like beings from a dream. It was almost impossible to catch sight of them directly. They were seen best from the corner of the eye, and if Grace quickly turned her head to gaze at one of them, all she saw was a silver shimmer on the air, then nothing at all.

There were a few times when they caught clearer glimpses of the ship's crew. Once she stood with Beltan near the stern, watching in the light of the full moon as a circle of goat-men pranced around a trio of slender women with twigs for fingers and leaf-tangled hair. When the shaggy goat-men closed the circle around the tree-women, Grace was forced to turn away, her cheeks hot. However, Beltan only laughed, his eyes merry as he watched a dance of a different sort.

There were a few other encounters. Once, when Grace was alone, the withered little creature with the mossy hair came to her again and touched her hand. Before it left, it looked at her with eyes like black stones in its knobby face, and it seemed to Grace a look of sorrow, and of hope.

Another time, a greenman—short and stocky, his beard grown of oak leaves and his eyes brown as acorns—brought a wooden cup to Falken on a day the bard was not feeling well, and the liquid within, though it seemed to be only water, brought color back to his cheeks. On several more occasions, the greenman brought a similar cup for Vani to drink.

The *T'gol* appeared to be sick often. More than once, from a distance, Grace saw Vani leaning over the ship's rail. Her skin often bore a greenish tint, and much of the time she walked with her hand pressed to her stomach and her shoulders hunched. Grace supposed the *T'gol* was seasick. Although the draughts brought by the greenman always seemed to restore her.

The sea through which they sailed was dreamlike as well. They passed floating islands of blue-green ice the elements had wrought into fantastic shapes that looked like castles and domed palaces, glittering in the sunlight. Then the ship veered southward, and the shore that appeared to port was more nightmare than dream.

Sheer black cliffs jutted three hundred feet out of the ocean, and the sea roiled and foamed about their base, as if cut upon the sharp rocks. From time to time, atop the cliffs, Grace saw jutting fingers of black stone. She assumed they were some kind of natural formation. Then she saw the yellow smoke pouring from the top of one of the spires.

"Watchtowers," Falken said behind her. "And foundries."

It was warm on the ship, but all the same she felt suddenly cold. "What land is that, Falken?"

"It's Imbrifale." The bard's blue eyes were grim. "The Pale King's Dominion."

After that she kept her gaze to the east and north, until finally they left the jagged coast behind.

Although it was always the same balmy temperature aboard the ship, Grace was sure the sea was growing warmer. They saw no more icebergs, and birds circled above the dense forest that lined the coast. All the same, she sensed winter had cast its spell over the land. Once the ship sailed close to the shore, and she could see that the forest was green because its trees were coniferous—spruce and pine. Often they were white as well, dusted with snow. However, no matter how close the ship sailed to land, she saw no keeps, no farms. It was a wild land.

Twice more as they journeyed, she spoke with Aryn over the web of the Weirding, marveling at the way the young baroness was able to reach across the leagues. Grace listened, fascinated, as Aryn described all that had happened to her since their parting—and all that she had learned. Grace knew she would have to tell Falken the knowledge Aryn had gained from Ivalaine's missive. But not just yet. After seven centuries of care and worry, the bard deserved a little peace.

As time went on, the travelers spoke less and less with one another. It was not due to weariness or strain; there simply seemed no need for conversation, as if the quiet conveyed their feelings with more clarity than words ever could. Sometimes Grace would sit with Falken and take his silver hand—warm and smooth—while they watched the forest slip by. At others she walked in silence with Vani, or rested on the deck with her head upon Beltan's chest. They never really slept anymore; they felt no weariness, although at times it was good to lie down and be still.

Often Grace saw Beltan and Vani together. It seemed their enmity for one another had been left behind in Toringarth. Now Grace saw something new blossoming between them. It was not romantic in nature. That was impossible; both loved Travis Wilder with all their souls. Still, there was a fondness between them, even a tenderness. What had caused this change of heart? Had the strange air of the ship had something to do with it? It was a mystery to Grace, but she was glad all the same.

Like speaking and sleeping, eating was something that was unnecessary. They drank the cool liquid the Little People left on the table at odd times, and that was more than enough to sustain them. Yet as strange as all of that was, there was another reason the journey seemed like a dream to Grace. The reason lay on the table in the center of the deck, cool and gleaming, and always eager for her touch. Fellring.

This must be a dream, Grace. It has to be. You can't be a queen, and this can't be your sword.

Only she was, and so was it.

Sometimes she dared to pick it up, and it seemed to hum in her hands. At some point its hilt had been fitted with a grip of polished wood—another gift of the Little People. The wood was pale and hard, but light; Falken said it was *valsindar*. The grip fit her hand perfectly, and the blade was so skillfully balanced it seemed to swing itself.

Each time she picked up the sword, questions filled her. What did the runes carved on it mean? Was she truly strong enough to wield it? And how—why—had Sindar sacrificed himself in order to forge it again?

"He knew, Grace," Beltan said one evening as stars appeared in the purple sky. He had been teaching her how to wield the sword again, and she was getting better.

She lowered the blade and looked at him. "Who knew?"

"Sindar. He knew that sometimes love means giving up everything you are."

Grace's knuckles went white around the hilt. No, it was too much. "Was this sword really worth a life, Beltan?"

"Drive it into the Pale King's heart, Grace. Keep his army from marching across the Dominions. Stop him from finding the Great Stones and giving them to Mohg. Then ask yourself that same question."

Beltan turned and left her then, and it was only as she watched his broad back fading in the twilight that she wondered if his words had really been meant for her. What if they had been meant for himself?

Sometimes love means giving up everything you are. . . .

"No, Beltan," she whispered. "Don't give yourself up. Not for anything. Not for anyone."

But her words were too quiet to be heard.

The ship sailed on into the east, until one day they reached a silver ocean. The ship turned southward, skimming past a rocky shore where gigantic trees reached twisting branches toward the muted sky. They came to the mouth of a great river, and on the north side of the broad estuary they saw a city.

The city was carved of white stone, and in its center rose a slender spire as silver as the ocean. At first they gazed at the city in wonder. Then the wind picked up, and a banner unfurled itself atop the tower. The banner was red as blood.

"Eversea," Falken murmured, his voice thick with sorrow.

Grace put a hand on the bard's shoulder. It was there those who fled the fall of Malachor had come, to the tower raised by King Merandon centuries before with the help of fairies. They had built a shining city, one to honor the spirit and memory of the kingdom which they had been forced to flee.

Then the runelord Kelephon had come, like a snake in a garden, and paradise had rotted from within.

For a time they held their breath, fearing dark ships would sail from the city and race after them, crimson sails full to the wind. However, the white ship passed into a bank of mist, and by the time the fog cleared they had sailed far up the great river, and the city was lost to sight.

Falken was certain the river was the Farwander, whose headwaters lay hundreds of leagues to the east, near Kelcior in the Fal Erenn. At first the river was so broad Grace could barely see the shores to either side of the ship. However, as the days and leagues slipped past, the banks drew closer and closer.

At last, on a snowy day, they came to a confluence where a river from the south poured its rushing waters into the Farwander. The ship turned and sailed up this river.

"It's the Silverflood," Falken said, as the ship navigated upriver, propelled by no means they could discern. "To the east lies Eredane."

The Silverflood was narrow and rougher than the Farwander, but still navigable by the fleet little ship. On the right bank of the river was a broad plain and, in the distance, the dark line of a forest that drew a bit nearer to the water each day. To the east they saw cities and castles. All were bleak, stained with soot and mantled by clouds of acrid smoke.

"By Vathris, Eredane was never like this," Beltan said, as they watched one of the dreary cities go by. "What's happened to this Dominion?"

However, their question was answered when they saw the long procession of people in black robes snaking its way toward the city. Grace could hear the chant rising on the air, but they were too far away to make out the words. However, she knew them all the same; in Omberfell she had heard a similar procession intoning the prayer to the Raven.

From time to time they saw more such processions. Where they were going and what their purpose was, Grace wasn't sure, but it seemed most of the people of the Dominion were taking part in the pilgrimage, for the ship constantly passed abandoned dwellings and farms where the crops had been left to wither in the fields. They glimpsed several bands of men in black armor riding along the road that followed the east bank of the river. It seemed Kelephon's knights were still in command of Eredane.

Sometimes Grace feared that the knights would raise up a hue and cry as the white ship sailed past. However, if the knights saw the ship, they showed no sign of it.

At last, thankfully, they left Eredane behind. The western forest drew close to the river, which became narrower yet, filled with jutting rocks and frothing rapids around which the white ship nimbly maneuvered. Then, small as the ship was, it could go no farther.

It stopped at a place where three small rivers joined, becoming the Silverflood. None was large enough for the ship to sail into. Instead, it drifted to the western bank. Dim forms scurried in the failing daylight, and the white plank reached to the shore.

Falken shouldered his lute. "We go on foot from here."

Grace picked up Fellring, and Vani and Beltan took packs of foodstuffs that had appeared when they weren't looking. Then they left the ship behind.

They tramped south on foot, keeping to the narrow strip of land between river and wood. It was not bitter as in Toringarth, but the air was damp and chilly, and a dusting of snow seemed to fall almost constantly. However, the clothes they had bought in Galspeth served well to keep out the wind, and walking kept them warm, as did the clear draughts of fairy wine they stopped to drink from time to time.

That first evening, as they camped in the shelter of the trees, they saw silver lights winking in the forest.

"We're not alone," Beltan said.

Vani peered into the night with gold eyes. "I've been watching them. They've been following us ever since we left the ship, keeping to the shadows."

But why? They had borne Grace to Toringarth. What more did they want?

"I think they want to make sure you reach your destination, Grace," Falken said in answer to her unspoken question. "This journey isn't over yet. And I think something's going to happen at the end of it. Something important."

Grace wondered what it could be. She polished Fellring with a cloth just to be ready.

Two days later, they reached the place where the tributary they had been following rushed out of a jumble of stones. Above rose a muted line of heather-gray mountains. The Fal Sinfath, Falken told them. They were almost there. By day they followed the line of low peaks south and east, keeping the mountains always to their left. At dusk, sparks of light danced in the forest to their right.

"What day do you suppose it is?" Beltan said as they gathered around the campfire that night.

His question completely startled Grace. Time had passed so fleetingly she had forgotten about it altogether. But time was important, wasn't it?

"It's hard to be sure," Falken said. "But I've been doing my best to count the days as we journeyed." He showed them a stick on which he had made a series of marks. "And I've been watching the stars, too. I'm fairly certain it will be Midwinter in two days. Which means tomorrow is Midwinter's Eve."

Panic flooded Grace. She started to rise. "We can't sit here. We have to go! We have to—"

Vani gripped her arm, pulling her down. She pressed a finger to her lips.

"What is it?" Beltan said quietly.

Vani gazed around them. "Do you see it?"

"I don't see anything but darkness," Falken whispered.

"Exactly."

The silvery sparks of light they had seen each night since leaving the ship were gone. The forest was dark and silent.

"Where are they?" Grace murmured, but no one had an answer for her.

Dawn came red as blood. The sky was clear, the air frigid, the ground blanketed with a hard crust of snow. None of them had slept; the darkness had seemed heavy, oppressive. All the same, they walked swiftly.

The day dragged on or flew by; Grace wasn't certain which. Beltan broke a path through the snow, and the others followed in his footprints. Each step Grace took was agonizingly slow. In contrast, the sun seemed to skip across the sky. Time. They needed more time.

The sun rose toward the zenith, then began its descent. There was not a breath of wind; the world was still. No birds sang, no animals scampered about.

"I don't like this," Beltan muttered more than once.

Vani vanished and reappeared like a shadow. Grace knew she was scouting ahead, but if the *T'gol* saw anything, she didn't say. The sun sank into the west, setting a bank of clouds afire. Fear rose in Grace's throat, verging on a scream. They had to hurry. She flung herself forward, trying to move faster, but her lungs burned, and the snow dragged at her feet.

Finally, exhausted and trembling, she lost her footing and went tumbling down a snowy slope. She heard Beltan's shout behind her, calling to her to dig her feet in to stop herself, but she couldn't do it, she was too tired. Rocks loomed beneath her. She was going to be dashed against them.

The slope leveled out; she skidded to a stop scant feet from the rocks.

Grace rose onto her knees. She was cold and wet, and her back ached, but the only thing that seemed to be damaged was her pride. Grunting with effort, using one of the rocks for support, she stood up.

And stared into hungry yellow eyes.

"Oh," Grace said.

She was so astonished she simply stared. The *feydrim* bared yellow fangs. A fetid reek washed over Grace. More spidery gray forms slunk across the rocks. The creature was not alone.

She thought she heard shouts behind her, coming closer. But they were too far away; they would never reach her in time. A growl emanated from deep in the *feydrim*'s throat; the others picked up the call. They tensed, ready to spring.

The sound of chimes shimmered all around. The *feydrim* snarled, raising their snouts to sniff the air, searching. The crystalline music grew louder, clearer. The *feydrim* hissed. They began to recoil, to scramble back over the rocks.

Silver light blazed to life all around them. It was so bright Grace was forced to covered her eyes with her hands. Through her fingers, she saw queer shapes moving against the glare. There was a chorus of high-pitched squeals, cut suddenly short. The light dimmed, and Grace blinked, trying to clear her vision.

"Grace!" a voice said beside her. "Grace, are you all right?" A strong hand gripped her. Beltan.

"The creatures are gone," Vani said. "I believe those who have been following us took care of—"

The *T'gol*'s words fell short, then Grace heard a gasp.

"Look," came Falken's soft voice.

Grace rubbed at her eyes, wiping the tears away. Then she gasped as well. The line of trees at the top of the slope must have blocked their view. Not now. It rose above them on a low hill: a spire of black stone.

"We're here," Grace said, and the feeling of relief that filled her was so strong she thought she would weep.

"By the Blood of the Bull," Beltan swore. "Look at that!"

Relief vanished, replaced by new fear. Dark, sinuous shapes slunk rapidly up the slopes of the hill toward the Black Tower of the Runebreakers. There were dozens of them. Hundreds. The sun was almost gone; the snowy ground was red as blood.

Falken clenched his silver hand into a fist. *"Feydrim."*

"But why are they here?" Grace said, shivering.

"Maybe we weren't the only ones who hoped to find Travis here," the bard said. "Maybe the Pale King knows as well, and he's sent his minions to gain Sinfathisar."

"There could be more *feydrim* behind us," Vani said, circling around.

Grace clutched at Beltan. "What do we do?"

"Follow them," Beltan said, pointing.

The sun vanished behind the trees; blue twilight descended over the world. In the gloom, the sparks of silver shone clearly, far too many to be counted. They streamed toward the tower from all directions, closing in on the shadowy forms that loped up the hill.

"Come on!" Beltan said, tugging her arm. "Travis is in there!"

They lurched into a mad run, Vani and Falken on their heels. It was hard to see; the gloom was deepening. As they started up the side of the hill, it seemed shadows closed in around the tower, surrounding it in a perfect circle of darkness. Beltan pulled harder, nearly yanking her arm from its socket.

She forgot her pain. The ring of sparkling silver lights grew brighter. It closed around the darker circle, engulfing it. Gangly shadows writhed against the light. Shrill cries of pain and release rose on the air as the light grew brighter yet.

"Grace!" Beltan shouted. "The key!"

She squinted against the glare. Then the wall of light seemed to part before them, and she saw it: the dark arch of a doorway, and in its center a small hole. Grace groped beneath her cloak and pulled out the iron key that hung around her neck just as the four of them slammed against the door.

Beltan beat on the iron surface with both fists. "Travis!"

The light still blazed around them, but the shadows surged against it, pushing it back. Then the light grew purer, brighter, pressing the shadows against the walls of the tower. Inhuman cries rang out, shattering the cold air. Grace fumbled with the key.

"Please, Grace," Vani said. "You must hurry."

"Let me help," Falken said, and his silver hand closed around hers, steadying it, guiding it.

The key slipped into the hole, then turned. As one, Beltan and Vani threw themselves against the door, and it flew open with a *boom!*

For one more heartbeat, the light shone all around. Then it dimmed, and Grace could see again.

Not five paces in front of them, a man clad in a black robe knelt on the tower floor. Either he had not heard the door open or he did not care. He pawed at a heap of brown cloth, then seemed to find what he was looking for. He stood up. In his hands was a disk of creamy stone. He turned it over, and for a second Grace saw the symbol carved into its surface: a dot with a line above it.

●

"Travis, Durge!" Beltan shouted. "Hold on!"

Grace looked up, and joy and terror pulled at her heart so fiercely she thought the feelings would rend it in two. A staircase spiraled up the inside wall of the vast chamber. At the top were two familiar figures. Durge swung his greatsword as a knot of *feydrim* hissed and leaped out of the way. Travis lashed out with his stiletto, the ruby in its hilt blazing like a red eye. Just above them on the stairs, Lirith and Sareth held on to one another.

The figure in the black robe seemed finally to have noticed them. He looked up, but it was impossible to see his face in the depths of his cowl. Beltan started forward.

"Sar," the man in the black robe said, holding out a hand.

The stone floor rippled beneath Beltan, softening, turning to mud. His boots sank in several inches, then the man lowered his hand, and the stone grew solid once again.

Beltan lurched to an abrupt halt; he tugged, but his boots were stuck in the floor. He reached out, but the man in the black robe had already turned to flee. He passed between two columns, reaching the far wall of the tower. *"Sar,"* he spoke again. A hole opened in the tower wall. The man slipped through, and like a mouth the gap shut behind him.

Beltan jerked his feet out of his boots. He dashed forward,

behind Vani, who was already bounding up the stairs. One of the *feydrim* whirled around and sprang at her. She grabbed its head in her hands and gave it a sharp twist. A crunching sound echoed off stone; the creature went limp.

Another *feydrim* sprang at Beltan. He ducked, then quickly rose as the thing sailed over his back. It flew into space, limbs flailing, then crashed to the floor twenty feet below, landing in a crumpled gray heap. It did not get up.

Durge pulled his greatsword from the corpse of one of the creatures, and Travis had wounded the last remaining one with his stiletto. Vani finished it with a precise blow just beneath its skull, on the back of its neck.

It was over. The last traces of silver light faded away outside the tower. Night closed in, quiet and empty.

Beltan took a step up the stairs, his chest heaving as he struggled for breath. "Travis," he said, his words hoarse. "I never gave up. Not even after the Etherion came crashing down. I never stopped believing I'd see you again."

Travis stared, amazement on his face. Then all at once he grinned. "I came as fast as I could."

Beltan laughed. Then Travis was racing down the last few steps. He caught the blond man in his arms, and they held on to one another with fierce strength. At last Travis tilted his head, his lips brushed against Beltan's—

—and the blond man pulled away.

Travis frowned, his gray eyes puzzled. Beltan took a step down, looking suddenly uncomfortable. He cast a glance at Vani, then nodded. She took a tentative step up.

Travis's smile returned, and in that moment Grace knew he truly did love them both.

"I am glad to see you," the *T'gol* said, her gold eyes speaking more emphatically than her words. "All of you."

Travis quickly closed the distance between them, enfolding her in an embrace that was gentler than the one he had given Beltan, yet no less urgent. She did not resist. However, even as he held on to her, Travis's eyes moved to Beltan. The knight did not meet his gaze, and again pain and confusion flickered across Travis's face.

Grace sighed. She would talk to Travis later. She would tell him what it was Beltan feared—and what Travis's actions had just confirmed. However, it could wait.

"I believe there are others here who would like some hugs," she said, hands on hips. "From all of you."

Then Travis and Durge were running down the stairs, the others following after. Durge actually dared to try kneeling before Grace, but she caught him before he could, wrapping her arms around him, pressing her cheek against his.

"Durge." She said the word like prayer.

"My Fairy Queen," he murmured, tightening his strong arms around her, and for the first time in a long time, she felt safe.

"Is Lady Aryn not with you?" Durge said when she finally let him go.

Grace smiled, thinking of the familiar voice she had heard over such a long distance. "In a way."

Durge gave her an odd look, but she could explain later. Then she was hugging Lirith. "Sister," the witch said, her voice warm with affection. Then, to her surprise and delight, Grace was twirled around by Sareth. He looked a bit gaunt to her, as if he had been ill, only now was much recovered. That was one more thing she would have to ask about. As well as where they had been all this time. Somehow she sensed much had happened to them.

As it has to you, Grace.

She turned and saw that Travis was gazing at the heap of brown cloth on the floor, the one the man in the black robe had pulled the stone disk from. Travis's eyes, bright before, were now muted with sadness.

"I don't know if you saw," he said quietly. "It was Sky."

Falken nodded. "I did see it for a moment. You're right, it was indeed the rune of sky."

Travis looked up, sadness replaced by puzzlement. "No, Falken. I don't mean the rune. I mean the person. It was Sky. You remember him, from the Gray Tower."

A needle pierced Grace's heart. It wasn't a heap of brown cloth. It was a brown robe.

Falken shook his head. "You must be mistaken. I saw it clearly. It was a bound rune. *Tal,* the rune of sky. The man in the black robe picked it up right there." He pointed to the fallen garment.

They all stared at the brown robe, then at one another, struggling to comprehend.

"But it was him," Travis said weakly.

Falken's eyes were thoughtful. "And it was a rune."

"Sky and sky," Durge said in his rumbling voice. "Peculiar as it seems, there appears to be but one logical conclusion. Both rune and man were one and the same."

Grace looked at Travis. "Sky showed up in Tarras the morning after Tira's star vanished. He was wounded, and he told us to look for you here at Midwinter. Then he disappeared."

"We saw Tira's star vanish," Travis said, his gray eyes surprised. "And we saw Sky that same night here at the Black Tower. He told us he was going to take a message to you, that he would be able to reach you quickly."

"Very quickly," Durge rumbled. "It seems it took him mere hours to reach Tarras. Although the *feydrim* surrounding the tower must have tried to stop him. He must have returned here today to help us."

Lirith knelt beside the fallen robe, her dark face troubled. "The man in the black robe, we saw him stab Sky with a knife. We saw him die."

"We only thought we saw him die, *beshala,*" Sareth said, placing his hands on her shoulders. "All we really saw was a flash of blue light, then Sky was gone."

She looked up at him. "What are you saying?"

"Maybe he didn't die when the other stabbed him. Maybe he was transformed."

"From man to rune," Lirith murmured. "But the man in the black robe—who was he?"

Grace felt weak, exertion and fear and joy all finally getting the best of her. She couldn't stop shaking. "He was Runebreaker."

Lirith's eyes went wide.

Travis gave her a sharp look. "But I'm Runebreaker, Grace. We know that. The dragon said so."

Grace gave a stiff nod. "And so was he. I can explain it later, but Aryn learned about him, and she told me while we were on the white ship that he would be here. I wanted to warn you, Travis, but I was too late."

"Warn me about what?"

She drew in a breath. "There isn't just one Runebreaker. There are two."

They gazed at her, stunned.

"You mean Kelephon, right?" Beltan finally said. "He's a runelord, and we saw him break runes. So he must be the second Runebreaker."

Falken shook his head. "It's more than just being able to break runes. Runebreaker is the one prophesied to break the First Rune and destroy Eldh."

"It can't be Kelephon," Grace said, thinking of the man in the black robe. "Kelephon was bigger than that man. And I don't think he could have gotten here before us. There's no way his vessel could have kept up with the white ship."

"Besides," Beltan said, "Kelephon means to betray the Pale King, take the Stones, and rule Eldh himself. He wouldn't want to destroy the world. It's got to be someone else."

Durge crossed his arms. "Then who is it?"

"I don't know," Falken said, his face haggard. "But whoever the second Runebreaker is, he has the rune of sky . . ."

". . . which he can use to open a crack in the world and bring Mohg back," Travis said, his gray eyes haunted.

Grace moved to him. "You know about Mohg? How he intends to get back to Eldh?"

Travis nodded. "And how he intends to use the Imsari to break the First Rune."

She touched his arm. "But how do you know?"

"It was Brother Cy. I saw him, Grace, in—"

Ruby light filled the tower. They all turned to see a small figure pad through the open door on bare feet. The girl wore the same simple gray shift Grace remembered, and her fiery hair was as wild and tangled as ever. In her hands was a stone.

Not a stone. The Stone. Krondisar. The Stone of Fire.

It was from the Stone that the light radiated. It danced on the air like crimson fireflies, its touch warm and gentle. So that was why her star had vanished. She was here.

Grace's heart melted. "Tira," she said, smiling, even as tears streamed down her cheeks.

The little girl laughed and padded toward her. No, not toward her. Toward Travis. He knelt before Tira, and the girl held out the glowing Stone.

"Runebreaker," she said, and laughed again.

Here ends *Blood of Mystery,* Book Four of *The Last Rune*. The story of the Final Battle for Eldh will continue in Book Five, *The Gates of Winter.*

ABOUT THE AUTHOR

MARK ANTHONY learned to love both books and mountains during childhood summers spent in a Colorado ghost town. Later he was trained as a paleoanthropologist but along the way grew interested in a different sort of human evolution—the symbolic progress reflected in myth and the literature of the fantastic. He undertook this project to explore the idea that reason and wonder need not exist in conflict. Mark Anthony lives and writes in Colorado, where he is currently at work on the next book of *The Last Rune*. Fans of *The Last Rune* can visit the website at http://www.thelastrune.com.

Don't miss

BOOK FIVE of
The Last Rune

THE GATES OF WINTER

by

MARK ANTHONY

Coming in spring 2003 from Bantam Spectra
Here's a special excerpt:

Deirdre Falling Hawk sat in a claw-footed chair that was older
than her by a good four centuries and stared at the closed mahogany door across the hallway.

*All right, Deirdre—blink already. You don't have X-ray vi-
sion. And even if you did, the room is probably encased with
lead shielding. Gods know, the Philosophers always think of
everything.*

With a sigh, she leaned her head back against glossy wood
paneling. She wasn't certain she believed in fate. All the same,
she had a feeling hers was being decided on the other side of
that door right now. She reached up and touched the polished

bear claw that hung around her neck, wishing she could muster some kind of clairvoyance, some kind of true vision. Wishing she knew what Hadrian Farr was telling them.

She wasn't surprised they had asked to see her and Farr separately. That was standard procedure in interrogation, wasn't it? Divide and conquer—convince each accomplice the other was ratting on him. Nor was she surprised the Philosophers themselves had wished to conduct this final *interview,* as they termed it. The fact was, compared to what she had witnessed on the weathered asphalt of Highway 121 outside of Boulder, Colorado, nothing in the three months since—the midnight phone calls, the endless question and answer sessions, the surprise early morning visits to the South Kensington flat they had granted her—could possibly have come as a surprise.

If she closed her eyes, Deirdre could still see it: the window rimmed with crackling blue fire, hanging in mid air. It was what she and Farr had joined the Seekers in hopes of finding—a gateway to another world. They had watched as Travis Wilder and Grace Beckett stepped through the gate, along with the wounded man Beltan and the spindly gray being that was, impossibly, a fairy. Then the window collapsed in on itself and they were gone. In silence, they had walked from the accident scene where Duratek's transport vehicles lay scattered on the highway. Not two hundred yards away, the Seekers were waiting to pick them up. So much for the policy of not interfering with those who had otherworldly connections.

Twelve hours after the Seekers picked them up, they had touched down in London; to Deirdre, it felt like traveling to another world. In the time since, she and Farr had both written detailed reports about their activities in Denver. They had been questioned and questioned again by Seekers at nearly every level in the organization. Deirdre was no psychologist, but she knew enough to be sure the subtle repetition was conceived to reveal any inconsistencies in their stories. However, she simply told them the truth; she guessed Farr did as well.

Maybe not all of the truth, Deirdre. Do you think he told them he really is following in the footsteps of the famed Seeker Marius Lucius Albrecht? Albrecht fell in love with Alis Faraday, the woman he had been sent to observe. Do you think Farr told the Philosophers what he feels for Dr. Grace Beckett?

Regardless, it was almost over. Deirdre knew the only ones

left to talk to were the Philosophers themselves—if they even really existed.

Evidently they did; the summons came that morning. Deirdre had actually dressed up for the occasion, donning a simple but tasteful skirt suit of black wool. However, she had kept her bear claw necklace, and she had been forced to grab her leather biker jacket against the chill January drizzle that slicked the London streets.

She had spent perhaps an hour in the room beyond that mahogany door. It had been dark and empty except for a single chair carefully placed in a circle of gold light. Then the voices had started, and she had seen the row of dim silhouettes just beyond the light. For a moment she thought they were really there. Only that wouldn't be nearly mysterious enough for the Philosophers, would it? After a minute, a crackle of static passed in front of the figures. It was a projection, that was all—their electronically altered voices coming through speakers, her replies returning to them by hidden microphone. They could have been a thousand miles from that room.

It was only at the end of the interview, after a long pause, that a different question finally came.

"Please tell us one last thing, Ms. Falling Hawk," said the anonymous vocoder tones of one of the Philosophers. "If you were given the opportunity, would you go there?"

She stiffened in the chair. "Go there?"

"Yes, Ms. Falling Hawk. To AU-3, the world some call Eldh. Would you go there, if you could?"

She leaned back, unsure what to say, and touched the silver ring she wore on her right hand. It was the ring Glinda had given to her at Surrender Dorothy—the London nightclub that had been a secret haven for people with fairy blood in their veins. Duratek had been controlling the folk of Surrender Dorothy, supplying them with the drug Electria, hoping to use their blood to help open a gateway to Eldh. Only then Duratek had captured a true fairy; it had needed the others no longer. The nightclub had burned to the ground, but not before Deirdre had gone there, not before she managed to talk to Glinda.

As she had a thousand times since that night, she thought of Glinda's purple eyes, and the impossible forest she had glimpsed when they kissed. A forest she was certain had not been anywhere in the nightclub, or anywhere in London.

"Please answer the question, Ms. Falling Hawk. If given the opportunity, would you go to Eldh?"

She twirled the ring on her finger and smiled. "I think maybe I already have."

The lights came up, and it was over. She had gone into the hall to wait while Farr took his turn.

Once again Deirdre sighed. How long had he been in there? There was no clock in sight—nothing that would mar the precisely engineered patina of age and tradition that permeated the London Charterhouse. The only concessions to modernity were an EXIT sign at the end of the hallway and electric bulbs in the brass sconces that once burned oil.

Built just before Shakespeare's time, the Charterhouse had originally been the guild lodge of some of London's most notorious alchemists. These days, passersby thought it some exclusive club. They weren't all that far off. The Seekers weren't so very different from the geographic societies of Victorian times, planning trips to exotic locales. That these locales resided not on other continents, but on other worlds, was merely a matter of degree.

Just as Deirdre contemplated getting up and pounding on the door, it swung open.

Farr stood half in the darkness beyond, so that she could see him only in stark black and white. With his chinos, rumpled white shirt, and before-noon five o'clock shadow, he looked as if he had been digitized right out of a Humphrey Bogart movie.

"Well?" Deirdre stood.

Without looking back, Farr shut the door and stepped into the light. "I wouldn't have thought it would go like that."

"Go like what?"

A camel hair jacket drooped over Farr's arm. He unfolded the garment and shook it out, but this action only seemed to encourage the wrinkles. Farr slung the jacket over slouched shoulders.

"Do you know how many of the Nine Desiderata we broke?"

"Yes, actually. Numbers One, Three, Four, Six, and Seven. Although I never could see the difference between Desideratum One and Desideratum Three. Do you think something was lost in the translation from the Latin?"

"And do you know how many other directives and regulations we ignored in our actions?" Farr went on.

"Let's see. There was the Vow, of course. Plus a dozen or so local, state, and federal laws applicable in Colorado. And as I recall, Hadrian, you only flossed once the entire time we were in the States."

He ran a hand through his dark hair, as if it could be any more perfectly mussed than it already was. "It doesn't make one whit of sense."

"No, Farr, you don't make one whit of sense." She plucked a bit of lint off his coat, noticed it had been covering a spot, and gently replaced it. "And nobody says *whit* anymore. Or at least they shouldn't. Now tell me what happened. They've taken three months to decide what to do with us. Are we to be censured? Exiled? What?"

Farr's brown eyes finally focused on her. Even dazed and disheveled, he was handsome. Deirdre realized he should have been a poet or an artist a hundred years ago; he would have looked absolutely beautiful dying of tuberculosis.

"They've invited us to rejoin the Seekers. All privileges and benefits restored. And each of us at one rank higher than we were previously."

Deirdre gaped, at last surprised.

"So what do we do?" she finally managed to say.

Farr stuck his gray fedora atop his shaggy head. "We go downstairs. The Philosophers have politely requested we stop by the main office before leaving the building."

"And what if we don't?" Deirdre said. She felt light-headed, as if the air all around had gone thin.

"What, Deirdre? How could you possibly think to disobey the wise and benevolent Philosophers?"

Farr's voice was strangely soft; nor was he looking at her. Instead he gazed down the corridor, brown eyes haunted.

Deirdre started to reach toward him. "Hadrian?"

He turned his back and moved out of reach. "Be a good Seeker and come along, Deirdre. We'd best see what wonders the Philosophers have in store for us."

A quarter of an hour later they stepped through the door of the Merry Executioner, a pub three blocks from the Charterhouse and their haunt of old.

Over the last few years, a shocking number of London's centuries-old drinking houses had been quietly replaced by chain-owned franchises—establishments that were not genuine English pubs but rather deftly manufactured replicas of what an American tourist thought a pub should be. Deirdre had mistakenly walked into one not long after their return to London. The too-bright brass railing on the bar and the random coats of arms on the walls couldn't hide the fact that the steak-and-kidney pie came out of a microwave and the bartender didn't know the difference between a black-and-tan and a half-and-half.

In a way, the bland commercialization of London's pubs reminded Deirdre of the workings of Duratek Corporation. That kind of thing was right up their alley—take something true and good, and turn it into a crass mockery in order to make a tidy profit. Wasn't that what they wanted to do to AU-3, to the world called Eldh? She could see it now: rollercoasters surrounding the medieval stone keeps, and indigenous peasants in the castle market hocking cotton candy and plastic swords imported from Taiwan in order to keep sticky-fingered Earther tourists from noticing the smokestacks rising in the distance.

Luckily, the M.E. hadn't succumbed to the scourge of commercialization in Deirdre's absence. The dingy stone exterior and slightly grimy windows were just unsanitary-looking enough to assure foreigners would hastily pass by, shrieking children in tow. Inside, things were as dim and warmly shabby as Deirdre remembered. A comforting drone of conversation rose on the air from a scattering of locals. She and Farr slipped into a corner booth and caught the bartender's eye. He nodded. Scant minutes later they sipped their pints: Newcastle for Farr, Bass Ale for Deirdre.

Deirdre gave Farr a speculative look over the rim of her glass. "Better now?"

He set down his own glass and leaned back. "Marginally," he said, gazing at the battered surface of the table and the pair of manila envelopes they had been given.

"So, are you going to open it, Hadrian?"

"Maybe. I suppose I really haven't decided."

Deirdre let out a groan. "Please spare me the I'm-too-cool-to-care routine. You know as well as I do, that for all the rules we broke, and for all the havoc we caused, we're the first Seekers in centuries—maybe even the first since Marius Lucius Albrecht was a Seeker himself—to report real, verifiable, and multiple Class One Encounters. We've done the one thing the

Seekers have always wanted to do: we've met travelers from other worlds." She leaned over the table, letting her smoky green eyes burn into him. "Admit it. You want to know what the Philosophers have planned for us now as much as I do."

Farr's expression was unreadable. He flicked a hand toward the envelopes. "Ladies first."

He had called her on this one. It was time to show she wasn't bluffing. Deirdre picked up the envelope marked with her name, tore off one end, and turned it over.

A laminated card fell to the table. On the card was a picture of herself, her name, her signature, and the sigil of the Seekers: a hand holding three flames. So it was a new ID card, that was all, a replacement for the one they had taken from her at the first debriefing months ago. She turned it over to look at the reverse side.

Farr sat up straight and drew in a sharp breath. Deirdre raised an eyebrow, glancing at him.

"What is it, Farr?"

"Those bastards. Those cunning, diabolical bastards."

Deirdre frowned and followed Farr's gaze to the back of the card. It bore her thumbprint—no doubt in ink laced with her DNA, taken from blood samples the Seekers had on file. The DNA signature in the ink could be read with an ultraviolet scanner, providing a level of authentication that was virtually impossible to counterfeit. However, as interesting as the technology was, that couldn't be the source of Farr's outburst.

Then, in the lower corner of the card, she saw the small series of dots and lines—a computer code printed in the same DNA ink. Next to the code was a single, recognizable symbol: a crimson numeral seven.

A jolt of understanding sizzled through Deirdre. She looked up at Farr, her eyes wide. When she spoke, it was in a whisper of wonder. Or perhaps dread.

"Echelon 7. . ."

Farr grabbed the other envelope, shredded it, and snatched his new ID card form the debris. He flipped the card over, then tossed it on the table with a grunt. Like Deirdre's, his card was marked with a red seven.

He slumped back in the booth, his expression stricken. "Now," he murmured. "After all these years, they finally give it to me now. Damn them to hell." He leaned over the table, voice hoarse. "Do you understand what this means? With this card, there's nothing that's barred from you. Every file, every artifact, every document and bit of data—this card gives you access to all of them. With this, the deepest secrets of the Seekers will be at your disposal. Everything but the private files of the Philosophers themselves. It's all yours."

"And yours, too, Hadrian."

"I don't think so."

Deirdre gave an exasperated sigh. "What are you talking about? I thought this was what you wanted."

Farr shrugged, running a thumb over his card. "I suppose I did want this once. But I can't say I really know what I want anymore. Except maybe that's not true, either. Maybe I do know what I want, only it isn't this." He flicked the card away from him across the table.

Deirdre snatched it up. "This is ridiculous, Hadrian. You're one of the most important agents the Seekers have, and they've rewarded you for your work. Why is that so hard to bear?"

Farr let out a bitter laugh. "Come now, Deirdre, certainly you're not that guileless, not after what we've witnessed. This is no reward. It's simply another ploy to control us, to make us behave in the manner they wish. Think of what we've seen, what we know. And think of who besides the Seekers might want that knowledge for themselves."

"Duratek," she said on reflex.

"Exactly. The Philosophers will do anything to get us to come back and to keep us out of the hands of Duratek—even if it means giving us what we've always wanted. But that doesn't mean we're anything more than the puppets we were in Colorado, when they cut us off from the order."

Anger bubbled up inside Deirdre, at Farr—and, she had to admit, at the machinations of the Philosophers. As much as she would have liked to deny it, there was a ring of truth to Farr's words. But it didn't matter.

"So what?" she said. "So the Philosophers are trying to manipulate us. The fact is, no matter why they gave them to us, these cards still work." She reached across the table and took his hand. "Think of what we can do with them, Hadrian, what we can learn."

"No." Farr pulled his hand from hers. "I'm not resuming my work with the Seekers, Deirdre. I'm resigning from the order as of this moment."

She glared at him. "You can't quit, Hadrian. I know; I tried it once. And you were the one who told me that leaving the Seekers isn't an option, that it's a union that can't be broken."

"It seems I was mistaken."

Deirdre hardly believed what she was hearing.

Farr's handsome face was haggard but not unsympathetic. "I'm sorry, Deirdre, I truly am. I know it's difficult. But you have to face the fact that we've lost."

"That we've lost what?"

"Our belief."

She sat back, staring as if slapped. In all the years she had known him, Farr had never wavered in his quest for other worlds, had never stopped believing in them. "I don't understand. You were there, Hadrian, on the highway to Boulder. You saw it all with your own eyes."

"You misunderstand me. I haven't lost my belief in other worlds. I know they exist, just as you do. It's my belief in the Seekers I've lost. And from everything you're telling me, you have as well."

She struggled for words but could find none.

"To Watch, To Wait, To Believe—that was our motto. We thought all we had to do was keep our eyes open, be patient, and one day it would happen, one day the Philosophers would reveal everything, and the door would open for us. Well, the door did open, only it wasn't the Philosophers who did it." He laughed, and the cold sound of it made her shiver.

"Stop it, Hadrian."

"I used to believe the Philosophers knew everything, that they were infallible. But it turns out they're not. They make mistakes just like the rest of us. Do you think our mission in Denver went even remotely as they had planned?"

"I said stop it."

"We don't have to be their playthings, Deirdre. And as we learned in Denver, we don't need them or the magic of their little plastic cards in order to find other—"

She hit the table with a hand. Beer sloshed, and patrons turned their heads.

Farr was watching her, one eyebrow raised. She drew a breath, steadying her will.

"Don't even think about it," she said, her voice low and dangerous. "I mean it, Hadrian. Leaving the Seekers is one thing. You're mad to do it, but that's your prerogative. If you want to start a nice quiet life as a shopkeeper or an accountant, that's fine. But leaving the Seekers and continuing your...work is something else altogether."

He started to speak, but she held up a hand.

"No—shut up for once in your life and listen to me. The Seekers have eyes everywhere, you know that better than anybody. And you also know how the Philosophers feel about renegades. If they can't be sure of your allegiance, they'll make sure no one else can either."

She locked her eyes on his and listened to the thudding of her heart. For a moment she thought she had him, that he had finally seen reason. Then a smile touched his lips—it was a fond expression, sad—and he stood up.

So it was over; the words escaped her anyway. "Please, Hadrian. Don't go like this."

He held out a hand. "Come with me, Deirdre. You're too good for them."

She pressed her lips together and shook her head. Farr was wrong. It wasn't just their belief they had lost. He had lost Grace Beckett to another world. And Deirdre had lost Glinda to the fire in the Brixton nightclub. To Duratek.

Yet Deirdre hadn't lost her faith. There was still so much to learn, and with the new card the Seekers had given her—with Echelon 7—there was no telling what she might discover. Maybe there was something in the Seeker's files about Surrender Dorothy and its not-quite-human patrons. Maybe there was something that would help her decipher the language on Glinda's ring. The pieces of the puzzle could all be there, waiting to be matched together in the Seekers' database, just like the Graystone and Beckett cases.

Deirdre gripped the silver ring on her right hand. "I can't go with you, Hadrian. I have to stay here. It's the only chance I have to learn what I need to."

"And that's the reason I have to go."

Farr's smile was gone now, but despite his grim expression, there was something about him—a fey light in his eyes—that made him seem eager. He had always taken risks—that was how he had risen so high so quickly in the Seekers—but he had never been one to recklessly thrust himself into danger. Now Deirdre wasn't so sure. In the past, she had been angry with Farr, had been awed by him, and even envious of him. Now, for the first time, she was afraid for him.

"What are you going to do?" she said.

He shrugged on his rumpled coat. "You're a smart girl, Deirdre, and you've got good instincts. That's why I requested you for my partner. But you're wrong about something."

"About what?"

"Before, you said that we've done the one thing the Seekers have always wanted to do. Except that's not quite true." Farr put on his hat, casting his face into shadow. "You see, there's still one class of encounter we haven't had yet. Good-bye, Deirdre."

He bent to kiss her cheek, then turned and made for the door of the pub. There was a flash of gray light and a puff of rain-scented air.

Then he was gone.

There was a package from the Seekers waiting for her when she stepped through the door of her flat. Deirdre set her keys next to the cardboard box on the Formica dinette table. The landlady must have let them in.

Or maybe the Seekers have a skeleton key that works for all of London.

She wouldn't put it past them.

The Seekers' box took up almost the entire table. There was no mark on it, not even a mailing label—only a small symbol stamped in one corner: a hand with three flames. What was contained within, waiting to be revealed?

Deliberately, she pulled her gaze from the box and picked up instead the wooden case that held her mandolin. It was too quiet in this place; every thought was like a shout in her head. Maybe a little music would help.

She strummed the mandolin and winced. The thing could never seem to hold a tune in this damp London air. She tightened the strings, then strummed again. This time she smiled at the warm tone that rose from the instrument, a sound as welcome and familiar as the greeting of an old friend.

Without thought or direction, her fingers began to pluck out a lilting Irish air. It was the first tune she had learned to play as a girl at her grandmother's house, after finding the mandolin on a high shelf. She supposed she had been no more than eight or nine, and small for her age, so that she barely had been able to finger chords and strum at the same time. Now the mandolin nestled perfectly against the curve of her body, as if it had been fashioned just for her.

More songs came to her fingertips, bright and thrumming, or slow and deep as a dreaming ocean, filling the flat with music.

Her mind drifted as she played, back to the days when she had been a bard and nothing more, wandering to a new place, earning a little money with her music, then moving on. That was before she had ever heard of Jack Graystone or Grace Beckett. Before Travis Wilder was anything other than a gentle saloon keeper in a small Colorado town with whom she had almost had an affair. Before she met Hadrian Farr in that smoky pub in Edinburgh, fell like countless other foolish women for the danger and mystery in his dark eyes, and found her way into the Seekers.

It was only as she thought how strange and unexpected were the journeys on which life could lead one that she realized it was a song about journeys she was playing. In a low voice, she sang along with the final notes.

> *We live our lives a circle,*
> *And wander where we can.*
> *Then after fire and wonder,*
> *We end where we began.*

It was a simple tune, yet with a sadness to it that made her heart ache. The words almost reminded her of something. Something that had happened in Castle City, something she had forgotten...

She set down the mandolin and moved over to the trunk where she had stowed her few belongings. After a bit of rummaging, she pulled out a leather-bound book—one of her journals. One lesson Farr had taught her early in her career as a Seeker was to take notes. Lots of them. She checked the label on the spine to make sure it was the right volume, then headed back to the sofa. she flipped through the pages, trying to remember.

Three words caught her eye, and her heart fluttered in her chest.

Fire and wonder....

Quickly, she read the entire entry. Yes, she remembered now. It was the day she had ridden alone into the canyon above Castle City to make a satellite phone call to Farr. There, by the side of a deserted road, she had encountered a pale girl in an archaic black dress. Only later did she learn that both Grace Beckett and Travis Wilder had encountered this same girl, that her name was Child Samanta, and that there were two others she seemed to travel with: a preacher named Brother Cy, and a red-haired woman named Sister Mirrim.

The Seekers had never been able to locate any trace of these three individuals, but that didn't surprise Deirdre. Because Deirdre had known in an instant this was no normal child.

Cradling the journal, Deirdre ran her finger over the conversation she had transcribed over a year ago. Again she read the girl's final words, spoken just before she vanished like a shadow in the sun.

Seek them as you journey, the child had said.

What do you mean? Deirdre had asked. *Seek what?*

Fire and wonder.

She set down the journal and found herself staring once more at the box on the table. Maybe it was a hunch. But she went to the box, broke the tape with a key, opened it, dug through layers of biodegradable packing peanuts, and pulled out something cool and hard. It was a notebook computer. The machine was sleek and light, encased in brushed metal; no doubt it was the latest-greatest money could buy. Was this another gift from the Seekers meant to bribe her?

She put the computer on the dinette table, opened it, and pressed the power button. A chime sounded as it whirred to life; the battery was charged. A login screen appeared, but there was no place to type her agent name or password.

Maybe you don't need to, Deirdre.

She turned the computer, studying it. There—inserted into the side was a silvery expansion module. The module bore a thin slit, about the width and thickness of a crdit card. Deirdre reached into the pocket of her jeans and pulled out her new ID card. It slid into place with a soft *snick*.

The login screen vanished, replaced by a spinning wheel. Just as Deirdre was thinking she should have plugged the computer into a phone jack, another chime sounded. The screen went black. Then words scrolled into being, as if typed by invisible hands:

**DNA authentication scan accepted. Seeker Agent
Deirdre Falling Hawk—identity confirmed.
Working...**

Deirdre let out a low whistle. So this thing was wireless; she could take it anywhere. More glowing words scrolled across the screen, and her breath caught on her lips.

Welcome, to Echelon 7.
What do you want to do?
>

The cursor blinked on and off, expectant. Deirdre sat back in the chair and ran a hand through her red-black hair.

What was she supposed to do? There were no menus on the screen, no windows to explore, no buttons to click. Just the glowing words.

It asked you a question, Deirdre. So why not answer it?

She swallowed a nervous laugh, then leaned forward and tapped out words on the keyboard.

I want to find something.

She pressed *Enter*. A moment later, new words appeared on the screen.

What do you want to find?
>

Deirdre hesitated, fingers hovering over the keys. Then, quickly, she typed three words.

Fire and wonder.

Again she pressed *Enter*. The words flashed, then vanished, and the screen exploded into a riot of motion and color. Dozens of session windows popped into being, each overlapping the next. Text poured through some of the windows like green rain, while in others images flashed by so quickly they were superimposed into a single blurred montage of stones covered with runes, medieval swords, pages of illuminated manuscripts, and ancient coins—each gone in less than the blink of an eye.

Deirdre leaned closer to the screen. Some of the data windows contained menus and commands she recognized; they belonged to various database systems in the Seeker network she had accessed in the past. But most of the windows bore interfaces like nothing she had ever seen before, their indecipherable menus composed in glowing alien symbols. Atop everything was a single flashing crimson word: *Seeking...* Trembling, she reached out to touch the computer.

The screen went black.

Deirdre jerked her hand back. What had she done? Had she damaged it somehow? Then her heart began to beat once more as glowing emerald words scrolled across the screen.

Search completed.
1 match(es) located:
/albion/archive/case999-1/mla1684a.arch
>

So it had found something. But where? Deirdre didn't recognize the server name; wherever this file was located, it wasn't in a database she had ever searched before.

What did the file contain? Text? Images? And concerning what subject? Deirdre had no idea, but she intended to find out. *Display search file. [Enter]*

The cursor flashed for several seconds, then the computer let out a beep.

Error. Unable to access file mla1684a.arch.
File does not exist.
>

Deirdre swore, then typed another command. *What happened to search file? [Enter]*

File mla1684a.arch has been deleted from the system.
>

Deirdre typed with furious intensity. *When was file mla1684a.arch deleted? [Enter]*

The computer whirred, chirped.

File mla1684a.arch was deleted from the system at timestamp: Today, 22:10:13
>

A coldness stole over her. It was hard to move, but she craned her head up and forced her eyes to focus on the art deco clock on the mantle. 10:12 P.M.

Two minutes ago. The file had been deleted from the system two minutes ago. But that had to be . . .

"Just seconds after your search query located it," Deirdre whispered to no one.

She pushed back from the table and reached for the phone on the wall. Fumbling, she punched the number of the flat where Farr had been staying. One ring, two.

She had to talk to Farr; he would know what to do. He knew everything, didn't he? Three rings, four.

"Come on, Hadrian, answer. Bloody hell, come on."

A click. The ringing ended, and a voice spoke in her ear. But it wasn't Farr's low, compelling tones. Instead it was a robotic drone.

"The number you have reached has been disconnected. If you feel you have reached this recording in error—"

Deirdre slammed the phone back onto the wall. No, it was no error. Farr had left. But where was he going? There had been something about him earlier—a power, a peril—she had never seen before. Then, with a shiver, she remembered his last words to her.

You see, there's still one class of encounter we haven't had yet . . . .

Deirdre sank back into the chair, staring at the computer screen. It was the first thing every Seeker learned upon joining the order: the classification of otherworldly encounters. Class Three Encounters were common—rumors and stories of otherworldly nature. Class Two Encounters were rarer, but well represented in the history of the Seekers—encounters with objects and locations that bore residual traces of otherwordly forces. And Class One Encounters were the rarest—direct interaction with otherwordly beings and travelers.

But Farr was right. There was one more class of encounter, one that had never been recorded in all the five centuries of the Seekers' existence. A Class Zero Encounter. Translocation to another world oneself.

Deirdre clenched her hands into fists. "What are you doing, Hadrian? By all the gods, what are you doing?"

But the only answer was the soft, ceaseless hum of the computer.